✝HE SOUL DRIΠKERS OMΠIBUS

SOUL DRIΠKER
✝HE BLEEDIΠG CHALICE
CRIMSOΠ ✝EARS

LIKE ALL OF the superhuman Space Marines, the Soul Drinkers Chapter are dedicated to their service to the Emperor. Their loyalty is second to none and their courage knows no bounds. But when the Chapter are betrayed and one of their most ancient relics is stolen, the Soul Drinkers face a terrible dilemma – betray the Imperium, or lose their honour?

BURSTING WITH ACTION, bloodshed and intrigue, *The Soul Drinkers Omnibus* brings together the first three novels about this proud and noble Chapter.

A WARHAMMER 40,000 OMNIBUS

THE SOUL DRINKERS OMNIBUS

BEN COUNTER

A Black Library Publication

Soul Drinker copyright © 2002 Games Workshop Ltd.
The Bleeding Chalice copyright © 2003 Games Workshop Ltd.
Crimson Tears copyright © 2005 Games Workshop Ltd.

This omnibus edition published in Great Britain in 2006 by
BL Publishing,
Games Workshop Ltd.,
Willow Road,
Nottingham,
NG7 2WS, UK.

10 9 8 7 6 5 4 3 2 1

Cover illustration by Clint Langley.

A CIP record for this book is available from the British Library.

ISBN 13: 978 1 84416 416 5
ISBN 10: 1 84416 416 0

Distributed in the US by Simon & Schuster
1230 Avenue of the Americas, New York, NY 10020, US.

See the Black Library on the Internet at
www.blacklibrary.com

Find out more about Games Workshop
and the world of Warhammer 40,000 at
www.games-workshop.com

IT IS THE 41st millennium. For more than a hundred centuries the Emperor has sat immobile on the Golden Throne of Earth. He is the master of mankind by the will of the gods, and master of a million worlds by the might of his inexhaustible armies. He is a rotting carcass writhing invisibly with power from the Dark Age of Technology. He is the Carrion Lord of the Imperium for whom a thousand souls are sacrificed every day, so that he may never truly die.

YET EVEN IN his deathless state, the Emperor continues his eternal vigilance. Mighty battlefleets cross the daemon-infested miasma of the warp, the only route between distant stars, their way lit by the Astronomican, the psychic manifestation of the Emperor's will. Vast armies give battle in his name on uncounted worlds. Greatest amongst His soldiers are the Adeptus Astartes, the Space Marines, bio-engineered super-warriors. Their comrades in arms are legion: the Imperial Guard and countless planetary defence forces, the ever-vigilant Inquisition and the tech-priests of the Adeptus Mechanicus to name only a few. But for all their multitudes, they are barely enough to hold off the ever-present threat from aliens, heretics, mutants – and worse.

TO BE A man in such times is to be one amongst untold billions. It is to live in the cruellest and most bloody regime imaginable. These are the tales of those times. Forget the power of technology and science, for so much has been forgotten, never to be re-learned. Forget the promise of progress and understanding, for in the grim dark future there is only war. There is no peace amongst the stars, only an eternity of carnage and slaughter, and the laughter of thirsting gods.

Contents

AUTHOR'S INTRODUCTION

THE SOUL DRINKERS start out ignorant and driven by pride. And, perhaps, that is how they finish, too – driven to the edge of destruction not by the enemies that surround them, but by their own refusal to back down while the Emperor's work is still to be done. They do not have obstacles thrown in their way, and they do not simply have deadly foes appear from nowhere. Everything that befalls them is their own doing. That is why they fight – because ultimately, they have chosen to.

I first came up with the Soul Drinkers in a novel proposal I sent to the Black Library after having some short stories published in BL's *Inferno!* magazine. Two of the stories I had written centred on Space Marines, the superhuman armoured elites of the Imperium. The Space Marines were tempting for a writer, because they were both very popular, and larger than life (literally – they top out at over two metres tall) in a way that made them suitable for epic myth-making and tales of spectacular derring-do. They were also difficult to write, because they are one step away from human. They do not feel fear, at least not in the way that a 'normal' man does, and they can endure stupendous amounts of punishment and horror. In another sense, they feel more than 'normal' humans – they have senses of duty, brotherhood and righteous hatred that go beyond what most people can experience. No one holds a grudge, obsesses about honour or makes spectacular sacrifices like a Space Marine. They are difficult to get right, but when it all clicks they earn their place at the top of the 41st Millennium's food chain.

It was inevitable, then, than my novel proposal to the Black Library would be based around Space Marines. I used the name 'Soul Drinkers' because it was the coolest Chapter name I had read, and because the Chapter was nothing more than a name and had no history or other background to get in the way of my making it all up. Similarly, the story I would tell was obvious to me, inspired by some of the colour text in the old Realm of Chaos rulebooks for Warhammer, which described the fall of two noble heroes into the clutches of corruption and Chaos. The Soul Drinkers would not just be an Imperial Space Marine Chapter who battle evil and win the day. They would gradually become corrupted by pride and hatred, be seduced by the Dark Gods, and end up a rage-filled, damned and utterly despicable Chapter of Chaos Marines. The Dark Gods would deceive them into pledging themselves to Chaos, and the Soul Drinkers would enter an eternity of damnation!

That, of course, was not how the Soul Drinkers turned out. The original proposal was pored over by Marc Gascoigne and Lindsey Priestley at the Black Library, and we sat down for a meeting at Games Workshop HQ. The proposal was picked apart, chopped up and reassembled, and what emerged was something very different. The Soul Drinkers would have their close encounter with the corruptive force of Chaos, but they would not end up Chaos warriors covered in skulls and spiky bits. Instead, they would renounce the Imperium and Chaos alike, going on their own way, and the first novel would detail the painful and extremely bloody process by which the Soul Drinkers would throw off the shackles of the Imperium.

The Soul Drinkers represent a sort of 'third way' between slavish obedience to the Imperium, and the hellish corruption of Chaos. This meant that they were opposed to the Imperium as well as dark forces of the galaxy, and that I could explore the Imperium as an enemy. This is perhaps the real reason the Soul Drinkers ended up the way they did – because the Imperium is such a wonderful bad guy.

The Imperium is my favourite aspect of Warhammer 40,000, because it is not just a heroic human empire valiantly defending itself from hostile outsiders. It is not even a deeply flawed but ultimately just empire that does grim things to survive. The Imperium is a ruthless tyranny, inspired by the worst excesses of real-world history and ramped up to such levels of darkness and hatred that it barely fits on the page.

These were themes that I was able to explore as Sarpedon (with the help of some Chaotic meddling) realised how hypocritical and corrupt the Imperium really was. And yet the Imperium is not just an evil empire to be destroyed, because without the structure of the Imperium and the ruthless way it crushes heretics and rebels, the human race would surely fall apart and be devoured. It is this cruel irony, central to the Warhammer 40,000 universe, that Sarpedon and his Soul Drinkers have to contend with as they try to find their way in the universe. Is it possible to help humanity, and do the will of the Emperor, while opposing the structures of the Imperium itself? Sarpedon thinks so, and this belief has all but led his Chapter to destruction.

Soul Drinker was written, rewritten, hammered into shape and published. When it came to the sequel, *The Bleeding Chalice*, the Soul Drinkers were out on their own and trying to cure the blight left on them by their close brush with Chaos in the previous book. The Imperium was now actively hunting them, and Sarpedon had to face not only old-fashioned enemies who wanted humanity's destruction, but also human foes who believed as strongly in the Emperor's will as he did. The third in the series, *Crimson Tears*, saw the Soul Drinkers tangling with the piratical dark eldar as well as their brother Space Marines of the Crimson Fists. The real enemy in *Crimson Tears*, however, was one of their own, twisted and driven mad by the events that Sarpedon set in motion. *Crimson Tears* perhaps tells the real truth about the Soul Drinkers – that no matter how many aliens, Chaotic hordes and Imperial armies they come up against, the Soul Drinkers' greatest threats come from within. The Chapter is trapped in no-man's land between all the forces of the galaxy, and eventually it must surely tear itself apart.

The Soul Drinkers are fighting a losing battle. Their numbers dwindle and they are hunted by the Inquisition and the vengeful forces of Chaos alike, all while they are trying to do the Emperor's work and defend humanity. The cracks are starting to show and Sarpedon's ability to hold the Soul Drinkers together is far from certain. But ultimately, they are not about winning. They are free, perhaps the only Space Marine Chapter to truly throw off the Imperial yoke without falling to some corruption in the process. If they are destroyed, then they will die free, which is more than almost anyone in the Imperium could ever say. Even if only one Soul Drinkers remains, there will be some freedom in a galaxy smothered by the Imperium and corrupted by Chaos. That is perhaps the victory that Sarpedon is seeking – a victory that only a Space Marine, with his depth of honour and refusal to despair, could ever really win.

Until that time, the Soul Drinkers will fight on, cold and fast just as the *Catechisms Martial* says, and somewhere in the galaxy the Emperor's work will be done.

Ben Counter
August 2006

SOUL DRINKER

CHAPTER ONE

IN THE SILENCE of the vacuum the corvus assault pod tumbled towards the star fort, the curved metal of its hull studded with directional jets that fired once, steadying the descent. The pod had been fired on a trajectory that took it halfway across the orbit of the planet Lakonia, which hung bright and cold below. The battle cruiser which had housed it, along with the half-dozen other pods glinting against the blackness of space, was on the other side of the planet. No one in the star fort would have any idea they were coming. And that was just how the Soul Drinkers preferred it.

Inside the drop-pod, Sarpedon could hear only the soft song of the servitor choir and the gentle hum of armour. The battle-brothers were quiet, contemplating the fight to come and the many years of warfare that had forged them into the pinnacle of humanity.

They were thinking of Primarch Rogal Dorn, the father of their Chapter literally as well as figuratively, and his noble example they strove to follow. They thought of the favour the Emperor had bestowed upon them, that they might travel the stars and play their part in a grand plan that was too fragile and vital to place in the hands of lesser men. They had thought such things a thousand times or more, readying their minds for the sharp intensity of combat, banishing the doubt that afflicted soldiers falling below the standard of the Space Marines; of the Soul Drinkers.

Sarpedon knew this, for he felt the same. And yet this time it was different. This time the weight of history, which refined the Soul Drinkers' conduct into a paragon of honour and dignity, was a little heavier. For there was more at stake than a battle won or lost. Soon, when the fight was over, they would have reserved a place in the legends that were taught to novices and recited on feasting nights.

The choir's delicate faces, mounted on brass armatures, turned to the ceiling of the corvus pod as the note from their once-human vocal chords rose. The Soul Drinkers Chapter used the mindless, partly-human servitors for all menial and non-skilled labour – those making up the choir were little more than faces and vox-projectors hardwired to the pod. Their presence was a tradition of the Chapter, and helped focus the thoughts of the battle-brothers on the battle to come.

They were close. They were ready. Sarpedon could feel the brothers' eagerness for battle, their concern for proper conduct and their scorn for cowardice, mixed and tempered into a warrior's soul. It shone at the back of his mind, so strong and unifying that he could receive it without trying.

The pod juddered as it encountered the first wisps of Lakonia's atmosphere, but the thirty battle-brothers – two tactical and one assault squad strapped into grav-ram seats, resplendent in their dark purple power armour and with weapons gleaming – did not allow their reverie to waver.

His brothers. The select band that lay between mankind's destiny and its destruction. The tune of the choir changed as the pod entered the final phase, almost drowning out the hiss of the braking jets. Sarpedon took his helmet from beside his seat and put it on, feeling the seal snaking shut around his throat. New runes on his retinal display confirmed the vacuum integrity of his massive armour. Every Space Marine had spent many hours on the strike cruiser observing the strictest wargear discipline, for they could be fighting in a near-vacuum before entry points were secured. He activated a rune on the retinal-projected display and his aegis hood thrummed into life. Handed down the line of senior Librarians of the Soul Drinkers, its lost technology warmed up to protect Sarpedon as he led his brother Space Marines into Chapter history.

Close. Closer. Even if the choir and the corvus pod's alert systems had not told him, he could have felt it. He could feel the star fort's bulk rearing out of the darkness, its bloated shape creeping across Lakonia's green-brown disk as they approached. The braking jets entered second phase, and the grav-rams flexed to cushion the Marines' weight against the deceleration.

'Soul Drinkers,' came Commander Caeon's voice over the vox-channel, clear and proud. 'I need not tell you why you are here, or what is expected of you, or how you will fight. These are things you will never doubt.

'But know now that when the youngest novices or the most scarred of veterans ask you how you spent your time serving this Chapter, it will be enough to tell them that you were there the day your Chapter proved it never forgets a matter of honour. The day the Soulspear was returned.'

Good words. Caeon could tap into the hearts of his men, use the power of those traditions they held sacred to will them on to super-human feats.

Lights flashed inside the corvus pod. The noise grew, the servitor choir matching its harmonies, a wall of sound growing, inspiring. The metallic slamming that rippled through the hull was the sound of the docking clamps forced out of their cowlings, ceramite-edged claws primed to rip through metal. Sarpedon could see the star fort fresh in his mind, planted there by the repeated mission briefings – it was ugly and misshapen, probably once spherical but now deformed. Docking corridors would be stabbing out from its tarnished surface, but the attack had been carefully timed.

There was no cargo on the star fort and no ships docked – no way out for defenders. The Van Skorvold cartel and its rumoured private army believed their star fort to be a bastion of defence, its weapon systems and labyrinthine interior protecting them from any attack. It was the Soul Drinkers' intent to turn the place into a deathtrap.

Long-range scans had only penetrated through the first few layers of the star fort. It had been difficult to plan an assault route when there could only be guesswork about what form the inside of the fort might take, so the mission was simple in principle. Go in, eliminate any opposition, and find the objectives. Where the objectives were, or what that opposition might be, would be discovered as the mission unfolded by the leaders of the individual assault teams. In the case of Sarpedon's squads, that was Sarpedon himself.

There were three objectives. Primary objectives one and two were means to an end – that end was Objective Ultima, and its recovery would emblazon the names of every Space Marine here on the pages of Chapter history.

Sarpedon checked his bolter one last time, and clasped a hand round the grip of his force staff, the psyk-attuned arunwood haft warm to the touch. Faint energy crackled over its surface. The other Space Marines were making a last symbolic check of their wargear, too – helmet and joint seals, bolters. The plasma gun of Givrillian's squad was primed, its power coils glowing. Sergeant Tellos's assault squad, stripped of their jump packs for the star fort environment, unsheathed their chainswords as one. Sarpedon could feel Tellos's face behind his snarl-nosed helmet, calm and untroubled, with a hint of a smile. All Soul Drinkers were born to fight – Tellos was born to do so with the enemy surrounding him at sword-thrust range, daring to take up arms against the Emperor's chosen. Tellos was marked for great things, the upper echelons of Chapter command had said. Sarpedon agreed.

The choir suddenly fell silent, and there was nothing in the Space Marines' minds but battle. The docking charges roared in unison, and they hit.

THE CORVUS POD'S doors blew open and the air rushed out with a scream. The flesh on the servitor choir's faces blistered and cracked with the sudden cold. There was silence all around, save for the hum of the power plant in his armour's backpack and the almost-real sound of his brothers' minds, washing back and forth like a tide as they snapped through the orientation/comprehension routines that had been implanted on their minds during psycho-doctrination.

Sight – the swirling smoke through the blast doors, fragments of ice and metal spinning. Sound – nothing, no air. Movement – none.

The Space Marines unbuckled their harnesses, ready to rush the breach. Tellos would lead them in, his men's chainswords primed to rip through the first line of defenders. Sarpedon would be in the middle of the tactical squads on their heels, ready to unleash the weapon that boiled within his mind.

Sarpedon only had to nod, and Tellos bolted through the breach.

'Go! Go! With me!' Tellos's young, eager voice broke the silence like a gunshot as his squad followed. Then the sergeant's breath was the only sound. Every Space Marine listened with augmented ears for the first contact with the enemy.

The tactical squads were unbuckled.

'Clear!' called Tellos.

The Tactical Marines plunged into the smoky breach, their power armoured bulks dropping through into the darkness. Givrillian was in the lead, Brother Thax with the plasma gun at his shoulder. Sarpedon followed, bolter ready, force staff holstered behind his armour's backpack. As he ducked into the breach he caught sight of Lakonia, a glowing sliver of a world framed in the gap between the pod's docking gear and the star fort's hull. The pod had come in aslant and the docking seal had not adhered, the atmosphere within the pod and immediate environment beyond venting out into the thin near-void.

An assault craft of lesser forces would have been forced to disengage then and there, its blast doors clamped shut, to drift vulnerable and impotent until second wave craft picked it up. But the Soul Drinkers cared nothing for such things – power armour's sealable environment made a mockery of the dangers of vacuum. And there would be no second wave.

The smoke cleared and Sarpedon got his first look at the star fort's interior. It was low-ceilinged to a warrior of his superhuman height, dirty and ill-maintained – they had hit a derelict section, of which there were probably a great many in the fort. Oil and sludge had frozen on the pipes that snaked the ceilings and walls. They were at the junction of two corridors – one way was blocked by a lump of rusting machinery, but there were still three exits to cover or exploit. Two curved away into the dimness and one ended in a solid bulkhead door, guarded by half of Tellos's assault squad, ready to blow it with melta-bombs.

The lack of immediate resistance was explained by the two bodies. Probably maintenance workers, they were unprotected when the local atmosphere blew out. One had been thrown against a stanchion by the explosive decompression and had burst like a ripe seed pod, his blood bright like jewels of red ice on the floor and walls. The other was stretched pathetically along the corridor floor, mouth frozen mid-gasp, staring madly up at the breach with eyes red from burst blood vessels. Sarpedon's keen eyes caught the glint of an insignia badge on the body's grease-streaked grey overalls, a retinal rune flashing as the image zoomed in.

Stylised human figures, twins, flanking a golden planet.

The Van Skorvold crest.

The Tactical Marines fanned out around him, bolters ready, enhanced senses scanning for movement.

'Breach the bulkhead, sir?' Tellos voxed.

'Not yet. Flight crew, get that seal intact. I don't want any decompressions throwing our aim.'

'Acknowledged,' came the serf-pilot's metallic voice from within the corvus cockpit. Vibrations ran through the dull metal grating of the floor as the clamps edged the docking seal true to the breached hull.

Sarpedon contracted a throat muscle to broaden the frequency of his vox-bead. 'This is Sarpedon. Squads Tellos, Givrillian and Dreo deployed. Nil contact.'

'Received, Sarpedon. Confirm location and move on mark.' The voice was Commander Caeon's from his position some way across the bloated bulk of the star fort. Along with Caeon, Sarpedon and their squads, six more corvus ship-to-orbital assault pods had impacted on the spaceward side of the star fort and disgorged their elite Soul Drinkers complements. Three more were following carrying the remaining apothecaries and Tech-Marines, along with a platoon of serf-labourers kitted out for combat construction duty, ready to support their brethren and consolidate the landing site bridgeheads.

Three whole companies of Soul Drinkers. A battlezone's worth of the Emperor's chosen soldiers, enough to face any threat the galaxy might throw at them. But for the prize that shone deep within the star fort, it was worth it.

Sarpedon pulled a holoslate from a waist pouch and flicked it on. A sketchy green image of the corridors immediately surrounding his position flickered above the slate, with lines of data circling it. The star fort was based on a very old orbital defence platform, and the platform's schematics had been supplied in case any of the assault pods hit a section of the original platform.

'Subsection delta thirty-nine,' he voxed. 'Redundant cargo and personnel route.'

'Received. Consolidate.'

Sarpedon's fingers, dextrous even within the gauntlet of purple ceramite, touched runes along the holoslate's side and the corridor system was divided into blocks of colour, marking the different routes out of their position. Crosshairs centred on a point that flashed red, indicating the convergence of the three routes two hundred metres further into the fort. Barring enemy concentrations elsewhere, their immediate objective was the primary environmental shaft head, a grainy green curve at the edge of the display. Once taken, it gave the Marines an option for a larger thrust into the oxygen pumps and recycling turbines, and then through the mid-level habs into the armoured core that surrounded primary objective two. A messenger rune flickered on his retinal display, indicating the docking seal had achieved integrity.

'By sections!' he ordered on the squad-level frequency, indicating the holo to his squad sergeants. 'Tellos, the bulkhead. Dreo, left, Givrillian right, with me. Cold and fast, Soul Drinkers!'

The squads peeled off into the darkness, leaving two Space Marines from each of the tactical squads to hold the bridgehead and cover the arriving specialists assigned to Sarpedon's cordon. There was the thud of melta-bomb detonations and the whump of air re-entering the area as the bulkhead fell.

Sarpedon led Givrillian's unit through the side corridor into a cargo duct, broad and square, with a heavy rail running down the centre for crate-carts or worker transports. Thax swept beyond the entrance.

'Nothing,' he said.

'Unsurprising,' said Sarpedon. 'They weren't expecting us.'

No one ever did. That was how the Soul Drinkers worked. Cold and fast.

They felt the faint report of bolter-shots in the thinned air. 'Contact!' came Dreo's voice.

Sarpedon waited, just a moment.

'Enemy down,' said Dreo. 'Half-dozen, security patrol. Autoguns and flak armour, uniforms.'

'Received, Sergeant Dreo. Proceed to rendezvous junction.'

'Mutants, sir.'

Sarpedon's skin crawled at the mere concept, and he could feel the disgust of his brothers. The evidence of illegal mutant dealing had been damning enough, but there had been stories that the Van Skorvold cartel had skimmed off the most useful of their illicit cargo and formed them into a private army. Now it was certain.

'Move the flamer to the rear and burn them. Squads, be aware, mutations include enhanced sensory organs. Some of those things might see as well as you. And there will be more.'

Degenerate, dangerous individuals but cowardly at heart. His powers would work well on such foes. But first they had to find them.

'Heavy contact, cargo hub seven!' Luko's callsign flickered. Luko's squad was part of the strikeforce from another corvus pod, one which had come down nearby and just before Sarpedon's. Sarpedon knew Luko would be itching to tear into some miscreant flesh with his power claws, and it was right that he should the first into the bulk of the enemy.

'Sarpedon here, do you request support?'

'Greetings, Librarian! Come on over, the hunting is good!' Luko always had a laugh in his voice, never more so than when the foe dared show its face.

Givrillian led them down a side-duct, cutting across the unassigned sectors delta thirty-eight and thirty-seven. A flash of the holoplate showed Luko's auspex data – red triangles, unknown signals, skittering across the edge of delta thirty-five.

'Dozens, sir,' said Givrillian.

'I can see that, sergeant. Suggestion?'

'Tellos'll be there first, so their first line will be engaged. We go in with light engagement fire pattern, get in right amongst them. Don't let them get dug in.'

'Good. Do it.'

They all heard Tellos as he called upon his brother assault troopers to slay for the Emperor and for Dorn, and the familiar sound of

Ben Counter

chainblade into flesh. The bolter-fire from Luko's squad stitched a pattern of sound into the air every Marine had heard a million times before. Givrillian burst through an open hatchway into the cargo hub that made up sector delta thirty-five, picked a target and loosed off a handful of shots from his bolter. Thax was a footstep behind and a pulse of liquid plasma-fire burst white hot from the muzzle of his gun, power coils shimmering.

Sarpedon cocked his bolter and followed, and saw the enemy for the first time.

The hub had once been dominated by the tracks at ceiling-level, which moved huge crates of cargo around the immense room between the duct entrances and pneumo-lifters. The forest of uprights which had held up the system had mostly collapsed or fallen askew with age and poor maintenance, and it was these that the mutants were using for cover.

In that split-second Sarpedon picked out a hundred unclean deformities – hands that were claws, facial features missing or multiplied or rearranged, spines cruelly twisted out of shape, scales and feathers and skin sheened with ooze. They had autoguns, some las weapons, crude shotguns. There were implanted industrial cutters and saws, and some with just brute strength, all in ragged stained coveralls in the uniform dark green bearing the Van Skorvold crest.

There must have been a thousand of them in there, crowds of baying mutants behind their makeshift defences. Their leaders – those with the most horrific mutations, some with massive chitinous talons or vast muscle growth – had either communicators or slits at their throats that indicated crude vox-bead implants. This was an organised foe.

Tellos's men were vaulting the first barricades and laying in with chainswords – limbs lopped off, heads falling. The sergeant himself was duelling with something hulking and ugly that wielded a recycler unit's harvester blade like a longsword. If it wasn't the leader the creature would at least form a lynchpin of morale for the degenerates that crowded around it – Tellos was good, seeking out the target that would damage the enemy most if eliminated, using his duelling skill to the maximum. If he took a fine trophy from the beast, Sarpedon would put in a word for him to keep it.

It took Sarpedon half a second to appreciate the situation and decide on his plan of action. The enemy had overwhelming strength and the Soul Drinkers had to neutralise the threat before a proper line of defence could form. Therefore they would attack the enemy's prime weaknesses relentlessly until they broke.

He loosed a couple of shots into a crowd of mutants and workers that were sheltering behind mouldering cargo crates from Luko's pinning fire. The bolter's kick in his hand felt good and heavy, and somewhere in the heart of the enemy two red blooms burst – a stream of autogun fire crackled towards him and he ducked back into cover.

First blood. Sarpedon had made his mark on the battle and could join with his brothers in pride at its execution, according to the Chapter traditions.

'Givrillian, sweep forward and engage. Watch for Luko's crossfire. I will follow.'

'Yes, sir.' Sarpedon could hear the smile in the sergeant's voice. He knew what was coming.

Sarpedon slammed back-first against an upright stanchion for cover while he focused. The enemy's weakness was moral – there might be many hundreds of them but they were degenerates and weak in mind, not least those untainted by mutation's stain but who nevertheless stooped to associate themselves with the unclean. His augmented hearing picked out the grind of chainblade against bone above the gunfire, as Tellos wore down the mutant he had sought out. The beast's death would weaken the enemy's capacity to fight. Sarpedon would finish it off.

Givrillian's squad flowed around him and he heard the plasma gun belch a wave of ultraheated liquid into the enemy flank, skin crackling, limbs melting.

What did they fear? They would fear authority, power, punishment. That was enough. He shifted the grip on his bolter so he had a hand free to draw the arunwood force staff from its leather scabbard. Its eagle-icon tip glowed as its thaumocapacitor core flooded with psychic energy. He concentrated, forming the images in his mind, piling them up behind a mental dam that would burst and send them flooding out into reality. He removed his helmet and set it on a clasp at his waist, taking a breath of the air – greasy, sour, recycled.

He stepped out into the battlezone. Givrillian's squad had torn the first rank of mutants apart, and they were now crouched in firepoints slick with deviant blood as return fire sheeted over their heads. Mutant gangs were scuttling and slithering through the debris, moving to outflank and surround them. Tellos had the beast-mutant on its knees, one horn gone, huge blade chipped and scarred by the assault sergeant's lightning-quick chainsword parries.

Sarpedon strode through it all, ignoring the autoshells and lasblasts spattering across the shadowy interior of the hub.

He spread his arms, and felt the coil of the aegis circuits light up and flow around his armoured body. He forced the images in his head to screaming intensity – and let them go.

The Hell began.

The closest mutants, at least two hundred strong, were thirty metres away, firefighting with Givrillian's Marines. Their firing stopped as they stared around them as tall shrouded figures rose from the floor, carrying swords of justice and great gleaming scythes to reap the guilty. Some bolted, to see hands clawing from the shadows, hungry for sinners to crush.

Bat-winged things swooped down at them and the mutants ran screaming, knowing their doom had come to punish their corruption at last. They heard a deep, sonorous laughter boom from somewhere high above, mocking their attempts to flee. The waves of fire broke as the mutants fled back through their own ranks, sowing disruption amongst their own for a few fatal seconds.

Sarpedon leapt the barricade with the nearest of Givrillian's Marines and stormed across to the mutant strongpoint. Most of the enemy still gawped at the apparitions boiling out of the darkness. A swing of his force staff clove through the closest two at shoulder height – he could feel their feeble lifeforces driven out of their bodies even as the staff tore through their upper bodies with a flash of discharging energy. The burst of psychic power knocked three more off their feet and they landed hard, weapons dropped.

The Hell. A weapon subtle but devastating, striking at the minds of his enemies while his brother Marines struck their bodies. In the swift storming actions that the Soul Drinkers had made their own, it bought the seconds essential to press home the assault. It worked up-close, in the guts of the fight, where a Soul Drinker delighted to serve his Emperor.

Three of Givrillian's Marines, more than used to Sarpedon's conjurations after years of training and live exercises, pointed bolter muzzles over the mutants' makeshift barricade and pumped shells into the fallen, blasting fist-sized holes in torsos. Several more Space Marines knelt to draw beads on the hordes of mutants thrown into confusion by the sudden collapse of their front line. Shots barked out, bodies dropped.

A tentacle flailed as its owner fell. Something with skeletal wings jutting from its back was flipped into a somersault as a shell blew its upper chest apart.

Sarpedon stepped over the defences and swung again, swiping a worker/soldier in two at the waist as he tried to scramble away. Givrillian appeared at Sarpedon's shoulder, his bolter cracking shots into the backs of fleeing enemies. Assault Marines leapt past them and sprinted towards the mutants ranged towards the back of the hub. Tellos's armour was slick with black-red gore.

A hand clapped Givrillian's shoulder pad – it was Luko. In an instant the two tactical squads had joined up to form a fire line and chains of white-hot bolter fire raked around the Assault Marines, covering them as they did their brutal work. Some mutants survived to flee – most died beneath the blades of Tellos and his squad, or hammered by the fire from Givrillian and Luko. Their screams filled the hub with the echoes of the dying.

The enemy had broken completely and the spectres of the Hell strode amongst the panicking mutants as the Marines slaughtered them in their hundreds.

It was how the Soul Drinkers always won. Break an enemy utterly, rob him of his ability to fight, and the rest was just discipline and righteous brutality.

Givrillian caught Luko's hand in a warrior's handshake. 'Well met,' he said. 'I trust your men are blooded?'

Givrillian removed his helmet, glancing around. 'Every one, Luko. A good day.' Givrillian had lost half his jaw to shell fragments covering the advance on the walls of Oderic, and he scratched at the swathe of scar tissue from cheek to chin. 'A good day.' He looked out to where Tellos's Marines were picking their way across the heaps of mangled dead. The kill had been immense. But now, of course, the whole star fort would know they were here.

'Sergeants, your men have done well thus far,' said Sarpedon. 'We must not give the enemy pause to recover. How are we for an advance on objective two?'

'The cargo ducts to port look better-maintained,' replied Luko, gesturing with his clawed hand. 'Enemy forces will be using them soon. If we bear to starboard we'll avoid contact and give them less time to form a defence around the shell.'

Sarpedon nodded, and consulted the holoslate on the speediest route to the sphere. As the other Soul Drinker units thrust deeper into the star fort their hand-held auspex scanners were piping information about the environment to one another, so each leader had a gradually sharpening picture of the star fort's interior. The holoslate display now showed a wider slice of the star fort, and several paths through the tangle of corridors and ducts were tagged as potential assault routes towards primary objective two.

Intelligence on the objective was slim. Its most likely location was a shell, an armoured sphere suspended in the heart of the station, two kilometres from their position. The star fort had once been an orbital defence platform, and the shell had protected its command centre – barely large enough for one man, the Van Skorvolds were probably using it as an emergency shelter.

Primary objective one was being dealt with by forces under Commander Caeon himself – responsibility for objective two fell to Sarpedon. This was to enable him to make command decisions regarding the use of his psychic powers, which were considered essential in an environment such as the star fort. Sarpedon absolutely would not countenance a failure to take objective two, not when the prize was so great. Nor when Commander Caeon had given the responsibility to the Librarian when he could easily have picked a company captain or Chaplain for the role.

Once the two primary objectives had been taken, the information gleaned from them should be enough to allow for the final thrust on to the Objective Ultima.

And if it was Sarpedon who took the prize… He fought here for the Chapter, for the grand plan of the Emperor of Mankind, and not for himself. But he would be lying if he told himself that he did not relish the chance to see the true object of their attack first, to take off his gauntlet and hold it as Primarch Dorn had done.

The Soulspear. For the moment, it was everything.

'We pull Dreo's squad back from the environment shaft,' he began, red lines indicating paths of movement on the holoslate's projection. 'They are our rearguard. Tellos takes the lead into the starboard ducts and through the habs.' The holoslate indicated a series of jerry-built partitions, possibly quarters for lower-grade workers, possibly workshops. 'There's a channel leading further in, probably for a mag-lev personnel train.'

'We could take it on foot if we blow the motive systems,' added Givrillian.

'Indeed. There's a terminus a kilometre and a half in. Our data thins out there, so we'll meet up with the rest of the secondary force and work out a route from there. Questions?'

'Any more of those?' asked Tellos, jerking a thumb at the steaming, bleeding hulk that he had left of the mutant-beast.

'With luck,' said Sarpedon. 'Move out.'

The secondary elements – an apothecary, Tech-Marine and dozen-strong serf-labour squad – were already arriving at the beachhead near the hull. Sarpedon voxed the Space Marines left stationed there to join up with Dreo at the rendezvous point and follow his advance.

The Space Marine spearhead moved out of the cargo hub at a jog, leaving thousands of mutant corpses gradually bleeding a lake of blood across the floor. It had been slightly over eight minutes since the attack began.

NEITHER THE SOUL Drinkers' Chapter command nor the Marines in the assault itself knew anything of the Van Skorvolds save intelligence relevant to the strength and composition of any likely resistance. Everything else was beneath their notice. The Guard units transported by the battlefleet knew even less about their opponents, knowing only that they were part of a hastily-gathered strike force readied to act against a space station. But there were those who had been watching the Van Skorvolds very closely indeed, and through a number of clandestine investigations and carefully pointed questionings, the truth had gradually emerged.

Diego Van Skorvold died of a wasting disease twelve years before the Soul Drinkers' attack on the star fort. His great-grandfather had purchased the star fort orbital defence platform at a discount from Lakonia's cash-starved Planetary Defence Force, and proceeded to sink most of the Van Skorvold family coffers into converting it to a hub for mercantile activity in the Geryon sub-sector. Succeeding generations gradually added to the star fort as the manner of business the Van Skorvold family conducted became more and more specialised. Eventually, there was only cargo of one type flooding through its cargo ducts and docking complexes.

Human traffic. For all the lofty technological heights of the Adeptus Mechanicus and vast engineered muscle of the battlefleets, it was human sweat and suffering that fuelled the Imperium. The Van Skorvolds had long known this, and the star fort was perfectly placed to capitalise on it. From the savage meat-grinder crusades to the galactic east came great influxes of refugees, deserters and captured rebels. From the hive-hells of Stratix, the benighted worlds of the Diemos cluster and a dozen other pits of suffering and outrage came a steady stream of prisoners – heretics, killers, secessionists, condemned to grim fates by Imperial law.

Carried in prison ships and castigation transports, these unfortunates and malefactors arrived at the Van Skorvold star fort. Their prison ships would be docked and the human cargo marched through the ducts to other waiting ships. There were dark red forge world ships destined for the servitor manufactoria of the Mechanicus, where the cargo would be mindwiped and converted into living machines. There were Departmento Munitorium craft under orders to find fresh meat for the penal legions being bled dry in a hundred different warzones. There were towering battleships of the Imperial Navy, eager to take on new lowlives for the gun gangs and engine shifts to replace crew who were at the end of their short lifespans.

And for every pair of shackled feet that shuffled onto such craft, the Van Skorvolds would take their cut. Business was good – in an ever-shifting galaxy human toil was one of the few commodities that was always much sought after.

And then Diego Van Skorvold died, leaving his two children to inherit the star fort.

Truth be told, there had been rumours about old Diego, too, and one or two of his predecessors, but they had never come to anything. The new siblings were different. The tales were more consistent and hinted at transgressions more grave. People started to take notice. The rumours reached the ears of the Administratum.

Pirate craft and private launches had been sighted sneaking guiltily around the Lakonia system. The star fort's human traffic was conducted under the strict condition that all prisoners were to be sold on only to Imperial authorities; allowing private concerns to purchase such a valuable commodity from under the noses of the Imperium was not to be tolerated.

And there was worse. Mutants, they said, who were barred from leaving their home world, were bought and sold, and the cream skimmed off to serve the Van Skorvolds as bodyguards and work-teams. There were even tales of strange alien craft, intercepted and wrecked by the sub-sector patrols, whose holds were full of newly-acquired human slaves. Corresponding gossip pointed darkly to the collection of rare and unlicensed artefacts maintained by the Van Skorvolds deep in the heart of the star fort. Trinkets paid by alien slavers in return for a supply of broken-willed humans? It was possible. And that possibility was enough to warrant action.

Matters pertaining to the star fort fell under the jurisdiction of the Administratum, and they were concerned with keeping it that way. The Van Skorvolds had been immensely successful, but the persistence of the rumours surrounding them was considered enough to constitute proof of guilt. The accusations of corruption and misconduct indicated that the control of the prisoner-trade lay in the hands of those who broke the Imperial law, and so it was deemed necessary that the Administratum should take control of the star fort and its business.

The Van Skorvold siblings were not so understanding. Repeated demands for capitulation went unanswered. It was decided that force was the only answer, but that an Arbites or, Terra forbid, an Inquisitorial purge would do untold damage to an essential and profitable trade. The flow of workers and raw servitor materials was too important to interrupt. It had to be done as discreetly as such things can be.

In the decades and centuries to come, Imperial history would forget most of these facts when relating the long and tortuous tale of the Soul Drinkers. Yet nevertheless, it was there that the terrible chain of events began, in the drab dusty corridors of the Administratum and in the decadent hearts of the Van Skorvold siblings. Had the Van Skorvolds picked a different trade or the Administratum persisted with negotiations and sanctions, a canny scholar might suggest, there would be nothing but glory writ beside the name of the Soul Drinkers Chapter. But, as seems always the case with matters so delicately poised, fate was not to be so kind.

'EVERYWHERE... FRAGGIN'... EVERYWHERE...'

'...crawling all over the sunside... armour, guns... monsters, all of them...'

On board the Imperial battle cruiser *Diligent*, the transmissions from the Van Skorvold star fort were increasing in number and urgency. The tactical crews clustered around the comm consoles on the bridge were tracking a dozen battles and firefights, as a small but utterly ruthless force cut their way through the mutant army of the Van Skorvold cartel.

They were the sounds of panic and confusion, of death and dying and shock. There were screams, sobs, orders shouted over and over again even though there was no one left to hear them. He could hear them fleeing – they were the sounds of bolter shells thunking into flesh and chainsword blades shrieking their way through bone.

They were also the sounds of Iocanthos Gullyan Kraevik Chloure getting rich. It wasn't about that, of course – it was about safeguarding the economic base of this sector and rooting out the corruption that threatened Imperial authority. But getting rich was a bonus.

And, of course, most of them were only mutants.

Consul Senioris Chloure of the Administratum could see little evidence of the carnage within the star fort through the viewscreen that took up most of the curved front wall of the *Diligent's* bridge. Magnified inset panels appeared in the corners to pick out something the cogitators decided was interesting – plumes of escaping air and squat ribbed cylinders of large ship-to-ship assault pods emblazoned with the golden chalice symbol of the Soul Drinkers Chapter.

Space Marines. Chloure had spent decades in service to the Imperium and yet he had never seen one, confined as he was in the drudgery and isolation of the Administratum. Grown men talked of

them like children talk of heroes – they could tear men apart with their
bare hands, see in the dark, take las-blasts to the chest without
flinching, wore armour that bullets bounced off. They were three
metres tall. They never failed. And yet Consul Senioris Chloure, in
charge of the mission to cleanse and seize the Van Skorvold star fort,
had managed to engineer their presence here and let them do the job
for him. Chloure had a three-cruiser battlefleet supported by one
Adeptus Mechanicus ship, and if he played this right, he wouldn't have
to use them until it came to cleaning up.

There was a moment of gloom as the screens and lights on the bridge
dipped to acknowledge the figure arriving on the bridge. Chloure
looked down from the observation pulpit to see Khobotov, archmagos
of the Adeptus Mechanicus, enter flanked by an honour guard of
shield-servitors, another gold-plated microservitor scurrying in front
paying out a long sea-green strip of carpet for the magos to walk on.
Three or four of those damned sensor-technomats droned in the air on
hummingbird wings, trailing wires like cranefly legs – Chloure hated
them, their chubby infant bodies and glazed cherubic faces. They were
sinister in the extreme and he felt sure Khobotov affected them to
inflict uneasiness on whoever had to meet him.

Chloure had spent long enough in the Administratum – that huge
and complex institution which tried to smooth the running of the
unimaginably vast Imperium – to know the value of politics. The
Adeptus Mechanicus had wanted a part in the subduing of the
rumoured heretics of the Van Skorvold cartel, and the representative
they sent to join the battlefleet was Archmagos Khobotov and his ship,
the *674-XU28*.

Chloure had been willing to suffer Khobotov's inclusion in the mission to grease the wheels between the Administratum and the
Mechanicus, but he had begun to wish he hadn't. The Mechanicus was
essential to the running of the Imperium, constructing and maintaining the arcane machinery that let mankind travel the stars and defend
its frontiers, but they were so damn strange that their presence sometimes made Chloure's stomach churn. The *674-XU28* was almost
entirely silent, so the first warning crews had that Khobotov was paying
them a visit was usually when the archmagos swept onto the bridge.

Chloure rose from the pulpit seat, smoothing down his black satin
greatcoat. He took the salute of Vekk, his flag-captain, as he trotted
down the main bridge deck with its swarms of petty officers and
lexmechanics. Khobotov himself was a complete enigma, swathed in
deep green robes with ribbed power cables leading out behind him
from beneath the hem. Tiny motorised sub-servitors held the cables in

silver jaws and whirred around, keeping the cables from snagging on the rivets and consoles jutting from the deck of the *Diligent's* bridge. This caused the cables to slither like long artificial snakes, which was another thing that struck Chloure as gravely unpleasant.

He supposed he should be grateful it was the Mechanicus who had insisted on coming along. The puritans of the Ecclesiarchy or inflexible lawhounds of the Adeptus Arbites would have been more hassle and less use.

Chloure did what the Administratum had taught him to do many years before – grin and bear it, for the good of politics.

'Archmagos Khobotov,' he said, feigning camaraderie. 'I trust you have heard the good news.' One of the technomats buzzed past his head, a leathered tome clutched in its dead-fleshed hands, and he resisted the urge to swat it away.

'Indeed,' replied Khobotov, his voxed voice grinding from within his deep green cowl. 'It is of concern to me that neither your crew nor mine detected their approach.'

'They have fine pilots, as does any Chapter. And I hear this is the Soul Drinkers' speciality, rapid ship-to-ship swashbuckling and all that. I'd wager the Van Skorvolds didn't realise they were coming either.'

'Hmmm. I take it this indicates your intelligence was accurate regarding the artefact's location.'

'We'll see soon enough. Hopefully by the time they've finished our Guardsmen will only be fulfilling an occupational role. Save us assaulting the place ourselves.' Chloure remembered he was still maintaining a big false smile, and hoped the conversation would be over soon.

'My tech-guard would have been willing to take part in a landing action, consul.' If Khobotov had taken any offence it was impossible to tell. 'My forces are compact and well-armed. But yes, for them to attack would have yielded casualties amongst my resources that could be used profitably elsewhere.'

'Yes. Good.' Chloure wished he could see the archmagos's face – was he smiling or glowering? Then it occurred to him that the tech-priests of the Adeptus Mechanicus were notorious for the levels of bionic augmentation and replacement they indulged in, and that there was no telling if there even was a face under that cowl. 'I shall… keep you updated.'

'There is no need. My sensors and tech-oracles are far superior to yours.'

'Of course. Good.'

Archmagos Khobotov swept around and led his unliving entourage off the bridge, doubtless towards the command crew shuttle bay where he would return to the *674-XU28*. The rust-red Mechanicus craft was designated as an armed research vessel, but it was a damn sight bigger and more dangerous than it sounded. Within the hold was a regiment of tech-guard, although it looked like there was room for a lot more.

Had it come down to it, it would have been those tech-guards now piling into the Van Skorvold star fort alongside the Imperial Guard units transported by the rest of the fleet. Stationed on the cruiser *Hydranye Ko* there was a below-strength regiment from Stratix, the 37th, most of them mother-killing gang-scum who joined up for no better reason than that it would get them the hell off Stratix. The second cruiser, the *Deacon Byzantine*, contained elements of the Diomedes 14th Bonebreakers and, owing to an administrative error, a strike force of assault and siege tanks from the Oristia IV Armoured Brigade. The *Diligent* itself contained a regiment of Rough Riders from the plains of Morisha, deeply unhappy at being separated from their horses who were wintering several systems away.

Three cruisers, not of the highest quality but recently refitted and with well-drilled crews. It wasn't much compared to the immense battlefleets that scoured the void in times of crusade or invasion, but it had been all Chloure could muster through string-pulling and favour-calling in a short period of time. He had to secure the star fort and its lucrative trade before some other Imperial authority came sniffing around. And if it paid off he would be in charge of the star fort for the rest of his life, content and comfortable, as a reward for the seemingly endless drudgery he had undergone, pushing papers and running errands in the Emperor's name.

And now it seemed the Guardsmen and tech-guard would be more than enough, for his biggest gamble had paid off. The information that the Soulspear was on board the star fort had travelled exactly as he hoped it would, straight to the ears of the Soul Drinkers Chapter. Judging by the displacement of the small Astartes fleet anchored on the far side of Lakonia and the number of corvus assault pods, their number was estimated to be above three hundred.

Three hundred. Smaller Marine forces had conquered star systems. Of course, officially their presence here was fortuitous and Chloure didn't have the authority over them that he did over the battlefleet. Space Marines were famous for their autonomy. But the Soul Drinkers were so honour-bound that their reaction to the information on the Soulspear could be predicted exactly. Chloure had known they would ignore his fleet and make their own attack, sweeping through the star fort as they searched for their antique trinket. When they found it they would leave as quickly as they had arrived, leaving the star fort filled with bodies and ripe for occupation by the Guardsmen.

Warming as these thoughts were, Chloure couldn't stop his skin from crawling as Archmagos Khobotov's technomats droned past. Soon the star fort would be taken in the name of the Administratum, the risk would be over, and his future would be secure. And he wouldn't have to talk to that Mechanicus spectre again.

YSER HAD HIDDEN as soon as the first shooting started. At first it had been relayed over the cull-team's communicators – scratchy, distorted screams and dull crumps of bullets spattering into flesh. There was confusion and anger, but for a change none of it was directed at Yser or his flock. Something new had appeared, something terrible. Giants, they said. Giants in armour, with guns and swords, swarming without number from the sunward side of the star fort. They were everywhere at once.

Yser peered between the mouldering packing crates where he had hidden in the corner of the maglev terminus. He had hoped to steal some food from the lumbering supply carts as they hummed down the maglev rail towards the heart of the star fort, but the cull-teams were out and he had been cornered. He had felt sure they would take him this time – they were brute-mutants, afflicted with a semi-stable strain of uncleanliness that let their muscles bulge out of control. They stomped across the sheet metal of the maglev deck, beetling eyes peering into the shadows, shotguns and spearcannon clutched in their massive paws. Yser hadn't minded that much – it was a worthy way to die, trying to keep his flock alive, striving to continue the dutiful worship of the Emperor. What else did he have?

Then the reports came in. Word was that Mirthor was down, which was in itself impossible – the Van Skorvolds had appointed Mirthor the chief of their close-knit mutant bodyguard solely because it was reckoned absolutely nothing could kill him. He was an immense horned monster, twice the height of the tallest man, and yet they said he was dead, cut to pieces by armoured giants who bled from the shadows and had the spirits of vengeance on their side.

Impossible. But for Yser to have gone from violent petty thief to a priest ministering to the faith of a flock of escaped slaves was also impossible. Yet Yser had done it, praise to the Architect of Fate. Yser wondered if there was a miracle unfolding in the depths of the star fort – or, indeed, if the Emperor would let him live long enough to see it.

The brutes began to select fire points as the reports put the attackers closer and closer, and suddenly the crump of gunfire was real, echoing from the cargo ducts and recycler shafts snaking away from the terminus.

More arrived. Danvaio's lot, mostly with minor mutations that made them ugly and bitter, and a bunch of unaltered humans from the dock work-gangs in the dark green uniform of the Van Skorvold army. Yser could hear the voices ugly in their throats – they had tooled up with whatever weapons they could find and mustered here, because the attackers were heading this way and they were damned if that bitch Veritas Van Skorvold was going to have their heads because they ran instead of fighting.

They were still arguing over what to do when an explosion ripped into the side of the great maglev platform.

Yser reeled in shock and slumped onto his back, ears screaming, a white patch blotting his vision. As it cleared he could see the wash of blood spattered over the platform where Danvaio's mob had caught the worst of it, their incomplete bodies slumping over the plasticrete rubble.

And he saw them. Clad in purple trimmed with bone, holding heavy squat guns or whining chainswords almost as long as Yser was tall. He thought there was some trick of the light, but no, these men really were that tall – they topped out as tall as the bigger brutes, and their armour gave them immense bulk. There were a dozen of them perhaps, sprinting across the terminal space to rush the makeshift defences. Someone fired back but the few shots that hit spanged off their armour. Guns opened up in reply and tore through plasticrete and flesh alike, a half-dozen normals shredded in a second.

He had seen them before, in the waking dreams when the Architect had first come to him and answered his plight. They were His chosen, the warriors of justice, whose unending battle would redeem humanity's sins and lay the foundations for His great plan. Could it be? He had thought it a legend, something that would come to pass long after he had died. Was it happening now? Was the Architect of Fate really sending his warriors here, to save Yser's flock?

More of them were pouring in at a sprint as the first wave slammed into the defenders, mutant and normal alike sliced or riddled with explosive shells. The warriors dived over barricades into the teeth of blades and work-axes. Amongst those now arriving was one without a helmet, shaven-headed with a battered, yet volatile face, around whose skull played a blue-white corona echoed by that around the top of the mighty staff he carried. The chalice symbol on the shoulder pad of every man's armour was echoed on this warrior, but chased in gold. Sparks flew as his feet hit the floor and he raced with his brothers into the fray.

As Yser cowered he saw more and more mutants pouring from the maglev tunnels. He knew the voice of Veritas Van Skorvold herself would be stinging the ears of those with communicators, demanding they make their lives worth something by giving them to defend her star fort. He saw crews from the hunt gangs, who tracked runaway slaves through the star fort with their stalked eyes or sensitive antennae, running right into the teeth of the warriors' gunfire and being shredded to bloody rags. He watched the bare-headed warrior raise his staff and unleash a storm of power, which coalesced into shadowy shapes that descended on the hordes of arriving mutants and put them to flight.

Yser had never seen such slaughter. Those of his flock who had been caught by the cull-teams had been surrounded and butchered or killed while they slept, and Yser had seen many of them die – and now it seemed they were being paid back a thousandfold by the righteous warriors of the Architect of Fate. It was the deliverance of justice as Yser had dared to believe it would be, swift and merciless. The screams of the dying and the stench of blood washed over his hiding place, and when he dared peek out again he could see mountains of mutant corpses piled up against the maglev platform. The warriors, not pausing to gloat over the dead, moved swiftly on into the maglev tunnels, the bare-headed one shouting orders. Yser caught his words – they were to press on, strike fast before the defenders could get properly organised and meet them a third time, find the objective and link up with their brothers.

Then they were gone, leaving only the dead.

THE EDUCATED GUESSES had been correct. The maglev line led deep into the star fort, past cavernous generatoria and parasitic shanty-towns, right onto the doorstep of the shell. Mutant strongpoints dotted the square-sectioned maglev tunnel, but the energy weapons to the fore had cracked open gun emplacements and grenades had blown apart huddling bands of mutants. Some had communicators, and the Space Marines on point had reported a screeching female voice yelling orders through the head-sets.

The Soul Drinkers had kept moving, posting pickets to guard the route into the heart of the star fort as the Chapter serfs moved in behind the Marine spearhead. With the mutant army scattered and broken, the Soul Drinkers had passed through the increasingly intact command sector of the ancient orbital defence platform, and reached the shell.

It was thirty-nine minutes since the attack had begun.

Sarpedon checked the vox-net for Caeon's progress. The larger force of Soul Drinkers had advanced on a broader front, for primary objective one was believed to be located in the Van Skorvolds' lavish private quarters – four floors of garish decadence that were well-defended and had required an assault from many angles. There were injuries, some disabling, but no deaths. Caeon had thrown a ring of Marines around the private quarters and was in the process of squeezing the defenders – fewer mutants, and more well-armed mercenary guards – to death inside.

Good, then. Caeon would get the job done – he was an experienced and trustworthy commander. Sarpedon himself, with what was his first true command, could concentrate on his own part of the mission. The part that concerned primary objective two.

Sarpedon watched the dozen-strong work-serf gang hurrying past, one of them carrying a needle-nosed melta-saw. They were some of the thousands of Chapter serfs maintained by the Soul Drinkers for tasks too menial for the Space Marines themselves. They were stripped to the waist and covered with a sheen of sweat from their work rapidly shoring up the assault pod breaches, and from the quick march along the trail of destruction the Soul Drinkers had blazed before them.

The serfs passed into the Marine perimeter – fifty of the Imperium's finest warriors had formed a cordon of steel around the exposed section of the shell. The rest of Sarpedon's hundred-strong command either formed rings of defence further out or were organised into hunting parties to eliminate knots of mutants skulking nearby.

There had been casualties – the sheer numbers of the opposition had made it inevitable – but every one hurt when each Space Marine was so valuable. Koro and Silvikk would never see another dawn, and Givlor would be fortunate to survive, his throat transfixed by a metre-long speargun bolt. There were scores of minor injuries, fractures and lacerations, but a Space Marine could simply ignore such things until the mission was finished. It had been cold and fast. Chapter Master Gorgoleon himself would be proud.

Sarpedon watched as the serf gang prepared to bore a hole in the shell. The exposed section of the shell was surrounded by crudely wired data-consoles, charts and maps, detritus of the Van Skorvold business. Doubtless the Administratum would make much of the information in the scattered files and cigitator banks, but Sarpedon cared nothing for it. Once the Soul Drinkers had secured Objective Ultima they would leave this place and let the Imperial battlefleet outside take it over and do what they willed.

There was one way into the one-man command module housed within the shell. It was sealed, and Sarpedon knew it would take time to crack the encryption locks. That was why they had brought the serfs.

One of the work-serfs, his arms replaced with articulated tines to fit the melta-saw, hefted the huge cutting device and let a thin superheated line bore into the smooth metallic surface of the shell. Slowly a red tear dripping with molten metal was scored across the metal as an entrance was carved.

The work-serf strained to drag the cutting beam the last few centimetres, black smoke coiling from where the bionics met his shoulder. The Chapter apothecaries and serf-orderlies often practised cybernetic surgery on the work gang augmentations, and they weren't always of the highest quality. But they sufficed here, for a large section of the shell wall fell away with a loud clang.

Sarpedon stepped forward, projecting a crackling aura of power around his head. It was a simple trick, but it worked surprisingly well in cowing the weak-willed. Several of Givrillian's Marines followed him in.

Inside, the shell was clean and well-kept. It was small, enough for one or two men, but it had been stripped of the command mind-impulse units and cogitator readouts, and kitted out as a luxurious bedroom. There was a four-poster bed, deep carpets, and a dressing table with a large mirror that doubled as a holoprojector. Antique porcelain decorated the shelves running around the room, and several original paintings lined the walls, along with a finely-decorated sword that had almost certainly never been drawn from its scabbard. It was evidently intended to ensure the notable forced to shelter here did so in the comfort he was accustomed to.

That notable lay cowering on the bed, trying to hide under sheets although he was fully clothed in a powder blue velvet bodysuit with gold lace trimmings. His periwig had fallen off and lay beside the bed. His face was thin and youthful, with a weak chin, watery eyes and lank blond hair dusted with powder. A faint odour of urine rose from him, plain to Sarpedon's enhanced senses.

Primary objective two: Callisthenes Van Skorvold.

Sarpedon was a transmitting telepath, not a receiver – a rare talent, and one that was of little use in dragging thoughts out of a man's mind during interrogation. But Sarpedon suspected he would not need such trickery here in any case.

'Callisthenes Van Skorvold,' he began, 'doubtless your crimes against the Imperium are many and grave. They will be dealt with later. For now, I have but one question: *Where is the Soulspear?*'

HALFWAY ACROSS THE star fort, amongst the tapestries and chandeliers of the garish inner sanctum of the Van Skorvold cartel, Commander

Caeon's force closed in on primary objective one. The assault had been near-perfect, storming the hastily prepared defences of the Van Skorvold private chambers from a dozen directions at once, isolating pockets of defenders and annihilating them with massive firepower or lightning assaults before sweeping on to the next opponents.

Hard, fast, merciless. Daenyathos, the philosopher-soldier of Chapter legend, might have written of such an assault when he laid down the tenets of Soul Drinker tactics thousands of years before.

Bolters blazed their way through the last few chamber guards. The guards were professionals, picking defensive points with care and trying to relinquish them in good order when they had been overwhelmed. But their quality as soldiers meant only that they were compelled to die to a man in the teeth of Caeon's advance.

Commander Caeon strode past Finrian's tactical squad, whose two melta guns had burned great dripping holes through the partitions between the drawing rooms, audience halls and bedchambers. His feet crunched through the glass of the shattered chandelier and the splinters of priceless furniture the defenders had tried to use for cover.

All around smoke coiled in the air and flames crackled around the wooden panelling. The opulence of the chambers was in ruins, strewn with bodies and riddled with bullet holes. The Soul Drinkers were rising through the gunsmoke as the echoes of bolter fire died away, sweeping the muzzles of their guns across the bloodstained corridors and hunting for survivors.

'Clear,' came Finrian's voice over the vox, as twenty sergeant's icons flashed in agreement on Caeon's retina.

Caeon was an ancient and grizzled man, three hundred years old, and he kicked the bodies of the fallen guards aside with the contempt appropriate to a Space Marine hero. He had fought some of the sharpest actions in the recent history of the Soul Drinkers and taken trophies of the kraken, the ork, the Undying Ones and a dozen other species besides. He peered through the wreaths of bolter smoke, searching for primary objective one.

A couple of parlour slaves were wandering about stunned, ignored by the Marines. A thin, aged woman whimpered as she stumbled over the wreckage, seemingly oblivious to the two hundred-strong Marine force stalking through the area. A pudgy child scampered here and there, as if trying to find a way out. A couple of others were huddled in corners, seemingly catatonic. They barely registered with Caeon.

The place was desolate. There were no reports of the objective being sighted, and he was running out of time. He wanted to secure his goal and get off the star fort before he had to deal with the Administratum minions who considered themselves to be in charge here. He wasn't about to waste time having his Marines chase around like children.

There was a sharp pain in his leg, where the greave met the knee armour. He thought it must be one of his older war wounds, of which he had a score – but glancing down, he saw the pudgy bat-faced girl withdrawing her hand, something long and glinting in her palm.

How had she crept up on him? A child! A heathen serving-girl! He would never hear the end of it – not to his face, of course, but every Marine would know...

He knocked her flying with a backhanded swipe, but though she landed hard she sprang up again, her ugly little face filled with hate.

'Filth! Hrud-loving groxmothers! This is my business! Mine! How dare you destroy what is mine?'

The pain in Caeon's leg hadn't gone. It was a spreading heat winding its way deep down into the muscle.

One of Finrian's Marines – Brother K'Nell, the bone and purple of his armour blackened with melta-wash – grabbed the child by the arm and held her up so she dangled, squealing. The thing in her hand was a heavy ring, chunky gold with a thin silver dagger jutting from it. 'Digital weapon. Xenos, lord.'

A needler. The child had a digi-needler. Where the hell had she...

'Butchers! Bilespawn! K'nib-rutting gorebelchers! Look what you've done!'

The pain had turned cold and Caeon felt himself beginning to sway. He had passed out from massive wounds on the battlefield more than once, but this was different. This time, he wasn't so sure he would get back up.

Before the eyes of Finrian's squad Commander Caeon's massive frame teetered like a great felled tree and slammed to the ground.

'Ninkers! Thug-filth! My home! My life!' screeched primary objective one, Veritas Van Skorvold.

CHAPTER TWO

IT WAS A massive inverted cone of compacted superconductor circuits that speared down from the room's ceiling like a vast stalactite. Though the hall took up a sizeable proportion of the Adeptus Mechanicus ship it somehow felt low-roofed and close, such was the presence of this most ancient of machinery.

Archmagos Khobotov paused a while before beginning the ceremony, as he always did before dealing with a hallowed device such as this, to appreciate its beauty and intricacy. His bionic eyes, faceted like an insect's with scores of tiny pict-stealers, picked out magnified images particularly pleasing in their intricacy and logic. To think that the hands of mere men had made this machine! It was such wonders that inspired the magi, and the tech-priests below them, to prepare the way for humanity's capacity to create them again. It would take many thousands of years of painstaking and dangerous work, but time and hardship were beneath the notice of the Omnissiah and so they were beneath that of the truest magi.

One day the Omnissiah's great masterpiece of knowledge would be complete at last. And this time, it would not be misused as the ancients had done, for it would be protected by the expertise and secrecy of the Adeptus Mechanicus, who did not feel the capriciousness of petty emotions. This was the dream – and a fragile dream it was, for with every scrap of knowledge that slipped into eternal obscurity, humankind stepped a little further from the Omnissiah's vision of a galaxy whose great and terrible forces were controlled by man through his machines.

Yes, there was much to do. There was so little time, it seemed, and he was so busy...

The chronometers reached the appointed hundredth of a second and the one hundred and ninety-eight ceremonial servitors snapped to attention, their puckered dead skin glowing amber in the warm halo of the machine. Khobotov's artificial joints whirred as he drifted to the gap in the deck floor where a section of plating had been removed to reveal a web of cogs and gears. Khobotov knelt – he felt nothing as he moved, for he had long since cut off nerve-responses from the motive parts of his artificial anatomy – and took a small pot of six-times-blessed engine oil from within his robes. With a finger of matt-grey synthalloy he placed a symbolic smear of oil on the teeth of the uppermost cog. The mouths of the servitors dropped open and from within their throats came a rasping, clicking sound – the sound of the Omnissiah's praises being sung in binary, the language that it was said most pleased the Machine God.

Khobotov straightened and glided over to the sub-control console wired into the floor. He made the sign of Mars over its verdigris-stained casing and depressed the large flat panel in its centre. The panel lit up and printed prayer-tapes began to chatter from twin slots in the casing, ensuring that the running of even this minor part of the machine was imbued with sacred gravity.

The cogs began to grind and an expectant juddering sound came from the large power conduit running around the edges of the room and into the root of the machine's conical projector. Such was the energy required by the machine that the conduit was to pump plasma into it directly from the Mechanicus craft's engine reactors. Once the coupling system was warmed up, the machine itself could be activated.

The servitors formed a line, then a triangle, then a square, with perfect geometry, as they had been programmed. This machine was old and could not be replicated with the current expertise of the Mechanicus, and so the Omnissiah's favour had to be sought before using it. Geometric shapes and meaningful numbers were pleasing to Him, for He loved the abstractness of logic above all things, and it was right that His pleasure be sought before using His most hallowed devices.

Now, a servitor with its exposed mechanical sections inlaid in gold approached from the shadows in the corner of the hall. It entered the sacred square and handed the control sceptre it carried to Khobotov. The sceptre was a solid rod of carbon inscribed with machine-code legends in delicate scrolling lines, topped with a perfect sphere in which spun twin hollow-centred cogs, symbolic of the Mechanicus and its work. Deep inside the cylinder was a tiny filament of silicon in which were set threads of an as yet unidentified element, which were as old as the machine and formed the key which allowed its activation. How it worked was a mystery to the tech-priests – doubtless this and all other mysteries would be revealed when the Omnissiah had judged their labour to be sufficient.

Khobotov pointed the sceptre at the activation rune on the surface of the machine's cone, and a gentle choral hum filled the air. The servitors stepped swiftly into a hexagon, then an octagon as the machine charged up. Faint gold and silver shimmers flickered along the super-conductor circuits, and the coils deep inside the cone began to thrum. It was these coils, it was believed, that generated the shield against the warp.

Khobotov made a gesture of command and servitor hands three decks below slammed the plasma seals open, sending torrents of ener-gised plasma coursing through the conduit. It was newer, this technology, far less refined than the machine itself, and there were alarming howls and rumblings as the plasma surged on. Drips of plasma oozed from overstressed joints in the conduit and landed hiss-ing on the deck. But the power coupling held and delivered its payload into the heart of the machine.

The sound was a song – a beautiful harmony of coruscating power. The machine was alive.

Khobotov turned and walked towards the ramjet elevator that would take him to the crew muster deck. It was time to fetch the Machine God's servants-at-arms and prepare them for His purpose.

The teleporter was ready. By the end of this day the Omnissiah's mas-terpiece would be one step closer to revelation.

THEY SAID CAEON was going to die. Looking at him, Sarpedon was forced to admit he believed them. The apothecaries had done all they could but the needler had been loaded with a cocktail of viruses and neuro-toxins. Caeon's mighty constitution had held off most of them but there were xenoviruses that had latched on to his nervous system and wouldn't let go. Caeon's immune system was fighting so hard it was beginning to reject the commander's augmentations – soon his replacement organs would fail, the apothecaries said, and Caeon would fail with them.

Caeon lay in a side chapel leading off from the Van Skorvold private quarters. It was a little-used place, for the Van Skorvolds were anything but pious, and it was considered unsullied enough for Caeon's deathbed. Sarpedon had taken Givrillian and Tellos's squad and headed across from the shell as soon as the news of Caeon's injury had hit the vox-net. The other units of his command were holding position around the shell, and guarding a broken Callisthenes Van Skorvold. Elsewhere in the fort the situation was good, considering Caeon's injury had forced a pause in the assault – the mutant army, robbed of Veritas Van Skorvold's caustic leadership, was pinned down in knots between the two Soul Drinker positions of the shell and the private quarters.

The boldest of them had led raids against the Space Marine defences. The boldest of them had died.

Inside the small, sparse chapel the commander had been stripped of his bulky armour, which had been arranged respectfully in the corner. Mighty arms that had torn at the battlements of Quixian Obscura lay immobile at his sides, the veins standing out purple-black with venom. Hands that had broken the neck of Corsair Prince Arcudros were curled into claws of gnarled flesh. His mighty face was sunken-featured with strain. The black carapace implanted just under his skin was livid and red at the edges.

The Soul Drinkers had been on the star fort for one hour and thirty-seven minutes.

'What are your orders, commander?' Sarpedon knew the time for sentiment and mourning would come after. For now, it was cold and fast and nothing else.

'Librarian Sarpedon, I am unable to discharge my duty to the Golden Throne.' Caeon's voice should have been a low rumble of authority, but it was faint and cracked. 'I cannot fight. I am dying and I must submit myself to Dorn and the Emperor for judgement. You will recover the Soulspear.'

The Soulspear. Truth be told, Sarpedon had entertained thoughts of the circumstances that could lead to him being the one to finally hold the sacred weapon. But he hadn't wanted it to happen like this. Caeon was too great a man to lose. 'I shall fulfil your wishes and my duty to this Chapter, commander.'

'I know you will, Sarpedon. This is an unkind way to discover whether you are suited to command, but I believe you will serve your Emperor well.' The corners of Caeon's mouth were flecked with foamy blood. 'May I ask that you commend my soul to the ancients?'

Sarpedon hesitated. Caeon was great and he was suffering, and everything should be done to let him know he was dying with honour. But…

'Yours was… yours was not a warrior's death, commander.'

'Hmm. Indeed it was not.' A hint of colour flared into Caeon's face as he recalled with anger the child who had mortally wounded him. 'A treacherous slay. A moment's distraction. Be vigilant always, Sarpedon. As you cannot pray for me, learn your lesson from this. What appears to be a wretched girl-slave may be more. What seems innocent may be deadly. Do not fail as I have done here, for if it costs you your life, too, the prayers of your brothers cannot accompany you to the Judgment Halls of Dorn.'

It was a sad fate. Caeon would be at the Emperor's side in the legion of Rogal Dorn when the final battle of the endless war took place, of that there was no doubt. But he would not enter their ranks with the glorious fanfare that was his due, for he had died not by the hand of a deadly foe, but through a second's lapse of concentration. Veritas Van Skorvold was not a worthy enemy to have killed any Space Marine, let alone a Soul Drinker, and still less one of Caeon's rank, and it had been Caeon's lapse far more than Veritas's needler that had felled him. It was a measure of the man that Caeon did not argue, but accepted the results of the insult done to him in death.

Apothecary Pallas entered the side chapel. With Pallas were two orderlies, Chapter serfs carrying racks of unguent jars which Pallas would use to ease Caeon's journey into the next world. Sarpedon took his leave and stepped out into the remains of the Van Skorvold's private chambers, in which the Soul Drinkers' headquarters had been set up. His headquarters now, he realised.

Veritas Van Skorvold was forty-seven years old. She had a rare and subtle mutation that inhibited her growth and gave her the appearance of a particularly spiteful eight-year-old child. Veritas was as ruthless as her brother was weak – she placed efficiency and profit far above morality and the laws of the Imperium, and had masterminded the many illicit dealings that had made the Van Skorvold business both very rich and destined for conflict with the Administratum. She was reaping the terrible harvest of her earlier sins – her punishment would doubtless be grave indeed, and she was in considerable discomfort at that moment, locked as she was in a small side pantry. Her screamed curses were of such venom and inventiveness that her guards had to be changed hourly to prevent their moral corruption.

Outside the chapel waited Sergeant Tellos and Brother Michairas, whom Sarpedon had requested attend upon him for the Rites of the Libation. Tellos was there by virtue of acquitting himself admirably with the slaying of the mutant behemoth in the operation's first stages. Michairas, as a novice, had been attendant upon Caeon for many years before his elevation to the status of full battle-brother, and so brought a measure of Caeon's honour and authority to spiritual matters. Michairas had fought as well as his brothers in the thrust into the Van

Skorvold chambers, but it was his connection with the dying commander that caused Sarpedon to seek him out.

Wordlessly, the three strode into a small cartographic chamber, where
a large star map glimmered beneath the glass top of a table. Other hand-
drawn maps were displayed on the walls or rolled up in racks, for
Callisthenes Van Skorvold had counted such things amongst his collecting passion.

Onto the star chart table Sarpedon placed the ceremonial golden chalice that hung at his belt. It was old and despite his dutiful care of all his
equipment there was a cordon of tarnish building up around the deep
carvings. It had been presented to him upon his ascension from scholar-
novice to Librarian, more than seventy years before – a time that felt so
distant that Sarpedon sometimes wondered if he had been the same
man at all. It was as if he had always been a Librarian of the Soul
Drinkers, his life a cycle of battle and honour-reaping, his driving force
a fierce devotion to the eradication of the enemy and an unbreakable
code of martial dignity.

Michairas took a canister from his belt, the type used by the
apothecaries when transporting samples of unusual xenos the Soul
Drinkers had fought. In it was a mass of pulpy tissue, taken from the
brain stem of the huge mutant Tellos had fought and slain. It would
have been improper for Tellos to carry it himself for he had already
taken one trophy – a massive horn shorn from the beast's brow.

The bloody, pulpy matter was poured into the chalice and Sarpedon
took it in his gauntleted hand.

'Know your enemy,' intoned Tellos. They were the only words permitted to be spoken in this ceremony, an ancient and hallowed one, yet one
kept small and simple to ensure clarity of mind.

As commander, it was now Sarpedon's right to observe the soul of the
vanquished foe. He tipped his head back and poured the semi-liquid
mass down his throat. Swallowing it, he placed the chalice back on the
table and ran through the mental exercises that would begin the rite.

There was a spirit's eye inside him that saw what the physical senses
could not. He imagined it opening, drinking in the light after so much
darkness, careful not to blind it with the glare of knowledge. There was
a warm electric sensation in his stomach and he knew it was working.

He felt a film over his body like dirt that wouldn't wash off. His limbs
were clumsy and ungainly – there was an unclean taste in his mouth
and a dull churning in his ears. He glanced around the room and saw
his two brother Marines as if through a gauze, their faces distorted, the
room's many maps shifting and untrue. His organs were tight and ill-
fitting – he felt wrong, completely wrong, like a picture of a man drawn

by a child, ugly and crude. A pressure bore down on him – the rest of humanity, this whole universe, that felt such revulsion at him that it had imprinted itself on his very soul and pressed like a weight on his shoulders. He was human, but less. He was alive, but didn't feel it.

He was unclean, bathed only in shadow where the light of the Golden Throne should be. He couldn't get out – he was trapped here in this tainted existence, trapped forever. He felt panic rising in him, for he would be like this forever until death, and after death there was nothing. Nothing, just the blank finality of knowing that he was not even supposed to have been born…

With a start, he slammed the eye shut again and his vision lost its dirty tint. Michairas looked worried, for he had not witnessed the ceremony of the chalice before and Sarpedon must have appeared weak and scared in a way not proper for a Space Marine. But it had been worth it. He knew his enemy that little bit more, and knowledge was power in war.

Due to the Soul Drinkers' gene-seed the omophagea, the organ implanted in every novice during his conversion to a Space Marine, was different to that of most other Chapters. Its purpose was to absorb racial memories and psycho-genetic traces from ingested organic matter – allowing the Marine to gain intelligence on how to use the enemy's weapons, into their beliefs and morale, sometimes even battle plans and troop locations. The Soul Drinkers' omophagea was overactive compared to those of other Marines, delivering an experience both more intense and less precise. It was one of the cornerstones of the Soul Drinkers' beliefs that they could experience the thoughts and feelings of their enemies and come out sane and uncorrupted, furnished as much with disdain for their inhumanity as with knowledge of their behaviour.

And it had served well here. Sarpedon had felt the mutant's uncleanliness, the sin inherent in its existence. Huge and mighty it had been, but without duty or purpose. It believed in nothing and survived only for the sake of existing. They were better off dead – he and his Marines had done them a favour this day by sending so many of them to the inky blackness of death.

'I am well, brothers. My gratitude for attending upon this ceremony. But though the victory has been won it is not yet complete.' He flickered a retinal icon and his vox-link switched to the all-squads frequency. 'Soul Drinkers, withdraw patrols and muster inside the primary defences. It is time.'

CALLISTHENES VAN SKORVOLD had not held out for long. Once Sarpedon had picked him up by the throat and held him up against the wall of the shell, he had told them everything – the many and various crimes committed by his sister in maintaining her profits, the illicit dealings made to assemble his collection, and many other things that Sarpedon would rather not have heard. Callisthenes had proven himself to be that particular type of criminal who commits wrongs through boredom and idle curiosity rather than the urge to survive, and whose depravations become gradually worse until he is no better than the heretic in the gutter.

Sarpedon wasn't interested in any of this. But in the middle of his garbled confessions Callisthenes Van Skorvold had mentioned the star fort's brig dating from its days as a PDF orbital defence platform, which had been refurbished and expanded by generations of Van Skorvolds into a solid vault for keeping prized valuables. It was this brig that eventually became the home to Callisthenes's collection of tech and alien curiosities. This was what the Soul Drinkers had come for. And though it had cost them the life of the commander, it was where they would enter the annals of the Chapter's glorious deeds.

Sarpedon had led a strike force through the tangle of conduits and machinery and into the location of the brig. The Chapter serfs went with them, cutting gear at the ready, along with Tech-Marine Lygris. The mutant defences were, as suspected, non-existent, but they were closing in on the location of the Objective Ultima and there was no excuse for laxity. The Soul Drinkers approached the great metal slab of the brig cautiously, and in strength.

When they arrived, the things they saw were enough to take even a Space Marine's breath away.

'Do you think we could take a prize of conquest, sir?' It was Luko's voice, breaking the hush as only he could. This was only the first vault of the star fort's brig and with one glance they had seen enough decadence to elicit horror and admiration in equal measure. There was no denying it – some of this was beautiful, and that was what made it dangerous.

The floor was carpeted a deep blue and the walls hung with tapestries. Spotlights in the ceiling picked out glass display cases in which glimmered some of Callisthenes Van Skorvold's beloved collection. One case held half-a-dozen antique pistols, one an extraordinary compact melta-weapon, another with multiple barrels and a chunk of glowing crystal for ammunition. There were statues of women with insect heads and semi-humanoid figures made from petrified vines like bundles of snakes. There was a composite bow of horn and matt grey metal as long as a Marine was tall, with a quiver of arrows tipped with barbed reptilian teeth, and a suit of armour made with sheets of diamond and silver links.

The Marines waited for Sarpedon's lead. He stepped through the massive brushed metal vault door and into the room, his psychically sensitive mind fairly humming with the cold, sharp resonances of rarity and high technology. He felt uncomfortable – there was too much unknown here, too much forbidden. He decided that much of this would be taken to the flamer as soon as they were done, and that Luko would be castigated for suggesting the Chapter sully itself with xenos tech and forbidden devices, even in jest. They were no experts in archeotech, and they had no way of knowing what was dangerous. Better destroy it all than risk impurity.

'Librarian Sarpedon?' came a voice over the vox-net, crackling with distortion as the signal passed through the massive bulkheads of the star fort's inner structures. 'Squad Vorts. We're encountering civilians here.'

'Civilians?'

'Cargo, sir. Slaves or prisoners.'

'I thought there was no cargo on the star fort. There were no transports docked.'

'Must be runaways, sir, escaped from the transports. We've got a civilian named Yser, seems to be some kind of priest for them. Sounds like they want to help.'

Vorts and about half the Soul Drinkers were deployed in concentric rings of mobile defence around the vaults. There was little danger of the shattered defenders mounting a concerted counter-attack but the Marines had already lost a commander to a treacherous slay and no more chances were being taken. The assault had taken place when there were no large prisoner transports docking to avoid cargo humans getting in the way, but it seemed like there were some on the station anyway – runaways who had made their homes in the guts of the station.

Sarpedon didn't have time for this. He wanted to end this now, before the dark clouds gathering over the mission began to rain further misfortune. 'Relay to all defensive units. Keep civilians clear. We shall be gone soon and we can ill afford complications. Leave any dregs for the Guard to deal with.'

A sequence of acknowledgement runes flickered. A troop of serf-labourers and Tech-Marine Lygris had filtered through the exhibits and were working on a couple of massive techno-locked doors at the far end of the first hall.

The labourers kept their eyes from the exhibits, knowing that undue curiosity would earn them the severest of reprimands. They were a good example of what even lesser-quality humans could do, thought

Sarpedon – owned by the Chapter from birth and schooled to respect their superiors in all things. A crypto-drone skimmed behind Lygris and settled like a fat insect on the glowing runepad of the first door, bands of light across its curved metal body flickering as it worked on the door code algorithms. There was a beeping sound and a deep thunk as the restraining bolt drew back.

As the serfs attached chains to the door and prepared to haul it open, Sarpedon glanced again at some of the objects Callisthenes had assembled. Beside him hung a banner seemingly woven from hundreds of shades of human hair, and a perfect replica human skull carved from deep crimson stone the lustre of jade. Callisthenes Van Skorvold had collected an astounding range of forbidden objects in his lifetime – how many alien slavers and noble degenerates had he dealt with to do it?

Sarpedon could not deny many of these things were beautiful, but he could feel the corruption that surrounded them. These trinkets would not deceive the Emperor's chosen warriors as they had Callisthenes Van Skorvold.

The door was open. At Sarpedon's signal the closest tactical squads stalked carefully through the vault, wary of traps or ambushes. He would not put it past the Van Skorvolds to sacrifice some of their prized possessions just to spite the Emperor's servants.

The door opened on a corridor lined with cages in which scuttled a small alien menagerie, hooting and chittering. Sarpedon stopped the tactical squads and waved forward Brother Zaen, flamer-bearer in Luko's squad. Zaen stepped carefully into the corridor past eight-legged monkeys and birds with feathers of glass. Sarpedon saw a pair of servitors trundling along the carpeted floor of the corridor, simple waist-high automata designed to deposit pellets into feed bowls and scrape the cage floors free of excrement. It had doubtless pleased Callisthenes Van Skorvold to have a private zoo beyond the doors of the brig, maintained by servitors, where even servants would not be permitted.

'Threat nil,' voxed Zaen.

Sarpedon followed him and felt the crude thoughts of the animals. He could not receive any impressions from intelligent creatures, for he was a transmitter rather than a receiver and intelligence was too complex and fluid for him to pick up. Nothing here had enough cunning to do them harm from within their cages. He considered flaming them anyway, but that would slow them down and he wanted the objective recovered as quickly as prudence would allow. A tiny pair of sapphire-blue eyes glared at him from within a symbiotic knot of snakes and something half-plant whumped at him dolefully. Callisthenes had strange tastes.

The corridor opened up into a room with walls of brushed steel, large but shadowy and sparse. A single spotlight shone down on a simple table in the centre of the room.

On the table was the Objective Ultima: the Soulspear.

THE STORY WAS carved into the walls of the chapels and meditation cells throughout the fortress-monastery that was spread out across the Soul Drinkers' fleet. It was the first thing the recruits learned before they were ground down by punishing training and volatile chemo-engineering until there were but a handful left fit to become novices. In the origins of the Chapter could be found the seed for the fierce martial pride that became a fundamental part of every Marine. Without it, they were less than nothing. With it, they could not be stopped.

Rogal Dorn, the perfect man created by the Emperor as the greatest of his primarchs, gave his genetic blueprint to the Imperial Fists legion that followed him like sons into battle. Ten thousand years before Sarpedon first shed his novice's habit and took up the armour of a full Soul Drinker, the Imperial Fists had fought on the very battlements of the Emperor's Palace on Terra against the besieging forces of the Traitor legions under Horus. Abbots taught children the tales of that terrible conflict in the schola progenia, and it became legend to the untold billions who swore fealty to the Imperium.

When Horus was slain and the rebellion broken, the remaining loyal legions were broken up into Chapters so no man would have power over so many Space Marines at any one time. Dorn knew the pride his sons took in the glory of the Imperial Fists, and fought to have his legion left intact. But he bowed to his fellow primarchs, and his Marines became a multitude of Chapters, one retaining the name of the Imperial Fists, the others taking on new names and heraldry, ready to forge new paths into Imperial history.

Crimson Fists. Black Templars... Soul Drinkers.

To each of them was given a symbol of their sacred purpose, gifted by Dorn himself so they would remember that his spirit was with them always, that his glory was theirs also. The Soul Drinkers, formed from the fleet-based shock attack elements of his legion, received the Soulspear. Dorn himself had found it on a dark and lonely world during the Great Crusade – with it he had speared great warp-beasts and from it had hung his banner on a hundred worlds reconquered in the Emperor's name.

Such a tale was taught to the recruits brought in by the Chaplains before they were put through the savage meat grinder of selection, so they would have some inkling of the ideals for which they were suffering.

Sarpedon had been taught it himself, as had all the Marines under his command. He had come through the fire and the agony of selection and training, received the Space Marine's new organs and psycho-doctrination. Through it all, the Soulspear had been a symbol to hold on to – and for his generation, something more: a reason for vengeance, a catalyst for the sacred hatred that served a Marine so well in the fires of battle.

For the Soulspear had been lost for a thousand years, since the Soul Drinkers' flagship *Sanctifier* had been lost on a warp jump. Now it had been found in the collection of a degenerate who had no comprehension of its true significance. With their commander dying, it was Sarpedon who would bring it back to his Chapter's embrace.

THE SOULSPEAR WAS as long as a man's forearm, gloss black, and inlaid with intricate circuitry that shifted and changed before the eye. There were smooth indentations where fingers far larger than a normal man's would fit, each one with a laser-needle surrounded by a ring of gene-sensitive psychoplastic.

Even Callisthenes had seen enough in its simple elegance to give it a chamber to itself. But to Sarpedon it shone like a beacon of hope, rage and righteousness, as if everything he had fought for – his Emperor, his primarch, the place of mankind at the head of the galaxy and the sacred plan that would lead to humanity's ascendancy – was embodied in this one sublime artefact.

Zaen froze beside him, and Sarpedon could sense he was holding his breath in awe. The Tactical Marines following were similarly dumb-struck.

'Prep the corvus pods to disengage,' he voxed quietly. 'We have found Objective Ultima and are ready to withdraw.' Then, on the local frequency – 'Squad Luko, Squad Hastis, with me. Honour guard duty.'

Then, the world turned black.

HE SHOOK THE darkness out of his head and tried to get his bearings – he was down on the floor, half-lying on his back with Zaen beneath him. He heard confusion welling up around him as his inner ear recovered from the massive shockwave of noise that had washed over him.

A bomb? That would be just like the Van Skorvolds. But the Tech-Marines had swept the place. It was possible but unlikely. What, then?

His vision returned and the dimness sharpened before him. Then light, bright and sudden. He hauled himself further upright and saw he had been thrown halfway back up the corridor – the cages were smashed and any alien creatures still alive were scampering about in confusion. He could hear the pinking of breaking glass as Marines picked themselves up from the glass-strewn floor of the first chamber, where they had been blasted back through the display cases.

There were figures moving ahead. Dark, cloaked, a dozen of them crowding the Soulspear room. Rust-red with hooded faces.

Not a bomb then… a teleporter – but how? Teleporter technology was rare in the extreme, and the Soul Drinkers' own such devices had not worked for centuries. Not only that, but this was a small, precise target in the heart of a large and complex space station. It was madness, no one could do it.

There was a greasy reek in the air and Sarpedon spotted knots of twitching flesh on the floor of the room, tangled with scraps of dark red fabric and twists of metal. Some of the arrivals had not arrived intact: whoever had activated the device had been willing to lose some men in getting them here.

Sarpedon was quickly on his feet, bolter in hand. Zaen had landed heavily and Sarpedon could hear Marines clambering over him to follow – the thrum of a plasma pistol sounded as one of Hastis's Assault Marines prepared for action.

'You!' yelled Sarpedon, rage boiling inside him. 'You! By the Throne, identify yourselves!'

The nearest figure turned. Blank augmetic lenses met his gaze. A wide ribbed cable snaked from a dead-skinned mouth, ferromandibles spreading out from the upper chest and neck like insect legs. Around the hood's edge was embroidered the cog-toothed motif of the Adeptus Mechanicus, and a black-panelled heavy bolter jutted from one sleeve.

Siege engineers. Mechanicus elite. They must have been stationed with the Mechanicus ship in the battlefleet, which had not seen fit to tell Chloure's intelligence of its teleporter array.

But why?

'Nobody move! We are Space Marines of the Soul Drinkers Chapter, the Emperor's chosen, and we are here to do His will.' Sarpedon levelled his bolter, and all the Marines crammed into the corridor behind him did the same.

The engineer's heavy bolter whirred level, pointing at Sarpedon's chest. Twelve others had survived the teleporter jump and as one they took aim with lascannon, multi-meltas, and stranger weapons besides, all fitted to hardpoints wired into their bodies. If they fired, Sarpedon and the Marines around him would be shredded.

But firepower had never decided a fight. It was strength of mind, and nothing else, that won victory. Sarpedon had known this all his life. He would not fail here.

'You will return to your ship,' he continued. 'This station is under our control now, and you will be permitted to enter once we have retrieved what is ours and left. I shall assume this is a misunderstanding. Do not prove me wrong.'

Could he use the Hell, if it came to that? What did these people fear? Were they even people at all? What he knew of elite Mechanicus troops had given him an impression of emotionless, cold-blooded warriors, who could march on unconcerned as their numbers were decimated or lay down a curtain of fire for weeks without rest or respite. Did they fear anything at all in the normal, human sense?

The nearest engineer turned away again. At the centre of their number dextrous mechadendrites slid from three engineers' hoods and wrapped around the Soulspear, lifting it from the table.

They had the most sacred relic in the Chapter's history in their cold, dead, wretched grasp. This was dangerously close to blasphemy.

A crackling corona of blue light flared and contracted around the room, covering the engineers with a layer of ice-cold fire. Then, with a thunderclap so loud it was felt rather than heard, they were gone.

IOCANTHOS GULLYAN KRAEVIK CHLOURE was asleep when he was woken with the news. For a depressing moment he thought he was back in the Administratum habitat on the agri-world he had served for fifteen years, and that he would have to drag himself through another mindless day reviewing production quotas from the continent-sized grox farm that formed the planet's reason for existing.

Then he saw the glint of Lakonia's bright disc through the porthole of his well-appointed but dingy cabin, and remembered he was on the *Diligent*, trying to secure a future and serve the interest of the Imperium. And someone was knocking very loudly on his door.

'What is it?' he shouted, hoping he didn't sound too groggy. He had decided he didn't like space travel – sleep was disturbed by the peculiar metabolic uncertainties created by constant half-light and the random vibrations from the *Diligent's* guts.

'Captain Vekk's orders, sir. Something's come up on the scanners. It's really big.'

Chloure struggled into his plain black Administratum uniform and threw his greatcoat over the top of it. He probably looked disgraceful, but it would be worse not to bother turning up. Vekk seemed a flag-captain of reasonable competence and if this was something important he wanted to know about it. Chloure was in command of the battlefleet and he had to make sure that he was there if decisions were to be made.

'Take me to the bridge,' he told the lad outside his door, one of those young men in a petty officer's uniform who had been suckered into running errands for Vekk's crew in return for a nominal rank.

'They're in the sensorium, consul.'

'Then take me there.'

The lower crew of the *Diligent*, gangs of rope-muscled conscripts and tarnished servitors, seemed rather more busy than usual, and petty officers barked orders at every turn. They seemed to be gearing the ship up for some kind of defensive station – gun gangs were to stow munitions and the engine crews were pulling another shift off rest to open up the coolant channels. Chloure began to get nervous.

The sensorium was a transparent dome bulging from amidships, braced with gothic ironwork. The view into the void outside was distorted by the many layers of filtration to protect observers when the ship was in the warp, and the stars outside were just grey smudges against the blackness. But there was something sharper – a blue-white blossom boiled sunwards. Even Chloure could appreciate it must have been something major.

Vekk was standing in full dress in the centre of the sensorium deck, surrounded by chattering knots of lexmechanics and logisticians. One of the ship's Navigators was there, looking worried, and Chloure wondered if he had seen the anomaly with his genestrain's warp-eye before the ship's sensors. Two of the ship's complement of astropaths brooded in their robes, sightless eyes wandering. A leisure-servitor, waist height with a broad flat cranium for serving drinks, was trundling around in the mistaken belief that the important crew gathered here represented a social engagement.

'Chloure,' called Vekk. 'Good job you're here. This might be rather important.' Vekk's voice was clipped and alert. Chloure wondered if he ever slept at all. 'We picked up this little curio twenty minutes ago.' He pointed at the anomaly above them. 'It's not on the visual spectrum but the warp-reactive layer lights it up like a firework.'

'What is it?'

'A rift.' It was the Navigator who answered. He was a tall, thin man as all Navigators were. Chloure had not seen him before as, again like most of his kind, he kept himself firmly cut off from the rest of the crew in the armoured shell of his private chambers. 'It's localised, not big enough for a ship. It is also centred on the craft of our Mechanicus allies.'

'Are they damaged?' Chloure didn't want to start losing ships now, not when he was so close.

'You misunderstand, consul. The rift was deliberately created. The archmagos himself caused it to come into being.'

'How?'

'Interesting you should ask,' said Vekk. 'DiGoryan here and I were discussing the same thing. We thought it might be a subspace propulsion rig at first, those solid-state numbers they had docked at Hydraphur a few years back.'

'But that, of course, would cause infra-quantum fluctuations far beyond the range of what we are currently acquiring,' said the Navigator, DiGoryan, folding his long, intricate fingers into a steeple below his chin.

Chloure nodded. He had no idea what they were talking about. He could organise the details of an entire planetary economy, but the vagaries of warp science were simply beyond him.

'We believed it was a psychoportive weapons system powering up,' continued DiGoryan. 'But, of course, the astropaths have detected nothing that might suggest such a thing.'

'Then we realised,' said Vekk conversationally. 'It was a teleporter. The Mechanicus have brought a teleporter along with them.'

Arcane technology might not have been Chloure's area of expertise, but he had some idea of the kind of influence required to acquire a teleporter, even within the Mechanicus. Emperor's throne, what was happening? Was Khobotov attacking? Was he being attacked?

'We've got the fleet on code amber,' continued Vekk, 'just in case. But it very much looks like the archmagos has plans of his own he's not telling us about.'

'I… I shall contact him. We'll find out what he thinks he is doing.' But Chloure didn't get where he was without being slightly sharper than the average wage slave, and in truth he had already guessed.

THERE WERE TWO kinds of operation in which Space Marines might be employed. One was much more common than the other – a surgical strike. A small but – in terms of quality, equipment and leadership – vastly superior force would be sent in, perform a particular task, and get out again. The enemy would be struck hard and the weapon withdrawn before they knew they had been attacked. A foe cannot retaliate if he does not know he is fighting.

Space Marines excelled at such operations – they could deploy in an instant, move with skill and confidence through any terrain, take fire and dish it out. They were the best assault troops in the galaxy. The Soul

Drinkers specialised in ship-to-ship and drop-pod actions of this kind, and soem even said there were few Chapters amongst the Adeptus Astartes that could claim to match them. Their tactics were based on their own speed and the enemy's confusion, and as the attack on the star fort had shown, they were savagely effective.

The second kind of operation was far rarer, and a far more serious undertaking. Sometimes in the thousands of wars the Imperium might be fighting at any one time, there was an objective so vital that it had to be achieved at any cost. A strongpoint that absolutely had to be held to keep the Imperial line from breaking. An enemy-held spaceport that could not be allowed to function one minute longer. A fortress that had to fall before the armies of the Emperor were bled white at its gates. These were times when the odds were grave and the enemy undaunted, but the might of the Imperium had to prevail, when strength of mind and faith in the Holy Throne were as decisive weapons as the chainsword and the bolter. Times when Space Marines took their stand and prepared to die to the last man if necessary.

Marines were trained for the first kind of mission. But they were born for the second.

It was this thought that prevented Sarpedon's rage from turning to despair. They had done everything they could have been asked – an assault of surgical precision, far beyond the clumsy posturings of lesser Imperial forces, cutting through the mutants and criminals the Van Skorvolds had put in their path. Caeon had been lost, and a terrible loss it was, but they had secured every objective in rapid time. The warfare tenets of the philosopher-soldier Daenyathos had been followed to the letter – they had been cold and fast, fearless and merciless, just and proud and deadly.

But it had not been enough. Their prize had been snatched from them by those who dared call themselves allies. And now what had been the first kind of mission was in real danger of becoming the second.

'The insult is not done to you.' Caeon's voice was no more than a whisper, for he was slipping away. 'You are the Emperor's chosen. An insult to you is an insult to Him, and is a heresy in itself.' It pained Sarpedon to hear him like this, when once his voice commanded Marines to superhuman feats.

Chaplain Iktinos was also at his side, watching his commander dying through the impassive red eyes of his permanently fixed rictus-mask. When Caeon died – and it was when, not if – Iktinos would help administer the rites due to any Soul Drinker in death while Apothecary

Pallas removed Caeon's gene-seed for transport back to the Soul Drinkers' fleet.

Iktinos did not speak. In a moment of crisis, when not battling the Emperor's foes with the crozius that hung at his side, Iktinos was required to observe and silently judge. It was he who would report to the Chapter's upper echelons on the quality of morale and leadership shown here.

'They shall suffer for it, Lord Caeon,' said Sarpedon. 'They will know how the Soul Drinkers answer to slighted honour.'

'This is no place for a final stand, Sarpedon, here amongst the filth and mutant-stench. Do not let them trap you here, and threaten you until you back down. If you must fight, remember what we are born to do, to strike hard and fast and never look back.' Caeon spoke as if with his last breath, and his eyes slid closed. His chest heaved with laboured breathing as the jagged red lines on the pict-screens of Pallas's monitoring equipment jumped alarmingly. The poison had already robbed him of movement, and Pallas said the old hero's lungs were next.

It would not be for nothing. Sarpedon vowed then, to himself and to the ever-watching Dorn, that the Chapter would prevail and honour would be satisfied. They were but a few thousand strong, substandard Guard and Mechanicus troops, and they would quail before the threat of the Soul Drinkers.

Stop. What was he contemplating? Fighting the forces of the battle-fleet? There would be little honour in that. He and his Soul Drinkers had to acquit themselves with honour here, for they were Space Marines, the best, and had to act like the best in all things. He could not just fight to get the Soulspear back, like a common soldier. There had to be another way.

The philosopher-soldier Daenyathos, the greatest hero of the Chapter save Rogal Dorn himself, had written of the strength the Soul Drinkers could have by virtue of their mere presence. They did not have to charge into the fray to win wars – sometimes the legend that had grown up around them was enough, and the threat implicit in their existence could force an enemy's surrender without a shot being fired. Such occasions were rare – the Imperium's foes were usually too degenerate and corrupt to countenance backing down. But the Adeptus Mechanicus and Chloure's battlefleet were led by Imperial servants, who would surely understand how dangerous an angry Space Marine would be.

It would not have to be a massive threat. The Administratum, who controlled the battlefleet, wanted the star fort and little more. The Soul Drinkers would hold the fort and demand the Soulspear, relinquishing the fort only when it had been returned to them. They would have to make sure the threat was real, of course, manning the star fort weaponry and preparing defensive positions. But the Guard units and the Mechanicus troops would never dare assault, not when they realised that the Soul Drinkers held the upper hand. There would be some posturing and red tape, but the Administratum consul in command – Chloure, Sarpedon recalled from the mission briefings – would never for one moment contemplate actually facing the Soul Drinkers.

Yes, that was how it would work. They would recognise their folly and give back the Soulspear with obsequious blandishments and the Marines could travel back in triumph, with Caeon's body in state. That was how the Chapter had maintained its place at the head of mankind, by refusing to back down or kneel before the weaknesses of lesser men. They were the Emperor's chosen, and to the Emperor they would answer, not to some half-machine tech-priest tinkerer or desk-bound Administratum bureaucrat.

There had been enough fighting here. All the real enemies were dead and the Soul Drinkers' losses, though few in number, had included one of the best of them. Now it was time to resolve the threatened conflict without bloodshed, and in a way that would ensure the Soul Drinkers retained their honour and returned with their prize intact. This place had cost them enough, and once this unfortunate matter was resolved they could leave as soon as possible.

Sarpedon saluted Caeon and left the chapel, leaving Iktinos to his vigil.

He had defences to prepare.

CHAPTER THREE

THOUGH MANY OF the fleet's officers gathered on board the *Diligent* were of old naval aristocracy stock and would never admit weakness in front of the lowly logisticians and petty officers, in truth they were quietly terrified.

A holo-servitor in the middle of the bridge, its torso opened like fleshy petals to reveal a pict-array, projected a huge image in front of the viewscreen.

It was the first Space Marine most of them had actually seen outside the stained glass windows and script illuminations of the schola progenia or cadet school chapels. His face was scarred, not with obvious wounds such as the sort many naval officers wore like badges of office, but with dozens of tiny wounds accumulated over the years to form a face battered by war like a cliff face battered by the waves. It was impossible to guess his age, for there was youthful strength there alongside the wear of a lifetime, eyes brimming with both experience and child-like fanaticism. The head was shaven and from the high collar of his massive purple-black armour curved an aegis hood. The chalice symbol of his Chapter could be seen on one shoulder pad, echoed in the cup emblem flanked by wings proudly emblazoned in gold across his chest.

'We have the star fort,' he was saying in a voice that filled the bridge like thunder. 'We can defend it indefinitely. I do not have to tell you how unwise any force on your part would be.'

He had called himself Commander Sarpedon, and though his booming voice was coldly disciplined, he was clearly beyond rage. His eyes

burned out from the viewscreen, pinning the assembled officers to the
deck, and the corded muscles of his neck strained with anger. 'If you
want your prize, consul, you have two choices. You can come and get
it, in which case you will fail. Or you can return our prize to us, which
was taken as our victor's right.'

Consul Senioris Chloure was a diplomatic man. He had spent a lifetime negotiating the most delicate deals where a whole planet's
economy might rest in the details. He hoped it would be enough now.
'Commander Sarpedon,' he began, trying and failing not to be awed by
the huge image glowering down at him, 'you must understand that the
Adeptus Mechanicus are but nominally under our–'

'Our attempts to communicate with the Mechanicus have failed!'
boomed Sarpedon. 'They stole what was ours, fled to their ship and
jammed all contact. This falls to you, consul. If you cannot control the
elements of your own fleet, that is your problem, not mine. Return the
Soulspear to us or return to port without your star fort. This communication is over. Do not make us wait for a reply.'

The image winked off and the holo-servitor whirred closed. For a few
seconds there was silence on the bridge of the *Diligent*, the after-image
of the huge grizzled face still bright in the officers' minds.

'Sir?' asked Flag-Captain Vekk. 'Your orders?'

A Space Marine. Chloure had been so proud that he had managed to
engineer their presence here. It was to have been the crowning achieve-
ment to justify the comfortable future he sought. And now he was
forced to accept the possibility that it was going very wrong, very
quickly.

But that did not mean he had to let it all fall apart. He had dealt with
conflict and stubbornness before, for many years. He had spent decades
negotiating the Emperor's share. He told himself he would just have to
do it one more time.

'They hold the star fort. But they have nothing else. Their fleet is tiny,
probably only a couple of strike cruisers. We have more, and a blockade should be simple. They will be without supplies and support, and
they cannot leave the place without our permission. If it comes to a
blockade they will have to back down eventually.'

'They are Space Marines, sir. They don't need supplies…' It was
Manis, Vekk's Master of the Ordnance, who spoke.

'We have all heard tales of how they can survive on nothing but thin
air and faith, Manis. But the Emperor has chosen not to make men who
do not need to eat or breathe – the fort is based on an old-pattern
orbital defence platform that requires new recycling filters and liquid
oxygen supplies to maintain a survivable atmosphere. If we must we will

simply wait until they see sense and ask to be allowed to return to their fleet.'

'It would be simpler by far, dear consul, if we were merely to return this trinket,' said Kourdya languidly. Kourdya was the captain of the *Hydranye Ko* and had, allegedly, won his ship with a particularly dazzling hand of five-card raekis.

'I am assuming that will be the solution we arrive at, Captain Kourdya. But I don't think any of us here can truly guess what these Marines are thinking, and there is no shame in planning for all eventualities.'

THEY WERE STILL there when a petty officer – the same flustered-looking lad who had woken Chloure several hours before – scurried up to the knot of officers in front of the holo-projector.

'Officer on the bridge, sirs,' he said. 'Archmagos Khobotov.'

The bridge blast doors opened apparently of their own accord and Khobotov swept in. He was flanked by a dozen tech-guards, in rust-red flak-tabards and toting weapons of exotic design. The drones were drifting above like fat loathsome insects.

'I trust,' said Chloure, interrupting Khobotov's entrance, 'that you heard all of that.' Chloure gestured at the space where Sarpedon's face had hung an hour before.

'Indeed,' droned Khobotov.

'Then you are aware we have some questions.'

Vekk, seeing the tech-guard, had silently summoned a squad from the *Diligent's* naval security battalion, who were silently filing onto the bridge. Chloure knew enough about the Imperial Navy to appreciate that captains didn't like anyone lording it on their bridge. Vekk might be insufferable sometimes, but Chloure was glad then he had the man on his side.

'We monitored the transmission,' said Khobotov. The tech-guards around him were tightening their formation as the black-armoured naval security troopers formed up. 'Commander Sarpedon's views have been noted.'

'Do you plan to do anything about it?'

'Commander Sarpedon's force is small and ill-supplied. They are not equipped for defence. It is unlikely they can hold out against a concerted assault from the Imperial Guard and Adeptus–'

'We are not going to *attack* them, Khobotov,' said Chloure sharply. As ever, he couldn't tell if Khobotov was serious or just stalling. Would he really throw the battlefleet's combat units against Space Marines? They said tech-priests started thinking differently when there was more machine in them that human, but surely Khobotov wouldn't throw away so many lives. 'We're going to give them what they want and then forget all of this. You are still under the command of this battlefleet, archmagos, no matter how you may wish otherwise. The next time Sarpedon contacts us I want to tell him where the Soulspear is and how long it will be before we give it back to him, so I ask those questions to you now.'

Chloure had dealt with awkward customers before. He had negotiated his way through whole planets full of hostiles. But he had never had to gauge the reactions of a man who might not have been a man at all in the physical sense. Chloure had gained a feel for the tone of voice and body language that very few could conceal, but Khobotov betrayed none of those things. He would have to be firm and direct, and hope that Khobotov's view of the situation approximated Chloure's own.

'Very well.' Khobotov looked right at Chloure, who could just pick out the gleam of a lens deep within the cowl. 'The Soulspear is currently on board a high-speed heavy shuttle within warp route 26-Epsilon-Superior.'

'Destination?'

'Koden Tertius.'

Koden Tertius was a forge world, a planet owned and run by the Adeptus Mechanicus as a centre of manufacture and research. Specifically, Koden Tertius was half a galaxy away and famed for the robustness of the war engines it supplied to the Imperial armies of the Segmentum Obscura. It was also the name stencilled on the side of the *674-XU28* and from which Khobotov's tech-guards were recruited. Archmagos Khobotov was sending the Soulspear to his home world.

'I see,' said Chloure coldly. 'Would it be pointless of me to demand its return?'

'It would, consul senioris. Communications are impossible with the vessel in the warp. Once at its destination the contents will fall under the jurisdiction of the Archmagi of Koden Tertius, not your battlefleet.'

'That's why you were here in the first place, isn't it?' said Captain Kourdya from somewhere behind Chloure. 'Sly dog. You only showed up so you could steal your little toy.'

'I had imagined Consul Senioris Chloure would have deduced this for himself and hence would not need informing of the fact.' Somehow the tech-priest sounded mocking even with his monotone voice.

Chloure couldn't keep the chill out of his blood – the Soulspear was gone and this situation was dangerously close to being more than he could possibly handle. The truth was that Khobotov could do pretty much anything he liked – Chloure could not monitor his communications or exert direct authority when the *674-XU28* possessed unknown but probably superior capabilities.

It would probably be beyond even Chloure's abilities to magic the Soulspear back from Koden Tertius. But he was here to do a job, to secure Administratum control of the Van Skorvold star fort. He would see it through to the end, no matter how long it took. And then, he told himself, he would truly deserve his reward.

'I don't think we need to know anything more,' said Chloure. Flag-Captain Vekk gestured and the security troopers took a step back as the tech-guards stomped off the bridge. Khobotov was already on his way out, moving deceptively fast. He didn't walk – he glided, his robes swishing along the floor behind him. The pudgy corpse-drones followed him, attentive cherubs trailing wires.

A heavy hand was laid on Chloure's shoulder, and he smelled stale smoke and age.

Druvillo Trentius, hoary and generally disagreeable captain of the *Deacon Byzantine*, glared down at him with liquor-shrunk eyes.

'Complete gak-up this, Chloure.' They were the first words he had spoken on the bridge that day.

As the fleet's officers gathered their lackeys and headed towards their respective shuttles, Chloure fought off the feeling that Trentius was right.

YSER DIDN'T LOOK like much. The man was on the wrong side of middle age, thinned and harrowed by malnourishment. His hair and beard were matted rats' tails, his nails blackened. He had evidently made some effort to keep himself clean, but the effect had been merely to highlight the pallor of his skin. He was dressed in rags, almost bare-chested. Yet around his neck was a heavy pendant, doubtless from some decoration scrounged and punched to accept a chain – an Imperial aquila, with an eye drilled through each of its two heads so it stared out in two directions. Forward and back, the past and the future. The icon lent the man an air of holiness and purpose that Sarpedon couldn't shake from his head.

They were standing in what Yser called his church. It was a supply hopper, a massive round-ended cylinder set into the very guts of the star fort, where light was sporadic and breathable air hung in pockets around recyc-line leaks. The place had once held towering stacks of food and other supplies which would be winched up by means of an enormous cargo crane, but the supplies had long been used up or reduced to a level of detritus that filled the bottom third of the hopper.

The great four-clawed metal hand of the crane, fallen from its mountings, formed the church itself, and cargo containers had been salvaged for pews and side chambers. Tattered banners, frayed wrappings sewn together and daubed with simple symbols like children's drawings, hung from the plasteel girders. The place was strangely serene, lit by the twilight of halogen work-lamps high above them, and with the soft breeze of convection currents tugging at the banners all around.

'You are Yser?' said Sarpedon. He stood in the shadow of the makeshift church and towered over the scrawny man, who seemed to show little of the fear that men normally did when confronted by a Space Marine.

'I am.'

'A priest, you say?'

'Yes, ministering to my flock. We are few, but the Architect turns His light upon us all.'

The Architect of Fate – the Emperor, it seemed. Aspects of the Divine Emperor were worshipped all over the Imperium, where He might be the god of the seasons on a primal agri-world or the Chooser of Warriors in a gang-infested underhive. Such things were tolerated by the Adeptus Ministorum as long as they acknowledged the primacy of the Imperial cult. To Sarpedon, such fragmentation showed the inability of lesser men to comprehend the true majesty of the Emperor and His primarchs. But this man did not seem at all feeble-minded.

'Our church is not much, I grant you,' continued Yser. 'It is all we could do to survive in the depths of this station, when the cull-teams were sent down. But no longer... you have come and swept them away in turn.'

Vorts's squad was searching through the church and debris piles. As the squad who had been approached by Yser in the first place, they had been given the church and its immediate area to search and appraise. There were many useful – if derelict – recyc-lines and cargo ducts radiating out from the supply hopper that made it worth fortifying. Most of the other Soul Drinkers were prepping and manning the many macrolaser emplacements and missile clusters that were still operational, and Sarpedon wanted to ensure that routes through the station were open and secure for redeployments.

It wouldn't come to that, of course. They were up against Administratum pen-pushers and Guardsmen, who would soon back down when they considered the quality of soldier they were daring to cross. But if the star fort was to be made ready for a battle, it was worth doing properly.

Givrillian's squad were in guard positions covering the many exits to the hopper. They were functioning as Sarpedon's command squad as he moved from one part of the star fort to the other – over the last few hours he had overseen preparations on the sunward and orbitside firing arcs, and in the maglev terminal where Tellos was in command of a mobile assault company to react to any boarding actions.

Not that it would come to that. But it was worth being sure.

'I have long known that He would send His chosen to save us, to complete His plan,' Yser was saying. 'I had never thought I would see it my lifetime – but the things I have witnessed in my dreams are coming to pass.'

'How many of you are there?'

'Perhaps four dozen. We make our homes in the dark corners of this place, and gather here to worship.'

'Escaped prisoners?'

'Mostly. And one or two Van Skorvold men who grew sickened by toil in the service of corruption.'

'Ah, corruption. It is good that you and I see it in the same places here. My men are to fortify this station and we need to know of any defences we may have missed. If you wish to serve your Emperor, you will share your knowledge of the star fort's layout.'

Yser smiled. 'You are the Architect's chosen, Lord Sarpedon. I have seen you when He places His visions in my mind. Anything you ask shall be delivered as far as we are able.'

Visions. Normally talk of visions and prophecy was dangerous – Sarpedon had seen the darkness of the psyker-taint when it ran unchecked in the weak-willed and malevolent. He had seen the arcs of green lightning spearing down from the heights of the Hellblade Mountains and heard the gibbering screams of a hive-city driven mad, and known that renegade witches were responsible. Such men claimed visions and voices from their gods.

But it seemed Yser was different – thrust into the belly of this dark place, he had responded by clinging to his faith until it granted him visions of holiness. Perhaps the years here had taken too much of a toll, or perhaps he really was blessed by the Emperor's light. For now, Sarpedon was glad only that he seemed to have an ally here at last.

'I shall consult with my flock. We should be able to divert power back to some of the guidance domes, and uncover some of the servitor emplacements. There may be more – you shall know shortly, Lord Sarpedon.'

'Good. Sergeant Vorts will send his men with you.'

Yser nodded and smiled, and hurried away through the debris. It was as if he had been expecting the Soul Drinkers, and was at last able to fulfil some goal now they had arrived. Sarpedon wondered for a

moment what would happen to Yser when the Marines had reclaimed
the Soulspear and left. He would probably be consigned to the fate he
had tried to escape – mind-wiping and incorporation into a
biologically-powered servitor. A shame? Perhaps. But he was only one
man, and protocol forbade anyone to set foot on a Soul Drinkers' ship
who was not a member of, or owned by, the Chapter, so he could not
come with them when they left.

A thought occurred to Sarpedon. 'Yser!' he called out. 'You were a
prisoner. What was your crime?'

'I was a thief,' replied the prisoner-priest.

'And now?'

'I am whatever the Architect of Fate makes of me.'

THE ADEPTUS MECHANICUS ship *674-XU28* was just under one thousand
years old. Every hundred years to the day it was refitted in the dockyards of Koden Tertius with the latest rediscovered and re-engineered
archeotech and machine-spirit augmentations. A fighting force was
maintained on the craft of tech-guard, siege engineers and other, more
exotic forces, that needed constant upgrading and replacement of parts
if it was to operate at full potential.

For some time this work had been done under the supervision of
Archmagos Khobotov, for he was three hundred years old.

He believed in the primacy of the machine as the building block of
human civilisation. Machines were efficient and tireless, and possessed
cold, analytical, unfalteringly loyal personalities of the kind that
Khobotov himself was proud to rejoice in. Their dedication to the com-
pletion of the Omnissiah's lost masterwork of knowledge was the equal
of his, and through their example he would create a microcosm of
human perfection.

Apart from the tech-guard units, the *674-XU28* was crewed entirely
by servitors and tech-priests whose industriousness and knowledge-
obsession reached Khobotov's exacting standards. Between them the
Mechanicus magi that crewed the ship had barely enough flesh on their
bodies for a single man – the rest was augmentation and improvement.
Khobotov himself had lost track of how much of him was real and how
much synthetic, and he was glad, for it was one less distraction from
the Omnissiah's work. In the massive crypto-mechanical entrails of the
ship, in the corridors of gleaming glass where the ancient machine-
spirit dwelt and amongst the forests of rail driver cannon and
sensorium tines, the map of human knowledge was rebuilt. Between
the magi and the servitors, Khobotov's own rigorously disciplined personality and the dark throb of the ship's machine spirit itself was built

a web of learning that would grow and mature until the Omnissiah saw in it a part of Himself. The critical knowledge mass would be reached, a point where the learning contained in the ship would render it capable of unlocking any secret, fearing nothing, travelling beyond the prison bars of the real universe. One day, one day, when the ship and the crew and the knowledge within it would be as one, that distant day when all that had been lost in the perversions of the Dark Age of Technology would be regained...

The ship was still young. A thousand years was not nearly enough to begin such a task. And he was always busy, so busy. Sometimes it seemed too far off to even contemplate.

But then, that was just the human in him.

Khobotov glanced across at the huge muscular piston array that stood poised to wrench a vast section of hull off the underside of the 674 and cast it bleeding into space. Sometimes he was sorrowful for causing such a wound in the craft of which he was an essential component, but he knew it was for the good. The machine-spirit agreed with him, rattling the hydraulic rams and breach-charges in eagerness.

There were few servitors in the area for the near-vacuum caused their tissues to degrade, and so it was tech-priests and more senior magi who performed the rites required. This was not as delicate an operation as the most holy teleporter's activation had been, but a job was still worth doing well. Some were dark, robed figures, hunched or inhumanly shaped. Others were bright and gleaming, with the bodies of young men and jewelled decorative attachments of glass and chrome.

Let it not be said that Khobotov was an unfeeling man who had lost contact with his human instincts. He knew well the ways of ordinary men – like children or animals, they were quick to anger and quick seek comfort. They needed encouragement to commit acts of logic, and in some cases, they needed fear.

They said the Space Marines knew no fear. But they were still human. Khobotov was a man of such immense knowledge that he had no doubt he could read their actions and resolve the situation they had stubbornly created. It was simple. Give them no option but to back down. They believed themselves to be the elite of the Imperium, and so the logical way to determine their path was to give them only one option that would not require them to take up arms against that same Imperium.

He could let it go. He could return to Koden Tertius to study the Soulspear, and leave Chloure to deal with the Space Marines himself. But that would leave the Adeptus Mechanicus looking like cowards to the Soul Drinkers, and like thoughtless thugs to the Administratum. These things were not important in themselves, but Khobotov understood that they were important to other Imperial authorities. He was not a politician but the ways of humanity were simple enough for him to grasp – if he forced the Space Marines to back down they would respect the Adeptus Mechanicus as brave and powerful. The Administratum would welcome the possibility of future alliances. But these results would be beneficial to the Adeptus Mechanicus overall. It was almost childlike the way they acted, but Khobotov had to remind himself that one day, before he had trod the path of the Machine God, he had been motivated by similar concerns of politics and saving face.

So he would not let it go. The Space Marines would relinquish the star fort and the Administratum would take it over, and Khobotov would help them do it, because that it what would be to the greatest benefit to the Omnissiah's servants.

His plan was simple. The Soul Drinkers would have no choice but to give up the star fort and return to their fleet under terms of truce. Any other course would require they fight Chloure's battlefleet or Khobotov's forces themselves. They would not choose these options. They would back down.

It was simple.

Satisfied that the necessary rites and preparations had been made, Khobotov impulsed his desire to return to the archivum and continue his manifold researches. This problem, having been set up to resolve itself, would require no more of his attention. And he was so busy...

'SENSOR SWEEP TURNED up something,' said Brother Michairas. 'What do you think that is?'

Michairas was one of the Soul Drinkers manning the sensoria that studded the surface of the star fort. For the past few hours he had pulled a shift in the tiny transparent bubble looking out onto the star field and great glowing disk of Lakonia. The Administratum and Mechanicus fleet was formed of glinting silver shapes hanging in space. The object of his concern was a bright burst of white against the black.

Brother Michairas had voxed for the Tech-Marine as soon as he had seen it. A flare, again centred on the Mechanicus ship, but different this time – purely physical, like an explosion.

'How long?' Tech-Marine Lygris clambered up into the cramped sensor shell, assisted by the clamp-tipped servo-arm reaching up from his backpack.

'Three minutes.'

'Hmm.' Lygris tapped the large curved surface of the clear bubble. 'If it is a secondary explosion from attack, it is catastrophic. But these are deliberately vented gases. Not air. Pneu-retros, or air rams. And a spray of ice crystals, there are hydraulics in there too.'

'Meaning?'

Lygris glanced down at the many tarnished instruments and read-outs, noting figures that confirmed his suspicions. 'Meaning they are launching something. Something big.'

CAPTAIN VEKK HAD a habit of yelling at the servitors on the bridge of the *Diligent*. They didn't answer back, so it didn't matter that the blank-eyed thing was merely delivering the best guesses of bridge logistician corps.

'I need more than that!' he shouted. 'Is the 674 hit?'

The explosion was bright on the viewscreen above him, the image inset with different views from the fleet's other craft. The Adeptus Mechanicus ship was spewing a white cloud of vapour from its hull, a huge mass of gas and liquid growing by the second. Then he saw it. First a tiny sliver in the brightness, then growing and gaining shape. Something huge and flat – a section of the hull? A huge, intact hull section, just ripped off by an internal blast? Or…?

'I want specs on that thing, now! Size, orientation, class!'

'It looks like wreckage, sir…'

Vekk glanced at the petty tactical officer who had spoken. A glare was all it took. 'It looks like nothing of the sort. I was at Damocles Nebula, boy, I know what it looks like when you blow a chunk off a ship. I want it scanned and classed, and I want it double-quick. Move!'

It was growing more defined now. Yes, he was sure. It could be good, it could be bad. It all depended on what that cyber-freak thought he was doing.

'And somebody wake Chloure!'

THE GERYON-CLASS orbital artillery piece found brief favour amongst the forge worlds bordering the halo zone, given that the form of warfare there often involved opposing or unknown forces blundering upon one another in the depths of space. In such a situation confusion and disruption are potent weapons with which a withdrawal can be covered, or a potential enemy can be stalled while more information is sought. The Geryon-class was conceived from the start to take advantage of this with the rapid and forceful deployment of electromagnetic and magna-frag weaponry alongside conventional munitions.

It was an ordinatus-level macro-artillery piece, a huge cannon that lobbed disruption shells through the depths of space to detonate in the midst of attacking spacecraft. When mounted on an orbital platform it was the size of a small spacecraft itself. However, the Geryon-class sadly lacked any edge in conventional engagements compared to similarly sized, less specialised pieces. Its use gradually declined with the increased tendency of commanders to simply blast their way out of uncertain situations and concern themselves with niceties only after the enemy was drifting and ablaze.

It seemed that Archmagos Khobotov, however, had some fondness for the Geryon-class. Because that was what had detached itself from the *674-XU28* and was now descending into geostationary orbit several thousand kilometres from the star fort, riding on a standard artillery platform as big as a medium-sized island.

Sarpedon speed-read this information from the data-slate handed to him by Tech-Marine Lygris, and brooded. They had been at an impasse – that was bearable, because he knew his Space Marines could hold out for as long as it took. But this changed everything. This meant the Administratum fleet had the upper hand.

They knew they couldn't take the star fort, not against the Soul Drinkers. So they were going to lob macro-shells into the station until the Soul Drinkers were broken and scattered before ramming hordes of Guardsmen in to take the place. They knew they couldn't face the Emperor's chosen, but they were so petty and preening that they couldn't back down and lose face – they would rather massacre humanity's finest than admit they were wrong.

'An insult to us is an insult to the Emperor, for we are His chosen and Dorn was His foster-son,' said Sarpedon.

'Agreed, commander,' replied Lygris.

'Then these men have insulted the Emperor.'

'Indeed they have, commander.' Lygris talked in the curt, clipped way of most Tech-Marines, his voice echoing slightly in the maglev terminal which was now cleared of mutant corpses. 'Have you spoken of this with Caeon?'

'Caeon is dying, Lygris. I cannot trust him to be in full possession of his faculties.'

'A bad death.'

Sarpedon snapped the data-slate closed. 'There are too few good ones.'

But what to do now? Their ships were was on the other side of Lakonia, and would never survive an engagement with the sub-battlefleet and the Ordinatus. Extraction was simply not possible – that, of course, was the plan the Administratum and Mechanicus had doubtless concocted, to trap the Soul Drinkers like rats and butcher them from afar. Curse them, that did such evil in the Emperor's name! The

Soul Drinkers were the best men of the Imperium, and yet the Administratum and Mechanicus had first stolen from them, then dared to threaten violence to keep their prize. What could they be thinking? Didn't they know what the Soul Drinkers were, what they stood for?

Was the Imperium truly the instrument of the Emperor's will, when it was peopled by such lesser men? When the battleships and fighting men were wielded in the Emperor's name, to humiliate those who most closely followed the Emperor's plan? Sarpedon had long known there was corruption and indolence in the very fabric of the Imperium, but rarely had he seen it so starkly illustrated, and never had it put his life and those of his battle-brothers at such immediate risk.

When the Geryon-class ordinatus cannon spoke, the Soul Drinkers could be lost, all so the Administratum and Mechanicus could save face. It couldn't happen. It wouldn't happen. But how would Sarpedon find a way out? They were effectively trapped on the star fort with a massive orbital artillery piece bearing down on them and several thousand Imperial Guard waiting in the bellies of the battlefleet.

There was little doubt that Consul Senioris Chloure and Archmagos Khobotov intended to do violence to the Soul Drinkers if they did not relinquish the star fort, Soul Drinkers would not back down, not while Sarpedon still breathed.

Would they have to die, to prove that they would not accept an insult unanswered? Was that as petty as stealing the Soulspear and refusing to return it? That was not the issue here. The Soul Drinkers were the superiors of anyone the battlefleet might boast. They expected to be treated like the elite that they were.

If the Soul Drinkers had to die to show the galaxy how seriously they took the martial honour that made them what they were, then so be it.

Yet there was hope. Not because he had hit upon a plan, but because a Space Marine is a stranger to despair. There would be a way, even if it would only let them face death as warriors. The legends were true – Marines never failed, even in death.

Givrillian, who was maintaining the terminal perimeter, jogged up to Sarpedon, breaking his thoughts. 'Commander, we have a communication from Squad Vorts.'

'Routine?' Sarpedon had better things to worry about.

'No, sir. The priest, Yser, was showing them some of the orbitside workings and… well, he remembered something. Something old. He suggests you and Lygris come immediately and see for yourselves.'

* * *

WHEN SARPEDON ARRIVED he found Tech-Marine Lygris surveying what Yser had shown the Soul Drinkers. Given the decadence and ill-maintenance of the star fort it was almost the last thing Sarpedon would have expected to find. It was a fully functional, fully stocked, flight deck.

Lygris was primarily an artificer, overseeing the maintenance of weaponry and armour in the forge-ships stationed with the Chapter fleet. But like every Tech-Marine he had been appraised during novicehood as possessing a certain skill with all manner of technology, and had been thoroughly schooled in myriad branches of combat tech. He therefore knew a thing or two about attack craft.

'Hammerblade-class,' he was saying, mostly to himself. 'And Scalptakers. Throne of Earth, these should be in a museum…'

And the place could have served as a museum – a flight deck within the orbital platform architecture, like a thin horizontal fissure through several decks of the star fort, low and broad. There was very little air here and Yser had been given a rebreather array by the serf-labourers, while the Marines wore their helmets.

Where breathable air had seeped in the metal was corroded and treacherous, but most of the flight deck was intact, scorched comfortingly black with blast scars that were still there after centuries. Vivid black and yellow strips marked out complex taxi routes across the gun-metal deck, and islands of refuelling equipment surfaced here and there, hoses coiled, some with tanks still marked full.

And all around stood the craft. Some were hulks of rust, others had been stripped of anything that could pried off the fuselage. But there were plenty that looked intact – sleek and noble compared to the blunt killing weapons of more recent times, with ribbed superstructures and swept-forward wings tipped with lascannon. The Hammerblade boasted a great underslung plasma blastgun while another variant bristling with close-quarter megabolter turrets was a Scalptaker-class superiority fighter. These marks had been flagged as obsolete more than a thousand years before, when the Soulspear had yet to even be lost, and had been relegated to patrol duty around Lakonia before the platform was acquired by the Van Skorvolds.

'There was some talk from the Van Skorvolds of using them again,' Yser was saying, his breath misting against the rebreather mask. 'But it would have cost too much, I suppose, and who amongst them could have flown one of these? I and my flock used this place as a shortcut sometimes, when the air was good.'

There were other variants, too – a bloated nearspace refuelling craft, a fighter-bomber with a single-shell payload bolted to its back. Great chains of ammunition were racked at intervals across the deck, and the noses of warning-marked missiles poked up from pods below decks. Ships, fuel, ammunition...

Sarpedon had thought they were trapped, and had been ready to defend every metre of the star fort against attack. But here was another option, and suddenly he saw the possibility of his Soul Drinkers doing what they did best. The philosopher-soldier Daenyathos had written that the surest way to defend a place was to attack the enemy until they were incapable of attacking what you wanted to defend. On the flight deck was the means to put Daenyathos's words into actions.

Sarpedon turned to the Tech-Marine, and saw he was thinking the same thing. 'Lygris? Can you do it?'

The Tech-Marine gazed at the mechanical playground to which Yser had led them. 'Not on my own. Pull the others off the weapons systems and give me all the serf units, and I'll see about making some of these spaceworthy.'

'It shall be so. Vox for what you need.'

'Yes, commander. May I ask what you are planning?'

'The obvious.'

As SARPEDON WAS assembling his force and the serf-labour units were breaking backs in the halogen glare of the fighter deck, Commander Caeon died.

Chaplain Iktinos delivered the death rites all but alone. There were few required to attend when the death had not been a glorious one, and there were preparations elsewhere that had to be made. Michairas was there, and Apothecary Pallas. The rites were simple given that they were on an active battlefield – a recitation of Caeon's condensed chanson in Iktinos's monotone, detailing the moments of Caeon's fine life that had been judged fit to be recorded in the epic that every Marine compiled to record his deeds. The ceremonial taking of Caeon's gene-seed, and the reclamation of his weapons to be sealed and archived in the armoury until it was their time to enter the hands of a novice. The weapon's history would be revealed to this novice when he ascended to the position of full Marine, and would serve to emphasise the gravity of his calling which bore him on his way into Chapter history.

There was nowhere Caeon could be buried, so a cairn of rubble and wreckage was erected, blocking the door to the chapel. There they left him, and returned to their posts.

LESS THAN TWENTY minutes after Lygris had given his word that the fighter deck would be operational within hours, Tellos and a full hun-dred Soul Drinkers were assembled around Yser's church in disciplined ranks. There was an air of reflection about them, for every one of them was fully aware of the star fort's situation and the lengths to which they would have to go to protect themselves.

But the death of Caeon and the loss of their prize had steeled their minds, and he could see the pride in their eyes. Perhaps they felt distaste at raising arms against those they had once fought with – but they were all certain that honour, and in this case their very survival, were paramount. Sarpedon felt they all hoped, as he did, that once the assault began the Adeptus Mechanicus would realise the gravity of their folly and relinquish their grip on the Soulspear. Then the Soul Drinkers would take their prize and return to the fleet, honour satisfied.

Sarpedon was grateful for Sergeant Tellos's presence. His exultation in battle was infectious, and he was a talisman for the assault squads who formed the core of this force. Givrillian, too, would accompany Sarpedon, a solid dependable voice at his shoulder in case the madness started. Most of the Tactical Marines would maintain the defences of the star fort – the attacking force, consisting of most of the assault squads and a handful of specialists, was amongst the most swift and deadly Sarpedon had ever seen.

And it was his force. He was in command. That Caeon had to die was a tragedy, but now he was gone and such things should not be dwelt upon. These were his brothers and he was leading them even if only to provide the threat of force, and he was proud. He had felt the swell of pride when he first joined the ranks of the Soul Drinkers, and to think that such men were now looking up to him as he had looked up to Caeon, and to Chapter Master Gorgoleon himself, was more than he could describe.

His psychic talents were not tuned to receiving from the minds of others but he could still feel that the men standing before him were eager to put the fear of the Emperor into their opponents. They had all felt the slight of the Soulspear's loss and wished nothing more than to send the Mechanicus crew quailing before them. And if a tech-guard or machine-priest dared resist them, they would use every ounce of force at their disposal to teach them what happens when you raise arms against the Soul Drinkers.

'Lygris here, commander.' The Tech-Marine's voice crackled in Sarpedon's comm-bead. 'The fighters are old but spaceworthy, and there's enough fuel for a one-way trip. We can take about one hundred and twenty Marines if we strip out most of the weapons systems.'

'We'll have about a hundred, spread out across the craft, so don't skimp on the firepower. And select pilots if you haven't done so already. How long do you need?'

'Two hours.'

In two hours borer shells could be gouging their way through the star fort's hull to explode, or magnacluster bombs could be raining frag torpedoes across its surface. 'You have one.'

'Yes, commander.'

'Sergeant Tellos!' barked Sarpedon, turning to the assembled Marines. 'I want squads of eight, at least one plasma weapon in each and as many melta bombs as you can carry. I leave squad organisation to your discretion. You will be prepared within the hour.'

Tellos saluted and began carving the assembled squads into self-contained fighting formations, each with its leader and many with a Tech-Marine or apothecary. They were facing possible combat in a largely unknown and unpredictable environment where each element had to be able to survive on its own unsupported.

It would be Sarpedon's first full command, and he knew there was a risk. If the Adeptus Mechanicus fought, there could be terrible bloodshed, and if that happened not all his battle-brothers would return.

But even if such an unthinkable thing happened, the Soul Drinkers would fight on, acquit themselves with honour, and win back the Soulspear. No matter what, there would always be hope that the insult would be redressed, that the affair would be put behind them and Sarpedon could return to the Soul Drinkers' flagship with the Soulspear in hand.

As Daenyathos wrote – *when all is darkness and every way out is lined with blood and lit with the fires of battle, there is still hope.*

But it wouldn't come to that. The Mechanicus wouldn't fight. These were Space Marines, the best of the best, no one would dare actually fight them face to face.

It wouldn't come to that.

IT WAS A man's life in the Sixers. The regiment's proper name was a twelve-digit string of letters and symbols that indicated its size, composition and base camp location on board the *674-XU28*. It was only the tech-priests and magi of the crew, and the senior officers who might one day be accepted into the tech-priest ranks, who could remember the whole thing in full. The logic-string happened to begin with the number six, and so it was as the Sixers that they knew themselves.

Kiv had been a Sixer all his life, as had most of the tech-guard. On his rare forays out onto inhabited worlds he would be alarmed and dismayed at how so many people seemed to have nothing around which they built their life. He had his grenade launcher, entrusted to him as a child when the neurojacks were first sunk into the back of his skull and he was upgraded to a member of the tech-guard. He had learned its exact rate of fire down to tenths of a second, and the range at which the electromagnetic pulses and photon glare would be effective. He knew that at that particular angle he could lob a haywire grenade over two partitions on the Geryon platform's muster deck and drop it right down the throat of an attacker. It had been stripped and repaired so often that none of the original components remained, yet it was the same because it was bound by the weapon's spirit, to which Kiv spoke thrice-daily as the Rites of Maintenance decreed. He knew that the shadowy figure of Archmagos Khobotov had a similar affinity with the unimaginably vast and complex ship itself, which must have given him a deep and holy understanding of the ordered universe the magi laboured to create.

It was something that tied him to the great spirit of logic that stood against the random chaos of the universe – the Omnissiah, Machine God, the defender of reason and knowledge. He assumed that the Omnissiah and the divine Emperor were different sides of the same coin, although the magi he had asked found some way of avoiding the question. The answer must involve concepts beyond his understanding, he guessed.

'Heads up, Sixers! Combat protocol ninety-three, defence in depth and repel!' Colonel-priest Klayden's voice was artificially amplified so every Sixer on the muster deck woke from their reveries. 'Action stations, dogs, action!' The klaxons started up a second later – Klayden's rank allowed him access to the simpler levels of the ship's own machine-spirit, and he was able to anticipate the more important decisions it made.

A whole Sixer battalion had transferred to the ordinatus platform before it had been launched. Every one of them was suddenly up and aware, throwing open ammo trunks and pulling on their quilted flak-armour. There were even units stationed on the Geryon itself. The huge barrel of the cannon was high above, jutting above the upper hull of the platform, but the immense recoil-dampeners and ammo feeds were housed in the centre of the muster deck and it was on this steel mountain that tech-guard squads were preparing defensive positions.

Combat. Kiv had seen it many times, and was chilled by the randomness of it. It was something akin to righteous determination with which the tech-guard and the other forces of the Adeptus Mechanicus would take up arms and strive to win the fight, so that the supreme logic they built could be preserved and the disordered tide of battle turned back. Kiv shrugged himself into the heavy flak-tabard and strapped up the knee-high boots that would protect his feet and legs from the backwash of haywire chaff released from the disruptive grenades he could fire. He hefted the cylindrical metal bulk of the grenade launcher that was as familiar to him as another limb. He drew the jack-lines from the targeting array and pushed them into the sockets in his skull, feeling the orientation of the launcher through his own sense of balance, the barrel temperature through his skin, the ammo count through the fullness of his stomach. The augmentation was a simple one compared to the near-total prosthesis of the tech-magi, but it gave Kiv a taste of how it was to be truly at one with the Machine.

'Subsystem nine! Muster and deploy!' came Klayden's amplified voice. Subsystem nine was Kiv's unit, a mobile defence squad, equipped to hunt down attackers and expel them.

The other tech-guard of Kiv's unit hurried past bearing melta-guns, plasma rifles and hellguns. Each one would fulfil a particular role in the fight, where the confusion of Kiv's haywires, destruction of the energy weapons and precision of the hellguns would combine to form an efficient combat machine.

There was fear. But it was a good fear, like a diagnostic rite, running through his mind and checking for flaws of cowardice. There were none. He had been a Sixer all his life, and Sixers never died. They just broke down.

'Multiple signals, tracking,' boomed the machine-spirit voice. The machine-spirit on the platform was a part of the *674-XU28* itself, and spoke with the ship's authority. 'Approach vectors confirmed. Prepare for boarding on platform twelve.'

The enemy, whoever they were, would probably think they were making a surprise attack. But the sub-spirit that controlled the Geryon platform was as cunning as its parent on the *674-XU28*, and no one could approach without the platform, and then the tech-guard, knowing about it. The attackers would be met by a fully-prepared tech-guard battalion and the weapons system of a fully-aware orbital platform.

High above the muster deck other tech-guard units were scrambling over the vast loading rams and ammo cranes, prepared to sell their lives rather than have disorder infect a masterpiece like the Geryon.

CHAPTER FOUR

THE GERYON ORDINATUS platform was a silver diamond against the star field, bright with light reflected from the planet Lakonia. Sarpedon watched it growing closer through the age-grimed glass of the port-hole, the Hammerblade fighter-bomber juddering around him as the Chapter serf-pilot flew Sarpedon's Marines towards their objective.

Sarpedon's craft held eight other Space Marines under Sergeant Givrillian. There were eleven other craft like it, Hammerblades and Scalptakers, speeding in scattered formation towards the Geryon platform. They would land all over the upper surface, and the Soul Drinkers would enter the upper decks of the platform from a dozen different entry points. Once inside they would link up as they swept through the structure, with the ultimate objective being control of the Geryon itself. Once they had the platform the Soul Drinkers could be sure the Adeptus Mechanicus would have no choice but to return the Soulspear. Then the two Chapter cruisers could swoop in unmolested and pick the Soul Drinkers up from the platform, along with the nearly two hundred Marines remaining on the star fort.

'Taking fire!' crackled a serf-pilot's voice over the vox – Sarpedon glanced at the holomat set up in the centre of the Hammerblade's cargo bay and saw the rune that flashed was that of Squad Phodel.

'Squad Phodel, give me details.'

'Magnalaser turret fire,' replied the serf-pilot, voice warped by sudden static. Sarpedon peered through the thick porthole glass and saw ruby-red lines of laser flashing out from the platform, lancing past the silver glimmers that were the Soul Drinkers' makeshift assault craft.

In spite of everything, of all honour and tradition and basic loyalty, the Adeptus Mechanicus would resist. This should have been little more than a show of strength, a lightning raid that would leave the Geryon platform in Soul Drinker hands and convince the Mechanicus to return the Soulspear – but instead, the tech-priests had seen fit to turn this into a battle.

Deep down, Sarpedon had feared this. Those willing to steal the Emperor's finest could have it in their hearts to fight them for it, too. He had thought it hardly possible that sane men would dare take up arms against the Soul Drinkers, and now it seemed that this enemy was not sane after all.

There was a sudden flash of sparks against the black of space and the vox-link to Squad Phodel filled with static. A glint of silver sheared away from a magnalaser beam and tumbled towards the fast approaching Geryon platform. Six good Marines died as the Scalptaker hit at an angle, its scything wingtip catching on the edge of a hull plate and flipping it over and over until it smashed into a support stanchion. It burst, spilling its guts of fuel and machinery against the structures supporting the gargantuan ordinatus barrel above.

Two of the runes were still lit – an Assault Marine from Squad Phodel and an apothecary. They clung to the hull, hard vacuum against their backs as the fuel evaporated around them, watching the rest of the attackers come down.

Sarpedon watched the half-dozen life-lights winking out on the command holo.

They were the first he had lost as a commander.

The Hammerblade juddered violently – Givrillian and the six Marines of his squad clung to the beams and struts of the cargo-passenger compartment. Through the porthole Sarpedon could now pick out the great metal plain of the artillery platform and the mountainous bulk of the Geryon cannon itself. The wide mouth of its squat main barrel could have swallowed a whole flight of attack craft, and Sarpedon had seen cities smaller than the web of recoil dampeners clustered around its base. He saw three more Soul Drinker craft swoop in low, aiming for the wide expanses of flat hull between sensorium arrays and thruster jet columns.

The Adeptus Mechanicus's apparent treachery had cost the lives of Space Marines, better men by far than any tech-priest. Every Soul Drinker would know it, in the star fort and the attack force. Their hearts would be steeled by the loss of their battle-brothers even as they whispered prayers to Dorn for the souls of the lost.

Sarpedon could feel their anger, for it was inside him, too, channeled into cold determination. This was war, it had been all along. The Mechanicus would have to kill to keep what they had stolen. Honour demanded that Sarpedon ensure they died for it, too.

Defences opened up all across the platform's surface, lasers and missiles. Bright bolts of power streaked across the porthole as servitor-emplacements took aim and fired. But there was nothing like the forest of fire they would have encountered had they gone for the platform's underside, where bombing runs would target the main thruster columns and ammunition holds. The Soul Drinkers weren't trying to blow the platform up – they were trying to get in.

A near-miss and the craft lurched violently, the Marines struggling to keep stable in the zero gravity. The platform loomed up ahead of them – they were heading for a wide expanse of metal with two craft going in beside them. Below the whine of the engines Sarpedon could hear the zips and crackles as las-bolts passed close and scored the hull.

Another Hammerblade was hit, one wing sheared off, and it angled sharply down towards the platform. Sarpedon didn't see how it impacted, but another eight lifelights turned cold.

Then the serf-pilot dipped the craft's nose and they were on their final run, hills and valleys of metal speeding by, explosions stuttering blooms against the blackness of space above them.

They hit shallow and belly-first, the pilot using the impact to slow the craft down given the Hammerblade's lack of retrothrust power. The noise was awesome – a screech of metal that felt like it would never end, stanchions snapping, hull peeling back like shredded skin. The floor buckled and ruptured, and the platform's hull plates could be seen scudding past below their feet as the compartment was shaken as if grabbed by a giant fist. Sarpedon glanced through to the pilot's compartment and spotted the Chapter serf wrestling with the attitude controls, void shield splintering in front of him. The atmosphere had gone by then and his rebreather hood was misted with perspiration.

They stopped. The lights had failed and the command holo was just a glowing green smudge in the air.

'Report!'

The squad counted off. They had all made it intact. The serf, should he survive, would be suitably decorated upon their return.

'The cargo door's jammed,' said the serf-pilot breathlessly.

'Get us out,' said Givrillian, glacing at Trooper Thax at the tail-end of the hold.

The gravity was normal now they were in the platform's gravitic field, and Trooper Thax stepped forward holding the las-cutter with which each craft had been issued. The only sounds as he carved a wide arc in the side of the craft were the tingling vibrations through the Hammerblade's hull, and the faint background hiss of the vox-link.

They needed to get into atmosphere soon. The Mechanicus were undoubtedly capable of jamming their vox-net and the Soul Drinkers needed the option of verbal communication.

The hull section fell away and Sarpedon looked out on this new battlefield. A rolling expanse of riveted hull plates, punctured by mechanical outcrops and bulky mech-shed hills. The mighty peak of the gun soared above them, brooding and dark, picked out in reflected light from the glowing disk of Lakonia and hung against the backdrop of stars.

Givrillian was at his side, bolter levelled as the squad deployed from the wrecked Hammerblade. 'Looks like a munitions supply tunnel half a kilometre west, commander. Good for an entry point?'

'Take us in, sergeant.'

The Marines moved swiftly across the platform deck, forming a cordon around Sarpedon. Thax and his plasma gun were on point and two Marines jogged backwards to cover the field of fire behind them. The munitions tunnel was a large square opening in the platform deck covered with metal slats of a shutter – there was a good chance the tunnel shaft led somewhere useful. There was an equally good chance the place had been marked as a likely entry point by the enemy and would be well-defended.

Good. Let them try. Let them find out what happens when they cross swords with the Soul Drinkers.

Sarpedon opened the command channel of the vox-net. The too-familiar broken chatter of battle flooded into his head.

'Squad Phodel down, I've got visual…'

'… hit hard, we have wounded and are heading into the secondary intake…'

'… pressure suits and energy weapons, taking fire…'

They were losing men already. But that was to be expected in such a high-risk deployment. When they were in the thick of the enemy and could fight back, it would be a different story. If there was another way, he would have taken it. But there was not. They had forced him into this, these thieves not fit to wear the Imperial eagle. And now they had shown the depths to which they would sink.

He held that thought and cherished it. Purity through hate. Dignity through rage. The words of the philosopher-soldier Daenyathos, written eight thousand years before in the pages of the *Catechisms Martial*, were a rock in the sea of war.

Purity through hate. Dignity through rage. Let the fire within you light the fires without.

The vox-net picture built up. The first craft had landed unmolested, with only a few injuries reported. The next flew into the defensive fire and two of these had been lost, with at least fourteen Marines dead and probably more. Amongst them the six members of Sergeant Phodel's assault squad and one of the Tech-Marines. There were no reports from the other two.

Tellos's squad, inevitably, was already inside, emerging in a main thoroughfare and blasting a great wound in the defenders they found with melta-bombs and bolt shells. In the background of his vox-frequency was the unmistakable thrum of chainblade through bone.

Las-fire stuttered soundlessly overhead as Sarpedon and Givrillian's squad reached the lip of the cargo-feed. Krak grenades blew off enough slats to provide an entrance, their small armour-piercing bursts imploding strangely in the vacuum.

'Go! Go!'

The Marines vaulted into the shaft in quick succession, Thax first, with Givrillian and Sarpedon in the middle. The shaft twisted alarmingly into the body of the platform and the Marines struggled to keep their footing. Sarpedon visualised their position – the shaft curled down alongside the massive machinery of the Geryon's loading and recoil mechanisms, right down to the muster deck where the Soul Drinkers would be able to move around the platform and secure it. They were heading in the right direction.

'Auspex is not transmitting,' said Givrillian from somewhere in the darkness. 'Interference.'

Deeper, through the guts of massive machinery. Through grilles in the shaft's side Sarpedon's enhanced eyes glimpsed immense cogs turning slowly, pistons thudding out a rhythm. The vox-net was fragmented – he could tell there were combats breaking out all over, but no more. Tellos's voice cut through for a second, bellowing triumphant.

'Contact!' came a yell from beneath, a split-second before a wall of air whumped up the shaft. An atmosphere. Somewhere for the tech-guard to fight.

The bright wash of Thax's plasma gun rippled up from the bottom of the shaft. Fire from both sides crackled. Sarpedon tore off his helmet, felt the oily air in his throat, and leapt downwards.

'For Dorn!' he yelled, force staff raised to stab and thrust.
Contact.

THE AIR HOWLED into the shaft when tech-guard Grik slammed the
intake lever down. The *674-XU28's* machine-spirit spoke to the
platform, which breathed atmosphere in the cargo feed so the Sixers
could fight there without fear of vacuum-death. As long as they
fought on this platform, the Sixers knew the very battlefield was on
their side.

The loader shaft the enemy was entering through emptied into the
throat of an ammo shifter, all huge blocks of brushed-steel
machinery chased with bronze icons and inscribed machine-prayers.
The great cogs beyond would move and the machinery would form
a great swallowing gullet, dragging shells down to be slammed into
the Geryon's breech. The shifter had reversed flow and brought the
Sixers up here, to meet the attackers forcing their way in from above.

The twenty-strong tech-guard fire-team drew up around the feed
exit, torchlights darting up into the twisted shaft. Klayden held up a
metal hand flat and they waited for a second or two, listening.

A voice, shouting from inside the shaft. Panic, without a doubt.
The attackers knew they had been found and they would probably
be scrambling back up, trying to find a way out of their trap.

The fist closed. *Advance.*

Both flamer-bearing Sixers hurried forward and aimed the spouts
of their weapons into the feed. After they had washed the feed with
flame the hellgun and melta-gun guard would follow, picking off
those fleeing from the firestorm.

Suddenly a plasma blast, a great bolt of white-hot liquid fire,
vomited from the feed with a brash roar, drenching the flamer
troops and dissolving one in an instant. The reek of burning metal
swept over Kiv, and his launcher racked a grenade to echo his revulsion.

Kiv caught a glimpse of the attackers – a sheen of purple ceramite
picked out in haloes of gunfire, the glint of jade green eyepieces, the
shine of bone.

The second tech-guard had lost half his body, dripping skeleton's
arm fragmenting, ribs burned clean. He had caught sight of the
attackers just as the plasma gun opened up.

'Space Marines,' he gasped, and died.

'Give me haywires!' yelled Klayden as bolter fire spat from the
feed, punching holes through tech-guard and ringing around the
shifter equipment.

Kiv knew he was their one hope – his haywire grenades could remove the Marines' advantage of armour and auto-senses. He would shout and his launcher would shout with him, sending electromagnetic waves billowing up into the Marines, shorting their senses, locking the joints of their armour. Tech-guards were dying, one decapitated as a round punched into his throat and blew his head clean off. Rounds snicked through the edges of Kiv's flaktabard and cracked around his ears as shrapnel spun and gunsmoke coiled in the air.

He took aim, ready to fire a haywire grenade through the shaft entrance and into the massive purple-armoured figures crammed into the metal throat. The launcher willed his finger to the trigger.

For order. For logic. For the Omnissiah.

A crackling shaft of arunwood speared out from the shaft and stabbed Kiv through the eye.

IT WAS SARPEDON'S first glimpse of the enemy here – a pale-skinned and shaven-headed tech-guard, clad in red-brown quilted flak-gear, his skin punctured with wires and interfaces. The determination on the face contrasted with the youthful features as the tech-guard slid off the force staff with a flick of Sarpedon's wrist.

There were about a dozen tech-guard still fighting, and Sarpedon wished for the hundredth time he had a better idea of the total techguard numbers on the platform. A hundred? A thousand? Five thousand? How many enemies would the Soul Drinkers have to fight before they could secure their honour and their lives?

He told himself it didn't matter. The tech-guard were just men. No more.

Sarpedon was now in the thick of the fighting, Marines spilling out around him with bolters blazing. His own weapon fired off three rounds into the chest of the nearest guard, whose left arm fell sheared at the elbow along with the hellgun he was carrying.

Givrillian barrelled forward into their half-bionic leader and crushed him to the floor, bolter stock slamming into the man's head. The bionic hand grabbed the sergeant's shoulder pad and began tearing handfuls out of the ceramite, deep enough to draw blood, before Givrillian drove a fist through his sternum.

Another brother Marine dragged Givrillian off the enemy's body so Thax could get a clean shot into the backs of the tech-guard now retreating between the massive steel buttresses. He caught one of them full on, the bolt boring right through him before spattering others with gobbets of superheated plasma. They fell, screamed, and caught fire. The Marines now advancing through the machinery picked them off before they could even start to scream.

Sarpedon despatched a wounded tech-guard with the butt of his staff. He was the last.

'Secure the entry point, commander?' said Givrillian.

Sarpedon pointed down the wide, dark metal tunnel that stretched downwards. 'No time, sergeant. Press on, remember the objective.'

A noise vibrated through the floor like thunder from a steel sky. Flakes of rust flittered down from the juddering walls and the huge chunks of machinery began to shift. Gaps between them opened up and Sarpedon could see those cogs slowly turning.

The machinery had activated. They were being swallowed by the offspring of *674-XU28*.

NIKROS, THE SINGLE Marine who remained of Squad Phodel, along with Apothecary Daiogan who had also survived the crash, somehow managed to find a way into the platform's secondary magazine chambers and set krak grenades to destroy the caches of macrocannon ammunition. Then their luck ran out, however. Pinned down by a siege engineer unit, Daiogan died under a hail of heavy bolter shells and Nikros was severely wounded.

Then the magazines went up, incinerating Nikros along with everyone and everything within a two hundred-metre radius, taking a huge chunk like a bite mark out of the platform's surface. Several dozen tech-guard were killed as the local atmosphere depressurised, failing to get their pressure-masks on. When the bulkheads closed and the leak shut down, Nikros and Daiogan had personally accounted for almost three hundred tech-guard.

ASSAULT-SERGEANT GRAEVUS linked up with two other units, one assault and one tactical, and threw a cordon around a huge docking emplacement that sprung from the platform's sunward corner. In a textbook move of which Daenyathos would have been proud, he stormed the emplacement as if it was a fortified town. Sweeping in and downwards half his troops cut their way through the tech-guard to reach the massively complex building-sized knot of wires and readouts, which contained the portion of *674-XU28's* machine-spirit. Several squads of tech-guard, their weapons silenced to avoid accidental damage to the sacred cogitators and knowledge-conduits, attacked with bare hands.

Graevus was a stone-cold killer with little time for such amateurish antics. He dealt with most of them personally with his power axe while Tech-Marine Lygris went to work on the link between the machine-spirit and the control systems for the Geryon.

TELLOS'S SQUAD HAD broken through the upper surface of the platform with melta-bombs, and leapt from the rafters straight into the heart of the tech-guard prepping for combat on the vast, high-ceilinged muster deck. His squad carved out a beachhead in the shadow of the Geryon's recoil-rams, and was acting as a focal point for the assault units making it through the hull and onto the platform's muster deck.

Tellos stood on a mound of tech-guard corpses, energy and las-fire like a halo playing around him, with Marines scrambling up to fight beside him, firing, slicing, dying. The tech-guard fed more and more men into the maw of the killing zone he was creating – he had taken upon himself the vital task of draining the tech-guard manpower and morale while the other scattered Soul Drinker units closed in on the real prizes.

THE MACHINERY DISGORGED Sarpedon and Squad Givrillian into the intake for the lubricant ducts. They came out halfway up the gargantuan recoil dampeners that dominated the muster deck. The metallic mandibles opened up before them and they tumbled into the slick trench of the intake, green-black lubricant sluicing over them. Brother Doshan was sucked into the yawning black oval of the intake before Givrillian dug the boots of his armour into the stained metal and halted the slide.

Sarpedon hauled himself up so his eyes were level with the edge of the intake trench, and looked down.

They were easily a hundred and fifty metres above the cavernous muster deck. From one corner billowed a great hemisphere of flame where the magazines had gone up minutes before. Smoke was thick in the air and straggling groups of tech-guard on the Geryon structure were trying to co-ordinate supporting fire. Below them the deck, partitioned into roofless rooms and corridors, was swarming with tech-guard streaming towards the centre.

Towards a charnel house. Bodies lay so thick the attacking tech-guard had to clamber up a slope of their own fallen just to get into sight of the Marine position. The tactical squads who had made it this far were sending sheets of disciplined bolter drill-fire down towards the tech-guard, scattering charges so they would break uselessly against the counter-charging Assault Marines.

Tellos was at their head, of course, his armour black with blood and his hair thick with it. It streamed down his bare face and rained from the whirring teeth of his chainsword. In the sharp relief of his augmented senses Sarpedon watched him take down two men with one swipe, ignoring the hellgun blast that raked channels into his armour like claw marks.

'Voxes coming in, sir!' called Givrillian. 'Lygris reports contact with the spirit-link!'

'Tell him to keep me updated. We're buying him time here.'

'Aye, commander!'

Lygris was good. He would know what to do.

Every battle was tough. The star fort was tough. This was tougher by far. The Van Skorvold mutants had been determined but ill-trained and of varied competence. The tech-guard, meanwhile, were quality troops equipped with some of the best weaponry the Mechanicus could forge. The star fort had been a rehearsal – this was the real fight.

'With me!' Sarpedon called, and Squad Givrillian clambered out beside him as the closest tech-guard stragglers spotted them and moved to fire.

THIS WAS WHY he had been born. This was why the Emperor had looked upon him and marked him out as a warrior, so the year-long Great Harvest of the Soul Drinkers had found him a strong and valiant youth, driven to excel, fearing not even the armoured giants who strode from their spacecraft to judge him.

To fight. To bathe in the blood of his enemies, to know that every cut and stab and bullet fired was for the good of mankind and the glory of the Imperium.

This was why Tellos had been born.

They were learning fast, these tech-guard, as does anyone who must learn to survive. Their advantage was the quick-firing high-impact energy weapons and they were sending fire-teams around all sides of his makeshift position to assault from many directions at once. Tellos, like any Soul Drinker, knew the power of psychology in the thick of combat – he picked out one enemy front, annihilated it totally, and left the others gazing into the gaping hole in their attack. They faltered, they turned. Then they died, for turning to flee is the most dangerous thing a warrior can do.

He dived in – literally, blade-first over the heads of a tight knot of tech-guard, two of their number manhandling a bronze-chased autocannon. He hit shoulder-first, buckling one man's ribcage underneath him, chainblade lashing out at the legs of another. His other hand held his combat knife and it jabbed up beneath the jaw of one of the autocannon crew. Tellos twisted it, felt the gristly wrench as the jaw came loose, and withdrew it in a fountain of blood.

Hot pain punched through his knife arm – a hellgun shot, thin and powerful. It went through the muscle and painkillers shot into his veins. The offending gunman was bisected with a wild upwards stroke, a novice's cut that would have left Tellos wide open to counter-thrust from any foe not shell-shocked and panicking.

He knew they would be defeated even now, nerves in tatters, unable to counter the most base of attacks. Elegance and duelling had its place in war – but the need here was for butchery.

He loved them both alike. The fine art of noble combat, and the glorious rush of righteous carnage. He had loved them both even before the ships of the Great Harvest had come to his world. It was why he had been chosen.

Behind him his squads followed up, firing bolter shells into fleeing backs and quickly slaying anyone still close. The Tactical Marines further back sent volleys of shells over their heads to explode against the partitions and machine-stacks, keeping tech-guard heads down.

A few energy bolts lasered down from a hidden position and a Marine was cut nearly in half by a thick crimson melta-beam. Another took a bad-looking abdomen shot from a lasweapon and had to be dragged as the assault squad regrouped before they were surrounded.

They were dying here. Tellos's squad was already down to half-strength. Only a couple of their fallen would ever fight again, for the formidable tech of their enemies inflicted grievous and unhealable wounds. Pallas, the apothecary who had made it to the position with some of the Tactical Marines, was busy collecting gene-seed from the fallen as well as patching up the brothers' wounds.

But they had taken down hundreds, maybe thousands between them, and there were only so many tech-guard on this platform. Marines were hard to kill and harder to beat, and though Tellos himself bled from a dozen wounds he was more eager for the fight than he had ever been. If they had to die, they would. But they would win.

Someone screamed, and Tellos was shocked to realise it was a Space Marine, for Squad Vorts was suddenly under attack. His auto-senses blocked out the flare but the shower of sparks was still spectacular, cascading from the sundered body of one of Vorts's Assault Marines. Attackers were storming the rear of the position, leaping from wall to console to corpse like inhuman things.

There were half-a-dozen of them and their skin was covered in swirling designs glowing blue-white so brightly the glare would hurt a normal man's eye. Flashes of lightning burst from their fingers and eyes, and rippled across their bare torsos. They were moving so quickly that Vorts's men hadn't had the chance to counter-attack.

Electro-priests. Tellos had never seen a real one – few in number but famously deadly, fanatical dervishes of the machine-cult. He faced them and readied that charge. This was why he had been born.

One was cut down by bolt pistol fire before he got there. Another was speared neatly by a chainblade as he landed. The others were suddenly in the middle of Vorts's squad – a helmet exploded under an electrified hand, a Marine was hurled twenty metres in the flash of energy discharge, trailing smoke from a ruptured chestplate.

Tellos picked out one and drew his assault, parrying blows from bare hands stronger than plasteel. The electro-priest's eyes were silvery and blank. He jerked and spasmed quicker even than a Marine's reflexes would allow. The priest whirled, one hand chopping low and clipping Tellos's knee, and the sergeant barely kept upright as the shock ripped through his leg. He felt the charred muscle and skin soldered to the inside of his armour. This thing would die.

He dodged, sliced, drawing a shower of sparks off the priest's torso. But the priest was still alive and grabbed the chainblade with arcing fingers. The mechanism shattered and teeth flew everywhere like shrapnel. Tellos countered with the knife, aiming for the space between the ribs where a heretic heart dared to beat, but the priest's other hand grabbed his wrist with inhuman reactions.

The power sliced through him. He couldn't get his hand away, the grip was too strong, like a magnet. He tried to slam the wrecked chainsword into the priest's face but it caught his other hand and the circuit was completed, power coursing free through him for a split-second before with one final effort he wrenched himself free.

Tellos landed heavily on his back and spotted the priest falling, recovering, standing again. Smoke coiled from the chainblade wounds. Tellos noticed that from somewhere it had picked up two purple gauntlets.

Then he looked to see if he still held his knife, and saw the charred stumps of his wrists. His hands. It had his hands.

The world was turning white around the edges and there was a thin keening in his ears. Something grabbed him and he caught the white shoulder pad out of the corner of his eye, knowing it was Pallas who was dragging him away by the collar of his armour and pumping bolt pistol shells into the electro-priest's face.

His hands.

This was it. He would die here. Just like he had been born to fight, he had been born to die here, maimed and broken, surrounded by his brothers and the corpses of his foes.

It wasn't bad. He would be remembered. But there was so much more he could have done, so much…

Something huge and dark dropped down in front of him. Power arced from its staff and around the aegis hood raised from his collar. And Tellos was glad, for as long as their commander was watching, he knew his death would be glorious.

SARPEDON DECIDED TO give the tech-guard what they deserved. He decided to give them the Hell.

What did they fear? Too simple. Go back a stage – what did they want? They wanted order and logic and a plan to the universe, a galaxy where the machine god's rules governed reality. And fear? They feared disorder and anarchy, confusion and madness, bedlam, impulse and rage.

That was *their* hell.

Somehow, the fact that these men had once called themselves his allies made it easier. Treachery felt worse that the mark of the xenos or the pollution of the mutant – it was more immediate, a thing of pure malice. Those who allied themselves with the foulness of Chaos were traitors too, against the Emperor and the rightness of the universe, and so it was treachery that Marines were raised to loathe more than anything else.

Put like that, it was simple.

He let the Hell boil up from the mound of corpses beneath his feet, and flood down from the shadows of the platform's superstructure high above. It was the screams of the dying changing to howls of blood-lust, the reek of brimstone and blood. Insane loops of colour coursed through the air and deathly stains of rust spread from the hands of great shadowy spectres of corrosion.

The tech-guard ran but the electro-priests just convulsed in confusion and anger, too far gone to flee but unable to fight on with sounds and smells and images of disorder surrounding them. The battered remainder of Vorts's squad took one down at chainsword length, sparks flying as the chainteeth bored through its skin and into its hyperactive organs.

Sarpedon went deeper. Groans of breaking machinery, like ice caps in thaw, rocked the muster deck, and the half-glimpsed shadows of falling cogs and masonry plummeted through the darkness.

'Advance!' The voice was that of Pallas, taking charge of the surviving forces in the strongpoint. Squads Volis and Givrillian levelled bolters and swept out, storming the surrounding positions of tech-guard now thrown into sudden disarray by the Hell. Walls of bolter fire tore through flak-tabards and augmetic torsos. Some way distant Squad Graevus arrived, dropping in from the overhanging ventilation channels onto the heads of reinforcing siege engineers. Graevus's axe blade could just be glimpsed, a bright blue diamond flashing up and down surrounded by crimson mist.

Sarpedon joined the three survivors of Squad Vorts as they sprinted after Volis and into the heavy weapons emplacement the tech-guard had been trying to set up. Two lascannon and an autocannon with six crew and about thirty tech-guard were crammed into a flak-board emplacement built around columns of cogitator-memory blocks.

'Lygris!' voxed Sarpedon as he ran. 'Does this platform run from the ship's machine-spirit?'

'Yes, lord.'

'Find out how it communicates with the crew. If it's verbal, I want a sample. You have twenty seconds.'

'Yes, lord.'

It took him fifteen.

By the time Sarpedon had vaulted over the flak-board behind Squad Vorts, he knew how the machine-spirit sounded over the vox-casters scattered throughout the platform and the Mechanicus ship itself. It was a cultured male voice with a hint of the aristocratic – reassuringly confident, calm and intelligent. Perfect.

He went deeper still. He hardly registered his force-staff swiping off the arm of a heavy weapons crewman about to fire. He was occupied with the Hell, going deeper still.

What did they fear?

'Die,' boomed the voice of the machine-spirit. 'Die. Die. Die.'

Most of them probably knew it was a trick. It didn't matter. They froze anyway, shocked to the core by the possibility that the beloved machine, the one thing in the universe that they could trust without question, was turning on them.

'Die.'

And they did. Volis's bolters chewed through dozens, the chainswords of Squad Vorts cut down more. Sarpedon must have bludgeoned and carved up a score of tech-guard as they fired blindly into the air or ran screaming. In the thick of the fighting they linked up with Graevus to form a body-strewn corridor into which Soul Drinkers poured and spread outwards, surrounding knots of panicking tech-guard and butchering them.

But even if they killed every single one of them, the battlefleet surrounding the platform could destroy them as soon as it was apparent the platform had been taken. It was time they were buying, nothing more.

ABOVE THE MUSTER deck, in the dark and cold mem-bank complex Graevus had captured in the assault's opening minutes, Tech-Marine Lygris and a dozen-strong Marine guard were pulling a cogitator stack apart. The complex was a tangle of cogitators and mem-banks, linked by metal-clad conduits and endless snaking lengths of cable. The moans of the dying and sharp cracks of gunfire filtered up from the muster deck below, echoing and eerie in the dim shadows of the complex.

The Marines' hands tore a tarnished metal plate away from the four metre-high obelisk of the cogitator stack, revealing a multicoloured tangle of cables. Lygris reached in and hauled a bundle of them out of the housing.

'We'll do this the old-fashioned way,' he said grimly, and the shears of his servo-arm cut through the waist-thick primary cable.

Electricity flashed violently and a hundred lights on the tangle of wires and cogitators above him went dark. The machine-spirit was cut off from the Geryon, for now at least.

Lygris drew the interface from his backpack – a snaking bundle of cables tipped with a sharp silver spike. He used it rarely, but knew it intimately. It was difficult to explain for someone who had not seen the machine-cult's teachings – this was something only the higher echelons had the right to do, and though he was a Soul Drinker and the best of men, he still recoiled at the horror the tech-priests would feel at his transgression. But it was the surest way. The only way.

He pulled down a likely-looking knot of mem-cables, pulsing with the information than ran through their filaments. He found a socket and snapped another cable into it, feeling it come to life in his hand.

'Cover me,' he said, glancing at the Tactical Marines. 'I'll be unconscious for a couple of minutes.'

'Yes, lord.'

Lygris took the interface cable and jammed the spike into the back of his head. His eyes must have rolled back and his arms flopped by his sides, but he didn't notice. His mind was full of the white light of knowledge – a standard mind-impulse unit link would disorientate an untrained man but this was anything but standard. The information from the Mechanicus craft and the platform was coursing through him, too much to filter, too fast to read.

He knew he couldn't interface directly. No one could – if such technology had ever existed then it had been lost tens of thousands of years ago. He had to focus, find the systems he was looking for, do his work and get out.

Remember what you are fighting for. For the Emperor. For Dorn.

He thought he would drown in the torrent of information. Finally he found a shape – a great shape of power and brutality, massive and terrible. Lygris could feel its intelligence burning as it loomed out of the hot white overload of information, could hear the deep throb of its virtual heart, taste its reek of old iron like blood in his mouth.

He looked for a name, and found it: *Geryon*.

He knew the machine-spirit would be furiously seeking a way through its secondary and redundant systems, trying to find a way in to challenge the interloper. Already a black beam like a searchlight was scouring the depths of the platform's mem-systems, hunting. Lygris had a few seconds here before the massive amorphous darkness of the machine-spirit found him, and knew also that it would all be over if it did. No one outside the Mechanicus had any idea of what a truly ancient and powerful machine-spirit could do to an intruder in its systems. Lygris could only be sure that he would be lucky if he got away with his mind wiped.

The Geryon yawned before him, huge and dark. Lygris scrabbled faster through the pale crystalline thought structures he had made to depict the mem-bank files, tore through the endless loops of cables that were control interfaces, battered down the plasteel doors his mind made from the hard-wired barriers. He sank imaginary fingers into the hard metal of the command program, forcing it to yield beneath his hands, feeling the vast machinery as great thrumming shapes against his skin. He felt immense ammo-haulers and forced them to move, slamming disruptor shells the size of tanks into the breech. The coolants, the recoil compensators, the propellant tanks – he rammed them all into position.

It was too late. The Geryon was upon him, powering up an information burst of such magnitude it would fill Lygris's mind to bursting and then drain away, leaving a brain scoured of all memory and intelligence. It was over. He was effectively dead.

He did the last thing the machine-spirit would expect. He dived right into it, down the black-smoke throat of the Geryon, feeling its reeking hot breath blistering his skin. He had to be quick, quicker than anyone could reasonably hope to be, before the Geryon caught him and crushed him with coils of information.

Lygris swept through the darkness of the Geryon and hurtled upwards, skimming the roiling black madness of the neural circuits that formed its brain. He sought out the tiny pinprick of light that was the link between the machine-spirit and the platform's sensoria, the conduit through which information about the outside void poured into the Geryon's brain.

Faster, so fast Lygris thought he would die of the effort. But the Geryon was behind him, breath hot on his back, teeth gouging at him even as he dived into the glowing portal and into the sensoria systems.

Lygris looked out onto space through Geryon's great eye. He spotted something, focused. The definition grew: conning towers and gun emplacements, the aquiline prow, the bright wash of its engines. An Imperial battleship, proud and strong, a large and tempting target.

He was locked. He was loaded.

He fired.

THE GERYON-CLASS had several classes of ammunition. One was a single titanic shell that had an immense starburst area, which would create an instant zone of interdiction through which attack craft and even lighter cruisers would be unable to travel.

Another contained a half-dozen void charges, which would spread electromagnetic chaff and pulse waves in all directions and create the equivalent of stellar minefields across a wide area.

Still another contained over a hundred disruption canisters, which would rain interference over an entire battlefleet, causing a temporary sensor-blackout. It was one of these that belched from the huge metal throat of the Geryon and burst just orbitwards of Chloure's sub-battlefleet.

One canister struck the underside of the *Hydranye Ko* and its momentum barged it through a full seven decks before it exploded, sending rivers of chaff-filaments rushing through corridors and pooling in cargo holds. More than thirty crew died in the explosion, and a further seventy or so from inhaling the filaments and fragments that flooded the lower decks. Half the light cruiser's air filtration system was clogged and the ship issued an all-points life support alert.

Several erupted between the star fort and the ships of the battlefleet. The *Diligent* and the *Deacon Byzantine* were in themselves relatively unaffected, but their view of the star fort was covered in a thick gauze of interference. Two scout craft on routine patrol from the *Deacon* became hopelessly lost as their unprotected servitor-guidance and comms failed completely. Several hours later they finally ran out of fuel and their crews froze to death.

The *Deacon* was quicker to respond to the sudden attack, firing several fragmentation torpedoes into the mass of interference discharge. The warheads malfunctioned as soon as they entered the electromagnetic fields and detonated piecemeal, adding more wreckage to the mess.

On the bridge of the *Diligent*, massive electrical feedback tore through the command systems and sent sheets of flame rippling up from the navigational consoles. For a few minutes all was black and hot and deadly – the screams of the dead and the roaring of flames mixed with the hiss of emergency saviour systems flooding the burning areas with fog and foam.

The damage control crew were there within three minutes, muscle-bound ratings with crowbars and rope hauling petty officers and nav-servitors from the burning wreckage. When the bridge was ordered enough for effective command, it had been established that the small craft tracked near the ordinatus platform were not obsolete fighters being used as maintenance craft after all, and that the platform was now under the control of the Soul Drinkers Space Marines.

It was also apparent that the Soul Drinkers had acted in a far more violent manner than Chloure had predicted. Chloure chose not to mention this.

Only the *674-XU28* was relatively unaffected, positioning itself to have a clear shot at the star fort and using its own jamming systems to counter the disruptive electromagnetic waves. Unfortunately its primary armament was currently under Soul Drinker control several thousand kilometres distant, and it had little more than defensive turret fire to boast in the way of firepower.

The tech-priests on board the *674-XU28* noted the puzzling fact that the defences on the star fort were powering down.

'GET ME DAMAGE reports! Now! And sensors!' Givo Kourdya hated letting things out of his control, and jumped from the deep leather upholstery of his captain's chair to bawl at the hapless petty officers and logisticians stumbling in the half-light of the bridge. Most of the lights had blown and the cogitator screens were flickering. Plumes of white smoke spurted from ruptured conduits and the viewscreen was full of ghostly static. The only sounds were sparks and steam, and the shouting of orders and curses. Otherwise there was silence, and this was significant because it meant the engines had stopped.

Lines of glowing green text chattered along the pict-slate set into the arm of the command chair. Damage reports – structural damage from the disruptor warhead was confined to a relatively small area, but the control systems for half the ship were haywire.

The engines had gone into emergency shutdown. Kourdya knew they wouldn't be back on-line for several hours, because priority for the damage control crews was the switching back on of the coolant systems before the plasma reactors overheated.

There were still no sensors. Sensors were the most delicate things on any ship and, annoyingly, the most useful. The *Hydranye Ko* was almost entirely blind. The most effective means of navigation, targeting and close manoeuvring was currently to look out of a porthole.

'Front sensorium's down, sir,' said the tech-adept whose unfortunate task was to liaise between the Mechanicus personnel and the command crew. 'But the rearward facing arrays are in some kind of shape.'

'And?'

'We've got energy signatures, sir, from the planet's far side. Two of them, cruiser strength, heading–'

'How fast?'

'Very fast, sir. Faster than our top speed.'

'Space Marine cruisers,' said Kourdya, mostly to himself. Wonderful. His ship was temporarily blind and crippled, but it didn't matter.

The real effect of the Geryon shell had been to prevent co-operation between the three cruisers of the sub-battlefleet. Between them they could have taken on the strike cruisers, which were probably light on weaponry to make room for attack craft bays. But one-on-one, the *Hydranye Ko* wouldn't have stood much of a chance even in full working order.

Kourdya sank back down into the command chair and pressed a control stud on the arm. If it still worked it would ring a bell somewhere below decks to indicate that a valet servitor should trundle up to the bridge bearing a decanter of eighty year-old devilberry liqueur and a shot glass. The *Hydranye Ko* wasn't going anywhere for a while, and in such situations Kourdya always tried to allow himself some little luxury to make sure it wasn't all bad.

'I wish I'd never won this ship,' he mused as he waited on the darkened bridge for his drink.

SARPEDON GLANCED AROUND him – he was in the flak-board corridor they had carved through the middle of the muster deck, daring the tech-guard around to attack, sending out counter-assault parties when they did. The Hell still burned all around – chains of glowing numbers formed equations in the air that fragmented and dissolved, and snakes of rust slithered along the bloodsoaked floor. The shock was dimmed by now but tech-guard still lost it here and there, screaming for machine-spirit's mocking voice to shut up. And the ordeal was taking the edge off even the stoutest of them, their aim thrown by shaking hands.

A voice came over the vox, strangled with static. 'Commander Sarpedon, this is the *Unendingly Just*. We are clear for pick-up.'

It had worked. Lygris had done it. If the Tech-Marine survived – and the Marines set to guard him said the interface had a taken its toll on him – he would be rewarded.

'Acknowledged, *Unendingly Just*,' replied Sarpedon, raising his voice to be heard above the static on the vox-net. 'Preparing to move out.'

Sarpedon had the majority of the Soul Drinkers with him, with the rest around Lygris's position. He loosed off a snap shot at a head that poked above a heap of wreckage, missed, guessed the position of the rest of the body and fired through the cover. Something screamed.

Treachery can never hide.

'Soul Drinkers!' he yelled. 'Prepare for withdrawal! Graevus, Vorts, meet up with Lygris's position and secure a route. The rest, fall back with me!'

THE GUNDOG AND the *Unendingly Just* swept in from the other side of Lakonia's orbit, where they had hung in the planet's sensor-shadow while the star fort and, later, the platform had been won. Their engines, overcharged for speed, were tagged as a larger-than-cruiser signal by the sensors of the closest ship, the *Hydranye Ko*.

The *Ko* made no move to intercept as they swept over the battlefleet, through fire arcs that would have destroyed even the tough Marine strike cruisers had the battlefleet been able to see them. Only the Adeptus Mechanicus craft tried to stop them, offering token turret blasts from its macrocannon batteries. The dark purple paint on the *Gundog's* hull was slightly scorched, nothing more.

The strike cruisers were run by serf-crews under the command of small Soul Drinker retinues who knew when to let their charges make the decisions and when to rein them in. Both ships had been refitted extensively for close-order manoeuvre and they tumbled elegantly towards the top of the platform, which was still wreathed in propellant wash from the Geryon's firing. Few of the defensive turrets were still functioning – the close-range lance batteries and light torpedo waves ensured that none continued to do so.

The *Unendingly Just* launched a wave of twenty Thunderhawks towards the docking emplacement that Graevus had assaulted less than an hour before. Marines were already gathering amongst the docking clamps and refuelling junctions, holding the landing sites against attack.

The *Gundog's* belly was empty, having held the corvus pods now dotting the hull of the star fort. Lacking a means of moving large numbers of troops it docked directly with the star fort, latching on to a wide ship-to-station thoroughfare through which millions of shackled feet had marched in the decades before. Chapter serfs made the docking secure and the Soul Drinkers withdrew from the star fort's weapons emplacements and muster points onto the strike cruiser.

Chaplain Iktinos, nominally in command of the two hundred Soul Drinkers left on the star fort, ensured that as per Sarpedon's standing orders, the personnel embarked upon the strike cruiser *Gundog* included the prisoner-priest Yser and the three dozen members of his flock.

WHEN THE SOUL Drinkers withdrew into the waiting Thunderhawk gunships from the ordinatus platform, it turned out there was more than enough room in the transports. Only sixty-three Marines of the original hundred were still alive.

The *Unendingly Just*, receiving its brood of Thunderhawks back into its flight decks, turned gracefully and gunned its primary engines, sprinting towards the system edge where it would meet up with the *Gundog* and escape into the warp. It left behind nearly forty dead Soul Drinkers, and uncounted thousands of Mechanicus tech-guard.

BY THE TIME the *Diligent* had recovered its wits and managed to focus its sensors beyond the interference field, the two strike cruisers had long since disappeared with the three company-strong Soul Drinkers' force. Chloure could do was sit back in his command pulpit, and watch the star fort die. The viewscreen was full of the ugly swollen bulk of the Van Skorvold star fort. It flashed like lightning as the first charges went off across its metal skin.

'Tertiary fuel stacks,' said Manis, the *Diligent's* master of Ordnance, as a blossom of fire burst against the scorched metal shell. 'They knew what they were doing.'

Chloure guessed the Soul Drinkers had planted bundles of grenades, or maybe explosives salvaged from the Van Skorvold arsenals, equipped with timers. Every Space Marine, he guessed, would have had extensive demolitions training and would know exactly where to plant a charge to hurt that star fort the most.

'Can we save it?' he asked.

'Not a chance,' said Manis.

Even Chloure could tell that the star fort was already tilting alarmingly towards the pale orb of Lakonia. The gravitic stabilisers, Manis informed him, had been the first to go. Probably melta-charges, but again bundles of standard grenades would do the trick if you knew what to look for.

Another explosion, the largest, tore a massive section out of the side of the star fort. The flaming wreckage scattered from the hull as if in slow-motion before winking out in the vacuum. It was moving quicker now, turning over ponderously as it fell into a terminal orbital decay.

His mission had been to apprehend the Van Skorvolds, dismantle their empire, and take it over in the name of the Administratum. He had thought he had done an extraordinary job, using just the right rumours to bring the Soul Drinkers into the operation, saving valuable resources and casualties by having the Space Marines clear the fort of resistance. But instead he had failed in his mission as completely as could be imagined – the fort was destroyed, his fleet damaged, the possibility of an Administratum-controlled human cargo business in flames. He might as well have left the Van Skorvolds in charge – the Administratum would have been far better off.

He tried to tell himself the worst thing was the billions of credits burning up before his eyes. But in truth, Chloure knew there were whole Imperial organisations devoted to publicly punishing men who had failed as totally as he had.

'Your orders, sir?' Vekk stood proud with his arms behind his back, as if nothing had happened.

'I suppose we'd better follow them,' said Chloure wearily. 'We'll lose them but there will be questions if we don't try.'

'Aye, sir.' Vekk turned and started barking out orders as if they were important.

All that revenue, he told himself. Bloody Khobotov. Bloody Marines. All that revenue.

CALLISTHENES VAN SKORVOLD never found a way out of the old defence station's command centre, let alone the star fort itself. When the friction with Lakonia's atmosphere melted the outer hull and sent flames gouting through the star fort, he died screaming as the skin and muscle was scorched from his bones. Finally he was reduced to a fine ash and scattered over Lakonia's rolling green countryside along with several million tons of flaming wreckage.

Veritas Van Skorvold found and launched one of the few saviour pods she had bothered to keep maintained on the star fort, and got far enough clear of the station to avoid being dragged down into its orbital decay. She drifted for three days and was picked up by the *Hydranye Ko*, which was stationary in high orbit while repairs were carried out. She was promptly arrested and thrown in the brig. The security systems had failed along with rest of the ship and keeping her incarcerated proved very tiresome, especially when she began biting whoever was assigned to guard her. Captain Kourdya was heard to voice on several occasions the suspicion that the Soul Drinkers had let her live deliberately for the sole purpose of annoying him.

Every warrior needs a funeral pyre. Commander Caeon got his when the flames roared through the hull of the star fort as it broke up in the atmosphere. Caeon was, perhaps inevitably, very difficult to burn. But by the time the star fort had disintegrated, this proudest of Soul Drinkers was nothing but dust.

CHAPTER FIVE

THE GUNDOG AND the *Unendingly Just* had been fleeing for six months, the last five of which had been spent hidden in the depths of the Cerberian Field. From a distance it was beautiful, a scatter of glowing dust clouds and sparkling asteroid fields, lit by the stars being born in its heart. Up close it was hideous – the outer regions were composed of chewed-up lumps of rock that span in random patterns, the largest the size of moons, the smallest still enough to degrade engine intakes and speckle portholes with cracks.

It was in this outer region that the *Gundog* and the *Unendingly Just* hung, powered down, hull paint almost stripped away by microme-teorite impacts. The sensor fuzz of the dust and rock clouds hid them from view and meant that monitoring their communications was worse. In fact, the only way the besieging battlefleet knew their quarry was there was for their crews to look out into the field and spot the tiny slivers of reflected starlight gleaming off the metal of their hulls.

It was a grim situation. Fuel was low and supplies were more so.

APOTHECARY PALLAS HAD been worried about Sergeant Tellos for some time. He had requested that he be the one to care for Tellos's griev-ous wounds, for he felt a strange sense of responsibility for the man. He had dragged him out of danger and hauled his bulk up to the platform surface, and duty had insisted he finish the process by see-ing to Tellos's recovery.

That had been then. Now, many months on, it was concern and not a little curiosity that spurred his interest in the mutilated assault sergeant. Of course, to allay his concerns about Tellos, he would first have to find him, for Sergeant Tellos had once more absconded from the secure infirmary bay where he was being kept until Pallas had worked out just what was happening to him.

Tellos would be hard to find, as he had been the last half-dozen times he had escaped. The *Gundog* was not the largest of the Soul Drinkers' ships – their faraway main fleet included immense battle barges and bloated supply craft – but its crew were elite and few in number, and hence there were whole decks completely deserted. Here, in the monastery wing where no brother Marines had dwelt for centuries, the footsteps of his heavy ceramite armour echoed through the cells and chapels. The place was kept spotless by the maintenance servitors which were occasional glimmers of movement in the long shadows, but somehow that made it seem more like a ghost town.

Pallas checked the auspex. Nothing. That in itself was worrying – Tellos's life-signature had been showing less and less on the auspex screen in the past few weeks. Pallas glanced around the high vaults of the ceiling and dark, matt-grey walls of the cells lining this thoroughfare. Lots of places to hide, if you knew what you were doing. Was Tellos treating this as a challenge? If so, he could evade detection for weeks down here. Maybe more – he was eating and resting less according to the latest data, and seemed to be existing on energy alone.

The thoroughfare opened into a librarium annexe. In years gone by some of the Chapter's Marines and novices had dwelt here, before the *Gundog* was refitted for ship-to-ship assaults. In the librarium they had maintained some of the Chapter's records, from the newest battlefield statistics to the aged chansons written by long-dead heroes to ensure their legends were not forgotten. Heroes had been made there, and new ones rediscovered.

Now the ceiling-high shelves were mostly bare with only a handful of texts. One was still perched on a lectern, from which a Chaplain would have berated the novices or inspired them with tales of their betters. Pallas had to take care not to crumble the yellow paper with the fingers of his gauntlet – the book was an elaborate epic of some crusade into a sector long since benighted.

One wall of shelves was not empty, but still packed to bursting with slim volumes – they were all copies of Daenyathos's *Catechisms Martial*, each one illuminated and annotated by the owner, each one recovered from his body after he had died in battle. This librarium had been designated their final resting place, and their removal had not been permitted when the *Gundog* was reassigned.

The auspex bleeped, and a warning sigil flashed up in the corner of Pallas's vision. A life-sign. It was faint, but it could still be Tellos.

Pallas backed up against a wall, knowing the shadows cast by the dim light would not mask his bulk from the senses of another Marine. One hand was encased in the injector/reductor gauntlet which would administer drugs or remove the gene-seed of the fallen. The other grasped his bolt pistol.

Not that he thought Tellos would attack. But Tellos had never been a predictable man and Pallas couldn't be certain.

He saw something moving some way off, across the wide space of the librarium, edging through the archway leading in from a side-chapel. The figure's raw muscles were twined around chunks of stained metal, twin glowing lenses jutted from a stripped-down head of sinew and bone. A drum-fed autogun was held in one hand, and a twin-bladed halberd in the other. It trailed bunches of wires and servos whined as it moved.

A combat servitor. As a novice, like any Soul Drinker, Pallas had despatched scores of the things with boltgun, chainsword, knife, bare hands, and all manner of weaponry he might use or find on the battlefield. They were designed to die hard, giving almost as good as they got – novices who failed combat assessments did not, by definition, survive.

Its artificial eyes scanned the librarium. Pallas knew the things had a limited range and it would not have seen him yet. Pallas hadn't even known there were any training facilities left on the *Gundog* – it must have been left here, like the books, when the monastery facilities were relocated.

The faint snick he heard was an autogun selector flicking to full auto.

Pallas raised his bolt pistol, drew a bead as the servitor's glinting eyes swivelled to fix on him.

A second figure, human this time, dropped all the way down from the ceiling, blocking Pallas's aim. Something long and silver flashed and the half the servitor's head flopped to the ground, wet and gleaming fresh-cut meat. The autogun drummed out a second's worth of shots in a fan that rang around the massive architecture, paused to re-acquire the target, fired again.

The attacker was quick. They all missed.

The servitor's halberd lashed out – it didn't have a power blade, of course, but that blue crackle of an energy field meant it was a shock weapon that would lock muscles and addle minds before the weapon's wicked point found its mark. There was a loud clash as the newcomer parried, whirled, drove his own weapon home.

Suddenly the servitor had been opened from throat to groin, cables and muscle loops spilling out. Then its gun arm was gone, then one foot. Then the remaining half of its head.

The pieces slid down the servitor's metal casings and flopped to the floor. There was the faint thrum of servos powering down, and the sound of the newcomer's breathing as it regained composure.

Stripped to the waist, broad-backed and pale, the man stood over the shreds of the servitor. His skin was translucent and Pallas could see the overdeveloped muscles of his back and upper arms slowly untensing as the battle-rage died down, and pick out the stark black plates of the carapace under the surface.

The weapons were blades from an air intake fan, a metre long and sharpened lovingly. They had been polished to a mirror silver, and thrust into the cauterised stumps where his hands had been.

'Greetings, Sergeant Tellos,' said Apothecary Pallas.

Tellos turned. The skin on his face was the same – Pallas could pick out the muscles of his jaw as he spoke. 'Apothecary. I didn't expect you to follow me this far in.'

'You are under standing orders, Tellos. You must remain in the infirmary. You have much healing to do.' Pallas could smell Tellos's sweat as he walked towards him. Pallas indicated the quietly oozing remains of the servitor. 'Practice?'

Tellos smiled. 'Re-training, apothecary. If the Chapter wishes me to fight on, I must learn to do so again.'

'Sergeant Tellos, you cannot fight. We have told you this, many times. The shock damaged the nerves, the augmeticists cannot connect any bionic–'

'I don't need bionics, Pallas. Just because I cannot hold a chainsword doesn't mean I cannot give my life to my Chapter as I have always done.' Tellos held up his home-made blades, edges shining in the half-light. 'I need more practice, I know that, but I was a novice once and I can be again.'

'No, Tellos. It is over. Talk to the Chaplain if you have difficulty accepting it. My concern is your physical well-being, for you are a brother and though your days in battle are over, I still have a duty towards you. We do not know enough about what has happened to you, Tellos. We are concerned that you are changing. Whether this is your gene-seed reacting to the trauma, we do not know. Until your condition has stabilised we cannot let you wander as you please.' He looked down at the servitor again. 'Where did you find that?'

'I went exploring. I've never done that before. All these years on one or another of our ships and I never thought to find out what lay beyond the next bulkhead. Why do you think that is, Pallas? Are we afraid? Under orders? Or does it just not occur to us to question?'

'These are matters for the Chaplain, Tellos. Let me examine you again and you can discuss them with him.'

'I will fight again, Pallas.'

'I know you will, sergeant. Now, will you come with me?'

The apothecary led the sergeant out of the librarium and back towards the *Gundog's* infirmary, where the serf-adepts and Chapter apothecaries would puzzle over what was happening to Tellos, and decide once again that they didn't know.

THE VIEWSCREEN IN the lecture theatre on board the *Diligent* showed the same unmoving image it had done for months – the scattered asteroids of the Cerberian Field lit by a glow from far within. Somewhere in the thick mass of floating rock were the two Soul Drinker cruisers.

The asteroid field blocked all but the most basic scans from the battlefleet. So far all the intelligence they had gathered told them only that the *Gundog* and the *Unendingly Just* had scarcely moved for the last five months. As to what the Soul Drinkers were doing, how many there were left, what they were planning, the state of their ships and remaining armaments – all they had was guesswork.

The Cerberian Field was a nightmare. Trying to engage the Soul Drinkers was suicide, for the cruisers would just coast deeper into the field while the Imperial battleships were torn up by the asteroids as they tried to pursue. But equally, the Soul Drinkers couldn't escape from their hiding place, since the battlefleet was now far larger than they could hope to evade, large enough to bring numbers to bear wherever the Space Marines tried to break out.

Consul Senioris Chloure never thought he would be glad to lose control of the most important mission of his life, but now he felt a curious strained relief that he no longer commanded the battlefleet in any meaningful way. His name might be tagged onto official communications to mark his nominal command, but his opinion was no longer worth anything.

It meant he was a passenger, an observer, unable to alter the events around him. It also meant he could absolve himself of any responsibility for what might yet become another bloodbath.

If Vekk hadn't suddenly decided to go all dashing and efficient they would never have picked up the warp-trail of the two strike cruisers. There would have been no astropathic communication with the sub-sector admiralty and the sub-battlefleet would not have swollen with every light year to become a mighty flotilla of the Emperor's Navy. The *Hydranye Ko* had stayed at Lakonia for repairs but there were now cruisers, escort squadrons, several fighter-bomber wings, a Departmento Munitorum hospital ship and innumerable support craft swarming around a stationary position outside the Cerberian Field. They had even been joined by the *Penitent's Wrath*, a Ragnarok-class that had seen better days but was nevertheless an immense capital ship bristling with more destruction than Chloure could comprehend.

'Five months,' he said to himself.

'Consul?' came a questioning voice from behind him.

Talaya must have been standing there for some time. She was a naval tactician, one of several dozen sent by the admiralty who had gradually eroded Chloure's authority until they were running the battlefleet by committee.

'Tactician. I thought I was alone in here.' He indicated the giant viewscreen of the amphitheatre – normally used for training lectures, it had been rigged to mirror the view from the screen on the bridge. 'Sometimes it helps to take stock of the situation away from all the noise and bustle.'

'Indeed. You do not have to explain. Your position must be one of great stress and tension.'

Chloure couldn't tell if she was being subtly critical, or if she simply wasn't much of a people person. She had a sharp, pale face that didn't seem designed for expressions and stood out spectrally against the dark blue of her uniform. 'You were saying, consul?'

'I was just thinking… they've been out there five months. Nothing has come or gone. We've had whole fleets of supply ships in and out, but they haven't had anything. Not one shuttle. What are they doing for food? Or fuel?'

'Our data regarding Space Marine resistance to privation is grievously lacking,' said Talaya. 'It is entirely possible they do not need food or water at all in the conventional sense. Even their life support requirements may not be the same as those of a normal naval crew given their resistance to hazardous battlefield conditions.'

'Maybe. Hardly encouraging if we're trying to starve them out.' It was the only way he could see to break down the Soul Drinkers and bring them in for disciplinary procedures. All offensive strategies had been ruled out given the density of the asteroid field and the probable attack capabilities of the strike cruisers themselves, not to mention the horror of another boarding action by the Soul Drinkers.

Of course, quite who would conduct the courts martial of three hundred Space Marines wasn't certain given the number of Imperial authorities that could claim wrongs done to them at the star fort and ordinatus platform. It wasn't even clear if there were brigs on the ships of the battlefleet secure or numerous enough to hold troops who they said could tear through bulkheads with bare hands and take hellgun shots to the chest and laugh. No one had thought that far ahead.

'A blockade is only one strategy. There may be others. It is being suggested that the arrival of further attack-configured craft would make a conventional attack feasible. A Golgotha-class factory ship has been requested, to be refitted for clearing a path through the field.'

'Talaya, that would take months. Years.'

'If that is what it takes, consul. These are renegade Space Marines of a famous and battle-proven Chapter. I am unable to name a more dangerous foe.'

She was right, of course. Somewhere within the grainy mass of the Cerberian asteroid field were two shipfuls of soldiers so deadly and dedicated they could hardly be called human any more. Whatever had driven them to stab their allies in the back – had it really been that freak Khobotov and their Soulspear trinket? – he knew enough of what was said about Marines to realise they would not give up on their treachery now, not ever. He could not imagine the Soul Drinkers forgetting their grudges.

'We'll have to kill them, consul. All of them. There is no other way.'

He looked at her. The woman's face wore no emotion. 'You understand what you're saying, Talaya. I mean, these are...'

'You cannot comprehend anything worse, consul. Renegades, free to do as they will. Banditry, idolatry, secession. All with the prowess and self-sufficiency of a Space Marine Chapter. If it took a century and led to the losses of all the ships of this battlefleet, it would still have to be stopped. We are fully aware of the consequences the extermination of such warriors will have. But we are also aware of what they will do if we are unable to act with complete ruthlessness.'

'I know, tactician, I saw what they left of the Geryon. But... in all my life, I never thought it would come to this.'

'Of course not, consul. And you should not blame yourself for the loss of the star fort and the treachery of the Soul Drinkers. You could not have been expected to cope.'

Evidently satisfied with her morale-boosting, Tactician Talaya walked neatly up the auditorium steps and back into the arteries of the *Diligent*, where officials and adepts from a dozen Imperial authorities combined to form the nerve centre of the mission. It even had a name of its own – the attempt to hunt down and capture – or, more likely, kill – the renegade Soul Drinkers was officially labelled the Lakonia Persecution.

Iocanthos Gullyan Kraevik Chloure wished very much that he was back on a backwater agri-world, pushing pens and drowning in a sea of boredom in the name of the Emperor.

YSER HAD A strong voice for such a weak-bodied man, and it filled the chapel of the *Unendingly Just*. The room was entirely carved of stone, from the lectern in front of him to the pews on which his flock sat, and the echoes of his voice were cold. It was a good place for inspiration, and they had needed it.

'You have all seen what can happen when the Emperor's name is taken in vain,' said Yser. 'When He becomes nothing more than an excuse for men to lay down laws which gain them power and riches, or He is used like a monster in a children's tale to frighten the weak into obeying the corrupt.

'You have seen it, for you have all lost brothers and sisters to such blasphemy, both Marine and the low-born of my flock. Now we are sorely tested – so great are the machineries of corruption and self-service built by such men that even the greatest of warriors, the chosen of the Emperor himself, are driven hard by their aggression.

'But the Emperor, the Architect of Fate, has seen these things and acted upon them. Has the true abuse of the Imperium been made clear to your eyes? Have the self-serving apostates not shown their hand by tarnishing the name of the Soul Drinkers and moved to do violence upon them? For though we are few and the enemies of the Emperor surround us even now, we know that knowledge of the Architect's true plans are a sounder weapon than the mightiest fleet of starships.

'Perhaps these words will be of little comfort to those of you who have lost much, or who are dying yourselves. But to be enlightened, even in death, is a thousandfold greater than to live for centuries in ignorance. We are few, and we are beset on all sides. But we are free.'

Yser looked across at the gathered flock. There were barely thirty of his original followers left – so many had been wounded or simply misplaced in the fall of the star fort, others had died of weakness or disease accelerated by the rationing. But alongside those few survivors were new worshippers welcomed to the light of the Architect of Fate – Space Marines, Soul Drinkers, over a hundred of them, kneeling giants in full armour repaired and gleaming.

It was daunting to think that such men were hanging upon his words, when he had once been a thief and lower than the low. But he knew he was right. He had heard the Architect calling to him, assuring him he had a part to play in the sacred plan, steering him from the debauched and idolatrous church of the Adeptus Ministorum and the superstitious oppression of its many cults. Now the Soul Drinkers had seen first-hand how the Imperium treated those who truly tried to follow the Emperor's path, they were open to Yser's teachings. Every Marine without immediate duties on the *Gundog* or the *Just* was here, silent, contemplating, gradually letting Yser's words mingle with the decades of teaching they had undergone. Even their Chaplain, Iktinos, who never removed his skull-faced helmet in their presence, listened to Yser, and found truth in the priest's words.

Yser could feel the power here. He had seen in his waking dreams the legion of warriors in purple and bone, who would take the plans of the Architect of Fate and make them real at last. That Yser should be there when it happened, that he should help show them the way… it would be pride, if he did not feel the Emperor's own hand guiding his thoughts.

'Be strong, brothers and sisters. Refuse to fail in His sight. Fill your veins with faith, disdain the foe, and prepare yourselves. For He will be our salvation, whether they take our lives or not.'

When the sermon was over the flock went about their duties – some to the sick, others to the ship, many of the Marines to their proscribed periods of contemplation when they would reflect upon the principles by which they lived. One approached him – Yser did not have to look up to know his name, for he could feel the power welling up inside him.

'Yser, I would speak with you,' said Sarpedon, the one the other Marines addressed as commander. 'Some of us are… changing. You have heard of Tellos.'

'I am ashamed that some rumours have reached my ears. My few followers hold your warriors in awe, Commander Sarpedon. They are curious, and they talk.'

'We do not know what has happened to him, or quite how he is changing. The details are complex but the chemistry of his body has altered and he refuses to accept his fighting days are over, crippled though he is. And there are others, but more subtle. The bone structure of Sergeant Graevus's hand is changing, and Givrillian says his eyesight is being altered. These are just two of many.'

'If you wish an explanation from me, commander, I must disappoint you. I can feel the presence of the Architect of Fate and, on occasion, I catch glimpses of what he wishes to tell us. But I know nothing more.'

Sarpedon turned to leave, but paused. 'Yser, there is something else.'

'Commander?'

'We have turned our backs on much that we once learned was sacred. We have seen the threat the Imperium itself presents to the right order of the universe. I think that when we realise just how little we know, and how different now are the reasons we fight... it will be much for us to deal with. I am not certain myself what will become of me. The whole universe will change for us.'

'Faith, Commander Sarpedon. There need be nothing more. But I think you know this already.'

'Of course, preacher.'

After Sarpedon had left, his image was burned onto Yser's vision for many minutes. He had never felt such power. Did Sarpedon himself realise what he could become? Could even the Emperor's own chosen warriors ever be truly prepared to do His will? He had seen, in his visions, what they must do – he had seen the world built from corruption, with a terrible intelligence at its heart, which must be cleansed to prove the warriors' worth. Would they be ready? Would anyone?

All his questions had the same answer. *Faith*. There need be nothing more.

No SUNLIGHT STRUGGLED through the purple-grey clouds on the forge world of Koden Tertius, but they were lit from beneath by the fires of the factory pits. Huge columns of flame, kilometres high, licked out from the exhaust ports bored into the rocky round, scorching the habs and control complexes, roaring with the fury that burned in the forge world's belly below. Most of the planet's habitable structures were set within mountainsides or underground, and the spindly metallic webs that stretched between pylons and mountain peaks were support struts and sensor mounts. A thick gauze of smoke hung in front of everything, making it washed-out and grey, punctuated by the great columns of fire gouting up from the planet's geothermal core.

Tech-priest Sasia Koraloth looked out on this scene through a port-hole in the side of her laboratory annexe. She knew that one day she would not think the darkness and fires of her forge world so ugly – such minor aesthetic distractions would be far beneath her when she was so occupied with the masterful logic that was the tool and creation of the Machine God.

Gradually she would be augmented and improved until there was so little of her original body left that her mind could become detached from the outside world and contemplate only the mechanics of reality.

She longed for that day, for this universe was a dark place and only the Omnissiah could make sense of it.

The stillness of her laboratory stirred and a servitor drifted soundlessly in. It was little more than a suspensor unit and a voice box. 'To Tech-priest Koraloth, the wishes of Archmagos Khobotov are to be known. One: that Tech-priest Koraloth is to commune with him on matters vital on the Route Cobalt. Two: that her laboratory and associated facilities are to be cleared and made ready for an examination temporal. Three: that he expects and will receive complete discretion on matters discussed and discovered. Awaiting reply.'

'I shall be there,' she said, and the servitor buzzed away. The idea that Archmagos Khobotov himself should have chosen her... her work here must have been noticed after all. The painstaking reverse engineering of trinkets brought by explorator parties took up all her time, as witnessed by the rows of disassembled and polished components on the work benches of her lab. But she had not thought she had discovered anything worthy of note, or that her diligence and dedication had been seen by any of her superiors.

Perhaps this was it. Perhaps this would mark the beginning of her ascent. Or perhaps it would end in nothing.

The data-mat set into the skin on the back of her left hand flashed up the location of Route Cobalt. She left her dingy lab and hurried through rock-walled streets populated by servitors of all sizes and functions, their only common link the presence of recycled human tissues to form their nervous and muscular systems. There was the occasional tech-priest too – recent initiates like herself and more venerable magi, some with small crowds of apprentices in tow.

Already she was beginning to see humans as machines of meat and bone. Already the underlying logic of the universe fascinated her, and she was increasingly repelled by the patina of corrosion that she had to clean off her technoclaves and data-thief probes every day. One day she would sweep through these rock-warrens with her own apprentices, enduring their unending questions and not caring about any of them. She would at last understand.

Route Cobalt was a little-used channel cut through the mountain to reach a shuttle terminus on the surface. A phalanx of servitors stood shoulder-to-shoulder across the street, before parting to reveal Khobotov himself, lens-eyes glinting within the shadows of his hood.

One day, she would be like that.

'Tech-Priest Koraloth,' said Khobotov in his wonderful metallic drone. 'I give you leave to select your research coven and conduct the rites of reverse engineering as you see fit.'

Something hummed behind her – a cherub-drone, dead-skinned face locked in a serene smile, arms replaced with dextrous mechadendrites that handed her something with great delicacy.

It was a scroll-case, simple and plain, rather longer than her forearm. Then she opened it, and saw what she had been summoned to investigate.

It was a cylinder, the surface of which gleamed with intricate golden circuitry, and which had what looked like impossibly miniaturised gene-encoders set into the handgrip. A small enough thing, but her experience with pre-Imperial technology told her it was something much more than it seemed. She could feel the power of its complexity flowing through her hands as she touched it.

'Archmagos, what…?'

'It is known as the Soulspear. There was considerable trouble involved in its acquisition. I will expect your preliminary data-sermon within the year.'

Koraloth couldn't take her eyes off the object, even to acknowledge the archmagos. What was this thing – a weapon, a shield, a transportation device – that by its mere presence could project such certainty in her that it was a masterpiece? And could she ever do such a creation justice?

She forced herself to look at Khobotov. 'Why have you chosen me, archmagos?'

'Your lack of status means few will care for your research, and your veneration of me and the values of the Omnissiah I represent mean you are unlikely to betray me. When much is at stake, it is always prudent to make use of the lowly.'

Khobotov swept away and his servitor-guard closed around him, striding away down the Route Cobalt and leaving Koraloth holding the Soulspear.

Lowly? She knew that. But not for long.

There were things not even Khobotov knew about her. The depth of her determination to do the work of the Omnissiah, the brightness with which her goal burned within her. And more besides.

Much more. There were others on Koden Tertius with the same devotion as her, and they shared a bond beyond their common calling. They would be her coven, and with the Soulspear they would begin their ascent to the ranks of the magi.

THE BATTLEMENTS OF Quixian Obscura had burned. The artillery had shelled for a solid week before the assault had begun, and the chemical fires they had lit raged across the crenellated stone of the cyclopean fortress wall.

Sarpedon had clambered from his drop-pod and saw theirs was one of the last pods to fall. Commander Caeon was already dragging his great armoured body over the lip of the nearest gate house, spraying bolter shells into the alien defenders below as energy bolts melted the stone around him. Squad Kallis, to which Sarpedon had been attached, hunkered down into a defensive position ready to cover the attackers who had landed before them. Fifty-strong, they had to take the gatehouse and force open the vast gates below so the storm units in the vanguard of the Imperial army could put these alien heathens to the sword.

Fire swept over them, fanned by the shrieking wind, but they had ignored it. Kallis took stock of the situation – hoary and old with a face that looked as if it had been stitched together out of battered leather, it was his calling to lead the newly-initiated into battle, to test what they had learned as novices. They had all taken part in the brutal live training regimes and fleet patrol duties, but few of them had been thrown into action as thick as it was there.

'I want plasma cover east! Flamer, Librarian, take down that weapons post!' Kallis had pointed towards an emplacement built into the stone where once a defensive lascannon or launcher had stood, but which was now being used by a half-dozen slender-faced aliens to fire a monstrous energy weapon into the backs of the Soul Drinkers ahead.

Vixu had led them in, flamer gouting, Sarpedon behind working up the energy for the Hell. Some within the Chapter's librarium could have cracked open the emplacement with telekenesis or psychopyretics, but Sarpedon's way was to crack open the minds of its crew.

And yet… what had been the point?

The thought in his head was like an intruder. He remembered Quixian Obscura in every detail, as he did every battle in which he had seen action, yet he had never thought any of it pointless. No, he had tried projecting every horror the aliens might fear, and lashed them with gunfire along with the rest of his brother Marines, all the while feeling righteous hatred coursing through him.

But really, what had been the point? After Quixian Obscura was claimed, what had become of it? It was probably just one more vacuous husk of a world run by the greedy and powermongering, populated by underlings who never knew the futility of their lives. To exterminate the aliens, that was a worthy thing – but when it was done to satisfy the whims of corpulent merchants and lying priests, was there anything truly noble in it?

The thoughts were new and strange. Suddenly, it was brought home just how much the universe had changed around Sarpedon – the deeds which had made him proud now seemed empty and futile, the hero-ism that propped up a regime of corruption. He tried to shake it out of his head, but it wouldn't go – the nagging voice at the back of his head stayed, bleating that it was all meaningless, that he had fought at the whims of the same self-serving bureaucrats that had tried to butcher his battle-brothers.

He tried, as he sometimes did when he needed to look long and hard at himself, to relive the battle and not just watch it played out in his head. He imagined the sharp-edged wind across the battlements and the reeking sulphuric clouds from the shelling below, the low rumble of shouted orders from a million Imperial Guardsmen and the flicker-ing in the air of a hundred shuriken rounds from alien guns shearing towards him.

Suddenly he was there as the Marines had burst into the emplacement and the energy weapon was a fiery shell, power cells crippled by a krak grenade. From just below the edge of the wall the ambush sprung, aliens with masks and bodysuits carrying glowing power-scimitars, cartwheeling and somersaulting with unholy speed.

It was no good. Sarpedon didn't care – gone was the warrior's rage at the enemy's deceit that had sent him wading into their midst, pump-ing bolter shells into their unarmoured bodies, cracking necks and splitting open heads within jewel-eyed masks.

A bolter blast caught the closest in the stomach and almost blew it in two – its grace dissolved instantly as it flopped to the ground. In the time it took the bullet to find its mark two more had come too close to draw aim – he slashed at one and it ducked, the other struck back and the tongue of its blade licked deep into his thigh. He stabbed at the head of the first, let it duck, stamped down on the back of its neck with a ceramite boot, felt it crunch beneath his foot.

But this time, living it all again, Sarpedon didn't care. He might as well have been breaking an eggshell or kicking an obstacle out of his way.

When the third staggered backwards, left arm torn off and still held in Sarpedon's hand, he felt none of the holy triumph that had filled his soul that day. When it fell from the lip of the battlements to land, hun-dreds of metres below, as a shower of bloody fragments, he did not cheer in victory, though he remembered doing so all those years before.

It had been the moment he had truly proved himself on the battle-field. The junior Librarian with the strange psycho-transmitter power, whose inclusion in the force had been little more than an experiment, had slain three of the treacherous xenos in close combat and held the rearguard of the assaulting force. He had been clapped on the back and saluted in the victory feast as the fortress burned, and known that he had finally earned his place at Dorn's side. Now it didn't matter. None of it did.

The Chapter archivists had even given him a line in the saga of Quixian Obscura. It had been only his third action since novicehood – Daenyathos's words must have impressed the Marine deeply, they said, for him to follow his creed so exactly. It had been an honour afforded few Marines of his status, but somehow, he just didn't care any more.

He knew that he would look around to see Sergeant Kallis slain by heathen power-blades, and would rally the squad's survivors to butcher the surviving aliens before they could carry their attack into the advancing Soul Drinkers. He knew that he would hear the earthquaking rumble of the gates opening and the cheer as ten thousand Guardsmen poured through to flood the fortress with vengeful steel and las-fire. He had been there, and recalled it all a hundred times over. But it felt different now, and he was distant and uncaring. Brother Marines lay dead – what had they died for? Alien vermin were slain beside them – why waste good Marine lives on them? And the swarming, idiot hordes of Guardsmen below – was there anything for them really worth fighting for, when the Emperor whose name was on their lips as they charged was thousands of light years away, His will distorted and ignored by the men who ruled in His stead?

All this waste. It was a hollow deep within him where his pride should have been.

Caeon, high on the battlements of the gate house and slick with alien blood, turned and fixed Sarpedon with war-honed eyes.

'Die,' he said in the voice of machine spirit *674-XU28*.

Sarpedon shook his head violently and the inside of his cell swam back into view. While Marines never truly slept, in their half-waking rest period they could dream, and there Sarpedon had visited the battlements on Quixian Obscura many times. But it had never been like this. He had never felt such emptiness in the face of battle, where a Soul Drinker should revel in the glory of the fight.

The fires of Quixian Obscura finally died down and he was alone in the cell. The walls were bare aside from the pict-slates for reviewing briefings and reports, and the shelf on which stood his volume of the *Catechisms Martial*. His armour was racked neatly in one corner and his bolter and force staff hung on a weapons rack. There was nothing else in the room, for what need had a Soul Drinker of anything else?

There was so much troubling him that he didn't understand. Seventy years a warrior, and yet what did he really know? He had lost himself in such a cycle of honour and battle and holy anger that he had nothing else.

Seventy years, and a hundred battles burned bright in his memory, but somehow they did not fill him with the pride they had done many months before. He looked down on his bare torso and saw the scars from surgery and wounds – a score of scalpel cuts around the edges of his implanted carapace, an ugly tear from an ork's chainblade, the slight colour mismatch of a skin graft and the dozen pockmarked memories of lucky shots. All these and more, and yet he felt that in gaining them he had earned nothing.

A tiny green cursor was blinking in the corner of the ship-comms pict-slate. Sarpedon focused on a retinal icon and the image of Tech-Marine Lygris appeared. He had suffered considerable neuro-trauma during his brush with the machine-spirit, and his facial muscles had been fixed into place with medical staples to stop them from spasming. It looked as if someone else's face had been nailed to the front of his head.

'Commander Sarpedon, we request your presence on the bridge. The serf-crew have picked something up.'

'Something?'

'We have some guesses, but none of us have the necessary clearance. These are some of the highest-level codes we have ever encountered.'

'Enlighten me.'

'Carmine, commander. Level carmine.'

'NOT EVEN OUR most senior tacticians can open level carmine encoding – we'll have to wait for them to come to us, consul, if we are to know who they are.' Vekk was getting the chance to be important for the first time in some months and had his chest puffed out and hands clasped behind his back accordingly. The long-service medals on his chest were probably kept polished just for chances like this.

Talaya looked up from the mostly meaningless data streaming across the screens in front of her. 'Agreed. Preliminary scans suggest a considerable power output potential. I suggest we prime the shields as stated in the standard fleet procedure for the approach of an unidentified ship.'

'And roll out the red carpet in one of the shuttle bays,' continued Vekk. 'Could be a visitor.'

'Very well. Do it all.' Chloure was under no illusions that the decision had been made already – he was barely a rubber-stamp any more. Two fighter wings from the *Epic* were even now showing as tiny tagged blips on the main viewscreen of the bridge, fanning out to surround the new ship and run guard-dog duty. Just in case.

'Comms down!' shouted someone and suddenly the dark blood-glow of the warning lights strobed painfully across the bridge. 'We've lost comms control!'

The security troops at the rear of the bridge stomped into the alert formation as several emergency tech-teams, lower-grade tech-priests and attendant servitors bristling with servo-tools, scuttled out of maintenance alcoves and began prying the panels off comm-consoles.

'They've hijacked our vox-casters and transmission network,' said Talaya tonelessly. 'Interdiction and exploitation patterns.'

'Why? Are they hostile?' Chloure had so far avoided participation in a proper pitched space battle and had no intention of breaking the habit.

'Unknown,' said Talaya predictably, the deep red lights picking out her sharp, precise face.

Vekk jumped down into the sensorium readout pit, sunken into the deck of the *Diligent*, which was populated by a gesticulating gaggle of tech-priests and petty officers trying to interpret the signals pouring in from the ship's sensors. Streams of printouts were spewing from data outputs. 'Here!' yelled Vekk, pointing at a stream of coordinates. 'Get this on screen!'

The ship appeared on screen. And what a ship it was. A bright swell in space, warping the light passing through it so the stars were drawn into long white streaks. The few sensorium traces that Chloure could understand implied the *Diligent* didn't believe there was anything there at all.

'Are they Imperial?' he asked.

'Probably,' called back Vekk from the sensorium pit. 'It may not be entirely good news for us if they are.'

The vox-casters screamed and Chloure tried to cover his ears, too late. He imagined the same sound screeching through every 'caster on every ship of the fleet, but fleet comms were still out and he couldn't be sure.

'Helm control lost,' said Talaya just before the lights went out completely.

The crew were silent. Only the viewscreen still lit the bridge of the *Diligent*, washing the faces of its crew with faint blue-white light.

'In the name of the Immortal Emperor and all His dominions,' spoke a sonorous, throaty voice from every vox-caster in the ship. 'This battlefleet is now under the command of Lord Gorgo Tsouras of the Ordo Hereticus. Your ships are mine, as are your bodies and minds, as tools with which to execute the Emperor's will.'

Chloure could hear the whispers from the petty officers below. In truth, he thought, he had known this would happen all along. Given the nature of their foe, and the principles at stake, it was perhaps inevitable that this would happen. Chloure would have given anything at that moment to be back managing the sector's largest grox farm, anything to get away from the organisation now claiming command of his fleet.

The image on the viewscreen swam as layers of sensor-shielding puffed away from the newcomer ship in layers of shimmering light. Below them was revealed dark, slick metal, beaten into sensor-deflecting triangular plates, with shiny black viewports like slitted eyes and sharp blades of projector weapons stabbing forward from its sleek bat-shape. The twin engine cowlings flared out behind it like fans of steel feathers, and from its sleek belly tiny gunmetal flakes broke off and sprang to life – drone-ships, tiny blue engines flaring as they formed a shimmering necklace of guard ships around their parent.

The ship was completely bare of paint save for one symbol carved in crimson onto its side. It was a simple image, but it was enough to confirm Chloure's fears and freeze the breath in the throats of the bridge crew. Few of them had ever seen it for real, but every one of them knew what it meant, even if only from stories that preachers told them as children to scare them into obedience.

A huge stylised letter 'I', with a sleek-toothed skull at its head.

The Lakonia Persecution was now officially under the command of the Holy Orders of the Emperor's Inquisition.

CHAPTER SIX

A SINGLE SHUTTLE, of the same bare angular metal and with the same sigil of the Inquisition emblazoned on its hull, weaved dextrously through the tumbling rocks of the Cerberian Field. It was unarmed and transmitting a truce-signal, keeping a respectful distance from the Thunderhawks the *Unendingly Just* sent out to escort it.

Sarpedon watched the shuttle approach from the bridge of the *Just*, knowing as soon as the visual became clear that it was an Inquisitorial craft. Chapter-serfs in vacuum gear hauled the docking clamps into place as the sleek craft alighted in the shuttle bay, and hurriedly backed off as its occupants emerged.

Sarpedon waited in the audience chamber, where tapestries of Chapter heroes hung on the age-darkened walls and the flagstones were worn smooth by generations of power armoured footsteps. He watched a holomat image as the shuttle's passengers emerged, always looking with an eye to evaluate potential opponents.

Though the shuttle had come under truce, there was no doubt that the Inquisition's representatives here believed in conspicuous strength. A phalanx of twenty Ordo Hereticus troops marched down the gangplank of the shuttle, clad in glossy dark red combat armour and armed with hellguns. Their faces were masked with veils of scarlet-linked chainmail and bundles of grenades hung at their belts. Towards the back of the group was a figure entirely shrouded in dark grey robes, a large shoulder-mounted hypodermic array pumping murky fluids into its neck.

An astropath, guessed Sarpedon, for rapid psychic communication with the main Inquisitorial craft. Probably an aged and experienced one judging from its stooped, laboured gait.

Flanking the Hereticus troops were two mercenary gunmen. One was a man dressed in battered leather with muscles swarming with gang-tattoos, carrying a shotgun and bearing a bionic eye worth rather more than him. The other was a woman in bulky padded armour, with three pistols at her waist and a burn-scar taking up half her face. Sarpedon had heard tell of the rag-tag miscreants that some less orthodox inquisitors could assemble as field agents and bodyguards, and these two low-lives were in stark contrast to the ordered ranks of Inquisitor-ial troops alongside them.

At the centre of the phalanx was a man in armour of brass, the barrel chest and gauntlets of his armour imposingly huge. His face was incongruously youthful, sleek-featured and dark-skinned. There was a sword slung at his back with an immense blade, nearly a metre and a half long and half a metre wide, surely too large by far for anyone to wield?

Around his neck hung a solid silver Inquisitorial symbol, a simple and definite badge of office.

There were protocols for this sort of thing. Sarpedon stood at the centre of the audience chamber with Givrillian and his tactical squad at the back of the room, to observe proceedings. The Hereticus troops waited at the opposite end of the room and the visitor strode up to meet Sarpedon.

The man's armour gave him almost the bulk of a Space Marine. The sword at his back still seemed impossibly huge – Sarpedon looked over the man's body and saw there was nowhere another weapon could be concealed.

'Librarian Sarpedon,' said the visitor, his voice slick and cultured. 'I am Interrogator K'Shuk, envoy of Lord Inquisitor Tsouras of the Ordo Hereticus. My master has sent me to convey his demands to you and your men. You have been accused of treachery, heresy by action, and the mutinous killing of the Holy Emperor's servants in the person of tech-guard stationed on the *674-XU28*.

'You will surrender your ships immediately to me. We shall bring in a containment team who will receive all your weaponry and armour. You will be incarcerated and subjected to an Interrogation Martial and full Oculum Medicae while you are transported to an Inquisitorial fortress-world for processing. You will co-operate with us in all these matters, and failure to comply in any particular of these demands will be considered an admission of guilt.'

K'Shuk folded his hands behind his back, waiting for the answer.

It was as Sarpedon had expected, as soon as it was clear the Inquisition were now involved. Tsouras would take the Soul Drinkers' weapons away, shut them up in a prison-ship, and use all manner of techniques old and new to get them to confess. No matter what the result of the Interrogation Martial, Sarpedon and his Marines would be taken to a planet controlled by Inquisitor Tsouras, tried, and executed. A verdict of guilty and the deaths of his men were inevitable, but that was not the worst. To be disarmed and rendered harmless while they were examined and tormented, unable to fight back and defend the honour that was stripped from them, would be worse than death for any Soul Drinker.

The insult was appalling, worse by far than anything the Chapter had ever suffered before. Tsouras and K'Shuk would be well aware of the reply they would get. But still, there were protocols for matters such as this.

'Interrogator K'Shuk,' began Sarpedon, 'The Soul Drinkers do not recognise the authority of Inquisitor Lord Tsouras or any agent of Imperial authority. The Imperium has been shown to be corrupt and self-serving, its actions a mockery of the most blessed God-Emperor's will. It has robbed this Chapter of its due, then moved to destroy us when we took steps to redress the slight, then pursued us in its anger and sent its agents to demand our humiliation.

'Your demands are refused, Interrogator K'Shuk. The Soul Drinkers submit only to the will of the Emperor, and you act only for yourselves.'

'Very well.' K'Shuk's face was impassive. 'Commander Sarpedon, it is my duty to inform you that the Soul Drinkers Chapter is hereby declared Excommunicate Traitoris, to be struck from the annals of history. The Chapter's name will be deleted from the scrolls of honour in the Hall of Heroes and wiped from the memories of the Archivum Imperialis. Your gene-seed will be destroyed and your bodies incinerated so that no more will your blood taint mankind. The Imperium of man turns its back on the Soul Drinkers.

'Confess now, Sarpedon, repent your misdeeds, and it shall be quick for your men. Either way, your lives will end for your sins against the Emperor.'

Sarpedon said nothing. He had known deep down it would happen, but somehow had never accepted it as a possibility. Excommunicate Traitoris. Banished from the human race, cast from the light of the Emperor. Though he and his Marines had learned the true sickness of the Imperium and refused to be a part of it any longer, the concept still filled him with horror. He was Excommunicated from mankind. For so long, there had been no graver fate.

He was horrified, but was also angry that the Imperium would pass such a judgement on those no one was fit to judge. Use that anger, he told himself. Use it, let it keep you sharp, do not turn numb with shock or cold with fear. Stay angry, because you will need it.

K'Shuk reached up the the hilt of the huge sword slung at his back. 'You understand, Commander Sarpedon, your conduct here has revealed you to be a dangerous man and a threat to the stability of the Imperium. The Inquisition cannot allow your sins to multiply with your continued existence. I am empowered by Inquisitor Tsouras to perform your immediate execution.'

Sarpedon had known they would try to kill him, just as they had tried before by launching the Geryon to shell the star fort. It was only logical – he had realised what the Imperium really was, and they would do anything to silence that truth. But now it had come to it, here in the age-hallowed audience chamber of the *Unendingly Just*, he let the anger grow in him again. That anyone would think themselves not just Sarpedon's equal, but his superior, that they could pass a sentence of death on him – that was an obscenity. Daenyathos had written that emotions are the enemy of the common soldier, but for a Space Marine, they were an ally. Use the hate, channel it, turn it into strength.

K'Shuk drew the sword. It seemed impossibly light in his gauntleted hand and Sarpedon's enhanced hearing picked out the faint hum of tiny gravitic motors as the immense blade swung over the interrogator's shoulder. Suspensor units, one in the pommel, one at the tip of the blade. The sword would be light enough to lift with a finger, but utterly unbalanced and so difficult to use that most martial treatises considered such weapons to be useless in combat.

But K'Shuk had been sent here as an executioner, and would be skilled beyond comprehension in the arts of the blade. The interrogator stepped forward, and lunged.

Squad Givrillian and the Hereticus troops didn't move. This was a duel between accuser and accused, and such things were not to be interfered with.

The blade thrummed past Sarpedon's ear, and he could feel the keenness of the edge as it cut through the air. He ducked back and drew his own force staff just in time to parry the blade's backswing.

K'Shuk was skilled to a near-supernatural level, with the kind of speed and finesse that comes from being trained from birth. Tsouras probably had a stable of infants he could have raised as interrogators, and every now and then, he would find one like K'Shuk.

Sarpedon was on the back foot, the blade slicing at him like an arc of lightning, K'Shuk's movements swift and slick. A cut down towards Sarpedon's throat was turned onto his shoulder pad and the blade bit deep through the ceramite, slicing through it as if it wasn't there.

K'Shuk dropped a shoulder, span, lashed a reverse cut towards Sarpedon's torso which was parried with a wild swing that left Sarpedon wide open.

K'Shuk span again and this time the sword hit home, the massive broad blade carving up into Sarpedon's abdomen. Red pain stabbed up from the wound, but Sarpedon knew he would survive, knew he would go on fighting. He had taken a thousand wounds, and knew which ones would slow him down.

What was more, he knew how he could win. K'Shuk was lightning-quick and his sword was a weapon of a type Sarpedon had never faced before, but his skill came at the expense of variety. Whatever ancient fighting system the interrogator followed, it was one which relied on intricate set patterns to allow its adherents to wield the suspensor-blade in anger. There must have been a million variations on a thousand patterns, but they were there in the movements of K'Shuk's feet on the worn flagstones and the bright shapes made by the lashing blade. A half-step back was a cue for a lateral cut, an overhead strike from the force staff was met with a broad circular parry leading into a counter-thrust to the solar plexus. There were basic principles built into every movement, and if Sarpedon could learn them...

Gradually, as Sarpedon met K'Shuk's blows, he saw the fundamentals of the suspensor-blade art. On an upward cut the blade could take flight thanks to its anti-grav units and spiral out of the wielder's hands, so K'Shuk's upward swings were limited. It was difficult to change the direction of the blade suddenly, so every sequence of attacks had to be made up of strikes that flowed into one another – it was fast and no doubt pretty to watch, but it cut down K'Shuk's options. The interrogator compensated with speed, but Sarpedon was fast, too.

Sarpedon reminded himself that though he had never fought anyone like K'Shuk, the reverse was also true. K'Shuk had probably killed hundreds of skilled opponents, heathen aliens and warp-strengthened heretics, but he had never faced anything as deadly as an angry Space Marine commander fighting for his honour.

The wounds were opening fast – a deep thrust right through the meat of Sarpedon's forearm, a lunge that put the blade's tip dangerously close to his secondary heart. The blade was broad and wounds bled terribly in spite of the Marine's rapidly-clotting blood, and K'Shuk could win simply by wearing Sarpedon down with debilitating cuts. Sarpedon's time was limited – he had to break the code of K'Shuk's skill soon, or he would be too slowed by his wounds to stand a chance.

Sarpedon blocked a blow to the side and knew what would follow – K'Shuk had the option of an upward cut that promised a killing strike up underneath the jaw. Sarpedon ducked back and sure enough the blade swept up a hair's breadth from his face.

K'Shuk needed a precious fragment of a second to arrest the blade's upwards motion, turn it and bring it swinging down. In that fragment of time he was open, and Sarpedon struck.

The hit to K'Shuk's stomach didn't penetrate the massive bronze armour, but the butt-end of the force staff left a massive dent that must have ruptured K'Shuk's organs. He was sent him stumbling backwards, blade dragged down to guard. Sarpedon followed up with a lunge over the blade ringing off the armour above K'Shuk's collar bone.

Sarpedon stabbed again, and struck home. The end of the staff passed right through K'Shuk's throat, spearing out through the back of his neck. Sarpedon stepped to the side, reached behind the interrogator, and grabbed the blood-slick end of the staff. He pulled, drawing the whole length of the staff through K'Shuk's neck, until the eagle-winged head of the staff ripped through the throat in a shower of blood.

K'Shuk tried to turn but his spinal cord was in tatters. His legs collapsed and he sent one final accusing glance at Sarpedon as, nearly decapitated, he clattered to the ground. The suspensor blade escaped his grasp and fluttered like a leaf to the floor where, with delicate slowness, the monomolecular blade sunk up to half its length in the flagstones.

There was only a faint oozing sound as K'Shuk's blood flowed. The rest was silence.

Sarpedon holstered the force staff at his back. He looked around the Hereticus troops and K'Shuk's warband, and the Marines of Squad Givrillian, arrayed around the room. This, it occurred to him, could be awkward.

'Cut the fuel lines of their shuttle,' he said. 'Set them adrift.'

He could hear the fingers easing off the triggers of the Hereticus troops' hellguns.

Squad Givrillian moved to surround the troopers and acknowledgement runes flashed in Sarpedon's vision to confirm that serf-labourers were heading to cripple their shuttle.

He could have killed them there and then, with the guns of Squad Givrillian chattering against the wall of the audience chamber as the Hereticus troopers and scum of K'Shuk's warband died for daring to set foot on a Soul Drinkers' ship. But they would have shot back and Sarpedon could have lost good Marines.

And, besides, there were protocols for this sort of thing.

* * *

IN THE LECTURE auditorium on board the *Diligent,* a holo display projected a room-filling image of the Cerberian Field, the asteroids a grainy haze of orange specks. The battlefleet of the Lakonia Persecution was represented by a host of blue icons at one edge of the large circular room. Between the fleet and the edge of the asteroid field were two dagger-shaped purple icons, the *Gundog* and the *Unendingly Just,* heading rapidly through the air towards the field.

Many of the *Diligent's* bridge crew were seated around the room, watching the display as it re-enacted the scene several months before as the Soul Drinkers had first been chased to the edge of the Cerberian Field.

Well separated from the crew was Inquisitor Tsouras, watching impassively from the back of the room. The inquisitor was grudgingly admiring of the skill the Soul Drinkers showed in keeping their cruisers ahead of a large and well-provisioned battlefleet for so long. Very grudgingly.

Twin shockwaves burst at the nearest edge of the cloud, sending the tiny orange specks tumbling out of the way. The daggers flew into the space created as the obstacles closed again behind them, just as several blue squares pulled up suddenly as the field knitted itself back together around the Soul Drinkers' cruisers.

'Gravitics torpedoes?' asked Inquisitor Tsouras.

'We do not believe so,' replied Senior Tactician Talaya, pausing the holo display. 'We suspect the torpedoes the Soul Drinkers used were improvised. Probably assault torpedoes loaded with munitions – the blast would spread in all directions.'

'Their flying was reckless indeed, then.'

'Insane,' agreed Talaya. 'It is likely they suffered minor damage once within the Cerberian Field but it is impossible to verify. The extremely hazardous nature of the manoeuvres evidently reflects the desperation of their flight.'

'Presumably your forces have been unwilling to replicate such hijinks, consul?'

'Their strike cruisers are much more athletic than any of our craft, my lord inquisitor,' said Chloure, with a touch of nervousness he couldn't hide from Tsouras's sharp ears. 'It would have been suicide for us to follow them.'

'Of course.' Tsouras didn't like Consul Senioris Chloure. He was wet, gutless, and utterly out of his depth. A decent commander, being aware of what was at stake here, would have sent an expendable ship in to test the waters and make sure there was no way a direct assault could have been carried out. There were enough captains and crews here that were only good for sacrificing.

It was good he had arrived when he had. An operation like this was more than capable of disintegrating completely. He had seen it happen, and incompetence had been the most common justification on his lips as he gave the order for execution.

Not this time, though. This time it had been treachery in the extreme, Grand Treason Imperial. And for the first time, his order had not been carried out. His executioner, Interrogator K'Shuk, had not returned or made any communication of success. It was a shame, for Tsouras had harboured some hopes for K'Shuk, who was as cold-blooded a killer as Tsouras had ever come across. But at least there was no doubt now as to what Commander Sarpedon and the Soul Drinkers really stood.

'As you can imagine, inquisitor,' continued Talaya, 'our current tactic is to enforce a blockade while exploring alternative options. It is very probable to our tactical corps that privation will eventually render the enemy defenceless, allowing us to begin a campaign of pioneering through the Cerberian Field to reach them.'

'And in this time there will be no actions taken by the enemy that could possibly catch you by surprise?' said Tsouras. 'No way in which they could bring the fight to you? Perhaps when your crews were so dogged by fatigue and indiscipline that their threat reactions will be slow and confused? Such things have happened to fleets far greater than this. They become lazy. Indecisive. Space Marines, on the other hand, do not. They will be razor-sharp right up until the end, when they are exulting over the burning corpses of your ships.'

Talaya was silent. Chloure squirmed uncomfortably, and Tsouras reflected that he had little reason to let the consul survive. 'We act now, and decisively. No matter how many we lose, every second we wait gives them further advantage. They do not sleep, gentlemen. They need to eat or drink only rarely, and even if for whatever reason they have no supplies they will have the underlings of their Chapter to live upon if necessary. They are not an ill-led rabble. They will not decide to break for your benefit. We must break them ourselves.'

'It is debatable,' said Talaya, apparently unflapped, 'whether entry into the Cerberian Fields will even be possible for either main craft or assault waves.'

'There is no debate, tactician. The Marines had to blast their way in without gravitic warheads. We do not have to suffer that hardship. My ship carries more than enough gravitic weaponry for our present purpose. In any case, having seen the quality of leadership here I shall be taking command of the operation personally. Every captain on this fleet will have every available assault wing fully bombed up and ready to launch. Perhaps you can claw back some semblance of dignity by refraining from screwing it up this time.'

Heresy. Why did they not understand? It was like a plague of vermin, near-impossible to eradicate unless you were prepared to destroy much of what you were trying to save. Once a world was tainted by unchecked heresy you could cover every square metre in smouldering craters a man's height deep, and still there would be some dark-thinking traitor ready to poison what was left. Inquisitor Tsouras knew this because he had tried it himself.

And now there was a Chapter of Marines that had fallen from grace, and these officers dithered here like nervous children while the cancer grew. At least the sentence of Excommunicate Traitoris had given him free rein to do whatever he wanted to bring the Soul Drinkers to the Emperor's justice.

He stood, drawing himself up to his full augmented three metre height. All of it, the skeletal elongations, the bronze ram's head shoulder pads, the thick studded leather cloak and tabard and the blank yellow-grey eyes, had been affected solely to intimidate weaklings like these. They were simple, cosmetic augmentations, far from the complex bionics that the Mechanicus were rumoured to have developed – but they seemed to work. Only Tactical Officer Talaya seemed unperturbed, from which Tsouras concluded she was a rather more stupid woman than her codex-quoting speech suggested.

He swept out of auditorium dramatically, leaving the tactical holo display frozen with the battlefleet's blips impotent outside the orange sparks of the asteroid field.

Marines. Soul Drinkers, no less, who by all accounts had never been the most genial of the Emperor's servants. He couldn't wait to see the faces of his allies and enemies when he brought a thousand grizzled heads back to the Ordo Hereticus conclave-sermon. This would make him. They would teach his example to interrogator pupils as how one man might defy a legion of the galaxy's most murderous warriors, if only he has faith and justice on his side.

But there was still much to do. He had to ensure the gravitational warheads were loaded and primed. They were delicate and ancient technology, not to be trifled with. He would not let carelessness rob him of his finest moment, not when the loss of his executioner had already illustrated the venom of the foe.

Even now, his astropathic choir would be transmitting the sentence of Excommunicate Traitoris throughout the Imperium, and not one inquisitor would be ignorant of the importance of Tsouras's mission. Behind him, the battlefleet's useless officer class would be watching him and quaking, knowing that to obey his every word might just be to secure their lives. They would be lost, frightened, disposable. Those few who knew anything of the Inquisition would have only heard tales of implacable crusaders, prepared to torture and kill whole populations at once, who let nothing stand in the way of the moral purity of the Imperium.

Most of those tales were true.

Inquisitor Tsouras smiled.

THE ORDERS WENT out immediately, with the highest Inquisitorial authority. The attack craft of the Lakonia Persecution were fully armed and fuelled within three and a half hours of Tsouras's declaration, ranked up with engines idling and crews on board, ready for their call signs to be broadcast.

The first bomber wing launched from the flight decks of the *Penitent's Wrath*. It was not anticipated that there would be any interceptors to oppose them, but they went with full fighter escorts anyway, just to be sure.

They were followed by dozens of other swarms, from Avengers and Praetorians with their bellies swollen with bombs, to control craft trailing salvoes of semi-smart torpedoes, to the delta-winged gloss-black nightmares that swept from the flight bays of the Inquisitorial ship itself. The flight assets of the Lakonia Persecution had not been accurately totalled, and the number of fighters and bombers launched was uncertain. Estimates made it a thousand, give or take.

The first waves, though they did not know it, were to test the density of the Cerberian Field. Their engines clogged with micrometeorites and their hulls were punctured by ice fragments or buckled by the gravitational forces of superdense ferrous asteroids. The fleet logistitians under Tsouras's orders used the data of their death throes to calculate where best to strike. When a hundred had been sent crashing against the wall of broken rock, the gravitational salvo erupted from the wedged nose of the Inquisitorial ship.

The torpedoes' size indicated their age, for they were ancient indeed, to the degree that the secrets of their manufacture had long since been lost. They had cost much both in funds and favours. But Tsouras had known they would be worth it.

Slowly, with the nearest bomber wings banking wildly to avoid them, the shoal of impossibly valuable torpedoes detonated and the edge of the Cerberian Field began to collapse. Ripples of electromagnetic power drew the tumbling rocks closer and closer in a gravitational trap. Clumps of asteroids dragged into the epicentres in turn drawing in more matter until a chain reaction had begun, the field contracting into single lumps of rock.

More warheads exploded further in and the effect travelled deeper, melting a path towards the Soul Drinkers' position in the heart of the asteroid field. Attack craft followed in their wake, and many had to sight their target visually as their nav-cogitators broke down amidst all the interference. To them, the *Gundog* and the *Unendingly Just* were barely visible, picked out by the sharp-eyed as twin patterns of silver against dark purple against black. They were both on all-stop so there was no engine flare to lock onto – the bombers would have to get in close and do things the old-fashioned way.

'WE ARE HERE for a reason, children.' Yser's voice was inspirational as ever, this time quieter and more reflective. 'The Architect has seen to it that all we do for good or ill has led us to this point. If we are to die here, we know it is because He has chosen it as our punishment or reward.'

It was first lesson of the Architect of Fate. Any who dedicated their life to following His plan would be sent through the Architect's weaving of fate to the end they deserved. Yser knew he had done his best, for the Architect had spoken to him and he had done all He asked – founded his church, protected his flock, enlightened His chosen warriors. If he was to die here, it was for the good. It was what should be.

The first bombs that hit sounded like rolls of thunder deep in the heart of the *Gundog*. The men and women of the flock shook with both fear, and with the cold caused by the reduction of life support to give the ship the lowest possible energy profile. Vapour steamed off them as they huddled in the armoury chamber, Yser at their centre, the focus of their faith.

The armoury housed no weaponry any more, and it was one of the toughest parts of the ship. But that would not save them if the ship's reactors went critical or there was a massive structural failure. Or the power could shut down completely and they would be entombed here, to freeze or suffocate.

And if, by some miracle, the ship was lost but they survived, they would each die a thousand heretic's deaths. Their crime, of associating with Space Marines declared Excommunicate, would doubtless require the ritual purification of their flesh before they died. They would be unlikely to remain sane under such punishment.

Could he bear that? Yser had undergone many privations as a poor man, a thief and a prisoner, but was there a point when he would give up on his faith again? Would he renounce the Architect of Fate and admit to the foulest of treacheries under the torturer's blade? He honestly didn't know. It was said that a man would be known by the manner of his death – Yser hoped his was quick and sudden, in a flare of nuclear light or the lethal shock of the void.

The child closest to him was crying quietly. A tough one, this, because she had to be to make it this far. But this was too much.

'It's alright,' he said, hoping he sounded like someone who could be believed.

'It's because she can't do anything about it,' said the child's father, who had buried her mother in the garbage spoil of the star fort a year earlier. 'You can deal with anything if you can fight it. But this... we all feel so small.'

'Faith,' said Yser quietly. 'There is nothing else.'

Another hit, and was followed by the huge crunch of an explosion which seemed to boom from everywhere at once. The shockwave threw many people to the floor and for a minute there was no sound, only a ringing white noise.

They were going to die. They were all going to die.

'THAT'S IMPOSSIBLE.' TALAYA'S face was lit by the ghostly green glow from the screens of data arrayed in front of her. Chloure had begun to think of it as her natural appearance. 'The route's been Interdictus for six hundred years.'

'Then what is that?'

Half the bridge viewscreen was taken up with the best image they could bring up of the *Gundog*, a blurry fractured purple-black shape pocked with tiny orange-white explosions as the first waves of bomber swept over it. The other half was full of complicated wavelength readouts that fluctuated violently. Chloure wasn't an expert in these things, but every officer on the *Diligent's* bridge had told him the same thing. It was the signature of a warp route, the entry/exit point of a rare and relatively stable path through warp space. It was pulsing with the energy of a large volume of shipping hurtling through it. This was unusual because all the charts said there was no warp route there.

'I don't know,' replied Talaya. It was the first time Chloure had ever heard her say those words. Perhaps she was human after all.

'Alright. Will Tsouras know about this?'

'Probably more than us,' said Vekk. 'Of course, you know what it is.' He paused for effect. Chloure glared at him.

'Six hundred years ago they closed warp route 391-C after something woke up inside it and ate a transport convoy. They lost about three hundred thousand souls. Their astropaths tried to get a signal out but all was left were a few echoes. Walls of flesh, they said. Walls of flesh closing in.'

'Why wasn't anybody told?'

'The route's been dead for centuries, consul. Besides, it's just some mariner's tale.'

'Only now it's got hungry again?'

'Could be, consul.'

Then one of the logistitians screamed and a shower of sparks burst from the mind-impulse link plugging him into the sensorium banks. He spasmed violently before the mind-jacks were thrown free and he convulsed to the ground. Petty officers barked orders and a couple of menials hurried forwards to drag away the smoking body. The rest of the logistitian corps did nothing, locked into the world generated by the sensor arrays.

'What now?' asked Chloure, trying not to gag at the wafting reek of charred skin.

'Feedback,' said Talaya. 'Something big.'

For the first time in six hundred years, warp route 391-C opened.

FIGHTER COMMAND ON board the *Penitent's Wrath* was a vast sheer-sided circular pit of iron in which rows and rows of flight controllers, lexmechanics, statisticians and tech-adepts were arrayed along rows of sensor screens and holo displays. Most of them never left. Some of them had been born there.

Snatches of comm-link transmissions from the fleet's attack craft rang through the air. The attack wings were in a ragged state – some were executing attack runs on the Soul Drinkers' cruisers, others were on their way into the maw of the Cerberian Field or limping half-strength back towards the fleet carriers. Every crew out there had been thrown into shock in the last few seconds as an immense warp rift had opened up just outside the Cerberian Field and started disgorging starships.

'–out of nowhere... starboard retros out...'

'Claw leader to all points! Break formation and bank fleetward, Now!'

'–down, going down, going...'

Tsouras strode between the mem-bank columns and star maps. All he heard were the sounds of a crisis beginning. Naval Chaplains intoned the death-rites over comm-links to crews who were bombed-up and burning. Vacuum seals popped, men screamed, igniting fuel ripped through hulls. Where there had been heartless efficiency just a few minutes ago there was now confusion and desperation.

Every display showed the same thing – a ship, yet to be identified – had emerged from warp route 391-C insanely close to the edge of the Cerberian Field, and charged into the waves of fighters heading for the Soul Drinkers position. Close-range ordnance and turret fire had torn through several bomber wings before they had the chance to break and scatter. Now the forward wings were trapped in the field, enclosed in the tunnel of rock created by the gravitic warheads, with a swift and well-armed ship blocking their path. Tsouras could hear the weapons battery-fire scything through them as they died. The attacking ship was huge – bigger than the *Penitent's Wrath* itself. It was fast, too, and loaded with close-range weaponry. Its pilots must be maniacs and its gunners trained to the point of inhumanity.

A hundred stories of heroism and disaster were unfolding at the edge of the Cerberian Field. Tsouras didn't care about any of them. The *Unendingly Just* and the *Gundog* were still intact. All other considerations were secondary.

'Lord inquisitor!' Hrorvald, captain of the *Penitent's Wrath*, emerged from the clouds of incense. He was a large-jowled man of greater bulk than had been allowed for in the naval uniform he wore. 'Disastrous! That route had been closed for hundreds of years! Hundreds! I have briefed my command crew on a full attack craft withdrawal followed by a fleet action…'

Tsouras held up a taloned hand to stop him. 'I want everything in space, captain. Everything. These could be pirates or opportunists, but they could also be heretics come to aid the enemy. If the Soul Drinkers escape then all is for nought. When the targets are confirmed destroyed, then they can regroup.'

Hrorvald looked around at the officers following him like pupils, looking for support. 'Our men will be butchered, inquisitor! We cannot just–'

'You know, Captain Hrorvald, it almost sounded as if you were questioning my authority. I do so hope you can prove me wrong.'

A satisfying wave of fear passed over Hrorvald's red, flustered face. 'Of course. Just for information, you see. They won't survive.'

'That has been allowed for. Now, I assume you are here to tell me the identity of our newcomer.'

'They're jamming us, lord inquisitor, and most effectively. But… well, the visuals are very sketchy, but our tactical officers have hazarded a guess. It's rather far-fetched, you see, and I… well, the long and the short of it… it's the *Carnivore*, inquisitor.'

There was silence, broken only by the faint background of prayers and screams.

'I see,' said Inquisitor Tsouras at length. 'My orders stand. Destruction of the *Gundog* and the *Unendingly Just* supersedes all other concerns. Including survival. Get to it, captain.'

THE CARNIVORE WAS followed by the *Sanctifier's Son* and the *Heavenblade*, both smaller but still deadlier than any ship of the battlefleet. The *Heavenblade* swept out towards the battlefleet, which was hastily organising a defensive line. Out of position and with attack wings already out, there was nothing they could do to prevent the *Heavenblade* closing. It drove an arrow-straight course towards the *Deacon Byzantine*, ignoring the nova cannon shot from the heart of the battlefleet that almost clipped it to starboard.

The *Son* launched a fighter wave of its own and the tract of void where the battlefleet's assault waves were regrouping became a seething cauldron of combat. The *Son* itself dived in, taking bomber hits all over, swatting fighters aside like insects.

'TARGETS, SIR?'

Captain Trentius paced the bridge deck of the *Deacon Byzantine*. 'Nose. Underside, around the cargo ports.'

'It's increasing speed, sir. Close to ramming velocity. Should we...'

Trentius glared at his master of ordnance. 'Your job is to acquire the targets I require, Bulin. Not tell me what I should and not shoot at. Nose, underside, cargo ports.'

'I just thought that a hit on the engines might...'

'Do a lot of thinking, do you, Bulin? It doesn't suit you. Get me targets and load torpedo tubes for a tight spread.' Trentius rounded on his chief of the watch. 'You, get those lazy buggers out of the boarding parties and get them on damage control detail.'

The *Heavenblade* loomed large, head-on, her bone-coloured prow like the point of a knife stabbing towards the *Deacon*.

'Perhaps,' came the slickly educated voice of Flag-Lieutenant Lriss, 'we should consider our options. Given the nature of the enemy and their known tactics, it might be the case that—'

'They are not going to board us, Lriss,' growled Trentius. 'They are not going to ram us or do any of the things they would normally do.

'Imagine, Lriss, your mission was rescue and not destruction. You want to get in and out as fast as possible. You are facing a numerically superior but low-quality enemy already in disarray. None of their ships are worth anything to you so there's no point boarding. You're not desperate to bash up a good ship with ramming. What do you do?'

Lriss knew better than to venture an answer.

'No?' Trentius took a thick cigar from the pocket of his nicotine-yellowed uniform. He lit it with a flourish. 'A fire ship, Lriss. You send a fire ship.'

The *Heavenblade* slewed sideways suddenly, presenting the side of its armoured hull.

Trentius saw it was painted dark purple, with the huge chalice symbol emblazoned in gold.

The torpedo spread hit and a tide of fire billowed from the underside of the *Heavenblade*. The entire lower decks must have been filled with nonoxidising fuel, the kind that didn't have to react with air to burn. A cloud of flame boiled off like the outer layers of a dying star, sprays of structural debris stabbed out through the massive rents opened by the torpedo blasts.

'Burn retros, and I mean now,' ordered Trentius as his bridge crew observed the spectacle. 'She's going to go critical.'

And she did. The screen was pure white for half a minute, the plasma cores hitting critical temperature and expanding catastrophically, before they collapsed to leave a shattered husk of a spaceship.

'Reload ordnance, move to engage, sir?' asked Lriss with a smile.

'Don't be bloody stupid, Lriss. You think we can actually fight them?'

THE BATTLE BARGE *Carnivore*, along with the strike cruisers *Heavenblade* and *Sanctifier's Son*, were more than enough. But they were joined by more – the interceptor cruiser *Animosity* scattered the battlefleet's flank merely by driving forward with its lance arrays charged. The carrier-fitted battle barge *Mare Infernum*, meanwhile, sported so many assault boat docks that they covered it like scales – the prospect of the ship launching a boarding action was so truly ghastly that the battlefleet fell into general retreat, Tsouras be damned. With the flaming wreck of the *Heavenblade* in their midst and the highest-quality ships now bearing down on them, the ships of the battlefleet were in utter disarray.

Only the *Deacon Byzantine* held its nerve, refusing to follow the rout though it was alone and effectively surrounded – as if it knew the new fleet had no intention of attacking it.

It was the *Mare Infernum* that fell back to escort the *Unendingly Just* from the Cerberian Field, battered but unbowed. Sarpedon watched from the porthole in his cell as the battle barge's near-inconceivable bulk gradually slid past against a backdrop of debris. The *Gundog* would be limping alongside the battle-scarred *Sanctifier's Son* – the first bomber wings had blown two of the main engines clean off the *Gundog*, but it was a tough cruiser and it would make it with help.

The communication flashed through the comm-systems of both cruisers.

'Fleet command orders to Librarian Sarpedon. Return to fleet ground immediately. Conclave Iudicaris to commence. Out.'

Simple and blunt. But it told him everything he had expected.

BY THE TIME the Lakonia Persecution's attack craft had begun to regroup at the edge of the Cerberian Field, the *Gundog* and the *Unendingly Just* were far out of their attack range, escorted by a vast and dangerous phalanx of ships into a warp route from which no bomber wing could hope to emerge. The Lakonia Persecution was scattered and useless, its attacking assets milling in confusion, its cruisers and battleships hopelessly out of position.

Warp route 391-C was contracting even as the *Animosity*, the rearmost of the fleet, slid through its shimmering gate and into the maelstrom of the immaterium. With dangerous rapidity the warp gate closed behind the cruiser, sealing off the new fleet from realspace.

This new fleet – two battle barges and three strike cruisers, enough to fend of the mightiest fleet – had been sent by Chapter Master Gorgoleon of the Soul Drinkers Chapter. Sarpedon had under his command three companies of the Soul Drinkers. Now the other seven had sought them out to get some answers.

CHAPTER SEVEN

SARPEDON LOOKED OUT into space, seeing for the hundredth time the blackness that hid the Soul Drinkers from prying eyes. He knew they were far to the galactic north-east, past the Qisto'Rol system and the warp storm they called the Emperor's Wrath, on the indistinct boundary where Imperial space gave way to the Halo Zone. But he knew this only from his memory, for there was no frame of reference in sight.

It was a dark sector. Nebula clouds that could swallow whole systems formed a featureless backdrop through which only the brightest stars could shine. It was abandoned and quiet, and it could take decades for anyone to find the Soul Drinkers here. It had been marked by the Chapter millennia ago as somewhere they could lie low in case of emergency. An emergency such as this.

Closer was the Soul Drinkers' fleet, the size of a sector armada, formed almost entirely of lightning assault craft – some pregnant with pods and boarding torpedoes, others weighed down with lances and nova cannons. The *Leuctra* was hanging in the blackness beside them, and on the other side was the *Carnivore* still bearing the scars of the Cerberian Field.

A battle barge was one of the most deadly creations that mankind could wield. And there were two of them here, detailed solely to guard the darkship on which Sarpedon and his Marines were being held. It was with a curious pride that Sarpedon realised what important prisoners they were. The rest of the Chapter considered them rebels whose conduct had brought a stain of suspicion to the name of the Soul Drinkers, and rogue Space Marines were not to be trifled with.

The rest of the fleet could be seen glittering further out. A silver diamond was the immense training platform on which novices and Marines made practice drops and dummy assaults, live ammunition and hard vacuum combining to force combat discipline into the brothers. The strike cruisers looked like a shoal of fish in the distance – amongst them would be the *Gundog* and the *Unendingly Just*, undergoing flame-cleansing by the servitor purge-teams in case Sarpedon's Marines had brought the stain of corruption back with them. Furthest away yet huge and bright, was the *Glory*. Immense: half as big again as a standard battle barge. Its hull was smothered in gold and the great gem-chased chalice on its side was visible even from the darkship.

For good or ill, Sarpedon's fate would all be decided on the *Glory*, in the hallowed gathering hall of the Chapter elders and the chambers of Chapter Master Gorgoleon. Perhaps Sarpedon and his Marines would be exonerated, perhaps they would be killed. But it would be easier now either way, for they were at least amongst brothers at last.

Sarpedon turned from the porthole and headed back towards the light of the autosurgeon, bright on the dim infirmary deck. The stained metal slab on which Sergeant Tellos lay gleamed with new blood as the sanguiprobes peeled back the skin of his abdomen and sunk thin shafts into his organs. Apothecary Pallas, standing over him with two serf-orderlies, watched the complex readouts on his holoslate flicker with the flow of information. The orderlies both had their mouths and ears sutured shut – they had been supplied by the Chapter infirmary and were not permitted to speak or to hear tainted words.

'Will he live?' asked Sarpedon.

'I am beginning to suspect that life and death are relative terms, commander,' replied Pallas. 'He will probably soon cease to be alive in the normal sense. But I do not think he is about to die, either.' He pressed a finger into the skin of Tellos's chest – it was greying and translucent, and beneath it could be seen the twin hearts beating and the tough third lung rising and falling. The skin puckered and rippled, like something gelatinous. 'His body chemistry has changed and his biorhythms are very erratic. He has sudden floods of energy.'

'And his mind?'

Pallas shrugged. 'As far as Iktinos can tell, he is convinced he will fight again. No matter what we do, he keeps training. A Marine with no hands is like a mockery of a warrior, but sometimes he almost has me convinced. I don't pretend I can know what he is thinking.'

The probe array, spindly like a skinny metal hand, rotated and a finger with a long transparent tube leading from its tip stabbed down into Tellos's stomach. A thin line of red ran up the tube as the blood was drawn out. 'The gene-seed itself shows no abnormalities, so the source of the changes is a mystery. I would endeavour to find out just what was causing all this but our facilities here are limited. We've given samples to the Chapter apothecarion in case they can help, but they won't.'

'They wouldn't. Not while there is chance they would be aiding traitors.'

The probe withdrew and began knitting Tellos's skin back together. But the blades of the tiny manipulators kept slipping through the altered tissue and the join was left ragged. Slowly, the ripped skin began to flow together, as if melting, until there was no trace left of a wound.

'The other battle-brothers are the same,' Pallas was saying. 'There is no obvious cause for those who are changing. Yourself included. You haven't eaten for weeks now – there should be some degradation in energy levels or muscle mass. But there's nothing.'

'I feel stronger.'

'It's hard for us to judge.'

'I mean psychically. I felt it on the Geryon platform. The Hell has never gone that deep, Pallas. It has served us well, but never that well. Yser says it is strength born of faith, now we have seen the truth. The Architect's blessing.'

Tellos stirred on the slab. The anaesthetics couldn't even keep him under for an hour at a time – as if something had woken inside him that struggled and fought any attempt to make him lose control. Sarpedon had forbidden him to be imprisoned, as he had committed no crime, and it was all Pallas could do to keep track of the assault sergeant. Several attempts had been made to take the twin blades Tellos had jammed into the stumps of his wrists, but he had always found new ones. It was eventually decided that it was best to leave them as they were.

'In any case, commander,' said Pallas, 'it can hardly put us in good stead. There will doubtless be an investigation of great thoroughness and any abnormalities will be noticed. But without facilities or power, there is little I can do.'

Power. The dim light and lack of working equipment on board the darkship was deliberate – no simple brig existed that could hold a Soul Drinker against his will, and so a whole ship was set aside for incarcerating Marines under investigation. Its plasma reactors were crippled so it could only travel latched on to another ship, preventing its use for escape, and the weapons systems had been torn out. Power was limited to the most basic life support requirements. This darkship had once been the strike cruiser *Ferox* – now it had no name.

A vox-icon flickered at the back of Sarpedon's eye.

Chaplain Iktinos's dour voice sounded in his ear. 'Your Chapter Master requests the presence of Librarian Sarpedon. A shuttle will be sent. You will come alone.'

'Tell him I will be ready.' Sarpedon switched to another channel. 'Sergeant Givrillian, make ready for diplomatic escort duty. We are going to the *Glory*.'

CHAPTER MASTER GORGOLEON adhered to one rule in war: the rule of despair. If an enemy despairs, if he does not believe there is any hope left, if he has seen his comrades dead and maimed by the hand of invincible foes, he has lost. When he is in such a state he cannot resist – whether he is to be captured or killed, or merely broken, there is nothing he can do. Battles are won when one side is rendered incapable of fighting, and that is best achieved by the massive and unrelenting infliction of despair. This was one of Daenyathos's prime tenets for the conduct of war, and it was one Gorgoleon had turned into a science. It was why he was Chapter Master. It was why he so rarely failed.

Despair was usually created by inflicting fatal or mutilating damage on an enemy, but there were other ways. That was why the walls of his private chambers had been stripped out and replaced with carved marble slabs depicting his life as a warrior – here he was, kneeling on a pile of tau dead, back-to-back with the long-dead Chaplain Surrian as the pulse shots blazed down at him. Here he strode into the halls of the Archfoul and looked it in the eye as bolter-fire poured into its corrupt flesh. Again, in the jungles of Actium, and again, in the shattered streets of Helsreach. Gorgoleon's entire chanson had been carved out here, an epic of his life chiselled into the stone.

He didn't really care for it personally. There had been careers more glorious than his in the long history of the Soul Drinkers, and he needed no picture-book to remember it all. But it inspired a measure of awe in those who saw it and, in the right circumstances, he had hoped it would inspire despair.

A servitor shuffled along the long gallery that led to Gorgoleon's chambers, past the carvings of his early heroics. 'The shuttle approaches,' it said in its the thin, feeble voice. The servitor had once been a Chapter serf, who had become too aged and decrepit to be of further use and had been rebuilt as Gorgoleon's personal valet. Gorgoleon took pains to make the menials in his presence especially wretched.

'Convey permission to board the *Glory*. Have Sarpedon leave his escort squad in the shuttle bay and send him to my presence immediately. Ensure he is not rested or fed.'

'Yes, Lord Gorgoleon,' lisped the wizened servitor, and limped off across the gilded tiles of the chamber.

Gorgoleon settled his armoured bulk into the ivory chair. Pict-slates set into the hardwood of his desk flashed images of Sarpedon and the officers now apparently under his command. He called up the Chapter command citations from Quixian Obscura, Karlaster Bridge and the Haemon Forest. Sarpedon had turned battles, buying time when all was lost, sowing confusion to crack open impenetrable positions. Gorgoleon switched to a list of active commands. There was only one – Van Skorvold Star Fort, joint command with Caeon. Librarians rarely took such roles in the Soul Drinkers, where combat-hardened regular officers were favoured to lead from the front. Caeon must have trusted Sarpedon's competence and integrity to have selected him. But everyone, even veterans like Caeon, can make mistakes.

He went further back, calling up Sarpedon's earlier record. Sarpedon was something rare – possessing both the mental qualities needed for selection as a Marine, and the great psychic potential required to use his powers without danger of possession. The unusual nature of his talents had not dissuaded the Librarium from taking him on, almost as an experiment.

As a novice his adherence to the tenets of Daenyathos had been something of note. As a new Marine he had proven capable of using his psychological advantage to take on opponents far superior in number. His should have been a fine career, an example of Daenyathos's teachings applied exactly to the practice of war. But instead, something had gone wrong.

Gorgoleon could find nothing that suggested instability or incompetence. In other circumstances he would have considered Sarpedon a good model for novices – an ideological soldier who wielded the beliefs and traditions of the Chapter like a weapon.

Yet he had rebelled. He had spilt the blood of his allies. His words to the Inquisitorial envoy he had slain were the most damning of all – it seemed Sarpedon had turned his back on the very Imperium the Soul Drinkers were supposed to shepherd towards greatness.

Gorgoleon was good at his task. He had rarely had cause to bring a fellow Marine into his chambers and subject them to that same despair he believed in, to see if they would break down and confess to some sin. And this time, the whole Chapter was at stake – nothing really scared him, but even he had felt the tension in his gut as he heard the ugly words of Inquisitor Tsouras grinding from the astropath's throat.

He had heard the stories – Astral Claws, Thunder Barons, Chapters who had fallen from grace and become everything they feared. The Soul Drinkers would not be added to that list. Not while he still lived.

The brass-banded doors slid open and a protocol servitor thrummed in. 'Into the presence of Dorn and the Emperor's sight, announcing Librarian Sarpedon.'

Sarpedon did not look like a man who had suffered months of privation. The darkship had been stripped of all supplies, and the few the Marines had brought with them had been squandered on the filthy ragtag prisoners they had insisted on bringing with them. As Sarpedon strode along the gallery, Gorgoleon saw he seemed as healthy as he had been on the eve of battle.

The chambers were designed to force anyone entering to walk past the great galleries of Chapter history and Gorgoleon's own deeds. Sarpedon was not distracted. He looked utterly determined.

Gorgoleon, still seated behind the desk, waited for Sarpedon to reach him, letting the silence last as long as possible. 'Librarian Sarpedon,' he said at length, 'there are matters we must discuss.'

Sarpedon stood proudly, hands behind his back, no fear in his face. 'Indeed there are.'

'Perhaps you have not yet been made fully aware of the consequences of your actions. Several months ago I received a communication from Inquisitor Tsouras on behalf of the lords of the Ordo Hereticus. We were commanded to down our weapons and submit ourselves to an Inquisitorial purge. We refused, as Dorn himself would have done. And then we ran.'

'My Lord Gorgoleon, I too have had dealings with–'

'We *ran*!' yelled Gorgoleon, standing and slamming his fist into the desktop. 'Do you understand what you made us? We were fugitives! Us! The best the Imperium can produce, and we ran like criminals! They would have taken our weapons, Sarpedon. They would have stripped us of our armour and entombed us in some prison-rock until they had decided not to kill us. We would have been treated like vermin, Sarpedon! They forced me to order this fleet to flee, as if we were nothing more than cowards. I cannot begin to describe the humiliation – to run when every word Daenyathos ever wrote extols us never to retreat. But that was not the worst, Sarpedon. That was not the worst.'

'It is a complex matter, lord–'

'No, Sarpedon, it is very simple indeed. After the insult of demanding we hand over our guns and walk in chains, I received a second communication far worse than any I have seen.'

Sarpedon paused, perhaps struggling to force out the unholy words. 'We were declared Excommunicate Traitoris.'

'Excommunicate!' Gorgoleon spat out the word. 'We are the lowest of the low, Sarpedon. We are the worst of the worst of the worst. I sent you out with Caeon to restore a terrible injustice, and you return bearing only dishonour such as this Chapter has never beheld. They can kill us on sight, Librarian! They can remove any trace of us! They can end our existence!' Gorgoleon stood suddenly, stopped for a moment, let his rage boil down. 'What happened to you, Sarpedon? What could have made you so abhor the beliefs you held dear that you let your brothers fall so far? Why did you fire upon your allies, and defy the highest authorities of the Imperium? Why did you stain us all with your taint?'

'Why?' said Sarpedon evenly. 'Because I believe, Lord Gorgoleon. I believe in justice and dignity, and in the will of the Emperor. I believe in the best of men being given their due. I believe that those who would deny us that due are our enemies, because they defy everything that makes us great. I am accused of shedding the blood of my allies. But the Imperium is no ally of mine.'

Gorgoleon shook his head, 'No, of course not. Because that vagabond preacher says so. Dorn's flesh, even your Chaplain kneels at his sermon! Sarpedon, you had such strength of mind. But now you have brought foulness upon us all. You understand, there is only one option left open to me.'

Sarpedon was silent. There was no trace of repentance in his face – he knew full well what Gorgoleon would have to do.

'The Ordo Hereticus want me to hand you over,' said Gorgoleon. 'With your head on a spike and your brothers burned to ash, they would rescind the order of Traitoris. I would be rid of a traitor and the Inquisition would have their heretic to burn. After enough purging and sacrifice, we might be free of the taint again. Hand you over, and we would eventually be free once again.'

'But you have not, Lord Gorgoleon.'

'No. Why would that be, when you have committed the gravest sins a Marine ever can?'

'Because only my brothers may judge me.'

Gorgoleon would have dearly loved to have thrown the Librarian to the wolves for the dishonour he had wrought. But he could not. Though his hate was cold in his veins, there were certain principles that made him a Soul Drinker and not just another man. 'Only your brothers. The Inquisition knows nothing of the standards a Marine must maintain, or the beliefs he holds dear. We are but one step removed from the Emperor, Sarpedon, for His blood ran in the veins of Dorn, and Dorn's in ours. No one can judge you but a fellow Marine, before the eye of the Emperor.'

'Such were the words of Daenyathos, Lord Gorgoleon.'

'And I intend to follow them. You have led us into a terrible place here, Sarpedon, but there is no excuse for failing to honour our traditions. The trial shall be in the Chapel of Dorn, in three days. The Emperor will lend strength to the arm of the righteous man.'

'I am ready, Lord Gorgoleon. I do only the Emperor's will.'

'So will I, Sarpedon. For the greater the sin, the greater the judge. And I am the greatest man of this Chapter. For your crimes, you must face me.'

'So it shall be.' Sarpedon was impassive. Was it denial of his treachery? Or was there genuine belief there? Had he really convinced himself that stabbing his allies in the back had been a right and honourable thing? Impossible. It was either mendacity or delusion.

'No fear? You know what I have done. You can see it carved into the walls of this chamber. You heard the tales when you were just a novice. I need just to think it, and you will be dead. You are tough, Sarpedon, but you're not that tough.'

'I have faith, Lord Gorgoleon. There need be nothing else.'

Gorgoleon fixed the traitor with a hard stare – but there was no fear there, or even anger at his imminent death. What had happened out there? Had the loss of the Soulspear really done so much to addle his mind? They said he was having visions, and there were even hints of physical corruption amongst them.

It was the only way. He had to die, and justice had to be done.

'Three days,' he said quietly. 'Hope that Dorn will forgive you, for I will not.'

Sarpedon turned and left, ignoring the intricate carvings of Gorgoleon reaping fields of the dead and pouring bolter-rounds into hordes of xenos.

He could have been so much, thought Gorgoleon. Something unique. And in a way he was, for the Chapter had never known shame such as Excommunication.

But the Soul Drinkers would not fall from the Emperor's light. Not while Gorgoleon was still alive. But before he could begin to heal the wound of dishonour, Sarpedon would have to die. And though he was a brother Marine, Gorgoleon would enjoy pulling him apart.

THE SHIELD-RITES TOOK many hours if they were unabridged. Normally a cut-down version of the rites was conducted in battlefield conditions, when time was at a premium on the eve of battle. But before a warrior set off on a crusade, or when he had ample time to contemplate the task ahead of him, they were to be observed in their entirety.

Sarpedon had nearly finished. In the half-light of the darkship his eyes picked out the sheen on the ceramite of his armour where he had scrubbed off the grime that had built up over the last months. It was easy to miss where it was ground into the seals and plate joins, and the gold was worse – it took so much care to keep it from tarnishing, and each bullet scar needed delicate reworking.

Sarpedon took a breath of the incense as he fitted the lens back into the eyepiece of his helmet. He wouldn't be actually wearing it, of course, but these rites were about preparing the spirit of the armour and every piece had to be included. He always felt strangely raw out of his armour, as if the armour was his skin and without it he was naked and bleeding. The faint stirring of the circulated air rasped against his back, and even when he breathed it seemed cold and harsh.

He placed the helmet to one side, satisfied that it was ready. Every piece of the armour – the greaves and kneepads, thigh-pieces, gauntlets, backpack, and all the rest had been checked by Lygris and cleaned by Sarpedon. At last, before the fight, it was a sacred thing again.

The door of his cell hissed open. Sarpedon heard the padding of bare feet and knew who it was.

'Father Yser. Thank you for coming.'

'Anything for the flock, Lord Sarpedon. There must be many things troubling you.'

Sarpedon turned to face the priest – without his matted beard and layer of grime he looked healthier in spite of the conditions. 'Yser, there is every chance I will die today. This has been the case for me many times and I have no fear of it, but… there are things I would like to know.'

'Ask.'

'I have seen things, Yser. In my dreams. I have seen a world steeped in filth, with something terrible at its heart calling out to me. My body is changing, too. I do not eat, and things have begun happening to my bones that Pallas cannot explain. I have never been afraid of anything, Yser, but this is different. I need to know what all this means. Why am I receiving these visions, and why am I changing?'

Yser smiled. 'Lord Sarpedon, we have all felt it. This is the hand of the Architect of Fate. The Emperor is preparing you. He has shown you the world you must be overcome to prove your worth. The trial you must undergo today is the same – the Architect saw the injustice done to you and turned it into a test that will make you stronger.'

'I have followed the will of the Emperor for many years, Yser,' said Sarpedon. 'I have never felt anything like this.'

'Because you never knew the truth, Sarpedon. You followed a lie. But now you know the truth, and you are at last truly doing His will.'

If it was true… the idea that he might actually feel the touch of the Emperor was more than Sarpedon could really comprehend. How many had been done such an honour in the ten thousand years since the Emperor ascended to the half-life of the Golden Throne? None?

'But none of this will matter,' Yser continued, 'if you are dead. Can you win this fight?'

'Gorgoleon is the finest warrior this Chapter has produced for centuries, Yser. Before, I would have said I had no chance of defeating him. But everything is different now.'

'No, Sarpedon. Everything is the same as it ever was. The only thing that has changed is you.'

Sarpedon stood and picked up the massive barrel chestplate, with its winged chalice wrought in gold and the collar where the aegis hood would lock. 'Thank you, Yser. Tell my brothers I shall be armed and ready, there is no need to keep them waiting any longer. And Yser?'

'Lord Sarpedon?'

'They will bring me my force staff. Bless them for me, father, and wish me well.'

IT WAS WHISPERED between the brothers, and spoken aloud only by the Chapter's higher echelons, that Dorn was the inheritor of the Imperium.

There had been twenty primarchs created by the Emperor as templates for the superhumans that would conquer the galaxy in His name. But there were dark forces watching Him and meddling through mortal tools, and the primarchs were born flawed. Fully half would be revealed as traitors in the fires of the Horus Heresy. The others were tormented vampires, hot-blooded butchers, barbarian thugs, power-hungry tyrants. All passed on their flaws to the Chapters who bore their gene-seed, and inflicted them with some stain of dishonour that was never spoken of, yet which had started wars.

All except Dorn. For the Emperor was wise and just, and outwitted the dark forces to make one of His sons the true model of perfection He had intended. Though Marines carrying the gene-seed of other primarchs would die rather than admit it, Dorn was the best of them all. He did not crave power, only justice. He fought not with savagery or malice, only with honour. His legion excelled in all things – doughty defence, merciless attack, cunning stealth and everything in between, skills which existed to this day in the many Chapters formed from the Imperial Fists.

Yes, Dorn was the best man who had ever lived save the Divine Emperor himself – by following only Dorn's example, the Soul Drinkers could ensure that they, too, could be nothing but the best. At the heart of the Chapter was Dorn, his words and deeds burning as bright as they had when he was alive. Matters of the greatest gravity were conducted before the gaze of Dorn, who watched from his halls of judgement in the afterlife, so he might see how his sons followed his example of justice and righteousness in everything they did.

And so it was that the Chapter Master and the traitor met in the Cathedral of Dorn in the heart of the battleship *Glory*, to settle the Chapter's greatest crisis in the only way they saw fit.

GORGOLEON IN FULL battle-array was as fearsome as Sarpedon had remembered. His armour was polished and gleaming in the light of a thousand candles, the crest of Rogal Dorn bright on one shoulder pad, the golden chalice glinting on the other. Gorgoleon still wore the bone-carved crux terminatus around his neck, from the days long before when he had worn one of the Chapter's few suits of terminator battle armour. The ceremonial armour he wore now was the same bulk as Sarpedon's, but shone with artificer's craftsmanship and the constant attention of the Chapter's Tech-Marines. One hand was massive and pendulous with the power fist he wore – the fist had a built-in power field which, when switched on, would let the Chapter Master punch through walls and tear through tanks, and certainly dismember Sarpedon with one good shot. The field could be flicked on and off at Gorgoleon's whim, leaving his hand dextrous one second, destructive the next.

In the centre of the vaulted cathedral, Gorgoleon waited as Sarpedon was marched in flanked by a six-Marine guard. Sarpedon had left his bolter for the ritual combat did not allow for guns – his sole weapon was therefore the force staff which would have to serve its master well one more time.

The Soul Drinkers were arrayed all around the cathedral, exercising their right to witness the honour-combat that was a tradition as old as the Chapter. Rogal Dorn himself looked down upon the scene, a titanic figure in stained glass rendered on the window above the altar. A faint gauze of incense hung far above, and the whole cathedral was bathed in the warm, pulsing glow of candlelight.

The place was quiet, the assembled Marines hushed to respect the few moments before the fight. This time was dedicated to the watching Emperor, because that was why this combat held the central place it did in the traditions of the Soul Drinkers. Now, more than ever, He would be watching, because He would be the true judge here, and His will decided the victor.

Then the moment was over. Sarpedon's guards stepped back and joined their battle-brothers around the cathedral. An ancient Chaplain, one of the very few who had survived long enough not to end his days on the battlefield, stood forward on servo-assisted limbs and intoned the ritual words.

'Lord High Emperor, to whose plan our brothers are bound, and Rogal Dorn, he whose blood is our blood. Observe with us this tradition, lend Your strength to the arm of the righteous, and through victory show us Your way.'

The Chaplain stood down, Gorgoleon activated the field of his power fist, and the fight had begun.

Sarpedon ducked Gorgoleon's first blow, but he realised too late he was supposed to. Gorgoleon's kneepad soared up and into the side of his face, snapping his head back. The cathedral's interior whirled as Sarpedon staggered – the vaulted gothic ceiling, the stained glass face of Dorn looking down fiercely, the rows of purple-armoured Marines that turned the nave into an arena.

He could feel their eyes on him, watching every move, fascinated and appalled by the magnitude of what would be decided here. Even a non-psyker could have tasted the tension in the air.

A lesser man would have flailed blindly. A Marine could think the world into slow-motion and see the next blow before it was struck – and so Sarpedon caught Gorgoleon's follow-up strike on his forearm, felt the ceramite buckle under the Chapter Master's strength, stepped sideways and brought his force staff up to parry the power fist uppercut. The power field and force-circuit clashed and a great shower of sparks erupted, pushing both men onto the back foot.

Gorgoleon was smiling. He knew he would win. The massive power fist flexed its fingers and Sarpedon could see the hundreds of golden rivets struck into its surface – one for every foe of note it had despatched.

'Give in, traitor,' said Gorgoleon, not even out of breath. 'We could make it quick for you.'

Marines in the crowd were yelling – demanding a fast end or a long and bloody one, making claims to parts of the dead traitor's corpse. Disciplined as they were, there was nothing like a good honour-scrap to get their blood rising. They said it was older than the Chapter itself, as old as Mankind – two men settling a matter of the deepest honour, armed with their favoured weapon, in holy combat ended only by death. So sacred an act was it that the Emperor himself would give strength to the fighter who was in the right, and the transgressor would be struck down by righteous power.

The Emperor knew. The Emperor was watching. And through this honour-combat, the Emperor would act.

Sarpedon stabbed with the butt-end of his force staff, aimed deliberately wide so Gorgoleon would dodge into the strike – but Gorgoleon had fought a thousand foes on a hundred worlds and turned the blow aside. Sarpedon realised he was left wide open as Gorgoleon shifted his weight, barged forwards, caught Sarpedon full-on and bowled him backwards.

The Soul Drinkers cheered as Sarpedon tumbled down the steps, down amongst the hardwood pews. All cheered save the separate section of the crowd – Sarpedon's Marines, brought here to watch their treacherous leader die.

When he was dead, they would follow.

No. It would not end this way. If Sarpedon lost here they would parade the few remaining body parts through the *Glory*, so the serfs and novices could see what happened to traitors, even as the Marines of Sarpedon's three companies were put to the sword. That would not happen. No matter how impossible it seemed, Sarpedon would survive.

Time slowed. Gorgoleon's bulk bore down on him, framed by the stained glass window at the far end of the cathedral and the crowds of watching Marines all around. The power fist's field was a halo of lightning, Gorgoleon's eyes flashed with triumph.

They would kill his battle-brothers, and Yser's flock alongside them. The Architect of Fate would be forgotten. The truth would die out and the Soul Drinkers would return to serving the whims of evil men.

Again, something deep inside him spoke. It would not end this way.

With a speed he didn't know he possessed, Sarpedon grabbed the nearest pew and wrenched it from its fittings, swinging in into the falling body of Gorgoleon, swatting him aside like a fly. Wood splintered as the Chapter Master crashed through the pews and hit a pillar.

They were shouting with anger now. They were hissing and yelling for his head.

If they wanted it, they could damn well come and get it.

Gorgoleon was quick but Sarpedon was quicker now. He strode over Gorgoleon's prone form and grabbed him by his arms, lifting him up and slamming him into the pillar at his back. Shards of stone flew and Gorgoleon's head snapped back and forth with the force.

'You dare call me traitor?' shouted Sarpedon. 'I am the only true man here!'

Gorgoleon's body slammed into the pillar again and a fracture ran up the stone surface.

'You are slaves to corruption! You are puppets of greed!'

Suddenly Gorgoleon's free hand was at Sarpedon's throat, and the two men's eyes met – frenzied, fanatical, all semblance of discipline gone. They were the eyes of men fighting for the survival of everything they believed in.

'Wretch!' snarled Gorgoleon. The power fist's energy field roared into life and Sarpedon dodged backwards as the fist's gauntleted fingers threatened to tear a chunk out of his torso. Gorgoleon grabbed the collar of Sarpedon's breastplate with his other hand and headbutted him square on the eye.

Sarpedon reeled. He sensed the battle-brothers had broken ranks and were swarming closer now, a baying crowd just metres from them, a wall of huge purple-armoured bodies. They would tear him apart.

Ha! They could try.

Gorgoleon's backhand swipe could have ripped Sarpedon in two – he turned just in time and it caught him on the back, throwing him into the crowding Marines. Armoured bodied pressed in on him as he clambered to his feet, expecting the pendulous weight of the power fist to tear through his body any moment.

Sarpedon recognised the men around him and realised he was among his own battle-brothers now, if only for a second. Dreo and Givrillian helped Sarpedon to his feet and spoke a few encouraging words. They had been stripped of their weapons, but they could still help him for their very presence gave him strength. He would survive.

His brothers. They had fought all these years, only to find they were fighting for a lie. He felt their anger, as the same anger raged inside him. He would use it, as Daenyathos had taught.

Purity through hate. Dignity through rage.

Gorgoleon hurled Dreo aside and the crowd parted to give the combatants room to fight.

Both were bruised and bleeding. Neither would ever give up. Gorgoleon's fist would be death if it got a good hit in – but Sarpedon's force staff could punch through even Gorgoleon's artificer armour if the Librarian timed his mind's focus with the blow. They ducked and struck, parried and dodged, the crowd following them as the fight flowed across the cathedral's flagstones. The ancient place, its peace usually broken only by the Chaplains' fiery words, echoed to the crunch of cracking ceramite and the cheers of the assembled Space Marines. The stink of sweat and blood mingled with the incense, and the candles guttered with the shock of the might brought to bear.

Sarpedon could feel the blood crusting around his eye, and knew the hit to his back had cracked his rib-plate and ruptured at least one of his lungs. Gorgoleon was bleeding from a gash to the cheek, but if he was suffering internally he did not show it.

Sarpedon's anger. That was the key. What had set it all off? Why had there been such bloodshed on the Geryon? Why had the inquisitor's executioner met with such a savage refusal? Sarpedon had been willing to meet death rather than back down, and his battle-brothers had followed him. Why had they done that? What had made their actions so extreme?

It had to be anger. It was the only force strong enough. But was it just the loss of the Soulspear that had driven them to such excesses? To tell the truth, Sarpedon had hardly thought about the Soulspear at all in the last few months. Its loss felt more like one thread of a whole web of injustice.

What could he tap into that would give him anger enough to win? He had to think quickly, for Gorgoleon would surely kill him soon.

Sarpedon realised his concentration had slipped when Gorgoleon suddenly jinked behind him and there was an arm around his throat.

Gorgoleon hauled Sarpedon into the air, hoisting him high above the heads of the cheering Marines. The soaring vaults of the cathedral ceiling span before him as Gorgoleon ran towards the altar end of the nave.

Sarpedon struggled. It didn't work. Gorgoleon reached the altar and lifted Sarpedon high above his head.

'For Dorn!' he bellowed, and hurled Sarpedon through the stained glass window.

The world turned into razor-sharp shards of colour. An iron floor slammed into him and Sarpedon felt something else rupture.

No. Don't go under. Not yet. Not when there is still hope.

He saw startled, young faces staring at him, their scalps newly-shaved, implants raw. Novices.

He was in the Hall of Novices, where the Chapter's new recruits gathered to contemplate the traditions of the Chapter and the magnitude of their task in becoming full Space Marines. Sarpedon had spent untold hours here as he was honed into someone fit to wear the chalice of the Soul Drinkers. Statues of saints and Chapter heroes glared sternly down from alcoves in the grey walls and fat prayer-drones hovered, belching incense from their bulbous bodies.

The purple-robed novices scattered, clutching copies of the *Catechisms Martial*. They must have gathered to pray for their Chapter Master – but they had never thought they would be blessed with witnessing the combat itself.

Sarpedon grabbed his staff and hauled himself to his feet. He could feel he was bleeding internally and his inner breastplate of fused ribs was shattered. His system was cutting out the worst of the pain but he knew he was badly hurt.

And for a second he was back on Quixian Obscura, an alien neck snapping in his fist, feeling a terrible futile emptiness...

He had fought across a hundred planets and been savagely wounded dozens of times. He had seen battle-brothers dead by the score and killed enemies by the thousands.

Why? Why had they died? Why had he killed?

Gorgoleon vaulted through the frame of the shattered window and landed nearby. The other Marines were swarming into the Hall of Novices, eager to watch the kill.

The servants of the Emperor had died on Quixian Obscura, on the star fort and the Geryon platform. And all across the Imperium – on Armageddon and Ichar IV, through the depths of the Sabbat Worlds, Tallarn and Valhalla and Vogen. At the Cadian Gate they had died, in the hives of Lastrati, on the plains of Avignon, and on sacred Terra in the final acts of the Heresy – millions of Space Marines and untold billions of men had given their lives to protect the sanctity of the Imperium, and yet the Imperium was built of lies.

But that was not the worst of it.

Gorgoleon's strides seemed slow and loping. Sarpedon could feel it, the power Daenyathos had written of – the sacred anger that drove a man's feats beyond the limits of possibility. It was filling him, coursing through his body and the aegis circuit. Sarpedon could feel the light of the Architect of Fate shining on him, and knew that there really was hope.

Because he knew what had been boiling at the back of his mind, something so terrible that he had not dared contemplate it. At the heart of all that futile death and meaningless war, the Soul Drinkers had fought braver than their brothers, kept purer than anyone, striven to be the best there was.

But they had won only shame, for they had held the decadence and corruption of the Imperium together. They had thought they were following Dorn's example with fanatical zeal, little knowing that all this time…

Gorgoleon's fist swung in a massive uppercut. Sarpedon caught it with the staff, turned it aside, and ripped the staff's head deep into Gorgoleon's torso.

'All this time,' yelled Sarpedon, 'we were nothing!'

He grabbed Gorgoleon by the arm and threw him through the wall of the Hall of Novices, sending him tumbling into the dormitories and study-cells beyond.

Had he ever been this strong? No, it was the Emperor, the Architect of Fate, filling him with such power that it felt like he could hardly contain it. Sarpedon strode through the shattered wall and saw Gorgoleon, battered and bleeding, pulling himself to his knees. The spectre of panic crossed the Chapter Master's face. He had never faced anything like Sarpedon. No one had.

What did Gorgoleon fear? He feared *failure*.

And so, the Hell.

Barren, scarred rock lay beneath their feet. Above was the pure black of space, the stars swollen and dying. Deformed alien craft streaked across the star field and warp storms opened immense weeping wounds in reality, bleeding formless hordes of Chaos out into the universe. It was a galaxy lost to the alien and the daemon, cold and evil, sucked dry by the foes of humanity. It was an image calculated to horrify the stoutest Imperial servant, a place where all their efforts had failed.

The sound was the worst. The cackling of alien slavemasters. The gibbering of mindless daemons. The distant scream of a dying mankind. Even Gorgoleon's face registered shock at the horror around him.

Sarpedon had never gone this far, never constructed a whole world of fear out of the Hell. But he knew that nothing less would serve against Gorgoleon, and he felt the Emperor's strength inside him, fuelling him until his psychic power was a white-hot star inside his mind, its power streaming out into the Hell. All that power was focused on Gorgoleon himself – the Hell was for him and Sarpedon only, utterly real to them but only a faint haze to the battle-brothers watching them.

'You can't win with witchcraft, Sarpedon!' shouted Gorgoleon against the din of a suffering universe.

Sarpedon could feel the power growing, building up inside him so he felt fit to burst. It pushed against his skin and the bones of his altered skeleton. He was full of fire. The power was ready to explode out of him.

Gorgoleon clambered to his feet and swung again with the power fist, gouging great rents from the ground. His face streamed with blood and his teeth were gritted – his was the face of a man confronting death, as he had many times before. Every last gramme of the Chapter Master's strength went into the assault, battering at Sarpedon, swiping the stabbing force staff away, desperately trying to keep the Hell around him out of his mind by letting himself fill with rage. But Sarpedon couldn't be beaten back – there was a boiling sea of fire in his veins, and the hand of the Architect of Fate was upon him.

The two Marines ducked forwards and locked, face to face, for a split second. Gorgoleon's face was lit from beneath and Sarpedon realised that light must be streaming from his own eyes, such was the massive build up of power within him. It rose impossibly high as the ceramite of Gorgoleon's armour fractured within his grasp – it was too much for him to contain, the screaming in his ears too great to stand, the fire inside him too vast to bear.

There was a shriek of tearing armour and the cracking of bones. A great burst of light erupted all around as energy discharged from Sarpedon's body. There was a bolt of pain through his legs and then something he had never felt before – growing, splitting, changing.

Suddenly they were back in the wreckage of the study-cells. Gorgoleon lay where he had been hurled against the cell wall, unable to disguise his horror. There were thick lashes of blood up the walls and scraps of purple ceramite scattered all around.

Eight segmented arachnoid legs jutted from Sarpedon's waist, chitinous, jointed, and each tipped with a wicked talon.

The pain was gone. The Hell was gone; he didn't need it any more. Here was the blessing of the Architect of Fate – a new form, swift and deadly, a symbol of how he had thrown aside all that had imprisoned him. Sarpedon reared up on his hind legs, fully four metres high, and crashed down onto Gorgoleon. The two front talons speared the Chapter Master through the chest and lifted him high into the air. Sarpedon hooked his fingers into the shoulder joints of Gorgoleon's torso armour, stared up into the glazing eyes, and pulled.

The power. The majesty. Sarpedon had never felt this strong before.

Gorgoleon's body tore in two above him, raining blood and coiled organs. Sarpedon cast the flailing remains down onto the floor of the cell, breath heaving, ears ringing.

The din in his ears died down. There was silence, broken only by the steady drip of the blood spattered across the ceiling and running off Sarpedon's shoulder pads.

He looked around and saw the Soul Drinkers were crowded in a circle around the bloodstained wreckage that remained of the cells. Gradually Sarpedon's hearing returned and above the dripping of the blood and the coiling of the smoke, a thousand voices grew louder and louder, filling Sarpedon's soul.

They were chanting.

They were chanting his name.

CHAPTER EIGHT

THE WARP WAS a dark and terrible place, a realm where fears and emotions were made real, where the nightmares of men found form, and evil things lived. There were malevolent forces that called themselves gods, and mindlessly violent predators. There were no safe paths through the warp, and only the guiding light of the Astronomican beacon and the skills of the Navigator caste could bring a ship home.

The risks of travelling the shifting ways of the empyrean were offset by the vast distances that could be travelled in a matter of hours, so that ships which sailed the warp for a few days could make several years' worth of distance in real space. But inevitably, when ships departed the safety of reality and ploughed the waves of the warp, some did not return.

Worse, some returned changed.

Ghost ships. Prodigals. Craft which had been gone sometimes thousands of years, suddenly spat back out into real space. The terrible forces of the warp could twist their structures or weld lost ships together, and sometimes – the worst times – they brought something back with them. Their original names forgotten, these ships were known as space hulks.

Sarpedon couldn't tell how old this particular space hulk was, but it must have been older than any he had heard of. It was not the first he had seen, for the Soul Drinkers were suited to storming hulks and destroying them before their inhabitants could pose a threat. But it was the most ancient, and by magnitudes the biggest.

His half-arachnid form let him clamber along the walls and ceiling, so any foe he found would suffer a moment's disorientation in which Sarpedon could strike. This particular part of the hulk was Imperial, as witnessed by the aquila and devotional texts on the bulkheads. It had been an Imperial Guard hospital ship, with wards running its whole length and a huge quarantine and decontamination sector in the stern. It was also in a sensor-shadow, a part of the hulk which had been veiled from the fleet's intensive life-sign scans. Which meant it had to be searched the old-fashioned way.

Sarpedon rounded a corner and looked down from the ceiling at the ward. It was perhaps a kilometre and a half long. Centuries ago the rows of beds and equipment stations had been lit by unforgiving strip lights, but now the lights were dim and the beds were mouldering. Shadows gathered too dense for even Sarpedon's eyes to pierce.

He dropped down onto the floor and flipped the closest couple of beds with a talon. The layers of grime had built up over the centuries – which was good, for it meant nothing had been here to disturb them.

'Sarpedon to control, waypoint nine reached.'

'Acknowledged, Lord Sarpedon,' came Givrillian's voice over the vox. Sarpedon had been happy to appoint Givrillian as the mission's tactical co-ordinator, where his level head would be put to best use. Givrillian was back on the *Glory* with the HQ, while Sarpedon led the search on the hulk.

Sarpedon recalled the four extra eyes that had opened in Givrillian's facial scar since the victory on the *Glory*. If they had bothered him, he hadn't shown it.

A couple of bulkheads down one of Luko's squad emerged, bolter at eye-level, sweeping the area for anything that moved. Three more of the fire-team followed. Luko himself would be at the far end of the ward with the rest of the squad.

'Anything, Luko?' said Sarpedon.

'Nothing,' came the voxed reply.

The squad moved into the ward in scattered formation, gradually moving down its length. There were trolleys of medical equipment standing here and there, and cabinets set into the walls containing jars of unguents and chemicals. A couple of autosurgeons were stooped over screened-off beds, their many blades tarnished, power feeds corroded to nothing.

'Luko?'

'Lord?'

'Why did they leave the equipment?'

Millions of creds' worth of medical gear, abandoned. More than that, if something untowards had happened in the warp then the crew would have tried to evacuate, probably into the quarantine decks or saviour pods. They would have at least taken some of the medicine and surgery gear with them, to treat the worst of the patients. It made no sense.

Unless whatever happened had been so sudden they had no warning before they died. In which case every bed should contain a human skeleton.

Sarpedon ran up the wall and onto the ceiling, splaying his chitinous legs to put his face close to the surface.

No scratches. No stains. He moved further, looking for any signs that something had been alive in here. Could attackers have used the air vents? Unlikely, given the number of sterile filters in the ventilation systems. What, then? And if something had taken the bodies, where had they gone?

Where were they now?

'Givrillian? I need data on the air filtration for this place.'

'Yes, commander. We don't know how old that ship is but we will see what the mem-banks can say.'

Sarpedon flicked to the squad frequency. 'Luko, stay alert. I think we've got something here.'

'Still no contacts, commander.'

The patients and crew, the Sisters of the Orders Hospitaller and the Guard Medical Corps – they were only human, and they could be manipulated like all humans. They could be herded like cattle into a slaughterhouse, and then…

'We've got something, sir,' said Givrillian. 'Hospital ships derived from that class had separate filtration systems for the wards, the command decks, the quarantine zones and the operating rooms. To prevent cross-infection.'

That was it. And it meant the attackers could still be here.

Sarpedon ran along the ceiling, the hooked talons of his legs moving him faster than even a Space Marine could run. At the end of the ward was the operating suite, where a pair of autosurgeons would have performed delicate procedures on the most badly wounded or, more likely, the most important patients. It was separated from the ward by a heavy pair of airlock doors. The edges of the doors were clean. But there was no other way.

'Luko! I want a fire-team with me, now! The rest, stay where you are, fire support pattern.'

'Yes, lord!'

The lead fire-team stomped up behind Sarpedon. Three Marines: Mallik, Sken and Zaen, with Zaen toting Squad Luko's flamer.

Sarpedon jabbed the talons of his two front legs into the gap between the doors. He forced them open, and realised they did not resist nearly so much as they should have done.

The airlock beyond was clear. The doors into the operating suite were set with glass panels but they were opaque with filth. Sarpedon drew his bolter and gestured for Vrae to take up position at his shoulder.

Sarpedon dropped a shoulder and barged through the doors, feeling them buckle under his strength.

The floor was crusted with excrement and the walls streaked with it. Against the walls were piled bones, some crumbled and grey with age, others gleaming white. Eye sockets stared blindly from the mounds of putrescence, fingers and teeth were scattered like maggots of bone. The autosurgeon arms were black with gore and filth where something had perched on them while it fed.

Warning runes were blinking at the back of Sarpedon's eye. The stench here was so strong and infectious it could have killed a normal man, but Sarpedon's armour and implants were blocking it out. For this he was grateful.

The attackers had cut off the air supply to the ward, or perhaps polluted it beyond use. The crew had moved the patients into the operating suite where the separate air supply should have kept them alive a little longer. Except that, packed into the operating room, they had been a sitting target, unable to run or fight back, when the predators came.

Herded into a slaughterhouse.

But not all the bones were that old. Some were of bodies that had decayed thousands of years before, but others were new. Had the inhabitants of this hulk been preying on backwater space lanes? There were tales of how treasure-hunters would board hulks in the search for cargo or archaeotech – but there were very few tales of them getting out again. Or perhaps the attackers had found some way of attracting ships, or even hunting them down?

Sarpedon took a step further into the room, talon crunching through an aged ribcage. He looked up at the ceiling, trying to see some way they had come in. The vents had been undisturbed, and they had not used the main airlock doors.

He realised it just before the first one attacked. It ripped through the disposal hatch set into the far wall, scattering sparks and debris. Sarpedon caught the flash of pulpy grey-beige flesh beneath a glossy black exoskeleton, a pair of tiny black eyes, a mouth like a mantrap. Claws lashed out and knocked off Sarpedon's aim as he put two bolter-rounds into the wall behind it.

Genestealer. A four-armed, parasitical predator – if it took you down you could look forward to an implanted pupa and a messy death. That was if its claws didn't tear you apart first.

Bolters chattered but the thing was fast – it picked up Brother Mallik by the face of his helmet and smashed him through the autosurgeon, scattering tarnished blades. Sarpedon swept up along the ceiling and stabbed down with his staff from above, spearing the stealer through the back. He reached down and grabbed it by the throat, hauled it up, flicked his wrist and felt the gristle in its neck snap.

A genestealer, in close combat. Sarpedon had always known he was formidable in battle, but had he ever been that strong?

'Flamer!' he yelled, dropping the foul alien corpse. Zaen was already at the opening and poured a gout of flame down the waste chute. Something let out a gurgling scream and thick brown smoke billowed up.

The stealers had come up from the disposal deck, where medical waste and the bodies of those who died on the operating table were sent. That was how they had got in – it made sense, really. Waste was ejected into space and the hatch would be an obvious entry point for a predator like a genestealer. Maybe they had been there for months before taking over the ship, breeding down there amongst the auto-mated incinerators and corpse-dumps. The hospital ship might well have jumped into the warp as it was assaulted, hoping to remove the aliens from real space. It was brave, and would have worked had the ship not become part of the immense space hulk.

'Sarpedon to control. Contact, xenos confirmed. Genestealers. Send fire-teams to disposal deck, form a cordon and prep kill-teams.' He glanced down at Mallik, who was struggling to pull his ruined helmet free. Blood was seeping from an eyepiece. 'One man down, request medical support.'

'Acknowledged.'

'And send Tellos in.'

'Yes, sir.'

THERE HAD BEEN a civil war. There was no other way of saying it. Chapter traditions had it that Sarpedon was judged to be in the right in the eyes of Dorn and the Emperor, by virtue of his victory over Gorgoleon. Most of the Space Marines who had watched Sarpedon tear the Chapter Master apart had sworn allegiance to Sarpedon on the spot – they said there had been a golden light shining around Sarpedon as he stood spattered in Gorgoleon's blood, and that the choirs of Terra were heard singing. Sarpedon became Chapter Master of the Soul Drinkers by the acclamation of the battle-brothers.

But there were those who had not believed. They had seen their leader slain by a half-monster, half-human psyker, and they had renounced Sarpedon as a corrupt and evil daemon-thing. They had loaded their guns and set up barricades, and fought their last fight against their brothers.

They had fought well, Sarpedon had to admit. The strange thing was, the veterans and specialists had sided with Sarpedon, while most of the novices had rebelled against him. It took weeks to reduce the most dug-in hardpoints, and to hunt down the guerrilla units striking from the labyrinthine depths of the *Glory*. The *Sanctifier's Son* had been lost entirely when rebels gained control of it and tried to flee – it had been shattered by combined broadside fire as it manoeuvred to warp jump position.

But the rebels had been rooted out, eventually. Those taken alive were rounded up and put onto the darkship, which was then destroyed with massed lance battery fire.

When the death toll was counted, between the operations on the star fort and Geryon platform, and the revolution of Sarpedon's victory, the Soul Drinkers had lost fully one third of their number. Sarpedon felt the loss of the rebels because on one level they were his brothers, but he celebrated their deaths as traitors. If they had to die to ensure the Soul Drinkers would be free of the Imperial yoke, then so be it. He had led men to their deaths before, and not regretted it. Sometimes, he realised then, a commander must be hard.

The only one that really stuck in his mind was Michairas, the Marine who had once attended upon Caeon, and who witnessed Sarpedon conducting the ceremony of the chalice. Sarpedon had faced him personally as he led a band of novices trying to flee off the *Glory* – he tore out Michairas's rebreather implants and threw him out of an airlock. For some reason that stuck with him. He could see Michairas's eyes even now, brimming with fear but tempered by defiance.

Brave boy. But he had to die. That was the price of truth, and nobody said the truth was an easy thing to follow.

When the dead were offered up to Dorn or cast out of the debris hatches according to their allegiance, the fleet had been in a grim position. An Imperial battlefleet would find them soon – if not the one led by Inquisitor Tsouras then another under an admiral hungry for the scalp of an Excommunicate Chapter. The Soul Drinkers' fleet was large and impossible to conceal forever, and the Imperial Navy could muster enough ships to destroy them in a decisive engagement or harry them to the ends of the galaxy. The Soul Drinkers were alone in the universe, with no allies or safe harbour, and it was a matter of time before they were hunted down.

It was Yser who had shown them a way. The Architect of Fate had appeared in his dreams wearing a crown of many stars – Yser had recalled the image in exact detail, and the crown had formed a star chart that led them to the hulk. Another miracle, and Yser seemed certain that the Emperor had seen the Chapter's suffering and was gifting them a new home and a new start. By now the Chaplain and Marine alike hung on his word and he was acting as Sarpedon's principal adviser. Without Yser, perhaps the Chapter would have torn itself apart completely, but he provided a spiritual leadership alongside Sarpedon's authority.

Huge, ancient, and devoid of life save the isolated stealer colony, the hulk had been perfect. It was formed of perhaps a score of other ships, crushed and fused into one – it was large enough to house the whole Chapter but, as only one ship, it would be more difficult to track than an entire fleet. With so many dead areas it could hide in debris fields or dust clouds, and the Tech-Marines had suggested that it possessed enough armament, once refitted and repaired, to create a formidable bastion. Its monstrous bulk was so twisted and deformed that it had been christened the *Brokenback*.

The *Brokenback*. The new home of an excommunicate and renegade Chapter. Somehow, it seemed fitting.

'SAD TO SEE them go, commander?' said Lygris.

'A little,' replied Sarpedon. 'But we should use this as an opportunity to start again. To refound the Chapter.'

'Perhaps.'

'Does this not grieve you, Lygris? As a Tech-Marine I would have imagined the loss of so many fine ships would be like losing a limb.'

Lygris smiled, his dead-skinned face just managing to turn up the corners of his mouth. 'With the loss of the fleet with Chapter will lose a part of its soul, commander. But we have lost so much already, it is perhaps better to destroy everything that ties us to the lies of our past. And it should not be forgotten what we have here in the *Brokenback*. We may have lost a fleet, but we have gained one of the largest space hulks ever taken intact. There must be thirty plasma reactors in the structure. The warp drive potential alone is astonishing.'

They were in one of the more recognisable parts of the *Brokenback* – a private yacht that had been owned a couple of centuries before by some rich noble or trading magnate. Whoever it was had not possessed a subtlety of taste, and every surface was covered with flowing scroll-work or gilt sculpture, now dark and tarnished with age. This was the yacht's viewing gallery, where parties of dignitaries would gather to witness some celestial phenomenon over a glass of chilled amasec – a great ocular viewing window swallowed the whole ceiling and looked out onto space.

The Soul Drinkers' fleet was drifting dark and powerless outside. Once the stealers had been cleared out – a swift and simple operation with Tellos at the fore, hand-blades slick with alien filth – the Chapter had been moved into the *Brokenback*. Now no longer needed, the fleet was a liability, large and easy to track. It had to be scuttled.

An explosion bloomed towards the stern of the *Glory*, where the fuel pods fed into the reactors. A white ring of fire suddenly burst from the heart of the ship and sheared it in two, spouting burning fuel and debris. Two of the strike cruisers were caught in the expanding disc of plasma-fire and had their hulls ripped open like foil. Another charge blew the prow off the *Carnivore* – with its structure terminally violated the ship imploded, the shock of its death spewing storms of hull fragments tens of kilometres into space.

Slowly, silently, the Soul Drinkers' fleet died. Charges carefully planted at the key points shattered power feeds and cracked open reactor cores. It took perhaps an hour for the destruction to unfold, and Sarpedon watched it all until the end.

They had saved what they could – records, equipment, the librarium and apothecarion, several serf-labour battalions. But there must have been so much lost that the Soul Drinkers Chapter that had once existed could be said to have died, and a new Chapter to have taken its place.

That was how it should be. They were not Imperial Space Marines any more – they were beholden to no one save the Emperor, who voiced His approval through the visions and miracles granted to them. At last, the Soul Drinkers were free. At last, they could begin to redeem themselves after centuries of pandering to the tyranny of the Imperium.

When all that remained of the fleet was a handful of burned-out husks, Sarpedon and Lygris watched them drift for a while, feeling the weight of history lifting off their shoulders. All these years, they had been nothing. But now they could start again, and this time they would carry the light of the Emperor into the darkness.

'Lord Sarpedon,' crackled a voice in a vox-interrupt burst. 'Sergeant Salk here, supervising labour unit secundus. We're working on a machine-spirit housing in the Sector Indigo and we've uncovered an anomaly. Requesting specialist assistance, technical and medical. And a Chaplain.'

'A Chaplain?'

'Yes, sir. I believe we are in the presence of a moral threat.'

Sarpedon snapped the link shut and opened another net-wide channel. He felt his pulse quickening. 'Sarpedon to all points. Specialists to Sector Indigo. Moral threat, moral threat.' The Soul Drinkers had done a thorough job in scouring the *Brokenback* for anything suspicious, but there had always been a possibility something had survived here. No chances could be taken.

'Lygris, with me,' said Sarpedon. 'I want to see this for myself.' His multitude of limbs gave him far greater ground speed than another Marine and he soon left Lygris behind as he hurried across the observation gallery and down along the ceiling of the corridor.

SECTOR INDIGO WAS a research ship, a squat blocky craft filled with galleries of man-sized specimen jars full of milky fluid. The markings of the Adeptus Mechanicus Xenobiologis were on every piece of equipment, and the bridge bristled with mind-impulse units for the crew. But there was nothing alive on the ship and everything had been perfectly preserved by the craft's sterilised air systems, even after the ship had been swallowed by the bulk of the *Brokenback*.

The machine-spirit was the prize here. It was held in a ceramo-plastic core just behind the bridge – a room-filling sphere of circuitry, its surface studded with valves and slots for punch cards. Initial inspection had suggested it was something beyond the scope of the Mechanicus to create from scratch, and if it could be made to work it might provide a means to control primary systems all over the *Brokenback*.

So Sergeant Salk went with labour unit secundus to open it up so the Tech-Marines could start working on it.

That was when they found the moral threat.

SARPEDON WAS QUICK but there was already an apothecary, Karendin, at the scene when he arrived, tending to the wounded serf-labourers in one of the specimen-cargo bays.

'What is our situation, Karendin?'

'Bad, sir.' Karendin was one of the youngest Soul Drinkers to side with Sarpedon – newly inducted into the ranks of the apothecarion, the Chapter war had been a baptism of blood for him. 'We've lost a half-dozen of the labourers.' He looked down at the body lying at his feet – its face had been half-scoured away by acid, which had left an ugly green-black crust around the edges of the wounds. The serf was breathing his last, and four others were lying beside the specimen containers with whole limbs, heads or torsos seared away. A dangerous, acrid smell drifted from the bow of the ship.

'And Salk?'

'By the machine-spirit core, sir. In case it tries to get out.'

Sarpedon hurried up the specimen gallery to where Salk was crouched by the sealed bulkhead, bolter ready, with two of the remaining labourers. Salk's armour was scored and pitted with acid burns.

'Bad, sergeant?'

Salk saluted hurriedly. 'We opened up the sphere and something fired. It took down half the serfs before we got out, nearly took me. It is not my place to suggest such things, commander, but I think it's possessed.'

Sarpedon glanced at the black metal bulkhead door – he could feel the wrongness beyond it, as strong as the reek of decay.

'Commander!' called Lygris as he sprinted down from the specimen gallery. 'Reinforcements are heading in. Three squads from Sector Gladius. Five minutes.'

'Too long. It's awake now, if we give it any more time it could break out or grow stronger.' Sarpedon drew his force staff. He had only just finished scrubbing the filth off it from the encounter with the genestealer, now it would taste corrupt blood again.

'Serf?' said Sarpedon, and one of the labourers hurried up. 'Open it on my mark.'

The labourer put his weight behind the black metal wheel lock. The surface of the door was creaking and bulging beside him.

'Mark.'

The serf rammed the wheel round and died, the door bursting open and vomiting a gout of grey-green acid over him. Sarpedon and Lygris were quicker by far, diving down and to the side as the billowing filth rolled over them.

The air inside would be toxic. But a Space Marine, with his extra bio-mechanical lung and rebreather implants, could hold his breath for many minutes. There were no excuses.

Sarpedon scuttled over the dissolving body of the serf and into the machine-spirit room, Lygris at his shoulder. The circuitry sphere was half-open, one hemisphere peeled aside. Inside, like the heart of a rotting fruit, was a pit of green-black corruption bubbling with heat and malevolence, spitting gobbets of corrosion and exuding a wave of toxic air.

Sarpedon ran onto the cylindrical wall of the room as Lygris threw a frag grenade into the corrupt core. The dripping filth swallowed the grenade and dissolved it before it could go off.

'Flamers to Sector Indigo!' voxed Lygris. 'Now!'

'Four minutes,' came the reply. Givrillian's voice, realised Sarpedon. Good.

The rear of the sphere was mostly intact, but the plates of its surface were beginning to work loose and green-brown rivulets of ichor were running from the card-slots. By the Emperor, he could feel it, the waves of hatred, the sheer malice of the thing. There was no intelligence here that could have been able to create an emotion – and yet it hated still, as if it was nothing but a receptacle for that hate.

He drove the force staff through the circuitry skin and into the thing's heart. He felt the semi-liquid machinery shredded by the staff's head, but the thing's hatred did not die.

Lygris was pumping shells into it. He must have known this was no mortal enemy that could be killed by bullets. He was trying to distract it, to give Sarpedon the time to kill it for real. Lygris, seemingly like all the Soul Drinkers, had utter faith in Sarpedon's abilities – they had seen the light of the Emperor streaming from him, and the gifts He had granted their new Chapter Master. Sarpedon hoped he could live up to their trust.

Sarpedon gripped the arunwood tight and channelled his psychic force into the staff, trying to break the thing's grip on life. The waves of malice shuddered, shifted, grew more powerful but less focused.

What was it? Alien? There were tales of creatures that could usurp control of technology. But would they project such horribly familiar, human hatred?

The arunwood squirmed in his grasp as it was repelled by the wrongness of the thing in the machine-spirit core. Sarpedon strode up the wall and onto the ceiling, dragging a long gouge in the core's surface through which bilious filth poured.

Lygris ducked to one side as a tongue of acidic gore spat out at him, lashing deep into the opposite wall with a hiss. The Tech-Marine rolled as he landed, crushing the sorry remains of the final serf-labourer before he came to his knees and pulled a wire from the back of his neck.

'Lygris, no! It'll kill you!' Sarpedon didn't want to risk using up his breath with speech, but he knew what Lygris was trying to do and he knew it would fail. He had barely survived the machine-spirit on the Geryon, and that was but a fraction of the *674-XU28* full consciousness. This was an alien infection or deliberate techno-heresy of some kind, and it would rip his mind apart.

'Hurt it for me, Lord Sarpedon!' came the reply, just before Lygris jammed the cable jack into an infoport and flopped insensible to the floor.

Sarpedon yelled, not caring if there was anything left in his lungs, and plunged his staff-wielding hand up to the elbow into the machine-spirit core. Ichor and entrail-like machinery wrapped around his arm and dragged him further in. Sarpedon twisted the staff head, felt the thing's scream of pain, and knew what he must do.

Lygris convulsed on the floor. Now it was Sarpedon's turn to distract the hideous intelligence, so Lygris might at least have a chance.

ARE YOU IN here? thought Lygris. Are you in here? For if you are not, then all is lost.

I am here, something replied through the din of blasphemous screams. *But I cannot fight it.*

It is hurting, replied Lygris. We are wounding it deeply, my lord and I. But we cannot kill it without your help, Sector Indigo.

I know. But it is so strong. When I was the research ship Bellerophon, *I mapped systems unseen by man and catalogued species never even comprehended before. Now I am small and frightened. It is nothing but corruption, Tech-Marine Lygris. It is a spectre of corrosion, utterly without remorse, and it has defeated me at every turn.*

But it can be beaten, said Lygris. I can show you the way. I can help you. While it is blind with pain, you can cut the primary power feed to the machine-spirit core, where its physical presence resides, and you will starve it to death.

Yes, I can, Tech-Marine Lygris. But if I do this thing, I will die too, for the core is where my mem-banks also reside.

But it will be dead. You can know that in ceasing to exist, you have destroyed a great and terrible thing. You can have revenge, Sector Indigo. Are you willing to make that sacrifice?

Tech-Marine Lygris, this creature is the enemy of everything for which I once strove. You should know, as a Space Marine, that when there is a choice between life and revenge, there is really no choice at all.

SARPEDON WRESTLED WITH the glutinous foulness that threatened to swallow him whole. He was up to his shoulders and his front two legs were thrust deep into the corrosive body of the spirit core, trying to hold his torso out of the quagmire. He held the force staff with both hands now, using both ends to gouge away while the thing fought to wrest it from him.

The armour on his forearms was mostly gone. Already his hands and wrists were burning where the armour seals had been eaten away and acid was leaking in. But the creature was angry now, focused entirely on him. If there was anything Lygris could do, it could be done now, for the monster's back was effectively turned while Sarpedon battled with it.

If it survived, it could escape and have the run of the rest of the *Brokenback*. The whole Chapter was at stake, then. That made the situation simple – Sarpedon would win or die.

Then there was something else. *Fear*.

The lights in the room guttered and died. And suddenly Lygris was beside him, the cable still snaking from his neck, slamming his bolter into the rents Sarpedon had opened up, firing explosive rounds into the core.

The thing screamed in terror as blackness opened up all around it, the bottom of its world falling away as the power drained from the core. It fought to the very end, but with its life force haemorrhaging it was no match for the combined anger of two Space Marines and its guts were shredded by bolter and staff.

Sarpedon and Lygris emerged from the machine-spirit room just over three minutes after they had gone in, covered in gore and acid burns, gasping for the relatively clean air of the specimen deck. They met the first of the reinforcements coming in, bearing flamers and plasma guns to cleanse the chamber. Karendin immediately left the dying serfs and saw to the wounds of his commander, as Salk directed the flamer troops in scouring the spirit core room.

Givrillian strode up to where Karendin was peeling the armour from Sarpedon's blackened arms. Givrillian's scar was a bright livid red and the old wound had opened up – from between folds of rent skin peered a half-dozen eyes which glanced here and there constantly. They gave the already grizzled Givrillian even more presence and importance – the sergeant's alteration was just one more of the many uncanny gifts the Architect of Fate had granted the Soul Drinkers.

'Commander, are you hurt badly?'

Sarpedon shook his head. 'A few courses of synthiflesh will suffice. I have had much worse.'

'Sergeant Givrillian,' said Lygris, his voice harsh from the rawness of his gas-burned throat. 'What we fought was in there for a purpose. I don't think it was xenos, either. If I may make a suggestion, I would have you gather the Tech-Marines and librarium adepts and find out what information remains in there.'

'Agreed,' said Sarpedon. 'If there is another force on the *Brokenback*, we must know of it.'

Givrillian saluted and moved off to prepare for the investigation.

Lygris turned to Sarpedon. 'It was trying to take over, commander. And it wasn't doing it for its own benefit.'

MUTANT.

A month had passed since the machine-spirit in Sector Indigo had been purged. In that time the exploration of the *Brokenback* had continued, the mem-banks salvaged from the fleet now being filled with information about the Chapter's new home. There had been sixteen separate component craft identified – some were rotted husks, others as clean and pristine as the day they sailed off their manufactoria docks. There was a flight of pre-heresy fighter craft fused and welded into a jagged starburst of metal, and an orbital generatorium platform that the Tech-Marines were activating and re-routing to power the hulk's myriad warp drives, and a ship-bound schola progenium habitat being divided into monastic cells. The hulk was gradually being mapped and adapted – soon, it would be as formidable a fortress-monastery as any Chapter could claim to possess.

Sarpedon's wounds had been severe but they had been quick to heal. The charred, blackened skin on his forearms had flaked away to reveal strong new flesh. The weeping acid burns that ran right up his arachnoid legs had been washed clean with the apothecaries' balms and now only tough ridges of chitinous scar remained. The sinews that had burned away grew back over a matter of days, and the rugged exoskeletal limbs were packed with new-grown muscle.

And that was, perhaps, the problem. As Sarpedon walked through the cavernous gun decks that formed a giant cavity within the body of the *Brokenback*, he knew that the strength he felt all throughout him was something not entirely natural.

Mutant. They had used the word to his face when the Chapter had fended off meltdown in the days following his victory over Gorgoleon. Michairas had gurgled it as Sarpedon strangled the life out of him – mutant: unclean, an aberration, a sinner by its mere existence. It was one of the gravest insults that could be slung at a fellow Space Marine, and Sarpedon had killed many of them for it. And yet on one level he could understand them, if not forgive them.

The gun decks had once bellowed the fiery rage of an Imperial battleship, the same craft that formed perhaps half the bulk of the *Brokenback's* forward sections. The ship's name, *Macharia Victrix*, was struck onto every bulkhead and stanchion, for this was once a proud ship which, judging by the kill tallies etched into the gun casings, had fought the misguided fight of the Imperial cause for many centuries. But at some point it had become lost and the *Brokenback* had swallowed it, leaving the guns to fall silent and corrode. There were powdery piles of bones dotted in the shadows of the immense tarnished gun casings, where stranded crew had gathered in darkness as the madness of the warp took them. Some of the bones had teeth marks.

Sarpedon broke into a run, feeling the steel-taut tendons in the joints of his legs and the bunches of muscles contracting. Eight talons struck sparks from the iron-grated floor as he sprinted and skidded, testing the limits of his altered body. There was no pain any more – it was as if the new-grown flesh was stronger still.

To an unbeliever's eyes, he must have been a monstrous sight – a spider-centaur; half-man half-arachnid. A Space Marine was fearsome enough, but Sarpedon knew he would look truly terrifying to those who had not witnessed his triumph at the Cathedral of Dorn. Those novices had not felt the true sacred strength of the Soul Drinkers, or seen the halo of the Emperor's glory that had surrounded Sarpedon at the moment of his victory. Their minds had still had room for doubt, where a true Marine knew none. They had seen a monster and assumed that Sarpedon was a monster indeed, without feeling the magnificent truth.

But Sarpedon knew he was no monster. He knew as surely as he felt the eyes of Dorn and the Emperor upon him. For he knew what it meant to live under the taint of the mutant. He had consumed the flesh of the mutant slain by Tellos on the star fort, and remembered every detail of what he had felt – the ugliness covering him like a film of dirt, the aura of loathing that the whole universe projected towards him. The curse of the mutant was something terrible and all consuming – and Sarpedon felt none of it now. He felt only the divine strength of the Architect of Fate coursing through him, directed through his altered limbs and the newfound power in his arm.

Sarpedon hurtled up the side of the closest gun casing, talons goug-ing scars against the surface of the ancient metal. He reached the apex of the casing and leapt upwards, finding the wall, then the ceiling, until he was scuttling upside-down, watching the shadowy depths of the gun deck flitting by beneath him.

The battle-brothers had no doubt, either. Ever since the violence of the Sarpedon's ascendance he had not felt one echo of dissent. Many of the brothers were themselves changing – Givrillian with his many eyes, Tellos with his strangely changed flesh and keener senses. Every day brought some new gift to light – Brother Zaen was growing sharp triangular scales down his back and upper arms, while the fingers of Sergeant Graevus's right hand were so long and powerful that he could handle his power axe as if it weighed no more than a combat knife.

Sarpedon flipped off the ceiling and dropped, his eight legs spread to cushion his landing as he slammed into the floor, denting the rusted metal.

Mutant? No, his new form and those of his battle-brothers were gifts from the Emperor, a sign that they had been set further apart from the mindless masses of humanity, that they were as different in body as they were in spirit. It was fitting that the weak-stomached inhabitants of the Imperium would mistake them for unclean mutants – it was just one more symptom of their feeble-mindedness.

In a chamber towards the stern of the *Brokenback*, the Tech-Marines would be routing the shattered remnants of Sector Indigo's mem-banks to the information feed cluster they had assembled in the sensorium dome of the yacht-ship. If there was anything left to find, it might tell them something about why the foulness had dedicated itself to winning control of the *Brokenback*.

THE PLACE HAD no name. But that made no sense – every planet had a name, even if it was only a number assigned to it by the navi-cogitators mapping the area. Here, there was nothing – every field in the readout was blank. The only information available was its location. That, and the image. But that was of little use, for the world was smeared with a layer of thick cloud, a swirling grey-white mantle that wrapped the planet from pole to pole. The milky glare of the image cast sharp-toothed shadows on the walls of the captain's quarters being converted into Sarpedon's chambers.

'There is nothing here that warrants our attention,' said Sarpedon, sitting back on the haunches of his newly blackened legs.

Tech-Marine Solun adjusted the servitor's holo-array and the image drew out, revealing a shattered grid of information – hundreds of panels of planetary data, all scarred and defaced until not one world was legible. It was the visual representation of a database that had been corrupted beyond redemption.

'The mem-banks to which the machine-spirit had access were in an appalling state,' said Solun. 'The infection had destroyed the information systematically. The mem-plates were nearly liquid when we opened them up.'

'So it left this one world. But why?'

Solun adjusted the servitor again and the image flickered into a complex map of Sector Indigo's navigational systems. Solun was, like all Tech-Marines, responsible for maintenance of the Chapter's battlegear and field engineering duties.

Unlike most Tech-Marines, however, his area of expertise was in the arcane and near-magical world of information, retrieving and storing it. Temporary mem-banks were ranged in black slabs on his armour's backpack and shoulder blades, while his servo-arm was tipped with a syringe-like data-thief probe.

'This is Sector Indigo's own navigational system,' said Solun, as a section of the map flickered red. 'It's been hooked up to the bridges of at least eight more of the *Brokenback's* components craft. Most notably, a high-capacity cargo freighter and a xenos ship currently in a quarantined sector. It is probable that controlled movement of these ships would have allowed the *Brokenback* to be flown very effectively.'

'So it was about control? It was taking over the ship and flying it to our mystery planet.'

Solus nodded. 'That would be our conclusion.'

'Very well. Good work, Tech-Marine.' Sarpedon looked towards another figure, half-covered in the shadows cast by the holo-array. 'Now, do we know what it was?'

The black-armoured bulk of Chaplain Iktinos loomed from the darkness. 'It was a daemon,' he said evenly. 'You say you felt its intelligence. It was a hatred you recognised, commander. That was no alien or man-made abomination. It was a servant of the enemy.'

A daemon. A footsoldier of the powers of the warp, a servant of the Dark Gods of Chaos. Chaos was the horror that the Emperor had died to thwart. It was the dread Horus, Warmaster of Chaos, who had been slain by the Emperor at the height of the battle for Earth, and who had grievously wounded the Emperor in return. It had been Chaos that had corrupted the weak hearts of the lesser primarchs and brought the foul traitor legions into being.

When Sarpedon had turned his back on the Imperium it was apparent to him how Chaos might thrive in such a tyranny – there were so many corrupt institutions through which Chaos might seep into the galaxy. Sarpedon had harboured visions of the Soul Drinkers battling the pure horror of Chaos, and even dismantling the Imperium to deny the enemy a breeding ground. But now, the touch of Chaos was here, on the *Brokenback*.

A thought came unbidden – at last, Sarpedon, you can get to grips with a foe worth fighting.

But there was more. A tiny incessant voice at the back of his mind…

You have seen this place before. You have been here in your dreams, and felt the stink of what lives there. Peel back the layers of cloud and the raw, bleeding planet revealed will be more familiar to you than your own battlegear.

'It was going to this place, wasn't it?' said Sarpedon. 'The daemon-disease was supposed to corrupt the *Brokenback's* guidance systems so it could be flown to this planet.'

'That would be my conclusion, commander. The Librarians concur. The question remaining is why?'

'Because it is an evil place, Iktinos.' Sarpedon looked from the milky sphere of the unnamed planet to the Chaplain's impassive helmet mask. 'This is the place Yser spoke of. This is where we are required to prove our worth to the immortal Emperor. I have seen the evil that is waiting for us here, and now the Emperor has delivered us proof. That evil sent a daemon to bring it the *Brokenback*, but we got here before it could complete its mission. And the *Brokenback* will sail to this world, but with us as masters.'

'I take it, Lord Sarpedon, that you would have me deliver the litanies of readiness,' said Iktinos, as if he had expected this all along.

'Indeed, Chaplain. As soon as we are warp-worthy, this is where we will be headed.' Sarpedon pointed at the unnamed world – and though it was clouded and obscure, he could see burning bright behind his eyes the nightmare that boiled on its surface.

Was there any greater blessing for a warrior? Here was something utterly evil that could be brought to battle and crushed. Something wicked formed not from betrayal or greed but pure, understandable sin.

Something he could face.

Something he could kill.

CHAPTER NINE

THE UPPER ATMOSPHERE was freezing and harsh, but even there he could feel the warm pulse of unholy life throbbing thousands of metres below. Yser knew that if he looked down he would see the same sight again, the same one that had threatened to strip his sanity away these last few months – but he also knew that he could not just shut his eyes and refuse to believe. He was here for a reason – for nothing would happen to him that the Architect of Fate did not will.

There was a hideous lurch as Yser dropped into freefall. He opened his eyes and saw the yellowing banks of clouds sweeping up towards him before he was plunged into a foul-reeking soup of pollution. It was thick against his skin, heaving like a diseased lung drawing breath. But there was worse, he knew. He had been here more times than he could remember, and knew the next layer was worse.

As always, he heard it before he saw it. A saw-like hum that cut through the howling winds and the sinister bubbling of the rot-cloud, an oath hummed by a trillion tiny throats. He braced himself, but knew it would not be enough. The horror was welling up inside him a second before he hit.

Flies. A near-solid slab of fat-bodied flies half a kilometre deep, a foul black choir of insect vermin. They burst against his skin and became a shell of thick liquid gore, forcing up his nose and into his ears, prying at his lips and eyelids. The roar of millions of ripping bodies flooded his ears as he tore deeper into the fly-layer, arms flailing.

And past that would be the worst of all. For a second he was almost begging for the stratum of insects to hold him forever, just so he wouldn't have to see what lay beyond. But their slimy grip was weak and he slipped deeper and deeper until the fly-layer thinned out and now it was heavy, clammy air that squeezed the sweat from Yser's frail body.

He opened his eyes. He had to. The Architect wanted him to see.

Yser knew it would not look like this. But this was how it would feel. To his eyes it was black shot through with purple, a mile-high bloom of dark flame. The heat billowing off it was damp and heavy. Its massive flickering form was watching him – Yser could feel that hard, cold, evil intelligence burning against his mind. It was speaking to him, taunting him in words he couldn't hear. It was laughing. It could see him, and knew how weak and pathetic he was in the face of such evil.

He forced his eyes down. The Architect wanted him to see.

A million million corpses were piled into a wet, pale landscape of suffering. Yser knew they were all good men and women, those whose souls the Architect of Fate wished to seek out and introduce to His light. This hideous darkness had taken them, enslaved them, butchered them in their millions and was living off them like a wily predator lived off carrion.

They were the fuel for the flame. This abomination lived by consuming their goodness and truth, and the black-hot fire rippled over the deathscape reducing the corpses to crumbling husks. It needed decency and honesty and purity to survive, for it fed by corrupting their purity into something it could live upon. These men and women were the last chance of humanity, the only ones with the strength to face the truth of the Architect's will, and the evil force here would consume them until there was nothing left.

One day, it would be Yser's turn to become fuel for the flame of darkness.

Unless it was stopped. That was the message the Architect was giving Yser by forcing him to see this horror. The vision was not of the present but of the future, a universe where evil had triumphed and the Architect's flock lay amongst the heaps of the dead. A future that could be prevented if Yser and the sacred warriors of the Emperor could find the nightmare and end it before it became that all-consuming flame.

A force seized Yser like a huge invisible hand, yanking him upwards away from the deathscape, ripping through the fly-slab and through the clouds of pollution. Then faster, further, into the raw cold of space.

The last sight was always the same – a glimpse of the world they had to cleanse. Clouded and pale like an immense cataract, it festered in orbit around a star that was bloated and dying as if the hell-planet had infected it with its evil.

Then blackness washed over everything, and the vision was over.

WHEN YSER TOLD Sarpedon of his latest vision, it was in the new Cathedral of Dorn, the air heavy with a mix of ancient engine oil and burning incense, and resounding with the echoes of prayers old and new.

'It was the same?'

'No. More intense, Lord Sarpedon, More real.'

'As if you were closer?'

'Yes. Yes, that was it. We are close, I feel it.' Yser held the copy of the *Catechisms Martial* in still-shaking hands – Daenyathos's masterpiece was never far from his side now. His voice sounded small and feeble in the high-ceilinged nave that had been selected as the new Cathedral of Dorn, and though Yser was far cleaner and healthier than when he had been found on the star fort it was still very apparent that he was a frail old man.

'Are you afraid, father?'

Yser's old, watery eyes looked up from the hidebound book. 'Lord Sarpedon, it does not matter if I am. I will do what I must. We all will.'

The nave had once held hundreds of torpedoes, racked up ready for loading into the tubes of a blocky, squat warship. The torpedoes had long since been looted leaving a massive pyramidal cavity with its apex lost in the shadows overhead. The statues of Chapter heroes had been transferred from the fleet before its scuttling and were now standing around the edges of the chamber, glaring and huge. In the centre was the colossal statue of the Primarch Rogal Dorn – his power sword was holstered but his combat blade was drawn, symbolising the potency of a compact, cunningly-wielded force like the Soul Drinkers. His noble, high-browed face was turned upwards and away from the half-formed spawn beneath his feet that represented the creatures of Chaos. Overlooked by the stone primarch was a lectern of black wood, where the Chaplains would hold their sermons, and from where Yser would preach the new, true faith to the Soul Drinkers. The Chaplains themselves were receiving instruction from Yser, so that it was with words of truth that they would inspire their men.

'Will they rebuild the window, do you think?' said Yser unexpectedly. 'The one that was broken.'

Sarpedon remembered the storm of shattered glass as he plunged through the stained-glass window of the first cathedral. The shards had been gathered from the floor of the Hall of Novices and transported aboard the *Brokenback* before the scuppering of the fleet. But Sarpedon somehow felt it would be inappropriate to reforge the window, symbolising as it did the Chapter bound to the whims of the Imperium. They had left the Imperium behind now, and every symbol of the Chapter would have to be reworked to reflect their freedom. 'The artificers will craft a new one. I shall see to it once we have returned.'

'You will be here one day, Lord Sarpedon,' said Yser, gesturing at the stern-faced statues ranged around the chamber.

Sarpedon smiled. 'I hope they include all the scars. I would hate to be remembered as a handsome man.'

'And the legs.'

'Of course.'

The silence of the cathedral was light and calming. It was hard to imagine the maelstrom of the warp that boiled around the *Brokenback*. For several weeks now the *Brokenback* had traversed the warp once more, but this time it was under human control, its massive array of warp engines linked up to the nav-cogitators of the *Macharia Victrix* and a half-dozen other semi-intact ship's bridges. The co-ordinates of the unnamed planet from the mem-banks of the *Bellerophon* were hard-wired into every system. Within a scant few days the *Brokenback* would arrive close enough to begin preliminary scans.

'And what about you, Sarpedon?' asked Yser. 'What have you seen?'

Sarpedon paused, recalling the depths of the dreams he had witnessed in half-sleep. 'Quixian Obscura again. But... there is something else. When I am up on the battlements and I cannot fathom why I am fighting, there is something new behind it all. Not just in the distance – I mean it is beneath everything, as if it was in layer of reality that I could not see before. It is huge and dark, like a black cloud. I can feel its hunger, Yser. I can hear it laughing at me. When I have fought off the aliens and Kallis is dead, Caeon looks round to me and his words are lost in the laughter coming from all around me.'

Yser smiled. 'And when it is done, you see the tainted world like a blind eye in orbit.'

'Yes, father. The same as you.'

'Then it is good, Sarpedon. You know what you must do. How many of us ever really know what our true purpose is? There are billions of men who are lost and stumbling, unaware of the truth or how best to serve their Emperor. But you – you have seen it. You know where you must go and you have seen the magnitude of the evil you must destroy there. Is this not a blessing, Sarpedon?'

Sarpedon looked up at the towering statue of Rogal Dorn. Soon, when the serf battalions had finished dressing the stone taken from the hold of the *Glory* and the artificers had completed their carving, there would be a new statue behind the primarch, towering over it. It would be the Emperor, the Architect of Fate, as He appeared in the scrawlings of Yser's flock and the fleeting visionary moments of the Marines – face masked, shoulders broad, great jewelled wings of truth spreading from His back. It would be the first properly rendered image of the Emperor as the Soul Drinkers now worshipped him.

And he would look down on them, eyes searching, accusing if they failed and proud if they succeeded. Never would they forget the Emperor's eyes on them.

'Yes, Yser,' said Sarpedon. 'I am blessed. Chances like ours are rare indeed. I know I can count on you for guidance, Yser and the brothers can too. But the Emperor will not have set us a simple task to prove our worth. I will be taking our finest warriors with me, and even if we are victorious you may have to counsel a Chapter which has lost many of its best to this evil.'

'I have given my life to service in the name of the Architect of Fate, Sarpedon. I may not hold a gun but I know I have my part to play.'

Sarpedon stood, flexing his legs. They were almost healed – the tightness around the joints was gone. He felt as if he could punch a talon through solid rock. 'Of course, Yser. But I would not be much of a commander if I was not sure you knew what you might have to do.'

'Don't worry about me, commander. This Chapter is my flock now, and I will give them my heart and soul if that is what they need.'

Sarpedon knew the statue of Dorn was mostly conjecture – the primarch was a legend, his deeds half-myth, and no one could claim to know what he had looked like. But a symbol of him was enough. Dorn was amongst them, watching over them, judging them, so that when the end came he would know the best of men were at his side in the final battle.

'And commander?'

'Yser?'

'Kill a few for me.'

IT WAS RAINING on the forge world Koden Tertius, which meant a total lockdown. Triple-layered armaplas shutters slid down over the viewports and doorways, and the sensoria were drawn into smooth white sheaths against the elements. The sulphuric acid rain and nuclear lightning-storms sheeting down outside would kill even the most unfleshed tech-priest in seconds, and every facility on the planet had to be sealed completely. Acid could get in anywhere and eat away essential power feeds, and any metallic contact could channel lethal shocks into the bodies of the laboratories and manufactoria. When the great storms of Koden Tertius were overhead, all manufacturing stopped, and the acolytes of the tech-priesthood withdrew into the habitats deep in the rock to contemplate their devotion to the masterpiece of the Omnissiah.

But even though a day of introspection had been declared, there were corners of the forge world where work continued. There were those for whom the desire to deconstruct the most sacred secrets of the universe overrode everything. Five of them were gathered in the reverse-engineering laboratory of Sasia Koraloth.

Perched over a bench scattered with servitor parts was Kolo Vaien – a pale adolescent with a permanent sheen of sickly sweat, he had been found on the streets outside a mechanicus lab-temple on a distant hive-city. An astonishing capacity to absorb and process reams of information at will had seen him taken in by the tech-priests and transferred to the forge world.

Beside Vaien, dwarfing him, was Tallin, once of the tech-guard Skitarii, who had been taken on as an apprentice engineer in the forge world heatsinks and had worked his way onto the fringes of the priesthood. He was scarred and scowling, his dextrous paws clenched with anticipation.

'You've seen it, Sasia? Come on, girl, show it!'

'It's not that simple, Tarrin. We never anticipated this kind of power.'

'There are ways,' said a dry, deathly voice.

They were the first words El'Hirn had spoken that day, and for many days before that. The only thing any of them really knew about El'Hirn was that he was old. He had joined the coven halfway through the study, without warning, and though they all suspected he had been watching them for several months before, none of them had asked how he had come to find out about them. 'Your laboratory is rigged with an electromagnetic field-cage, Tech-Priest Koraloth. There is very little that can escape.' El'Hirn gestured with a hand draped in the tattered strips of mottled fabric that covered him from head to toe.

'You are very observant,' said Koraloth, aware as ever that El'Hirn could be anything, including a spy for the tech-magi of Koden Tertius. 'But I am beginning to understand the magnitude of power we are deal-ing with. I have taken all the precautions I can, but it will never be enough if something goes wrong, or if this artefact is something other than we first believed.'

'What sort of power are we talking about?' asked Gelentian, the savant, loose-fleshed and ugly, who stood against the wall of the lab supported by a basic augmetic framework that took the place of his withered legs. 'Powerful like a bomb? Like a bullet? Something that could hurt us or something that could give us away to the priesthood? We have seen very few results, Koraloth, yet it has been almost a year. Time is running out.' As a savant Gelentian had been altered by the magi to increase his capacity for information gathering and storage, but while Vaien was raw, Gelentian was experienced and disciplined. He functioned as the coven's archivist, with all their findings sealed within his memory – it was too volatile a set of information to entrust to any mem-bank.

'Gelentian,' said Koraloth, 'have you ever seen a vortex grenade explode?'

The coven were silent for a moment. Vortex weapons had not been manufactured for thousands of years – there were theories that they had not been made since the mythic days of the Dark Age of Technology.

'He hasn't,' said Tallin. 'I have. A vortex missile on an Imperator Titan, back when we supported the Guard at Ichar IV. Just one, that was all it took. One of them great big tyranid bio-titans got hit – there was this huge black explosion and then nothing. Nothing where its head had been.'

'Seventeen thousand rounds of standard Titan battery ammunition to kill one Vermis-class tyranid bio-titan,' said Vaien with something approaching awe. 'Twelve hellstrike missiles. But only one vortex charge. Is that what we have, Priest Koraloth?'

Sasia Koraloth shook her head. 'A vortex grenade or missile creates a one-time reality-break effect, an area of null-space. Anything inside the effect is dislocated from this layer of reality and annihilated. This is all anyone really knows. You will also know that anything as short-lived and uncontrolled as an explosion is of strictly limited use.'

'Ah, Koraloth, we begin to understand,' hissed El'Hirn. 'It is not about power at all. It is about control.'

Koraloth stepped into the centre of the lab where the brass-banded cryochamber stood. She slid a finger across the clasp's print-reader and lid swung open, sighing out a fog of frozen air. The Soulspear had been measured emitting low levels of radiation, and it had to be kept completely inert to avoid detection. Koraloth slipped an elbow-length thermoglove onto one hand and lifted the artefact from inside the cask – no matter how many times they saw it, the coven who had been studying its intricacies for almost a year still felt that thrill of power when they saw the Soulspear.

It had proven remarkably resilient, being composed of alloys and high density ceramo-plastics with properties they could not find on any database. They had managed to pry off some of the outer sections and attach data-thief lines which dangled like bloodless veins from the cylindrical shaft. The tiny apertures on the grip had lit up in red shortly after the study had began and were still winking brightly, as if protesting at the invasion.

'We thought these were gene-encoders,' said Koraloth, indicating the lit apertures. 'I suspected they were something else. I think now they're measuring not just genetic information but chemical balance, acidity, even temperature.'

'And you tried to bypass them?' said Tallin. 'Gene-coders are a piece of skrok to short-circuit. Our magos commander had a gene-lock on his liquor cabinet but it never stopped any of us.'

'I tried,' replied Koraloth. 'And it almost worked. But it doesn't like being messed around with. The circuitry structure changes when you so much as look at it. Every route I found around the encoders, the Soulspear closed it. I don't have the cogitator power here to keep one step ahead of it. I had it active for a couple of tenths of a second at most, not long enough for a full reading.'

'You sound like you think it's alive,' said Gelentian. He sounded unimpressed.

'I do, savant. If a machine can have a soul, and the Omnissiah teaches us it can, then the Soulspear has a cunning and powerful one.' Koraloth turned to Vaien, who was fidgeting nervously in the presence of such power. 'Vaien, we cannot crack this artefact with raw power. We must outthink it. That is why I brought you amongst us. Do you know what you have to do?'

Vaien silently rolled up a sleeve of his simple adept's tunic and removed the prosthetic left hand. It was merely cosmetic – beneath it was the real augmentation. Fused into the boy's elbow was a simple but elegant neuro-bionic attachment composed of two long, thin, blunt-ended metal tines. A knot of servos at the elbow chattered as the tines juddered and warmed up.

Koraloth unfolded a broad keypad from one of the lab benches, and connected its info-feeds to the data-thief lines running into the Soulspear. Immediately lines of glowing green text and numerals ran rapidly through the air above the pad's holo-projector. Vaien's eyes followed them, his pupils a blur, as the raw data generated by the sleeping Soulspear flowed into his prodigious brain.

'Ready?' asked Koraloth. Vaien nodded almost imperceptibly, the streams of numbers reflected in his glazed eyes.

'Very well.' Koraloth made a complex gesture with her free hand and the control studs wired into her fingertips activated the field-cage. A deep thrum opened up as the coils built into the lab's walls came to life and projected a web of electromagnetic lines to contain the power generated by the Soulspear. They all knew that if something really went wrong it wouldn't be enough.

Needle-like manipulators slid from Koraloth's fingertips and she began to work on the first encoder, bypassing the Soulspear's defences to force the activation signal deeper into the labyrinthine circuitry.

At once it fought back, the crypto-electronics squirming and shifting against Koraloth's invasion. Vaien's tine-hand typed information at an astonishing rate into the keypad, firing up a data-war against the Soulspear, immeasurably ancient archeotech against raw human brainpower.

The first encoder went down, then the second as the Soulspear was blindsided by the novelty of a worthy opponent. It rallied and Vaien fought it at the speed of thought, Koraloth's activation commands breaking past the third barrier. Silver sparks were dancing around the glowing ends of the Soulspear and the air was turning thick.

El'Hirn was backing off slowly. Gelentian scribbled notes onto the data-slate hung around his neck, and Tallin stood arms folded, daring the Soulspear to defy them.

The fourth took longer and the sheer volume of processing power coursing through the interface between Vaien and the Soulspear robbed the local systems of power – the lab's lights dimmed further; attentive servo-arm arrays slumped powerless.

Then the fifth went down and the Soulspear was activated for the first time in a thousand years.

ALL ACROSS KODEN Tertius, klaxons wailed in alarm. Monitoring stations were bathed in pulsing amber light and the menials manning them jumped into full alert mode. Any forge world was in constant danger of suffering a massive industrial disaster, such were the magnitudes of forces involved in the manufactoria and the sheer levels of power the planet had to manage, and vigilance was heightened during Koden Tertius's regular death-storms.

At first it was assumed by most that the shielding had somehow failed and acid rain had sheeted through some vital component in the power grid, or that lightning had been conducted away from the earthing towers and seared deep into some crucial control system. The first hurried diagnostic rituals showed an immense power spike at a point on the equator, in the research and theoretical engineering sector commanded by Archmagos Khobotov.

The closest tech-guard garrison was alerted and rescue/retribution teams scrambled. The history of Koden Tertius was punctuated by industrial catastrophes and occasional massive loss of life amongst the menials and even tech-priests, and it was not always entirely accidental. The sector was to be surrounded and the tech-guard were to move in around the source of the readings, letting nothing escape, and hold the position until some answers could be found.

They hurried through the tunnel-streets and across the great gantries crossing chasms of generators, until four hundred men surrounded the laboratory of Tech-Priest Sasia Koraloth.

THE FIRST THING Sasia Koraloth saw when she regained consciousness was the closest lab bench sheared in two, the edges dripping and melted. The equipment bolted to its surface had overloaded and was belching acrid smoke. One wall was spattered with black coolant spray fountaining from a severed hydraulic line – it was mixing with the blood on the floor, seeping from the bodies of her tech-coven members that had been thrown around the room.

'Tallin? Anyone?' Koraloth hadn't been out for more than a couple of seconds, she was sure, but in that time her lab had been reduced to a ruin. She tried to haul herself to her feet but the pain was making her groggy. The bones of one hand had been pulped by the violent vibrations of the Soulspear as it tried to break free from the field-cage. She coughed and peered through the stinking smoke of burned plastic.

Gelentian must have died instantly – there was a clean, round wound right through his chest. Vaien had probably taken a moment longer, for one arm and shoulder had been sheared neatly off when the Soulspear had swung wildly in her grasp as the field-cage began to fail. All around the lab chunks had been sliced out of the lab benches, the equipment, the walls. The Soulspear itself lay on the floor, white smoke coiling off it.

'Here, girl,' said Tallin. Still a soldier at heart, he had hit the floor the instant the Soulspear had come on line and owed his life to it. 'I think it all worked a little too well.'

'Omnissiah preserve us…' gasped Koraloth with a shudder, staring at Vaien's lopsided corpse. 'Did you see it?'

It was… magnificent. Twin blades of pure blackness, two tears in reality, shearing out from either end of the Soulspear. It was as she had suspected – the Soulspear generated a vortex field just like a vortex missile or grenade, but it could maintain the integrity of that field instead of just unleashing it as an explosion. If they could unravel the inner working of the Soulspear, think of the wondrous things they could make…

'In time, perhaps,' came that sinister hissing voice. 'But for now, Tech-Priest Koraloth, our objectives are rather less lofty. We must flee.'

El'Hirn caught Koraloth's uninjured arm and pulled her to her feet with surprising strength. 'The tech-guard will be coming. If they find out you have not been working alone then Khobotov will find out our true purpose here. You understand that cannot happen.'

Tallin pulled himself upright. 'Where can we go? They'll have us surrounded.'

'There are places,' said El'Hirn. 'I have been on this planet some time. I know many of its dark corners where a fugitive might hide.'

'Not just hide,' said Koraloth, her face pale and sheened with sweat as she fought off the pain. 'We have to finish this. We know what the Soul-spear can do. It is what we have been looking for all these years, it is why I gathered you and Vaien and Gelentian. We have heard the true word of the Omnissiah, and we must offer up a sacrifice in return.'

El'Hirn headed towards the lab's entrance. 'Indeed we have, tech-priest. The Omnissiah appeared to me, too, in his guise as the Engineer of Time, and told me all those things that you believe. And I know that he demanded you prove your worthiness to receive that truth. We will offer up to him the Soulspear, but first, we must ensure that we survive.'

El'Hirn took up the Soulspear in one hand and led the survivors of Koraloth's coven out of the lab. Glancing around at the sound of approaching tech-guard, he levered a panel away from the wall with his fingers to reveal the rusting hollow of a humidity shaft. Wordlessly, he dropped into the darkness. Tallin followed and, faint with pain but determined not to fall when she had got so far, Koraloth was last.

If they could find a place to hide, if they could survive, then they could complete the task that had been planted in the heart of Tech-priest Sasia Koraloth when the Engineer of Time had appeared in her dreams and begun to tell her the truth. She believed all his whisperings of how mindless and hidebound the Adeptus Mechanicus had become, of how an entire universe of arcane technology was gleaming beneath the surface of reality, begging for an open mind to uncover it. Since she had been given the Soulspear to study the certainty inside her had hardened until she knew what she must to.

She would offer the Soulspear to the Engineer of Time, and see the truth for herself.

At first, all the sensors could come up with was a web of contradictions. The unnamed planet was in far orbit around a near-dead star, and yet it was warm and teeming with life that showed brightly on the carbon scans even from the range limit. The atmosphere was theoretically human-breathable but, in all probability, practically near-toxic. That there was oxygen at all was an anomaly for the planet's surface was almost entirely ocean, broken only by scattered archipelagoes and island chains, and there were no forests or jungles to act as the planet's lungs. The closer the *Brokenback* got the more it seemed that there was a prosperous civilisation on the planet, but that the swarms of life were not a part of it – there were negligible artificial energy signatures, no communications net, and the one or two orbital installations were cold, ancient and corroded.

Now the *Brokenback* was the closest an unexpected craft could get and not run a severe risk of detection. The Soul Drinkers had turned to their Chapter Master for a decision.

'Even if we could be sure of landing the *Brokenback* safely, there is no land mass down there isolated or stable enough to serve as a landing zone.' Varuk, the Tech-Marine who had been supervising the scans from the multitude of sensorium spines that stabbed from the *Brokenback's* hulls, was pointing out the few islands of any size on the giant holo of the unnamed planet. The sensors had had some luck penetrating the freakishly dense cloud layers and could generate an image of the surface stripped of its pale shroud. 'We know that these are volcanic and active, they'd collapse under the hulk's weight.'

The Chapter's most able combat leaders were assembled in the audience hall of the noble's yacht that had evolved into Sarpedon's quarters and the centre of his command. Most of them, like the glowering Graevus or the ever-present Givrillian, were from the force that had been alongside Sarpedon since the star fort. They had earned his trust directly and he knew their strengths. Some others were from the rest of the Chapter who had acclaimed him Chapter Master after the victory over Gorgoleon, and were all Marines who Sarpedon had fought alongside before.

Sarpedon sat back in the throne that had once belonged to the noble whose chambers he had adopted. 'Landing the *Brokenback* was never an attractive option,' he said. 'Could we use the Thunderhawks? Or the drop-pods?'

'Not to strike directly at the enemy, commander,' replied Varuk. A section of the globe lifted off the image and was magnified. It showed an archipelago, a chain of volcanic islands strewn across the ocean. The image was misted by clouds of interference. 'The librarium believe this is the origin point of the psychic emanations,' said Varuk. 'If we are to defeat the force that holds this planet, this is where we will find it.'

Sarpedon knew even before Varuk had pointed it out – that was where the black flame burned.

'But it is also the point where the atmosphere is the most volatile,' continued Varuk. 'You can see, the scans can hardly get through it. It is thick and stormy and completely impassable from the troposphere down. There's a layer that is effectively semi-liquid. It would be like trying to fly a Thunderhawk underwater.'

'Then we will have to land them somewhere else,' said Sarpedon. 'Any ideas?'

It was Sergeant Luko who stood up, smiling. 'Commander, I believe I may have an answer for you. The atmosphere thins out in patches further across the globe, specifically here.' The view switched to a sickly scattering of islands. 'You will have been briefed that there was once a civilisation on this world, probably human. These islands formed one of its centres.'

'If they were human, are there any left? And what are they like now?' asked Graevus gruffly. Sarpedon noticed he was flexing and unflexing his unnaturally long, powerful fingers.

'It's not them I'm interested in, sergeant,' continued Luko. 'It's what they left behind.'

The scans were more accurate through the thinner atmosphere so the view could be zoomed in. Contours appeared, gnarled knots of basalt and cold, rippled lava flows. Luko picked out a section of coastline on the second-largest island and shifted the holo into a close-up of a large natural harbour.

'Commander, we have no logistical structure on this planet and the Thunderhawks cannot stop off for fuel if they are over the ocean of a primitive planet. But whoever lived on this world before it fell to the dark powers had their own ways of getting around. These.'

They could all see them. Ships, three of them, large and dark, singularly ugly vessels built for stability and resilience rather than speed. Each was big enough to have been a major cargo vessel or troop transport.

'There look to be some very basic settlements on the islands,' continued Luko, 'but it's clear they're devolved far from the people who built them. We won't know until we get closer but the ships still look intact.'

'So we sail in,' said Sarpedon with a smile. 'Well done, Luko. Trust you to come up with the must unorthodox tactics possible.'

'One which will leave us on an enemy-held planet an ocean away from the nearest support,' said Dreo from the other side of the room. 'What happens afterwards?'

Sarpedon gave him a withering look. 'It does not matter, sergeant. Even if there will be no afterwards, if there is a way we can get there we must take it. I relinquished our choice in this matter when I took the

Emperor as my guide.' He turned to Varuk. 'We could refit the ships with engines from the Thunderhawks and travel under power. Can it be done?'

'We would have to take a number of serfs with us to accomplish it, and they would be unlikely to survive for long given the environment. But yes, it could be done.'

'Good. Varuk, Luko, I shall require a full tactical sermon in eight hours. If the details are sound we shall proceed. I want some better scans of the archipelago and a full survey of potential drop zones. Fall out, brothers.'

THE CHAPTER LIBRARIUM was as old as the Chapter itself, and in many ways older, for it had stemmed from the conclave of Librarians in the Imperial Fists legion in the time of Rogal Dorn. Every novice who showed psychic potential was tested rigorously by the librarium – those who passed were trained in the control of their powers, more art than discipline, alongside the combat skills of a Space Marine. What happened to those who failed was irrelevant, for failure equalled death. It was a gruelling process that none ever mentioned but none ever forgot – novices kneeled before a council of three Librarians and had to keep their mind closed against the most brutal psyk-interrogation. Sarpedon himself had gone through this process, and had passed with some distinction, for instead of just shutting his mind against the assault he had reached out and woven a web of confusion amongst the interrogators. Every novice who made the grade did it differently, some blasting their tormentors across the interrogation chamber, others building an unbreakable wall of mental power. More than one had immolated themselves with mental fire and let the pain block out the probing, to wake up in a synthiflesh incubator with the assembled librarium applauding their success.

When not in battle the Librarians acted as an independent advisory body to the Chapter Master, and it was in this capacity that Sarpedon had commanded them to build up a picture of the threat that awaited the Chapter on the unnamed planet. There were seventeen Librarians left in the Chapter, not including Sarpedon himself, who had survived the violence the Chapter had done to itself in the past months, and in their days-long meditative sessions they had carefully probed the psychic maelstrom that lay beneath the storm-laden clouds.

It was a nightmare. Aekar had died, his eyes pools of streaming jelly and his organs burst and ruptured, when he had peered with the psyker's sixth sense into the boiling mass of madness. The others suffered hideous nightmares, sometimes waking visions, of purple-black firestorms and canyons brimming with corpses. When they probed the darkness they could make out a location, the largest of a string of black coral islands forming an archipelago. There was something down there, burning bright with malice, wallowing in a pool of life. They could not give it a form or divine its powers, except that it was strong, and held the planet under its thrall by force of will alone. Its will extended from the highest wisps of atmosphere to the depths of the oceanic trenches, and every living thing was corroded until it was mindless or enslaved.

There was one thing more, gleaned even as Sarpedon and Yser were addressing the assembled strikeforce in the new cathedral of Dorn. Tyrendian had found it as he forced his consciousness deeper into the wailing madness than any had dared go save Aekar, risking his sanity in the hope he would find something, anything, that might give them a clue as to what they were facing.

He heard them, millions of them crowding the black coral cliffs, chanting. Chanting its name: *Ve'Meth*.

SOMEWHERE ACROSS THAT half-sighted horizon lurked Ve'Meth, a daemonic power of vast brutality, corrupt and merciless. Commander Sarpedon had told them of its evil and of the Architect's wish for them to put it to the sword, but none of them had really needed telling. They could feel it, a great horror throbbing beneath the deck of the Thunderhawk, watching them. For months it had been disturbing their dreams.

Brother Zaen saw the unnamed planet for the first time through the open rear hatch of the Thunderhawk gunship as it screamed down low over the dark waves. The sky was purplish grey, like an old bruise, a massive heavy ceiling of rain-laden cloud. The sea roiled beneath in sharp waves, breaking against the scattered black rocks as the gunship roared at full tilt towards the island that formed their objective.

Zaen had made airborne drops before, dozens of times in his still-short career as a Soul Drinker. But not like this. They had always known something about the foe they were facing, even if it was only who they were – unclean hordes of orks holding the refineries on the ice caps of Gyrix, secessionists who had taken over the manufactoria of Achille XII. Here, they had only a name, and an assurance that the foe was terrible indeed.

The air swirled in the back of the Thunderhawk and Zaen instinctively checked the survivability readouts reflected onto the crystal of his helmet's eyepiece. He could breathe the air but his lungs would have filled up with phlegm and his eyes would have started streaming after half an hour – armour discipline was to be made paramount and helmets were to be worn.

Closer now, and the dead volcanic peak rose like a broken tooth from the crags of the island. Half-formed ruins, rotted by corrosives in the air, clung to the rocks. They had once been majestic, but now they were like the mouldering skeletons of civilisation.

One last check of the seals around his flamer's fuel cylinder. One last whispered word to the ever-watchful Emperor, and to the vigilant Rogal Dorn whose blood flowed in Zaen's veins.

Squad Luko would be first out, and Zaen had the point where his flamer could buy a half-second if they found themselves facing danger. Zaen had been in the same position when they dropped into the demiurg positions at the Dog's Head River, and two aliens had died in the wash of his flame before Squad Luko's bolters had began to open up.

Was there fear? No, there was none. What lesser men felt as fear, a Space Marine felt as a high-tensile readiness, a state of rarified awareness that let him act faster, think quicker, hit harder where it counted. So were written the words of Daenyathos – for a Space Marine shall know no fear.

The razor-sharp rocks hurtled by beneath as they headed over the coast, black-grey shot through with streaks of quartz. The Thunderhawk lurched to one side and flew in a broad curve as it descended, losing speed, dropping over a ridge on the final approach.

The landing zone was a broad bowl of broken rock, a short run from the harbour but far enough away from the nearest ruins. The Soul Drinkers would have to secure the landing zone before the Thunderhawks could land, which meant the gunships would have to stay in the air while the Space Marines swept the area. The engine pitch dropped as the Thunderhawk reached bale-out level, four metres above the ground. Zaen jumped.

They were still travelling at a fair pace when he landed but he had done this many times before, rolling on and coming up on one knee, flamer braced, head jerking as he swept for contacts. For a second or two he held fast as the remaining nine Marines of Squad Luko hit all around him, the sergeant coming down halfway through, lightning claws spread like skeletal wings as he fell.

'Squad Luko down, no contacts,' he heard the sergeant voxing to the command Thunderhawk. The acknowledgement blip sounded and Luko raised a hand for them to follow.

The storm-swept island seemed devoid of life. Indeed, it seemed hard to believe that anything could survive here. Zaen could see nothing moving save the Marines and the incoming Thunderhawks, and could hear nothing beneath the white noise of the ocean, the pounding of boots and his own double heartbeat.

Squad Luko moved at a jog towards the harbour, careful to keep their feet on the cracked strata of rock. The harbour itself was like a bite taken out of the rock, and beyond it the ocean reflected the grim dark grey of the sky. The volcanic peak of the island loomed to the rear of the landing zone, the sorry ruins zigzagging up the dark rock. Everything was covered in sea spray, glistening in the weak light.

'Movement!' called Brother Griv on the squad vox. 'North-north-east!'

Zaen saw it a second after, something pale and spindly darting amongst the rocks in front of them. He knew that Squads Graevus and Dreo would be dropping some distance away to form the two ends of the Marine line. Squad Luko was in the centre, and the next squads would fill in the rest of the line. They had twenty seconds, perhaps, on their own before the rest arrived.

'First blood, men!' shouted Luko.

Griv fired on the move and missed. Three more bolters took his range and hit – something thin and humanoid flailed in pain and another shot took off what must be its arm.

The name of Squad Luko would be inscribed in the Chapter records as taking first blood of the enemy on the unnamed planet. Zaen knew Luko took pride in such things, and to tell the truth Zaen felt the same. His hands were fairly itching to get close enough to use his flamer.

'Command, this is Squad Luko. Positive contacts, repeat, contacts.'

Zaen glanced back and saw Lord Sarpedon himself disembarking with Givrillian leading his command squad. Sarpedon was majestic, his strong taloned legs carrying him swiftly over the rock, bolter barking at the figures scurrying towards the Marines.

Zaen saw the enemy properly for the first time – humanoid and perhaps technically human, but shambling, with sloped gaits and lolling mouths. Luko slid into cover behind a lip of rock and fired a burst from the bolt pistol worked into the back of his right lightning claw gauntlet. The squad followed him into cover.

'I want bolter discipline, men, and I'm counting every bullet!' he yelled. 'Fire!'

There were more now, a dozen, reaching out from deep furrows in the rock where they had taken shelter. Their eyes were wide watery saucers and their skin streaked with blood and filth.

This was what had happened to the human peoples that once called this planet home. They had perhaps been proud and noble, until

Ve'Meth came. Now, maybe generations later, the daemon's influence had robbed them of intelligence and left them slack-jawed primitives, cannibals clutching clubs of human bone and chunks of sharp flint.

Bolters chattered and a dozen fell, their soft, light-starved flesh coming apart. Zaen heard their moans of pain and anger beneath the gunfire. With their dead as cover still more poured from the cracks in the ground: twenty, fifty, a hundred.

'Hold, brothers, and close on my lead!' called Luko, the vox cutting through the jabbering of the humanoids and the crackling bolter-fire.

The creatures were within a half-dozen strides, clambering over the dead and jabbering with anger, their teeth gnashing and eyes glaring wetly with fury at the invasion of what passed for their home.

Luko vaulted over the ridge of rock and three of the enemy were dead before he landed, their torsos sliced to thick bloody ribbons with a swipe of his lightning claw. A follow-up swipe tore another one into strips lengthways in the flash of a discharging power-field. The howls were screams now, the creatures a wall of sallow flesh rearing over Luko on a tide of broken bodies.

By then, Brother Zaen was at his side, and Luko stepped back, dripping with watery blood, to let him do his work.

Zaen took the split-second to check range and target density. Close and packed. Perfect. The pilot light on the tip of the flamer nozzle flickered hungrily, and Zaen issued a silent prayer to the watchful primarch as he squeezed the trigger handle in his gauntleted hand.

The blue-white cone of flame ripped through the closest bodies sure as any bullet, rending four or five hapless subhumans into shrivelling, flailing limbs half-glimpsed in the flamewash. Those further away fared even worse, coated in a cloak of burning petrochemical that ate through their skin and left screaming, flaming skeletons spasming as they died.

The closest survivors, many half-aflame, screamed in pain and shock and ran. They took their fellows with them and soon the subhumans opposing Squad Luko were in full rout, Luko himself laying into the closest with his shining claws, the squad's bolters thudding shells into the disintegrating flesh of the fleeing pack. Zaen washed the ground with flame, scouring the few survivors into burning ash, melting the flesh of those who had fallen in their flight.

'Squad to me, regroup!' came Luko's order, and the squad strode over the sticky, burning remains of the cannibals to where their sergeant stood, the power field around his claws flickering as the residue of muscle and bone burned off. Zaen knelt to the squad's fore, ready to answer another ambush with a burst of burning justice.

He could hear the crackle of gunfire as the fleeing creatures blundered into the fire zones of the other squads, and were cut down in short order. There was a flash of light as the psyker-lightning lanced out and shattered a swathe of fleeing bodies – it was Tyrendian, the Librarian, lending his mental artillery to the fire of his battle-brothers. Zaen knew the fleeing subhumans wouldn't return, not after so many of them had suffered the white heat of his flamer, the speed and savagery of Luko's claws and the massed gunfire of the Soul Drinkers.

They had taken first blood. The omen was good, one of the best, for it promised the Soul Drinkers would meet the enemy face to face and bring their superior quality to bear. But these cannibal creatures were no kind of resistance. Just looking at the bruised sky and the murderous, polluted ocean promised that the real test was ahead, and the sternest of tests it would be.

Zaen might not survive. Zaen didn't care. To die while partaking in the destruction of such evil was a victory in itself, and whatever happened, his name would be inscribed along with his brothers in the tales of the first true battle of the only free Chapter in the galaxy.

He checked his flamer tanks. They were still nearly full of fuel – the weapon had barely cleared its throat yet. But he did not need the words of Daenyathos to tell him that soon, he would need every drop.

SARPEDON SCUTTLED UP a rise of rock, watching the patrol squads cutting down the few straggling half-humans with placed gunfire. Assault squads saved ammunition and used their combat knives – Tellos, easy to spot even at a distance with his bare pale-skinned torso, was using them as practice for the complex twin-sword techniques he had found in the ancient combat records of the Chapter archives.

Sarpedon was pleased. It hadn't been much of a fight, truth be told, but his Marines had responded with every bit of discipline and sharpness a Chapter Master of the Soul Drinkers could expect of his men. Squad Luko had faced the largest mass of them and Graevus had found his unit nearly surrounded, but in each case the enemy had been broken rapidly and totally, then pursued to destruction.

That had been three days ago, in which time Sarpedon had kept up aggressive patrols against the island's natives. He knew that activity as much as rest was needed to keep his troops battle-ready, and they would need nothing less than total focus. The Soul Drinkers were heading into an uncertain enemy, who might well have control of the battlefield in the most literal sense if the librarium conclave was to believed. It was not a situation he had not faced before or that his Marines were not trained and experienced for, but they all knew those uncertainties multiplied the danger a hundredfold. This was an operation that, if it were not carried out by the Soul Drinkers, could not be carried out at all.

He could see the three ships in the harbour, lit by showers of sparks as serf-labourers fitted the power systems of the Thunderhawks into the hulls. The ships were well-made and the years had done surprisingly little to rot their hulls – they were made of some splendidly light hardwood and banded with quality iron. The sails had long since disintegrated in the foul winds but the Soul Drinkers didn't need them, and indeed the masts themselves were being felled to reduce the profile of the ships against the horizon. These craft were a testament to the sophistication of the peoples that once called this world home, and to the utter degeneracy that Ve'Meth's influence created.

Tech-Marine Varuk was in charge of the engine conversions. Under his watchful eye the Thunderhawk propulsion systems were becoming powerful waterjet propulsion rigs that would send the ships carving across the ocean faster than the winds had ever sent them. The Thunderhawks, four of them stripped down for parts, stood on the open rocks, lashed to the stone with heavy chains.

Sarpedon had brought four hundred Soul Drinkers onto the unnamed world, well over half the Chapter's remaining strength. There was a very real chance that none of them would return, a chance every one of them understood. They would be vulnerable on the ocean – they were vulnerable now, not least because the dark power they were here to destroy could well know they had arrived. And even if everything went right they would still be attacking what was in all likelihood a well-defended and fortified position, facing doubtlessly fanatical and even daemonic resistance. And there was always the problem of whether they would even be able to get back to the orbiting *Brokenback*, regardless of their success on the ground.

None of it mattered. They were here because they owed the Emperor, the Architect of Fate, for showing them the truth, because He demanded they prove their worthiness to count themselves as His divine warriors. If they had to die, then die they would. The only fear that death held was that they would die without having accomplished their life's work of service to the Emperor – but to die here, for a Marine to give his life facing such a foe for such a reason, was to accomplish more than the longest-lived of the weak-willed Imperial servants could ever hope to achieve.

The low, throaty rumble drifted across from the harbour as the engines were tested. They sounded healthy enough – no doubt within a couple of hours the Soul Drinkers taskforce would be heading across the ocean towards the lair of Ve'Meth.

Sarpedon headed down the rocky ridge to supervise the Marines' embarkation onto the ships. Soon they would be gone from the island, leaving only a handful of serf-labourers guarding the Thunderhawks, and two hundred subhuman corpses.

CHAPTER TEN

IMAGINE A MAN. Now imagine him with no skin. Muscles wet to the open air, crowded onto slabs of pulpy pink tissue. Veins snaking, arteries squirming like snakes. Take his eyes and multiply them, like those of a spider, studding the upper half of his face, translucent blue-black. For a mouth, give him a pit lined with a dozen mandibles that could open like the tendrils of a grabflower.

Hammer a chunk of pitted metal, one edge honed sharp, into the bony club of one hand for him to wield like a sword.

Armour him, but not in iron. No, in chunks of more muscle, grown into his own until his body was massive and huge-shouldered, spines jutting from the corded tendons. Mould it into a high collar of gristle and gauntlets of bone. Have him leave footprints of gore wherever he goes, and let clear grey liquid seep from his every surface.

Gelentius Vorp knew what he looked like. He rejoiced in it. Not least, his leathery seven-valved heart swelled to think of how even the mightiest chieftains of Methuselah 41 would have quailed at his very approach.

The peoples of the outer hills on Methuselah 41 had never been tamed. Though the men of the Imperial Guard fought them with guns and the Missionaria Galaxia battled with faith, the horsemen of the outer hills had never relented. They had made it their livelihood to raid the Imperial settlements and refinery outposts, as much to prove the manliness of their way of life as to steal weapons and livestock. They had struck like thunder and killed like lightning, and never stooped to pity the foes who fell before them.

It had been a good life. Gelentius Vorp had been proud of his people, who had raised him on the banks of the nitrogen rivers and sent him out strapped to a warrior's saddle before he had learned to walk. He had tasted a man's blood while he was still suckling mother's milk, and taken a man's head while he could still count his years on his fingers.

As he stood on the beach of broken black coral, he tried to remember – would he have loved that life on Methuselah 41 had he known what really lay beyond his homeworld's yellow-green sky? No. He would not. A thousand heads piled outside his groxhide tent would not have sated his lust to serve a power worthy of his subservience. When Ve'Meth had come to his world, he had learned so much and seen such wonders that he could never have gone back to the horse tribes of Methuselah 41.

Not that he could – as with every world Ve'Meth had visited on his travels, he had left Methuselah 41 a blighted place, brimming with poisons and inimical to human life. A beautiful world, thought Vorp, but not one where he could leave his mark upon the universe as he desired. This new planet was better by far, hard and cold. It was one of the few worlds that could both be a home to Ve'Meth, and remain survivable enough to be a base for an army of his followers. Gelentius Vorp was the greatest of those followers, leading the plague hosts deep into the surrounding star clusters and preying on the foolhardy space traffic. One day, Vorp too would ascend to daemonhood, take a world for himself, forge an empire of malice and kill until the stars died around him.

Vorp's thoughts were broken by a messenger-thing, a dried-out tangle of tendons and skin that flapped lopsidely towards him from along the beach. In the distance Vorp could see the slave-gangs hauling sharp chunks of coral to form barricades and hardpoints, and the cult-legions of Ve'Meth marching to the tune of discordant screeches from attack beasts that dogged their steps. Daemons, skin sallow and wet, malformed warp-flesh glowing faintly in the dusklight, clambered on the rippling peaks of coral and stone, befouling everything with their touch. Every living thing here was malformed, withered by disease or torn by mutation – everywhere limbs ended in clubs of bone and skin sloughed off by the handful, skeletons were racked by uncontrolled growth and mouths lolled with madness.

And beyond the beach, the ocean. Vorp's warp-attuned senses could hear the huge, mad creatures wallowing in the deeps, waiting for the call of their prince to bring them up to the surface. Shoals of malicious things swam around them, picking bites from their flesh, laughing at their agony. The planet was steeped in life, and that life was wielded like a weapon by Ve'Meth.

A wonderful world, to have taken so much to the touch of the Daemon Prince Ve'Meth.

'Gelentius Vorp, heed us,' hissed the messenger. 'Our lord would speak with you.'

Though he had been long in service – ten years, a hundred? – Vorp had rarely had the pleasure of an audience with the daemon prince himself. Lord Ve'Meth chose only those who pleased or displeased him the most – the first for reward, the second for a fate not even his own followers could divine.

'Do you know fear, Gelentius Vorp?' asked the messenger insolently.

'No, creature. I fear nothing. I serve my lord and have never failed in his eyes.'

The creature smiled – though it was hard to tell given its loose-skinned and rotting face – and flapped away.

Daemons. They had no respect for the mortal. No matter – eventually Vorp would himself wear the flesh of a daemon prince, and would toy with the lesser daemons as he wished. He knew Ve'Meth often hurt them for amusement, as he did the hapless hordes of slaves brought in from Vorp's raiding parties, and Vorp would do the same when his time came.

He headed back up the beach towards Ve'Meth's fortress, grown from the once-dead coral like a massive black stone pustule topped with a crater from which watery pus bubbled and flowed in steaming streams down its living sides. Vorp felt the shards of coral sand digging into the raw soles of his feet, and was proud that he could take the pain like it was nothing.

Onto the foothills of the fortress, through the orifice-gate and into the innards of Ve'Meth's palace, where the floors were paved with the half-living bodies of worn-out, plague-wracked slaves and the walls sweated bile. Up the tortuously twisted spiral staircases, upwards through the halls where shock troops, hardened cultists with sheets of metal nailed to their pustuled bodies, ran through the drills that had billhooks and morningstars slashing through imaginary foes. Through the viewing gallery where visions of the planet's polluted clouds scudded across the room, past the moaning huddles of disease-stricken slaves who had displeased their master, and into the audience chamber of the Daemon Prince Ve'Meth.

'Vorp. Good.' The voice that spoke was a woman's, sharp and clipped. Then, in a deep and slovenly masculine voice – 'Our world is less wearisome, for the hunting will soon be good.'

The chamber was an immense abscess beneath the pus-filled tip of the fortress-blister. And in the chamber stood eight hundred human bodies, male and female, all shapes and appearances, dressed in rags or finery or spacer's boiler suits. The only things they had in common were that they all bore the mark of some disease plain on their pasty skin, and they looked towards Gelentius Vorp as one.

'Something clean and unpestilent has come to our world, my champion,' said yet another of the bodies, for every sentence came from a different mouth. 'Unblessed! Cleanlisome! Four times a hundred of them, Vorp, and even now they ride the waves of our world in the hope they can face me and destroy me.'

Vorp smiled, if it could be called a smile. 'You cannot be destroyed, Lord Ve'Meth.'

All who were graced by the favour of Ve'Meth knew it to be true. The daemon prince had been blessed by the Plague God with a form most pleasing to those who revered pestilence and decay – he was a sentient disease, a colony of industrious microbes that infected the hosts of his choice and rotted their senses until they belonged completely to him. The eight hundred bodies of Ve'Meth, knitted together by the prince's infectious colony-mind, formed the blighted heart of the unnamed world, and the crusade of corruption that would one day soon sweep out from this planet and into the soft underbelly of the universe.

The eight hundred mouths of Ve'Meth scowled. 'Destruction, Vorp? Such a base, crude, unbotheratious thing! Do we fear destruction? How much of the flesh you wear now were you born with? None, I feel. You have been destroyed, Vorp. So have I, a million times over as I scaled the ladder of His pestilent Grandfathership's favour. No, I think of what they could do to the future. The potential I have created, Vorp, the bepustulated, filthificatious future! And they would make us nothing, rob us of our power, scrape our beautiful world clean of its vileness and make us just one more meaningless drop of nothing!

'Destruction, Vorp? Destruction is nothing. We will survive. But nothingness – that is something to fear.'

A little under sixteen hundred eyes glared. Ve'Meth rarely admitted to any weakness, much less fear. But Gelentius Vorp, champion of the plague god, felt it too. They had come so far, from the scattered warbands following Grandfather Nurgle through the stars to the perfection of this world, shaped by Ve'Meth's will, a seed that would grow into an empire of glorious fecundity and decay. They were so close now, but perhaps an enemy dedicated and deadly enough would have a chance of fatally upsetting their preparations.

'What do you wish of me, Lord Ve'Meth?'

Ve'Meth paused, and eight hundred faces seemed to consider this question. 'Ah, what to do? You are but a soldier, Gelentius Vorp, but one whom I have raised to be my right hand. If the enemy have lost their way, they will die no matter what they do, for my oceans are vomitorious and grave. But if they find their way here, they will surely attack with every last cleanlisome one of them. Therefore I give you, Gelentius Vorp, the task of marshalling an army on my shore, to fend off the uncorroded ones. You have the enlightened of my cults and the creatures born of my daemonhood, and the slaves if you can find a use for them.'

Gelentius Vorp felt the maggots in his entrails writhe with pride. To think that the Daemon Prince Ve'Meth himself had chosen him for such a task! He had captained daemon-fuelled plague-galleons into the cosmos to raid the space traffic foolish enough to stray too close, but he had longed to wield a true army in the field against a worthy enemy. Now he had got his wish – and on the doorstep of the fortress, under the very eyes of Ve'Meth himself!

'Lord Ve'Meth, it is a most plaguesome honour to–'

'Do not fail me, Gelentius Vorp, General of Chaos.' The voice this time was hard and commanding. 'To waste energy creating a punishment for you would not please me. Now leave, and prepare your defences.'

Eight hundred backs were turned to him. Ve'Meth was not in the habit of granting such audiences and when he did, they were short. Vorp turned and left the chamber, to feel the hundreds of eyes suddenly against his back.

'Vorp? Am I not stenchsome? Am I not the fulgurating glory of Grandfather Nurgle's joyous corruption?' said eight hundred voices.

'Yes, my prince. As always.'

One day, thought Vorp as he strode through the ichor-crusted halls of Ve'Meth's fortress, he would take on the mantle of daemon in the hordes of Ve'Meth's crusade, and this planet would bloom into a cancerous empire smearing corruption across the stars.

But first, the interlopers would die. Muscles tightened around the pitted iron of his bastard sword and the grimworms squirmed down his spine with anticipation. Once he had been proud to lead a dozen warriors on horseback against the outposts of the Missionaria Galaxia – now he would have gibbering daemon-spawn beneath his lash, and ten thousand slave-filth crushed at his whim, all for the purpose of fending off those who would violate this world with their purity.

He found himself wishing the invaders would survive this far, so he could face them across the black coral beach and hurl them back screaming into the sea.

THE FOG ROLLED in like an enemy. Sarpedon was perched on the bow, talons dug into the iron-hard wood, the blade of the ship's prow cutting through the waves beneath him. The pulse of the engine throbbed through the hull as it powered the ship forwards at a speed even the exacting Tech-Marines had been pleased to reach.

The air was fouler the longer they travelled – it had got steadily worse over the last two days, and Sarpedon was sure it was because they were closing in on the source of the planet's sickness. Every Marine was still under orders to wear his helmet, and the serf-labourers were already developing lesions on exposed skin no matter how hard they tried to keep covered and stay below decks. The skies ended in an impenetrable ceiling of yellow-grey cloud even when there was no fog, and the waves were tipped with unhealthy foam. Fish with too many fins attached themselves to the sides of the hulls with vile round suckermouths, and titanic dark shapes slid into the depths in the distance.

The unnamed planet was against them. Every time one of the Soul Drinker lookouts spotted land, the damn fog swept in again. It was as if it knew they were here and blinded them as soon as there was anything worth seeing. It made it difficult in the extreme to navigate, not least because communications with the *Brokenback* had, as expected, been lost. Tyrendian, stationed on the second ship half-glimpsed through the fog, was responsible for navigation, and had filled a cabin below decks of the second ship with orbital scan printouts covered in scribbled routes and sightings. It had been hoped that Tyrendian and Sarpedon could navigate by psychic means, but the menacing darkness of the black flame burned so intensely that they feared it could poison their minds if they stared too far with their minds' eyes.

Sarpedon had put Captain Karraidin in command of the second ship – Karraidin was a respected force commander who had shown total loyalty to Sarpedon ever since the fires of the chapter war. Chaplain Iktinos was at his side, crozius in hand, along with several tactical squads and the few serf-labourers the taskforce had taken with them. The first of the three ships had been christened the *Hellblade*, after the Hellblade Pass where the Chapter had made one of its most celebrated stands.

Sarpedon's own ship – the *Ultima*, after the operations around Ultima Macharia – included his command squad under Givrillian and rather more than a hundred Space Marines. The third ship, hanging just behind the other two, was commanded by Sergeant Graevus and contained the bulk of the assault squads under Tellos. Even Sarpedon had to consider the wisdom of putting Tellos in charge of anything – he had changed so much in body and mind that a more hidebound commander would consider him unstable. But his enthusiasm was such that the battle-brothers would feel something was missing if they launched an assault without Tellos, twin hand-blades flashing, at its head. Graevus's ship would be the first onto the shore when they reached Ve'Meth's archipelago, and Tellos would be the first into the face of the enemy.

Graevus had wanted to call his ship the *Quixian*, but Sarpedon had suggested otherwise. Instead, it was named the *Lakonia*. This name Sarpedon approved of – it was good omen, to name the ship after the Soul Drinkers' first true victory.

Four hundred Marines, packed into three ships. Three arrows speeding towards the heart of corruption? Maybe. Three pens of animals, herded into killing pens? Definitely. They had never been more vulnerable. No matter that the augmented musculature and the nerve-fibre bundles of power armour made a Marine a strong swimmer – anyone who ended up in the water would have minutes to live, and that was assuming he could struggle out of his heavier armour sections before he sank like a stone. A ship that went down might take every fighting man with it.

Something huge and mindless lolled just beneath the water's surface. Its flesh was grey and rubbery and Sarpedon thought he could see a massive pale eye through the swelling waves. He glimpsed great flapping things through the fog and thought how deformed and unnatural they must be to breathe the air here. Every Marine's internal rebreather implant was already furring up. When they got back to the *Brokenback* the apothecaries would be on constant duty replacing the pre-lung filters.

If they got back at all.

But it didn't matter. None of it mattered, as long as they cut out the cancer that was Ve'Meth, or did themselves the honour of dying in the attempt.

Gunfire chattered. One of the flapping creatures spasmed and fell into the sea, the sound of its death drowned by the rumblings of the waves and the creaking of the ship's timbers. Sarpedon glanced back over the deck and saw Sergeant Dreo holstering his boltgun, his squad gathered around him with guns still drawn, scanning for targets. The game was the same – any Marine who could bring down a target before the sergeant would be excused menial tasks for one day, spending it instead in contemplation and research in the archivum. This had

happened twice since Dreo had been made sergeant, and that was
twelve years ago.

Dreo was a hell of a shot, one of the best in the strikeforce. He had
just brought down a creature that the rest of his squad had hardly been
able to see. But it was guts, not a good eye, that made Dreo officer
material, and it was guts that would win this battle.

Sarpedon watched Dreo turn to head back below decks. Suddenly
the sergeant paused and stared back out to sea. He took off his helmet,
exposing himself to the polluted air, squinting into the fog-shrouded
distance.

The vox crackled and an alert rune lit up.

'Commander, we have a sighting.'

'Dreo? Give me details. A ship?'

'I think calling it a ship would be far too kind.'

'There, brother. See it?'

Zaen peered from the stern of the *Ultima* into the murk, in the direction that Keldyn was pointing. There was little more than a smudge of
darkness deep into the brown-black gloom that rose and fell with the
swell of the waves. It was maybe five hundred metres from the *Ultima*,
and closing. 'Just,' he said.

The rest of Squad Luko was emerging from below decks to join the
fire-team on the stern of the *Ultima*, even as the general alert runes
were beginning to blink on the eyepieces of their helmets. The
sergeant had the blades of his power claws folded back and was loading the bolter fixed to the back of his gauntlet. Brother Griv was
lugging a missile launcher, one of the few heavy weapons the strikeforce had. Soul Drinkers rarely used heavy weapons, preferring to use
speed and surprise, but even the proudest commanders admitted they
had their uses.

'Griv, hit them as soon as they're within range. And aim low,' said
Luko. Griv took up position at the edge of the stern, with the ship's
wave boiling beneath him. There were several more squads up on the
deck now, checking their weapons and pulling loose deck equipment
into crude barricades. Captain Karraidin, resplendent in one of the few
suits of terminator armour the Chapter owned, stood proud amidships, watching the Marines under his command run through the
mind-drills and wargear rites to prepare themselves for the fight.

The enemy ship was close enough now to pick out some details. It
was a strange bloated shape, something that should never have been
seaworthy. Splintered masts stabbed up from its deck like stumps of
rotted teeth, and a filmy darkness played around it as if a permanent

shadow followed it. Zaen thought it might be interference in his helmet's auto-senses – but when he heard the low, dark buzzing he realised it was a swarm of insects drawn to the ship as if to a ripe corpse.

Zaen was very aware his primary weapon, a flamer, would be of no use in a long-range firefight such as one they could expect here.

'Take mine,' said Griv, who was loading the rocket launcher. He handed his own bolter to Zaen.

'My gratitude, brother,' said Zaen as he took it.

'I want that back, Zaen. And you'll owe me for the bullets.'

The all-squads vox-frequency crackled into life. 'All points, this is Graevus! We have sighted another enemy ship.'

'Understood, Graevus,' came Karraidin's voxed reply. 'You handle yours. We'll deal with this one.'

'You heard the man,' said Sergeant Luko, nodding at Griv. 'Blow them out of the water.'

Griv shouldered the missile launcher and fired.

The missile streaked over the waves and slammed into the ship, a ball of flame erupting from just above the waterline. It was close enough now to see something pouring out of the hole in the hull, lumpen and semi-liquid.

'Throne of Terra…' whispered Keldyn.

Cargo? Ballast?

No. Maggots.

The enemy ship lurched forward as if affronted by the attack. Return fire thudded from its bow, large-calibre and low-velocity. Shots peppered the sea in front of the stern and a couple impacted on the hull. The *Ultima* was made of sterner stuff than that, though.

'Sergeant Luko, give me a range,' voxed Karraidin.

'We'll be in bolter range in thirty seconds,' replied Luko.

'Good. You give the word.'

'Yes, sir.'

Griv had another missile loaded and had the launcher up to his shoulder, drawing a bead on the lower prow.

A black shadow was thrown over Griv and several Marines of Squad Luko. Too late. Zaen realised it wasn't a shadow but the wings of some immense gliding creature that had slammed onto the deck. It shrieked as bolter-rounds tore through it from underneath, its skeletal head jabbing downwards, beak seeking Griv.

Zaen dropped the bolter, tore his flamer from its holster on his back and pumped a gout of flame over the beast, hearing it howling in pain. There was a flash of near-blinding light as lightning claws sheared its head clean off. Another flying creature was diving towards the prow but bolter-fire tore it to rags as the Marines underneath the first creature hauled its body over the stern.

There were flies in the air now, turning the sky darker, a storm of tiny black bodies. The enemy ship yawed closer and Zaen was not surprised to see it was festooned with human body parts nailed to the hull. The hull bulged hugely amid ships like the abdomen of a huge insect, the splintered boards barely holding together, as the pulpy white mass of maggots poured through the missile rent and plunged foaming into the sea. Shadowy shapes flickered at the deck rail, half-glimpsed crew with no form of substance as if the horror of the ship had sucked the reality from them. They were of no consequence, Zaen felt, they weren't the threat here. It was the ship that was the enemy, bulging with malice, its hull limned with tattered mould like the rind of an old fruit, desiccated limbs and wizened heads nailed to its prow.

Bolter range.

'Fire!' yelled Zaen and the fire line assembled on the stern opened up as one, their bolters sending a layer of hot shrapnel shrieking into the enemy ship. Shells tore the deck apart, shredding the splintered wood at waist height, ripping cover apart, felling the masts like rotten oaks. Vaguely humanoid figures jerked and came apart. A great tear opened up in the wall of flies, like a dark cloud blown away by the wind.

In the time it took him to put down his flamer and take up Griv's bolter, Brother Zaen had a closer view the river of maggots and bile pouring from the hole in the enemy ship's hull. There were a dozen runes flashing warnings in his peripheral vision – atmospheric tolerance levels exceeded, lethal toxins measured, infectious agents present – all set off by the concentrated foulness inside the ship.

This time Griv got another missile off and shattered the enemy ship's hull on the waterline, so the ship would scoop up water as it advanced and be dragged prow-first downwards.

Something erupted from the new rip in the hull. Not a limb, not a tentacle, but something both jointed and flexible, tipped with a slavering lamprey's mouth, an ugly mottled grey and studded with barnacles. The pseudopod lashed out and Zaen heard, even above the massed gunfire, the crunch as it crashed through the hull of the *Ultima*.

'Damnation, what is that thing?' shouted Keldyn.

'I don't care what it is, I want it dead!' came the reply from Luko, even as a Marine from Karraidin's veteran squad arrived at the stern and fired a superheated blast from his melta-gun into the rubbery flesh of the writhing limb.

But the monster in the ship had got a grip on the *Ultima* now and was dragging itself closer. Its stench was so great it was clogging up Zaen's helmet pre-filter and the reek of rotting flesh and excrement was getting through the auto-senses. What kind of monster survived sealed in the hull of a rotting hulk of a ship, wallowing in maggots and filth?

The Chaos kind. The great enemy had many faces, and this was one of them – the monstrous and deformed, mindless and destructive. They called them Chaos spawn, and they were constantly mutating, idiot engines of destruction. It stood to reason that one of them should have made this ugly world its home.

Zaen lent his fire to those of his brothers, sending shells into the hull of the enemy ship and hopefully into the body of the monster it contained. The return fire was feeble – the humanoid crew were mostly dead or thrown off their feet by the violent lurching as their ship was dragged through the waves towards the *Ultima*. It was the beast that formed the real threat.

Above the gunfire pouring into the body of the ship there was a shriek of tearing wood. The whole side of the enemy ship was rent open and – *something* – erupted outwards, bloated and foul, its sagging flesh bubbling into new shapes. A massive spasm cast it out of the plague ship's hull, ripping the deck open, and across the closing distance between the two ships.

It was huge, the size of a spacecraft shuttle. Impossibly, the horror thudded wetly onto the starboard deck of the *Ultima*. Two squads were trapped beneath its immense bulk – some were mashed into the hardwood of the deck, some dragged themselves out with help from the battle-brothers, others were stuck fast but had the freedom to point their bolters and empty their magazines into the heaving flesh.

The beast reared up in pain, half-limbs reaching from its guts and dashing Marines aside. Zaen ducking the flying bodies and flailing tentacles, stepping round to the beast's exposed side and sending spurts of flames over its blistering skin.

He saw Luko's claws flashing and a tentacle as thick as a Marine's waist fall charred to the deck. He saw Karraidin, like a walking tank in his huge terminator armour, punching a power fist into a descending globe of flesh and bursting it like a bubble of pus. He saw Marines lining up on the opposite side of the deck and forming a firing squad that sent a sheet of hot bullets carving deep into the spawn's body, soaking the deck in something watery and brown that might have passed for blood. He saw the black-armoured form of

Chaplain Iktinos and the power that fountained off the crozius he swung into the boiling flesh of the spawn.

The flesh flowed back over the wounds and the beast kept changing, horns of bone shearing out from its side and spearing Brother Keldyn through the thigh.

'Pin it down! Keep it pinned!' shouted Karraidin over the din as a mess of toothed tendrils lashed against his massive purple armour.

As the bullets poured into it and blasts of energy weapons bored deep into the spawn's hide, Zaen realised it really didn't feel pain or fear, or any of the things that might drive it back. It would soak up the bullets until every Marine was dead, and then it would nest in the hull of the *Ultima* until it drifted upon another meal. Keldyn screamed as the flesh flowed over him like water and sucked him up into the belly of the monster.

Sometimes, thought Zaen, a stupid enemy was the most dangerous of all.

The beast thrashed and knocked half of Squad Vorts into the ocean as the *Ultima* pitched wildly. Zaen's flamer and a plasma gun from Karraidin's squad razed another layer off the spawn's skin, but entrails that spilled out plastered themselves across the wound. The serf-labourers – barred by the Chapter from combat in all but the most dire circumstances – were clambering up from the hold with power spanners and crowbars, ready to die alongside their masters.

The Soul Drinkers would have to kill this creature bit by bit. Before it did the same to them.

VARUK WAS IN the hull, screaming at the Marines assisting him to swing the *Hellblade* around so they could lend fire to the *Ultima*. Sarpedon could hear him from the deck – but he was more intent on listening to the screams over the vox as Karraidin and Luko desperately tried to keep the spawn at bay. He could see the scattering of muzzle flashes and the pulse of energy weapons, and the rearing amorphous mass that had swallowed up a large chunk of the *Ultima*.

'Moving now, commander,' said a breathless Varuk as the prow of the *Hellblade* turned towards the stricken *Ultima*.

'Good. Keep us at half bolter range, I don't want it taking us down with it. And I want a ten-man reserve to take men out of the water.' Sarpedon switched a channel. 'Dreo?'

'Commander?'

'You are in fire command. It'll be mayhem on the deck but the target is large. Go for the central mass, we'll have to bleed it dry.'

'Understood, commander. Kill it for the throne.'

'Kill it for the throne, sergeant.'

Sarpedon tried the vox-channels for the *Ultima* again. Iktinos was chanting on the all-squad channel, bellowing prayers to inspire any Marine who tuned in. Karraidin was leading from the front but most of his squad were dead and only his terminator armour had kept him alive for this long. Luko was in close, too, skirmishing his squad around the monster's flailing limbs and hitting it where it hurt. Even over the static he could hear Luko's lightning claws slicing through flesh, and the growl of the squad's flamer.

But even without the vox he could pick out the tortured howls of the *Ultima's* hull as it began to break apart.

'Sarpedon to Graevus. The *Hellblade* is moving to support the *Ultima*. What is your situation?'

'One ship, closing fast,' replied the gruff-voiced Graevus. 'Full of troops, heavily armed. We're taking fire and gearing up for boarding.'

'In short, then, your situation is excellent.'

'Never better, commander. Graevus out.'

SERGEANT GRAEVUS HEFTED his power axe in his altered hand and switched to the all-squads vox.

'Here they come, lads! We don't just sit here and take it – you follow me and board 'em back!'

The assault squads cheered throatily. The Soul Drinkers had long claimed excellence in spaceship boarding actions and that included defence, where the preferred tactic was to let the enemy do the hard work in closing with you and then launch a counter-boarding action to cut down the attackers and lay into the vital crew. This would be no different in principle – confined spaces, fearsome enemy, and woe betide any man who went overboard.

The Chaos ship bore out of the mist and they saw it wasn't a ship at all. It was a sea monster, an immense shark perhaps a hundred and fifty metres long, a gargantuan living corpse with dark blue-grey skin covered with scars and bite marks, tiny blank cataracted eyes and a mouth big enough to swallow a tank and filled with sword-like teeth. The middle section of its back had been hollowed of flesh leaving the ribs exposed, between which stood the readied ranks of Chaos shock troops on a deck of desiccated organs. The shark's massive ragged tail propelled it forward through the waves towards the *Lakonia*.

The enemy boarders wore armour of black iron and carried vicious billhooks and halberds, with swords sheathed at their sides. Their bodies were misshapen and every one had its face covered, as if to spare the universe their ugliness. They would have looked like backwards savages

from an evil-hearted feudal world were it not for the haloes of sickly
energy that played around the power weapons of their leaders. There
were perhaps two hundred of them packed onto the beast-ship.

Pistol fire crackled towards the *Lakonia*. Graevus ignored it. The few
that hit were turned away by the power armour of the Soul Drinkers,
one hundred and thirty of whom were ready to take whatever the
enemy could throw at them and then throw it right back.

Graevus saw Tellos leaning out over the water, first in line, daring the
Chaos vermin to take him on. He was unarmoured from the waist up,
but somehow he seemed twice as deadly as any Marine – the
determination in his eyes, the shocking pallor of his skin, the keenness
of the blades with which he had replaced his lost hands.

Close now. He could see the swarms of mites living off the shark-
ship's eyes and the chunks of metal and bone embedded in its raw,
pink gums. The beast slewed, presenting its side to the *Lakonia* as it
made the final approach. The warriors on board grabbed the polished
ribs to lean out over the side, ready to catch the *Lakonia* with the hooks
of their halberds and drag her close enough to be boarded.

Close enough.

'Fire!' yelled Sergeant Graevus and a hundred bolt pistols erupted.
The warriors were better-armoured than they looked, perhaps clad
more in infernally tough hides and resistance to pain than in mere
iron. Half a dozen fell, torsos pulped by the bullets, and two more were
rent open by the blasts of plasma pistols.

Tellos was the first off the *Lakonia*, as Graevus and everyone else had
known he would be. He leapt the gap between the ships, whirling as he
went and decapitating the closest hulking warrior with his trailing
blade, shearing the arm clean off another. His teeth were bared, but
Graevus felt it was through joy and not anger. Tellos loved a good fight.
That, at least, had not changed.

For the few seconds that Tellos was alone on the shark-ship, maybe
twelve of the enemy were cleaved apart, stabbed through the gut, sliced
through face or simply pitched over the side to sink. The blades were
extensions of his body as Tellos fought with a swirling, lightning-fast
style, a swing that parried the blow of one attacker while taking the
head off another. The Chaos troops clambered over the falling bodies
of their dead to get close, and died in turn.

The shark-beast slammed into the side of the *Lakonia*, the hard wood
gouging rotting flesh from its side.

'Charge!' yelled Graevus, and leapt over the side.

The Assault Marines charged as one, chainswords biting deep into the
first enemy they found, slashing down the first rank of Chaos warriors

like a hurricane felling a forest. The beachhead forged by Tellos let those nearer the prow thrust deep into the mass of Chaos troopers, running past their gore-drenched sergeant to lay into those warriors reeling from his attack.

Graevus landed with a dozen Assault Marines at his back, the dried loops of the monster's compacted entrails spongy beneath his feet. There was a mass of black iron all around him and a hundred halberd heads stabbing down at him. He blocked one, pivoted, swept his power axe one-handed up into a soldier's torso and clove a grimacing face-wrought visor in two. Chainblades lanced in from behind him and carved limbs and heads away. The Soul Drinkers yelled their battle-cries and the Chaos warriors howled in anger and pain, punctuated by the report as a bolt pistol was brought to bear and the hideous grinding of chainsword teeth against bone.

Graevus paused and glanced around to see a bolt of Chaos-stuff lance down from a flying figure's finger and explode deep in the seething mass of combat towards the prow. The flying creature was humanoid but cloaked in ragged shadows, and was held aloft by a near-solid halo of flies. As Graevus watched, Tellos reached up and hooked an elbow over the shark-beast's spine, using it to lever himself up level with the magician. Tellos lunged and impaled the magician on his hand-blades, ignoring the black lightning that arced into him from the magician's hands, and held him aloft and helpless.

Bolter-fire from the supporting Tactical Marines on the deck of the *Lakonia* thudded into the spasming magician's body. He was ripped apart until all that remained of him were shreds of shadow drifting feebly on the wind, and dark charred stains on Tellos's blades. With a glance of acknowledgement at the Marines on the *Lakonia*, Tellos vaulted back down into the fray.

Graevus allowed himself a smile and swung his axe back into the iron-clad warriors, knowing that with every blow another of the Emperor's most hated foes would die.

Every Marine was brimming with the fire of battle, the white-hot glorious surge that made men into heroes and Marines into something more. Graevus felt himself becoming lost in the glare of battle, and knew that the Soul Drinkers would not take a step back until every single Chaos-loving piece of filth was dead.

ZAEN WAS BACK-TO-BACK with Chaplain Iktinos. The deck beneath them was slick with the blood of Squad Vorts, of whom not one Marine survived, mingled with the steaming foulness that poured from the Chaos spawn. The beast had extruded a huge club-headed limb which arched over their heads – from its tip barbed whips of sinew were lashing. Iktinos was parrying them with his crozius, sending showers of sparks cascading, while Zaen kept up the stream of flame into the side of the monster.

They were cut off, surrounded by walls of flesh. They had to fend off the beast themselves, for they could not rely on the battle-brothers cutting their way through to rescue them.

Zaen had been in awe of Iktinos as a novice and some of that still remained – to think that anyone could be picked for their piety and strength of mind from amongst such devoted men as the Soul Drinkers fascinated him. Now, Zaen would die alongside the Chaplain who had so mesmerised him during his novicehood, and he was proud.

He could barely tell what was happening elsewhere on the *Ultima*. The deck was smashed to pulp and the spawn's growing bulk had poured into the hull. Gunfire came from all directions, sometimes in massive walls of shrapnel, sometimes single shots from battle-brothers trapped or stranded by the beast's always-changing limbs. The vox was a mess, with only Karraidin's booming voice cutting through the yells of the dying and the howling battle-oaths.

'We will go to the Halls of Dorn together, Chaplain,' said Zaen breathlessly as he blasted at the limb arching over them with Griv's bolter, pausing to slam his last fuel canister into the flamer.

'There is no place there for me yet, Brother Zaen,' replied Iktinos, slicing through a writhing spear of tendon. 'When my task here is done, then I can die.'

The spawn reared up over them, a wave of flesh. It roared like nothing alive could, and crashed down on them like a landslide.

The flabby slabs of fat and slippery loops of entrails closed over Zaen as he tried to dive out of the way, a massive liquid weight slamming down onto him and driving him into the wood of the deck. Everything was black and hot, and foul ichor was forced through his helmet's pre-filter. His arms were pinned down, one leg folded under him in a gunshot of pain, he felt the plasteel of his armour's backpack fracturing and his breastplate bending out of shape. His shoulder pads split and there was a white-hot shock as his skull fractured.

His trigger finger spasmed and bolts from Griv's gun spun into the pressing mass of flesh. It would do no good. He tried his flamer hand but the pilot light had been smothered.

It was a rare Space Marine who retired from combat duty. In many ways they existed to die in battle. Brother Zaen had not just been trained and altered to fight the Emperor's foes across the stars – his purpose was also to give his life to the fires of war, so that his death would form a part of that monolithic legend of the Chapter, which would inspire its future Marines to their own feats of arms and sacrifice.

This is what Zaen told himself as his abdominal armour gave way and his organs began to burst under the spawn's weight.

A blue-white gash opened in front of his eyes and a black-armoured hand reached in, grabbing the lip of his shoulder pad and dragging him out onto the deck. Pain ripped through him as his mangled leg was twisted further, but he was alive – the huge inspiring form of Iktinos was bent above him, hauling him from the sucking flesh.

A thick leathery mass shot out and caught Iktinos square in the chest, hurling him backwards. Zaen glanced round and through the gauze of pain he saw a cavernous orifice opening in the wall of flesh. It was a mouth, and he was staring down the wet quivering tunnel of the spawn's throat. Iktinos had been batted aside by the beast's tongue, a thick leathery stalk tipped with a knotted club of meat.

The blubbery mass of its body slid underneath him and Brother Zaen was washed towards its mouth. He tried to brace himself with his hands but the skin was slippery and the shadow of the spawn's jaw passed over him. Past his shattered foot he could see the ribbed shaft of its throat convulsing as it swallowed, hungry to contract around him and squeeze him to crimson paste.

Teeth slid from the pulpy gums as Zaen slipped over the threshold. One speared into his groin and out through the small of his back, and another stabbed down from above through the top of his shoulder, ripping through one of his lungs and deep into his guts.

He had his left arm free. Everything else was broken. In that hand he held his flamer but he needed another hand to flick on the nozzle's pilot light. He tossed the useless weapon into the maw of the spawn, which was darkening as the mouth closed behind him.

He reached round to where his right hand dangled feebly. His hand had clenched as the nerves were severed and it still held Griv's bolter. But it was too far away. His left didn't reach.

Come on, novice Zaen. What are you? A child! A weak, useless child! So there is pain? You have had pain before. You survived. Survive it again. Move your hand, novice. Move your right hand and stop complaining like a scolded stripling.

Zaen moved his right hand and snatched Griv's bolter from it with his left before the tendons snapped. Was Griv still alive? Would he ever know how his weapon met its end?

Zaen could just see the dull glint of the flamer's fuel canister in the failing light, lodged in the throat of the spawn.

The jaws closed and the monster's teeth sliced through Zaen's body. Out of the corner of his eye he saw the right side of his body flopping away. A knee was forced up into his throat.

Everything went black as the jaws closed.

Zaen fired.

SARPEDON SAW THE collar of flame that burst out through what must have been the beast's throat. The *Hellblade* was closing fast – he was close enough to see the Soul Drinkers on the *Ultima's* deck illuminated in the flame, still spitting gunfire into the rearing spawn that now took up about three quarters of the ship mass. Already Sarpedon's men were pulling Soul Drinkers out of the sea and hauling them gasping onto the deck of the *Hellblade*. Many of them had discarded most of their armour to stop them from sinking into the black depths, and some were completely unarmoured.

They said that the whole of Squad Vorts was dead, and maybe thirty others, either torn apart by the spawn or pitched into the sea to drown.

The Marines cheered as the head of the beast was all but torn off by the explosion, burning fuel streaming from the huge wound. Sarpedon's Soul Drinkers, and those from the *Ultima* who still had their weapons, formed a three-rank firing squad in the prow of the *Hellblade*. Sarpedon took his place amongst them, bolter drawn. 'Captain Karraidin, this is Sarpedon,' he voxed. 'Tell your men to get their heads down and hold tight. We'll get them out of there.'

'Yes, lord!' came the reply through a haze of static and gunfire.

'Soul Drinkers!' yelled Sarpedon to the Marines around him. 'The beast is hurt! It is blind and confused. If we hit it now we can kill it!' He took aim at the rearing bulk of the Chaos spawn, which was now belching smoke from the massive charred wound. 'Open fire!'

This time the monster had no hope. Its nerve centre was shattered by the explosion, and all it could do was sit there on the deck of the *Ultima* and take the hail of gunfire. Before, it had been sheltered by the hull of the enemy ship or fired at by scattered opponents. Now it bore the full weight of sustained bolter-fire from nearly one hundred and fifty Space Marines, each one thirsting for revenge against the good men they had lost.

Its skin blistered and cracked against the heat from within and without. Chunks of bloody fat were thrown into the air and fountains of ichor spurted as its organs ruptured. It lost what little shape it had and reared up in its death throes, scattering storms of muscle and ragged skin, before it toppled back and dragged its massive semi-liquid bulk into the sea. The *Ultima* yawed violently with the beast's weight, the Marines still on board clinging desperately, but as the spawn's body poured into the water it righted itself and stayed firm.

Sarpedon's Marines cheered the spawn's death even as Varuk gunned the *Hellblade's* engine to sweep in and rescue what they could.

THE SHARK-SHIP KNEW its crew were dying and it was starting to thrash, its massive tail sending sheets of filthy water into the air, its huge mouth biting at the air.

The Chaos dead were two bodies deep on the deck, and the Soul Drinkers had effectively taken half the ship. The Chaos survivors had closed ranks and were keeping the Soul Drinkers' chainswords at bay with halberds and hooked spears. The Space Marines were replying with pistol fire, keeping the Chaos warriors pinned and wearing them down. Tellos was up close, stabbing into the black-armoured mass, weaving between the thrusting blades. He was red to the shoulders in blood, and had a score of Chaos dead to his name.

'Marines, prepare to fall back! We've got to kill this thing!' called Graevus over the vox. The Chaos troops might be beaten but they were now riding on the back of a huge and angry sea monster. The *Lakonia* was locked to the side of the shark-ship and could easily be brought down if the monster dived.

Graevus pointed at the three closest Marines. 'You! Give me your frags, now!' They handed him their frag grenades and, gesturing for them to follow, he ran towards the head end of the ship, where a wall of leathery muscle pulsed. Graevus's power axe flashed and a gash opened in the thick membrane, exposing the roiling pink mass of the shark's brain stem beyond.

'Soul Drinkers, disengage and cut the ship free! Now!'

Instantly, the Marines were falling back, keeping up fire. Tellos had to be physically dragged away from the slaughter and hauled back onto the *Lakonia*.

Graevus took the bundle of frag grenades in his altered hand and thrust it deep into the shark's brain stem.

'Fire in the hole!' he yelled and ducked to the side. The explosion was deep and muffled and sent a shower of pink blubber raining down over the deck. The shark spasmed violently, throwing two of the Marines off their feet. Graevus looked up and saw the *Lakonia* was free but still close and sprinted towards it, lashing out with his axe at the Chaos soldiers who stood in his way and cutting them down in short order. The shark thrashed as it died, its brain stem destroyed, Graevus kept his feet and reached the edge of the deck.

He leapt, and found the solid wood of the *Lakonia's* deck under his feet. He turned in time to see the shark-ship rolling over, exposing its mottled white belly, before it slid under the waves.

He looked round at the Marines who were watching the monster die. He didn't think they had lost any of them. Every one of them was spattered with gore, and Tellos was thick with it, shocking red against his pale skin. Graevus looked down at himself and saw he was spattered with clots of brain matter.

'Graevus to Sarpedon,' he voxed. 'Enemy ship destroyed. No losses.'

'Understood, sergeant. The *Ultima* is lost. Return to assist.'

So it had not all gone well. But they knew it would be bad here – they knew they would be fortunate if any of them got off alive. Now they had lost their first battle-brothers on this world.

'Acknowledged, commander. Graevus out.'

CHAPTER ELEVEN

ARCHMAGOS KHOBOTOV KNEW she was here. He could hear the machines whispering to him. The rogue Tech-Priest Sasia Koraloth had chosen a poor place to hide, for there was nothing in this place but machinery, and the machines here were like his children. The forge world of Koden Tertius was falling under the archmagos's mantle, like the *674-XU28* before it, to the extent that when the Omnissiah was with him he could hear the generatorium depths like old friends telling him their secrets.

She was down here. She was wounded – the walkways tasted the blood where she had stood. She was desperate, for the coolant regulators heard her sobbing. And most importantly, every system in the sector told him that she had with her an item of such power that the energy readouts spiked wherever she went. That could mean only one thing: Sasia Koraloth had the Soulspear.

The mechadendrites slid back from the generatorium readout console and the mundane world swam back into view. Khobotov and the tech-guard strike team he commanded were at the top of the generatorium stack – a massive turbine sunk vertically into a cylindrical pit in the rock of Koden Tertius. The great silvery bulk of the turbine was bounded by a spindly network of walkways and control centres where tech-priests, menials and servitors would keep the generatorium at optimal power output. All those personnel had been evacuated, and the only living things in this area now were Khobotov's men and Sasia Koraloth.

Even powered down, the turbine's latent energy output was massive. It swelled Khobotov's iron heart to be in the presence of such power.

Captain Skrill adjusted the readout on his auspex and turned to the archmagos. 'We've got biomass, sir, but not much of it. Probably dead. Think it could be her?'

'Unlikely. Tech-Priest Koraloth had very limited augmentation, her bio-readings would be higher. It is likely your auspex sensors will be blinded by the artefact when we get near, in any case.'

'Understood. Shall I have the squad begin the sweep?'

'Proceed.'

Skrill was a good man. Blunt, simple, with an acceptable head for logic and little compassion. He and his dozen-strong tech-guard unit were clad in heavy rust-red flak-armour and carried high-calibre autogun variants. Khobotov had witnessed the effectiveness of the unit's mass-reactive ammunition in police actions against wayward menials. When Sasia Koraloth's gene-signature had been flagged up by a servitor cleaning up a bloodstain in the generatorium sector, Khobotov had personally selected Skrill's squad for the search. His tactics were crude but well-suited to the mission. There was little fear that Koraloth would be left alive, which suited Archmagos Khobotov very well.

'Vilnin, cover us with the longrifle,' ordered Skrill. 'And don't fire until I give the word. I don't want you wasting any more servitors, we're the ones have to pay for 'em.' The thin-faced Vilnin nodded, uncased a long, slim sniping rifle, and took up a vantage point at the edge of the gantry.

'The rest of you, with me. There's only one of her but she's cornered, so you stay alert. Move!'

Khobotov skimmed just above the walkway on his grav-dampeners, drifting down the spiralling gantries after the advancing squad, watching the fractals they formed as they spread out through the web of walkways. Their angles of fire were good, he noted. Most mathematical. Skrill would go far. In fact, the *674-XU28* had lost a number of security components in the unfortunate altercation off Lakonia. The ship was still short-handed, and Khobotov resolved to have Skrill and his men transferred to the *674-XU28* as soon as Koraloth was apprehended.

A gunshot rang out, sharp and illogical. Not one of Skrill's squad – it was a las weapon, power setting high.

'Shots fired!' voxed Skrill as his men dropped down. 'Anyone hit?' Eleven beacon pulses sounded. The shot had missed. 'Vilnin! Target, now!'

'Think I saw a las-shot,' replied the sharpshooter. 'Somewhere underneath us.'

Skrill waved a hand and the squad split up, scattering quickly to approach the target area from a number of angles. Below them the generatorium output had created a dim fuzz of smoke and shadows, where the exposed inductor coils bled the light out of the air. It would have been a good place to hide, reflected Khobotov, if there had been a way out other than through the advancing tech-guard.

'Found our biomass, sir,' voxed one of the troopers. Khobotov's vision zoomed in to where the trooper was standing over a pathetic bundle of rags. A thin, stringy hand reached out feebly.

Ah, El'Hirn. Of course. There had been rumours the old ghost was still alive. He had been a promising magos in his day, before he fell victim to some insane heretical notions about the Omnissiah and had been cast out of the tech-priesthood. Without the support of his Mechanicus brethren his augmentations would have failed and his flesh withered until there was nothing left. Khobotov wondered how El'Hirn had survived this long and had the energy to team up with Koraloth in her schemes, but it was of little matter. Evidently the two had had a falling-out as they fled, judging by the high-energy las-burns on his robes.

Khobotov reached out with his hyper-augmented senses and latched on to the emergency vox-caster system. 'Tech-priest Koraloth,' he said, his voice booming from a score of speakers dotted throughout the generatorium structure. 'You are surrounded and alone. Escape is a logical impossibility. Give yourself up to us, Sasia Koraloth, deliver up the artefact you have stolen, and we will not have to risk damaging the holy machinery of this place in a firefight.'

Another shot, hitting the trooper who had found El'Hirn's corpse and throwing him onto his back. His torso armour fizzed with the heat of the shot, as bursts of auto-fire rattled down from the troopers on the gantries around him. Koraloth fired again from somewhere in the darkness below, hot las-bolts lancing up at the tech-guard.

'Suppression fire!' called Skrill, aiming his own autogun over the gantry railing and spraying fire downwards. 'Krik, you alright?'

'Think I took a lung shot, sir,' groaned the wounded trooper. Khobotov saw another tech-guard scurrying along the walkway to help him. Skrill's men might be tough, but there was still far too much flesh in them for Khobotov to truly respect them. If he had taken a wound like that he would just have shut down one pneumo-filter and switched to another one. This man would probably die, because the Omnissiah had not touched him with the same metallic blessings.

Vilnin's voice crackled over the vox. 'Think I got her, sir. There's an observation platform about four hundred metres down. I've got someone moving on the infra-red.'

'Good,' replied Skrill. 'Put a bullet through her.'

'She's got hard cover, sir, I can't get a shot. It's... there's something else down there. Looks like a shrine.'

'A what?'

'You know. Sacred stuff. Altar, bunch of books. She's got cover behind the altar and I can't take her from this angle. I can move around the turbine to the other side but it's a long walk.'

'Stay put, Vilnin. Put a couple of shots her way, get her scared. Then shut her down her if she moves.'

'Yes, sir.'

Interesting, thought Khobotov as he listened in. A temple. It seemed El'Hirn had found another convert to whatever half-baked belief system he had created for himself. 'Sasia Koraloth, your false religion can offer you no hope. Whatever El'Hirn told you was a lie. There is only one Omnissiah, and He is most jealous.'

Khobotov drifted further down, keeping gantries and girders between him and Koraloth, blocking her aim. It would not do to have his components tarnished with lasburns.

'You're wrong!' yelled a small, frightened voice from far below, audible only to Khobotov's hypersenses. 'He has spoken to me! He has shown me the way!'

'Then why did you find it necessary to kill your fellow unbeliever?' Khobotov could see the renegade tech-priest now. She was cowering behind a slab of carbon upon which were set two candelabra and a number of books, on a hexagonal observation platform hung with banners covered in scribbled equations. The place would normally be deserted apart from the occasional mindless maintenance servitor, and so it made a deceptively good choice for a hidden place of worship. Koraloth herself was pale and drawn with fatigue and fear, her tech-priest's robes torn and unclean, the barrel of the laspistol still glowing red in her hand.

'He couldn't face knowing the truth!' she shouted. 'When it came to make the offering, he was afraid! Everything we know is wrong, Khobotov! The Engineer of Time has told me in my dreams!'

Quite insane, thought Khobotov. A shame. There was a slight chance that Sasia Koraloth could have been a tech-priest of some note, and in any case her skill at reverse engineering would have had its uses. Instead, she had to die. But while the Omnissiah disliked the waste of good material, he abhorred the corruption of His sacred name far more.

Khobotov stepped off the gantry and floated downwards, the immense metallic curve of the turbine stack sliding by beside him. He rarely engaged his grav-dampeners so overtly, thinking it a rather vulgar way to travel, but he wanted a closer look at Koraloth and her temple before the tech-guard killed her.

Koraloth held up a hand, and from the sudden power-glare in Khobotov's eyelenses he knew the hand held the Soulspear. The arte-fact had just as strong an aura of power as when Khobotov had first seen it. He would find someone else to study it, and when they had made some headway in the dangerous and unpredictable process of unlocking its secrets, he would take over the research and add the Soul-spear's majesty to the Omnissiah's masterpiece of learning. Koraloth was no loss. The Soulspear was what mattered.

'See!' she yelled. 'See how much you know!'

She slammed the Soulspear into the carbon altar, end-first. For a split second Khobotov's senses shut down in the face of massive overload, the synapses parting to prevent the surge of sensory energy coursing into the archmagos's brain.

An energy spike so vast even the archmagos's blessedly augmented body could barely cope with it. A discharge of power so far off the scale that the first thing he heard when his aural senses came back on line was the shriek of the generatorium stack coming apart beside him.

Critical mass.

There was a great disc of light where only the grimy depths of the generatorium sink had been before. It was white and blinding, the glare swallowing everything else, even the tumbling sheets of metal pouring from the ruptured turbine. Khobotov was dimly aware of a strangled vox-traffic, screams and howlings of pain, from the tech-guard somewhere above him. The normally dominant, analytical part of his brain told him their skin would be dry scraps fluttering upwards on the column of light, just as his own robes were burning away around him. But most of him just gawped at the fantastic output of power. Machine-discipline had served him so well these last centuries, but the Omnissiah's logic faltered in the sight of such madness.

Sasia Koraloth stood on the platform that floated at the heart of the light, the Soulspear a blazing thunderbolt in her hand. She was scream-ing something at him but the only sound was a wall of white noise.

The light rose up and began to swallow her, and beneath its surface something moved. Something humanoid but gargantuan, its features swimming beneath the curtain of light, reaching a hand upwards. Nails like jewels broke the surface, pale perfect skin. Symbols flashed in the air, numbers, letters, strange sigils that throbbed with power.

Sasia Koraloth sank into the light, taking the Soulspear with her. Beside her, the giant's face, still half-obscured by the glare, looked upwards with burning eyes. The arcane symbols solidified, and suddenly the air was full of sorcerous equations, leading rings of power around the upstretched hand. Bright bolts of energy swirled in great circles as the hand opened and the fingers spread to surround Khobotov.

His motor systems burned out, Khobotov hung paralysed as the fingers closed around him. Scrabbling around inside his own head, he managed to disconnect his few remaining sensory inputs before he was crushed.

THE SOUL DRINKERS had lost more than fifty of their number. Over a quarter of the strike force down in a matter of minutes, trapped on the *Ultima* or dragged beneath the waves. Many of those they had pulled out of the water had discarded much of their armour and there were many Soul Drinkers who would have to fight on with parts of their armour missing. There weren't enough backpacks and without a power source others would go almost completely unarmoured, for even a Soul Drinker would struggle to move in an unpowered suit of Space Marine armour. Their augmented physiology would resist the pollution of the unnamed world's seas, but that would be of little consolation when they found what Ve'Meth had planned for them, and would have to face it almost naked.

Not unarmed, though. For not one of them had dropped his gun.

The night was clammy and cold at the same time, the brutal jagged ocean stretching out around them, bleak and endless. It was worse than the fog, for here a man might feel how small he was compared to an entire planet that knew they were here and wanted them dead. Ve'Meth had seen them arrive, of that he could be sure. The ships they encountered were probably part of a cordon thrown around the daemon's fortress island, a lifeform's reaction to foreign bodies. Sarpedon could feel the baleful heat of the black flame that Yser had described, the horrible mocking laugh he had heard in his dreams of Quixian Obscura. He was not just closer to Ve'Meth – the foul thing was watching him, scrying by some sorcery or watching through the eyes of the monstrous fish and distant flying creatures.

He looked round to see the survivors of Squad Luko taking over the watch at the stern of the *Hellblade*. Sergeant Luko and his few remaining men were some of the Marines who had been accommodated on the *Hellblade* and *Lakonia* after the shattered remnants of the *Ultima* had sunk beneath the waves.

Sergeant Luko saluted Sarpedon. Sarpedon left his vigil in the stern and picked his way across the shifting deck.

'Sergeant Luko, Chaplain Iktinos told me of what you did on the *Ultima*.'

'And I could tell you something of him, too, and of every Marine there. We all fought.'

'He told me how Brother Zaen died.'

Luko nodded slowly. 'Zaen. An excellent death. Something to remember.' Luko could put on a good face, never fazed by the fires of battle. But like every leader amongst the Soul Drinkers there had been a fair few men lost under him, and it always left him reflective. Few would recognise the fiercely joyous Luko save those who really knew him. 'Vorts gone, too, and all the serfs. I heard Graevus's mob did better, though.'

'They left nothing alive, and took no loss.'

'Just how Daenyathos would have liked it.' Luko looked round and Sarpedon saw how old he looked bare-headed. Sarpedon had relaxed the helmet-discipline, if only because so many Marines had lost their helmets in the ocean. He realised that he was old, too – ninety years, if he stopped to think about it, seventy of those as a fully-fledged Soul Drinker. But those seventy years seemed like a solid slab of memory, one long apprenticeship of battle he had to complete before his real life started. He had dreamed of living out a glorious career in the service of the Imperium of Man, but now he realised he had just been a child, making mistakes he had to learn from.

'They say Tellos took half of them down himself,' said Luko.

'They say right. It will be some time before I can give Sergeant Tellos an independence of command, though. Graevus's men had to drag him back on board the *Lakonia*.' Sarpedon had often asked himself the question of Tellos's future. He had lost the discipline that had made him a sergeant, but doubled the ferocity and bravery that had made him all but idolised by the Assault Marines around him. Grim as it may sound, Sarpedon suspected the problem would solve itself – there was little doubt Tellos would be the first off the *Lakonia* onto the shore of Ve'Meth's fortress, and it was unlikely he would survive forging the beachhead for the Marines deploying behind him. It would be a good death, one of the best.

There was the sudden flash of an alarm rune at the edge of Sarpedon's vision. He peered through the twilight to see the lookout in the prow of the *Lakonia*, pointing to the dim horizon as Marines gathered behind him.

'Sarpedon here. What do you see?'

It was Iktinos's rune that flashed. The Chaplain had taken his turn in the watch, just like the ordinary Marines who made up his congregation. 'Land sighted, sir. We're closing in.'

'Understood, Chaplain. The *Lakonia* can lead, we'll follow you in.' Sarpedon saw it now, too – a hard black scab just visible on the horizon.

He would have Graevus prepare the assault troops, and know that Tellos would be doing the same on the *Lakonia*. The black flame was burning bright now, the mocking laughter loud in his head. The final run had begun, and he had seen too much of this world to believe any of them would survive.

TECH-PRIEST SASIA KORALOTH was dead. There was only Sasia the child, her mind blasted backwards as she was bathed in the sea of power that had swallowed her.

She was alone. She was afraid. There was light and noise all around her, filling her, too much for her to cope with. There was heat against her skin, and currents of power pulling her this way and that, like a thousand hands snatching at her. She opened her eyes, the white light nearly blinding her. But she wanted to see. She wanted to know where she was, what had happened to her, who was doing all this.

The light solidified, and the Engineer of Time stood before her.

He was a thousand storeys tall. His skin was white crystal. His thoughts were magic, and the symbols of that magic were orbiting him in wide circles of sigils, spelling out impossibly complex equations of power.

He held out a hand the size of a city and, with incredible grace, plucked something from her grasp. It was a tiny thing the little girl had been clutching in her woman's fist, and dimly, Sasia remembered that she had wanted the Engineer to take it, and that perhaps now he had it he might be happy.

It held the thing up in front of his face and examined it with eyes like twin gas giants.

'Such a small thing,' said a voice in her head. 'So much anguish. Most satisfying.'

The Soulspear. It was called the Soulspear.

And suddenly she knew that the Engineer had everything he needed now, and that he had forgotten about her already.

He looked away from her and suddenly the forces he had created to hold her intact were dismissed. The light exploded and gargantuan islands of madness rolled in, oceans of tears, malicious lumps of thought looming dark like kraken.

Little Sasia was torn apart by the sudden storm of experience the human consciousness wasn't supposed to comprehend. She lost her mind a split-second before her body was dissolved by the forces of the warp.

* * *

IN THE FADED splendour of the pleasure-yacht's viewing gallery, Tech-Marine Lygris looked out through the huge oculus. The great blinded eye of the unnamed planet glared back at him. Lygris knew Sarpedon and his battle-brothers would be down there, probably fighting, probably dying. They had been down there for several days now – probably halfway through the mission at the best guess. Communications with them had, as expected, been cut the instant the Thunderhawks had dropped through the thick layer of bone-coloured cloud. There had been nothing but static over the comms.

Part of him said he should have been down there. But, with so little known about Ve'Meth and his capabilities, Sarpedon had needed a level head to stay on the *Brokenback*. They were here to prove the Chapter's devotion to the Emperor's will, and if that was the part Lygris had to play, then so be it.

He wanted to fight. He wanted to feel a bolter in his hand and fires of battle all around him. But he was needed here, just in case.

He felt the rumble in the deck through his feet and heard it a split-second after, rolling through the *Brokenback's* cavernous body. The image of the unnamed world shuddered as the crystal of the oculus shook and somewhere a klaxon sounded as a component ship's alarm system activated. There was a jolt and Lygris only just kept his feet, tortured metal wailing through the walls.

He switched on his vox. 'Engineering, what was that?'

'The sensors say it's a warp fluctuation, sir. Could be something arriving.'

'I'm in the viewing gallery, sector green. Route it to the oculus.'

The huge round viewing screen above him flashed and an image was cast onto it, a composite of the region of nearby space taken from the hundreds of sensoria all over the *Brokenback*. The disturbance was a boiling mass of blue-white against the star field, pulsing like a beating heart and sending out the pulses that shook the space hulk even now. Lygris called up the damage report – the *Brokenback* was made of tough stuff, though, and there had been little more than a few nuts and bolts shaken loose.

Could it be another ship? Unlikely. But they were orbiting a world saturated with Chaos, and everything about it was unlikely.

'This is Tech-Marine Lygris,' he announced over the vox-casters. 'All personnel to weapons stations.'

With so many Soul Drinkers on the surface the *Brokenback* was effectively on a skeleton crew of Marines and serfs, and every man would be heading to his weapons stations, ready to launch the racks of torpedoes they had found intact, or fire the macrocannon and magnalasers that studded the hulk's surface.

As Lygris watched the disturbance rippled and faded, sinking back into the blackness of space. The *Brokenback* stopped shaking, and the sensorium data streaming along the top of the image returned to normal. Background radiation was up, but there was little more.

Could be a simple ripple in the immaterium, to be expected in a place as horribly linked with Chaos as this. Or it could be something more sinister, that didn't show up on the *Brokenback's* myriad scanners. Such a thing was, effectively, impossible, but Sarpedon had not given Lygris command of the *Brokenback* to take needless risks. He would keep the hulk on alert for a couple of hours, until he was satisfied any danger had passed.

He had the oculus blink back to the image of the unnamed planet, and the blinded eye kept on staring.

THE ISLANDS OF the archipelago rose all around them as they approached, midnight spires of broken black coral jabbing from the ocean. Ve'Meth's influence was so strong every battle-brother felt it and the pollution was stronger and viler here – there was a sickly rainbow sheen, like oil, on the surface of the water, and the coral was crusted with residue where the waves lapped at them. The air was heavy with toxins, the light feeble, the cloud a dirty dark slab of pollution in the sky like a ceiling. The lookouts saw islands floating in the air, and squat amphibian daemons on top of the coral spikes, vomiting gore into the breakers beneath. They glimpsed the distant fins of giant sharks and the mottled bodies of kraken.

They sighted other ships – a ghastly spidery thing that skimmed across the water on wooden legs, a bloated galleon with sails of skin – but the *Lakonia* and the *Hellblade* were hidden by the poor light and mist. Sarpedon wondered why they were not attacked again. Perhaps they had proved their valour in ship-to-ship combat to such a degree that Ve'Meth would rather face them on land than at sea again. Or maybe this place was so wholly Chaotic that the Soul Drinkers were simply too few to spot amongst all the madness.

There were flies everywhere. They got into armour joints, helmets, bolter actions. Wargear rites had to be doubled. Iktinos led the men in prayers for deliverance and strength in the face of such all-pervading corruption. Sarpedon had asked Tyrendian, the strike force's other psyker, what he could tell of Ve'Meth. Tyrendian's nightmares had been of a huge serpent, wrapping itself round a world and crushing it to death, then swallowing it whole along with billions of souls.

There was no need to navigate. Ve'Meth was like a dark beacon, shining evilly. Tyrendian, in the *Lakonia*, took them in. The engines were little more than idling as the ships swept almost silently through the shadows of the archipelago, the lumped black coral reefs becoming more frequent until they stood in rows like the ribs of something huge and dead.

Nine days after they had departed in their ships, and five after the loss of the *Ultima*, they came within sight of Ve'Meth's fortress.

It was the size of a mountain. Great pustules dotted its surface, opening and closing like dumb mouths weeping bile. Noxious yellowish steam rose in clouds from cracks in the scarred coral surface, and flocks of winged creatures flapped blindly around the fortress's distant pinnacle. Rivers of pus ran down the mountain's sides, clotted thick and squirming with creatures. Far above, thunderstorms raged in the solid black slab of flies that hung in a thick layer in the sky.

It was as if the black coral had been alive and then infected by something so terrible that it had flared up into this immense tumor. Even from here, the Soul Drinkers could see the columns of men marching out of it – armoured warriors such as Graevus's men had faced, shambling monstrous things, bent-backed slaves, daemons with flesh of pure disease.

Sergeant Dreo had been on lookout when the fortress was sighted, and had summoned Sarpedon right away. Sarpedon looked upon the fortress and wondered how they could assault such a place. It was not just a huge and well-defended strongpoint, but it would be alive – malevolent and deadly, more an enemy than a battlefield. He decided to keep it simple – beach the ships, pour out, and use all the speed and hitting power of the Soul Drinkers to break into the fortress and storm through it until they found Ve'Meth.

Simple. Like all the best plans. Of course, Ve'Meth's plan would be simpler still – throw waves of Chaos troops at the attacking Soul Drinkers until every one was dead.

Sarpedon voxed down to the *Hellblade's* hull. 'Varuk? Gun the engines. We're making our approach.'

'Yes sir!' The refitted Thunderhawk engines growled beneath Sarpedon's feet and the *Lakonia* darted forward, driving an arrowhead of rippling water in its wake. The *Lakonia* took the lead, sweeping fast through the waters, peeling off to one side as the approach began. The Marines on the deck scuttled into the hull to make the final battle-rites, leaving a couple of lookouts to spot the forces that would oppose the landing.

The two ships would land close together, but far enough apart so they wouldn't get in each other's way. The Marines from each one would act as an independent force, meeting up in the fortress if all went well but not relying on it. Sarpedon would be in command of the *Hellblade's* complement – Karraidin had command over the *Lakonia*, but he would be as aware as anyone that Tellos and Graevus would be leading the assault.

Sarpedon checked the mechanism of his bolter, letting the well-practiced motion act as a trigger to shut out the rest of his thoughts so he could think only of war. It was a trick he had learned when only a novice, when the universe had been much simpler. He switched on the aegis circuit and felt the old power spiralling around him, through the same armour that had clad his body every day of battle for seventy years.

Then he went below deck, to see that his battle-brothers had readied themselves for the fight.

'ONE MINUTE THIRTY!' called Graevus from the prow. The one hundred and seventy-odd Soul Drinkers in the hold of the *Lakonia* would be making their final entreaties to Rogal Dorn, that he might keep his gaze upon them and see the valour they would display.

The *Lakonia* was really moving now, carving towards the broad beach of black coral sand that stretched in broad crescent, beneath the shadow of the fortress-mountain above. The fortifications were crude – chunks of black crystal and sharpened bone jutting from bunkers of piled-up rocks – but they would be effective enough against a force without heavy weaponry or artillery to break them open.

But that wasn't the worst.

The worst was that there must have been five thousand of the enemy waiting on the shore, waiting for the *Lakonia*. In front were slaves, pale-skinned, sickly and chained. Behind the slaves were ranks of huge man-beasts using pikes and halberds to herd them forwards into the surf. Even at this distance Graevus could hear the screams of the drugged slaves and bellowing of the beastmen that drove them on.

'Thirty seconds!' yelled Graevus over the vox. He heard the reassuring sound of one hundred and seventy bolters cocked in unison.

The *Lakonia's* hull scraped the sea floor as the shore swept closer. Graevus could see the slave-soldiers herded into a defensive line – they were chained together by their collars, and had crude clubs in their hands. Their mouths lolled and their eyes were half-dead and hooded – the beastmen held spear-points at their backs and pressed them forward into the surf. A sick and cowardly tactic, but it would work – the Soul Drinkers would be mired in slave-fodder troops, giving the defenders more time to redeploy and fall upon the attacking Marines.

The solution was obvious. They would just have to kill them all.

'Ten seconds!'

The *Lakonia* ground deep into the broken coral sea bed, jarring to a halt a pistol shot from the shore. This close the ranks of slave-things seemed without number, and Graevus could see them drooling. They had been mind-wiped, or simply bred for idiocy and kept for food.

Close enough.

'Move!' yelled Graevus, swinging his power axe out of its backpack holster. There were twin thunderclaps as the shaped charges in the hold blew a huge section of the hull outwards in a shower of splinters, and hollered battle-cries as the Soul Drinkers vaulted out into the surf. As the gunfire started Graevus jumped off the prow, drew his bolt pistol, and started firing.

The slaves were like a wall of moaning flesh pressing all around him as soon as he hit the water, glazed-eyed and gibbering, swinging makeshift weapons at the Soul Drinkers pouring in amongst them. Graevus put a clip of bolt pistol shells into the closest, saw them reel and still keep fighting as they died, and knew they must have been pumped full of Frenzon or combat drugs.

'Forwards!' bellowed Karraidin over the vox, and the Soul Drinkers surged on, pistol shots and chainblades carving through the frenzied slaves as the surf around their knees turned frothy pink with blood. Karraidin's storm bolter chattered and the flash of the power field was like sheet lightning as he landed a blow into the press of bodies.

Graevus didn't pause to reload – his altered hand swung the power axe in great arc through the attackers, shearing through limbs and bodies. Assault Marines were at his shoulder, helping gouge through the slave ranks, forcing an opening through which the Soul Drinkers could charge onto the beach. A club rang off Graevus's shoulder pad and a heavy blade cut into the joint of his armoured knee but he stepped further into the fray, knowing that his battle-brothers would be doing the same at his side. There were mounds of dead on the coral beneath his feet, and the water was thick with gore.

'With me!' he voxed on the squad channel, swinging the shining power axe blade high so all could see it. 'Keep close and keep moving!' He risked a glance around and saw Karraidin's massively armoured form behind him, a walking bastion that sprayed storm bolter-fire into the baying hound pack being driven towards the rear of the Soul Drinkers. The half-rotted dogs bounded through the frothing waves but Karraidin was pumping volley after volley into them, then snapping off shots into the beastmen packmasters.

A good plan – mindless cannon fodder to the front to slow them down while fast-moving attack dogs surrounded them. Against any normal enemy, it might even have worked.

Tellos. He couldn't see Tellos.

Graevus tried the vox-channels and got the din of battle filtered through disciplined Space Marine comm-drills. Two Marines from Squad Hastis were down, trampled beneath the waves by a teeming mob of slaves who were cracking open their armour with chunks of coral. Squad Karvik was bogged down around Karraidin, shoulder-deep in the blood-choked water, trapped between the slaves and the hound packs. But most of the Soul Drinkers were bunched behind Graevus, jostling for a chance to get bolter muzzle and chainsword into contact with the mass of slaves, and that was what mattered now. Karvik and Hastis would have to fend for themselves – it was break out or die.

Graevus couldn't pick out Tellos and had no time to search for him – he blocked the downswing of an outsized club and slammed the butt end of the power axe into the attacker, feeling the strength of his massively altered arm driving the axe through the upper chest of the slave. He pushed forward and the pull of the water was gone – his feet were on land, on the black coral sand of the beach, and the slave line broke around him.

Tellos.

Sergeant Graevus had charged into a thousand battles in a hundred warzones, but he had never seen anything like it. Tellos must have dived into the slave-pack and writhed through the wall of bodies, despising the crude tactic of using cannon-fodder and determined to get to grips with the real enemy. He had reached the beach alone and been surrounded by the beastmen – for a soldier it was suicide, a quick and brutal death. But this was not just a soldier. This was Tellos.

By the time Graevus had reached him, Tellos was high up on a mound of the dead, butchered bodies beneath his feet, howling beastmen jabbing at him with spears whose tips shone with venom. There must have been twenty or more able to get at him and he was duelling with them all, blades flashing too fast to see, turning aside spear shafts and lashing deep into mutated beastman flesh. Where he had been cut his pale skin puckered and closed before the wound could bleed.

Sarpedon had his arachnoid legs. Givrillian had his multitude of eyes, Graevus his hand, and the other battle-brothers all manner of blessing the Emperor had bestowed on them in His role as the Architect of Fate. And His blessing to Tellos was to turn him into a man designed solely for war – reflexes like quicksilver, flesh that weapons could sail through without causing damage, a mind that yearned for one more fight.

Graevus was at Tellos's side and lent his axe to the slaughter, the grotesque equine faces of the beastmen grimacing in pain and hatred, cloven-hoofed legs and claw-fingered hands flailing. Gunfire whipped

into the beastmen who tried to run as the ferocity of the Soul Drinkers'
assault slammed into the Chaos line, throwing the beastmen onto the
back foot and grinding them into the blood-slicked coral.

The momentum of the assault bought Graevus a couple of seconds to
glance up the beach towards Sarpedon and the *Hellblade*. The *Hellblade*
was still some distance from the shore, and Graevus knew for the
moment the Marines from the *Lakonia* were alone on the beach.

There was room to move now, time to stop and take stock. Karraidin
was still somewhere behind, fighting hard to link up with the beachhead, but most of the Soul Drinkers had made it to the shore. Losses
were in double figures. A good start, thought Graevus, but through the
murk and shadows beneath the immense fortress he could see the coral
slopes teeming with Chaos reinforcements.

'Fire point!' he called over the vox, sprinting to a set of abandoned
rock fortifications. 'Regroup on me, now!' They had to move with speed
but there was no point in running headlong into a counter-attacking
force flooding down from the fortress slopes. They would have to hop
from one strongpoint to another, overwhelm one set of fortifications,
regroup on it and strike out to the next until they reached the fortress,
ran out of enemies or were all dead.

No problem. It was what they had been trained, engineered, and educated to do. What they had been born to do.

Soul Drinkers were forming fire arcs to cover those still struggling
through the surf, bolters and bolt pistols barking at the darting packs of
beastmen retreating in disarray. Graevus could see the goat-headed
beastmen and black-armoured warriors swarming down the fortress
slopes – even now the Soul Drinkers were snapping off ranging
bolter-shots at them, ready to open up when they were within range. A
minute or two, and then the killing would begin again.

Graevus loaded a fresh clip into his bolter. He had never been one to
hold with visions and portent, relying instead on the gut instincts built
up over a long campaigning career. But even he could feel the pure malice that boiled within the fortress high above him. He had heard that
everyone saw Ve'Meth differently in his dreams – Graevus couldn't
avoid getting the image of an immense parasitic insect, squatting on a
throne, with bristly black skin and huge segmented eyes, mandibles
filthy with blood.

He shook the picture out of his head. If they were here to kill that
thing, then he would be proud to have a part in it.

THE STENCH WAS almost too much – dank, mossy, a reek of decay and
death, rolling from the shore over the stricken *Hellblade*. A hundred

metres beyond was the beach, obscured with noisome mist, through which Sarpedon could just glimpse half-human figures scurrying, eager to fight the invading Soul Drinkers.

The ship lurched as it tried to power over the obstacle, the engines screaming, the water behind foaming. Sarpedon ignored the stench and voxes below deck. 'What's the hold-up, Tech-Marine?'

'Hit a rock, lord!' came the short-breathed reply. 'We're taking on water. I'm sending everyone topside.'

The hatches were opening and the Soul Drinkers were clambering out as the *Hellblade* began to list. Sarpedon glanced below deck and saw the water foaming up around a massive black stone spike that had punched through the hull. Varuk was struggling through the waist-deep and quickly rising water – Sarpedon reached down and grabbed the Tech-Marine's hand, hauling him up onto the deck.

If they stayed, they would be trapped, and the defenders would doubtless have some way of reaching them given time – ships of their own, or those gargantuan sea monsters they had glimpsed during the voyage. Maybe something that flew. There was only one choice.

'Soul Drinkers, over the side!' he voxed. 'Stay together and keep moving!' With that he vaulted over the side of the *Hellblade*.

The water was about two metres deep – drowning point for a normal man, but a Space Marine could keep his head above water as he moved. Sarpedon's many legs helped keep his footing on the uneven coral rock underfoot but Marines around him were stumbling beneath the waves as they landed, helped back up by their battle-brothers. The *Hellblade* lurched brokenly and rolled onto its side as the last few Marines jumped into the water.

The sea was warm. Somehow, that made it far worse.

Steadily, Sarpedon strode towards the shore, the coral crumbling beneath his feet. He ordered the squads under him command to sound off as they made their way towards the beach. Givrillian, Dreo, Corvan, Karvik, Luko – there were a dozen squad sergeants and their men, plus the remnants of the squads who had survived the *Ultima* along with Tech-Marine Varuk, Chaplain Iktinos and Sarpedon himself.

The mists were rolling back from the shore, exposing the open wound that was the waiting force. Pale ragged skin, dark rotting flesh, hunched shoulders and singly glowing yellow eyes.

Daemons. Ve'Meth's will made solid, living embodiments of Chaotic power. The sight of them was grainy with the haze of flies that clung to them as they gambolled along the black sand or lay crouched in wait.

Would the Hell work here? They said daemons felt no fear. But then again, they had never met Sarpedon.

'Something in here with us, commander,' came the gravelly voice of Sergeant Karliv, one of the sergeants who had not gone to the star fort but who had proved loyal enough in the Chapter war.

'What do you mean, Karliv?'

'There's something moving in the water.'

'Kill it and keep moving.'

Sarpedon glanced backwards in time to see something thrashing in the water in the midst of the advancing Space Marines, and heard the yells of one Marine as he was dragged under.

'It's got Trass!'

Gunfire stuttered as the members of Squad Karvik held their bolt pistols above the water and fired shells into the body of the thing that had already swallowed one of their number. Tentacles flailed wildly, something pale and mottled rolled in the water.

There was a sudden flash and a cloud of steam rose with a hiss. The thrashing stopped, and Sarpedon could make out the slashes of light that were Sergeant Luko's lightning claws.

'Got it,' voxed Luko calmly. His voice was still uncharacteristically grim – he understood as well as any of them how little chance they could succeed here. But they had no choice. Ve'Meth represented everything that the Architect of Fate stood against, and if there was a chance to kill him then that chance had to be taken no matter what the risk.

They were close enough now to see the enemy lookouts staring at them, turning to gibber instructions to their brother daemons. Somewhere far along the shore gunfire flashed as Karraidin and Graevus's men stormed their section of the shore. Sarpedon listened in to the other force's vox for a second or two – bolter-fire, orders yelled, cries of pain and anger.

Sarpedon didn't have time for any of that now. He heard a bolter shot, saw the head of something on the shore snapping back in a shower of dark green blood, and knew that Dreo had found his range.

There was a roar from the beach and suddenly the daemons were charging as one, turning the water green-black with filth as they splashed into the surf, sharp lengths of iron wielded as swords. They weren't a random-willed pack, intent only on violence – something was leading them.

'Mark targets and covering fire!' Sarpedon voxed to the tactical squads behind him as he strode into the shallower water. 'Assault squads on me!'

Then he was close enough to see the loops of rotting entrails through the rips in the daemons' stomachs, the hideous leering single eyes glaring from their foreheads, their lolling mouths and stumps of rotting teeth. The reek was like a solid wall in front of him but he broke into a sprint and pressed on for the charge, firing into the advancing bodies as he strode within bolter range. Bolt pistol shots blazed in from around him, blowing lumps of putrescence out of the shambling bodies.

He could feel Ve'Meth laughing at them, peering down from the rotting coral mountain above them. Ve'Meth wouldn't be laughing for long.

The Soul Drinkers and the plague daemons clashed in the shallows, chainswords ringing sparks off ugly two-handed blades. Sarpedon whipped the force staff from his back to block a crude downward swipe, followed up with an upswing that ripped a leering daemon's head in two. The daemons were rotting and deformed but they were quick, with slack muscles unnaturally strong. The ruined face howled and the blade swung at Sarpedon's waist, smashing sideways into the ceramite breastplate and knocking Sarpedon onto two of his knees. The blow had left the daemon wide open and Sarpedon lunged forward, hooking the staff round the back of its shattered head and pulling it onto the muzzle of the bolter in his other hand, so he could blast its torso apart at point-blank range with half a magazine of bolter shells.

They had an utter contempt of pain. Their bodies were unnatural bags of disease which ignored injuries that would kill a mortal thing – to kill them you had to dismember them completely.

That was fine by him, Sarpedon thought.

He dodged another blade and darted his two front legs forward, impaling the daemon on his front claws and ripping it clean in two. The Assault Marines of Squad Karvik were around him and Karvik's power sword darted over his shoulder to shear the arms off the closest daemon. Sarpedon nodded his thanks – Karvik's helmeted head glanced at him in acknowledgement, then turned back to lead his Marines in the killing. All around was a swirling, brutal combat, plague daemons charging through a cloud of flies, Soul Drinkers meeting them with chainswords and battering them into the unclean surf. But the daemons were strong and there was a horde of them here – Squad Dreo had gone in on one flank and were four men down already, the spearhead was blunted and Sarpedon could see more daemons piling in from the shore.

The beachhead would fail. The Soul Drinkers would be trapped in the surf and surrounded.

Time for the Hell.

What did daemons fear? Nothing? No, they had minds of a sort, even if they were something a decent human being could never wish to comprehend. They had desires and hates and obsessions like everything else. They had fear, too. But of what?

All Sarpedon had were his fellow Marines, battling in the surf. The greatest warriors humanity could produce, proud soldiers of the Emperor's will. They were warriors worth fearing for even the most degenerate mind. That was what the Hell would be.

Sarpedon felt the aegis circuit pulse white-hot against his skin as he let the psychic power inside him flood out, a torrent more powerful than he had ever gathered before. Every day he had felt his powers reach greater heights and now he unleashed it all at once, the tide of the Hell rising up around him.

His battle-brothers' eyes glowed with righteous hatred. Their swords were flashes of lightning, their guns belched bolts of fire. They were five metres tall, twenty-five, fifty. The cloud-filled sky shrunk back from them in fear and the waters receded in terror. Sarpedon let the power rage through him, channelled into his fellow Marines. The chalices on their shoulder pads were brimming with traitors' blood, the masks of their helmets grim and forbidding. Those forced to fight without armour had skin that glowed with strength, as if it would turn aside bullets and blades like ceramite.

Sarpedon rose from the surf, power arcing off the force staff in his hand. He was a hero of mankind, venerated in the annals of humanity long after the corrupt Imperium had decayed and the enemies of the Emperor purged from the galaxy. He was Rogal Dorn battling the traitorous hordes of Horus on the battlements of Earth. He was huge and terrible, a demi-god of vengeance striding into the midst of the plague daemons.

The butchery faltered as the plague daemons' diseased minds struggled to comprehend the majesty of the warriors before them. Their blades stopped swinging for a second, and in that second the Soul Drinkers charged forwards as one, Sarpedon at their head, his staff ripping through deformed bodies. They tore through the daemon pack and sent them scurrying in shock, run down by the Assault Marines and massacred by supporting fire from the tactical squads.

Some tried to rally and amongst them Sarpedon saw the leader who had directed the daemon horde. He was a nightmare – a giant of bare glistening muscle and a face that was a mass of sharp mandibles and gleaming eyes. He had a huge slab of metal stabbed through one clubbed hand for a sword and was surrounded by baying daemon-things.

Kill this monstrosity and the daemon front would fail.

Sarpedon ran on to the beach at full tilt, outstripping the Assault Marines charging into the faltering daemons around him, focused on the champion of Chaos who dared stand before him.

GELENTIUS VORP SAW the invading commander and gave thanks to Grandfather Nurgle that he should have this opportunity. Oh, glorious decay, his hand would be slick with the blood of the clean ones and his body blessed with Ve'Meth's pestilent reward!

This enemy was tall and clad in massive purple armour trimmed with bone and gold, a chalice symbol picked out on one shoulder pad – a Space Marine, the most stubbornly misguided of mankind who refused to look upon the majestic corruption of Nurgle, a fine scalp for Vorp to present to Ve'Meth. This one was different, though – he had eight legs, like those of an insect or a spider, sprouting from his waist, which sent him bounding up the shore far faster than his fellow Marines advancing behind. The Space Marine had a long staff in one hand – he wore no helmet and was shaven-headed, and his eyes burned with anger. Vorp saw there was some trick that this enemy had used to throw the daemons into disarray, but Vorp himself was above such things, for Ve'Meth had shielded his mind against trickery.

His simpering daemon-pack of plaguebearers bounded alongside him as he strode towards his prey, their lips drooling at the prospect of the kill. Vorp swung his huge blade at the Space Marine but the enemy was quick and turned the pendulous sword with a shoulder pad, jabbing with the staff and spearing it through the head of the closest plaguebearer. The staff flicked and the daemon's gristly spine came apart.

A worthy opponent. Vorp made a note to offer up thanks to Ve'Meth and the Grandfather for such an opportunity to prove his devotion to the Lord of Decay.

Vorp stepped in close and rammed a clubbed fist into the enemy's chest, denting the ceramite and throwing the Space Marine back a pace. But suddenly the staff was entangled in his legs and Vorp was pitched off his feet, slamming into the sharp black sand on his back. The Marine saw Vorp was wide open and a massive downward swipe of the staff tore deep into Vorp's shoulder, narrowly missing bisecting his skull.

The arrogance! The nerve!

Vorp rose to his feet and slashed with the sword, biting into the Marine's shoulder pad and into his arm. The Marine stumbled back again and caught Vorp's descending blade with the staff – Vorp reached down and grabbed one of the strange arachnoid legs, twisted and pulled, and felt the leg come away with a snapping of tendons.

The Space Marine bellowed with rage as he saw the mangled stump of his leg spurting vermilion blood over the sand.

Vorp had hurt it. Now Vorp would kill it.

A WHITE-HOT PAIN flared bright in Sarpedon's mind, flooding through him from the bleeding socket of his left mid-leg. The leg itself was held in the paw of the skinless monster standing over him, triumph in its multitude of insect eyes. Even though the battle was raging all around him, the gunfire and howling of daemons was blocked out by the white noise of agony.

The pain would pass. Sarpedon had suffered worse. And he still had seven legs left, damn it.

The Chaos champion barrelled forwards, doubtless hoping to capitalise on its small victory and finish Sarpedon for good. Sarpedon dodged to the side and weaved between the huge swinging blows of the champion's tarnished sword. Sarpedon was favouring his left side but knew he could not let up for an instant – the champion was inhumanly strong and seemed as immune to pain as its attendant daemons.

The sword stabbed at head height and Sarpedon caught a huge fleshy knee in the throat as he ducked. He slashed upwards with a talon, following with the staff, and as the champion stepped back he slammed the heel of his free hand into the side of its leg. A bone snapped somewhere deep within the slimy muscle. The champion didn't notice, pivoted on a heel, brought the blunt pommel of its blade down on the back of Sarpedon's neck.

It was fast as well as strong. It had no finesse – there was no method here, only brutality and anger. Sarpedon couldn't outfight something like this, because every trick or flourish he might bring out would be beaten down by the champion's sheer relentless strength. The only way was to be stronger than it was.

There was no art in this fight. The champion made a wide arcing downward swing, hoping to decapitate Sarpedon. Sarpedon took the blow on a shoulder pad, swung back with his staff. The champion blocked the attack but Sarpedon struck again and again, slamming the staff into the champion's guard, battering it slowly backwards. With its free arm it slashed a spined elbow into Sarpedon's face and tried to close its gnarled fingers around his throat. But Sarpedon had to focus everything on attack, never back down or pause for breath, and hope it would be enough.

The force staff, crackling with psychic power, ripped downwards and the champion met it with a wide circling parry, driving the head of the staff deep into the sand beneath its feet. Sarpedon's assault was fended off, and in that moment, both combatants were wide open to the counterattack.

Sarpedon was a split-second quicker, reflexes honed by decades of training and battle outstripping the instincts of a life in service to the Dark Gods. Sarpedon reared up on his back legs and stabbed down, spearing a talon through the wrist of the Chaos champion's sword arm. Its foul mandibled pit of a mouth yawned wide and it howled as Sarpedon dropped the force staff and grabbed the monster's head, jabbing his gauntleted fingers into its eyes. With his free hand he drew his boltgun from its holster and jammed it under its throat. He pulled the trigger and blew a corona of filthy bilious blood out of the back of its head.

It wasn't dead. But it was close.

The champion reeled wildly, segments of skull flapping from scraps of skin. Sarpedon lunged into it, knocking it backwards and landing astride of it. He put the rest of the bolter magazine into its chest, blasting the ribcage open and spraying ragged chunks of organs. When the magazine was empty Sarpedon punched down and split the ruined ribcage clean open, plunged his hands into the pulpy mass beneath, tore out leathered lungs and a foul still-beating heart, knowing that a creature like this was harder to kill than anything he had faced before. But it still bellowed and thrashed beneath him, massive corroded sword swinging wildly even as brackish blood sprayed across the sand.

Sarpedon grasped the champion's ruined head with both hands and ripped it clean off the abomination's shoulders. He cast the hideous head into the black sand, its mandibles still writhing, its glossy eyes glaring.

As the thing fell still, Sarpedon took up his gun and staff again, glancing behind him to see how his squads were faring. The daemons were in flight and the Soul Drinkers were making a break for the rugged slopes of the mountain-fortress, where the broken landscape would afford some cover for the ascent towards Ve'Meth's sanctum.

He stood up, blocking out the pain from his severed leg. He joined the forward elements of the spearhead as they sprinted through the remains of daemonic defences, raking the distant Chaos forces with bolter-fire as they ran, the Hell still burning around them.

* * *

GELENTIUS VORP LAY there for some time on the black coral sand, trying to force the parasites infesting him to knit together his sundered organs. He could probably survive without his head, or with his chest cavity blasted free of organs, but maybe not with both.

Would the Grandfather help him? Almighty Nurgle blessed His followers with durable bodies that scorned injury – but as he stared up at the sky with his remaining eyes Vorp speculated that perhaps even the Ve'Meth, most powerful vessel of Nurgle, might have trouble saving Vorp now.

The Space Marine would pay, of that Vorp was sure. If the fortress didn't kill him then Ve'Meth himself would. But he had so longed to feel the Marine's naively clean blood on his hands and look into his eyes as he tore his heart out…

Dismembered on the beach of Ve'Meth's island, Gelentius Vorp died at last.

CHAPTER TWELVE

THE DIN OF death echoed up the bile-slicked slopes of the fortress to reach Ve'Meth. The screech of ended life, the low keening of pain, the roar of anger. The dim crackling of gunfire was drowned out by the delicious racket that living things made when they suddenly became living no more.

That there was so much death, however, was tempered by the fact that so much of it was of Ve'Meth's own servants. Space Marines had died, and their passing was most satisfying – but daemons had been torn asunder and their spirits banished to the warp, and slaves and beastmen had died in droves. Gelentius Vorp, champion of Nurgle, had actually been killed, which was something Ve'Meth had considered to be effectively beyond the capability of anything mortal.

Ve'Meth sent out a command through the living stone of his fortress. Every servant who dwelled within his walls snapped to attention and ran, slithered or wallowed towards its designated position within the organic warren of the fortress, ready to receive and repel the invaders in corruption's name. Even if the Imperial weaklings got within striking distance of Ve'Meth's abscess-chamber his bodyguards should deal with them quickly enough.

And if they didn't? Well, then Ve'Meth would have to handle things personally.

A host-body broke ranks and strode towards the rear of the chamber where Ve'Meth kept a shrine to himself. Images offered up from cults and worlds under his domination were piled up against the sweating coral

wall – crude idols of an insect-god, a beautifully wrought reliquary in the
form of a golden snake, totems of shrunken heads and human bones,
and hundreds more. Ve'Meth swept them aside to reveal the wooden box
he kept there, burned with runes to keep the unworthy from opening it.
The host lifted the lid, reached a hand in and removed Arguotha.

It pleased Ve'Meth to savour the memory again of all those centuries
ago, when he still had a single mundane body. On his long pilgrimage
through the Eye of Terror he had been beset by the Daemon Arguotha,
who flew into a rage when he saw the suppurating marks of favour the
Plague God had bestowed upon Ve'Meth. The daemon set his thousand
offspring on Ve'Meth but the young champion had faced them all and
won, scattering them in combat. Then Arguotha himself attacked, yet
Ve'Meth had shown no fear and defeated the daemon. He wrestled it to
the ground and intoned the canticle of binding, making the daemon his
own to do with as he wished. And Ve'Meth had wished to bind the daemon into his favourite weapon.

Arguotha had brooded over the centuries and his anger was marked
upon him. His barrel was gnarled and toothed, the metal of his casing
twisted into faces that ground their teeth and screamed from time to
time. In the magazine slung beneath, the thousand young of Arguotha
writhed in captivity, eager to be released.

If the Space Marines dared cross Ve'Meth's threshold, they would get
their wish, and Arguotha would speak once more.

'MEDIC!' GRAEVUS GLANCED up to see Apothecary Pallas ducking through
the scattered gunfire towards where the Marine from Squad Hastis was
trying to pile the oozing mass of his lung back into the massive rent in
the side of his chest. The Marine knew he was dead, but he wanted to
make sure Pallas took the gene-seed organ from his body for transport
back to the Chapter apothecarion.

Brave lad, thought Graevus. They all were.

Graevus's spearhead had made it across the beach, clearing out the
black stone fortifications of the mutants and cultists who were sheltering
there. Karraidin and Squad Hastis had made it up there too, leaving a
gory trail of the dead across the sand. Now the Soul Drinkers were at the
foot of the cave-riddled mountain fortress, taking fire from hundreds of
murder holes and firepoints studding the slopes above them. The
weapons were crude and badly aimed but there were scores of them,
pouring fire down onto the Soul Drinkers.

'Give the word, Graevus,' said Karraidin as his hugely armoured bulk
clambered over the stone outcrop of the fortification in which Graevus
was taking cover.

Graevus peered out at the Soul Drinkers still arriving through the gunsmoke. 'Give it a moment. If we make a break for it now we'll leave half the lads strung out under fire.'

Karraidin risked a long look at the firepoints above them, his aristocratic features profiled against the corpse-strewn battlefield. 'The fortress is teeming with them. There must be thousands.'

'It'll be in our favour, captain. Enclosed spaces, up close. Like a boarding action.'

Karraidin smiled grimly. As a Soul Drinker who had distinguished himself in spacecraft boarding actions, for which the valuable terminator suits had been designed, he knew full well the intense, half-blind butchery that the Soul Drinkers would have to wade through.

'Can't wait,' Karraidin said, and Graevus knew he meant it.

Another purple-armoured body dived into the cover of the rock, bullets snickering into the sand beside him. It was Sergeant Karvik, chainsword in hand.

'My squad's in position sir,' he gasped.

Squad Karvik had been trapped in the shallows when the spearhead had first advanced, and must have sprinted through both the regrouping beast-cultists and the fire from the slopes. 'Good work, sergeant. Captain, that's all of them. We move.'

'Soul Drinkers, with me!' called Karraidin over the vox and vaulted over the stone wall. All around the Soul Drinkers squads broke cover and ran, snapping shots at the openings overhead. Graevus saw Marines fall, some to be helped by their battle-brothers as they passed, others to pick themselves up and carry on, others to lie where they fell.

Karraidin had spotted an opening at foot-level – a ragged cavern entrance from which ran a runnel of sickly brown ichor. Through the shadows inside Graevus saw Chaos troops, hunched figures clad in rags, manoeuvring an autocannon to cover the entrance. A volley from Karraidin's storm bolter caused them to duck so that by the time they had squeezed off a burst of shots the closest Assault Marines were upon them, Sergeant Tellos in their midst. Three Marines fell, large-calibre autocannon rounds punching through their bodies, before the gun crew were cut to pieces and the Soul Drinkers were inside.

Graevus's eyes adjusted instantly to the darkness, and he realised that this was something that had not been built; it had been grown. The tunnel stretching into the heart of the fortress was ribbed and puckered, the internal organs of something long-dead or dormant, something that might wake or be revived at any moment. And this particular monster's brain was Ve'Meth.

The assault squads were fifty metres down the tunnel with Tellos and Karraidin, spraying bullets at things that dared move in the shadows.

'What do you think, Graevus?' voxed Karraidin.

In any normal situation Sergeant Graevus, with the decades of experience feeding a honed combat instinct, would have carefully weighed up the routes likely to bring them within striking distance of a tactical objective. But this was not a normal situation, and Graevus knew exactly where they had to go to exterminate the pollution that had deformed this whole planet. 'I think we go up,' he said.

THE HELL WAS still with them. Sarpedon couldn't have turned it off if he'd wanted to. It made them ten metres high, striding angels of death with guns that fired thunder and swords that slashed lightning. They lost a dozen men to heavy weapons that raked the broken ground with fire; another ten to the dripping, tentacled things that thumped down from the ceiling of the cave they had charged into.

But they had not slowed down. It was the classic Soul Drinkers' assault, fast and deadly, heedless of danger, cutting through everything that moved. Hunch-limbed slaves fled, hulking black-armoured warriors were sliced and blasted apart. With Sarpedon at their head they ran through tunnels and broad chambers packed with heaps of rotting meat, crevasses full to the brim with corpses, crossed bridges made of human bones.

The fortress was teeming with life – tunnels were knee-deep in insects and there were colonies of skeletal flapping creatures that hung like bats. Most living things fled instinctively at the Soul Drinkers' approach, such was the aura of righteous death surrounding them. Some stood and fought, directed by the fanaticism with which Ve'Meth had infected them, but the blubbery eyeless monsters and crooked-limbed humanoids that ran along the walls were shredded by bolter and chainsword, and the Soul Drinkers pressed on. Squads Dreo and Givrillian must have picked off a hundred enemies between them with snap shots. The assault elements in the lead, led by Sarpedon himself with talons slashing, carved their way through twice that number by the time they reached the huge subterranean lakes of bile with their islands of folded skin, and the towering cathedrals with pillars of coagulated blood.

Ve'Meth knew they were there and his fortress was coming alive around them. The walls quivered and oozed and the defences became more and more organised the higher they got. Slave-packs blocked orifice doorways with piles of their dead. Serried ranks of warriors filled caverns with rows of pikes. Heavy weapons were dragged by deformed pack beasts into corridor junctions, studding the walls with gunfire before the weight of the Soul Drinkers' assault slew the gunners, turned the weapons around, raked the path ahead with fire and moved on.

Sarpedon knew they were close. The volcanic cupola of boiling pus was raging above them, and the black laughter echoed through his mind. He could feel a massive responsibility bearing down on him, oppressive as the fortress's stink – they were within striking distance now, and suddenly the possibility that they might get this far and fail was bright in Sarpedon's mind.

But he must leave no room for doubt. He was a commander, responsible for the most vital mission in his Chapter's history. They would kill Ve'Meth or they would die – either way they would not go back to the *Brokenback* having failed.

Sarpedon rounded a corner and saw the library before him. The cavern was as big as the Cathedral of Dorn had been back on the *Glory*. It walls were of bleeding veined meat, and gargantuan cases of books were piled on top of one another in crumbling towers. In a glance Sarpedon's augmented vision and quick mind saw the millions of volumes bound in daemon's hide with pages of skin and clasps of bone, the tablets of black rune-carved stone, and scrolls of tattoos cut from the backs of cultists. He could hear them whispering, gibbering their secrets in a thousand tongues, crammed mouldering into every space and lying in great rotting heaps in every corner.

This was the accumulated vileness that every perverted tongue had preached in the name of Ve'Meth, the vast tomb of blasphemy that fuelled the daemon prince's influence.

Sarpedon was about to call the flamer Marines forward when the first shell grazed a knee joint and slammed into a Marine from Squad Givrillian behind him.

A bolter shell. Sarpedon would recognise it anywhere – but it was different, a low-velocity mark that had not been issued to Space Marines for thousands of years...

'Traitors!' he yelled in warning, diving to the side as the fusillade opened up. A wall of bolter-fire tore across the library, shredding the tainted books and thudding into the Marines pouring in through the arched entrance. Twenty or more life-runes winked out at the edge of Sarpedon's vision as chunks were blasted out of the fleshy walls all around him.

Chaos Marines. The traitor legions. Those who turned from the Emperor's light and betrayed Mankind ten thousand years before, when the Emperor still walked among men and Rogal Dorn's Imperial Fists had yet to be split into their component Chapters. It was a sign, of course – the Architect of Fate had directed them to this place not just to kill Ve'Meth but to confront a symbol of what could happen when faith is lost and perverted, when the tendrils of the enemy reached into men's hearts and they forgot the sacred will of the Emperor.

He could see only the muzzle flashes from their positions hidden amongst the towering shelves and mounds of books on the other side of the chamber. They were disciplined and accurate – they had lost nothing of their martial prowess, for a Space Marine's quality as a soldier remained where loyalty and dignity did not.

'Charge!' rang the cry of Chaplain Iktinos and he led Squad Karvik's Assault Marines out into the library, hoping to rush the Traitor Marines under the covering fire of their battle-brothers. But the traitors seemed to ignore the fire tearing into the mouldering books and worm-ridden shelves around them, and Squad Karvik was cut to pieces, the survivors minus their sergeant scrambling into cover as the compacted meat of the floor erupted all around them. One of them grabbed the power sword of the fallen Sergeant Karvik. Sarpedon knew Karvik had carried the weapon for twenty years, and would have wanted nothing more in death than to know it would carry on his work in the hands of another.

'If we have to die, then we will,' voxed Iktinos on the command channel. 'But if there is an alternative, commander–'

'We need to flank them,' replied Sarpedon, thinking fast. 'Givrillian!'

'Unlikely, commander,' replied Sergeant Givrillian, who clambered through the debris to Sarpedon's side. 'They have an elevated field of fire and excellent cover. We will be impeded and exposed all the way.'

Givrillian was right. The Soul Drinkers would have to forge on right through several tottering bookcases, ten metres high or more – they would either break through them and bring tonnes of rotting debris down on their heads, or climb them which would be like scaling a sheer cliff under fire. Either way the Traitor Marines would have free rein to pour fire into them as the Soul Drinkers moved, and would probably redeploy as soon as Sarpedon got into any kind of flanking position.

But all was not lost. There was always hope, even if that hope was merely for a good death in battle with the Enemy.

'Iktinos?'

'Commander?'

'I believe we shall die. Pray for us, then lead the charge.'

GRAEVUS KEPT GOING as the rushing torrent of blood threatened to close over his head. His feet crunched through piles of bones on the bed of the channel, and there were tiny, sharp things zipping past him with the flow.

He was in the heart of his spearhead, with Tellos and the assault squads ahead of him and Karraidin in the rear. They had known the instant they entered the fortress that they were in some living thing, and had soon found themselves wading through the sludge in its intestines, shielding themselves from the noxious fumes exuding from the pulpy walls of its lungs, and now struggling through the gushing tunnels of its veins. They could feel its evil heartbeat through the floor and hear its slow breathing rumbling through the walls. And Graevus could hear the buzzing of the corpulent insect-god that brooded at its peak, waiting for them, thirsting for the prize of a Space Marine's blood.

'Opening ahead!' came the vox from Sergeant Hastis, whose assault squad was on point.

'Take it!' replied Graevus, knowing that even Space Marine power armour would suffer from immersion in this caustic, befouled gore that passed for the fortress's blood.

Ahead of him the Soul Drinkers pulled each other out of the sucking blood flow. A hand reached down and a Marine – one of the half-armoured battle-brothers, hauled Graevus's bulk upwards onto the shelf of slick rock that led into to an upwards-curving inlet.

Storm bolter-fire sounded above the rush of the blood torrent. 'Something on our tail,' voxed Karraidin by way of explanation.

The gunfire kept stuttering.

'Karraidin? Is that still you?' asked Graevus.

'Negative, Graevus. Killed it.'

Bolter fire. Bolter fire, without a doubt – but not theirs, maybe Sarpedon's...

The first Graevus saw of the Chaos Space Marines was a severed head. It span back down the inlet, past Graevus as he followed Sergeant Tellos who, inevitably, was the first to sprint towards the gunfire. It wasn't a helmet, but a head – in the shape of a Space Marine helmet but covered with skin, with eyepieces that were not photoblocker lenses but wet, cataracted living orbs.

Tellos had carved his way through the first and Graevus barrelled past him into the next one. It had doubtlessly once been a Marine, but its skin had grown outside its armour, pink and bleeding from sores and tears. Some of its organs were outside, too, loops of necrotic entrails and pulsing, sputtering valves. Its face mask had sharp stained teeth instead of a filter grille, and its bolter muzzle had a fleshy mouth that spat that mark four bolter ammunition across the room. Tattooed onto the skin of one shoulder pad was a three-orbed symbol that Graevus had seen daubed onto the vehicles of turncoat armies and carved into the hides of victims massacred by Chaos cultists.

Graevus hardly noticed the towering piles of volumes and the great drifts of rotting books. He was only dimly aware of the bolter fire replying from below, where Sarpedon's Marines were trying to engage the Traitor Marines. His whole vision was filled by the Chaos Marine as he slammed the blade of his power axe into the enemy's midriff, carving right through the dead-fleshed torso.

The Chaos Marine tried to turn his bolter on his assailant, but Graevus's hand speed had increased so greatly since his axe arm had changed that the return stroke had already sliced the Chaos Marine in two through the spine. The axe whirled and the blade slashed down, hacking the Chaos Marine through the collar bone down to the mid-chest.

Tellos was already in the heart of the Chaos Marine position, killing all around him, with the Assault Marines beside him relishing the chance to follow him in forging a trail of the dead.

Bolter fire was raining down on them but all was confusion – the Chaos Marines were on the back foot now, breaking ranks to form a new firing line, but the Soul Drinkers were in no mood to stand around and let the enemy shoot at them.

Graevus looked through the mist of blood and saw the next target – a leader of some kind, wielding a sword edged with gnashing teeth.

He brought his axe blade out of the quivering body at his feet, and charged back into the fray.

'WE'VE GOT THEM pegged back, commander! Move while they're down!'

It was Karraidin's voice, but it might as well have come from the throat of Rogal Dorn himself.

'You heard the captain,' yelled Sarpedon. 'Move!'

The fire that came down onto them was broken and panicked. The sounds of blades through power armour rang from above as Sarpedon's spearhead crossed the foetid expanse of Ve'Meth's library to where the exit in the far wall was a raw, open wound.

Sarpedon leapt over the tumbled heaps of books and into the ribbed throat that curved upwards beyond.

Losing a leg hadn't slowed him down. And the laughter was so loud now it was drowning out his own thoughts. The aegis hood's protective circuitry was white-hot against his body as it struggled to protect his psyker's mind.

'This is it, sir?' said Givrillian at his side. It wasn't really a question.

'Stay close,' voxed Sarpedon. 'Fast, disciplined, and no one runs.'

He didn't need to say it. But they needed to hear it – words that had been drummed into them as novices, reminding them that the training and values that they had extolled all their lives as Soul Drinkers would still serve them here.

They didn't know how they would kill Ve'Meth. They didn't really know what Ve'Meth was. The few of them who had seen a daemon prince on the field of battle each carried a violently different memory, for Chaos was ever-changing and never rose twice in the same form.

Ve'Meth could be anything. But there wasn't much that bolter and chainsword couldn't kill.

The throat was steep but none of them stumbled. The muscles shifted and contracted, trying to throw them off, but they dug their fingers into the rubbery flesh and held on.

At the top a clenched fist of flesh blocked their path. Chainsword slashed through it and Sarpedon ripped his way through with his talons, staff in hand, ready to shred whatever he saw on the other side.

It took a split-second for his eyes to adjust to the darkness. The whole fortress had been pitch-black but this was something else, an abysmal pit of darkness, as if the magnitude of evil here had sucked up the light and devoured it.

Then his augmented eyes forced an image out of the darkness, and he saw Ve'Meth's true form for the first time.

Ve'Meth was a multitude of bodies – between seven and nine hundred at Sarpedon's first count, standing rigid in square formation. There were men, women, in finery and engineer's overalls, primitive rags and camouflage, some squat and muscular from high-grav environments, some life-spacers with willowy limbs and thin faces. Every one had the same expression of intensity. Every one was looking at him.

Something stirred in their midst and Sarpedon saw one of them was holding a weapon – something old and crusted with runes, glowing with power. A gun.

The first bullet buzzed through Brother Nikkos's chest – and then it hit him again and again, whipping through the air in wide looping orbits to punch again and again through the Marine's armour. Nikkos toppled and came apart, armour joints clattering to the floor, slopping his sliced body onto the polished black coral.

Another shot barked from the weapon even as the return fire tore apart the first rank of Ve'Meth's bodies, riddling another Marine. Another, and another, each one singling out a Soul Drinker and piercing him a dozen times before he died.

Every mouth opened. Eight hundred voices laughed.

Marines were flooding into the chamber around Sarpedon but they were dying all around. Sergeant Dreo hurled himself to the ground as the bullet-daemon skimmed past him and dismembered one of his squad. Chaplain Iktinos strode forward, diving between two dying Marines to sweep his crozius arcanum through the three closest bodies – they were thrown through the air with a flash of the power field. More were dying with the bursts of return fire but the Soul Drinkers were dying faster and the air was filled with the hideous buzzing flight of the daemon-bullets.

A well-placed shot took the gun-wielding body in the throat but another stepped into its place in the ranks, took up the weapon and fired again. Time and time again the ancient gun barked and with every shot another battle-brother died, and every time the firer fell another took its place.

'Discipline! We have to kill them all!' yelled Sarpedon. Glancing to the side he saw Givrillian, the many-eyed Sergeant Givrillian who had been his most trusted and level-headed soldier, being speared by a tiny glowing monster even as he loosed a salvo of bolter shells into Ve'Meth.

Above the screams and the gunfire was the laughter, loud with the voices of Ve'Meth and louder still inside Sarpedon's head. He looked through the mayhem and saw Sergeant Dreo trying to form a firing line. Half his squad were dead.

They had to kill every body at once. That was how Ve'Meth ultimately defended itself – not with its soldiers or its daemon gun, but with the fact that it was formed of host bodies, hundreds of them, and Sarpedon was certain it could survive with just one. It could take more, too, and Sarpedon knew it would be pleased to take one of his battle-brothers if it could.

There was one way. He had seen it done often enough, but never like this. If enough of them stayed alive, if that discipline would hold even when every single one of them could die in the blink of an eye…

'Sergeant Dreo!' yelled Sarpedon. 'Execution duty!'

'Execution duty, line up on me!' bellowed Dreo. The surviving Soul Drinkers had all lined up for execution duty many times before, when traitors to the Emperor had been taken alive and sentenced to death, or when battle-brothers had committed some grave transgression for which death could be the only penalty. There had been enough executions following the Chapter war, when unrepentant rebels had been put to death with a massed bolter volley in the nave of the Cathedral of Dorn.

More died, a dozen at once. Gaps formed in the firing line even as it was formed. But Sergeant Dreo, the crack shot, didn't rush. He had been given charge of the execution on many times and knew full well that a clean kill needed one concentrated wall of fire. Many died in the seconds he paused. But it was one concentrated volley, or nothing.

The guns were in position, a line of bolters stretching two deep across Ve'Meth's chamber, the front rank kneeling.

'Fire!' yelled Dreo, and the front rank opened fire.

As one, a hundred of Ve'Meth's bodies fell, bodies punched open by the explosive bolter shells that ripped through them. The front rank emptied their magazines into a sheet of shrapnel that tore into the host bodies. The gun wielder fell and another bent to take up the weapon, to be torn apart in turn.

The front rank paused to change magazines and the rear rank came in flawlessly, keeping up a steady stream of fire that swept across the chamber. By the time the first rank took up the fire again they were pouring bolter shells into the mangled remains of eight hundred bodies, oozing tainted blood onto the black coral.

'Cease fire!' barked Sergeant Dreo. 'Good kill.'

The silence was shocking. Sarpedon lowered his bolter and through the gunsmoke stared at all that remained of Ve'Meth – a room full of broken bodies, blood spattered up the walls, torn limbs and bodies heaped across the floor.

A screaming began – quiet at first, but growing louder and louder. A grainy cloud of pestilence rose from the bodies. It solidified and darkened, and in its depths Sarpedon could see movement – huge shapes, filth-caked, daemon-plagued worlds, plunging away through space, falling into the darkness, hurling away from him and out of sight, faster and faster.

The screaming reached a pitch so loud Sarpedon could hear nothing else. He knew what he was watching – this was the empire of Ve'Meth, the kingdom it would have built in the name of its god, the empire that Sarpedon had destroyed before it could be forged. Unable to survive outside its host bodies, the daemon prince didn't mind dying, but its dreams of domination were dying with it, and that it could not stand.

The horror. The agony. Everything Ve'Meth had feared was coming to pass and it poured its hatred and terror out into the chamber, filling it with a screech of rage and the huge dark image of a universe cleaned of his presence. Then the scream became weak and the image pale, as Ve'Meth's lifeforce dissipated. The dark miasma dissolved and the chamber fell quiet.

The aegis circuit was calm. The vast oppression of Ve'Meth was lifted and suddenly the ugliness was bleeding away from the world – the darkness was not quite so complete, the stench was bearable, the weight of evil was lightening.

'Mission complete, my brothers,' said Sarpedon. 'Count the dead and regroup.'

SERGEANT GRAEVUS WATCHED as the Plague Marine dissolved. It was screaming, but the sound was dulled by the layers of ceramite and muscle that covered it. Graevus had been sure his Marines would battle the traitors to a standstill in the towering library, and that they would grind each other down until there was nothing left. The assault had swept through the Chaos positions but the enemy were undaunted and supremely resistant to injury, and Soul Drinkers were beginning to die. If that was the way it had to be, then that was how Graevus would have died – but then there had been a terrible keening from the otherwise silent Plague Marines and the traitors had convulsed with a sudden shock.

The Soul Drinkers had not paused to ponder their luck. Instinctively, Graevus knew that Sarpedon had done something magnificent at the fortress's peak, but most of his mind was concentrating on driving his axe blade through the enemies before him.

Now the Plague Marines were dead or dying, dismembered by the Assault Marines or riddled with bolter shells as they reeled. Some had pitched over the edge of the towering bookcases and been broken on the floor far below. Those who did not die by the hands of Soul Drinkers were dying all the same, their bodies liquefying as the Marines watched.

The Plague Marine was on his knees – his lower legs were gone. Alternate layers of skin and metal were flaking away and the skeleton was started to be exposed, gnarled and twisted, riddled with wormholes. The body collapsed, losing all shape as heavy metal implants rolled out onto the ground.

Graevus turned from the stinking mess, feeling something suddenly different in his mind. The buzzing was gone.

The bloated insect-god was dead.

FROM ORBIT, THE unnamed planet turned dark and clear as the clouds dissolved. The thick layer of flies dissipated and the banks of yellowing pollution faded. Suddenly the sensoria aboard the *Brokenback* mapped out every detail of a world dominated by oceans and scattered with rocky islands – for the first time the crew could see the towering coral stacks and blood-soaked beaches of the archipelago, and pick out the rotting ships, suddenly pilotless, which foundered and broke up in the rough seas.

Communications were back. Commander Sarpedon requested transport immediately. Lygris authorised a wing of Thunderhawks to land on the body-choked shore in the shadow of the fortress – the auspex arrays found the island completely dead, where hours before it had teemed with unholy life. Sarpedon and Graevus met up on the beach, compared scars, and embarked onto the Thunderhawks.

As on the ordinatus platform so long ago, there was plenty of room on the gunships for the return flight. Of the four hundred Marines who had landed on the unnamed planet, half were dead, slain in the assault on the fortress-island, or lying at the bottom of the great ocean that girded the planet.

When they reached the huge dark bulk of the *Brokenback*, the first welcome they received was the screaming of a thousand sensors all over the space hulk. Lygris's anomaly had returned, and this time, it was vast... and closing.

SARPEDON SPRINTED DOWN the corridor, the stump of his severed leg trailing bandages where Apothecary Pallas had been dressing it when the alarms sounded. Lygris caught up to him at the next bulkhead, his anxious face picked out in the strobe of the warning lamps.

'We picked it up about six hours ago, but it faded out,' Lygris was saying. Serf-labourers ran past them, heading for damage control stations. 'I doubled the sensorium watch but it seemed just an anomaly. Now it's of a higher magnitude than most of our sensors can measure. We're using Sector Indigo to track it.'

'Where is it now?' Sarpedon had come straight from the apothecarion, which was packed with the Soul Drinker wounded. His armour was still crusted with unclean blood.

'Seventeen thousand kilometres at the last count. It's closing, but it's erratic.'

'Not natural.'

'No.'

'Ve'Meth's dead. The planet died with him. I want to know what this thing is before we're within turret range, and it's going to have to be one hell of an explanation to stop me opening fire.'

'I'm with you on that, commander.'

Sarpedon and Lygris reached the viewing chamber, its lavish décor crudely inappropriate. Several of the Chapter's Tech-Marines were directing servitors to aim their image intensifiers at the great nimbus of light that filled the whole oculus. The whole room was bathed in its silvery light, and at its heart something was solidifying, lithe and serpentine.

'Targets!' called Lygris.

'Not yet, sir,' replied Tech-Marine Varuk, who had lost most of a kneecap to bolter-fire in the fortress and had yet to visit the apothecarion. 'Half the sensors say it isn't there and the other half say it's a black hole. We're aiming guns by eye but it's a fraction of what this ship's got.'

Sarpedon was well aware of the kind of offensive force the *Brokenback* could muster, wielding as it did the armaments of several cruiser-sized Imperial craft and the arcane weaponry of sinister alien craft. But if there was a foe who would only be seen when he wanted, who could get up close...

Ve'Meth? No. Ve'Meth was dead. What, then?

The shape in the light shifted and became real – smooth skin, long and powerful limbs, twin silver stars for eyes. Occult symbols flashed in concentric circles which stayed imprinted on the eye. A hand reached out towards the oculus, and suddenly the figure was much, much closer.

'INCOMING-INCOMING-INCOMING...'

The voice, activated by early warning systems on one of the ancient component ships, boomed through the space hulk as something huge and powerful landed on the upper surface. The sensoria that should have seen it all overloaded simultaneously, burning out a hundred hard-wired servitors in a heartbeat.

The *Brokenback* shut down. The engines died, the life support systems reverted to failsafe and large areas of the hulk were flooded by hard vacuum. All helm control died and the *Brokenback* drifted helpless, as if awed by the power of the being that stood astride it. It reached down and long, graceful fingers dug into blackened metal. With a rippling of serpentine muscles, it ripped the top six decks off the *Brokenback*.

It looked down at the armoured humans that teemed in the corridors and gun decks. It shone a bright silver light down on them and opened the gate to his silver city, letting his beautiful minions drift down like falling stars onto the ship below.

'I am the Architect of Fate,' it said in a voice like music. 'I am the Engineer of Time. I am Abraxes, Prince of Change, and you are all my children.'

SARPEDON STARED UP at the towering figure shining against the blackness of space. He had seen some things in his decades as a Soul Drinker, not the least of them in the last few days. But none of them compared to this.

It was several kilometres tall. Wings of light spread out from its back, framing its beautiful face and flowing hair. Its body, muscular yet slim, was clad in a toga of flowing white silk, and arcane symbols glowed in wide circles all around it. Glowing figures were pouring from a disk of light that hung in space behind it – strange-shaped things made of pastel-coloured light and birds with feathers of amethyst.

Sarpedon had to tear his eyes away to see the desolation around him. The roof of the oculus room was gone, along with several decks of the space hulk, exposing a huge raw wound of broken metal to the vacuum of space that cut across countless sector and component ships. Gases vented from ruptured plasma conduits. Fractured capacitor spines flashed as their energy bled into the void.

The Soul Drinkers were hastily donning their helmets against the vacuum. In the distance a tiny white shape that was Father Yser convulsed as the air was dragged from his lungs and his limbs froze. Suffocated and ravaged by cold, the pressure drop tearing at his organs and with the sight of the Architect of Fate flaying his mind, Yser died in a dozen different ways at once.

Father Yser, who had taught the faith in the Architect to the Soul Drinkers Chapter in the depths of the Cerberian Field, what seemed a lifetime ago. He had been the vessel for the greatest revelation in the Chapter's history, he had guided the Soul Drinkers to the *Brokenback* and the unnamed planet. He had seen the terror that was Ve'Meth. And now he had been destroyed at the first sight of the being he worshipped.

'Weak,' said the musical voice again. 'See how weak it is? For one such as this, Commander Sarpedon, my mere presence is death. But you are different, are you not?'

Sarpedon knew the vox was nothing more than static and his voice wouldn't sound outside his own helmet. But he spoke anyway, certain that the thing that called itself Abraxes could hear him.

'What are you?' he asked. 'How do you know who I am?'

'The second question first, commander. I have watched you for so long, searched the galaxy for someone who could make himself more than the dullards who infest your worlds. You burn so bright, Sarpedon. I could not fail to notice you even from the Silver City where my lord holds court.

'And what am I? I am Abraxes, herald of the Lord of Change. I am your salvation. I am the glory that Yser saw in his dreams, and that turned him into a beacon for you and your battle-brothers. I am the one who granted you visions, Sarpedon, of the foulness I would have you destroy. I gave you this beautiful ship, and see how easily I could destroy it. And

I am he who blessed your body and the bodies of your brothers, forged the strength of your mind so the daemons of the warp fled before you.

'I am your prince and you are my subjects, for you have done my will ever since you saw the folly of your Imperium. I am the Architect of Fate, the Engineer of Time. I am the glory and the essence of what the smallest of minds call Chaos.'

It wasn't true. It couldn't be. But…

The daemon prince brimmed with power the like of which not even Ve'Meth had possessed. Abraxes was the figure Sarpedon had seen daubed by Yser's flock, and carved into the statue that stood alongside the primarch in the Cathedral of Dorn. And the shimmering creatures that were teeming down onto the mangled surface of the *Brokenback* were surely daemons. Yes, this was a great and powerful prince of Chaos that bestrode the space hulk, the same one who had spoken to the Soul Drinkers in the guise of the Architect of Fate.

Sarpedon had thrown aside ten thousand years of service to the Imperium, because he saw honour in the Emperor where there had been none in the Imperium. But now he saw that what they believed to be the Emperor's will was nothing more than one more lie – the machinations of Abraxes, who had wished only to rid himself of a fellow daemon.

The knowledge was flooding over Sarpedon, and it was more than he could bear. He had been so sure they had achieved something magnificent, that they had thrown off the shackles of weak humanity and become the true soldiers of the Emperor – could they really be nothing? Could they really be worse than nothing, the foulest of traitors not through malice but by ignorance?

The star fort. The ordinatus. The Cerberian Fields and the *Brokenback*. Ve'Meth. What had the Soul Drinkers done? Try as he might, he couldn't help but remember the words of Inquisitor Tsouras's envoy and Chapter Master Gorgoleon – words like treachery, heresy, daemonancy. Sarpedon had killed both men, and now the horrible realisation was dawning that both had been right.

The Soul Drinkers had performed the will of Chaos. They were as much a part of the armies of the enemy as the Traitor Marines they had battled in the fortress of Ve'Meth. They had been pawns in the game of the Dark Gods, soldiers in the army of corruption. That they did not know what they had been doing was irrelevant. No true servant of the Emperor considered ignorance a defence. The Soul Drinkers were Chaos Marines.

'Ah, he understands,' said the voice like a thousand choirs. 'He knows what he is. He has thrown away the purity he held so dear, and done it willingly. He has turned his back on his allies, slain my enemies at my behest, accepted his mutant form as a blessing. And he has done all this without coercion. Sarpedon understands what he is, and he understands that there is no turning back.'

'It's not true,' Sarpedon heard himself gasping.

Abraxes smirked. 'You know yourself, mutant. I do not lie.'

Mutant. That word... and then Sarpedon felt it once more, the vile oppression of uncleanliness, the mantle of loathing that draped over him. It was just as he had felt when he had consumed the flesh of the mutant on the star fort, a crushing weight of the universe's loathing. His blood was impure, his flesh corrupt, his skin tainted. Every eye that looked upon him would do so with hatred. He was the lowest of the low – mutant, inhuman, vermin.

It would be falling on his battle-brothers, too – Graevus with his executioner's hand, Tellos with his heightened senses and strange metabolism. Even Givrillian, steadfast Givrillian slain in the grand chamber of Ve'Meth, was a deformed mutant. As Abraxes lifted the illusion of nobility from their minds the vileness of mutation would be sweeping over them as it was over Sarpedon.

Sarpedon sunk to the twisted deck, his unholy, unnatural insect legs splayed around him. Mutant. Traitor. Soldier of Chaos.

Abraxes was standing right over Sarpedon. He reached down and Sarpedon looked up through tears of rage – there was something in the daemon prince's hand, like a needle held between the gargantuan fingers.

'But Sarpedon, it pains me to see you so distressed.' Abraxes's face was troubled and sincere. 'Can you not see what you could be? You and your Chapter have achieved astonishing things. You have thrown aside the shackles of the Imperium, and you did it yourselves, for I merely stood back to watch. You proved your strength of mind when you turned your back on the tradition of mindless authority that threatened to make you weak. And with my guidance you destroyed Ve'Meth, who was a twisted parody of the glories of Chaos.

'Chaos is a wonderful thing, Sarpedon – it is freedom incarnate, where all things can change and the universe is subject only to the will of the strong. It is what you have been seeking all along, a release from the hypocrisy and dishonour of the Imperium. You sought the Emperor's blessing, because you were still naïve in the ways of the universe. The Emperor is nothing, Sarpedon, a corpse on a throne, to whom you were devoted only because you did not know what true Chaos could give you. But now I have shown you, and can you honestly say that you and your Chapter can truly follow anything other than Chaos and the glorious lord of change?'

It was true, all true. Had he really believed it was the Emperor who had granted him this foul mutation and the heretical visions that guided the Chapter to Ve'Meth?

The object Abraxes was holding was about the length of Sarpedon's forearm, a gleaming cylinder of microcircuitry that shone in the starlight. 'My lord is the only power in this galaxy worth fighting for. Join me, march as my soldiers across the stars, and give yourself to destruction in the name of the changeling god. What else is there? Your Emperor is nothing, your Imperium has excommunicated you. The only purpose you have left is the pursuit of Chaos, which you have executed so well already. There is no need for you to live a lie any longer, Sarpedon. You can have what you wanted at last – a lifetime spent in the service of a power you can believe in, towards a goal you can achieve. And in the name of my God, I wish to show you my gratitude for slaying my enemy.'

The Soulspear. A lifetime ago, it had been the only thing that mattered. It had torn the Chapter apart and set in motion a chain of events that had left the Soul Drinkers broken and heretic, with nothing left but to throw their lot in with the power which had shown itself to be a true god. The Soulspear – ancient and powerful, the artefact that should have cemented those Chapter traditions that had, instead, been thrown away.

Sarpedon reached up and took the Soulspear from Abraxes. It could be a new beginning. The Soulspear could be the symbol of a new Chapter, formed from the ashes of the Soul Drinkers, following a god that could reward them for their devotion. Sarpedon could lose himself in the eternity of battle, wielding the Soulspear as a mark of how he had broken away entirely from the lies of the Imperium and the corpse-Emperor. He could exult in the slaughter of the change god's enemies. He could blaze a trail of death against the stars, and have a purpose in slaughter that he had sought for so long.

From the back of Sarpedon's mind rose, unbidden, the snippets of history he had learned as a novice, when the story of the Soulspear had been one of pride and anger at its loss. It had been given to the Chapter by the Primarch Rogal Dorn, to show that he held them in no less esteem than the great Imperial Fists legion from which the Soul Drinkers had been founded. The custody of such an artefact had shown that the Soul Drinkers had their place in the grand plan of the Emperor, that they were beholden to His will.

Something stirred in Sarpedon's mind. Why had he turned the guns of his Marines on the tech-guard, and slain the envoy of Inquisitor Tsouras when he had declared the Chapter Excommunicate? Was it pride? Anger? Or something else, something he only had to realise?

He glanced across at his brother Marines. He saw Tellos, unarmoured as always, and it was somehow no surprise that the hard vacuum didn't seem to affect him. He saw Graevus and Karraidin, Tech-Marine Lygris, Apothecary Pallas and all the other Soul Drinkers who had followed Sarpedon through everything. Most had witnessed the catastrophe of the star fort and the hell of Ve'Meth, and all had fought through the horror of the Chapter war. Sarpedon could have led them through hell and every single one of his battle-brothers, he was sure, would have followed. If he bowed before Abraxes, they would follow him again. And they would follow him to the death if he did not.

Sarpedon's fingers tightened around the Soulspear. He found the row of pits in the cylinder's surface, and felt the tiny lasers punch through the skin of his gauntleted fingertips.

Rogal Dorn had resisted breaking up the Imperial Fists legion until he risked being branded a rebel. When forced to relent he had taken great pains to ensure each of the Chapters who bore his gene-seed were held in equal esteem, infused with the belief in independence and nobility that had characterised the Imperial Fists. Why had he done so? Was it just fatherly pride, for the Imperial Fists and their successors were in many ways his sons? Or was there something else?

Rogal Dorn had realised something that was beginning to dawn on Sarpedon, too. And as it did so Abraxes's spell was breaking. Would the other Soul Drinkers realise in time? Perhaps they were already lost to Abraxes. It some ways it didn't really matter any more.

His blood seeped through the pinprick holes in his fingertips and touched the gene-encoders built into the Soulspear. It was one of the weapon's secrets that it was attuned to the blood of Rogal Dorn, who had first discovered it. Only those whose veins flowed with Dorn's blood – the Imperial Fists or their successor Chapters, like the Soul Drinkers – could wield it. The weapon was hot and thrumming in Sarpedon's hand.

Abraxes stepped back. The shimmering daemons were gathered around his feet. 'Choose, Sarpedon.'

But Sarpedon had already chosen.

Twin spikes of pure vortex leapt from the Soulspear, infinitely darker than even the black backdrop of space. Sarpedon flexed his unholy mutant legs and prepared to run. He would have to be fast, and hope that the ship's gravitic field wasn't damaged. He would need to be strong and accurate, and would have to rely on his battle-brothers to do what was right.

He fixed the Daemon Prince Abraxes with a determined eye. 'This Chapter,' he said grimly, 'is owned by no one.'

Sarpedon charged. There was no way to communicate with his fellow Soul Drinkers, but he didn't need to.

Karraidin closed the fastest, barrelling into the closest daemons, shining creatures of pink and pastel blue light with serpent-fingered hands and huge gaping maws. His storm bolter chattered silently in the vacuum, shells ripping into the luminescent bodies. Tellos was right behind him and literally dived into the fray, blades swinging through daemonic limbs. Streaks of light flickered soundlessly against the blackness of space as every Soul Drinker opened fire, engaging the daemonic horde that had descended onto the *Brokenback*. Dreo waved the closest Marines towards him and was forming a firebase from which he could send volleys of fire raking across the landscape of twisted metal. Luko was charging across the broken deck, gathering Marines as he did so.

All they had to do was to keep the daemons occupied, while Sarpedon struck.

The missing leg didn't slow him. He propelled himself towards the towering figure of Abraxes, the Soulspear in his hand. The daemon prince's face showed shock and anger as the battle erupted around his feet. The rings of arcane symbols that shone around him turned to angry reds and yellows, his shining eyes turned dark, and ruddy veins stood out against his alabaster skin as he channelled his rage into strength.

'Fools!' Abraxes roared. 'You are nothing! Nothing!'

Sarpedon ignored him, and the only sound was his own breathing. He would have to be fast, and he would have to be accurate. He didn't know if he could do it. But it didn't matter if he couldn't – for if there was one thing that had not changed, it was that to die fighting the Enemy was an end in itself.

Fungus-bodied things, whose arms ended in flame-belching orifices, bounded into Sarpedon's path. Triple slashes of light darted and Luko's lightning claws felled two of the monstrous daemons, chainblades lashing out from the Soul Drinkers at his side. The daemons came apart, their shining flesh disintegrating. Sarpedon ran through them, swinging the Soulspear and carving the scattered daemons in two as he passed.

He drew his arm back, focusing on the huge pale-skinned torso of Abraxes. Silver fire rained from the daemon prince's outstretched hands, punching through Sarpedon's armour like bolts of molten metal but Sarpedon couldn't afford to falter now.

He flexed his seven mutant legs and jumped, tensing his arm. The fire was ripping through him now, shards of pain shearing into his torso.

He felt one lung puncture and another leg torn and useless. The glare from Abraxes was blinding – there was bolter-fire stitching across Abraxes's chest and shafts of light were bleeding out into space.

Everything slowed down. There was nothing in the universe but Abraxes, Sarpedon and the sacred weapon in his hand. There was only one sound now, a rhythmic thumping that was getting faster and louder as Sarpedon hurtled closer. It was Abraxes's heartbeat, quickened by anger, pumping silver fire through the daemon prince's veins.

Sarpedon hit, jabbing his talons into the glowing skin of Abraxes's chest. Clinging to the daemon prince, burning with magical fire, Sarpedon drove the point of the Soulspear through the skin and into the huge beating blasphemy of Abraxes's heart.

AFTERWARDS, FOR MOST of the time Sarpedon would remember very little. But sometimes, when before he had dreamt of the battlements on Quixian Obscura, he would dream of a massive flare like the birth of a new sun, a beam of light that ripped from Abraxes's ruptured heart. The pure madness of the warp that was the daemon prince's lifeblood flooded out into space, hurtling Sarpedon away on a tide of fire, pouring out onto the shattered decks of the *Brokenback*.

He would recall the daemons of the change god drowned in liquid fire, screaming and gibbering even in the soundless vacuum as their flesh dissolved. Then, as the dream faded, the ball of white fire that had been Abraxes would implode into a ball of blackness that sucked in the many-coloured flame and disintegrating daemons. Soul Drinkers clung to the battered metal to avoid being dragged into the vortex. A gauntleted hand – Sarpedon would never discover who it belonged to – grabbed one of Sarpedon's flailing legs and hauled him down to the deck.

Then silence would fall, the light would die, and Sarpedon would awake.

SARPEDON LIMPED ONTO the new bridge of the *Brokenback*. It had been several months in the construction – a hard armoured bubble in the heart of the space hulk, which acted as a focus for all the many control systems that ran throughout the various component ships. On the cavernous front curve of the sphere was set a huge viewscreen, displaying a composite image taken from all the sensoria studding the hulk's hull.

The place was silent aside from the distant rumble of the engines and the gentle thrum of the control consoles. Sarpedon hobbled across the metal deck of the bridge and up onto the command pulpit. The prosthetic strapped to the stump of his missing leg clacked on the floor as he walked – the replacement bionic would take some time and was providing a learning experience for the Chapter apothecarion. Two other legs were badly fractured and were still splinted – a Space Marine healed quickly but it would still be weeks before Sarpedon lost his lopsided, limping gait.

The control lectern in front of him flashed with readouts and weapons runes. The Tech-Marines kept on finding new directional thrusters and weapon arrays, and it was a race to keep them all connected to the bridge as quickly as they were discovered. It would take years to explore the *Brokenback* fully, and there were doubtless places and systems aboard that would never be properly explained.

This was the home of the Soul Drinkers now – a space hulk that had been found drifting and polluted, now cleansed and made holy. It was indicative of the Chapter as a whole – they had been cleansed, too, of all the millennia of lies that had afflicted them. It had cost them terribly, with losses bordering on the irreplaceable. But that would not be enough to break the Chapter – the great harvest would begin again, where the *Brokenback* would descend on scattered backwards worlds and select the bravest youths for induction into the Chapter. It had been Sarpedon's first order when he had woken in the apothecarion, burned and broken – the Soul Drinkers would gather a new generation of novices and begin to replace all that they had lost. It would take time, but they had been lost for so many thousands of years that time was not a worry.

Perhaps some of what Abraxes had said was true. Perhaps the Emperor was nothing more than a corpse on a throne, dead and powerless. Such a thought would be the pinnacle of heresy for a law-abiding Imperial citizen, but the Soul Drinkers had long since ceased to care about such things. Perhaps the Chapter really was alone, without any power to lend them strength and show them the way.

But it didn't matter. The Emperor might be dead, but there were still principles He symbolised that were worth fighting for. The horror of Chaos was very real, and just because the Emperor didn't guide their hand it didn't mean that the Soul Drinkers couldn't follow the ideals He represented. Chaos was worth fighting, not because the Emperor was telling them to but because destroying the enemy was the right and noble thing to do.

The Soul Drinkers had been lapdogs of a corrupt Imperium for thousands of years, and then the slaves of Chaos. But they had thrown aside both these masters – and in any case, they had destroyed two terrible princes of Chaos, and was that not something they could be proud of, no matter that else might have happened?

This was the Soul Drinkers' fate – they would fight Chaos wherever they found it, spurning all masters, renegade and alone. They had been born to fight and fight they would – they didn't need the Emperor or anyone else to give them a reason to take up arms. When Sarpedon had recovered and the Chapter was rebuilt, there would be nothing to stop them. It was a lofty ambition, to be devoted to the destruction of Chaos, when they were hated by Chaos and Imperium alike and could never rely on allies from anywhere. But if that was the only way the Soul Drinkers could fight the good fight, that was how it would be.

Perhaps it was ridiculous, or ironic. Sarpedon was past caring. He would die fighting to fulfil the principles the Emperor had founded the Imperium upon, and which had been betrayed by the liars who ruled in his name.

And so on the bridge of the space hulk, the mutant and excommunicate Space Marine vowed to do the Emperor's work.

†HE BLEEDING CHALICE

CHAPTER ONE

THE YEARS LAY SO heavily on the corridors of the Librarium Terra that the very air was thick with age. The endless tottering rows of bookcases and verdigrised datastacks seemed chained down by the weight of the thousands upon thousands of years of history. The librarium was deep within the planet's crust but even som the indistinct hum of activity droned through the labyrinthine corridors, just as it did everywhere else on the holy hive world of Terra. It was the sound of billions of souls grinding their way through the bureaucracy that kept the Imperium of Man together.

Even the captain of the deletions unit felt the sheer importance of the information that filled the librarium. He had lived on Terra all his life, immersed in the endless repetition of the myriad tasks that made up the government of the Imperium. He had done his job since birth, just as his forebears had done, and the shadows beneath Terra comprised his whole world.

But even he, after the decades spent performing his thankless task, had some instinctive understanding that the Librarium Terra held a repository of particularly pure, dangerous history.

The captain glanced around the next corner. The gallery he saw was lined with shelves of books so old they were little more than banks of rotting paper, lit by yellowed glow-globes that picked out the faint silver spider's webs that had been there, undisturbed, for as long as some of the books.

No one knew the full layout of the Librarium Terra. Estimates of its size varied, as no one had been to its furthest extents and returned – the deletions team had taken three days of forced marching to get this far. But, by the best estimates of the adepts who gave the unit its orders, the objective was close by.

The captain waved his ten-strong unit forwards. They wore black bodysuits with hoods that left only the eyes visible, rebreathers built in to keep aeons of dust out of their lungs. Their gloved hands held narrow-nozzled flamers connected to fuel canisters on their belts. But the captain carried a silenced autogun with a flaring flash suppressor. They moved quickly and almost silently, each one covering the other. They had always been members of the same unit, just as the captain had always commanded them. The captain didn't need to actually give them orders – they just did as they had always done, as generations had done in the endless predator's game beneath Terra.

The captain hurried down the gallery until it opened onto a landing overlooking a tangled knot of bookcases and datastacks. The cases held huge leather-bound volumes, tarnished infoslates, crumbling scrolls and reams of parchments, crammed onto shelves that had collapsed here and there into drifts of tattered paper. The datastacks, blocks of smooth black crystalline material that could store remarkable amounts of information, ranged from sinister glossy black obelisks to elaborate info-altars covered in filigree decoration and crowned with clusters of statues. Several of them bore images of the Adeptus Astartes, the armour-clad Space Marines who formed the elite of the Imperium's armed forces, battling aliens and corruption across the distant stars.

The captain peered into the gloom that flooded the labyrinth below. He spotted movement – a scholar worked in an alcove formed by the cases. Surrounded by discarded books he was leafing rapidly through another. His face was incredibly wizened and his arms had been replaced with jointed metal armatures that flicked through the book's pages with incredible speed. The scholar could have been a servitor, a mind-wiped automaton that was human only in the sense that it was formed from a rebooted human brain. Or it could have been a sentient human, a loyal servant of Terra like the captain himself, acting out some task that was probably redundant and meaningless but which represented the loyalty of everyone on Terra to the immortal God-Emperor.

The captain raised his autogun close to his face and focused on the hairless, tight-skinned skull of the scholar. The autogun coughed once and the scholar's skull crumpled suddenly as if paper-thin. The body slumped and fell, sprawling against the shelf behind it and disappearing beneath a cascade of books.

There were to be no witnesses to a deletion. That was the way it had always been done. Had the scholar been aware of it, he would have understood why he had to die.

The captain vaulted from the balcony down into the shadows below. The rest of the unit followed him, their feet padding on the tarnished wood of the floor as they landed. Down here the air was so heavy with age and knowledge that moving around was like walking through water. The faint, sickly glow from the electro-lanterns dotted here and there served only to make the shadows harder. The captain spotted some titles and dates on the volumes on the shelves. These books held details of the Imperium's armed forces, regimental histories of the Imperial Guard and accounts of long-forgotten battles. The deaths of billions of men were glossed over in those pages, and the captain could almost hear them screaming from the same pages that praised their sacrifice to the Emperor.

A simple hand signal, and the deletions team spread out, each taking a section of bookshelf and pulling out volumes at random, glancing at the covers and contents and then casting them to the floor. A servitor appeared without warning, its deformed splay-fingered hands spinning along the floor in a fruitless attempt to keep it clean. The nearest of the unit turned, sprayed a lance of flame through its vulnerable soft human core, and turned back to his work as the servitor shuddered and died in a burst of sickly smoke.

Another unit member hurried up to the captain. He was holding a book of red leather, its pages edged in gold. On the cover was a raised symbol of glittering black stone – a chalice surrounded by a spiked halo. It was the symbol they had been ordered to look out for.

The captain tapped the nearest deletions trooper on the shoulder. The trooper then tapped the nearest to him, and the signal passed through the whole team in a heartbeat. They dropped whatever they were holding and drew their flamers.

They fired plumes of flame into the bookshelves, filling the power-charged air of the Librarium Terra with the stink of flame and smoke. The protective clothing of the team reflected the worst of the heat but the labyrinth was still a furnace, with walls of superheated air billowing between the burning cases.

The captain removed the magazine of his autogun and replaced it with a single round picked from his belt. He aimed at the closest datas-tack, which was shaped like a three-panelled altarpiece with its mem-crystal worked into heroic images of battle. The gun fired again, with barely a sound, and the explosive round shattered the crystal into a flood of broken black glass.

Wordlessly, with an efficiency born of generations of toil, the deletions unit moved through the whole section of the library, burning and shattering anything that might hold the information they had been ordered to destroy. Already the energy suppression drones were hovering in from around every corner, projecting dampener fields that held back the heat of the fires and kept them from spreading. When the team left, the drones would move in and their overlapping fields would smother the flames – but not before the books and datastacks were reduced to smoke and ash.

Centuries of history were lost. Whole planets and military campaigns vanished forever from the Imperial memory. But more importantly by far, the deletion order had been carried out, and all official record of the Soul Drinkers Chapter was erased from the history of Mankind.

LIKE MOST OF the rest of the Imperium, no one really knew when Koris XXIII-3 had been settled. The grey-green, mostly featureless world had supported continent-spanning grox farms for longer than the Administratum could accurately record. The agri-world supported barely ten thousand souls, but was a subtly critical link in the macro economy of the systems that surrounded it, for grox formed a commodity as vital as guns or tanks or clean water.

Grox were huge, lumbering, reptilian, unsanitary and foul-minded. Crucially, however, they were almost entirely edible, each producing a mound of colourless, tasteless, stringy but nutritionally sound processed meat. Without the grox that were lifted from Koris XXIII-3 in vast-bellied cargo ships every three months, the billions of workers and gangers on the nearby hive worlds would starve, riot, and die. The shipyards of half a segmentum would find their human fuel faltering.

The Administratum knew how important the grox were. They administered the agri-world directly, circumventing tax-dodging governors and grafting private enterprise by keeping their own adepts as the sole power and, indeed, the whole population.

Very little of interest happened on Koris XXIII-3, a situation the adepts of the Administratum had worked hard for. The roaming herds of grox and the small islands of adept habitats went centuries with scant incident, the passing years marked only by the arrival of the huge dark slabs of the cargo ships and the occasional desultory deaths, births and promotions amongst the handful of humans.

So when a ship actually landed at the planet's only spaceport at Habitat Epsilon, carrying something other than another adept to replace a stampede death, it was a rare event. The ship was small and very, very fast, mostly composed of a cluster of flaring engines that tapered to a sharp wedge of a cockpit. There were no markings and no ship name, whereas an Administratum ship would bear the stylised alpha of the organisation. Adept Median Vrintas, the highest-ranking adept in the habitat, guessed that the ship carried someone or something important. She quickly donned her black formal Administratum robes and hurried across the meagre, dusty streets of the habitat to greet the ship's occupant.

She didn't know how right she was.

Habitat Epsilon, like every other structure on the planet, was formed of gritty brown rockcrete, pre-moulded and dropped from low orbit. The buildings were ugly and squat, the architecture featureless and windowed with dark reflective glass that kept the glare of the orange evening sun from the offices, workrooms and tiny living quarters. The spaceport was the only feature that made Habitat Epsilon remarkable, a prefabricated circle jutting from the edge of the habitat. There was a small unmanned landing control tower and a few unused maintenance sheds, indicative of how very few ships landed there.

A section of the ship's hull lowered with a faint hiss of hydraulics. Feet tramped down the ramp and three squads of battle-sisters marched out. Soldiers of the Ecclesiarchy, the church of the Emperor and the spiritual backbone of the Imperium, they wore ornate black power armour that clad them from gorget to foot and carried enough firepower in their boltguns and flamers to reduce the habitat to smoking rubble. Their leader was more stern-faced than the rest of the Sisters, and old in a way that suggested she was a damn good survivor. She bore a huge-bladed power axe. The armour of the Sisters was glossy black with white sleeves and tabards – order and squad markings had been removed.

The sister superior said nothing to Adept Median Vrintas as the Sisters of Battle filed out onto the spaceport's ferrocrete surface. They flanked the ship as an honour guard, weapons readied – as if anything in Habitat Epsilon could threaten them. Adept Vrintas had heard of the Sisters of Battle, of their legendary faith and skill at arms, but she had never seen one of them in the flesh. Was this some priestly delegation, then? The Missionaria Galaxia, or a confessor come to see to the planet's spiritual health? Vrintas mentally congratulated herself on having the habitat's small Ecclesiarchy temple swept out just three days before.

The next figure to emerge from the ship was a man. He was not particularly tall but his considerable presence was aided by the carapace armour that covered his torso and upper arms and the floor-length blast-coat of brown leather lined with flakweave plates. His face was long and lined, his jaw pronounced and his nose slightly lumpy as if it had been broken and set a few times. His eyes were a curious greyish blue, larger and more expressive than eyes set in that face had a right to be. His black hair was starting to thin. Subtle implants in one temple and behind the ear were for neuro-jacks, simple as far as augmetics went, but far beyond the means of any planet-bound adept. His hands were gloved – one held a data-slate.

He strode past his honour guard of Sisters, glancing at the sister superior with a barely perceptible nod. The watery sunlight of Koris XXIII-3 glinted off the rings on his free hand, that he wore over the black leather glove. The stiff breeze fluttered the hem of the blastcoat.

'Adept?' he asked as he walked up to Vrintas.

'I am Median Lachrymilla Vrintas, the chief adept of this habitat,' said Vrintas, tingling with the realisation that this visitor must be far, far more important than anyone she had ever met before. 'I oversee the planet's second most productive continent. We have five hundred million head of grox in nine…'

'I am not interested in the grox,' said the stranger. 'I ask only a few hours of your time and access to one of your adepts. There need be minimum disruption to your important work here.'

Vrintas was relieved to see a subtle smile on the man's face. 'Certainly,' she said. 'I shall need to know your name and office, for the records. We can't have just anyone wander around our facilities. And of course you and your colleagues will need to walk through our disinfectant footbaths. There will be quarantine protocols if you wish to leave the habitat as well, so once I know under whose authority you are acting…'

The man reached into his blastcoat and took out a small metal box. He flipped open the lid of the box and inside Vrintas saw a stylised 'I' of gleaming ruby in a silver surround. 'Authority of the Emperor's Inquisition,' said the man with the same smile. 'You need not know my name. Now, you will kindly direct me to Adept Diess.'

INQUISITOR THADDEUS was an extraordinarily patient man. It was this quality, above all others, that had kept him doing the Inquisition's work when men more violent, or brilliant, or strong-armed had found themselves lacking. The Ordo Hereticus, the branch of the Emperor's Inquisition that rooted out threats amongst the very men and women it was sworn to protect, needed all those qualities. But it also needed the understanding that the Imperium could not be healed of all its sicknesses at once.

It needed men who could see the enormity of a task that stretched well beyond their own lifetimes, and not give way to despair. Thaddeus knew that, as just one man, even with the magnitude of the resources he could command he could do but little in the grand scheme of the Imperium and the divine Emperor's wishes for mankind. At present he had a full company of Ordo Hereticus storm troopers and several squads of battle-sisters under Sister Aescarion, but he knew that even with their guns he could not hope to end the corruption and incompetence that threatened the Imperium from within – just as aliens and daemons threatened from without. The whole Inquisition had that responsibility. If the task was ever to be finished, it would be finished by men and women of the Ordo Hereticus, many generations distant.

Thaddeus understood all this, and yet was willing to give his life to the cause, because if he did not, who would?

It was precisely because of his patience that Thaddeus had been given his current task. The first inquisitor to have taken on this mission, a bloody-minded and morbidly stubborn soul named Tsouras, had been selected because he happened to be the only one available at that time. He had failed because he had no patience, only a burning determination to win visible triumphs to terrify and amaze those around him. Tsouras, and inquisitors like him, had their uses, but that mission had not been one of them. When there was time, the lord inquisitors of the Ordo Hereticus had selected Thaddeus to take over, because Thaddeus could succeed by picking away at the layers of lies and confusion until the truth was uncovered before its captors realised.

At that moment, Inquisitor Thaddeus wished he had not been given the mission at all. Though the higher purposes of the Inquisition were burned into his remarkably resilient mind, he was still ultimately just a man, and he knew a dead end when he saw it. The few available leads had dried up, and the man now sitting across the untidy desk opposite him was, grim as it sounded, possibly his last hope.

'I do hope I am not inconveniencing you,' said Thaddeus, who never saw any reason to be impolite no matter what his state of mind. 'I understand the importance of the work done here.'

'The numbers aren't important,' said Adept Diess. 'I just stamp forms all day.' Diess had, until recently, been a fit man, middle-aged but wearing well. Now he had given up on himself and was putting on weight, though he still looked sharper than anyone on this planet had a right to be.

Thaddeus cocked an eyebrow. 'You sound as if the Emperor's grox farms do little to inspire you. Median Vrintas would be discouraged to hear that.'

'If you had spent as much time as I have balancing the books for this place, you would know that Median Vrintas can hardly count. She can have her opinions but I keep this planet making the Administratum tithes.'

Thaddeus smiled. 'You speak freely. A rare thing, believe me. Refreshing, in a way.'

'If you have come here to kill me, inquisitor, you will do it no matter what I say. If you have not, you won't waste the bullet.'

Thaddeus sat back in the uncomfortable chair. The other adepts had shown the sense to leave the office before Thaddeus had to ask for them to be removed, so the only sound was the grinding of a cogitator somewhere in the back of the low-ceilinged room. Dust motes floated in the thick light from the setting sun outside.

The office was home to maybe thirty adepts, each at a partitioned workstation. Every wall and surface was covered with paper – statistical printouts, graphs, charts, graphic depictions of the many diseases that plagued the common grox, and grim notices reminding the adepts of the ceaseless sacrifice they were compelled to make for the Imperium. The Administratum tried to foster the same atmosphere whether it was running a palace or a workhouse – its members dedicated their lives to the work that kept the Imperium running, the unending mundanity of jobs without which the macro economy of the Imperium would collapse.

'You are an intelligent man, adept. Not many men of your station would know an inquisitor when they saw one. Median Vrintas certainly didn't. I have heard men swear blind we don't exist, or that we're all fighting evil gods and don't bother with the likes of mortals such as yourself. But you seem to know rather more than them. Am I right, consul?'

The adept smiled bitterly. 'I am glad to say I no longer hold that office.'

'I think we understand one another, Consul Senioris Iocanthus Gullyan Kraevik Chloure. You know what I am here to talk about.'

'It's been a long time since anyone called me that.' Chloure seemed almost nostalgic. 'I could have had command of a whole sector, if I'd just toed the line for a few years more. But, I wanted too much too fast. You've probably seen it before.'

'You understand,' said Thaddeus without changing his tone, 'that Inquisitor Tsouras condemned you to death in your absence.'

'I assumed so,' said Chloure. 'How many of the others got out?'

'Not many. Captain Trentius was spared, although he will never pilot anything larger than an escort. A few menials that Tsouras decided were sufficiently minor to be incapable of true incompetence. But most of the rest were executed. I must say, though Tsouras is not the subtlest of my colleagues, you have showed great resourcefulness in evading him for as long as you have.'

Chloure shrugged. 'I planet-hopped for a while. Faked up some references, I talk the talk so there weren't too many questions. I got posted here eventually, and I wasn't intending to go anywhere else. Not many people look on a place like this for a wanted man. At least, I thought so until you turned up.'

'You should know, consul, that you don't do anything in the Administratum without someone writing it down. Your paper trail was long and winding but I have associates who could follow it.'

'Well,' said Chloure. He looked more exhausted than frightened, as if he had always known this day would come and just wanted it over with. 'The Soul Drinkers.'

'Yes. The Soul Drinkers. In light of your cooperation, I shall let you begin.'

Chloure sat back and sighed. 'It was three years ago, you know the dates better than I do. Anyway, we had been detailed to take over the Van Skorvold star fort. We knew Callisthenes Van Skorvold had some alien trinket that was particularly valuable. We fed it into a couple of databases and found out it was the Soulspear.'

'The Soul Drinkers artefact?'

'The very same. It was a legend the search turned up, some poem about how it could level cities and kill daemons and such like, and how they'd lost it.' Chloure sat up sharply and leaned across the desk. 'I am a greedy man, inquisitor. I am ambitious. I could have let the Imperial Guard do it but I wanted it finished quicker and cleaner. I know I could have left the Soul Drinkers out of it entirely. If I had just played it by the book I would have saved us all a lot of grief. But like I said, I'm greedy. I mean, we all want something.'

'There are far graver sins, consul,' Thaddeus said, with a veneer of understanding that surprised many. 'You let the word go out that you had found the Soulspear. The Soul Drinkers would arrive, eliminate all resistance, and take the item, leaving you to march into the star fort unopposed. Is that the case?'

'If it had happened like that I wouldn't be shovelling grox dung for the rest of my life. But you know all of this.'

'What can you tell me about Sarpedon?'

Chloure thought for a second. 'Not much. I only saw him on the bridge screen. We had an Adeptus Mechanicus ship with us. They sent a teleport crew into the star fort and snatched the Soulspear right from under Sarpedon's nose.'

Thaddeus could imagine what Sarpedon must have looked like to the gaggle of naval officers and Administratum adepts – a Space Marine commander, a psyker, an angry man burning with betrayal.

Chloure was calm, having imagined his final reckoning with the Inquisition for some time, but even so the fear he must have felt when he first saw Sarpedon played briefly over his face. 'Were you able to judge his state of mind?' asked Thaddeus. 'His intentions?'

Chloure shook his head. 'I wish I could help you more, inquisitor. He was angry. He was prepared to kill anyone who got in his way, but you know that. You haven't found them, have you? That's why you're here. Not for me.'

Thaddeus's face betrayed nothing. 'The Soul Drinkers will be found, consul.'

'You must be desperate to have gone to the trouble of tracking me down. I was just along for the ride, Inquisitor Tsouras was calling the shots and presumably he couldn't help you. What did you think I could tell you?'

Chloure was a sharp man. In many ways he was the first decent adversary Thaddeus had encountered for some time. It was difficult to threaten a man who was perfectly resigned to his death sentence. He had guessed what Thaddeus was loathe to admit – the Soul Drinkers' trail had turned cold. There were barely any leads left from the debacle at the Cerberian Field when Tsouras and the battlefleet, nominally under Chloure's command, had been outfoxed and eluded by the fleet of the renegade Space Marine Chapter. Sarpedon and his Chapter numbered less than one thousand men, and such a force was barely a speck in the vastness of the Imperium, almost invisible against the boundless galaxy.

Chloure was, in a very real sense, one of Thaddeus's last hopes.

'You are one of the few surviving individuals to have had any contact with the Soul Drinkers,' continued Thaddeus. 'There is a chance you picked up something that Tsouras did not.'

Chloure smiled, almost in triumph. 'To think that a humble agriworld adept should cause the mighty Inquisition such woes! I can only tell you what you already know. Sarpedon won't give up, not ever. He cares for his honour more than his life or those of his men. He'll run if you make him and attack whatever the risks if there's a principle at stake. That's all I know. From the sound of it, that's all anyone knows.'

Thaddeus stood up grandly, letting his blastcoat sweep around him. 'The Inquisition knows where you are, consul. You do the Emperor's work much better here than if you had attained a higher rank, I feel, and for this reason you can consider your execution indefinitely stayed.

But should your standards fall, I can ensure the sentence is carried out. We will be watching the tithes with great care.

'So, until then, consider my presence here nonexistent. Continue the work of the Administratum, Adept Diess.'

The man who had been Consul Senioris Chloure, gave a sardonic salute and returned to the thankless task of sifting through the mountain of forms on his desk.

Thaddeus swept out of the office, down the darkened stairway, and out into the grim exterior of Habitat Epsilon where the evening sun was now setting and the endless rolling fields beyond the habitat were dark with the herds of sleeping grox.

The Sisters were still waiting by the ship.

'Prepare for takeoff, sister,' said Thaddeus to Sister Aescarion.

'There is nothing here?' she asked. Sister Aescarion talked to Thaddeus as if she was his equal, for which Thaddeus was grateful.

'Nothing. Tsouras left us precious little when he put half the Lakonia Persecution to death.'

'Have faith, inquisitor. The Soul Drinkers have committed blasphemy in the sight of the Emperor. He will guide our hand if need be.'

'I am sure you are right, sister. But I imagine the Emperor does little to help those who cannot prove their worth and we have proven very little so far.'

Thaddeus and Aescarion walked up the ramp and into the body of the ship. The Sisters trooped in behind, filing into the personnel compartment. The ship was clean and new, requisitioned by the Ordo Hereticus from the shipyards of Hydraphur and a rare example of craft both small and fast, with the manoeuvrability and firepower to look after itself. The inside was simple: glossy, black and bare metal, decorated with devotional texts to the Emperor that the Sisters had pinned up on bulkheads, walls and small shrines. Thaddeus had kept the trappings of faith from the cockpit, but gradually the Sisters had taken over everywhere they were stationed and had turned it into a mobile chapel to the Emperor.

Aescarion joined her battle-sisters in the grav-couches inside, and the Sisters murmured a prayer of respect as she took her seat beside them.

Thaddeus headed for the cockpit, which he had upholstered with dark maroon tharrhide. His co-pilot's seat nestled next to the installed pilot-servitor – once human, its facial features had been replaced with an array of scanning devices. One of its hands was now a set of gold-plated compasses that scritched out trajectories and geometric shapes on the data-slate jutting from its ribcage. The other hand was hard-wired into the instrument panel of the cockpit, and sent messages

from its once-human brain into the ship's cogitators and engine controls.

'Launch,' said Thaddeus to the servitor. The remnants of its brain
recognised the command and the ship lurched as the thrusters on its
underside kicked in. The featureless landscape of Koris XXIII-3 yawed
and was replaced by the clear bright sky. Suddenly, the ship's primary
engines roared, and Thaddeus was thrust into the deep upholstery as
the ship tore through the planet's atmosphere.

Thaddeus didn't know if anyone else would go to the trouble of
hunting down Consul Senioris Chloure. He hoped they didn't – Adept
Diess was doing far more for the Emperor's flock than Chloure ever
would have done.

Finding him, and letting him live, passed for a small victory, and
Thaddeus anticipated few enough of those. The Soul Drinkers were
tough and resourceful, and their intentions were unknowable. Though
a Space Marine Chapter could conquer just about anything, it still con-
sisted of just a thousand men, and the Soul Drinkers probably
numbered significantly less. Thaddeus's own staff numbered more and
he did not wield the massive household armies of some inquisitor
lords.

The Soul Drinkers could disappear, if they wanted to.

But they would not. That was Thaddeus's best hope. Sarpedon was
still, in many ways, a Space Marine, and he would not just sit tight in
some far corner of the galaxy waiting to be forgotten. He still believed
in something, no matter how twisted, and he would keep on fighting.
The Soul Drinkers would do something to make themselves visible
again. Thaddeus would be there, and he would find them. He would
trap them and kill Sarpedon, if he could. Then he would coordinate
whatever resources he needed to shatter the remnants of the Soul
Drinkers Chapter for good.

He had faith, like Sister Aescarion. And even if that was all he had,
for an inquisitor, it was enough.

THE SOUL DRINKERS Chapter had disappeared in its entirety at the climax of the Lakonia Persecution, when the Chapter's fleet had fled
through a long-forgotten warp route leaving Inquisitor Tsouras's battlefleet grasping at nothing. The events leading up to the Persecution
had been enough to mark the Chapter as rebels of the most dedicated
and dangerous sort – an attack on the Adeptus Mechanicus, the
destruction of the Lakonia Star Fort, the refusal to submit to Inquisitorial examination, and the killing of the interrogator sent by Tsouras to
deliver his ultimatum.

When the smoke cleared, the Soul Drinkers had vanished from the face of the Imperium.

Well over a year later, salvage crews in the far galactic east reported a huge find: a massive graveyard of ships, some battleship-sized, that had all been destroyed by scuttling. The investigating Imperial authorities soon ascertained that this was the Soul Drinkers' fleet, including the mighty battle barge *Glory* and a shoal of strike cruisers and support craft. Of the Soul Drinkers themselves there was no sign. No one knew where they were or how they were travelling, but the fact that they had destroyed their own fleet – one of the most powerful independent forces for some sectors around – indicated that they were determined to make life difficult for anyone trying to follow them.

The fleet could have been tracked. But these mere thousand men could not be tracked – not when they had the immeasurable vastness of the Imperium to hide in.

And so it came to Inquisitor Thaddeus of the Ordo Hereticus. There was no question of letting Tsouras carry on with the task of hunting down the Soul Drinkers – he had let them slip by once and that was once too often. Thaddeus had few leads left to follow from the wreckage of the Persecution and the burned-out remnants of the fleet. Chloure was the last to be exhausted and like the others – Archmagos Khobotov of the Adeptus Mechanicus, killed in a generatorium explosion on the Forge World Koden Tertius, Captain Trentius of the Cardinal Byzantine and a few others who had survived Tsouras's enthusiasm – he had yielded nothing to indicate where the Soul Drinkers were or what they were planning. But Thaddeus did not despair at the magnitude of his task. He was reliable and thorough. He would get the job done eventually.

He knew hardly anything about the Soul Drinkers. He had studied their history in great detail, of course, and it indicated a zealously loyal Chapter, independent of will but ready to throw its valuable Marines against insane odds in the Emperor's name. There was barely a taint on them. But that was not the Chapter he faced now – the Soul Drinkers had broken so violently with their faith in the Imperium that their heresy left nothing of the Chapter's previous personality. Thaddeus knew that Sarpedon, who had taken command of the rebellious Soul Drinkers, would be the primary force behind the Chapter's new, blasphemous existence. Sarpedon was a psyker, one of the Chapter's Librarians and highly decorated throughout his seventy-year service. He would be tough to crack. Probably impossible.

Thaddeus knew he would have to kill him. Sarpedon would have to die before the Chapter could be broken. Thaddeus might be unable to do it himself and might have to call in other inquisitors with their own resources, perhaps agents of the Officio Assassinorum or even the planet-scouring Exterminatus, once he had located the Soul Drinkers and driven them into a corner.

Messy and costly. But every drop of spilt Imperial blood would be worth it. A rebel Space Marine Chapter was a danger too great and unpredictable to forgive.

All these thoughts, as they often did, occupied Thaddeus as he sat in the darkened navigational chamber on the *Crescent Moon*. The circular chamber formed an auditorium of upholstered reclining couches that could have held a couple of hundred, but Thaddeus was usually the only one there, silent in thought as he sunk into the deep padding. The seating was reclined because the navigational display was projected onto the vast glowing disk of the ceiling, shining down on the chamber like a full moon.

The *Crescent Moon* was Thaddeus's own ship, a ribbed gunmetal-grey cylinder with vast particle scoops like the fronds of an anemone sprouting from the bow. These fuelled the four enormous engines just behind them, leaving the rest of the ship to house the bridge, living quarters, cargo holds, machine-spirit chamber, and all the rest of the many places that a spaceship needed to function. Thaddeus' own quarters, and those of his Interrogator, Shen, were armoured sections in the heart of the ship. The inside of the ship was furnished to Thaddeus's taste – simply and darkly. The ship was a rare creature, the sort of craft the shipyards of the Imperial Navy couldn't make any more, assembled centuries before from parts millennia old by one of Thaddeus's mentors. It was fast and comfortable, and it only needed a crew of a few dozen, which gave Thaddeus some valued privacy. However, with the storm troopers and Sisters occupying the refitted cargo sections, the ship was feeling rather more crowded of late.

'Sector map,' Thaddeus said, and the vox-sensor switched the star map from the shining star field to a map of the sector, with the many star systems and planets flagged with names and coordinates. The *Crescent Moon* was still orbiting around Koris XXIII-3, and Thaddeus had to give some thought to where he would head next – probably towards the nearest Inquisition fortress or subsector headquarters to relate the paltry scraps of information he had found to the Ordo Hereticus. The cluster of agri-worlds was surrounded by a ring of populous hive worlds and manufactoria planets, many of which had their own permanent Inquisitorial presence. Thaddeus was trying to decide which one would be the least grim place to explain his lack of progress when the vox-casters chimed in alarm.

An incoming transmission. The astropathic choir, the half-dozen telepaths who received and transmitted messages between Thaddeus and the rest of the Imperium, spoke in unison over the vox, their voices whispering and raspy. 'From subsector command Therion, sector Boras Minor, Ultima Segmentum. Ordo Hereticus naval liaison staff report rogue space hulk, possible Adeptus Astartes activity. Report to follow. Have faith lest your unbelief consume you.'

Thaddeus pulled himself upright and walked through the darkened auditorium towards the door that led towards the bridge. To tell the truth, he had held little hope that the requests he had made of the Hereticus command – that he be informed via astropath of any unusual discoveries that matched certain criteria, including the possible presence of Space Marines – would bring in much information of value. Now a space hulk had been found by the Imperial Navy, and the find had become known to the section of the Ordo Hereticus that kept watch on the fleets of the Ultima Segmentum. For whatever reason they had suspected the superhuman warriors of the Adeptus Astartes were involved. It was a thousand to one shot that the Soul Drinkers were the Marines in question (literally, for they said there were a thousand Chapters of Marines, though Thaddeus suspected the true number could be anything), but it was a better lead than anything else he had.

The bulkhead slid open and instead of the corridor beyond, Thaddeus was confronted with the sight of the Pilgrim.

Tall and shrouded and surrounded by a cloud of thick, sickly incense, the Pilgrim's face was hidden by the tattered dark grey hood of his robes. His hands were wrapped in heavy bandages. Thick cables ran from within the hood down to the quietly humming respirator clipped to the leather belt at his waist, to assist whatever was under those robes to breathe. The bulky power pack on his back, which ran the Pilgrim's portable life support systems, gave him a crippled and hunchbacked look. The ever-present incense was billowing from the twin censers that topped the pack, and a faint glow burned through the rents and frays in the shroud as if the Pilgrim was fuelled by a furnace.

Thaddeus permitted the creature to be referred to as the Pilgrim because he professed to be an utterly devoted follower of the Emperor, and he served Thaddeus as an expression of this fervour.

Although Thaddeus valued him greatly, the Pilgrim had a habit of acting in the most sinister manner, occasionally seeming to anticipate Thaddeus's movements.

'Inquisitor,' it said with a heavy, monotone, half-mechanical voice. 'The hulk. Will we go?' The Pilgrim turned and followed Thaddeus as he headed past it towards the bridge.

The Pilgrim must have been monitoring the information Thaddeus was receiving. Thaddeus knew the upper echelons of the Hereticus must be spying on him most of the time, but he was not happy that the Pilgrim was doing it too. Still, Thaddeus knew better than to risk a rift with the creature. 'Perhaps,' said Thaddeus. 'We are duty-bound to follow up any clues. But the chances of the find being relevant are...'

'It is them.'

'Unless you have some intelligence I have not received, Pilgrim, it would not do to get our hopes up. We have received more promising leads than this before.'

'Think on it, inquisitor.' In the Pilgrim's voice, the rank sounded like an insult. 'One craft is more difficult to track than a fleet. A hulk is large enough to house a whole Chapter. And what loyal Chapter would sink to taking up residence on a space hulk? The perversion of such an idea would suit Sarpedon perfectly.'

The Pilgrim knew the histories of the Soul Drinkers in depth, and had read of the many great victories they had won in the Emperor's name, from the dawn of the Second Founding to the eve of their heresy. It had instilled in him a hatred of what the Chapter had become; it was a hatred that rivalled Sister Aescarion's religious faith. The Pilgrim was a profiler, and expert in the means and beliefs of the Soul Drinkers, and he could be the most valuable individual in Thaddeus's entourage if it all came down to guessing which way Sarpedon would jump.

'We can't be sure,' said Thaddeus. 'The Ordo Xenos was tracking more than seven hundred hulks and suspected hulks at the last count, and they were only the ones they were willing to mention.'

'You are right of course, inquisitor,' replied the Pilgrim. 'One ship amongst hundreds gives us long odds. Perhaps you are pursuing a better lead at the moment? One strong enough to negate the value of optimism in our mission?'

Thaddeus had decided long ago not to rise to the Pilgrim's baiting. If he wasn't so useful, Thaddeus would have refused to accept him into the strike force when it was first assembled by the Ordo Hereticus. But the feel the Pilgrim had for the soul of the renegade Chapter was one of the few edges Thaddeus had.

They came to a bulkhead in the form of a massive set of bronze double doors. Thaddeus spoke a codeword and the doors swung open. Thaddeus and the Pilgrim stepped through into the cavernous space. The bridge of the *Crescent Moon* was suspended above the engineering decks, so the navigational consoles and command pulpit looked down on the massive spinning plasma turbines that churned away a hundred metres below. The engine-gang, pale-skinned red-eyed men who rarely emerged from the depths of the ship's engines, could be seen scuttling between the turbines, making adjustments in anticipation of the *Crescent* leaving orbit and putting into the warp.

Thaddeus had no flag-captain. He commanded his own ship. Servitors were slaved into most of the consoles so they could relay his commands directly. The platforms of the bridge held only the servitors, Thaddeus and the Pilgrim, Sister Aescarion, and Colonel Vinn of the Hereticus storm troopers.

'Sister, colonel,' said Thaddeus briskly. 'Our course is for the Subsector Therion. Have your troops make ready for warp travel.' At his words the servitors twitched as they fed his commands into the *Crescent's* machine-spirit. 'A space hulk is an environment not to be taken lightly. You may be required to put your troops at considerable risk.'

'We have chased ghosts for too long,' said Aescarion. 'My Sisters will give thanks for the opportunity to bring some purity to the place.'

'The men of the Hereticus Storm regiment will be ready,' said Vinn. Vinn had been mindwiped several times owing to the things he and his men had seen as they fought the Hereticus war against witchery and corruption. He had been forced to learn the ways of fighting several times in the course of his life and the result was a wealth of experience and battle instinct that he did not remember receiving but which made him an effective leader and an unquestioning Imperial servant. His bland features hid utter ruthlessness and beneath the black and red storm trooper fatigues he was covered in scars from the many near-suicide missions he had led.

The regiment, actually a vast body of men dispersed across uncountable Inquisitorial retinues and fortresses, had been seconded to the Ordo Hereticus for so long that they now had nothing to do with their parent Imperial Guard at all, instead being raised at Hereticus's request and trained in Inquisitorial facilities. Thaddeus had five platoons, over two hundred men, in the *Crescent Moon's* cargo holds, every one of them rigorously conditioned to face any horror with their assault-patterned lasguns, and perform the most gruesome of tasks at Thaddeus's request.

Thaddeus ascended the short flight of steps to the command pulpit that overlooked the banks of servitor-manned consoles and monitors. He tapped the subsector code into the glowing lectern display and a line of coordinates flashed up, streaming into the half-minds of the servitors as they in turn input the commands that would have the *Crescent Moon's* machine-spirit direct the ship through the warp. The ship's lone Navigator, a recluse named Praxas who had not left his cramped quarters in the ship's prow for months on end, would even now be preparing to gaze onto the warp and guide the ship through its treacherous currents.

'Has he had some insight?' Sister Aescarion enquired. She was standing by the pulpit and watching the Pilgrim, who was looking down on the rumbling engines as the engine-gang got them started.

'He seemed confident the hulk has something to do with the Soul Drinkers,' replied Thaddeus. 'I have reason to trust his judgement.'

'I understand that I am under your command, inquisitor, and that he and I will be called upon to fight the same battle. But it makes me uneasy that I have so little idea of who or what he is.'

Thaddeus smiled. 'Sister, do you think me a radical? You should not believe the rumours you hear. We are not all daemon-baiting madmen in the Inquisition. The Pilgrim is not a monster.'

Sister Aescarion did not return his smile. She had gained a reputation as a dependable commander of battle-sisters working alongside the Inquisition, and she would have heard more than enough rumours. Many of them were true – Thaddeus had himself been involved in clearing up the mess left by the Eisenhorn heresies and the destruction of the rogue Hereticus cell on Chalchis Traxiam. 'The Sisters wonder, inquisitor,' she said. 'That is all. They must be certain they are commanded by those who have the same depth of faith as they do. Idle chatter undermines the purity of faith and it would be better for me if you were more open about your companions.'

'The Pilgrim can be trusted, Sister. You have my word on that and this is all you need. Now, you should make sure your Sisters are prepared for departure, we will be in the Empyrean for some weeks.'

Sister Aescarion nodded curtly and strode off the bridge, the boots of her black lacquered power armour clacking on the metal floor of the bridge. Colonel Vinn followed her, stepping smartly as if on the parade ground.

The preparations took little time. Thaddeus valued the *Crescent Moon* partly because the procedures for beginning a major warp journey, which on an Imperial battleship could take days of tech-priest ministrations, could be handled in hours. Soon the massive engines roared and lit the bridge from beneath with the bright orange plasma glow. The flaring particle scoops folded into the cylindrical body of the ship and blue-white bolts of energy arced off the hull. The *Crescent Moon* drifted out of high orbit and the warp engines fired.

The inhabitants of the agri-world looked up to see a tiny bright star winking suddenly in the sky and then disappear. One of them, Adept Chloure, sighed a prayer of gratitude to the Emperor that the visitors had not taken him with them, and turned back to the never-ending mountain of paperwork.

CHAPTER TWO

THE SKY HAD turned dark over Eumenix. The whole hive world was locked in a perpetual twilight, lit only by the weak orange glow of the heatsink exhausts and the flickering, dying lumospheres that were winking out one by one as the planet died. Over Hive Quintus, home to a rapidly decreasing population of almost a billion, it rained greasy ash as the pyres of the dead begin to tower over the looted palaces of the nobles. The hive city's screams could be heard for kilometres around – wailing sirens of Arbites riot control tanks, the shriek of collapsing tunnelways as hordes of citizens tried to flee the latest hotspot, roars of explosions as looters tripped booby-traps or overladen tramp shuttles crashed on takeoff from makeshift pads.

And the smell. Burning, certainly – it could hardly be otherwise when fire was the only thing that could keep anything clean any more. And spilt fuel. And panicked sweat. But there was something else, sweet but caustic: a smell that made noses wrinkle and eyes water. It steeped the entire city from the pleasure-galleries to the underhive, to the endless maintenance warrens and the gold-plated halls of trade. It seeped out into the barren wastes between cities. Even in the wilds outside the city, those who tried to flee by land could smell it, and just before the seething pollution flats claimed them they knew it was the stink of death. And not just the ordinary death that wandered Hive Quintus constantly – this was the stench of the plague.

Some had called it the white death, or the underhive pox, or spirit rot. The doctors who tended to the city's ailing aristocracy invented long, complex High Gothic names for it. But by the time old Governor Hugenstein had succumbed, his body a mass of seeping welts, along with his family and most of his staff, it was known simply as 'the plague'.

No one knew how to cure it. Everything from full blood transplants for the super-rich to folk remedies, devised when the city was young, were tried and failed. In desperation, the people looked for a cause – and scores of innocents were burned as pox-spreading political agents or witches. By the time the pyres of plague dead broke the city's skyline, even being uninfected was a death sentence. But no one could tell where the infection came from. And trying to understand it just made it kill quicker.

Some got out. The Administratum offices cut through enough red tape to get the higher echelons to safety. Some of the manufactorium owners made the most of their razor-sharp business sense to buy themselves passage out of Hive Quintus as passengers on fleeing pleasure-yachts or human ballast on smugglers' scows.

Others could have run but did not – the governor had done the most noble thing of his reign and presided over the death of his city. The Adeptus Arbites decided without debate to stand their ground and preserve the Emperor's laws even as the city fell apart. The preachers of the Adeptus Ministorum stayed, and bellowed the Emperor's praises from temples crammed with desperate infected citizens. But the hundreds of millions who filled Hive Quintus's thousands of layers all wished they had the chance to flee in one of the pitifully few craft that were escaping. Any craft large enough to carry a significant number of people was shot down by orbital defence lasers maintaining the quarantine order against Eumenix – those who escaped did so in a tiny trickle, barely a dent in the massive, doomed population.

That, of course, did not stop larger ships from taking off and being turned into long burning streaks in the sky – more omens of death for the people below. But there were some smaller ships in the city that might run the quarantine blockade. Some spaceports were still operational, and whenever word went round that there was a ship about to launch, hordes of half-dead victims piled up around the launch pads and ship hangars.

Most of the time there were no ships. But as the plague reached its height, on Ventral Dock 31, Cartel Pollos managed to salvage a small research vessel just spaceworthy enough to get the House patriarch and his immediate family off Hive Quintus. Sure enough, masses of plague victims swarmed against the walls around Ventral Dock 31, held at bay by the private army of Cartel Pollos. Shotgun blasts ripped down into the crowds as the ship fuelled and prepped for takeoff. It was perhaps the last hope for anyone to escape the plague.

Hope was the rarest commodity of all. But when a massive explosion tore out a section of the east wall, all hope disappeared.

THE AUTOSENSES IN Sergeant Salk's helmet snapped his pupils shut as the glare of the explosion burst across the east wall. From his squad's vantage point in the ruins of a hab-block like an island in the centre of the heaving plague-infected crowd, he could see chunks of ferrocrete hurled into the air with a massive thunderclap. Pollos's guards were thrown off the battlements and a ripple ran through the crowd as the front ranks were blown backwards by the force of the explosion.

Karrick's demolition charge had done the job. Separated from his squad, Karrick would be lucky to survive to meet up with the rest of the squad, if any of them got inside the spaceport at all. But that didn't matter now. Captain Dreo was dead and Salk was in charge. The squad had secured their target and he understood that if he had to cash in the lives of his battle-brothers to complete his mission, then he would do so.

'Go!' he yelled into the vox and the six remaining Soul Drinkers vaulted from the burned-out windows of the shattered hab-block. They landed in the thick of the crowd and Salk felt festering limbs pushing against him as he sunk into the crowd as if into an ocean. He clambered to his feet and saw the rest of the squad battling against the human tide – Space Marines were a clear head and shoulders taller than the tallest unaugmented man and Salk easily spotted the Marines of his squad: Krin with the plasma gun, Dryan, Hortis, Aean and big Nicias hauling the squad's sole prisoner.

Nicias had been forced to abandon his missile launcher after the mission's bloody early stages, where Dreo was lost, and had fought on with knife and bolt pistol. He had accepted responsibility for hauling the prisoner, head covered and wrists bound, with his free hand.

Salk forged a way through the heaving crowd. Lolling-mouthed, mad-eyed faces loomed from the masses and hands grabbed at him. They were lit by the fires that burned in the hive-spires rising all around like mountain ranges, and the searchlights directing the fire of the soldiers on the breached walls of the spaceport. There must have been ten thousand crowding up against the east wall alone, and Salk could see where they were piled up, living and dead, against the barricades beneath the walls.

Salk pushed through them, his power armoured body barging bodies aside. He picked up and threw those in front of him. He didn't want to hurt these people – they could not help the madness of the

Imperium into which they had been born – but if they put themselves in his way, he would crush them underfoot. This mission had turned ugly from the outset, and it would end ugly, too.

The crowd surged forward as the front ranks recovered from the blast and began to pour into the breach. Gunfire stuttered from up ahead as the Cartel Pollos troops poured their fire into the plague victims that clambered over the rubble onto the landing platform of the spaceport.

A missile streaked down from the closest watchtower and blew a hole in the surging crowd. Salk pushed against the crowd and burst out into the smouldering crater, ringed with blackened bodies, a short sprint from the yawning breach in the wall. The wall was twenty metres high and several thick, but the charge had torn a huge section out of it. Autogun fire was already spraying from behind the fallen chunks of masonry, with shotgun blasts barking beyond the rubble as Cartel Pollos troops hunted down the plague victims that had got through.

'Nicias, Krin, with me!' voxed Salk as he fired a couple of bolter shots at the gaudily dressed Pollos troops ducking behind the masonry. 'The rest, covering fire!'

The huge form of Nicias tore out of the crowd beside Salk, followed by Krin. Already some of the troopers had spotted the massive purple-armoured Marines and were directing their fire towards them, rightly singling them out as the biggest threat to the east wall. Autogun fire spanged off Salk's shoulder armour and he returned fire, almost blind, as he put his head down and ran across the open ground towards the cover of the rubble in the breach.

The two Space Marines back in the fringes of the crowd opened up on full auto with their boltguns, spattering the walls with miniature explosions. Troopers on the walls jerked and fell, some tumbling over the lip of the wall onto the barbed wire and barricades below, their bodies mingling with those of the fallen plague victims.

Salk slid into cover as a heavy stubber in the watchtower stitched fire all around him. Nicias was seconds behind him, firing up at the watchtower. There was a missile launcher and a heavy stubber up there, and by now the Pollos troops would have marked Salk and his Marines as priority targets.

And with good reason. A spear of white heat ripped up from the open ground behind Salk and the top of the watchtower billowed open, the blast of the plasma impact compressed within the firepoint and incinerating whatever men and munitions were inside. Krin, plasma gun shimmering with haze as the heat rose from its charging circuits, stumbled under the impact of autogun fire from the walls but slid into cover beside Nicias.

Nicias's prisoner had given up struggling by now. Dressed in simple rust-red coveralls, blackened with grime and the residue of bolter fire, the prisoner simply hung on as Nicias hauled the rag-doll figure around with one hand while his other held his bolt pistol.

Salk ducked to one side to see what lay within the breach. A sergeant of the Pollos troops was organising his men into a firing line across the breach, most of them armed with autoguns, but there were a few shotguns mixed in. There were about twenty men, all dressed in the emerald green of Cartel Pollos with bright gold buttons and buckles and shiny black knee-high boots. Most of the time they were used by the cartel for show, hence the garish uniforms, but the cartel had built itself on the intimidation value of a private army and these were well-trained and motivated men.

Salk nodded at Nicias and Krin, then cast a handful of coin-sized frag grenades past the slab of rubble he lay against. A series of low whumping explosions sounded and Salk scrambled up the slope of rubble towards the firing line through the falling dust kicked up by the grenades.

His first few shots were sprayed on full auto to keep the troopers' heads down. Then he switched to semi-auto and fired as he ran, bolts kicking up crimson spray as they snapped back heads of those soldiers firing back. Shells impacted all around him, a couple registering as flashes of pain as they penetrated the ceramite of his armour. Salk ran through the bursts of pain and leapt into the heart of the firing line.

This was how the Soul Drinkers fought. Cold and fast. A Space Marine was safest at the very heart of the battle, face-to-face with his enemy where his armour, weapons, physical strength and valour were magnified and the resolve of his enemy could be shattered. As Krin's recharged plasma gun burst liquid plasma over the far end of the line, Salk clubbed the stock of his bolter into the first face he saw. Streaked with grime and lined with fatigue, the trooper stared in disbelief at the three-metre killing machine that reared over him even as Salk's gun cracked into the side of his head. Salk pulled the body beneath him, drawing his combat knife and slashing at the trooper behind the first.

Salk's second victim fell, clutching at the deep wound across his torso scored by the monomolecular edge of the knife. Nicias's bolt pistol spat shells into the troopers along the line and many were already running, to be cut down in turn by Nicias.

Nicias was still hefting the prisoner as if the quivering body weighed nothing. If the prisoner died, the whole mission would fail.

But Nicias was using his massive, barrel-chested body to shield the prisoner from incoming fire. He was a huge man even for a Marine, which was why he was one of the Chapter's few heavy weapons troopers, and the few shots that hit him burst against his armour in showers of sparks.

Salk pulled a third body off his knife and pumped half a magazine of bolter shells through the breach, showering the threshold of the spaceport with fire. The troopers' officer was trying to rally them into a new firing line on the smooth surface of the spaceport itself – Krin vaporised him with a gout of superheated plasma and the Pollos troopers broke and ran.

'Squad Salk, report in!' voxed Salk hurriedly to the Marines who had stayed behind to cover his assault. 'Aean, Hortis, Dryan!'

The only reply was broken fragments of speech cut up by static. Whichever of them was still alive was swamped by the masses of the crowd so heavily that his vox equipment had been damaged. Since the receiver was implanted in the ear and the transmitter in the throat, that meant a fractured skull at least. It was no way for three good Marines to die, pulled down by a baying, half-mad mass of dying civilians. No way to lose Soul Drinkers, who in their entirety were down to about seven hundred battle-brothers. The mission was a costlier one than the Chapter could really afford, but if it succeeded Commander Sarpedon had assured Dreo and Squad Salk that it would be doing the Emperor's work in an immediate and valuable way.

Salk didn't know what Sarpedon's plan was. Dreo had, but he was dead, far beneath Hive Quintus. But Salk believed in Sarpedon, the mutated, visionary Librarian who had rallied the Soul Drinkers against the evils of Chaos and the blindness of the Imperium alike. If he had to die here to ensure the prisoner was delivered as Sarpedon commanded, then Salk would die.

Salk waved the two Marines with him forward as he slammed a fresh magazine into his bolter. They had to move now, while the troopers in front of them were scattered and the crowd had yet to surge forward behind them. Even now he could hear the masses pouring towards the newly cleared breach. Three men, even Space Marines, could drown in the human tide.

Salk clambered over the crest of the rubble and saw the Ventral Dock 31 spread out before him. Lit by makeshift landing lights of burning fuel drums, it was a wide expanse of blast-stained ferrocrete with landing zones marked out all over it. Massive maintenance sheds and building-sized docking clamps broke up the surface, and many of these had been transformed into firepoints by Cartel Pollos. Emerald-uniformed troopers manned heavy stubbers and artillery pieces, nervously waiting for the hordes to burst in.

There, several hundred metres away, was Salk's immediate objective. An ugly, crouched craft, like a huge metal fly, squatted on one of the launch zones. Bulky servitors lugged thick fuel lines towards the craft as the maintenance crews tried frantically to prep it for takeoff. A gaggle of exotically dressed men, probably the leaders of Cartel Pollos, were being escorted across the spaceport by shotgun-wielding troops with crimson as well as emerald on their uniforms. Household troops, bodyguards of the cartel heads. No match individually for Space Marines, but they could be guaranteed not to give up.

The ship was the only way off Eumenix, and the Soul Drinkers had to ensure they were the ones who took it. They had been dropped onto the planet what felt like a lifetime ago by drop pod, because the risks from the orbital batteries were too great for a Thunderhawk gunship to bring them down. The plan had been for Dreo to lead them out into the barrens outside the city so they could be picked up later, maybe months afterwards, but the risk from the plague extended even there and the prisoner would not have survived. Ventral Dock 31 was the only choice left.

Salk ducked back down beyond heavy stubber fire from the closest hard point. A pair of two-man teams was hiding amongst the huge metal claws of a docking clamp, covering the breach.

Salk charged again, sending a volley of shots tearing into the heavy stubber position. Heavy chains of fire ripped into the ground all around him, one catching him on the greave and almost pitching him onto his face. He spotted Nicias out of the corner of his eye, taking shots to the torso as he tried to shield the prisoner. A plasma blast washed over the docking clamp and a couple of the gunners were turned to bursts of ash, but the fire kept coming, pinning down Salk and Nicias on the edge of the spaceport concourse.

A sudden explosion ripped the docking clamp apart, sending chunks of metal spinning, split sandbags fountaining the earth, broken bodies flying. Stubber rounds cooked off like chains of firecrackers. From the wreckage a single black-clad figure ran, gun in hand. Salk was about to open fire when he realised that the figure was as tall as he was, in power armour charred black but still with the chalice symbols picked out in bone on one shoulder pad.

'Good work, Brother Karrick,' voxed Salk.

Karrick crouched into a firing position, keeping troopers away from the firepoint. Salk sprinted to his side, Nicias behind him, and another plasma blast burst amongst the next firepoint along the line as Krin broke cover behind.

Fire rattled over the Marines' heads and Salk realised the fire from the spaceport was being drawn into the crowds now swarming over the rubble behind him. 'Now!' he voxed, and the surviving Marines outran the approaching edge of the crowd, charging towards the lone spacecraft. Salk sprayed bolter fire at any glimpse of emerald and Krin ripped a plasma shot into the ground by the Pollos heads' entourage, forcing them to delay embarkation as they scattered from the incoming fire.

Salk felt small arms fire impacting against the ground all around him as he ran, ringing off his armour. He switched to semi-auto and flicked shots off at the bodyguard trying to drag the dignitaries towards the ship. Two fell, and another spasmed as bolt pistol shots from Nicias tore through him. Karrick sprayed shells around the rear of the ship and the bodyguards fell back, trying to put themselves between the incoming fire and the dignitaries.

Salk could see the heads of Cartel Pollos now, clad in impractical aristocratic dress with so many layers they looked corpulent and farcical as they scrambled around the rear of the ship, trying to shelter behind the sternward landing gear. The bodyguards were opening fire at the Marines and the crowds spilling over the concourse, but they didn't have the range of the Marines' disciplined bolter fire. A quick volley of snapped shots from Salk took one man's head off and knocked another off his feet like a punch to the gut. Karrick kept the rest pinned down and Krin vaporised a handful of troopers trying to bring a missile launcher to bear.

Salk reached the prow of the ship, firing all the time, switching magazines as Nicias covered him with pistol fire and then sniping at the bodyguards through the landing gear.

'Get aboard!' voxed Salk to Nicias. Covered by Karrick, Nicias ran round the side of the ship and threw the prisoner over the extended boarding ramp and into the passenger compartment. A spray of fire sparked off his armour, tearing chunks from the ceramite as he vaulted his huge form into the ship.

Krin was next, then Salk and Karrick firing a full-auto volley as they clambered into the ship.

Inside, the small compartment was luxuriantly upholstered in the deep, clashing greens and reds of Cartel Pollos. There was room for about a dozen back here, and seemed cramped when filled with the bulk of four Space Marines and their single prisoner. Salk glanced at the remains of his squad – Karrick's armour was charred and the purple paintwork had almost all blistered off. His helmet was gone and one side of his face was badly burned. Krin's gauntlets were smoking from the overheated plasma gun, and Nicias's armour was riddled with bullet scars. Many of Nicias's wounds were bleeding, his blood clotting almost instantly into dark red crystals.

The prisoner was slumped on the carpeted floor, motionless except for shallow breathing.

Salk turned and saw the hatchway leading into the cockpit of the shuttle. It was shut. He slung his bolter, dug his fingers into the edge of the door and ripped it clear out of its frame, metal shrieking. In the cockpit were two pilots in emerald uniforms, young and terrified, shivering with fear. They had neural jacks plugged into sockets in the backs of their shaven heads. Salk glanced at the readouts on the instrument panels in front of them – the shuttle was fuelled up and ready to go.

Salk removed his helmet, feeling sweat running down his face. The smell of gun smoke from his bolter, burned skin from Karrick and the ever-present miasma of hive city pollution, flooded his senses.

'Launch,' he said. The two pilots paused for a second, mesmerised by the immense armoured figure that had just torn its way into the cockpit. Then they turned to the shuttle controls and, almost mechanically, began switching on the main engines and direction thrusters. The rumble of the main engines cut through the background noise of gunfire and screams.

Salk turned back into the passenger compartment. Past the closing boarding ramp he could see the crowd swirling just metres away, emaciated plague victims dragging down Cartel Pollos bodyguards and the heads of the cartel themselves. Krin lined up a shot into the crowd but Salk pushed his plasma gun aside – there was no need. Within a few seconds the shuttle would be aloft. There was nothing these people could do to them now.

The boarding ramp swung shut and there was a hiss as the interior pressurised. Salk looked through to the cockpit and saw, through the frontal viewscreen, the spires of Hive Quintus burning and the smoke-laden clouds boiling up ahead.

The primary thrusters kicked in and the craft lurched forward, away from the burning nightmare of Eumenix and Hive Quintus. Salk was leaving many good Soul Drinkers in the hive city, including Captain Dreo, none of whom the Chapter could easily afford to lose. But as long as their prisoner survived and was brought off the planet, any losses were ultimately acceptable. Commander Sarpedon had made that very clear to Captain Dreo, and Salk had been compelled to carry out those same orders when Dreo was lost.

Salk returned to his squad. Karrick and Nicias both needed medical treatment and Salk had been apprenticed to the Chapter apothecarion as a novice, before he had been selected as a squad sergeant and then taken into Sarpedon's confidence after the terrible Chapter war. More importantly, the prisoner was in shock and would have to be properly looked after.

They would have to search the shuttle for supplies. It would be some time before they could expect pickup and they would have to keep the prisoner alive. But for the time being, he would have the squad enter half-sleep and take turns watching the prisoner, and settle into the routine that would keep them alive until they could return to the Chapter.

Salk didn't know the details of Sarpedon's plan. But he knew enough to guess that this mission was only the start.

SUBSECTOR THERION WAS a near-empty tract of space, notable only for the scattered asteroid fields that yielded rare minerals to the hardy prospectors who mined them. It was these prospectors who first had alerted the Imperial Navy salvage teams to the presence of something strange and truly immense that appeared without warning, as if cast randomly out of the warp.

It was huge. There were parts of it that were still recognisably Imperial warships, aquiline prows jutting from the mass of twisted metal. Smaller ships, fighters and escorts, were welded into nightmarish starbursts of jagged steel. Other parts were completely alien, with scythe-shaped hulls or bulbous organic engine pods. No one could hope to count how many spacecraft were mashed into the space hulk, only that there were craft from every era and from civilisations that could not be identified. The hulk had clearly been in the wars, and recently – there was a new scar, silver and raw, where an enormous section of the hull had been torn open as if by a giant claw. The hulk was one of the ugliest things even the Imperial salvage crews had ever seen.

Inquisitor Thaddeus agreed with them. The monstrous space hulk was huge even from his vantage point on the bridge of the *Crescent Moon*, where the bridge holos projected a curved viewscreen several stories high above the engine room. The wide slice of space that Thaddeus looked out on was dominated by the grey-black mass of the hulk. The light of Therion, the subsector's primary star, picked out jagged metal edges and left the corners of the hulk in pitch black shadow. A few bright slivers hovering around the hulk were Imperial Navy salvage craft, which were transmitting their comms signals to the nearby escort cruiser *Obedience* and then on to the *Crescent Moon*.

The captain of the *Obedience* had accepted Thaddeus as the commander of the salvage operation without having to be asked. From the logs of the first few days of the operation, it seemed seventy-four salvage engineers had boarded the space hulk so far. Thirteen had got out.

The survivors had reported that the craft seemed devoid of the dangerous organisms that normally inhabited space hulks, but was instead rigged with well-hidden booby traps. Bundles of frag grenades were wired to bulkhead hatches. Gun-servitors guarded intersections. Airlocks opened into hard vacuum.

But there had been glimpses of what was beyond. There were areas partitioned into monastic cells, and a library crammed with leather-bound books. One man reported a deck of fighter craft and vehicles. That had been before the news of the hulk's recovery had been passed on to Thaddeus, and the exploration of the hulk had been halted at his request until he arrived to oversee it personally.

Space hulks, ships which were lost in the warp and drifted after centuries back into realspace, were frequently home to savage aliens, insane cultists, and worse. But this hulk, enormous as it was, did not seem to contain any such monstrosities. Rather, it appeared to have been inhabited until recently.

Thaddeus's fingers ran across the controls of the navigation pulpit and several inset images appeared on the viewscreen. They were jerky, low-res transmissions from cameras mounted on the shoulders of salvage team officers, who were now waiting with their men in Navy landing boats attached to entry points on the near side of the hulk. There was no hope that they could explore anything like the whole mass of the hulk – such a task would take years given its size – so Thaddeus had ordered them into some of the more stable-looking, recognisable areas, like an early-pattern Imperial hospital ship and an escort destroyer from the time of the Gothic War.

Imperial Navy salvage teams were hard-bitten veterans of some of the most dangerous environments deep space could offer. They knew men had died on the hulk, but they were prepared to go that bit further in than anyone else to make sure their crew got credited with a find that could be spent in the dives of the next port they put into. Armed with shotguns and sheer guts, most of them would be pirates or black marketeers if the Navy hadn't press-ganged them from the hives and frontier worlds. It would be a shame to have to mindwipe them if they found anything they shouldn't know about, but they understood that risk, too.

'Captain?' said Thaddeus.

'Lord inquisitor?' replied the clipped voice of the captain of the *Obedience*.

Thaddeus couldn't claim the status of a lord inquisitor, but he didn't correct the man. 'You may begin.'

The transmissions from the *Obedience* filtered through a film of static that came from the bridge speakers. The images on the viewscreen juddered as the salvage crews, each a dozen strong, moved from their landing boats into the outer body of the hulk.

One team moved past the devotional plaques and shrines of the hospital ship, now dark and empty where once Sisters of the Orders Hospitaller had tended to the wounded from some unknown Imperial battlezone. Another was in the cavernous entrails of a starship's engine room, keeping their weapon-mounted torches probing into the shadows beneath the plasma generators. The corridors were dark and deserted; the only sounds the footsteps and orders of the salvage crews and the creaking of the hull. Transmissions from the crews informed Thaddeus that the hulk seemed to be empty and, sinisterly, far too clean. The gravity was working and the atmosphere, most remarkably, scanned as safe on the teams' crude auspexes. The youngest member of each team was ordered to remove his respirator and the fact that he didn't drop dead meant that there were no airborne toxins.

Moving further into the hulk, one team found a brig that looked like it had been used recently, with new locks and cells with devotional High Gothic texts on the walls. A ship's bridge had been opened up and the complex electronics of the cogitators and comm-links spilled out across the deck, with monitoring devices hooked into the workings. The plasma generators encountered by the team in the engine decks had been restored to working order. Someone had lived in the hulk, cleaned up the useable parts and even, it seemed, tried to make the hulk spaceworthy. If they had succeeded, the hulk would have been a formidable weapon indeed, a fortress capable of carrying a massive number of personnel, along with the firepower of several of its constituent ships.

Thaddeus was now seriously entertaining the possibility that the Pilgrim was right.

'Coming up on Leros's crew,' came the voice of one of the team leaders. 'What's left of them.' The corresponding image showed the bloody remains of several men, blown apart as if by explosives or large-calibre gunfire, spattered around the corridor.

'Keep your wits about you, team seven,' ordered the *Obedience's* captain. Team seven, Thaddeus thought, probably didn't need reminding.

Thaddeus pressed an icon and the image from team seven was magnified on the viewscreen. They were in one of the warships, one with Low Gothic mottos scratched into the walls by a devoted crew. Leros's crew was scattered: an arm here, a head there, a weapon broken and thrown aside.

Something moved up ahead, a glint of metal.

'Halt!' barked the team's leader. 'Fall back! Lorko, you cover…'

A sheet of stuttering gunfire ripped down the corridor. The image swung wildly and a gauze of static shivered over the scene. Thaddeus could make out a man thrown back against a wall, the chest of his dark grey coveralls shredded and sodden with blood. Another man fell backwards, the upper part of his body blown apart.

Shotgun fire ripped back. Bright trails of an automatic gun spattered across the corridor. The team leader was yelling orders to fall back to the next junction.

Thaddeus caught sight of what was shooting at them.

'Team seven,' he said calmly, knowing his voice would be relayed directly to the team leader. 'It's a gun-servitor. What explosives do you have?'

The leader was running back with his squad. 'Just signal flares,' he said breathlessly.

'Use them. It will be blinded.'

Thaddeus heard the team leader gathering a handful of flares from his men. The screen burned scarlet as they were lit and thrown back down the corridor behind them.

The shooting stopped. The image filled with thick red smoke from the flare as the team ran towards the blinded servitor. A volley of thudding shotgun blasts came a second later.

'It's dead,' said the team leader. He had doubtless lost many men from his team on previous missions and his voice did not sound shaken in the least.

'It was never alive,' replied Thaddeus. 'Show me.'

The leader kicked the closest flares down the corridor and waved some of the smoke away. Thaddeus could make out, on the floor, the remains of the servitor – its lower half was a hover unit. Its arms had both been replaced with twin-linked autoguns connected to large cylinder box magazines. Its face was just a jutting mass of sensors. Presumably it would have been difficult to make and would have been set to guard something important – a task it had succeeded in with the first team to come across it.

'Proceed,' said Thaddeus.

The squad moved past the junction the servitor had been guarding. The leader glanced about, but Thaddeus saw that one of the corridors led to an arched doorway.

'That one,' he said.

The team assembled at the threshold. The room beyond was large and unlit, and nothing could be seen past the doorway.

'Auspex?' asked the leader.

'Nothing,' came the voice of one of his surviving crewmembers.

The leader shone his weapon torch through the doorway. The light played across a floor laid with smooth black marble veined in white, and across the foot of a bookcase. As the squad moved in they could see more in the light of their torches – cases of books that reached right up to the high ceiling. The shelves were full of books, most of them small volumes that could fit into the palm of a large man's hand, but there were a number of larger books, scrolls, and even stone tablets alongside them. A pulpit of stone stood before several rows of hardwood benches.

'Team seven, are there signs of habitation?'

'No, sir,' said the leader.

'Movement!' came a shout from behind. The leader spun around to bring his gun to bear and his camera showed a squat shape drifting along the floor – another servitor, but not a combat pattern this time. It was an autoarchiver, its legs and arms replaced with long, thin jointed metal manipulators which removed and replaced volumes from the shelves as it moved along on the wheels set into its back.

It was still functioning. That meant this place – this library – had been used recently and had probably been abandoned in a hurry.

'Leave it alone,' said Thaddeus. 'I want this place intact.'

'Understood,' said the team leader. 'Don't shoot it!' he yelled to his men. 'And don't touch anything. The bosses want it clean.'

A faint mumble of discontent from the other men indicated that they had been looking forward to seeing what they could loot.

Thaddeus glanced at the other images. One inset screen was blank – the team had stumbled into an explosive booby trap in the hospital ship, a set of tripwires strung across the entrance to one of the surgery theatres. Another had lost three men when a gantry over an engine room gave way under their weight. The team in the brig were rifling through the contents of an armoury locker – they were taking out wicked combat knives the size of short swords, power mauls and large-calibre ammunition for which the corresponding guns were missing. Gradually the teams were moving further into the hulk, and most of them were finding signs of a recent, organised and presumably human presence. One or two had reached parts of the hulk evidently of xenos design. But here their orders were to halt.

Thaddeus looked back at team seven. The library seemed huge – several bulkheads had been removed to form a large enough space.

Mem-slate blocks stood like glossy black monoliths in rows between the bookshelves.

'Get me one of the books,' said Thaddeus.

The team leader took one of the small volumes from the nearest shelf.

'*Catechisms Martial*,' read the team leader from the gold lettering on the book's cover.

'Thank you,' said Thaddeus, and switched from the team back to the officers on the *Obedience*.

Thaddeus was a well-read man – an inquisitor had to know a great deal about the various histories and philosophies of the Imperium to be able to root out the heresies that infected it. But he had only recently become acquainted with the *Catechisms Martial*, a work of tactical philosophy that espoused a swift, shattering form of warfare where speed and overwhelming focused strength were the primary weapons.

It was written by the philosopher-soldier Daenyathos. Daenyathos of the Soul Drinkers.

The Pilgrim had been right, again. The Soul Drinkers had made the hulk their home but they had left suddenly and recently. The hulk was the single biggest clue Thaddeus could reasonably have hoped to find, but it was still just a clue and not a part of the goal itself. The Soul Drinkers were somewhere else in the galaxy, pursuing some perverse plan while Thaddeus took tiny steps towards them.

'Captain,' Thaddeus transmitted to the *Obedience*, 'have your crews secure a landing zone. I shall oversee the exploration from the hulk.'

By the time the captain replied to object that the hulk was still not safe, Thaddeus was already gone from the bridge.

CHAPTER THREE

THE FIRST SIGHT *of the enemy was a scarlet streak through the upper atmosphere, glimpsed from the porthole of the Thunderhawk gunship as it plummeted from orbit towards the landing zone.*

'Gunners, can you lock?' voxed Captain Korvax as the xenos craft flashed past.

In response the Chapter serfs who manned the gunship sent lances of heavy bolter fire chattering through the air, the report of the heavy weapons sounding through the hull and over the din of the ramjets decelerating the Thunderhawk. There was a flash of orange as the alien craft broke apart at speed, scattering a black drizzle of debris behind it.

One down. The serf gunners were good; the Soul Drinkers had trained them well. But the fact that the alien fighter had closed with them at all indicated that the Marines were coming to the battle late. These aliens were fast, and the outpost could be lost in minutes if the Soul Drinkers weren't faster.

'Fleet command, how's our landing zone?' voxed Korvax to the strike cruiser Carnivore, *in high orbit far above the force of six Thunderhawks.*

'Contested,' came the reply. 'Vox-traffic indicates xenos landfall of light troops, three hundred plus.'

'Understood,' replied Korvax. He knew that for this particular variety of heathen alien, the eldar, 'light troops' meant lightning-quick, skilled, and well-armed specialist soldiers.

'Prepare for rapid deployment,' ordered Korvax as the Thunderhawk's deceleration ramped up a notch and the G-force kicked in.

The engines flared and the Thunderhawk was hovering about thirty metres above the ground. Korvax glanced out of the porthole – he could see two of the other gunships alongside. The shape of the outpost – a low building set into the hard frozen earth of the tundra – was broken by the Adeptus Mechanicus troops firing from the roof at the eldar moving rapidly towards it. Small arms fire from the strange eldar shuriken-firing weapons spattered against the Thunderhawk's hull.

The rear ramp of the Thunderhawk opened and the sound of the engines flooded in, punctuated by explosions and gunfire from below. Cold air rolled in, too, for the outpost was on a planetoid of frozen tundra too far from its parent sun to be hospitable. The restraints on the grav-couches snapped open and with practiced speed the ten-strong squad of Soul Drinkers Space Marines dropped out of the ship on rappel lines, bolters slung.

Korvax was amongst the last to drop out of the Thunderhawk. He saw Marines from the force's other gunships doing the same – he counted five ships in total and a small black shape trailing smoke and heading upwards, meaning one of the Thunderhawks had sustained damage and was heading back to the Carnivore. That still left fifty Space Marines making landfall.

Fifty against three hundred plus. Though pride was sinful in the eyes of the Emperor, Korvax still admitted to himself that those were the kind of odds he liked.

The battlefield yawed below him, and as the rappel line hissed through the clip he grasped it with his right hand. The outpost was surrounded by smoke and gunfire. Tech-guard on the roof had formed fire points and were firing at the eldar now moving to surround it.

The Mechanicus had access to the most advanced of weapons, Korvax saw a form of rapid-firing missile launcher send volleys of frag missiles into the eldar lines, and glimpsed the unmistakable liquid fire of a heavy plasma gun bursting amongst the aliens. The eldar were in many forms – as was the way of this heathen species – some wore bone-white bodysuits with tall masks which shrieked horribly as they cartwheeled through the gunfire to use their power swords against the tech-guard up close. Others had plumed helmets and shuriken weapons, and were covering green-armoured eldar with buzzing heavy chainswords and masks with mandibles that spat laser fire at the tech-guard manning the forward defences. The first wave of eldar had easily swarmed over the first lines of sandbags and barricades and, though many of their number lay broken and burned by the tech-guard fire, several hundred of them were surrounding the outpost and moving in for the kill.

Korvax hit the ground in the centre of his squad. A quick hand signal told them all they needed to know – advance and engage. The safest place on the barren battlefield was toe-to-toe with the eldar. The aliens were quick and skilled, but pile on enough pressure and they would break. Korvax had fought them before on Quixian Obscura and broken them, too.

The squad rapid-fired as they ran, spattering bolter fire into the defences. Blue-armoured eldar, seeing this new threat landing behind them, turned to man the defences they had just overrun. Their shuriken guns spat volleys of shining silver at Korvax and his squad, studding the Soul Drinkers' purple armour with razor-sharp discs. One Marine – Solus, the squad's flamer-bearer – went down, crimson spurting from the disk embedded in his knee joint. The bolter and shuriken fire met in a storm of metal, the Soul Drinkers closing quickly as the other squads did the same along that whole side of the defences.

The night sky above was clear and cold, and through it streaked a missile from Squad Veiyal, cracking in a flash of fire into the centre of the eldar sword-bearers. Two of them died, blown apart. Bolter fire ripped into them as they tried to regroup, and by the time Squad Veiyal reached the defences the xenos manning it were dead.

Korvax's squad hit the eldar on their section of the line. Korvax tore up the edge of the sandbag parapet with full-auto fire and deftly drew the power sword from its scabbard on his armour's backpack. The power field jumped into life as his gauntlet closed around the hilt and it shrieked as he brought it down towards the first eldar he saw. Eldar reflexes were notoriously quick and the alien jinked to the side, but the blade still caught its shoulder and sheared the arm clear off. Korvax vaulted into the ditch behind the parapet, kicking the eldar to the floor as he did so and bringing his bolter, like a club, cracking into the side of its skull.

Bolter fire spattered like rain into the ditch. Eldar died, or stopped firing to scramble out of the way. The ditch was deep but the far edge had collapsed into a crumbling slope where the frozen earth had been pulverised by explosive fire – the eldar retreated up this, attempting to fire as they went.

One of them moved with sudden, supernatural speed, seeming to flip over trails of bolter fire. It had a sword that looked like it was made of bone in one hand and a shuriken pistol in the other – the pistol flashed and a shuriken took Brother Brisias through the eye.

Korvax crunched through the body of the eldar he had killed and drove up the slope towards the eldar with the sword – part of their leadership caste, he guessed. They said eldar followed many paths of war, each type of soldier the result of a different path – those who became trapped on those paths became their leaders on the battlefield. They were considered priority targets in assaults.

The eldar saw Korvax approach, and fixed the black glass of its helmet eyepieces on him for a moment. As if acting on some warrior code, the alien paused for a split second, raised its blade, and somersaulted towards him.

Korvax followed no code save that of the Emperor and the sacred place of the Soul Drinkers in his plan for the Imperium. In the shadow of the beleaguered outpost he duelled with the eldar leader, matching the alien's speed with his own strength. Many times the eldar struck home with a blow that would have killed a normal man, but Korvax knew the protection that power armour offered and he knocked each blow aside with a shoulder pad or an armoured forearm.

The alien tried to flip away from him, but Korvax reached out with his free hand, grasped the plume of its helmet, pulled its head down and slammed his knee into its faceplate. The eldar reeled and Korvax slashed a deep gouge across its torso, cutting through the armour plates set into its deep blue bodysuit. He felt its thin ribs give way and drove forward, hacking at it as each parry from its bone sword became weaker. With one final slash Korvax brought the blade down through the eldar's guard and the power blade cut right through the alien's torso, shearing the spine. The alien froze for a moment, then fell limp. The sword dropped from its hand.

The power field around the blade burned away the tissue it touched and the corpse slid off the sword with a flick of Korvax's wrist. The blue-armoured eldar were dead. The Soul Drinkers had taken the aliens by surprise, catching them as they themselves were trying to storm the outpost with speed and skill. Korvax saw Squad Veiyal was almost at the outpost's front blast doors – he also saw that the doors were wide open and smoking. The xenos must have got inside.

The Adeptus Mechanicus Biologis outpost was a crucial research station. The experiments it housed were vital to the Imperium. Korvax did not know the exact nature of the work done here, but for the Adeptus Terra to ask the Soul Drinkers to defend it from alien raiders must mean that the work was of the greatest importance. If the eldar got inside and destroyed – or, worse, stole – the Mechanicus research, the consequences would be great.

They were too late. The heathen xenos had breached the outpost. It was time to make amends.

Korvax quickly voxed round his squads. Veiyal was the furthest forward while two other squads were busy pinning down the eldar reinforcements landing nearby. Assault Squad Livris was on Korvax's flank, clashing chainswords with the green-armoured eldar. They had lost a couple of Marines but they had cut their way through most of the eldar. That left Korvax three squads for the assault, with two more keeping the emerging eldar support units at bay.

'Veiyal, Livris, rush the doors!' voxed Korvax on the all-squads channel and he waved his squad forward, the Tactical Marines firing volleys sweeping across the defences in front of them as they advanced. More blue-armoured eldar tried to dig in and hold off Korvax's squad, but he led his men charging into their flank and drove them against Squad Livris. Many more eldar died between Korvax's bolter fire and Livris's chainswords.

That was how the Soul Drinkers fought. Hard and fast, never stopping.

Korvax saw Squad Veiyal at the doors, using the massive plasteel construction of the blast doors as a firepoint, as they gave covering fire to the two squads approaching. Explosive fire suddenly streaked over from the eldar heavy weapons units trying to reach the outpost. Bursts of fire and shattered earth fountained up where they hit, and several Marines were thrown off their feet. The autosenses of Korvax's helmet cut out for a second then juddered back. A warning icon flashing on his retina told Korvax the pict-recorder on his backpack was damaged, and was no longer recording the view over his shoulder for the mission's debriefing.

Korvax would have to survive. He ran on through the pall of falling earth as a rune winked out, indicating Brother Severian's lifesigns had ceased in the midst of the barrage. Korvas ducked into the doorway and his squad barrelled in behind him. Blue-armoured eldar fired shuriken shots after them but were shredded by Livris's charge, and the Assault Marines joined the rest of the spearhead at the outpost entrance.

Korvax checked the runes on his retina display. There were about half a dozen Marines down, maybe dead, but definitely out of action. Not bad losses. But the eldar had got inside the outpost and could even now be wrecking research vital to the Imperium.

Korvax slammed a new magazine into his bolter and heard half his squad doing the same. He glanced at Sergeant Veiyal – his helmet had been damaged and he was bareheaded, his breath coiling white in the cold.

'The others have our backs,' said Korvax. 'Sergeant Livris, your squad has the point. Veiyal, with me. Advance.'

Korvas levelled his bolter and followed the Assault Marines as they charged into the darkened heart of the outpost…

THE IMAGE WINKED out to be replaced by static. Thaddeus frowned and tapped the controls on the data-slate, rewinding the recording past the point where the feed cut out. It was the view over the Space Marine commander's shoulder from a recorder on his backpack, showing a screen full of showering earth and sharp white lines of gunfire. The recording rewound and the Soul Drinker commander's charge played out in reverse. Implosions sucked Marines back onto their feet.

The holomat was set up in the centre of the librarium. Salvage teams and tech-priests from the *Obedience* had carefully swept the librarium and lost several men rooting through trapped bookshelves. Once it had been established that the librarium was that of the Soul Drinkers

Chapter, Thaddeus had ordered the salvage teams to be confined to the hulk and to secure the immediate area. Corridors had been sealed off with rockcrete to prevent decompression traps from emptying the librarium sector of air. The teams slowly spreading out into the hulk were locating dormitories and meditation cells, weapons lockers and infirmaries, all converted from ancient, empty sections of Imperial ships welded into the mass of the hulk.

The datacubes recovered had mostly been wiped. The truly crucial information had probably been portable enough for the Soul Drinkers to take with them before they abandoned the hulk. But there was some residual information in the glossy black monoliths of data-slate and the cogitators of the various intact ships. The Soul Drinkers had referred to the hulk as the *Brokenback*, and had clearly adopted the craft as a home after the scuttling of their fleet. There were records of journeys across the galaxy, often to apparently dead sectors, and hints of massive Marine losses in a battle on some unnamed world.

And then, there was the pict-file that Thaddeus had just played, showing the assault.

'It had been accessed repeatedly,' came a voice from across the library. It was Interrogator Shen, a tall and handsome man who still carried an air of the tribal warrior about him in spite of the archaic carapace armour he wore and the inferno pistol holstered at his waist. His voice was clipped and somehow artificial, for he had been sleep-taught Imperial Gothic relatively late in life. 'Whatever its significance, the Soul Drinkers scrutinised this file extensively before they left. That was why the tech-priests were able to piece it together from the various cogitators.'

'Do they know what it depicts?' Thaddeus was cycling slowly backwards through the file, watching the assault unfold in reverse.

'We presume it is some former operation. The location is uncertain. It could be the event that cost them so many of their own, but the Adeptus Mechanicus were the first organisation they turned against and here they are helping them.'

Thaddeus shook his head. He pointed towards the weapon now sucking bullets back out of the eldar aspect warriors. 'That's a Centauri pattern bolter. The Soul Drinkers' equipment was well up to date when they turned, this file must have been shot a decade ago at least. Before their heresy. We need to find out where this is, have the tech-priests begun forensic scrutiny?'

'They have begun, Master Thaddeus,' replied Shen. 'But there is little to work with. The outpost building is apparently a common STC construction and there are no landmarks. It is a Mechanicus outpost and the world is one of tundra, but there are thousands such. And if the events are as old as you say, it may not even be there any more.'

Thaddeus paused the image. The recorder captured the instant when the tactical squad had leapt over the first barricades into the Dire Avenger defences. Dire Avengers were the most disciplined of the eldar aspects, diligent and dependable, the mainstay of the eldar elite. But the Soul Drinkers had smashed through them and other aspects alike, though outnumbered and unsupported. They had been most admirable in their time, thought Thaddeus. Great warriors, and fearless, but they had been proud. Their pride had led them to a terrible heresy, to break with the Imperium itself. It was a shame that they would have to be destroyed, but Thaddeus would see that they were.

'If it was important to them,' said Thaddeus, 'then it is important to us. If we find the location of this recording we may well find the Soul Drinkers. Shen, you may have to follow up other leads on your own. It is no little responsibility.'

'I accept, Master Thaddeus.' Shen had served Thaddeus for seven years, the latter few as a solid interrogator. Unlike Thaddeus, Shen was a warrior first, but Thaddeus had put most of his efforts into training the man's mind, and Shen could be trusted to look after himself.

'Good. Bring the astropathic choir aboard the *Brokenback* and have them take up their vigil again. I want to hear of any further sightings of the Soul Drinkers, no matter how trivial or unlikely. We may be able to use them to pin down this location. Take some of the *Obedience's* astropaths, too. Use my authority. The *Brokenback* will be our base of operations until I say otherwise.'

Shen bowed neatly to the inquisitor, and strode off to fulfil his duties. Thaddeus wondered if Shen ever really thought he would be an inquisitor one day. In truth, Shen didn't have the patience or imagination to hunt down the enemies that threatened mankind from within. Thaddeus knew his own strengths, and Shen didn't come close. He was, however, as fine an interrogator as Thaddeus could wish for – loyal, diligent, and able to summon a deadly streak of violence in a tight spot.

Thaddeus looked once more at the holo image, where purple-armoured giants charged fearlessly into a storm of gunfire. He had never truly understood how Space Marines, particularly the assault-oriented Soul Drinkers, could make a tactic of a headlong, suicidal attack and somehow attain victory after victory when mere men would be cut to pieces. It was as if their conditioning and sheer faith carried them through when physics and logic should bring them low.

And now that faith had been perverted until a whole Chapter of such giants had declared themselves the enemies of the Imperium. Thaddeus found it difficult to imagine a more dangerous enemy.

IT WAS A beautiful day. It was always beautiful in House Jenassis. The dome under which the habitat was built had been constructed of electroreactive materials that always created a flawless blue sky overhead no matter what the conditions on the planetoid outside. The atmosphere was permanently stabilised at an even summer's day, allowing the impressive alien plants of the gardens to flourish. Phrantis Jenassis always made time every day to walk the gardens, until he lost sight of the palace's golden minarets between the spreading boughs of imported alien trees.

House Jenassis was a colony several kilometres across, housed in an atmospheric dome and consisting of the palace itself, the grounds with their lakes and greenhouses, a cluster of simple rustic habs for the retainers, and the temple-like complex that housed the Grand Galactarium. House Jenassis was also the name of a Navigator family that had served the Imperium for more than ten thousand years, since before the Horus Heresy. Phrantis Jenassis, the current patriarch of the House, had himself taken the Emperor's starships through the warp where only his warp eye could see the way, but had returned after a long career to take over the House. It was a good life, especially considering how so many less fortunate billions suffered to survive. But it was a life deserved, of that Phrantis Jenassis was sure, for without the Navigators the Imperium would be no more than a vulnerable collection of isolated star systems at the mercy of its enemies.

The duties for the day were many. Phrantis had to negotiate with the Departmento Munitorum to contract Imperial Guardsmen to guard the many scions of House Jenassis on their travels. There were reciprocal arrangements to make that bound Navigators to particular individuals or Imperial organisations. New births would have to be registered and Phrantis would have to sign the examiners' reports to confirm that the new bearers of the Navigator gene were free from corruptive mutation. The House's accounts were due to be reviewed and a long and tortuous process that would become. Yes, the House retainers would doubtless thrust many sheets of parchment under his nose to be read or signed or acted upon, but that was for the rest of the day. The morning would be spent enjoying the gardens, for why else would Phrantis Jenassis have worked so hard if not to earn some deserved leisure time in old age?

Past the old summerhouse was one of the habitat's prettiest lakes, where crested devilfish swam between trailing branches of silver-barked fingertrees.

Phrantis wandered across the quaint little bridge that spanned the lake and watched a captive flock of jewelbirds wheeling beneath the clear blue dome.

The jewelbirds scattered as if in fright. Then the sounds reached Phrantis – reverberating booms like some huge hammer striking the surface of the dome. Ugly black cracks suddenly ran across a section of the dome and, with a sound like thunder, the section shattered.

Huge sheets of glass like giant knife blades fell, embedding themselves in the ground within sight of the lake. There was a growl of rushing wind as the heat within the dome rushed out into the cooler atmosphere beyond. A massive tear had been gouged out of the dome and Phrantis saw with horror the roiling grey-white clouds of the planetoid outside. The trees shook and the water rippled. Phrantis's jewelled robes ruffled in the wind and he felt a sudden cold wash over him.

A tiny black shape dropped from the storm clouds towards the tear in the dome. As it plummeted closer Phrantis could see that it was like a bulb of metal, ringed with restraints, segmented like the unopened bud of an ugly grey flower. Bright flares ripped from its underside to decelerate it but when it landed, maybe three hundred metres from Phrantis, it still hit the manicured lawn in a fountain of earth. Two more followed, then a fourth, and Phrantis realised the last one was heading for the lake.

He turned to run, but his old frame had barely lurched a few steps when something massive thudded into the lake, drenching him in a wave of spray. He turned to see the metal seed pod bursting open and the purple-armoured soldiers inside – ten of them – snapped off their restraints and waded out into the water of the lake. The lake was quite deep but their heads still showed above the water, indicating they must be a good metre taller than Phrantis himself. Phrantis knew of the Adeptus Astartes – he had occasionally come across those superhuman warriors in his career – and he had no doubt that Space Marines were invading House Jenassis.

The House had been loyal. It had served the Imperium with all its energy, asking only gratitude in return. Why would Space Marines be attacking a House that had helped the Imperium maintain its grip on the galaxy?

The Marines were already clambering up the bank, each with a pistol in one hand and an outsized chainsword in the other. Each wore the emblem of a chalice on his shoulder pad. One had some kind of attachment for a hand – Phrantis realised with a start that it was not a bionic but the grotesquely warped hand itself, with long muscular multi-jointed fingers gripping the haft of a power axe. The helmetless Marine wielding it was a grizzled veteran, face battered and scarred, and he had spotted Phrantis.

Phrantis didn't run. He was old, and they would easily outpace him. Either that, or his long and distinguished life would end with a bolter shell in the back. The closest Marine clambered up the bank, covered the distance in a few long strides, and dragged Phrantis to the ground by the scruff of his neck.

The sergeant with the mutant hand ran over. The power field around the blade of his axe was activated and droplets of water were hissing on the metal.

'You. What is your name?'

'Patriarch Phrantis Jenassis of House Jenassis.' Phrantis was amazed he had been able to answer.

'A Navigator?'

Phrantis nodded.

'Bind his hands,' said the sergeant to the Marine holding Phrantis down. 'Don't let him take his turban off. His warp eye'll kill you.'

Phrantis's hands were pulled behind his back and a plastic restraint tied around his wrists.

'What do you want?' gasped Phrantis. 'We are loyal here. We have been loyal since the days the Emperor still walked amongst us! Our warrant of binding was signed by his hand! We are loyal!'

The sergeant grinned, showing broken teeth. 'We're not,' he said.

Phrantis was hauled to his feet. Not loyal? Phrantis had heard dark tales of Space Marines who fell from grace and joined the great enemy, the powers of Chaos that could not be named by righteous lips. Chaos Marines, all the pride and vigour of Space Marines turned to cruelty, bloodlust and desecration.

A warzone, where the Chaos Warlord Teturact was carving out an empire, was only a couple of subsectors from House Jenassis. Phrantis had been assured that the warfleets massing on the border of the warzone protected House Jenassis from Chaos raiders, but perhaps those raiders had found a way through. Had these Marines come from the Teturact's hordes? What could they want with House Jenassis? Navigators for their fleets? Slaves? Or just the despoiling of somewhere beautiful?

Phrantis saw other purple-armoured giants moving away from the other pods that had fallen, taking up firing positions amongst the trees.

With the breach in the dome the sky was darker and a chill wind was blowing down from above. Beautiful House Jenassis was already imperfect.

'Commander?' the sergeant was saying into his communicator. 'We've taken the patriarch. I'm heading to your position now. No other contacts. Over.' There was a pause as someone made a reply Phrantis couldn't hear. 'I see you. Graevus out.'

Phrantis followed Sergeant Graevus's gaze, and saw a nightmare.

COMMANDER SARPEDON, Chief Librarian and Chapter Master of the Soul Drinkers, was a half arachnid mutant renegade. His eight legs – seven chitinous limbs and one bionic – skittered rapidly as he moved with Squad Hastis across the rolling lawns towards where Squad Graevus was advancing with their prisoner. The boots of Hastis's Marines churned up the manicured grounds.

Sarpedon met up with Graevus in the shadow of a spreading alien tree with scarlet leaves that cast a dim shadow beneath the darkening sky. Graevus, like most of the Chapter, was a mutant – his hand had deformed to give him greater strength and reach with the power axe he carried. Squads Hastis and Krydel were setting up a perimeter in case the planet's Arbites or Navigator House retainers arrived quickly. Tech-marine Solun, the Marine whose machine-skills would make the difference between success and failure here on Kytellion Prime, was with Squad Krydel, the mem-plates covering his armour glinting black.

Phrantis Jenassis was a grey-haired, thin-faced slip of a man in ruby-red robes embroidered with gold and gemstones. A turban wrapped around his head concealed the third eye, the warp eye, in the centre of his forehead. It could look out on the warp itself but also, they said, kill a man with a glance.

'He's unhurt,' said Graevus. 'We found him alone.'

'He will not be alone for long,' said Sarpedon. He turned to the shivering patriarch. 'Where is the Galactarium?'

Phrantis looked up blankly for a moment. 'I will not yield, Chaos filth,' he stuttered.

Sarpedon reached down and grabbed Phrantis by the chin. 'Do not waste our time, old man. We do the work of the Emperor. Where is the Galactarium?'

'The… the Arbites will be here, we have a precinct dedicated to our protection…'

Sarpedon cursed the fragmented intelligence he had been able to muster on House Jenassis. The Soul Drinkers knew the Galactarium was here – one of the wonders of the Imperium, by all accounts – but there had been no map of the house environs to plan the assault properly. 'We will kill them all if we have to,' said Sarpedon, knowing they would if it came down to it. 'That does not have to happen. All we want is access to the Galactarium, then we will go. House Jenassis can run back to the Imperium in safety if you just give us what we want.'

Phrantis Jenassis closed his eyes and whimpered, trying to shut out the cold, dangerous place his home had suddenly become.

'We have no time for this,' said Sarpedon, irritated. Time was an enemy here, as were so many factors. He switched to the all-squads vox. 'Squads Hastis, Krydel, spread out and find me the Galactarium building, then report back and hold tight. Squad Graevus, hold this location with me. Post forward troopers to spot contacts. Move out.'

HOUSE JENASSIS WAS located on Kytellion Prime, a planetoid with a superdense core (and hence Earth-standard gravity). Other settlements, undomed and exposed to the planetoid's cruel weather, dotted the barren landscape, mostly isolated trading settlements that had been founded by retainers released from House service. One of them, however, was a massively built compound with walls of sheer ferrocrete and watchtowers on every corner. This was the Kytellion Prime Adeptus Arbites precinct, where several squads of Arbites judges and suppression units were responsible for the protection of House Jenassis. Their presence next to the habitat was one of the many ways in which the Navigator House was repaid for its diligent service to the Emperor's fleets.

There were several events that would cause the Arbites to be mobilised. The breaching of the dome over House Jenassis was one of them, signifying as it did a potential meteorite strike or other disaster, or even an almost unthinkable direct assault on the House. Within minutes of the alarm going up, a column of riot control vehicles and APCs, loaded with heavily armed Arbites officers and judge commanders, was snaking rapidly along the short road towards the entrance to the dome ready to defend the estate of the Navigator House they had sworn to protect.

The precinct astropath, as per the protocols that had been in place since House Jenassis had come to Kytellion Prime, transmitted the distress call across the ether, alerting the highest authorities that the ancient and holy House Jenassis was violated.

A few scant minutes afterwards, it was answered.

SQUAD HASTIS HAD come across a few retainers with hunting rifles, and scattered them with a volley of bolter fire before moving into the palace itself. Without engaging the palace's automated servitor defences, the squad ascertained that the palace contained plenty of marbled galleries and lavish quarters, but no Galactarium.

Squad Krydel, heading the other way, had located the low building of marble with deep crimson lacquered panels and battlements plated with gold. It was located in a shallow depression in the landscaped gardens, surrounded by a ring of trees and with a marble-paved road winding to its collonnaded entrance.

The Soul Drinkers' enhanced senses had picked out handfuls of retainers from families bound into service by House Jenassis, straggling from their picturesque village on the other side of the grounds. They would be little more than a nuisance if any of them proved brave enough to attack, but they were not the ones Sarpedon was worried about.

'Ready to secure the structure,' said Sergeant Krydel. His squad was crouched by the columns at the front of the building. Techmarine Solun was beside the sergeant.

'No time,' replied Sarpedon. 'We'll go in together.'

Sarpedon, Squad Graevus and the captive patriarch moved rapidly through the trees and up to the threshold of the temple-like building.

'Squad Hastis,' voxed Sarpedon to the squad by the palace, 'advance to this position and maintain a perimeter.'

An acknowledgement rune flashed on Sarpedon's retina. Hastis was a good, solid soldier, and Sarpedon feared the assaulting squads would need backing up soon.

With a gesture, Sarpedon sent the three squads into the building. It was dark and cool inside, and with the breach in the dome there was a new chill in the air. The walls were of huge blocks of multicoloured marble bordered with plated gold and shiny lacquered panels. Banners representing the branches of the Jenassis family hung from the ceiling, which got higher as the floor sloped downward. Most of the building was beneath the level of the surrounding landscape.

Sarpedon skittered on his altered legs close to Sergeant Krydel. Krydel was a tactical squad sergeant whose squad had distinguished itself when the Daemon Prince Abraxes had manifested on the *Brokenback*, and he had a reputation for utter unflappability. From the front Sarpedon could see the huge marble architecture opening up into a central gallery, exposed to the darkening sky and surrounded by elegant columns of jade. The open space was several hundred metres across, and in the centre was a raised circular structure of white stone.

'Solun?' voxed Sarpedon.

'The auspex reads plenty of activity,' replied the Techmarine. 'There's a lot of electronics beneath us. This place must have its own power source.'

Sarpedon led the Soul Drinkers across the stone, leaving a handful of Marines as a rearguard. Graevus hauled Phrantis Jenassis to the front alongside Solun.

'Open it,' demanded the Techmarine.

'What do you want with it? What are you?' gasped the patriarch.

'Permission to do this the old-fashioned way?' said Graevus, unclipping a handful of anti-armour krak grenades from his belt.

'Granted,' replied Sarpedon. Phrantis was hauled away as Graevus planted the grenades at seams between the blocks of the circular structure, then fell back.

The grenades went off with a sound like a string of gunshots, kicking a haze of marble splinters into the air. Phrantis whimpered as the stone shell of the Galactarium, wonder of the Imperium, fell away.

The Galactarium was an extremely complex construction of strange dull grey metal and glistening black psychoplastics, nests of concentric circles and spinning globes on delicate armatures. Slowly it unfolded like the legs of a spider, rings spinning, sections rotating, like a huge armillary sphere that blossomed to fill almost the whole courtyard. Beneath the gathering clouds the rings and armatures spun faster and faster until points of light began to shimmer in the air as if conjured. Strange shadows played around the assembled Space Marines as stars and constellations bloomed into existence above them.

'Hastis, secure this structure,' voxed Sarpedon. 'Solun, get to work.'

The Techmarine ran beneath the spinning mechanisms towards the centre of the Galactarium. Already the map was solidifying in the air – a star map, the largest and most comprehensive ever constructed. The Imperium was too vast to ever be properly mapped, and no one had ever managed to even catalogue its inhabited worlds. But attempts had been made, and the Galactarium was the closest thing to success the Imperium had. There were few places not represented on the immense stellar map now spherically projected around the Galactarium.

The Galactarium was the pride of House Jenassis; it was spoken of with reverence amongst fellow Navigators and the Adeptus Mechanicus Explorator commands alike. It was a dangerous target because taking it left the Soul Drinkers momentarily visible and vulnerable, but it was the Chapter's only hope.

'Commander?' came a vox. It was Sergeant Hastis, leading his squad back across the grounds from the palace. 'We've got contacts. Arbites, coming in from the dome entrance. I count seven vehicles heading for the palace and five moving towards your position.'

'Understood. Do not engage, get back here and help maintain our perimeter.'

'Acknowledged. Hastis out.'

Sarpedon did not want to kill anyone here. There was no need. But if he had to, he would, and he knew his battle-brothers would do the same.

Solun drew threadlike cables from the interfaces in his armour and plugged them into the base of the Galactarium. The huge map display was flickering and a new image was ghosting over the starscape. It showed a low building set into frozen tundra, obscured by gun smoke and ringed by ditches and barricades. It moved jerkily as the recorder moved closer, explosions flashing, armoured alien figures returning fire and spasming as silent bullets hit them.

Purple-armoured Marines moved across the battlefield. They were Soul Drinkers, from the lost days before the break with the Imperium. The Marine carrying the recorder glanced up at the night sky…

…The night sky above was clear and cold, and through it streaked a missile from Squad Veiyal…

Solun paused the image. The night sky of the planet was transposed over the Galactarium map to form a smeared mess of stars. The Galactarium stars suddenly whirled and Solun's eyes went blank as the mem-plates on his armour filled up with stellar data and his mind was flooded with star maps.

Solun would have to be quick. Sarpedon didn't even know if he could do it. Techmarine Lygris was one of Sarpedon's most trusted companions, and Lygris himself couldn't have done it. He had recommended Solun for the mission instead, knowing the younger Techmarine was an expert in information and its manipulation. If Solun's mind was unable to cope with the storm of information flooding through it, he would be reduced to a drooling infant in a Marine's body.

'Taking fire,' came a vox from Hastis. Light automatic fire chattered in the background.

'Squad Krydel will cover you from the temple,' replied Sarpedon.

'I see them,' voxed Krydel from amongst the columns at the front of the temple. 'We've got a hundred plus, Arbites riot officers with five riot control APCs and light vehicles.'

Sarpedon grabbed the cowering Phrantis Jenassis and hauled him with him as he sprinted towards the sound of bolter fire, the seven chitinous talons and single plasteel bionic clattering on the marble.

He saw them through the columns, a dark line of Adeptus Arbites lining the crest of the depression, spread between the trees. Adeptus Arbites officers maintained the laws of the Imperium and were equipped with fearsome anti-personnel weaponry and body armour. They were well drilled and ideologically motivated. They could not just be broken, they had to be thoroughly defeated.

Gunfire flashed down towards Squad Hastis, the ten-man tactical squad running down the tree-lined path towards the temple. Sergeant Krydel yelled an order and his squad's bolters opened up as one, sending lances of fire stripping leaves from the trees and keeping Arbites ducked below the ridge.

Squad Hastis reached the temple and added their fire to Krydel's. An Arbites APC, based on the Rhino APC pattern, rode over the crest and opened fire with twin heavy stubbers. Bullets kicked fragments from the marble columns and rang off Marines' armour.

Sarpedon watched as a command APC emerged from between the trees, a large antenna dish revolving on its roof and twin banners flying – one for the Arbites, one for House Jenassis. The top hatch opened and a judge emerged, eagle-crested helmet silhouetted against the grey sky.

'Cease fire!' yelled Sarpedon. The gunfire stopped.

A vox-caster was brought out of the APC and mounted on the vehicle's roof. The judge took the handset.

'Intruders!' boomed the voice from the vox-caster. 'Cast down your weapons, release your captives, and surrender to the Emperor's justice!'

Sarpedon glanced back into the temple. The Galactarium map was pulsing, closing in on one star system at a time and then wheeling to show a different one. Solun was twitching as information seethed through him. The battle-brothers had to buy him more time.

Sarpedon strode out from between the columns. He knew what he looked like – the Arbites would see a mutant. And they were right. He wore the gold-chased armour of a Space Marine Librarian and carried a nalwood psychic rod in one hand, with an artificer-crafter bolt gun and the Imperial eagle still emblazoned across his chest – but Sarpedon was still a mutant. He hoped the Arbites wouldn't open fire on principle alone.

He motioned for Squads Hastis and Krydel to stay in cover as he moved into the open, still dragging Phrantis. He counted about thirty Arbites sheltering in the trees, with many more doubtless waiting on the reverse slope. Another APC rumbled into sight, this time with a breech-loader that would fire a shell large enough to leave even Sarpedon a smouldering crater.

'We will fight you if you make us,' called Sarpedon, his voice booming through the heavy silence. 'Every single one of you will die. Or you can turn around and leave. You have no business with us, we are no longer beholden to Imperial law.'

'Release your prisoner and come out unarmed,' replied the judge on the vox-caster.

'Graevus?' voxed Sarpedon quietly. 'Do we have a match?'

'Solun's close,' replied the assault sergeant. 'He's got a lock on three stars.'

Sarpedon glanced over his shoulder. He could just see the whirling circle of stars that filled the Galactarium chamber. Turning back to the assembled Arbites, he dragged Phrantis Jenassis out from behind him and held him down on the ground in front of him with his front two legs. He took his boltgun from its holster and pressed the tip of the barrel against the back of the Navigator's head.

'This man is worth more than all of your lives put together,' called Sarpedon. 'If we leave, he will survive. If you bar our way, he will not.'

The judge did not reply. He ducked back into the APC for a moment before the hatch opened again. This time, it was not the helmeted judge who appeared but an astropath, one of the powerful telepaths who provided faster-than-light communication across the Imperium. Sarpedon's enhanced sight picked out the man's blind, sunken eye sockets and the puckered, prematurely aged skin of his face.

The astropath's voice wavered as he spoke into the vox-caster. It was clear from the artificiality of his tone that the voice he spoke with was not his own.

'Commander Sarpedon,' spoke the voice. 'Do not end it with such futility. These men are under my authority and will kill you at my order. You and your battle-brothers are under arrest by the authority of Inquisitor Thaddeus of the Ordo Hereticus.'

CHAPTER FOUR

For all they cared, Teturact had always been there. There had never been anything else. If they had any recollection of their lives before the plague took them, it was just a washed-out memory, whereas now their lives were illuminated by the light from Teturact, the saviour, the way.

On a hundred worlds he had come to them, and saved them from the ravages of disease. He had taught them not to fight it but to accept the plague, to make it a part of themselves and draw on its power. The agent of their death had, with Teturact's word, become the foundation of their life. To forge worlds, hive planets and feral worlds he had come and saved them all. And they would follow him to the end of the galaxy. Because of him they were no longer dying but brimming with life, so full of seething vitality that it wept from their pores and seeped from the cracks in their skin.

Teturact had first appeared to them on the Imperial Navy dockyard world of Stratix. Now, all those who could be spared made the pilgrimage to the seat of his power. It was a world of gargantuan spaceship docks supported on great stone and metal columns riddled with hive settlements, and now followers poured from the cultist-held spaceports towards the throne plaza of their saviour. Millions passed his throne in a seething pestilent throng, gazing up with their cataracted eyes to the top of the black stone pillar that lifted him above the masses. Teturact looked back down from a palanquin held aloft by four massively muscled bearers, immense muscles rippling, their bodies subsumed to Teturact's will. The brute-mutant bearers contrasted with Teturact's own frail, wizened body, and yet power seemed to flow from him. His thin, ancient-looking face radiated wisdom and his long, fragile fingers reached down benevolently as he bestowed his blessing on the masses.

Teturact ruled an empire a dozen systems across, and he ruled them utterly. His servants carried orders to whole worlds of the faithful, who obeyed as one, without question. The Imperium, who had betrayed and abandoned them, was trying to reclaim their worlds but Teturact, in his awesome wisdom, was calling upon his followers to mire the Imperial armies in planet-wide battlezones and give up their lives for the glory of their saviour. The fleets of warships docked at Stratix had been turned into groups of fast raiders and fireships, breaking up the Imperial Navy spearheads. The Imperial armouries were stripped and used to turn hordes of grateful infected into loyal armies that rose up to slaughter the Imperial Guard that approached their cities. With their deaths, they would keep the empire of Teturact inviolate. There was no better way to die.

The empire included the Stratix system itself, and the forge worlds of Salshan Anterior and Telkrid IX. It encompassed the mineral-rich asteroid fields that circled the blue dwarf star Serpentis Minor. From naval shipyards, to agri-worlds that produced enough to feed those of his followers who still needed to eat, Teturact controlled enough resources and manpower to force the Imperium into a war that could last for centuries. The empire of Teturact was not due to fall for a very long time.

THE EMPIRE OF Teturact flickered by on the grand Galactarium, its diseased star systems whirling around the superimposed image from the pict-recording. Gradually individual stars locked in place over the image, until the star map and the night sky recorded over the outpost were identical.

Sergeant Graevus ran over to Techmarine Solun, who was reaching feebly for the wires plugged into the back of his head. Graevus unplugged the wires and Solun's eyes flickered back into focus.

'Did you find it, brother?' asked Graevus.

'Stratix Luminae,' said Solun. 'Outlying the Stratix system. It's still there untouched, it was never settled.'

'The Arbites have caught us up. Can you fight?'

'Always.'

'Good. Follow me.'

Sergeant Graveus and Techmarine Solun were still heading from the Galactarium chamber towards the front of the temple when the gunfire began.

SARPEDON HAD KNOWN the Inquisition would find them eventually – the Soul Drinkers were excommunicate, and Sarpedon had personally killed the Inquisitorial envoy who had delivered the sentence to the Chapter. But if the Ordo Hereticus could only have stayed off the scent just a little while longer, instead of finding the Chapter at their most vulnerable.

But they were implacable and intelligent. Inquisitor Tsouras, who had been outwitted by the Chapter in their escape at the Cerberian Field, had been little more than an enforcer, a thug who used his authority to bully and coerce. Thaddeus, though, must be a subtler and more patient man. It was an enemy Sarpedon did not need, not now when the whole Chapter needed to act with speed and secrecy. But Sarpedon had always known he would have to face the Inquisition again.

The first shot was from an Arbites sharpshooter, a cold-blooded killer and a good officer. His sniper-fitted autogun sent a bullet through the right eye of Phrantis Jenassis, blowing the back of the old man's head apart and leaving him a dead weight in Sarpedon's hand. The order had probably come from Inquisitor Thaddeus himself – the hostage represented Sarpedon's sole advantage, and that advantage had to be removed. The authority of the Ordo Hereticus exceeded even that of the Navigator House to which the Arbites precinct was bound.

Now the other officers had no reason not to open fire on the mutant who faced them. The pintle-mounted weaponry on the APCs sent shots raining down and Sarpedon scuttled to the side just in time to miss a cannon shot that ripped a hole in the ground and nearly blew him clean off his talons. The Arbites were mostly armed with short-ranged shotguns designed to break up riots, but those with longer range used them – sniper fire and shrapnel from grenade rounds spattered off his armour and lacerated the skin of his legs as he dropped the twitching body of Phrantis Jenassis and ran to the cover of the temple.

The body of Phrantis Jenassis flopped to the ground. His ragged turban fell off and his glossy black warp eye, now blind and harmless, stared blankly at the sky.

'Thin them out and fall back!' Sarpedon ordered Hastis and Krydel as he headed back towards the Galactarium.

Gunfire ripped out of the front of the temple and scoured the slope as the Arbites advanced. Their shotguns were useless over open

distance but once in the temple they would be ideal for blasting
around cover, so the riot details advanced through the bolter fire
coming from the two Soul Drinker squads. Sarpedon had given his
Marines time to pick their targets, but a cannon shot blew one of
Squad Krydel to pieces and volleys of small arms fire from the
sharpshooters and APCs soon made it impossible to size up targets
at will. As the first shotgun blasts sent splinters of marble showering
from the pillars, Hastis and Krydel yelled at their men to fall back
into the body of the temple, following Sarpedon towards the
courtyard.

The Galactarium was frozen, its sphere now showing only the night
sky of Stratix Luminae. It was strange to finally give the place a name.
But if the Soul Drinkers could not get that information off Kytellion
Prime, it would mean nothing.

Graevus's squad was at the edge of the courtyard, with Solun alongside them. Solun was apparently alive and capable of fighting, which
was just as well. If the Arbites judge had any sense he would send officers with grenade launchers onto the roof of the temple to rain frag and
krak grenades onto the Soul Drinkers as they fought the Arbites coming in through the front. And in a spot like that Sarpedon needed all
his battle-brothers fighting.

'We will defend this space and try to break them. Hastis and Krydel
will be the front line – Graevus, you are our reserve.' Sarpedon pointed
towards the machinery of the Galactarium. 'Destroy it.'

Graevus yelled an order and an Assault Marine ran towards the Galactarium, unhooking a large metal canister – an anti-armour melta-bomb
– from his backpack. Squads Krydel and Hastis were assembling at the
entrance to the courtyard, shotgun shrapnel following them as Hastis
stopped his squad, turned them, and began to direct their fire against the
Arbites storming in between the columns. Sarpedon added his own fire,
snapping a shot into the stomach of one officer and sending others ducking back behind the columns with a volley of bolts.

A series of massive explosions ripped from the front of the temple,
throwing a cloud of earth and marble dust into the interior. Squad Krydel was caught in the storm of shrapnel and fell back, purple armour
chalked with the white dust.

'Demolition charges,' voxed Hastis. 'They've brought down the front
of the temple.'

'More cover for the advance,' replied Sarpedon. 'We have no fields of
fire. We'll have to fight them toe-to-toe. Graevus?'

'Commander?'

'Counter-attack on my word.'

'Understood.'

There was a pause as the dust cleared. In the pause Sarpedon could hear the creaking as the melta-bomb's detonation seared through the machinery of the Galactarium and sent the huge metal construction sagging. The image twisted and flickered, and suddenly the star field was gone, to be replaced with the marble architecture of the temple. Sarpedon quickly scanned the edge of the roof around the opening to the courtyard – no Arbites waited there, but they would appear soon, to keep the Soul Drinkers pinned down while the other officers engaged them through the rubble.

Gunfire erupted between Squad Krydel and Arbites using the fallen chunks of marble to close with the Marines. Sarpedon saw Sergeant Krydel, power sword flashing, wading into the fight. Squad Hastis was backing them up, snapping bolter shots into the Arbites who ducked out of cover to loose off shotgun blasts.

Sarpedon holstered his bolter even as a scattering of blasts scored the floor armour him. He gripped his nalwood force staff with both hands and felt the psychic fire spiralling around him, forming a circuit of power that ran from the heart of his brain to the squirming nalwood in his fist. He was still a little nervous of the power inside him – he had always been strong but since the terrible events on the unnamed world and the *Brokenback* his psychic powers boiled hotter than ever, bubbling away in his subconscious and demanding a release.

A release like this. Like the Hell.

He focused his psychic power and forced it outwards, trained by the lens of his mind into images created to inflict pure terror. Shrieking, bat-like shapes dropped from above to tear through the Arbites on trails of crimson fire. Sarpedon concentrated and forced more from his mind until a whole swarm of them coursed through the Galactarium temple.

'Daemons!' someone yelled. The Inquisition probably suspected the Soul Drinkers were worshippers of Chaos, and had warned the Arbites to expect a daemonic threat. If they feared daemons, that was what Sarpedon would give them.

The Hell, the psychic power that had caused Sarpedon to enter the ranks of the Chapter's librarium, ripped into the Arbites. It was a storm of nightmares, drawing images of terror from the minds of its targets and sending those terrors swarming around them. Sarpedon was a telepath who could transmit but not receive, and his power had been honed by the librarium and his own willpower into a mental weapon the likes of which few Librarians had ever possessed. Physically it was harmless, but psychologically it was devastating. In the wreckage of the temple the effect was magnified, as Arbites out of sight of their fellow officers were pounced on by flying horrors that howled as they whipped their coils through the air above them.

Arbites were firing into the air. Many were panicking – Arbites were ideologically trained to a degree that the best Imperial Guard units could not boast, but few of them had faced daemons. Or, for that matter, a psyker as trained and powerful as Sarpedon.

'Graevus!' yelled Sarpedon 'Attack!'

Squad Graevus ran through Squads Hastis and Krydel, and Sarpedon went with them. Sarpedon had seen to it that all Soul Drinkers had been trained against the Hell through simulated battlefields on the *Brokenback*, so they would not be broken by it as their enemies were. Graevus sprinted into the enemy, power axe flashing in his mutated hand. His Assault Marines sent sprays of bolt pistol fire into the Arbites that was followed up with their chainblades, cutting through riot armour as if it wasn't there.

Sarpedon was in a split second later, his altered legs carrying him over a chunk of fallen marble and into the Arbites sheltering behind. He focused his power into the force staff and swiped the weapon through the first knot of Arbites he saw. He saw himself reflected in the black glass visors of their riot helmets as he sliced right through two of them at once. One officer still stood – Sarpedon impaled him with his forward leg, the bionic one, punching through his chest and flinging him back over his head.

Sergeant Graevus darted round the slab of marble and cut down the officer trying to bring his shotgun to bear on Sarpedon. All around bolter shells were blazing, cutting orange traces of fire through the air. The din of battle was hot in Sarpedon's ears – he could hear Arbites officers yelling, trying to find one another, give orders, or just scream at the monsters hurtling at them from the air.

Squad Graevus cut through the Arbites savagely. Arbites on the roof fired down not into battered, pinned Marines but into Squad Hastis, who returned fire instantly and sent the broken bodies of launcher-armed Arbites falling to the floor of the courtyard. By the time Squad Graevus reached the front of the temple, well over a hundred Arbites were dead, wounded, or hopelessly scattered.

The Soul Drinkers followed the fleeing Arbites out of the temple and into the grounds, knowing there were still enough officers left to regroup and attack again if they were given the chance. Squad Graevus quickly disabled the Arbites APCs with krak grenades while Squad Krydel took pot shots at the Arbites scattering into the gardens.

'Leave the crews,' said Sarpedon. 'I don't want more dead than there have to be.' He spotted the command APC on the slope near the ridge and quickly crossed the bullet-scarred earth. He holstered his force staff and ripped the side hatch off the side of the APC.

Inside sat the astropath. The old man showed no fear.

'You have one more message to send,' said Sarpedon. 'Tell Inquisitor Thaddeus that we are not what he thinks we are. I know he cannot let us go free, but ultimately he and I are on the same side. If it comes down to it, I will have to kill him in order to continue our work. He will understand what drives us, because it is the same thing that drives him.'

The astropath nodded silently. Sarpedon left him in the APC and voxed his squads in the temple.

'The fighters cannot reach us in the dome. We need to get out onto the surface for pickup. Follow me.'

Sarpedon let the lifesign runes for the three-squad force flash onto his retina. Squad Krydel had lost two Marines, while Squad Graevus had lost one in the thick of the fight with the Arbites. Three more that could not be replaced within the foreseeable future. Sarpedon knew that many more would be lost before the harvest could begin and the Soul Drinkers could rise again.

But now they knew, at least, where they had to start. Stratix Luminae. With that information, they were one step closer to survival.

THE MAP OF the empire was an arrangement of precious stones, torn from the necklaces and earrings of Stratix's wealthy and handed as tributes to the court of Teturact. They were set out on the floor of south-western dock three, which had been appointed as the seat of Teturact's rule. South-western dock three was several layers down into one of Stratix's hive-stacks and was draped in tapestries of gauze torn from infected wounds, their patterns of gore and pus a gift from the legions of grateful plague-ridden. The corners of the cavernous space, beneath the docking clamps and control towers, were crammed with huddled figures that had made pilgrimages into the very presence of their lord and yet were so awed by him they could not approach. The floor was heaped with the bodies of those who had died of that awe, and pure liquid pestilence wept from the walls and dripped in a fine drizzle from the ceiling.

Teturact leaned forward on his palanquin. The four brute-mutants, so muscular even the features of their faces were obscured by folds of brawn, tilted the platform forward so Teturact could get a better look at the map. Stratix, in the centre like the star in the middle of a system, was a single blood-red ruby the size of a fist. The forge worlds were sapphires, blue as dead lips. The worlds of the front line, where Imperial Guard regiments were pouring into killing grounds swarming with Teturact's followers, were fiery yellow-orange opals. Loyal worlds were diamonds, hard and clear in their devotion to their saviour. There were hundreds of gemstones, each one a major world under Teturact's control, each crammed with souls who owed their lives to him.

Teturact had been dead for several years. His heart was just a knot of dried flesh somewhere in his dusty ribcage. Only his mind was truly alive, pulsing away beneath the tight skin of his skull and behind the rictus face with its horrible dried-out eyeballs. His body, thin and wizened with jaundiced yellow skin, was animated by will alone – his muscles had long since wasted away. Teturact was, in a very real sense, a being of pure willpower. He dominated those around him directly. Take the simple bovine minds of the brute-mutant bearers – he barely had to think to control them. Others he controlled by manipulating their circumstances until they had no choice but to obey his every wish.

The diseases – and there were many, to keep any one cure from harming his cause – were just a part of it. They were the catalyst. It was the force of Teturact's will that was his real weapon. And that force of will had won him a mighty empire such as the Black Crusades themselves had rarely won.

Many of the worlds on the chart were emeralds, green with potential. They were worlds that had only just begun the traumatic process of bending to Teturact's will. On some, the plague was only just making itself known, spread by Teturact's agents devoted to bringing enlightening disease to governors and hive-scum alike. Others were nearly ripe, and Teturact would soon leave the seat of his power on Stratix to bestow life upon the infected through the sorcery he could wield over disease.

One emerald caught his eye. It was near the front line, and would provide a great strategic advantage in anchoring a stretch of space that could easily be turned into a massive warzone if he wished it.

Colonel, he spoke to the shadows, his voice a rich psychic boom since he could not speak with his own rotted vocal chords.

A human form shambled towards Teturact, and bowed before the palanquin. It was draped in bloody bandages but beneath them tattered crimsons showed, with the glints of silver bullion trim and a chest full of campaign medals. Colonel Karendin had been little more than a butcher even before the plague had taken him – Teturact had left his mind mostly intact and he served to oversee the military situation in the empire.

What of this world? Teturact pointed a spidery finger at the strategic emerald.

'Eumenix?' replied Karendin, voice hissing thick with spittle. 'It is nearly ready to fall. The governor is dead, they say. The Arbites have fallen. No ship has left for many weeks. A billion have drowned in blood and bile already.'

Then I will go there next, said Teturact. *I want this world, and with as little delay as possible.*

'If you leave now, saviour, the planet will be ripe when you arrive. I could have your flagship prepared at once.'

Do so. Teturact settled back into the upholstery of the palanquin. *Our empire grows, colonel. Like the disease, our worlds multiply. Do you see how we infect?*

'Oh yes, saviour!' hissed Karendin. A faint gaggle of agreement came from the pilgrims huddled in the shadows. 'Like the plague itself, a plague on the stars!'

See to it that the court can be embarked within the day, said Teturact, losing interest in the colonel's blandishments.

Eumenix. A fine world to take, a hive world teeming with infected who would rise up and worship him when he promised them release. Such a fine world, indeed, that would greet him as a saviour, and die for him as a god.

SISTER BERENICE AESCARION was sixty-three years old. She had spent fifty-three of those years consecrated as a daughter of the Emperor, her body conditioned and her mind purified with diligence and atonement so she could serve as a soldier of the Emperor's church. She had been taken from the Schola Progenium where orphans of Imperial servants were raised, then brought into the presence of the preachers and confessors of the Adeptus Ministorum. They had filled her mind with the revelations of the Emperor, but she had not been afraid. She had heard of the horrors of apostasy and unbelief that opened the doors to sin and corruption, but she had not despaired.

The hellfire confessors had not reduced the girl to tears. The words of the preachers had left her inspired, not cowed. She had the willpower to join the ranks of the Sisters, and during her novicehood amongst the Orders Famulous it had become apparent that she also had the physical endurance and zeal to join the Orders Militant.

Her faith had never left her. Never, though she had fought across the galaxy, following the banner of the Order of the Ebon Chalice from the abbey on Terra itself to the edge of Imperial space. In her later years she had tracked down and killed the Daemon Prince Parmenides the Vile, and in doing so had acted in a precarious alliance between the Sisters of Battle and the Inquisition. She had acquired a reputation as one of the few Sisters who could navigate the tangled question of church and Inquisitorial authority without losing sight of the ultimate enemy – Chaos, the darkness the Emperor still fought with the strength of his spirit. So when Inquisitor Thaddeus had requested a taskforce of Sisters to be assembled from a number of Orders Militant, it was Sister Aescarion he had asked to lead it.

Canoness Tasmander had asked Sister Aescarion to take on leadership of the Ebon Chalice, but she had turned down the office of canoness. Aescarion had fought her whole life, and she was too old to do anything other than keep fighting. It was the only way she knew her faith could become something more than mere words – that same faith that had made her a Sister in the first place, that had driven her to vanquish Parmenides and countless other enemies of humanity. It was the same faith that was being sorely tested in the depths of Eumenix.

Eumenix. If ever the Emperor's light had been taken from a world, it was this. She had never seen a world so utterly desolate of hope, and she had seen some terrible things. Eumenix was a grim illustration of what could happen in the absence of faith.

Aescarion watched as Interrogator Shen, his massive bronze carapace armour tarnished by the week-long trek through the filth and horror of Hive Quintus, moved warily down the steep shaft that led deeper into the lower layers of the hive. The air was infernally hot for the geothermal heatsinks were nearby, and everything stank. On the surface Sister Aescarion and her squad had seen mouldering mountains of corpses and their diseased reek seemed to permeate the whole planet – sweet and sickening, pure rot and corruption.

Down here, the heat made it worse. For several days Shen and the Sisters had been moving into the depths of the hive and now they were dozens of levels down, near the last possible Imperial institution in Hive Quintus. The Arbites and the governor's palace had fallen, the cathedral was a burned-out shell and the offices of the Administratum had been the first to fall when the madness began. The Adeptus Mechanicus geological outpost in the lower reaches of the hive was the last possible nugget of resistance, and last place where the reports of escaping Soul Drinkers might be confirmed.

That had been weeks ago. Thaddeus had passed on the news as quickly as he could, but had entrusted the actual investigation to Interrogator Shen while he himself sifted through the *Brokenback* and the wreckage of House Jenassis. Both Shen and Aescarion held out little hope for finding anything alive in Hive Quintus – at least, not alive in the normal sense.

The architecture this far down was cramped and twisted: the compressed, distorted relics of the settlements on which Hive Quintus had been built. Discoloured moisture ran down the walls, filtered down through a hundred floors of decay. Ruptured power conduits covered everything in a dank mist. Plague-rats the size of attack dogs writhed through the twisted metal. The groaning of the settling city was punctured by the screams of yet another life being snuffed out, one amongst billions on the nightmare of Eumenix.

The corridor angled downwards and bent sharply up ahead. Shen drew his inferno pistol from its holster and moved up to the corner, the boots of his carapace armour crunching through the crystallised filth that encrusted the floor. Sister Aescarion followed, bolt pistol drawn, as did the Seraphim she had chosen to accompany her on the mission. One of them, Sister Mixu, had been at her side for over a decade. The others had been supplied by their own Orders, and all fought with twin bolt pistols in the tradition of the Seraphim squads.

Shen led the way round the corner. The corridor flared out into a ragged cavity, like a hole torn by a bomb blast clean through layers of the warren-like lower levels. Murky water pooled on the uneven floor and pale vapour gouted from ruptured pipelines overhead.

'Geothermal must have gone up,' said Shen as he scanned for targets. His inferno pistol was an exceedingly rare weapon that packed the power of a melta gun into a relatively small pistol, and at short ranges it could carve through anything. 'Without maintenance half the hive is probably ready to explode.'

Sister Mixu pointed up at a symbol, half a stylised metallic skull and half a square-toothed cog, grinning lopsidedly down from the mass of twisted metal. 'The symbol of the Mechanicus. Looks like we're close, sister.'

'Movement!' shouted one of the Seraphim. Sister Aescarion turned to see one of the Sisters opening fire into the shadows. Shen followed her aim, firing a bolt of superheated matter that briefly lit the twisted, sub-humanoid shapes that were massing in the gloom.

The enemy weren't bandits, because they didn't steal anything. It was as if they pounced on anything living just for the novelty of killing something alive. They were the shambling remnants of the underhivers who had been reduced to walking corpses by the plague, and they had dogged the heels of Shen and the Seraphim for whole hellish journey to the underside of Hive Quintus.

In the brief burst of light, Aescarion counted fifty plus of them. The inferno pistol claimed three, scorched to cinders, and bolt pistol fire stitched a bloody path through several others.

'Fall back!' called Aescarion and drew her Sisters around her, adding her bolt pistol fire to theirs. The hive-scum surrounded them, clambering from the ragged walls, moaning their death-rattles. She could see their peeling skin and the runny whites of their eyes, their lolling jaws and the gnarled, blackened fingers that held crude clubs and blades.

If there was proof that Eumenix was cursed by Chaos, it was this. A disease that not only killed, but turned the bodies of its victims into mindless predators to stalk the survivors.

The Seraphim backed off slowly, pumping bolts into the shambling wave of the dead that was pouring in ever-greater numbers into the cavity. Shen's inferno pistol was recharged and sent out another hissing lance of fire that tore through a dozen scum at once.

'We're surrounded,' said Shen with a calm that struck Aescarion as most admirable. He indicated the Mechanicus symbol. 'We'll have to cut our way out. Head that way and we may hit the outpost, it'll be easier to defend.'

Aescarion nodded in agreement and drew the power axe from its holster on her back. She had fought with that same axe for decades, always refusing more refined weapons because the brutality of the axe was a befitting tool to bring down the Emperor's unflinching justice.

The weapon's blade hummed to life and a shimmering blue power field played around it.

'With me!' yelled Shen and fired his inferno pistol into the knot of plague-scum beneath the Mechanicus symbol. He charged into the remainder, barging their rotting bodies aside. The Seraphim behind Shen blew bodies apart with their twin bolt pistols. Sister Aescarion ran past Shen into the underhivers, hacking at the wall of flesh in front of her. Gnarled hands reached towards her and she hacked them off with her axe, punching her gauntleted fist into the mutilated faces behind. She stamped down and felt bodies crunching beneath her feet. Bolt pistol fire raged past her into the plague-dead, thinning them out around her as she and Shen barged their way through their attackers and out of the explosion site.

They plunged deeper into the darkness, snapping off shots at anything that moved. At Shen's lead they kept moving, knowing that if they stopped, their slower but massively more numerous attackers would be able to surround them and cut them off in the narrow, twisting tunnels below.

Age-darkened brass and heavy gothic mechanical architecture began to surface amongst the grime of the underhive. Massive industrial cogs lay here and there and the symbols of the Machine-God were tooled into every girder. The Adeptus Ministorum were privately wary of the

Adeptus Mechanicus – the tech-priests worshipped the Omnissiah, the Machine-God, which they claimed to be an aspect of Emperor, but the Ministorum had their secret doubts. That said, Sister Aescarion was grateful that at least they knew how to build.

The Mechanicus outpost was a solid cube of brass, its surface knotted with pipes, strong enough to survive the crushing weight of the hive above it. The entrances were massive blast doors sealed tight and Shen stepped back warily when he saw the sentry guns and the bullet-riddled bodies of plague-dead that had been unfortunate enough to shamble into range.

The squad scouted around the outpost, finding scores of dead – most of them infected but some in the rust-red coveralls of Mechanicus menials, along with one or two servitors hurriedly refitted for combat. Corpses lay draped over makeshift barricades, set up to funnel the shambling hordes into kill-zones now choked with their bodies. The outpost must have held out for weeks as Hive Quintus slowly turned into hell.

One door was not sealed. The underside of the outpost was blackened with scorch marks from a massive explosion that had ripped the lower hatch open. Jagged metal ringed the opening overhead like torn skin around an open wound.

Shen waded through the knee-deep murky water that filled the tunnels beneath the outpost. The opening overhead was dark and the walls were riddled with bullet holes.

'Bolter fire,' said Aescarion. She had seen the results of bolter weapons more often than she could remember. 'Disciplined. Tightly grouped.'

The final reports off Hive Quintus had been of the last shuttle out being stolen by purple-armoured monsters, leaving the wealthy Cartel Pollos on the hive to die. Shen and Aescarion had been sent to find out if there was any truth to them, but the outpost was the only place on the planet where Imperial personnel might survive to verify them. Now it seemed that not only had the outpost fallen, but that the Soul Drinkers might have been the ones who attacked it.

Shen reached up and grabbed the edge of the wrecked blast door above him. He hauled himself up through the opening and switched on the light mounted on the collar of his armour.

'Nothing,' he said. 'There must have been a hell of a firefight here. Small arms and grenades. There are bodies everywhere.'

'Follow me,' said Aescarion to her Seraphim, then followed Shen into the body of the outpost. She was reminded of her age as she clambered up beside him – it would have been much easier with the jump packs

Seraphim usually fought with, but they had left the packs behind since a hive city was hardly the most appropriate terrain for their use.

Shen was right. The straight, metal-walled corridors of the outpost had seen ferocious fighting. Blade marks on the floor and walls told of hand-to-hand butchery, the bullet-riddled walls of massive weight of fire. The corpses of menials lay where they had fallen defending the breached entrance.

The rest of the Seraphim climbed up into the corridor. 'No life signs,' said Sister Mixu, who carried the squad's auspex scanner. 'But there's a lot of interference. This place is pretty solidly built.'

'The underhivers didn't do this,' said Shen.' And if the Soul Drinkers didn't then it was somebody capable of bringing down a similar level of firepower. We need to find out what they wanted with this place.'

'Agreed,' said Aescarion. 'Could the Mechanicus have been working on something here? A weapon?'

'We'll find out. This outpost will be built along standard template construct lines. There'll be a control post at the centre and a testing bay not far above us. We'll try those first, then scour the rest.'

The outpost was a combination of massive industrial workings and the sort of oppressive gothic architecture that Aescarion was familiar with from the convent prioris on Terra. Fluted columns separated banks of cogs like giant clockwork, frozen by the outpost's shutdown. Turbines lay beneath vaulted ceilings. Shrines to the Machine-God were everywhere, stained with libations of machine oil, scrawled with prayers in binary. Everything the Mechanicus did needed the correct rites enacted to the Machine-God – and judging by the abundance of offerings and prayer-tablets in the empty armoury, it seemed that included fighting.

The testing bay held hundreds of geological samples in various stages of examination under powerful brass-cased microscopes, or lying in chemical baths now dried out. There was nothing there that suggested anything valuable enough for the outpost to be attacked. The control room that overlooked the bay was empty, too, its cogitators ritually sealed with runes of inaction to appease the machine-spirits as they were shut down.

'We should take what information they still hold,' said Shen. 'At least we'll have some idea of what work they did here and who was involved. They might even have pict-recordings from the sentry guns, so we could see who attacked them.'

'I am no tech-priest,' said Aescarion. 'Do you know how to operate all this?' She indicated the banks of cogitators that covered the walls of the control room, with blank readout screens.

'We'll just take the memory units,' said Shen. 'Thaddeus has men who can open them up.'

'Movement,' said Mixu, glancing at the auspex screen. 'Somewhere above us.'

'Probably more underhivers,' said Shen, drawing his pistol.

A hand plunged down through the ceiling of the control room, grabbing Shen by the collar of his armour and dragging him up sharply, slamming him into the metal ceiling. The hand was encased in a gauntlet of purple ceramite.

'Fire!' yelled Aescarion and bolter fire ripped up into the ceiling beside Shen, who was trying to bring his inferno pistol to bear. Before he could get a shot up he was dragged through the ceiling completely, the metal tearing as his armoured body disappeared from view.

Sister Aescarion was the first after him. The hole in the ceiling led to what must have been the outpost's main shrine, where ranges of pews carved out of solid carbon faced an altar formed from the casings of a giant cogitator. Pipes and valves knotted the walls so the chapel was contained entirely within the body of the cogitator, and when operational its readouts would have bathed the shrine in a glow of information. Now it was dark, so the scene in front of her was lit only in the flashes from the light mounted on Shen's armour.

It was a Space Marine. Its armour bore the chalice symbol of the Soul Drinkers on one shoulder pad. It carried no weapons.

Aescarion caught a glimpse of its face. In life the skin had been dark but now it was pasty and mottled grey with disease. The eyes were gone and dark ragged holes stared blindly. The lower part of the face had been gnawed away and the bleached white of jawbone and teeth grinned out. Nothing living could look like that, and nothing dead could stare with such blind madness and hate. Sister Aescarion only had the briefest glimpse by the swinging light on Shen's armour, but in an instant there was no doubt.

A Soul Drinker, claimed by the plague. The bullet scars on its armour suggested that it had been mortally wounded in the battle for the outpost, that it had been left behind by its colleagues, and succumbed to the terrible plague that had savaged Hive Quintus. It was the first time Sister Aescarion had actually set eyes on a member of the Chapter.

As she watched, trying to get a clear shot, the dead Soul Drinker tore Interrogator Shen's arm off at the shoulder in a crimson crescent of blood. The arm holding the pistol was flung to one side of the chapel and the rest of him to the other, his armoured body crashing limply into the wall.

Sister Mixu was beside Aescarion, firing her twin pistols. She snapped off two rapid head shots, blowing a hole in the Marine's forehead, but the Soul Drinker seemed not to even notice the massive wound. Aescarion couldn't claim to know a great deal about fighting the living dead but she hazarded a guess that it would take more than just a killing wound to fell the Soul Drinker – nothing but dismemberment would stop it. And dismemberment was something at which Aescarion excelled.

She drew the power axe and charged the Marine. It was a full head taller than her but she was much quicker. Her blade flashed down and she hacked deep through the Marine's collar and into his torso, the axe's power field splitting his fused ribcage and carving through dead organs.

The Marine gripped the haft of the axe, pivoted, and flung Aescarion into the brass-cased altarpiece-machine. The casing buckled beneath the impact and components rained down as Aescarion slid to the floor. Telltales flashed on her armour's retinal display and a brief flash of pain dulled to an ache as painkillers flooded her system.

The Soul Drinker stood above her, staring blindly down with its dried-out eye sockets. Bolt pistol fire ripped into its back from the Seraphim emerging into the chapel behind it, punching through the tarnished armour and kicking chunks from its skull. Its broken face grinned down as it reached for Aescarion.

Aescarion tried to roll out of its way but her body wouldn't respond – she must have shattered a shoulder and maybe a hip. The Soul Drinker picked her up by the shoulder joins of her breastplate and began to pull, trying to crack her open like a predator opening up armoured prey to get at the flesh inside.

Aescarion could feel her armour coming apart. Her good arm still held her axe and she felt its power field humming. As the telltales flashed red on her retina she dragged the blade into the waist of the Soul Drinker. She used every ounce of her strength to cut through the ceramite power armour, but she had no leverage and her system was struggling to cope with the pain.

One of the Seraphim wrapped an arm around the Marine's neck from behind, trying to saw its head off with her combat knife. The Marine turned and drove an elbow into the Sister's midriff, knocking her backwards. It let go of Aescarion with one hand as it did so. She planted one foot onto the floor of the chapel and swivelled on it, ripping the axe blade through the waist of the Space Marine, cutting clean through the ceramite and the Marine's spine.

Aescarion slumped to the floor. The upper part of the Soul Drinker's body fell beside her. Its legs stood for a moment, then fell to one side, clattering against the metal of the chapel.

The Seraphim picked herself off the floor and stood over the upper half of the Soul Drinker. It looked up at her, head jerking as the end of its severed spine flopped like a beached fish. Aescarion handed her the axe, and without switching on the power field, the Seraphim cut off the Soul Drinker's head.

Mixu was on the other side of the room, tending to Shen.

'He's dying, sister,' said Mixu. Two of the Seraphim helped Aescarion over to where the interrogator lay. Gore pumped from the torn shoulder socket, forming a thick pool beneath him. His eyes were open but they couldn't focus on anything and though his jaw worked no sound came out. Mixu opened up the breastplate of the carapace armour and Aescarion saw right away that the interrogator was beyond hope. The ribs had been broken and separated by the force of his arm being torn off, and then crushed when he hit the wall. The organs inside must have been torn to shreds.

As Aescarion watched, Shen died.

'He was a soldier of the Emperor,' said Aescarion, grimly aware of her own injuries. 'We cannot let him rise again.'

The Seraphim carried Shen's body down to the turbine floor, where they placed a long-fused krak grenade in his mouth and reduced the corpse to a rain of ash.

Aescarion was no tech-priest and only knew enough of the Machine-God's dogma to maintain her own battle-gear. She had the Seraphim lever off the casings of cogitators in the control room and remove what she took to be the datacores inside. Aescarion herself removed a plaque on the wall of the control room that recorded all the adepts who had ever worked in the outpost – hundreds of names inscribed in tiny letters on a sheet of brass. As an afterthought she took the head of the dead Marine, and sealed it in a specimen box from the lab, along with the Marine's bolt pistol that was still in its holster with its golden chalice symbol.

There was nothing else of value in the place. She only hoped that she had found something worth Shen's life. Mixu saw to Aescarion's injuries as best she could and Aescarion gave her the authority to lead the squad out to their extraction point.

It had been difficult for Shen to arrange for a naval salvage craft to pick them up from the wastes outside Hive Quintus – the Officio Medicae had banned all travel and few crews wanted to risk the polluted wastes. Inquisitorial authority had barely cut through the red tape in time to get Shen and the Seraphim onto Eumenix in the first place. If the squad wasn't there for the pick-up, the crew would abandon them there, and they would never escape. It was a good few days' travel to reach the barren inter-hive wastes and with Aescarion injured it would take even longer than she had feared.

Sister Mixu took them off as quickly as she dared, through the darkness and danger of Hive Quintus.

FAR ABOVE THE polluted wastes, a ship from the dockyards of Stratix approached the thinly-stretched quarantine line around Eumenix. Orbital batteries fell silent at its approach, crews suddenly riddled with the most virulent plagues. Officio Medicae craft fled from it like shoals of fish before a shark as their survival instincts set alarms ringing. Plague and madness had come, concentrated into the force of one being.

For the plague-damned of Hive Quintus, their saviour was almost upon them.

CHAPTER FIVE

A SHADOW, LIGHT years across, was cast like a dark halo around the warzone. The Imperium had quarantined the tortured worlds under Teturact's rebellion, establishing a firebreak of locked-down star systems. Whole worlds were under house arrest, their fleets grounded, their populations prevented from leaving without permission from the warzone's military command and the Officio Medicae. Cathedrals of the Imperial Faith offered up prayers for deliverance, begging the Emperor in his wisdom to let victory come to the Imperial war effort before the plague visited their worlds. Dark rumours circulated about Teturact, and the horror that would unfold if he ever broke through the Imperial fleets that were massing around his rebellious empire. Governors reassured their people that the Navy and the Guard would soon blaze into the warzone and puncture the heart of Teturact's pestilent realm. They were also in the throes of preparing hermetically-sealed bunkers in case the plagues reached them.

The Imperium was, in many ways, constantly at war – but around the empire of Teturact, war was a stifling, sinister shroud draped over hundreds of worlds and billions of people. Fear swamped the minds of billions. They said that Eumenix had fallen, so who knew where would be struck next?

Interstellar traffic was quiet and the space lanes heavily monitored. Travel between systems had to be sanctioned by the Imperial authorities, with no exceptions. But there were always those who tried to make themselves exceptions – smugglers running supplies between quarantined worlds that they would sell for a huge mark-up, deserters escaping from the warzone, and the usual criminals and degenerates who fled from the Imperium during routine times. Most were picked up or destroyed, but some as ever got through.

And some were almost completely invisible. It was difficult enough to catch massive cargo ships slipping in and out of the warp in the quarantined systems. It was next to impossible to see them when they were fighter-sized craft – a fraction the size of the smallest Imperial warp-capable ship. But the shoal of craft that slipped through the darkness around the Stratix warzone were not Imperial.

They were alien fighters; their faintly sinister organic lines contained powerful vortex reactors that could push them into and out of the warp. It was dangerous, there was no doubt about it. No one really knew which xenos species had built the fighters, and the handful of captured Navigators who directed the squadron through the warp were, through necessity, not the best. But it was worth it. If they achieved what they set out to do, the risk was worth it.

Sarpedon looked out on the star-scattered darkness from the first fighter's cockpit. He wasn't even sure it was a fighter – when Techmarine Lygris had shown Sarpedon the fleet of bizarre craft on one of the *Brokenback's* many flight decks, the ships were empty of any ordnance or weapons save those that could be extruded from the ships' hulls. Instead, Lygris had fitted out the ships with grav-couches so each could carry a payload of Marines. It was an enormous risk, transporting almost the entire Chapter on ships that traversed the warp by means the Techmarines couldn't begin to understand. But it was the only way – the *Brokenback* couldn't have hoped to slip into the warzone.

Inside the fighter the cold, bulbous forms of the bridge were an odd silvery colour with a sheen of sinister purple. The Chapter serfs at the controls – some of the few survivors of the Chapter's break with the Imperium and the battle on the *Brokenback* – worked the fighter's instruments by moving their hands through pools of molten metal like strangely-hued quicksilver. The basic readouts had been translated from amorphous alien runes, but most of the information that ran across the irregularly shaped readouts was indecipherable. The ship was almost crushingly non-human – corridors twisted and the mysterious vortex generators were strange organic shapes like seed pods or the shells of sea creatures. The air was only breathable because of the filters and purifiers that pumped oxygen through vents that had once held gases toxic to humans. The inhabitants had evidently been taller but thinner than humans, as the ceilings were high and everything was narrow.

'What are our coordinates?' Sarpedon asked the Chapter serfs.

The serf at the navigation controls didn't look round as he replied. 'We're on top of the meeting point, Lord Sarpedon.'

'Give me the fleet vox.' Another serf dipped a hand into a shimmering pool of metal and Sarpedon was connected to the other nine fighter craft. 'All craft, be on the lookout for Dreo. We cannot wait here long.'

Somewhere in that band of stars across the sky was the corrupt heart of Teturact's empire. Somewhere far more distant was Terra, the equally corrupt heart of the Imperium. The galaxy out there was utterly immense, and beyond it was the warp, a whole dimension of horror that bled into real space every time mankind jumped between the stars. Against it all the Soul Drinkers stood, utterly alone, a little less than seven hundred warriors who were, even after all their alterations and training, still ultimately men. It was almost liberating for Sarpedon to look on the sheer vastness of the fight, and to know that he had made a conscious decision to go on fighting.

'Signals, commander,' came a voice over the vox. It was Techmarine Lygris, who had managed to activate some of the strange sensor devices that jutted from the prow of his fighter. 'It's weak. They must be low on fuel.'

'Do you have a visual?'

A few moments passed, and then a film of liquid metal bled across the air and an image swam onto it. A shuttle limped painfully through space, one of its engines flaring as it died. Its hull was pitted with corrosion and streaked with burns from laser fire. It was a private craft designed for short hops between planets – not agonising hauls between systems. It must have taken months to get this far from Eumenix. There was no guarantee that any normal human could survive such conditions.

'Lygris, direct us in. I'll dock with them.'

'Understood. You realise any one of them could be infected.'

'If they're infected then the prisoner will be dead, and we might as well be. Besides, I need to debrief them myself.'

Lygris directed the serfs on Sarpedon's fighter to fly towards the battered shuttle. A section of the fighter's hull bulged outwards and burst like an ulcer; globules of liquid metal flowing into one another until they formed a smooth tunnel that latched onto the side of the shuttle like a hungry leech.

The metal formed a sharp, biting edge and began to bore through the hull of the shuttle.

A pressurised pocket formed in the hull of the fighter as the metallic bridge became airtight, and the wall formed an airlock. Sarpedon was there as soon as it had fully formed. 'Squad Hastis, Squad Karvik, meet me at the airlock. You too, Pallas.'

The smell of stale sweat exhaled from the flower-like airlock as it opened and the two Marine squads joined Sarpedon. The air inside the shuttle must have been barely breathable.

'Any communication from them?' voxed Sarpedon.

'None,' replied Lygris from his own craft. 'They're not receiving, either. Their comms must have gone down.'

Sarpedon peered into the darkness at the end of the airlock tunnel. A figure moved from the shadows, and slowly limped into the tunnel.

It was Sergeant Salk. His face – usually youthful compared to the Chapter's battle-scarred veterans – was now sunken-eyed and emaciated. His armour was tarnished and he walked as if it weighed him down.

'We lost Captain Dreo,' he said hoarsely. 'Karrik and Krin made it. Nicias died in the shuttle. We lost Dreo and the rest on the planet.'

Sarpedon had seen dozens of good Marines die, but his heart still sank. Captain Dreo was perhaps the best shot in the whole Chapter, and a fine level headed soldier. It was his nerve that had held in the confrontation with the Daemon Prince Ve'Meth, and his command that had riddled Ve'Meth's host bodies with bolter fire. That was why Sarpedon had trusted him with the Eumenix mission. Now he was gone, and another Soul Drinker would never be replaced.

'And the prisoner?'

'Survived.'

Salk waved forward another Marine – Sarpedon recognised it as Krin, who normally carried Squad Salk's plasma gun. Now he carried the sleeping body of a woman, tiny in his arms. Her clothes had once been the rust-red robes that signified the rank of a Mechanicus Adept but now they were charred and filthy. She was short and boyish with a square face mostly obscured by the pilot's rebreather unit she wore.

Apothecary Pallas took the limp body from Krin. He consulted the medical readouts on the back of his Narthecium gauntlet, the instrument that would enable a blood transfusion and, if necessary, administer the Emperor's mercy to those beyond help. Now it gave him an overview of the woman's condition.

'She's badly malnourished,' he said. 'Semi-conscious. We have enough of an apothecarion on Karendin's ship to help her.'

'Can she speak?'

'Not yet.'

Sarpedon recognised her as the much younger woman from the Stratix Luminae files. In them she could be seen ducking in fear from the bolter fire as the Soul Drinkers of a decade ago stormed the labs to drive out the eldar pirates. Now she was much older, with lines around her eyes and her hair shaven at the back of her neck to accommodate the sockets drilled into her skull.

Somewhere in Captain Korvax's mission reports there was a staff roster for the installation, and from these records Sarpedon had learned the woman's name – Sarkia Aristeia. She was then an adept inferior, just one step up from a menial but one of the only staff members that the Soul Drinkers could locate. It was strange to finally see her when acquiring her had cost so many lives – she seemed such a small and inconsequential thing. Sarpedon had fought daemons and monstrous aliens for over seventy years as a warrior, but she was a vital part of Sarpedon's plan, and without her the Chapter was lost.

Was Sarkia Aristeia worth the deaths of Captain Dreo, of Aean, Hortis, Dryan and the giant Nicias? If a hundred other vital victories were won, then yes. But there was so much still to do, and the hardest fights were always ahead.

'Stabilise her and take her to Karendin,' said Sarpedon to Pallas. 'I need to question her as soon as possible.'

'Perhaps it would be wisest if Chaplain Iktinos...' began Pallas, with slight awkwardness.

'Of course,' said Sarpedon, realising the Apothecary's point. 'She must have seen enough monsters on Eumenix, there is no need for her to see another.' Sarpedon had been imposing enough before he had become a mutant and the sight of him now would probably have knocked Aristeia unconscious again. 'Let Iktinos talk to her.'

Pallas carried the woman to the crew compartment so he could examine her properly. Karrik emerged from the shuttle, his armour charred black. His face was burned badly and, like Salk's, emaciated in a way that was uncharacteristic of a Marine.

'How was Dreo lost?' asked Sarpedon.

'Sentry gun,' replied Salk. 'He blew open the lower entrance of the outpost and was the first in. The Mechanicus had stepped up their security, the whole planet was on the slide by then.'

'And the others?'

'Nicias died on the way here. He had multiple internal injuries and there were only emergency medical supplies on the shuttle. We used those for the woman. Nicias went into half-sleep and never woke up. The rest were killed in the assault or lost when we broke into the spaceport.'

'How long have you been adrift?'

'Three months. According to the mission plan it should have been longer, but Eumenix went downhill fast and we had to get off. Then again, I don't think she'd have survived the shuttle any longer. The food ran out a week ago. The air had been excessively recycled so she couldn't breathe properly and we were down to our last rebreather filter.'

'The astropathic traffic we have seen suggests there was a plague on Eumenix. Do you or your Marines show any symptoms?'

Salk shook his head. 'Nothing. The conditions were bad there but we haven't brought anything back with us. And it was more than a plague, commander. It was something that rotted the mind. The whole hive had gone mad. Maybe even the whole planet. The dead were walking the streets and the living were butchering one another. It was as well we moved when we did. We would never have got Aristeia off the planet otherwise.'

'You have done well, Salk. With Dreo gone your chances were very slim.'

'I cannot help but feel his death was too high a price to pay, commander.'

'High, but not too high. I cannot tell you what we are fighting for, Salk, but you must trust me when I say it is worth anything we sacrifice. Dreo will be remembered for his part in our coming victory, but if we do not win it then none of us will be remembered. You and your men should transfer to Karendin's ship with the prisoner. He and Pallas will fix you up.'

The two squads returned to their quarters and the ragged remains of Squad Salk headed for the docking bay where they, along with Aristeia would be transferred to the infirmary.

Maybe Salk was right. Perhaps Sarpedon's mission was impossible and he was throwing away the lives of his men. But he could not falter now, when so much was at stake. They trusted him completely, even when he could not tell them what they fought for. To give up would be to betray that trust, and with the whole galaxy intent on wiping out the Chapter their trust was one of the few advantages Sarpedon had left.

The next stage could be the riskiest of all. While Pallas and Karendin tended to Aristeia's health and Iktinos interrogated her, the makeshift fleet would have to puncture the dark heart that lay past the Imperial cordon. The Soul Drinkers would be lucky to ever come out again.

'Piloting?' he voxed.

'Commander?' came the voice of the Chapter serfs on the bridge.

'Wait until the transfer is complete, then take us to the next waypoint. Cut the shuttle free. Report any contacts and have the other fighters keep formation.'

Sarkia Aristeia would have to know the information Sarpedon needed. The fleet would have to make it to the next stage and every Marine would have to fight harder than ever before. The Inquisition would have to stay a step behind for just a little while longer. So much could go wrong, but Sarpedon would have to accept those risks. It was enough that he would fight until the end and never turn his back on his mission. Everything else was down to the grace of the Emperor and the strength of his battle-brothers.

Sarpedon turned on his eight chitinous legs and headed back towards the bridge. They were close enough now that the fleet would not have to make another risky warp jump. However in real space there were sharp-eyed battleship captains and pirates to avoid.

The strange alien fighters lanced through space in formation, carrying a cargo of the Emperor's finest warriors, with one of the most dangerous places in the Imperium as their destination.

TETURACT'S FLAGSHIP WAS a vast flying tomb. Billions had died on Stratix before Teturact saved the survivors and bound them to his will. That had left mountains of corpses heaped from the undercities to the palaces and cathedrals, a festering monument to the power of Teturact's disease and the fate of those who opposed him. Such a volume of death was an end in itself – a great and glorious reminder of how Teturact could wield death like a king's sceptre. He wanted to surround himself with death at all times, to take it with him when he left Stratix so he would always be immersed in it.

The dark, heavy sensation of being drowned in death was an inspiration to Teturact and a reminder to all in his presence that he was not just their leader, he was their god. He decided who would die and who would live, and the form those lives would take.

The flagship itself had once been an Emperor-class battleship, a wedge-prowed slab of a ship that had rained fire on the enemies of the false Emperor. It had been taken to Stratix for refitting and was a stripped-down hulk in the naval dockyards when Teturact saved the planet. It was as if the planet had presented the ship to its new lord as a gift, and Teturact had accepted it. It had been refitted with masses of weaponry and shielding devices, replacing the life support systems and accommodation decks that were of no use when the crew needed neither air nor rest.

Then the dead had come – wrapped in their shrouds. They were entombed in their thousands, along the walls of the corridors and the cavernous spaces of the fighter decks. Teturact's loyal servants had broken bodies apart and used the bones to decorate the bridge and

Teturact's own chambers. They had flayed skin off corpses to cover the walls and hang as curtains. The instrument panels were inlaid with human teeth. Columns of vertebrae ringed the bulkhead doors. The corridors leading to the bridge were paved with fragments of skulls. The ship was a magnificent monument to death, and death coursed through it like lifeblood.

The circular hall in which Teturact now stood had once been a briefing theatre, where the ship's captain would deliver his battlefield command to his underlings. Now it saw something far greater – a conclave of Teturact and his wizards.

Every system had its rogues. Amongst these were psykers, the witches and shamans that were hunted by inquisitors, Arbites, witchfinders and law-abiding Imperial weaklings. When Teturact's empire began to spread he had sought out these psykers and made them the most loyal of all his followers. Through them, his mastery of disease was complete. Their powers could let him raise a plague on a world light years distant – so it had been on Eumenix, where his touch had made the world ripe for conquest even while he was on distant Stratix.

The wizards were from a hundred worlds and they now all wore the filthy robes of Teturact, and were cowled like monks of an order devoted to him. Beneath their robes their bodies had changed: some had become bloated, others emaciated, and many sported tentacles or segmented clawed limbs. Each one was a receptacle of immense psychic power, and they were so subjected to Teturact's will that they couldn't even remember what names they had carried before he found them.

The seating of the auditorium had been replaced with benches of carved bone. The spotlight that fell on Teturact at the centre was tinted yellow by the corruption that seeped through the ship. The wizards were shambling, seeping things, and yet in the eyes that peered from underneath their cowls Teturact could still see their devotion.

None of them dared to be leader, so they all spoke in turn.

'Eumenix is ready,' one of them slurred.

'We have seen it,' said another. 'The only living things are nomads in the wastes, and they will be gone soon enough.'

Have any others visited my world? asked Teturact, speaking with his mind rather than his rotted vocal chords.

'Few, my lord. There were some fanatics who came to spread the word of their Emperor, but they did not survive. There were others who looked like the Emperor's warriors, but they carried the taste of rebellion and anger with them. But there were few and they were the last to escape the world.'

Teturact plucked an image from the head of the wizard who had spoken. It had been gleaned by the wizard from the collection of dying minds of Eumenix. Space Marines had visited his world – probably to find out what was happening on the planet. He saw them sprinting across one of the spaceports in Hive Quintus, swapping fire with the desperate citizens of the hive as they headed for the last off-world shuttle. They had fled like frightened children when they had seen the scale of death – such was Teturact's power he could even send the vaunted Space Marines running.

How long until my arrival? he asked.

'The warp looks on you with favour, my lord. Seven days more and we will return to real space.'

Good. Make them seven days of very particular suffering.

The wizards bowed as one. Then one of their number shambled forwards. It was a horribly misshapen, bloated creature with a bundle of dripping tentacles where its face had once been. The wizards began to chant, a low, atonal drone that filled their air with the sound of a billion plague-flies. The wizard's body opened up, it was a hideous tentacled maw of miscoloured flesh, with internal organs pulsing. A thousand eyes were set into its innards and they rolled madly, seeing across the warp all the way to the depths of Eumenix.

As the wizards worked their magic, Teturact could see the images the central wizard projected. Endless layers of hive were knee-deep in gore. The dead had risen and were wandering, waiting for a purpose. The view panned across battlefields where factions fought in the vain hope of securing supplies or transport, or just to give voice to their horror through combat.

The wizards drew more and more dead from their graves. Whole mounds of mouldering bodies writhed like nests of worms as the corpses dug their way out. In the barren toxic wastes between the hives, nomads watched in horror as columns of the dead marched from the cities. Soon there would be no trace of life left on the planet to spoil the pure magnificence of death.

For a moment, Teturact could feel the whole planet simultaneously, projected into his mind through the wizards. It was a beautiful thing – it was as if the whole of Eumenix was composed entirely of suffering and fear, an imprint so intense that it still drove the walking dead to prey on one another in desperation. He had seen a hundred worlds reduced to such a state, but it still filled him with pride.

The images faded as the wizards finished waking all the dead they could muster. Eumenix seethed to new levels of horror as it disappeared from Teturact's mind, and its aftertaste was like pure victory.

Teturact mentally ordered his bearers to take him back to his quarters to wait out the rest of the journey. There was much to contemplate before he became the god of yet another world.

THE INQUISITORIAL FORTRESS on Caitaran would, in saner days, have served to coordinate the efforts of the Ordo Hereticus for several sectors around, so the ordo could effectively face threats that spanned worlds and systems. But now it formed the wartime headquarters of the Inquisitorial effort against Teturact, with a quarantined halo around it. It was now the gathering point for information submitted by inquisitors and their agents throughout the warzone.

Lord Inquisitor Kolgo had assumed overall authority, having rose to high favour after coordinating the Lastrati Pogrom decades before. Up to three hundred inquisitors and interrogators answered directly to him and his staff, with many more forming a secret network even the Inquisition itself could not unravel.

Many were embedded in the Imperial Guard units sent to claim back disputed worlds; others tried to determine which planets would be the next to fall. Some were even reporting back from worlds that now belonged to Teturact. They sent brief transmissions hinting at unimaginable horror, of the building-sized piles of corpses and plagues that rotted men's minds. The Ordo Malleus searched for daemons and the taint of Chaos amongst the thousands of reports from across the warzone. Even the Ordo Xenos, whose authority extended to the activities of aliens within the Imperium, examined the possibilities of xenos technology in Teturact's methods.

The Inquisitorial fortress was carved into the peak of the tallest mountain on Caitaran, so high the clouds rolled past below the fortress's spaceport. It was a remnant of a civilisation the Imperium had absorbed thousands of years before. It had been a martial society with kings, lords and barons, one of whom had expended untold fortunes to carve an impregnable palace from the mountains that no army could take. He was right – no invader took its walls, but the Imperium dropped a virus bomb on it when he refused to pay fealty to the explorator units that arrived on Caitaran when the world was on the frontier of Imperial space. The planet fell almost overnight once word spread that the fortress was now protected only by a legion of corpses.

It was a good story, the sort told to initiates in the Adeptus Terra about how a concentration of effort on one selected target could do more than a massive assault on all fronts. Perhaps it was even true, and it was certainly relevant here – the majority of the Inquisitorial effort was devoted to locating Teturact and killing him so that, just like the indigenous primitives of Caitaran, the empire of pestilence would crumble in short order. Unfortunately no one knew who, what or where Teturact might be, let alone what might kill him.

Strictly speaking, it wasn't Thaddeus's problem. He was lucky Lord Inquisitor Kolgo had given him use of the facilities on Caitaran. Thaddeus had little more than pure instinct to suggest that the Soul Drinkers might be in the warzone, or at least heading for it. The Soul Drinkers had been on Eumenix, of that there was little doubt, but Eumenix had only recently become off-limits through the plague and there wasn't even definite proof that Teturact was involved – worlds had fallen to disease before without agents of Chaos being responsible.

But it made a strange sort of sense in Thaddeus's trained mind. The Soul Drinkers might even be serving Teturact. But perhaps it was more complicated than that since the forces of Chaos fought one another as often as they fought the Imperium. Though the Soul Drinkers could be anywhere, there seemed a likelihood that they were tangled in the hideous mess of Teturact's fledgling empire. So that was where Thaddeus would look for them.

Thaddeus would soon try to push his luck by receiving an audience with Lord Inquisitor Kolgo himself. But for the moment, he was just trying to eke some comfort out of the quarters the fortress staff had given him. The outer parts of the fortress had not been modernised and the mountain cold blew through them with little resistance. The furnishings were sparse and the floor freezing. The view across the mountains was extraordinary, though, and Thaddeus had been lucky to requisition quarters for himself. The storm troopers and Sisters were in the spaceport barracks, and he had obtained an infirmary suite in which he could examine what Sister Aescarion had brought back from Eumenix.

It had been six months since he had landed on Koris XXIII-3, believing that he had run out of leads on the Soul Drinkers. Now he had part of one of their corpses, and the chalice symbol on the dead Marine's pistol was testimony to his allegiance. Along with the reports from the survivors at House Jenassis, he had found the first concrete proof of the Chapter's activities since the Cerberian Field. To find it, he had paid with the life of Interrogator Shen and several dozen Arbites at House Jenassis. The inquisitor in him said that the trade had been worth it – he was surprised to find that the man in him agreed.

Thaddeus opened up the trunk at the foot of the chamber's four-poster bed. Inside was the meagre collection of hard evidence he had accumulated – a datacube and viewer containing a copy of the pict-file from the *Brokenback*, a charred volume of Daenyathos's *Catechisms*

Martial salvaged from the Soul Drinkers' scuttled fleet, and data-slates containing transcripts of witness interviews. The bolt pistol lay on top in its holster.

Thaddeus picked it up – the weapon was so huge Thaddeus could only hold it in two hands, but a Space Marine carried it as a sidearm. It had an ammunition selector and twin magazines, and its casing was chased in gold. The chalice symbol of the Soul Drinkers was stamped on the handle.

'A fine weapon,' said a grimly familiar, grating voice. 'Terrible that it should be used for such evil.'

Thaddeus looked round to see the Pilgrim entering the chamber. Instantly the bare stone of the room seemed to darken and the air became even colder. The Pilgrim bore such strong determination to see the enemies of the Emperor dead, that its hate infected everything around it.

'The medicae are ready,' the Pilgrim said, and left the room. Thaddeus dropped the pistol back in the trunk, and followed.

THE OFFICIO MEDICAE personnel stationed at the Caitaran fortress had been seconded to the Inquisition to study the various plagues that sprung up wherever Teturact cast his gaze. Thaddeus had secured the services of the Medicae pathology team consisting of two orderlies and an Adeptus Mechanicus Biologis adept. These individuals were waiting in the small infirmary when Thaddeus and the Pilgrim arrived, the faceless orderlies standing as if to attention. The adept – a stocky middle-aged woman with a very serious face and wearing a white lab suit – stood with folded arms at the head of the slab of polished granite that served as an operation table. There was a Space Marine's battered head lying on it like an offering on an altar.

'I apologise for the delay, inquisitor,' said the adept in a clipped, no-nonsense voice. 'We had to ensure the specimen was fully irradiated and quarantined.'

'Understood, adept. May we begin?'

'Certainly. The specimen is of an oversized male humanoid cranium, partially fleshed, severed at the axis vertebra...'

Thaddeus watched as the orderlies took scalpels and forceps from the implement trays by the side of the slab and began to pare away the rotten flesh from the skull. The adept recited the initial findings, confirming that the head was from a Space Marine and a veteran at that, judging by the single silver long service stud in the forehead. The bones of the face and cranium were scored with old scars from blades and bullets, and a bullet wound that had blown a chunk from the forehead had evidently been caused after death. The adept had the orderlies reveal tell-tale implanted organs: larraman's ear – the inner and middle ear enhancement that gave a Marine sharper hearing and perfect balance. The occulobe – the organ that sat behind the eyes and gave the Marine a heightened sense of sight. The remains of the gene-seed in the throat – the sacred organ that controlled all the Marine's other enhancements and bolstered his metabolism.

'The state of the specimen suggests accelerated decomposition followed by a suspension of natural decay, similar to other specimens recovered from worlds within the disputed systems around Stratix.'

An orderly turned the head onto its side and began to remove the jaw. He struggled to break the strengthened bone around the joint.

With a snap the jaw gave way, and like a fountain, a thin jet of glittering liquid arced onto the front of the orderly's smock.

The orderly began to scream as the liquid burned through the smock and into his chest. The other orderly pushed him to the floor and began to tear off the burning clothes as an eye-watering acid smell filled the air and grey smoke coiled upwards. The adept grabbed an emergency medikit from one of the infirmary's wall cabinets and began to work on the orderly, washing down the hissing wounds with an alkali solution before it ate into his lungs.

'Inquisitor, you must leave,' said the adept sharply as she pulled a field dressing from the kit. 'We have possible contamination.'

'There is no contamination,' said the Pilgrim, its grating voice cutting through the orderly's gasping for air. 'The acid is a weak solution designed only to blind; your man will survive. It is produced by the Betcher's gland.'

'That's impossible,' said Thaddeus, watching the trail of greenish liquid spluttering on the granite surface. 'The Soul Drinkers are a successor Chapter of the Imperial Fists Legion. The Fists' gene-seed never allowed Betcher's gland to develop, it was only a vestigial organ.'

'Exactly,' said the Pilgrim, reaching towards the dissected head with a bandaged hand. It plucked the scrap of knotted flesh, the gene-seed, from the throat. 'Corrupt,' he said, holding up the gene-seed. It was mottled and discoloured. 'The Soul Drinkers carry the stain of mutation upon them. The gravest mutation of all, for their very gene-seed is degenerating and the organs implanted in them are themselves being changed.'

'Mutation,' repeated Thaddeus.

The survivors from House Jenassis had reported a monstrous creature leading the Soul Drinkers, with legs like a giant spider and vast psychic powers. He had been sceptical about such talk, but now he could not dismiss the image so easily. The Soul Drinkers were mutants, and with their gene-seed affected they would slide downhill fast.

That made them desperate. And desperation bred atrocity. Whatever their plans, the Soul Drinkers were heading faster and faster towards a state where they were mutated beyond all semblance of humanity.

Thaddeus had always known that his patience would have its limits. But now time had suddenly begun to press on him more strongly. Everyone was running out of time.

And Thaddeus had next to nothing to go on. But he would have to make it do.

He left the infirmary at a jog, heading towards his chambers through the cold, draughty stone corridors of the fortress. He heard the Pilgrim following him but had lost the strange creature by the time he reached his room. He flung open the chest again and pulled out another piece of evidence. It was something he had thought useless when Sister Aescarion had presented it to him – a thin brass plaque with the names of hundreds of adepts tooled into it, the adepts who had worked at the Hive Quintus outpost for the last few decades. There were hundreds of names in tiny, precise type, from the overseers of the menials and servitor engineers to the series of adepts senioris who had commanded the outpost.

The Pilgrim arrived at the door. 'Inquisitor? You have found something?'

Thaddeus looked round. He wished very much that he could have conducted this investigation without the Pilgrim, but he had to tolerate the creature for the insights it had into the renegade Chapter.

'Perhaps,' he replied. 'The Soul Drinkers were at the outpost for a reason. They left at least one of their own behind. Why? Why go to a planet consumed by plague, and journey into the heart of its worst city to fight a battle? Why break into a Mechanicus outpost that produced nothing of any real interest or importance? The rock samples were worth nothing. They had no specialised equipment or weapons. What *did* they have, Pilgrim?'

The Pilgrim tilted its head slightly, and Thaddeus had an unpleasant feeling that it might be smiling somewhere under there. 'They had people, inquisitor. A hundred Mechanicus adepts. Adepts who had not always worked at that one outpost.'

Thaddeus sat back onto his bed, still holding the plaque. 'One of them knew something. And it was enough for the Soul Drinkers to go down there and capture them. If they took a prisoner and got them off the planet they could have everything they need to know.'

Thaddeus stopped. The Imperium was so immensely vast, and the Adeptus Mechanicus such an insanely complicated organisation – from the Fabricator General on Mars to the lowliest menials and servitors labouring on forge worlds and in workshops across the known galaxy. How could he ever hope to track a single adept, even with the resources of an inquisitor? One tiny, meaningless worker who was no Chaos cultist or rogue secessionist, but a nobody in a galaxy of nobodies?

'No,' he said out loud to himself. 'I'm not letting this lead slip.' He flicked on the vox-bead on his collar. 'Colonel Vinn? Assemble your best infiltrators and scouts, ready for review at the spaceport in half an hour. See what you can do about commandeering us a shuttle for loading into the *Crescent*, it doesn't need much range but it will need stealth and assault capabilities. The best crew, too. Pull strings if you have to. Out.'

Thaddeus had not been in the warzone sector for long, but had done basic research into the sector's power structures. He knew that the information he needed might just be available if he was fast, skilled and lucky. It had been some time since he had last used a weapon in execution of his duty as an inquisitor, and he was mildly surprised to find that he was looking forward to doing so again.

CHAPTER SIX

IT WAS QUIET to the galactic west, a wasteland tract of space where few but hardy prospectors and driven missionaries bothered to go. The thick band of stars that marked out the galactic disk was empty for light years ahead, and pilot second class Maesus KinShao knew that without staging posts or spaceports there was little chance of an assault coming from that direction. But it was his duty to be here – he was a servant of the Emperor cocooned in the cockpit of his Scapula-class deep space fighter, a member of a squadron with orders to defend the western frontier of the warzone.

The Scapula had a six-man crew – KinShao, a navigator, three weapons officers and an engineer. There were seventy such craft spread out across this section of the frontier, each armed with sophisticated intruder detection sensors and a bellyful of ordnance.

KinShao called up the HUD screen to show an overview of his squadron's positions. Twenty fighters, each the size of a small cargo ship, hung in space with their sensor fields overlapping so nothing could get through. If any craft tried to escape from the warzone, or to break into it, the craft would be spotted and challenged. If it was remotely suspicious, it would be destroyed with a hail of guided munitions. The Scapulas were some of the most complex and valuable assault craft the sector naval command could muster, and KinShao loved the feeling of the massive metal structure all around with him. For now, though, everything was quiet, and the blazing war a few light hours to the galactic east seemed much further away.

'Squadron, sound in,' came the crackly voice of the squadron commander over the comms. The commander was young and aristocratic, but he seemed solid enough. KinShao hadn't flown under him in anger yet.

'KinShao, red seven. What's the problem?'

'Blue five is reading anomalies. Anything else on anyone's scopes?'

KinShao relayed the communication to his navigator, Shass.

'Nothing here,' she replied. 'All dead.'

'Keep alert, squadron,' said the commander, and signed off.

'You don't want to lose your nerve out here,' said Korgen from in the missile control pit amidships. 'Blue five had better not be getting the jitters. I've seen it happen, and when you can't think straight in deep space they blow you up just to be safe.'

'Stow it, Korgen,' said KinShao. Korgen had been a weapons man on deep spacers for decades, and had seen firefights at Patroclus Gate and St. Jowens's Dock that KinShao (though he wouldn't admit it) never tired hearing about. But he was also full of portentous stories of how crews went mad in deep space, light years from any support craft and with only their fellow crews for company.

'Wait, wait,' crackled another voice on the all-craft channel. 'This is red five. I've got something too.'

Red five's navigator was the squadron's best. He wouldn't have his captain jumping at ghosts.

'It's a small signature,' continued red five's pilot. 'Probably just junk. But it's emitting something, could be a rogue satellite or–'

A thin film of static, then silence.

'Red five?' came the commander's stern voice, as if admonishing red five for disappearing. 'Come in red five.'

KinShao kicked the ship's systems into combat alert almost as a reflex. 'Korgen, stand by to get me targets. Lovred, I want intercept speed on my mark.' Somewhere in the stern Lovred, the ship's engineer, would be readying the Scapula's engines to burst into intercept speed.

'Red five is off the map,' said Shass from the navigator's helm beneath the cockpit, with almost improper calm.

'Visual!' cried a voice on the squadron channel, 'I've got vis–'

'Blue ten's gone,' said Shass.

'Targets, Korgen, get me targets! Waist gunners, are you charged?'

'Check,' said a voice in one ear from the Scapula's starboard pulse laser battery. 'Check two,' said another in the other ear, from the port guns.

'I've got nothing,' said Shass. 'Just the remains of red five.'

There was a terrible pause. Pilots gabbled on all channels and the commander's voice tried to cut through it all and organise a proper sensor sweep as Scapulas disappeared one by one.

'Wait,' said Shass. 'Red five, it's moving.'

'Fire! Full spread!' yelled KinShao, and the fighter juddered around him like a bucking horse. Korgen sent half the fighter's missile payload in a glittering stream towards something that looked like red five's remains on the scanners. But it was moving towards KinShao's red seven faster than intercept speed.

Then he saw it. Lancing from the velvet black of space: a dart of silver that trailed a spray of stars. It rippled like mercury, shifted shape and widened, and a score of pure white laser bolts spat from the front edge of its glistening wings.

Red seven lurched and KinShao knew right away it was a hull breach. The artificial gravity kicked out of kilter and KinShao felt himself pressed against one side of his restraints.

'Count off! Damage report!'

'Nav, OK,' said Shass.

'Engineering, OK.'

'Ordnance, OK.'

'Gunnery? Gunnery sound off!' KinShao realised he was shouting. The silver streak flashed past, leaving a searing afterimage against the blackness of space.

'The shot took us amidships,' said Korgen. 'Waist guns gone.'

'I've got a target. It's faster than us. It's turning back to finish us,' said Shass.

'Korgen, give me everything. Short fuse, I want us screened.'

Korgen emptied most of the remaining torpedoes into space, their fuses cut so they detonated in a spread in front of the Scapula. A screen of electromagnetic radiation and debris was thrown up between red seven and the intruder, enough to screen the fighter from any attacker of Imperial-equivalent technology.

But the attacking fighter could see them. It darted up to red seven and stopped impossibly suddenly, hanging in space right in front of KinShao's cockpit. It was a shard of liquid metal with sharp edges that rapidly flowed into one another, reconfiguring the whole fighter. It was probably smaller than the Scapula but its highly reflective liquid surface shone so brightly it seemed to fill KinShao's sight completely. A dark slit towards the ship's knife-like prow looked in onto the bridge but KinShao couldn't make out anything inside. He was almost completely dazzled by the light, and the graceful effect of its delta wings folding in on themselves to become multiple fins rippling along the fighter's hull.

KinShao kicked the Scapula's retros on, but the engines were still geared to intercept speed. Too late he realised his mistake and the Scapula lurched forward before its retros could take effect. The screen of debris pummelled red seven's hull and billowed an brief orange flame across the viewscreen.

A storm of light ripped through the Scapula. KinShao could see the pure white lances as they seared past the cockpit. He could feel them tear through the hull as if it wasn't there. A booming sound was followed by a sharp silence, that told him the ship's midsection had explosively decompressed. Korgen was dead, probably the engineer, too.

Smoke and the chemical stink of burning plastics filled the cockpit, and heat billowed up from beneath. Shass was probably dead, too, incinerated down there.

The engines collapsed with a crump that washed through the Scapula's superstructure and the fighter lurched backwards as the retros gained a purchase. KinShao could see the enemy fighter wheeling, its body flattening like a manta ray's as it swam through the void, bolts of light spitting from it in an incandescent spray.

Every warning light on the instrument panel lit up. KinShao knew he was going to die, but the screaming sirens and roaring heat around him seemed to blot out any panic. He jammed his thumb onto the manual fire control and the twin gatlings spattered gunfire from beneath the Scapula's nose. They wouldn't hit and they didn't have the range, but KinShao had to go down fighting.

Warning lights winked in desperation. One of them was for the saviour pod behind the cockpit that KinShao was supposed to use if the Scapula was lost. The heat around his feet was unbearable, and flames licked from the instrument panels. The viewscreen started to blacken.

The silver wings rippled again as the fighter wheeled around and twin dark eyes opened up in its leading edge. Bolts of silver lightning burst from the apertures and punched through the cockpit of red seven, spitting the Scapula on a lance of light.

THE CONTROLS AROUND Sarpedon's hands squirmed as he sent fire ripping from the fighter's primary weapons, and punched ragged holes through the wounded craft in front of him.

The cold liquid metal seeped into his gauntlets and connected him with the ship. He only had to think and the fighter's weapons would fill the void with bolts of laser and plasma. The craft in front – a deep-space fighter, part of a cordon around one of the warzone's quieter frontiers – came apart in a blossom of shimmering debris. Sarpedon's fighter flew right through the clouds of wreckage; the fighter's liquid surface absorbing the thousands of impacts.

Beside Sarpedon two serfs still held the flight controls. But Sarpedon had taken over the weapons helm himself – none of the serfs understood weaponry and destruction like a Marine who had been a warrior for more than seventy years.

Karraidin's ship had gone in first and taken out three of the fighters. Sarpedon's had just destroyed two more. The deep space fighters seemed unwieldy compared to the Soul Drinkers' alien fighter fleet, even though the Scapula-class were actually highly sophisticated by Imperial standards. It was a sign of how much the Imperium had stagnated – the development of their technology had slowed to a crawl. Soon it would be at a standstill and its enemies would race past it, conquering and burning.

Sarpedon called up the fleet display. The ten Soul Drinkers' fighters had got through unscathed and had left the cordon well behind them. Sergeant Luko's ship, with the infirmary and Chaplain Iktinos on board, was safe in the middle of the formation since it carried the prisoner Sarkia Aristeia. The fighter at the rear was captained by Tyrendian, one of the Chapter's few remaining Librarians, apart from Sarpedon. His ship flew through fields of spinning debris and never took a shot.

Sarpedon always felt a faint pang of remorse when he was forced to take the lives of Imperial citizens. He had even felt it when Phrantis Jenassis died. The tragedy of the Imperium wasn't that it provided a breeding ground for the galaxy's evils – it was that the untold billions of people locked in its authority fought as if it was their only salvation. The people were the Imperium, and if they could only understand the error of that tyranny they could dissolve it overnight and make it into something that could truly eradicate the darkness of Chaos. But they could not. People were too blind to look beyond what surrounded them. Sarpedon himself, and every single Soul Drinker, had once been the most fervent defenders of the Imperium, believing its existence to be part of the Emperor's great plan to shepherd humanity towards something better.

But in truth the Emperor hated corruption, sin, and Chaos, and all those things were made possible by the Imperium. That was why the Emperor had given the Soul Drinkers a chance of redemption. They answered to no one but him, and Sarpedon knew that he wanted nothing more from them than to fight Chaos wherever they found it. Perhaps the Emperor was dead and was now no more than an idea – but that idea was still worth fighting for. And fighting was all the Soul Drinkers could do.

But the Soul Drinkers had to survive. And that was the purpose of this mission – survival. It seemed a petty thing alongside the war against Chaos, but it had to be done before the Emperor's commands could be fulfilled.

The alien fleet slipped through the void, leaving behind a squadron of vaporised fighters. Silently they slid into the Stratix warzone, into that place of death on a mission of survival.

LORD INQUISITOR KOLGO was an old man. It was all but impossible to rise to any position of authority within the Inquisition without having weathered decades of persecuting the Emperor's foes. Kolgo's rise within the Ordo Hereticus had taken a relatively short time – about eighty years.

Lord Inquisitor Kolgo was like a giant of a man, wearing the impossibly ornate ceremonial power armour that rivalled the Terminator armour of the Space Marines in size. Gilded angels danced across the barrel-like chest plate of ceramite. A power fist adorned each massive arm, with litanies of faith on the knuckles to symbolise how faith itself destroyed the Emperor's enemies, not simple raw strength. Sculpted friezes on each shoulder depicted infidels crushed beneath the boots of crusading knights. Red purity seals studded the armoured limbs, trailing ribbons of parchment inscribed with prayers.

Lord Kolgo's face, with nut-brown wrinkled skin and tiny inquisitive eyes, seemed utterly out of place on such a gilded monster. But the armour was the ceremonial garb of the lord inquisitor of the Stratix sector, and Kolgo could hardly hold audience without it.

At that moment he was giving an audience to one Inquisitor Thaddeus, in relative terms not long out of his interrogator training. It was something of a stretch for the man to have asked for an audience at all, since he was not directly involved with the warzone effort to which Kolgo had dedicated his waking hours. The circular audience chamber with its deep scarlet carpet and oppressively huge chandeliers was designed to remind everyone of Kolgo's authority, but to his credit Thaddeus didn't seem to be cowed by Kolgo's presence.

'Inquisitor Thaddeus,' began Kolgo. 'You understand that, given our current situation, I cannot allocate any real resources to you. It is fortunate that there is enough room in this fortress for you and your staff.'

'I understand,' replied Thaddeus. 'But my mission does intersect with yours. The Soul Drinkers may well be in league with Chaos, and a renegade Chapter in the employ of the enemy would be a major factor in Teturact's favour. The Soul Drinkers' presence within the Stratix warzone is surely a matter of some concern.'

'Perhaps you are right. But you must understand my priorities. Tetu-ract has killed billions already, and if we do not maintain our focus on destroying him the sector may be lost for good.'

'The favour I have to ask you, lord inquisitor, is not a great one.' Thaddeus was following the correct form for an audience with a lord, but he was not obsequious. Kolgo was quietly impressed. 'My staff and I are very close indeed to cornering the Soul Drinkers. What I need now is information. The Adeptus Mechanicus will have records of all their staff members that were on the outpost on Eumenix when the Soul Drinkers attacked...'

Kolgo held up a hand, the massive power fist whirring with servos. 'What you ask I cannot deliver.'

'But my lord, the Mechanicus must bow to your authority. It is not much that I ask. I regret only that my own authority does not stretch as far as to force the hand of the archmagi. If I could learn what I needed by myself I would have gladly done so, but your word carries far more weight than mine so I must ask that you do this for our mutual good.'

Kolgo sighed, as if weary. 'Thaddeus, the Mechanicus supply the ordinatus which inquisitors under my remit will use to destroy the targets they identify. The Mechanicus maintain our ships and the weapons we carry. Most importantly, it is their magi biologis who are being used by us to examine all aspects of the plague and the horrors that follow them. This operation requires closer cooperation with the Adeptus Mechanicus than any I have commanded before.

'When this Inquisitorial command was formed, I had to ensure that cooperation would not fail. Archmagos Ultima Cryol met with me to confirm that we would do all we could to help one another. He promised me the ordinatus, weapons and support we desperately needed. I promised him in return that the forge worlds of Sadlyen Falls XXI, Themiscyra Beta and Salshan Anterior would not fall to Tetu-ract.

'Salshan Anterior is already gone. We believe its servitor stocks were infected and were scrapped rather than incinerated – they returned to life, rose up and killed every living thing on the planet. This is bad enough, I am having to make concessions I cannot afford just to keep Inquisitorial warships in space. But Themiscyra Beta is showing signs of infection, too. I have flooded the place with inquisitors and their staff, but they cannot find the source of the infection and are having precious little success in stopping its spread. You understand, Thad-deus, that I simply cannot ask for any more favours from the Mechanicus.'

Thaddeus shook his head, more sad than angry. 'Lord Kolgo, we are so close. The Soul Drinkers are a step ahead of us but I could stop them if I could only pre-empt their next move. I could do that with your help. If we could get the Mechanicus to allow me just a few minutes' access to their databases…'

'Thaddeus, if what you want is information concerning Eumenix then it is more difficult than that. Eumenix would have fallen under the jurisdiction of the subsector command on Salshan Anterior, which is impossible to access if indeed it even exists any more. The only repository for the information you seek will be the Mechanicus sector command itself, and the archmagos ultima considers the information it contains to be a sacred relic. At the best of times it could take years of politicking to get an inquisitor inside. As you are no doubt aware, these are not the best of times.'

Thaddeus was silent for a moment. Then, he spread his hands as if utterly resigned. 'I fear, then, that I will have to look for some other way to find the Soul Drinkers. I appreciate your audience, Lord Kolgo. It has taught me a great deal that I did not expect to learn.'

'I am a politician, Thaddeus. I accepted that role when I took the title of lord inquisitor. It is my task to ensure that the holy orders of the Emperor's Inquisition are able to do their jobs, and sometimes that requires some reciprocity. I have the authority to have Archmagos Ultima Cryol executed and the Mechanicus command raided for the information you need, but then who would repair the warp engines on our ships? Who would find us a cure for Teturact's plagues? It is this cooperation that holds the Imperium together, Thaddeus. If you are lucky you will never have to deal with it, but someone must and that someone in this instance is me. I wish you the best of luck, inquisitor. Continue with the Emperor's work.'

Thaddeus bowed slightly, and turned to leave.

'I do hope,' added Kolgo, 'that you are not planning on doing anything rash.'

'I would not dream of it, Lord Kolgo. You have made your position clear, and it is my duty to see that your commands are respected.'

Thaddeus left the audience chamber, head held a touch too high. Kolgo smiled and considered how Thaddeus had a great future ahead of him, if he survived.

SARKIA ARISTEIA WAS forty-three years old. She had been born in the hives of Methalor, a dark, hot place where generations lived out pointless lives in machine shops or sank into the nightmare of the underhive. Sarkia broke out. She had a keen mind and a keener sense of duty. The

Imperium needed every single nut and bolt that Methalor produced, but Sarkia could do more for her Emperor. She was quietly religious, intelligent, and terrified of a life of mediocrity. She needed the Adeptus Mechanicus as much as they needed her, and recruits like her.

Sarkia was taken in by the temple of the Machine-God on Methalor and told the first truths about the Omnissiah, the spirit that permeated all machinery whose thoughts were pure logic and whose worship was the gathering of knowledge. She made a competent and useful adept, and by the time she had been transferred to the Stratix sector she was considered a potential tech-priest, on the verge of completing her apprenticeship as an adept inferior.

Then she had been given a post on the research outpost on Stratix Luminae, a tiny cold planetoid barely even visible above the dockyards of Stratix itself. The work suited her; it was away from the immense masses of humanity, and from here she could begin to believe that she was a part of something meaningful. In the rarified environment of the labs she could achieve something that would have some impact on the Imperium. She began to touch on the mysteries of the Omnissiah, and the religious power of unadulterated knowledge gained for its own sake.

Then the eldar marauders had made a daring raid into the Stratix system, running the gauntlet of the sector battlefleets in a cycle of attack and flight that seemed closer to a game than to war. The eldar, in their lighting-quick ships that sailed the solar winds, chose Stratix Luminae for the next round of their game. But this time, the Soul Drinkers Space Marines were in their way. The distress signal from Stratix Luminae found a Soul Drinkers strike cruiser at Stratix for repairs and the result was the mission which had been recorded in corrupted, incomplete files in the Chapter archives.

Sarkia Aristeia had lived through the eldar raid and the brutal reply by the Soul Drinkers. She had seen what had happened at Stratix Luminae and the horrors that followed it. Then, along with the few other survivors she had been granted a quiet posting at Eumenix. She had seen Eumenix die, too, die screaming around her until the same purple-armoured warriors of the decade before came and whisked her away. It was no wonder she had been found near-catatonic with fear and shock.

The room set aside for her interrogation had been made as comfortable as possible. The walls were draped in fabric to cover up the strange alien architecture. She had been given fresh clothes – loose-fitting Chapter serf garb, but at least it was clean. Pallas had examined her and fed her intravenously until her health was recovered and her cheeks less hollow. But she was still on an alien spacecraft, about to be interrogated. And it was still Chaplain Iktinos who was doing the interrogating.

Iktinos, as a guardian of the Chapter's faith and spiritual strength, had been at the heart of the Chapter war when Sarpedon led the Soul Drinkers away from the Imperium. He had sided with Sarpedon, for he had witnessed the treachery of which the Imperium was capable and watched as Sarpedon defeated Chapter Master Gorgoleon in ritual combat. The terrible events of the Chapter war had been orchestrated by the Daemon Prince Abraxes who had nearly turned the Soul Drinkers over to the purpose of Chaos – but the Soul Drinkers' faith had held nonetheless. Iktinos was one of the reasons. Even when doubt had been sown in the heart of every Marine, Iktinos had remained resolute. The Chapter followed the Emperor, not the Imperium, partly because of Iktinos's spiritual leadership.

He was sitting across a table from Sarkia Aristeia, dwarfing the woman completely. All Space Marines were intimidating to a normal human – and a chaplain's black armour and skull-faced helmet were more intimidating than most. Sarpedon watched from the shadows beyond the drapery and wondered if Sarkia was too deep in shock to be useful. Could anyone open up to an armoured monster like Iktinos? If Sarkia were to see Sarpedon it would probably kill her, but the skull-faced chaplain couldn't have been much better.

Iktinos reached up and released the collar catches on his helmet. He lifted it off his head and felt the breath of stale spacecraft air on his face for the first time in days. He hardly ever removed his helmet, and never in front of witnesses. Faith should be faceless and the battle-brothers should consider him the Emperor's hand guiding them, not a human being. Sarpedon had very rarely seen Iktinos's face, and it surprised him to see it now.

His face was the colour of dark polished wood. It was slim and open compared to most Marines, with large dark eyes, and was completely hairless. There were two silver studs in his forehead and two ebony studs, to represent twenty years of service as a battle-brother and twenty as a chaplain. Faith and confidence seemed to radiate from him, and Sarpedon understood why he kept his face covered. He wore the skull-helmet because he wanted the battle-brothers to follow him as a faceless icon of faith, not as a man. He could have been a charismatic leader, but that was not his job. He was there to guard the souls of the brethren – the leadership he left to Sarpedon.

'Sarkia,' said Iktinos in a deep, sonorous voice that was normally a mechanical drone inside his helmet. 'You understand why we have brought you here.'

Sarkia was silent for a moment. 'Stratix Luminae,' she said quietly.

'Ten years ago my battle-brothers came to your lab on Stratix Lumi-nae. Now we need to go back there, and we need to go soon. You were an adept, you had access to the upper levels. We need that access.'

Sarkia shook her head. 'No, that was ten years ago…'

'The Stratix Luminae lab was abandoned. You know that. Everything will be the same. We know what happened afterwards, Sarkia. There would have been no recovery teams sent. The same protocols that you knew will still work today and we need to know them.'

'Why?' Sarkia looked up suddenly, right into Iktinos's eyes. 'Why would anyone want to go back there?'

'We have no choice and neither do you.'

'It won't be enough. I was just an adept, only the magi knew how to get onto the containment levels and they never came out. We never saw them, we didn't even know a fraction of what they were doing down there. I'm useless, don't you understand? I only know the upper support and lab levels, there's nothing there…'

'We know all we need to, Sarkia. Just tell us, and when this is over, you will go free.'

Sarkia choked back a sob. 'You're renegades. You'll kill me.'

'You don't know what we are. At the moment the only thing you have is my word as a soldier of the Emperor. Tell us what we need to know and you will eventually go free.'

Sarkia shrugged. 'I am going to die. Stratix Luminae will kill you, too.' She paused, staring at the table. 'The grids are keyed to phrases from the revelations of the Omnissiah. There's a copy in every workshop and lab-oratory. There's an algorithm that'll pick out the code words, I can write it down. That'll open up the first level. The hot zone you'll have to get through yourselves.'

'You have been very helpful, Sarkia.'

She smiled bitterly. 'Are you trying to be comforting? You're a mon-ster. You all are. You can't make this any easier. You're going to kill me, Marine.'

'You can call me Iktinos.'

'I won't call you anything. I've only told you what I have so you won't have to break me for it, now I'm worth nothing to you. I'll be lucky if you just throw me out of an airlock.'

Iktinos stood up and picked up his rictus-faced helmet from the table. 'I say again, Sarkia, you have my word that when our work is done you will be freed. We have no interest in harming you. If we were still at the beck and call of the Imperium we would probably be required to hand you over for mindwiping. But we do not play that game any more.'

Iktinos strode out of the room, leaving Sarkia at the table. In a while the serfs would bring her something to eat and drink, and show her to the bunk that had been squeezed into one of the corridors they were using as a dormitory.

To anyone else, the successful questioning would have been a triumph. But Sarpedon was all too aware of the further risks the Chapter would have to take to survive, let alone succeed. In many ways it would have been a relief if Sarkia had known nothing. At least he would be able to banish any hope, and direct the Chapter's efforts elsewhere. Instead, Sarkia had just opened the gate for the Chapter to head into the heart of corruption and face both the horrors of Teturact's empire and the wrath of the Imperium. It would almost have been better if Sarkia had never been found, but Sarpedon had to lead his Chapter to do the Emperor's work, no matter what the risks.

Sarpedon watched her for a moment. She wasn't crying or trembling. She just looked very tired, and he imagined that facing up to an alien environment and the very real possibility of interrogation and death had been draining for her.

Sometimes, Sarpedon thought, watching unaugmented humans was like observing members of a different species. The Soul Drinkers were so isolated from the Imperium that the only normal humans Sarpedon saw regularly were the Chapter serfs: men and women so conditioned and loyal that they were more like intelligent servitors than people. Sarkia was Sarpedon's only contact with an Imperial citizen for a very long time apart from the short-lived Phrantis Jenassis, and no matter how curious he was about her he could not speak to her himself because she would probably go insane at the sight of him.

Sarpedon walked away from the shadows back towards the bridge, leaving Sarkia to the Chapter serfs. If she heard the talons of his arachnoid legs clattering on the metallic floor, she didn't look up.

ONE OF THE things that Thaddeus had begun to notice was that the Soul Drinkers were becoming officially nonexistent. His requests for astropathic traffic monitoring had been more and more difficult to implement, even when he brandished the small Inquisitorial symbol that carried the weight of immense authority. The warzone had been divided into military administration zones so the Departmento Munitorum could have a hope of wrestling with the logistics of such an immense operation, and Thaddeus had ordered alerts if astropathic transmissions were made with certain keywords – Astartes, renegade Marines, purple, spider, psychic and dozens of others. But there were several sectors that had not cooperated as Thaddeus had expected.

Imperial monitoring was impossible in areas completely controlled by Teturact, such as the space around Stratix that had been designated target sector primary, so Thaddeus could not expect much reply from the scattered recon ships and Inquisitorial operatives skulking between the plague worlds. But the Septiam-Calliargan sector had replied to Thaddeus's requests with red tape and misdirection. Aggarendon Nebula sector hadn't replied at all, yet there was little military activity around the nebula's scattered mining worlds. Subsector Caitaran, a tiny tract of space but one that included the Inquisition fortress and several Imperial Guard command flotillas, was worst of all: the communications Thaddeus received from the astropathic monitoring stations seemed stilted and contrived, and he had little doubt they were doctored.

That was only one symptom. Thaddeus's previous attempts to access historical records from worlds the Soul Drinkers had once fought on had yielded no information at all about the Chapter. The cathedral of heroes on Mortenken's World, for instance, no longer held the carved stone mural depicting Daenyathos, the Soul Drinkers' legendary philosopher-soldier who drove the alien hrud from the planet's holy city. Almost all the Soul Drinkers' marks since the Cerberian Field had been erased. Only Inquisitorial sources retained any cohesive history of the Soul Drinkers and their glorious history – glorious, at least, until the betrayal at Lakonia and the Chapter's excommunication. If there were aspects of their history not held in the Inquisition archives on the fortress-worlds in sectors where the Soul Drinkers had fought, then as far as the Imperium was concerned that history never occurred.

Thaddeus had never seen a deletion order in action before. He had heard of them of course, and been a part of some operations where they had been enforced. But he had never been aware of such a stain of ignorance across the Imperium, that burned books and wiped data-slates. Perhaps mindwipings were being carried out on people who had encountered the Soul Drinkers. Thaddeus, as an inquisitor must, understood the importance of information, and how knowledge could rot the souls of those unable to cope with it.

Renegade Chapters were not unknown – how many children had been told the grim stories of the Horus Heresy, when half the Space Marine Legions were corrupted by the great enemy? But that it could happen now, and without any great Chaos presence to blame for it, could cause disillusion and panic; a situation the Imperium could ill afford. And the Soul Drinkers' disappearance from the memory of the Imperium made Thaddeus's job a damn sight harder.

He didn't know which sub-ordo of the Inquisition enforced the order. Neither did he know which operatives in astropathic nexus outposts and planetary archives were fuddling communications about proscribed topics. But they were effective, and without the authority of an inquisitor lord Thaddeus felt he could do little to get round them. He was feeding on scraps, and it was getting worse. He only hoped that his last remaining lead – an investigation of Eumenix outpost and the reason they had attacked it – would lead to some breakthrough. Otherwise his investigation would be starved of information until it died.

The Inquisition could be obsessed with blinding one part of itself to the activities of another, and Thaddeus sometimes wondered if it could one day push back the darkness and learn to trust itself. But there were enough dark rumours of Inquisitors who had become dangerous radicals or gone mad in their pursuit of corruption, so perhaps keeping members ignorant was the only way to stop it from rotting inside.

'Inquisitor?'

Thaddeus looked up from the data-slate. He had been reviewing the potential hits on the astropathic traffic, but there had been nothing promising, yet again. He saw – inevitably – the Pilgrim waiting at the door to the cold stone chamber. It was night on Caitaran and the filmy pale blue light from the cloudless night sky coloured blue and grey. Thaddeus had been so intent on sifting through the paltry astropathic data that he had failed to notice Caitaran's twin suns going down.

'Pilgrim.'

The Pilgrim bowed slightly, as if in mockery. 'Colonel Vinn has assembled his men and has them ready for review.'

'Good. What do you think of them?'

'Me?' The Pilgrim paused. 'They are mostly veterans of reconnaissance formations or counter-insurgency on primitive worlds. They are skilled and determined soldiers. They will probably die well, but not much else.'

'You think this is insane, don't you?'

Thaddeus had the feeling that the Pilgrim, if it possessed a face, was snarling under its cowl. 'When you have seen the things I have seen, inquisitor, insanity has no meaning. I think it will fail, if that is what you mean. Better soldiers than your storm troopers have tried such ventures before and have not made it past the laser grids.'

'I haven't actually told you what I need the troops for, Pilgrim. You seem very certain I will fail, so you must know what I am going to attempt.'

'You are going to Pharos, inquisitor. There is no other way. And if I can guess it, Lord Kolgo can.'

'Lord Kolgo,' said Thaddeus, rising from his bed and dropping the data-slate into one of the trunks he had nearly finished packing, 'would like nothing better than to see me try. If I fail, I will have tested the defences for him. If I succeed, he will know how to crack that particular nut and will probably try to put me under his direct authority so I can do it again if needs be.'

'Perhaps. But you are going to Pharos, inquisitor, that much is so obvious to me there is no reason for your secrecy. If you are found out and survive you could make enemies who will never forget.'

'Are you trying to discourage me, Pilgrim? Don't you want to see the Soul Drinkers found?'

'More than you do, inquisitor. More than you. Never forget that.' A note of irritation crept into the normally inscrutable mechanised voice. 'You asked my opinion. I believe you will die. But if I were in your position, I would choose probable death too, for otherwise the chances of ultimate success are nil. I am simply saying that your mission is impossible.'

'The Emperor slew Horus at the dark one's moment of triumph. That was impossible, too. They say Inquisitor Czevak saw the black library and lived. Impossible, again. Protecting the Imperium from a galaxy of evil is impossible, too, but it is an inquisitor's duty to try. My duty. The only weapon I have now against the Soul Drinkers is information, and if I must do the impossible to gain it then that is what I will do.'

'Of course, inquisitor.' The Pilgrim, as ever, was being obsequious. 'Colonel Vinn has his men awaiting inspection.'

'Tell Vinn I trust his judgement. If his men are as dead as you think then I hardly need to inspect them. Have them embark onto the *Crescent* and make sure it's fuelled up. I'll be at the spaceport in an hour.'

The Pilgrim melted into the darkness beyond the door. Even though he was essential to Thaddeus's hopes of ever finding the Soul Drinkers, there was a constant nagging voice that told him he shouldn't have brought the Pilgrim along with him. Treachery seemed to ooze from him like a stink – and it lingered in the chamber after he had gone. But then again, inquisitors had always dealt with the foulest of mutants and aliens as long as they were useful. But the Pilgrim at least was no heretic or daemon, so Thaddeus would have to endure his company for a while longer.

Thaddeus finished throwing his few clothes and possessions into the trunk. He travelled light, and had not followed the holy orders of the Inquisition long enough to build up a library or collection of artefacts as longer-serving inquisitors had. His only possessions of note were the *Crescent Moon* itself, his copy of the *Catechisms Martial* and the heavily modified autopistol he kept on the ship. The pistol had been given to him by the citizens of Hive Secundus on Jouryan after he had wiped out the genestealer cult in the depths of the hive's heatsink complex. He had felt like one of the heroes from the Imperial epics then: a crusader crushing corruption and evil wherever it broke through to threaten the blessed Imperium. He felt very different now.

Had the Ordo Hereticus chosen the right man? Thaddeus was certainly good, there was no doubt. He was intelligent and tenacious, and had the patience to marshal his resources until he could execute a final, critical strike against his opponent. But there were so many inquisitors with more experience. There were some who even specialised in dealing with the Space Marine Chapters – which though they were amongst the Imperium's greatest heroes – possessed an attitude of individuality and autonomy that meant they had to be constantly watched. Was Thaddeus up to the task of finding the Soul Drinkers? Had he been picked for some political reason, by an inquisitor lord like Kolgo who had to balance a million interests against one another?

It didn't matter. He had the job, and he would do it. A thousand inquisitors were working in the warzone on a hundred different missions, and even agents of the Officio Assassinorum were creeping across the stars towards targets in Teturact's empire. And that included Teturact himself. Thaddeus had his own mission, and it was no less important than any of the others. He would hunt down the Soul Drinkers or die trying. Was there any greater devotion than his? No, there was not, he told himself.

He called for one of the fortress staff to take his trunk to the *Crescent Moon* and left the cold, draughty fortress quarters for the spaceport. He would leave for Pharos as soon as possible – that was where the final pieces had to lie. He would find what he needed there. Because if he did not he would fail, and that was not going to happen.

CHAPTER SEVEN

FOR THE MOMENT, the fleet was silent. The fighters had paused in a quiet system, waiting for a break in the heavy traffic of Imperial warships and transports between them and their objective. The system was dark and silent, its sole human structures the mine heads on a burned-out mineral world, its star mottled and dying.

The alien fighters hung in orbit around the system's gas giant, the blue-white strata of gas swirling beneath them in an unending storm. The star's sickly light cast the other half-glimpsed planets and moons in a faded greyish glow. The light muted the bright silver of the fighters, so they looked like just one more handful of mining debris thrown into orbit and left behind when the humans departed.

It was only after the rebellion of the Soul Drinkers that Sarpedon had begun to appreciate the galaxy. In some ways, it was a marvel – every remote corner held something new and extraordinary. Even in this washed-out system there were sights of beauty, like the constant torments of the gas giant below or the endlessly complex orbits of the planet's moons. But it was also a terrible and dark galaxy. In every one of those corners darkness and corruption could be waiting, hidden and frozen, ready to wake and ravenously hunt the stars.

Chaos could be anywhere, and by its very nature it was never in the open but hidden in the galaxy's corners like filth that could never be washed away. That was why the Imperium was such a malevolent thing – it was a part of the galaxy that provided so many hiding places for the

Enemy, and most of the best places were within the corrupt structures of the Imperial organisations themselves.

When Chaos had most threatened mankind, it had not sent a tide of daemons from the warp, but had corrupted its greatest heroes – fully half of the Space Marine primarchs – and ripped the galaxy apart in the wars of the Horus Heresy. It had only been men like Rogal Dorn, the Soul Drinkers' primarch and hero of the Battle of Terra, that had kept mankind from falling completely. Now Sarpedon saw what Rogal Dorn really was – a heroic man created as such by the Emperor, but a hero who found himself trapped in the decaying hypocrisy of the Imperium when the Emperor was confined to the Golden Throne and the Adeptus Terra turned His master plan into a mockery of humanity.

The porthole looking out onto space was located amidships on Chaplain Iktinos's ship, where Apothecary Karendin had set up the apothecarion. Pallas, the Chapter's most senior Apothecary, and Karendin worked here tirelessly, because the Soul Drinkers needed their expertise now more than at any time in their history. Pallas had just completed an examination of Sarpedon himself, the Soul Drinkers' first and most obvious mutant.

'Commander?' came a voice from behind him.

Sarpedon snapped out of his reverie and turned to see Apothecary Pallas reading analysis off a data-slate connected to an autosurgeon. The apothecarion set up in the fighter was comprehensive but cramped, packed into what had probably once been quarters for the alien crew. The autosurgeon, servitor orderlies and monitoring consoles were crammed in alongside the bulbous organic ripples of silvery metal. Wires and equipment hung from the abnormally high ceiling.

Pallas looked up from the data-slate. 'You are getting worse,' he said.

'I know,' replied Sarpedon. 'I felt it at House Jenassis. The Hell is… changing. If we do not succeed, the day is coming when I will not be able to control it any longer.'

'Nevertheless,' continued Pallas, 'you're not the worst. Datestan from Squad Hastis has increasing abnormalities in his internal organs that will kill him, or turn him into something different. We've had to take two Marines from Squad Luko off-duty entirely – one has claws that can't hold a bolt gun and the other is growing a second head.'

'And you?'

Pallas paused, put down the data-slate and removed one gauntlet and the forearm of his armour. Ruddy scales had grown from the skin on the back of his hand and spread up past his elbow. 'They go up to my shoulder,' said Pallas, 'and they're spreading. Marines like yourself and Tellos have the most obvious mutations, but there's hardly a Soul Drinker left who isn't changing in some way. Most of them are getting worse quicker and quicker.'

Sarpedon looked down at his spider's legs. There had been a time when, his mind clouded by the Daemon Prince Abraxes, he and his fellow Marines had thought his altered form to be a gift from the Emperor. Now he knew he was just another mutant, no different in many ways to the numberless hordes of unfortunates who were enslaved and killed in the Imperium to protect mankind's genetic stability. Sarpedon had killed enough mutants himself and, if any servant of the Imperium were to so much as look at him, they would try to kill him, too. 'How long do we have?' he asked.

Pallas shrugged. 'Months. Certainly not more than two years before the Chapter ceases to exist as a fighting force. We're already losing Marines to unchecked mutation and that number will only increase. I don't know what you're planning, commander, but it must be our last chance.'

Sarpedon knew what happened to the Soul Drinkers who could no longer function properly. Most were put down when they lost their minds, taken in chains to the plasma reactors on the *Brokenback* to receive a bolt round through the brain before being incinerated. There had been few so far, but Sarpedon had felt every one as keenly as the needless deaths of the Chapter war. 'Our last chance in more ways than one,' agreed Sarpedon. 'Teturact's empire is sustained by forcing the Navy and the Guard into battles that neither side can win, because Teturact has the numbers and the capacity to raise the dead. And we're heading right into the middle of it. From the information Salk brought back from Eumenix it'll be a meat grinder wherever Teturact's armies fight. This Chapter won't die out to mutation, Pallas, it'll die in battle or it will be cured.'

'We can't carry on like this, can we?' said Pallas unexpectedly. 'We have no support. The Imperium will destroy us if it can and Chaos will see us for the enemy we are. No Chapter can survive like this.'

'Carry on with the tests, Apothecary,' said Sarpedon. 'Let me know of any changes.' He turned and left the apothecarion, eight talons clicking on the metallic floor as he headed back towards the bridge.

THE SHUTTLE COCKPIT was bathed in eerie blue-grey light. It shone on the brass fittings of the servitor-pilot and turned the deep red upholstery a velvet black. The viewscreen swam with swirls of white, blue and grey as the servitor applied a touch of pressure to the engines, nudging the shuttle forward. Many of the cockpit's alarm readouts were incongruous beads of red on the instrument panels – the shuttle had not originally been designed for these conditions, but Thaddeus knew it would hold together. Colonel Vinn had pulled a few of the right strings with the Guard units seconded to the Caitaran command and acquired an exceptional craft for the mission. The shuttle had been fitted with reactive armour plates that even now were flexing under the abnormal pressure and cold, and the stealth mode of the engines worked on a jet propulsion principle that enabled the shuttle to be propelled underwater.

Or, in this case, under liquid hydrogen.

'Surface?' asked Thaddeus quietly.

'Three hundred metres,' came the mechanised voice of the servitor-pilot. The armatures plugged into its shoulder sockets eased into the controls in front of it and the shuttle's steering fins were angled upwards a touch, sending the craft on a gentle upwards arc through the unnaturally cold ocean.

Thaddeus switched on the ship vox. 'Lieutenant, to the bridge,' he said. A few seconds later the door at the rear of the cockpit slid open and Lieutenant Kindarek looked in.

'Inquisitor?'

'We'll hit the shore in about seven minutes. Are your men ready to go?'

'Standing by, sir.'

'Keep the grenade launchers slung until we get well away from the edge. There'll be dampening fields to prevent the liquid exploding but we'll still have a hell of a bang if it goes off. I don't want us losing anyone to accidents, it's dangerous enough in there.'

'Yes, sir. Hellguns only until your order.'

'Good.' Thaddeus paused, watching the liquid swirling in front of him. 'What do you think of this mission, Kindarek?'

Kindarek barely thought for a second. 'High-risk and vital, inquisitor. Our kind of operation.'

'And why do you think that?'

'Because Colonel Vinn selected us, inquisitor. He doesn't risk his recon platoon without a good reason, and good reasons always involve risk.'

'No one has ever done this, Kindarek. Some have tried, but no one's ever succeeded.'

'I'd imagine no one has ever tried taking this way in, sir.'

Thaddeus smiled. 'You're quite right, Kindarek. I hope.'

'Two hundred metres,' said the servitor.

'Prepare your men, lieutenant. I want men on point as soon as we hit the shore.'

Kindarek saluted briskly and headed back towards the crew compartment. Since Thaddeus wasn't an officer the gesture was inappropriate, but Thaddeus didn't point it out. It was probably force of habit. Kindarek seemed a soldier who learned his habits early and never strayed from them – it had made him a soldier trusted by Vinn to lead his recon platoon, as professional and unshakeable a body of men as the Ordo Hereticus could make out of mundane troops.

Shapes loomed past, half-glimpsed through the near-opaque liquid, picked out briefly by the floodlights mounted under the nose of the shuttle. Leaning columns and shadowy, submerged structures, set in precarious shapes by the extreme cold, formed a lattice of obstacles for the servitor-pilot to negotiate.

The light became paler as the shuttle ascended. An undersea shelf composed of drifts of silvery machine-shavings rolled out of the gloom – where it broke the surface was a shining horizon, the beach on which the shuttle would land.

Perhaps the shuttle had already been spotted. Perhaps combat servitors were writhing their way through the ocean or were waiting for the shuttle on the shore, ready to turn the liquid hydrogen into a localised, short-lived inferno that would incinerate the shuttle and crew. But these were the risks you took when you tangled with the Adeptus Mechanicus head-on.

PHAROS WAS AN asteroid, part of the remains of a world that had been destroyed millions of years before. It hung in a broken necklace around a dead, blood-orange star. Across those asteroids were scattered mining colonies and hard-bitten missionary outposts; the system was almost completely forgotten.

A thousand years before, the Adeptus Mechanicus had followed their complex fate-equations and tech-priest divinations and arrived at the asteroid chain. They selected the region to be the seat of Stratix sector command, which in an emergency would serve to coordinate Adeptus Mechanicus troops, spacecraft and expertise. But information was most critical of all – the Adeptus Mechanicus was a priesthood, and its religion was knowledge. Information was the stuff of holiness, and the sector command had built a cathedral to learning that would hold all the information generated by the many adepts throughout the sector.

The cathedral jutted from the surface of one of the largest asteroids, the iron-heavy Pharos, bored out by giant tunnelling machines and plated in sacred metals – purest iron, solid carbon, bronze and zinc. It took the form of a cluster of immense cylinders, arranged like the pipes of an organ, connected by thousands of glass bridges.

Several floors were below the surface of the asteroid, rooted into the super-dense core. Endless floors of knowledge and chapels of unfettered learning filled the cavernous spaces, and a regiment of combat servitors were hardwired into the structure to keep out the ignorant.

The delicate datastacks had to be kept cold to ensure their stability and the immutability of the information they contained. A whole ocean of liquid hydrogen flooded the lower levels, drowning the underground portion of the cathedral in the impossibly cold depths, fed by giant intakes that opened onto the asteroid's rocky surface. The captive ocean was regularly refilled by Mechanicus tanker craft in the never-ending cycle of holy maintenance that formed an act of worship for thousands of adepts and menials.

Inside, galleries of data-cubes were arranged above the freezing lake, almost alive with the immense volume of information they contained. A small body of tech-priests was permitted to live inside, sharing the cathedral with the maintenance servitors, bathing in the holiness of so much knowledge. They were adepts blessed for their devotion and service to the Machine-God with the opportunity to live out their extended lives in the icy splendour of Pharos.

When circumstances required, Pharos was a repository of vital knowledge that sector command could plumb for the good of the Imperium – the archives of its medical tower were at that moment being combed for solutions to the terrible plagues erupting throughout the Stratix warzone. But only tech-priests understood its real purpose – holy ground, created by the Mechanicus as a monument to the Omnissiah and a model of the Machine-God's ideal universe where immutable knowledge was the only reality.

There was no Chaos here, no evil randomness to pollute the sacred knowledge. And the Adeptus Mechanicus intended to keep it that way. No one was permitted access to Pharos except on the express order of the Archmagos Ultima, and he was known as a man not to be hurried. Only a handful of the Emperor's most trusted servants had been given access to the holy ground of Pharos, and then for the briefest periods of research under strict supervision. Some misguided souls and outright heretics had tried to force their way in, of course, but the holy ground had been kept inviolate with combat servitors and monitor ships.

No one had successfully stolen information from the cathedral of Pharos. But then again, no one had tried going in through the liquid hydrogen vents before.

'THE SEAL IS loose. Let me.' Lieutenant Kindarek reached over and adjusted the seal between Thaddeus's helmet and the neck ring of his hostile environment suit. Normally issued to explorator pioneers or engineers working on ships' hulls, the suit could keep extremes of temperature or noxious atmospheres from harming the occupant. All members of the recon platoon wore them, their faces appearing subtly warped through the square, transparent faceplates and their bulk increased by the thick, spongy dark grey material of the suits.

There was a hiss as the seal tightened and Thaddeus felt the air around his face turn cold and chemical.

'My thanks, lieutenant.'

The suited-up platoon was crammed into the rearward deployment airlock in front of Thaddeus, hellguns at the ready. Four storm troopers had grenade launchers slung on their backs and heavy garlands of frag grenade rounds looped on their belts. Neither the HE suits nor the fatigues underneath bore any Inquisitorial insignia, and Thaddeus himself didn't carry his Ordo Hereticus seal of authority – if the mission failed, there would be little to suggest that the Inquisition had been behind the infiltration.

None of them spoke. Thaddeus's own voice had sounded unwelcome and incongruous. How many battles had these men fought in? How many times had they waited in a Chimera APC or a Valkyrie airborne transport, not knowing if they would be dropped into a fire-fight?

Thaddeus knew several of these men had been at the Harrow Field Bridge where daemons of the Change God were emerging from the ground with the summer crops. Many had been part of the path-finding force that had found the tomb of the Arch-Idolator on Amethyst V. Some had scars and low-grade bionic eyes visible through their faceplates – all were silent and grim. Thaddeus's own nerves were tempered by his faith in the Imperial vision and the critical nature of the mission. Each man coped with the tense last few moments in their own way.

The shuttle tilted as the servitor-pilot in the cockpit turned it around. There was a metallic grating on the underside of the hull as the shuttle beached itself, braking jets pushing it up onto the shore.

'In position,' came the servitor voice over the vox.

'Open us up,' ordered Thaddeus. There was a squeal of hydraulics and the back wall of the passenger compartment dislocated, hissing downwards as the deployment ramp lowered.

Bright, cold, fluorescent light flooded in. The hydrogen lake filled the lower levels of this particular cylinder of the cathedral, and heaps of metallic cast formed piles under the surface that became sandbanks of silvery filings. It was against one of these that the shuttle beached. The beach glowed silver in the light and the ripples on the surface of the lake were as bright as knife blades.

The pointmen jumped onto the beach before the ramp was down, the huge boots of the HE suits splashing in the liquid hydrogen at the shore's edge. The photoreactive faceplates darkened in the glare as they panned the barrels of their hellguns over the area.

Kindarek's head tilted to the side for a moment as he received their voxes. 'All clear,' he voxed on his squad frequency. 'Move out.'

The platoon poured rapidly from the shuttle, boots kicking up the drifts of metallic shavings as they moved. Thaddeus followed, autopistol heavy in his hand and his mouth and nose already raw from the treated air. The light surrounded him as he stomped down the ramp onto the shore and he saw that the far wall was a single vast light source, phosphorescent gases trapped behind panes of transparent crystal, wrapping around the inside of the cylinder.

This cylinder of the cathedral was three kilometres across and perhaps ten high, with the lit section a hundred metres high. Access ladders wound their way in double helixes up to the first gallery levels. Columns hung from the distant ceiling, matt-grey so they drunk the abundant light. Between them were webs of glass walkways and platforms, thousands of filaments that turned the light flooding from below into a bright shimmering forest. It was like being inside a polished diamond, with a million faces looking up at the broken light of a new star. Clustered around the pillars and forming starbursts of light at the intersections of the web were intricate crystalline sculptures in complex geometric shapes, mathematical prayers coded into the angles and faces, each sculpture a crystal information repository holding enough information to fill a hundred cogitator engines.

Further up, the curved walls were hung with banners, rust-red cloth embroidered with binary prayers in gold thread. The brightness gave way to shadows towards the ceiling, incense-stained darkness swallowing the cathedral's light where Thaddeus could just make out the control structures looking down on the cathedral, where tech-priests might even now be watching intruders violating the Omnissiah's temple.

The technology of this place was the old kind, the kind they couldn't make any more, salvaged from the forgotten madness of the Dark Age of Technology and put to a new use in the worship of the Omnissiah. This was a sacred place indeed, where the Adeptus Mechanicus kept technology they could not – some said would not – replicate.

To Thaddeus, it was beautiful. To Lieutenant Kindarek and his men it was just another warzone. Kindarek barked an order and the platoons fanned out behind the pointmen, who were rapidly scanning the ridges of the metal sandbar. The platoon dissolved into its component squads, each overlapping fields of fire.

'What's our entry point, sir?' came Kindarek's voice.

Thaddeus glanced around. They couldn't spend more than a few moments down here, where they had no cover and where gunfire could make the hydrogen lake erupt. There were several maintenance stair-wells hanging down from the columns above, where adepts or servitors could descend to the lake surface. Thaddeus pointed towards the clos-est. 'There. Keep it simple.'

'Sir.' At Kindarek's order the platoon jogged towards the stairwell, a spindly spiral of pale silver metal that seemed impossibly fragile against the sheer size of the cathedral cylinder.

The pointmen ascended rapidly, taking two of the grenade launcher troopers with them. The squads went up after them, Thaddeus jogging alongside them as they took the stairs two at a time in their hurry to get out of such a vulnerable position. Thaddeus glanced down and saw the rear of the shuttle disappearing from view as it slid back under the sur-face to minimise the chances of detection.

The webs of light above fractured and reformed as Thaddeus ascended, as if the whole cathedral had been constructed to appear rad-ically different from each possible angle, mirroring the billions of facets of information it contained. He almost stumbled as he stared up at the sight and remembered that he was a soldier, too, just like these men who were ignoring the splendour, their minds only on the mission.

The pointmen were at the first level of the web-like walkways, pick-ing their way warily along the transparent crystal. The base of one of the suspended columns was nearby and they gathered there, one con-sulting an auspex to check for movement, others checking cautiously around the giant smooth pillar.

Kindarek waved the first of the platoon's squads onto the walkways. They spread out into a mobile perimeter, hellguns ready to fire, mov-ing around the abstract geometric shapes that formed the crystalline information vaults.

Several men carried bundles of equipment slung at their waists or backs – basic interface equipment, guaranteed to survive the intense cold, that would enable the user to jack into a simple information sys-tem. Many of the more technically-minded storm troopers had been quickly trained in its use, and Thaddeus himself could perform the vital task if need be.

Kindarek himself had got to the walkways. For a moment he paused and looked towards the troopers by the pillar – Thaddeus saw one of them, one of the pointmen with an auspex, mouth a single word as he voxed the lieutenant.

Movement.

That was all the warning Thaddeus had.

The trooper turned as he tried to gauge the source of the movement signal on his auspex scanner. He faced the pillar behind him and dropped the scanner to bring his hellgun to bear as he realised the movement was inside the pillar.

The pillar's surface fractured into hundreds of dark grey ceramic tiles. The column broke apart and the tiles were revealed as the flexible armoured carapaces of giant metal-limbed beetles that hung in the freezing air as a host of glowing metal eyes lit up on the scanner arrays jutting from their thoraxes.

The lower half of the pillar had broken into more than twenty combat servitors, each three times the bulk of a man, highly advanced and hovering with in-built grav-units. Metallic limbs folded into multilaser barrels and circular diamond-toothed power saws emerged on metallic armatures. In the few seconds before the servitors were battle-ready Thaddeus realised they had indeed been observed as soon as they had made it to the shore – the cathedral's defences had waited until the storm troopers were spread out between the walkways and the stairwell, vulnerable and out of formation.

Stupid. How could Thaddeus have believed he could succeed in infiltrating the Pharos archives when it had been proved impossible so many times?

No. That was the thinking of someone without faith. Fight on, for death in service of the Emperor was its own reward.

'Open fire!' yelled Kindarek over the squad vox. 'Launchers, now!'

The frozen air erupted into laser fire, searing red streaks from the overcharged power packs of the hellguns lashing from every trooper able to shoot, multi-lasers pumping volleys of white fire through the bodies of the troopers closest to the pillar. The screech and hiss of laser fire filled Thaddeus's ears and the vox was suddenly a mess of static and din, men shouting as they opened fire or screaming as they died. Men were shredded, their blood freezing into a hail of red shrapnel, chunks of flesh shattering against the crystal. One fell backwards as his leg was sheared clean off by the slash of a power saw, beads of frozen blood glittering as he tumbled off the walkway down towards the hydrogen lake. Another was picked up by the razor-sharp mandibles of the beetle-servitor and pulled apart, his body erupting in a shower of crimson shards.

White-hot laser fire slashed through the stairwell and the man directly above Thaddeus was hit, his torso shattering as a laser bolt punched through his chest. White fire screeched through the stairs beneath him and the structure came apart, metal steps raining down along with half of the last squad.

Thaddeus reached out and grabbed the railing as the steps under his feet disappeared. The bulk of the dead man above buffeted him as it fell, and Thaddeus was dangling one-handed nearly a hundred metres above the lake. The blinding light swallowed the men as they fell, reducing them to ripples in the silvery surface as they hit the lake.

Grenade rounds exploded above, sending clouds of shrapnel ripping through the servitors. The damage was minimal but the explosions scrambled their sensors, and one of the insectoid servitors fell wreathed in strange blue flame as a dozen high-powered hellgun shots tore up into its underbelly.

'Paniss! Telleryev! Make for their flank, pin them down!' Kindarek was yelling – Thaddeus saw Kindarek, back against one of the information-sculptures, firing with his hellpistol as he shouted orders over the vox.

A hand reached down and Thaddeus grabbed it – a trooper hauled him up onto the still-stable top end of the stairwell. Thaddeus was about to breathe a word of thanks when a laser shot seared through the air between them and sliced a deep furrow through the trooper's faceplate – Thaddeus saw him choke as the cold air he inhaled turned his lungs to chunks of ice. The man's eyes froze into white crystals and his body turned rigid, the heat fleeing from inside his suit and his muscles turning solid.

Thaddeus pushed the dead man to one side and let the corpse fall. He stumbled forward a few steps and pulled himself onto the walkway, the dizzying drop still yawning beneath him. The passage was only wide enough for a couple of men abreast and troopers were scrambling for the junctions where they could gather in gaggles of three or four, using sculptures as cover and concentrating hellgun fire on one servitor at a time.

Thaddeus drew his autopistol, feeling it click as an executioner round chambered itself in response to his hand around the grip. He sprinted the few steps towards the closest sculpture as laser blasts scored deep gouges into the crystal of the walkway beneath him.

He slid into cover beside two storm troopers, one of them hefting a grenade launcher and using it to lob occasional shots over the sculpture towards knots of servitors.

The trooper with the hellgun nodded curtly at Thaddeus as the inquisitor scrambled to a half-sitting position, back against the crystal.

'Musta lost half the lads!' shouted the trooper, voice muffled by the HE suit's faceplate. 'Do we have extraction?' Thaddeus recognised Trooper Telleryev, one of the platoon's sergeants.

Thaddeus shook his head. 'We break out the hard way.'

Telleryev spat a word from his homeworld that Thaddeus assumed was profane, then flicked his hellgun onto full power and sent a bright lance of laser into the body of a servitor drifting ominously over to flank them. Thaddeus took aim with his pistol and loosed off three shots, the microcogitators in the rare executioner rounds sending the bullets curving as they flew, punching into the servitor with mechanical accuracy.

The servitor juddered and listed suddenly as one of its grav units burst in a shower of sparks – Thaddeus sighted down the barrel at the bundle of sensors that made up its head and pumped the rest of the autogun's ten-round magazine into it. Like swift metal insects the rounds looped towards their target and shattered the servitor's metal face, sending arcs of electricity spitting from the broken machinery and exposing the biological core of the machine, the part that had once been human.

Without anything to guide it, the servitor yawed aimlessly, exposing the underbelly to which its jointed limbs were attached. The other storm trooper swung the barrel of his grenade launcher around and fired a single frag grenade into the servitor's belly, ripping it clean open and spilling machine parts and pulped flesh down towards the lake.

The grenade trooper allowed himself a grim smile of triumph as he racked another round into his weapon.

'Get us to Kindarek!' shouted Thaddeus. Telleryev nodded and the two men broke cover at a run. The grenade trooper waved them forward, pumping a volley of grenades into the walkways above them to send hot shrapnel bursting through the air and momentarily blinding the servitors as Thaddeus and Telleryev ran.

Kindarek was trying to organise a strongpoint around a couple of sculptures and a length of walkway that had fallen down from above, with seven or eight troopers keeping up fields of fire and preventing the servitors from surrounding them. There were still a dozen of the machines left, spraying multilaser fire across the width of the cylinder – but they were avoiding blasting directly at the sculptures, and so they had to close to use their power saws while keeping the walkways between clear. Kindarek was trying to punish the servitors that drifted towards them and, though he would probably not succeed, he was at least buying time.

Thaddeus reached Kindarek's position, Telleryev beside him.

'We need to get men upwards,' voxed Thaddeus breathlessly. 'We have to get a link set up.'

Kindarek paused as his soldier's mind rifled through the possibilities – stay here with at least some cover and a plan, or throw men through the gauntlet in an attempt to drag some information screaming from the cathedral's archives.

'We're dead here anyway,' he replied. Then, on the squad frequency – 'Suppression fire and break cover! Head for the upper walkways and concentrate fire:. Move, move!'

Thaddeus slipped a single shell from one of his waist pouches into the breech of the autopistol. A single heavy shell, it was more expensive than many spaceships and a handful of them had cost Thaddeus a lot of favours. Now, he was immensely grateful he had shown the prescience to have brought them along.

Thaddeus ran alongside the storm troopers and fired once at a servitor turning to spray fire at them. The autopistol barked and a glittering trail followed the bullet. Its armour-piercing tip and micro-guidance systems let it punch repeatedly through the glossy carapace of the servitor before running out of propellant. Its concentrated explosive core detonated in the heart of the servitor and blew it apart in a shower of frozen flesh and shimmering metal.

Adeptus Mechanicus specials, the pinnacle of personal armaments technology. Now Thaddeus was using them to get him out of a spot where it was the Mechanicus that wanted him dead. There would be a moral in there somewhere if Thaddeus survived long enough to work it out.

Thaddeus managed to spend two more priceless rounds of ammunition blowing another servitor out of the air, and the frantic hellgun fire accounted for three more as the storm troopers ran to the closest junction that would lead them upwards towards the next levels.

'Telleryev!' yelled Kindarek as the storm troopers made it to the next level and took cover behind a huge sculpture. 'Take three men and keep them occupied! The rest watch the boss's back!'

Thaddeus nodded at the lieutenant and took the hook-up equipment from a hip pocket of his suit. It was a simple portable cogitator linked to a data-slate by a thick bundle of wires, with various interfaces leading off on yet more wires. Thaddeus fumbled with the device as he crouched by the sculpture feeling the sudden hot flashes of laser blasts passing close by.

He couldn't find an interface. He passed his hands over the clear, angular crystal surface but there was no way in. Would he fail here because he had been stupid enough to assume the Mechanicus would use standard interfaces?

No – there was something, at the base of the crystal. A metal panel was bolted to the surface, an ugly flaw in the crystal. A data-thief probe extended from the plate into the body of the crystal and provided a low-tech way in. The data-sculptures were technology from a previous age and the Mechanicus had obviously lacked an equally elegant way of using them – they had been forced to make do with the technology they had, and that was the same technology used across the Imperium.

Thaddeus plugged one wire into the crude interface. There was a pause and suddenly the data-slate was full of solid information, dense columns of binary pouring across the screen.

The program loaded onto the cogitator had been almost as expensive in its own way as the bullets in Thaddeus's gun, taken from a tech-heretic that Thaddeus had helped capture back in his interrogator days. The Hereticus had ordered that the heretic be left alive so the Inquisition could make use of his skills – the man had escaped and Thaddeus had been a part of the mission that had finally killed him. The program he had given the Inquisition before his escape was a decoder, powerful enough to crunch through the encryption of just about any secure information source but simple enough to fit onto almost any computation device.

Skrin Kavansiel had been the man's name. A madman who had turned servitors and industrial machinery into rampaging monsters across half-a-dozen worlds in the Scarus sector, all in the name of the Change God. Thaddeus had shared the kill himself with two other interrogators on an agri-world near the galactic core. That Kavansiel had been allowed to live the first time had sowed the doubts in Thaddeus that Lord Inquisitor Kolgo had confirmed – the Inquisition was not the single, focused instrument of the Emperor's justice that he had learned of when he was first groomed as an interrogator. Half the time, it might as well be fighting itself.

The cogitator broke the mass of information down into categories and homed in on the records of Adeptus Mechanicus installations and personnel throughout the Stratix sector. There were still trillions of scraps of information in there – at least, thought Thaddeus as laser fire spattered around him and short, gargled screams told of troopers dying, the information vaults were all connected. He only hoped that the sculptures shattered below them had not contained the information he needed.

'Gak me sideways!' someone shouted. 'Company!'

Thaddeus glanced upwards. There were lights now in the darkness at the top of the cylinder, powerful spotlights swinging through the shadows. The lights picked out ropes coiling downwards and figures rappelling down them, troopers in rust-red jumpsuits, guns slung on their backs.

'Frag, tech-guard!' said Kindarek.

Half the storm troopers were still pinned down by the servitors. Thaddeus didn't hold out much hope that those who remained could deal with crack tech-guard troops firing on them from above.

He spotted a couple of tech-priests directing the tech-guard, robed and hooded adepts armed with shimmering power axes and exotic weaponry that sent bolts of power burning down at the storm troopers.

The data-slate began to sort through the information according to the same codewords that Thaddeus had used to filter astropathic traffic – Soul Drinker, purple, Marine, spider, a host of others.

As the screen seethed with information Thaddeus switched to the vox frequency he had reserved for the shuttle.

'Thaddeus to shuttle. Target above us, multiple hostiles. Make it count.'

'Received,' came the servitor's mechanical voice, the signal warped by the intervening liquid hydrogen. 'Shuttle out.'

A fountain of hydrogen burst out of the lake and with a roar the shuttle's stealth engines kicked in, ripping it out of the lake and sending it hurtling upwards like a bullet from a gun. Once clear of the lake the main engines erupted and the shuttle rose on a plume of flame, past the lowest walkways and upwards.

The data now rushing through the uplink device still poured through the cogitator in awesome amounts. Every Mechanicus outpost from the present day back to the time of the Great Crusade was listed, with staff lists, schematics, work rotas, research reports, accounts, tech-prayers, and all the ephemera of the Mechanicus's immense operation.

Thaddeus keyed in the last command he had – the order to sort the data by the staff list Sister Aescarion had recovered from the outpost on Eumenix. A few hundred names that represented the last hope – maddeningly, everything Thaddeus needed to know was probably streaming past in front of his eyes, he just had to pick it out from the ocean of information.

The datastream thinned. A blinking green light on the frame of the data-slate told Thaddeus that the information was concise enough for the cogitator to hold. Thaddeus pressed a switch and the information was seared onto the cogitator's memory.

Maybe it was enough. Maybe there was nothing there but trivia. Thaddeus would have to take the chance, if he survived. That was a big if.

The shuttle soared upwards shattering its way through walkways as it went. Mounted guns on the half-glimpsed structures above pumped a stream of shells into the shuttle, ripping through the armour plates and sending sudden, shocking gouts of flame bursting from the engine housings.

The first tech-guard were landing on walkways high above, sending down hails of rapid-firing autogun shots. The freezing air was full of shrapnel and vapour. Thaddeus saw Sergeant Telleryev ripped clean in two by one of the last servitors, his insides turning to a mist of crimson shards even as two of his men were shot off the walkway by tech-guard fire. Thaddeus blasted twice, three times, and three tech-guard were picked off their rappel lines by ammunition they could only have dreamed of using one day.

The shuttle's engine blew and clouds of vapour bloomed around it. Its rise peaked and it began to fall, just a few metres beneath the levels the tech-guard were now landing on.

The servitor-pilot, working to hardwired protocols Thaddeus himself had installed, switched the shuttle's fuel cells into reverse, pumping high-grade prometheum derivative backwards until it flooded through the ignition chambers.

The fuel ignited and incinerated everything in the cockpit and crew compartment in an instant. The servitor-pilot was atomised, metal components melted to gas, flesh disappearing.

The hull of the shuttle failed under the stress of the explosive forces within. With a thunderclap and a flash of flame that turned the crystal cathedral a blazing orange, the shuttle exploded, and boiling flame filled the top half of the cylinder.

Vapour, like a falling sky, billowed downwards and washed over the storm troopers. Thaddeus was blinded, bright white turning dark.

The vox was a mess of static. For a few seconds he was alone, encased in cold and confusion, fumbling blind as he tried to stuff the data-slate into the pocket of his HE suit. The shadowy shape of a storm trooper stumbled by then fell out of view, slipping over the edge of the walkway as random autogun fire spattered down through the darkness.

Something huge was falling. The sound of shattering crystal cut through the din, a high fractured crash growing rapidly closer. Shards of crystal, like huge glass knives, plunged through the darkness and the air was full of filaments. Spikes of icy cold jabbed at Thaddeus as fragments of crystal punctured his suit and cold air jetted in before the fabric tightened around the tiny wounds.

The huge burning hulk of Thaddeus's transport ripped down from above, trailing ribbons of flame, carving through the dense vapour like a comet. It took half the walkways with it, countless strands of the crystal web snapping, information vaults shattering into a blizzard of fragments. Men were screaming as they fell. Thaddeus expected any second to be dragged down with them, or to have his HE suit sliced open and his muscles turned to slabs of frozen meat.

The transport impacted far below, and a fraction of a second later the top layer of liquid hydrogen ignited.

The containment fields, designed to divert the energy of any ignition away from the information vaults above, compressed the heat and shockwave downwards and outwards. But the hydrogen kept burning as the transport plunged through it and then its plasma drive imploded. Without the containment fields, the whole lake would have burned and turned the cathedral into a column of flame, incinerating everything inside. Instead, the explosion was forced down into the root of the cylinder, where the ferrofibre walls met the rock of Pharos.

The walls of the cylinder fractured catastrophically, great black fissures rippling up the walls. The air shrieked out into the hard vacuum beyond, sucking men and debris with it. Thaddeus grabbed the datavault beside him as razor-sharp crystal shard whipped past. Storm troopers and tech-guard tumbled past, flailing hopelessly.

The hydrogen lake, designed to keep the information vaults stable, had instead led to the whole cathedral being destroyed. The Adeptus Mechanicus, in their obsession with technical perfection, had missed the obvious danger. It had never occurred to them that anything hostile could survive the extreme cold and the servitor-warriors, or that anything could detonate the lake with such ferocity that the confinement fields could not cope. It was holy ground, and holy information was inviolable.

The upper echelons of the Mechanicus could not imagine that a desperate, lone inquisitor would invade the Omnissiah's sanctum and would bring with him all the random, chaotic factors that could destroy it.

The irony was momentarily lost on Thaddeus as the columns broke away from the ceiling and swung around him, churning up the broken crystal into a storm of razors. Thaddeus's section of walkway broke away and suddenly the cylinder was whirling around him. The fissures tore on upwards and suddenly the whole top half of the cylinder boomed open, the stresses in the structure building up until the whole cylinder split like a seed pod.

Thaddeus tried to control his movement but he couldn't. He kicked fruitlessly against nothing, and glimpsed surviving storm troopers and tech-guard doing the same. The fires from below went dark as the air rushed out and there was nothing but darkness now, the ruins of the cathedral below him and the blackness of space above. The tide of escaping air carried him upwards and out of the cylinder and, as he span out past the limits of Pharos's artificial gravity field, he saw the damage inflicted on the rest of the cathedral. The fires had burst up into the neighbouring cylinders and flames boiled around the base of the cathedral.

Thousands of years of priceless information was burning together with the menials and adepts trapped inside. Thaddeus saw one or two storm troopers and tech-guard who were suffering the same fate as him, struggling helplessly as they were thrown further and further into space. Ejected crystal debris glittered like shooting stars, streams of bright silver fragments spinning against the blackness. Bodies and body parts span amongst the debris, broken and helpless.

Thaddeus's mind raced through the situation. He tried to think objectively, like a good inquisitor should when first presented with a problem. His HE suit could survive hard vacuum but the air filters would fail soon without an atmosphere from which to draw oxygen and nitrogen. He had no means of propulsion and nowhere to go even if he could move.

The data-slate was in his pocket. That, at least, was something. With luck, he had completed his objective. Now he just had to survive.

There was nothing around him now but space. Pharos was a brightly-lit city-temple behind him, the remnants of the cylinder a darkening mass of twisted metal. The searing unblinking eye of the dying red star burned to one side, and to the other was just cold vacuum. Thaddeus had seen space only through viewscreen or portholes, or as the night sky from the safety of a planet's surface. He had never been surrounded by it. For the first time, he realised just how delicate the Imperium truly was – an infinitely thin layer of tenacious life clinging to the dead rock that made up a minuscule fraction of the galaxy. No wonder mankind had to fight. No wonder it saw extinction around every corner.

The Soul Drinkers were out there somewhere, between those stars. Thaddeus might even now have the information he needed to find them, but he was cruelly aware of just how close his death was. An inquisitor was not afraid of death, but he was afraid – and proud to be afraid – of dying with his service to the Emperor left incomplete. As Thaddeus drifted, that fear grew and grew, until it surrounded him as completely as the uncaring galaxy itself.

CHAPTER EIGHT

SEPTIAM TORUS WAS a garden world. Its two main continents were cov-ered in temperate grasslands and deep, lush forests. The faint rings around the planet lit up the sky in shimmering rainbows, with sunsets of a million colours. Crystal-clear rivers wound their way through breathtaking countryside and plunged down spectacular waterfalls before joining a great shining ocean teeming with coral reefs. The planet's ecosystem had never evolved far beyond plant life, and so there were no animals to act as predators or scavengers save for the species introduced to pollinate the planet's small crop of soulfire flowers – flocks of birds with green and blue plumage that streaked across the skies like comets.

Soulfire stamens were the source of some of the most potent combat drugs the Imperium issued to its penal legions and more expendable Guard regiments, and so Septiam Torus was accorded special status. Its tithes were paid in the soulfire crop alone and the ruling family – descended from the first rogue trader to find the planet and annexe it in the name of the Emperor – was granted perpetual rights over the world.

Septiam Torus remained unsettled and unspoilt apart from its sole city, a sprawl of marble, like a vast colonnaded palace, with a barracks and brig for its private law enforcement regiment and endless tile-roofed streets housing the crop workers.

One day a ship's lifeboat was glimpsed in the upper atmosphere, its distress beacon bleating that it contained a sole occupant severely injured. The pod thudded home into the middle of a field, kicking up a

391

plume of purple-black petals. The Septiam Torus Enforcement Division sent a paramedic team to recover the occupant and bring him for treatment to the city. They found a body badly charred but alive, and brought it back to the infirmary in the shadow of the senate house.

For three weeks the infirmary staff tried to coax life from the victim. Eventually they caused their patient – they couldn't even tell if it was a man or a woman – to flicker an eyelid in recognition.

At that moment one of Septiam's senators was visiting the facility. It was the sort of duty expected of all senators, representing as they did a loose family group expected to outdo one another in service to their world. The senator disliked the infirmary but it was crucial to keeping the crop workers secure and happy on Septiam Torus, and she blandly absorbed the facts and figures the medical staff handed out as she followed them around the wards.

She rounded a corner and saw the charred form of the crash victim, suspended in a wire harness and wrapped in bandages that were yellow and stained even though they had been changed barely an hour earlier. Monitoring equipment blinked and chirped. The perfumed curtains that hung around the patient couldn't mask the faint odour of cooked meat.

'Ah, our visitor.' The senator smiled – ostensibly to show a friendly face to the unfortunate, but really because the seeping raw body was the first interesting thing she had seen all day. 'Our stranger. How long before you can tell us who you are? We are much concerned to find out about you and your ship.'

'The patient has only just awoken, my lady,' said one of the orderlies. 'We hope for a return to consciousness very soon.'

The patient stirred and stared out at the senator with pained, rolling eyes.

Then, as the senator watched, the patient dissolved, bandages unravelling as skin sloughed off, looping entrails slithering and hissing to the polished floor, organs bubbling away into a foul brackish pool. The spine came apart and the skull plopped onto the floor, brains liquefying, eyes running down the cheeks, teeth bleached cubes in the stinking mess.

The senator was hurried out of the infirmary and the orderlies hosed the gory mess into the drains. But the senator had breathed in a good lungful of noisome gases from the dissolving patient, and in this way contracted a disease which she then transferred to the senate house at the next meeting.

Within two weeks, the senate and half the population was wiped out. The tens of thousands of dead were heaped into pits and the beautiful sky of Septiam Torus turned dirty grey with fatty smoke from the pyres. The survivors tried to set up a sterile zone within the walls of Septiam

City but charred skeletal fingers tore down the barriers and the dead walked again, the perfection of the garden world turned into a blood-stained nightmare of shambling corpses.

The few living dead that could speak spoke the name of Teturact.

GUARDSMAN SENSHINI COULD swear he heard the crunch of bone beneath the tracks of the Leman Russ Executioner as the tank lurched over a wooded ridge, churning up the cratered mud that stretched across the land where once fragrant fields of soulfire flowers and lush woodlands had thrived. Beyond the main cannon's targeting array Senshini could just pick out the jumble of shapes on the horizon, past the broken lumpy landscape of chewed-up forests and churned mud. Septiam City was dug in against the landscape, pockmarked slabs of marble and log-jams of toppled columns forming huge barricades and rows of tank traps ringing the city's outskirts.

Senshini knew enough about the short history of the conflict on Septiam Torus to guess this was the big push. The first attack on the planet had taken place just a few weeks after Septiam Torus had been confirmed as having been tainted by Teturact. A regiment of Elysians had dropped onto the world from Valkyries by grav-chute. They had died almost to the man, finding themselves surrounded by masses of walking corpses where they had expected a handful of rebel private troopers. The Elysian Drop Troop regiments were considered elite formations but no amount of training would make a lasgun shot kill something that was already dead, especially when some of those living dead were former comrades.

The Imperial Guard had pulled out those Elysians they could and had sent in a regiment of more conventional ground-pounders, the Jouryan XVII. They besieged Septiam City. The Stratix XXIII, hard-bitten hive ganger conscripts itching for a chance to avenge their dead world, had been sent in to support them once it had become clear that the twenty thousand Jouryans couldn't take Septiam City themselves. The governor's own Gathalamorian Artillery were brought in to soften up the entrenched defenders prior to the inevitable assault.

In total, including the support and supply formations, Army Group Torus numbered just shy of a hundred thousand men.

Senshini, if he were being honest, didn't think it would be enough.

He had been with the Jouryans on Septiam Torus for three weeks. During that time he had heard some of the stories that patrols and kill-sweep teams had brought back. There were dead men out there, walking like the living. Some of them had once been Elysians. Some of them now were Jouryans. At least now the waiting was over, but, like everyone else in the armour section, Senshini feared what they might find inside the city.

He saw foot troops at the edges of his target viewer, figures hurrying past in the dark grey fatigues of the Jouryan XVII, black helmets and body armour already spattered with mud, lasguns held close to their chests.

The armour and infantry were to support one another as they closed in on the perimeter, the tanks breaching the walls and the infantry swarming through the gaps. Demolisher siege tanks were rumbling towards knots of shattered trees where they could scrounge some cover as they opened up at long range. Leman Russ tanks would close in, their medium-range guns shattering masonry and throwing defenders from the walls. The Executioners, of which there were only a handful amongst the Jouryans, would have to venture in further so their guns could fill the breaches with liquid fire before the infantry went in.

The Executioner was armed unlike any other Imperial Guard tank. Its Leman Russ-pattern chassis was topped with a massive plasma blastgun, most of the crew compartment crammed with the hot, thrumming plasma coils that fuelled the gun. An Executioner was a rare beast, hardly ever seen outside the forge worlds where the Adeptus Mechanicus jealously guarded the secrets of their manufacture, and the Jouryan XVII was fortunate indeed to have acquired any at all. It was Senshini's duty to fire the blastgun, and he knew that it would light up the tank to enemy spotters like a firework display.

Still, it could be worse, thought Senshini as he spotted broken figures moving between the shattered columns that broke the jumbled silhouette of the walls. He could be riding a Hellhound, the notorious and often ill-fated flamethrower tanks with external tanks full of promethium, which had to go into the teeth of the enemy to support the infantry with waves of fire.

Kaito, the Executioner's commander, swung open the top hatch and hauled himself up so he could see out. The awful battlefield smell rolled into the tank, cutting through even the electrical stink of the plasma coils – a stench of sickly rotting flesh and the heavy, charred smell of burning bodies.

'Hang left, Tanako!' called Kaito, 'Keep them beside us!'

Senshini, like Kaito, was well aware of the need to keep the infantry close alongside the tank. The Executioner had no sponson weapons to cover its side arcs, and it needed supporting infantry to minimise the chance of a lascannon or krak missile punching through the side armour.

Tanako, in the cramped driver's compartment below Senshini, swung the steering levers and the tank swerved to the left – Senshini could see through the targeter as the tank crept closer to the hunched Jouryans hurrying over the cratered mud.

Kaito dropped back into the tank and pulled the hatch down. 'Artillery's coming over,' he said. Senshini saw that already the tank commander's face was streaked with engine grime and the shoulders of his officer's greatcoat were spattered with kicked-up mud. Kaito was a veteran who had lost his previous tank, a Vanquisher tank hunter, to enemy fire on Salshan Anterior and had only taken over the Executioner a week before. To both Senshini and Tanako, the man was a mystery – quiet and reserved, rarely speaking without reason, with a calm face that showed little sign of having witnessed the fiercest action on Salshan Anterior.

Even with the hatch down Senshini could hear the first salvoes of the artillery attack shrieking overhead. The Gathalamorians' guns fired heavy, armour-cracking shells to shatter the walls, and high explosive rounds to wreak havoc in the city behind them. Senshini watched them as they hurtled over the advancing Jouryan line like falling constellations. The first of them hit home a split second later. He felt their impact through the lurching hull of the tank as they detonated with a sound like an earthquake, a dozen shells ripping into Septiam City, lighting up the walls and throwing the makeshift defences into harsh silhouettes against the flame.

Manticore artillery tanks to the rear of the Jouryans' armour added bright streaks of rockets, like claw marks against the dark sky, and one of the Gathalamorians' Deathstrike launchers sent a fat missile thudding into the city just beyond the wall where it erupted into a blue-white ball of nuclear flame.

Answering fire spattered back from the walls, a dusting of glitter that was distant small arms fire, autoweapons and lasguns.

'Squadron Twelve is giving us a ranging shot,' said Kaito through the tank's intercom, his voice punctuated by explosions growing closer.

'Understood, sir.'

Squadron Twelve was a few hundred metres to the left, consisting of two Leman Russ tanks with lascannon sponsons and a Vanquisher tank hunter; the squadron functioning as a nugget of anti-armour firepower in the infantry line.

Senshini swivelled the targeter to get a view of Squadron Six's Vanquisher tank firing a tracer shell towards the walls. It fell just short of the walls in a crimson starburst.

'Squadron Twelve, this is Squadron Six gunner,' said Senshini into the tank's primitive field vox unit. 'We got that. Make it three hundred metres to blastgun range.'

'Squadron Six, this is Squadron Command,' came the voice of the artillery's command section, mounted in a Salamander command vehicle a few hundred metres back. 'You have the short range, move forward for combined long range firing.'

'Yes, sir. Squadron Six out.' Kaito flicked off the vox. 'Get us closer, Tanako. We need to get into range the same time as the Vanquishers.'

'Let's just hope some of those footsloggers follow us up,' said Tanako bleakly as he gunned the Executioner's engines and accelerated.

The Jouryans in front of them would be in the first wave to hit the walls. Senshini had heard that such a thing was a great honour to many soldiers, but then he had also heard that there were a lot of crazy men in the Guard.

The thin, dark line of Jouryans crept closer to the city outskirts as the fire from the walls increased and the next waves of artillery hit home. Somewhere on the other side of the city the Stratix XXIII would be doing the same, gang-scum conscripts hurrying to get to grips with the defenders in the close-quarters butchery at which they excelled. And inside the city, defenders would be manning the walls even as they died, then rising from the dead again, if there was enough left of them.

Two hundred metres. Senshini could see barely human silhouettes, some limbless or even headless, many toting weaponry looted from the Enforcement Division armouries, others just shambling along the broken stone. Whole marble-tiled roofs had been tipped on edge to form walls, stacks of toppled pillar sections made huge obstacles. Whatever had been knocked down in the previous shelling had been carted to the edge of the city and piled into treacherous slopes of pulverised marble and brick, with fire points on the top to rake troops with gunfire as they struggled upwards.

One hundred metres.

Small arms fire was spattering in the mud around the troopers – the Jouryans knew better than to try to engage in a fire-fight at this range but one or two still fell, the steel rain cutting them down as they advanced. A couple of shots rang off the hull of the Executioner, sharp steel dints against the grinding of the engine and the crunching as the tracks rode over the remains of previous assaults. There were dead men in the mud below them, Elysians and Enforcement Division troops mixed with gnarled Septiam limbs, along with weapons and equipment dropped by dead hands. No matter what happened, there would be a new layer of Jouryan dead added to it before long.

Fifty metres.

If this had been a normal city the fleet would have obliterated it from orbit. But previous experience with Teturact's followers had shown that would just have given them a ruined warren of hiding places for the corpses to rise from. It had to be done the old-fashioned way, with troopers on foot bayoneting every one of them and burning the remains.

Senshini could just make out the yells of front-line officers as they lined their squads and platoons up with their designated attack points on the defences. Some would try to climb vertical marble rooftops with ropes and had climbing gear slung over their shoulders. Others would slog their way up crumbling slopes. Sapper units would try to go through or under, their task considered the most dangerous of all.

The targeting reticule showed the range in the bottom corner. Senshini knew he was close enough. For a second more he let the Executioner trundle on, bringing a few more metres of wall within the blastgun's reach.

'Squadron Six gunner, in range,' said Senshini.

'This is Squadron Six command,' echoed Kaito into the vox. 'Ready to fire.'

'Squadron Six, fire,' came command's response.

'Fire!' yelled Kaito, and Senshini slammed the firing lever down.

The reticule was filled with light, streaming from above and behind as the coils emptied their massive charges through the blastgun barrel. The energy was focused into a compacted bolt of superheated plasma, white-hot and liquid, which was spat with tremendous force towards the wall of column sections in Senshini's sights.

Huge column drums toppled, forming a landslide of carved stone, the sections rolling into the mud at the foot of the wall, kicking up great crescents of filth. Liquid plasma burst into a storm of lethal droplets, seething through the gaps between the stone. Figures tumbled down the ruined wall, bodies breaking or dissolving as the plasma hit them. Shells from the other squadrons nearby, and the longer-ranged tanks behind, slammed into the stone, splintering the marble and kicking more column sections down into the mud.

The troops to either side sped up, squads holding back to cover the advancing units. Lasgun fire spattered up towards the walls and heavy weapon units sent frag missiles and airburst mortars filling the air on the battlements with shrapnel.

The enemy took just a few moments to recover. The column stacks were broken but not completely breached. Senshini could see dozens and dozens of small dark figures dressed in rags, like insects swarming from under the bark of a tree.

The coils behind Senshini thrummed as they recharged and the tracks groaned in complaint as Tanako forced the tank over the churned earth by the walls, following the units that were running for the cover of fallen masonry as autogun and lasgun fire rattled down towards them. Shots were spattering off the Executioner's front armour, and components were sparking and shorting out in the crew compartment.

Tanako spat an ancient Jouryan curse as tiny flames licked from his control consoles. A cold chemical smell filled the compartment as Kaito smothered the fire with a handheld extinguisher.

Senshini watched as a vicious, swirling fight was born amongst the fallen stone of the broken wall. The enemy had the numbers, hundreds of ragged pasty-skinned men and women clambering over the blocks and taking cover amongst the crevices, but each Jouryan carried better firepower and had far better discipline than his opposite in the city. Officers formed fire lines to support the units advancing into the rubble. Assault teams hurled demo charges into knots of enemies, before charging with bayonets and feeding a brutal, swirling, close-order scrap that swelled at the base of the wall.

The old-fashioned way. No matter what the Mechanicus could cook up or the Navy could send into orbit, when it came down to it you needed a bayonet and some guts to win a war. For the briefest moment Senshini wished he were down there in the heart of the fighting, lasgun in his hand – but he could see men stumbling with limbs severed or entrails spilling, and he knew he should be glad there were several layers of armour between him and the hail of fire raking down into the Jouryans.

'This is Squadron Command,' crackled the vox. 'I need a visual on Squadron Twenty.'

'Twenty?' replied Kaito. 'This is Squadron Six, they won't be this far up front yet.'

'We've lost contact with Squadron Twenty. Report in a visual, we need them deployed at the wall.'

It made no sense. Squadron Twenty was a rear echelon squadron, consisting of three stripped-down Chimera transports crewed by medical corps officers. They would race up to the front line when the first wave of the attack had gone in, picking up the wounded and taking them back to the casualty stations to the rear of the Jouryan lines. Senshini hated to think what would go through the minds of the assaulting troops if they knew their only hope of any kind of rapid medical attention had been lost somewhere in the rearward echelons.

'Gunner! Emplacement, thirty degrees high!'

Senshini yanked on the vertical lever and the viewpoint swung upwards, framing a precarious section of the wall where several enemies were loading shells into a field gun that fired almost point-blank into the Jouryans battling to get a foothold in the rubble below. Senshini took a ranging, correcting up a few metres, and fired. The plasma discharged with a roar and the emplacement disappeared in a bursting blister of plasma.

Armour was coming up beside the Executioner, a Demolisher to help crack the wall open further and an Exterminator, twin autocannons barking rapidly as they sent shrapnel bursting amongst the enemy scrambling down the rubble slope. A pair of Chimeras streaked by, tracks kicking up sprays of dirt, and a Valkyrie roared overhead, belly compartment full of storm troopers to exploit a full breach further up the wall.

'Gak me sideways,' said Tanako from below. 'That's Squadron Twenty!'

Senshini swung the targeting array down to catch sight of the rear of a Chimera as it drove headlong for the walls, the staff-and-snake symbol of the medical corps stencilled on its rear ramp. A third Chimera with the same markings drove by a moment later, its driver recklessly gunning the engine and crunching through the gears as it rode over the crest of a shell crater.

'Take us closer, Tanako,' ordered Kaito. 'Senshini, close support fire, they're pinned down. And get onto command, tell them we've found Squadron Twenty.'

The Executioner lurched forward. The stink of the recharging coils surrounded Senshini, and he could feel the greasy grime caking on his bare hands and face. The viewpoint swung violently and he caught a glimpse of the top hatch of Squadron Twenty's closest Chimera swinging open.

Heavy-calibre fire spattered from the open hatch. Senshini spotted dark figures tumbling down the rubble slope. The volume of fire was massive and shocking, ripping into the Septiam's on the slopes. It was accurate, too, and Senshini saw Septiam's fall. No lasgun could blow a man apart like that, not even the hellguns of the Guard elites.

'That's not medical corps,' said Senshini, mostly to himself.

The Executioner was within easy small arms fire of the wall and shots rang loudly off the upper plates, kicking chunks of armour from the hull. Senshini caught glimpses of the closest enemy, sheltering in the cover of fallen column sections as they swapped fire with the Jouryans – dressed in rags, skin pale and torn, covered in old open wounds that didn't bleed. He saw tatters of finery and Enforcement Division uniforms. Opaque grey eyes took aim. Hands with missing fingers held hunting rifles and salvaged Elysian lasguns.

Every single dead man was walking again, and fighting too – the whole of Septiam City and half a regiment of butchered Elysians, lost

Jouryan patrols, workers from the now-ruined soulfire fields. The commanders had expected a fraction of the city's inhabitants still to be waiting at the walls. But now Senshini could see there were thousands of them, streaming down the breach into the advancing Jouryans like bloodants from a nest.

A storm of laser fire was like burning red stitches between the fallen blocks. Lascannon shots streaked from Jouryan armour moving up and explosions stitched the rubble slope where mortar and anti-tank volleys hit home.

The Executioner juddered to a halt. Senshini lined up another shot, paused to check the coils had charged, and sent another blastgun shot ripping into a knot of Septiams huddling in the cover of a fallen marble block. Two squads of Jouryans, no longer pinned down by the enemy fire, ran forward through the falling debris.

The Chimeras of Squadron Twenty skidded to a halt in a slew of mud. The top hatches and rear ramps swung open and the occupants leapt out, guns blazing.

'Looks like we got some glory boys,' said Senshini. 'They must've given Squadron Twenty to the storm troopers.'

But they weren't storm troopers, Senshini realised. They were huge figures, much larger than a man, and in the few seconds before grime and flying mud turned them into a spattered dark grey he saw that they wore purple, not the dull fatigues of the Jouryans.

'Shenking gakrats,' swore Senshini. 'Marines.'

Kaito opened the observer hatch and dared to poke his head up into the shrapnel-filled air. He pulled a pair of field glasses from inside his coat. Senshini was sure he heard a cheer go up from the Jouryan attackers, even over the din of gunfire, as the Space Marines charged into battle beside them. Every Guardsman had heard of the Adeptus Astartes and some even claimed to have seen them on the battlefield, superhuman warriors who could strike like lightning into the heart of the enemy, wore massive powered armour and had the best weapons the Imperium could provide. Preachers extolled them as paragons of humankind. Children swapped stories about their exploits. They decorated a million stained glass windows and sculpted friezes in temples and basilica across the Imperium, and now they were here on Septiam Torus.

After a long couple of seconds Kaito dropped back into the tank. 'Right, Command have sent us some Space Marines. It's the first and last time we'll see these buggers so we're going to close in and support them. If that breach can fall, they're going to be the ones to take it. Tanako, as close as you can. Senshini, I want plasma at the top of the wall, give these freaks nowhere to run. Fire at will, Now!'

The Executioner roared into the shadow of the walls, rumbling past the fallen column sections and crunching through the dead of the assault, heading for the maelstrom of the breach where the Space Marines were weaving a new kind of hell amongst the Septiams.

Jouryans were rallying all around, following the Executioner into the storm of fire, officers yelling at their men to follow in the Marines' wake. Senshini sighted the heart of the breach where the corpse-like Septiams were massed, thrown back by the shock of the renewed assault.

Senshini fired the blastgun and plasma erupted as if from beneath the rubble. He spotted the Marines scrambling up the burning slope, boltguns chewing through the swarming Septiams, and he knew the battle for Septiam City was on.

EVERYTHING WAS COLD. Thaddeus couldn't feel his hands or feet. For a horrible moment he thought he might have lost them to frostbite or shrapnel flying from the disintegrating cathedral, but then a prickly, electrical pain flashed through the nerves of his arms and legs and he knew that he was whole.

He tried tensing the muscles he could feel, expecting a sunburst of pain to tell him of a broken limb or a ruptured organ. He couldn't find any obvious injuries, but he was constricted. He thought he might be lying down but he couldn't sit up or turn his head. Although the numbness from the cold kept him from being sure, it felt like his hands were encased in something that stopped him even moving his fingers.

He smelled chemicals. Preservatives, disinfectants, a substance that smelled rusty and metallic like something distilled from blood. Ruthlessly clean and sterile.

At first he thought there was no sound – but gradually he picked out layers of soft noise, fluorescent buzzing, the faint irregular ticking and scratching from some machine near his head, a faint dripping of liquid.

Finally, he tried to pry his eyes open. A slash of light burned across his vision and it was several minutes before he could begin to see – he must have been unconscious for some time and his eyes were barely able to adjust to the light. He seemed to be looking up at a square of pure light, until gradually a pair of glowstrips coalesced in the centre of a white-painted ceiling.

The walls were also white. The floor was polished metal with channels leading to a central drain to bleed away unwanted fluids – this alone told Thaddeus he was in a medical facility. The machine by his head was a medical servitor, a biological brain somewhere in its chromed casing telling the armatures jutting from its front to scribble

Thaddeus's life-signs onto a long strip of parchment that spooled from the machine. Several cylinders were racked on one wall, thin transparent tubes feeding odd-coloured fluid into the gauntlets that covered his hands and wrists. The gauntlets were medical contraptions that kept veins in his hands and wrists open to keep medication flowing into him. The pains he had felt were the occasional probing of neurosensors adhering to his skin, triggering pain receptors intermittently to check his nervous system was still working.

Thaddeus listened harder. Beneath the faint thrum of the lighting and the ticking of the medical machinery, there was a distant rumbling, like a thunderstorm over the horizon. Engines – he was on a spaceship, then. It made sense, seeing as the last place he remembered being was in space.

There was a faint chiming as the light on the life signs machine blinked in response to Thaddeus's waking. A few minutes later the room's single featureless door slid open and Lord Inquisitor Kolgo walked in.

Kolgo seemed weak and wizened outside his ceremonial armour. He wore shapeless dark robes like a monk's habit, and the neuro-interfaces were red and raw on the back of his head where his armour was normally connected. To anyone else he would just look like another old man – but Thaddeus could see the authority Kolgo still carried with him, the indefinable quality that made even fellow inquisitors accept his command.

Kolgo pulled a chrome-plated chair close to the bed, and sat down.

'You are most determined, Thaddeus,' he said. 'I confess we really didn't anticipate you going this far.' There was a faint note of amusement in his voice.

'The Hereticus gave me a job to do,' replied Thaddeus, his voice raw and painful in his throat. 'Any inquisitor would have done the same.'

Kolgo shook his head, almost sadly. 'Our mistake was both underestimating and overestimating you, Thaddeus. Underestimated because we thought that your skills were not yet well developed enough to allow you to pursue the Soul Drinkers as closely as you have. Overestimated because we thought you would be quicker to develop a sense for the consequences of your actions. The Inquisitorial remit is theoretically limitless, but Thaddeus, for the Throne's sake – Pharos? After I told you how delicate our situation with the Mechanicus was. The damn place only blew seventy-two hours ago and already sub-battlefleet Aggarendon has lost three ships to the withdrawal of tech-priest support. Ordinatus units on Calliargan and Vogel are about to fall silent. The Mechanicus are convinced that Teturact somehow got at Pharos and the tech-guard presence there has been tripled.'

'You have your objectives, Kolgo, I have mine.'

'Ah yes, the Soul Drinkers. Presumably you know why you were given the task of tracking them down.'

'Because I could do it. And because I work differently from Tsouras.'

Kolgo reached up to the life signs machine and made an adjustment. The medi-gauntlets around Thaddeus's hands cracked open and there were several pinpricks of pain as the sensors and needles were withdrawn. Warmth seeped back into Thaddeus's body and he felt he could move again – he flexed his fingers and arms, and gradually sat up. He was aching and tired, but there was no more pain than there should be.

'We chose you, Thaddeus,' said Kolgo with an unforgivable twinkle in his eye, 'because we knew you would fail. We knew you would keep your distance, tailing the Soul Drinkers and gathering information without actually striking. You are a watcher, Thaddeus, a listener. A good one, too. But not a victor.'

'You didn't want them stopped.'

'Oh, we did. I and the inner circles of the Ordo Hereticus recognise the Soul Drinkers as a grave threat and it is entirely our intention to corner and destroy them. But not just yet. Think about it, Thaddeus. We estimate the Soul Drinkers Chapter is between half and three-quarters strength, with no chance of reinforcement. That gives us a maximum of seven hundred and fifty Space Marines with barely a handful of surviving Chapter serfs if the evidence from the scuttled fleet is anything to go by. My household's own staff numbers more than three times that. The storm troopers attached directly to my command outnumber the Soul Drinkers tenfold.

'Space Marines from preachers' sermons can take on entire armies on their own but the truth is rather different. Without the support of other Imperial forces, or hordes of cultists or secessionists, or legions of daemons, they are alone and vulnerable. There is no point being the head of the spear if there is no haft or driving hand to back you up. The Soul Drinkers are dangerous but compared to someone like Teturact, they really are of little consequence. And there are many creatures like Teturact loose in the galaxy, I am afraid to say.'

'So you sent me after them because they aren't important.'

'On the contrary, Thaddeus. They could be very important. Regardless of the truth, Space Marines are legends. Traitor Marines are a nightmare. There is something so inherently heretical in the very concept that it carries with it far greater power than the actual Marines in question.'

Thaddeus should have felt betrayed and used. But he felt neither in particular – he just felt small, like a tiny wheel in a huge machine. It was a strange, dry feeling, as if his blood had been drained and replaced with dust. All his life he had worked for the Inquisition, battling against the vastness of the galaxy in a quest to make a difference. But now, with Lord Inquisitor Kolgo sitting next to him and explaining how he was just a pawn in better men's games, the galaxy seemed vaster than ever.

'They are a weapon,' said Thaddeus, his voice tired. 'A political weapon.'

Kolgo smiled, almost like a father. 'I knew you would realise it eventually. It surprised me you didn't get it more quickly. The Soul Drinkers are political capital – an enemy with the symbolic power of a renegade Chapter is not to be destroyed lightly. There will be times when the Ordo Hereticus must fight its corner against the rest of the Imperium, for the Imperium is almost as likely to harbour enemies as the ranks of the heretic and the alien. When that happens, we need the power of such symbols to prove our worth in the eyes of the lesser-minded of the Emperor's servants. The Soul Drinkers are to be destroyed when it would bring us the most benefit, and when that time comes we will bring more and better minds to bear than yours.'

'I understand,' said Thaddeus. 'I am expected to track the Soul Drinkers but not to move on them until you give the word.'

'It will be a long time before you really understand.' Kolgo stood up and, as if on command, a pair of valet servitors trundled in, their low bodies sprouting long, thin manipulators that held the simple, dark leather bodyglove and blastcloak of an interrogator. 'You will be taken back to the fortress at Caitaran and reassigned. We need competent minds like yours in the warzone. The trip will take about three weeks – I'm afraid I can only offer clothes such as these and few comforts, I keep a very simple ship.'

'The data I collected. It was in a data-slate in a pocket of my HE suit. Do you have it?'

'Everything you were wearing was lost. Only your sidearm was robust enough to survive. A very nice piece, if I may say, particularly the ammunition. I have it in my armoury here.'

'No matter,' said Thaddeus, hoping Kolgo couldn't tell when he was lying. 'It didn't contain anything important.'

But in a way it was true. Thaddeus only remembered two names from the reams of data he had salvaged, but they were the most important information of all. The first was Karlu Grien, a Magos Biologis who was the only surviving adept to have worked in a certain isolated genetor facility. The second was the name of the facility itself: Stratix Luminae.

SEPTIAM CITY BURNED. The Gathalamorian artillery had lobbed incendiary charges into the presumed hotspots of defenders – the palace quarter, the senate buildings, the Enforcement Division barracks – and raging firestorms had engulfed the flammable hovels that crowded against the city's once-grand buildings. But far worse were the fires the defenders themselves had set. They didn't need to breathe as normal men did, so tottering piles of plague dead were lit to fill the streets with banks of greasy, stinking smoke. Ammunition and fuel dumps were rigged to blow and the first elements of the Stratix XXIII through the defences to the north found themselves in a nightmare of booby-traps and flaming debris. The Jouryans entered through the southern quarter, which was composed of the more spacious gardens and townhouses of Septiam Torus's middle classes, so they moved faster and further when the breaches were taken.

At their head were their unexpected allies, the Space Marines who had arrived at the largest breach at the critical moment and punched through the defences like a dagger. Few Jouryans asked what had happened to the crews and medics of Squadron Twenty – all they saw were purple-armoured warriors a head taller than any Guardsman, who charged ahead with insane speed and seemed almost desperate to come to grips with the enemy face to face.

The Stratix XXIII found themselves bogged down in the sprawling dwellings to the north. The homes of dead soulfire harvesters became room-to-room battlegrounds where dug-in weapons teams shredded Stratix troopers at intersections and in open spaces, where tripwires rigged with demo charges blunted assaults long enough for the Septiams to counter-attack.

But the Stratix XXIII had all lived out childhoods in the vicious underhives of their lost homeworld, and were happier fighting with bayonet and guile than out in the open. For many of them it was like coming home, and the Stratix were slowly, savagely, bleeding the Septiams dry, drawing more and more enemies from the south of the city into a meat grinding killing zone. Most of their officers were dead – but they had mostly been outsiders brought in by the Guard to tame the savages, and the Stratix fought this battle better on their own.

The Jouryans made good speed through to the palace quarter, which had formed the elegant marble core of the city before death and disease turned the place into a charnel house mockery of splendour. Grand buildings stripped of their roofs formed sheer-walled canyons of priceless marble, often with gilded decorations still coiling gracefully along the scorched stone. Tanks rumbled through the broader streets and blasted the ill-disciplined Septiam snipers off the tops of the walls.

A brutal jungle fight erupted between several Jouryan platoons and the blood-streaked retinue of a corrupted Septiam noble in the lush botanical gardens of a senator's villa. The noble hunted Jouryans with a silver-chased groxrifle in his rotting hands while the Jouryans waded through a tiny square of death-world terrain. One of the city's forums became a critical objective for staging armoured thrusts towards the senate-house, and Guardsmen fought almost toe-to-toe with thousands of Septiams over a space barely a hundred metres wide. Leman Russ tanks formed mobile strong-points to hold courtyards and gardens as Jouryan platoons leapfrogged from one shattered residence to the next. Wounded men drowned in ornamental pools. Shells airburst in the boughs of trees in the city parks and killed dozens with splinters of exotic hardwood.

And at the front of the slowing tide of Jouryans were the Space Marines, charging into labyrinthine villas with bolters blazing and chainswords sparking on the stone, flushing concentrations of walking dead out into Jouryan fire-zones and taking strong-points for the Guardsmen to occupy behind them.

The Jouryans followed them, because any man who valued his life chose to consolidate the path of destruction they blazed rather then venture into the enemy-held quarters.

When the Marines veered to one side and began to fight their way towards the Enforcement Division barracks instead of the senate house, the Jouryans backed them up with little argument from senior officers who were having trouble following the rapid advance anyway. The smooth, towering walls of the barracks formed a formidable barrier between the attackers, and the plan had been for the Jouryans to bypass the fortified compound entirely, leaving it to elements of Gathalamorian artillery to move up and hurl high explosives over the wall until the barracks were dust.

The Space Marines had other plans. When they went into direct assault against the most fortified structure in Septiam City, the Jouryans began to wonder why the Space Marines were actually here.

'OVER THE WALL! Now!' yelled Captain Karraidin, a huge tank-like figure in his Terminator armour, waving the Assault Marines forward with his enormous power fist.

Tellos knew that was his cue. He wasn't a sergeant any more – he had no rank at all, not even battle-brother, officially. But the Assault Marines of the Soul Drinkers followed him anyway, because to them there was no better symbol of the resolve that had taken the Chapter so far. Tellos was more severely mutated and crippled than any of them, and yet he loved nothing better than to be at the forefront of the assault where he could do the Emperor's work in destroying His enemies. He was an inspiration. He was the very tip of the spear.

Tellos broke cover and sprinted from the shadows of the collapsed Administratum building across the corpse-littered road from the barracks wall. He wore no armour on the upper half of his body and the wind was hot and grimy against his skin, sharp and painful against the stumps of still-red flesh where his hands had once been. He had lost both hands during the betrayal when the Soul Drinkers had first been forced to turn against the Imperium. Now he had replaced them with twin chainblades from the Chapter armoury, old-pattern chainswords with broad, curved blades like machetes.

Gunfire spattered down from the Septiams manning an autocannon post on the wall, surrounded by razor wire. Shrapnel and a couple of shots hit Tellos but they passed right through his shockingly white, strangely gelatinous flesh, cutting through skin and muscle that knitted itself back together again leaving scores of tiny white scars.

A burning Leman Russ tank had crashed into the wall, its blazing form reaching halfway up the wall. Tellos ran through the rain of gunfire and leapt onto the tank, scrambling quickly up onto its turret, chainblades scoring gouges in the armour. He could hear the footsteps of twenty Assault Marines as they followed him and they felt exactly what he did – the enemy were just a few steps away, crowded into the barracks, practically begging for the Emperor's justice.

Tellos leapt onto the crest of the wall. It bulged outwards at the top to prevent anyone climbing it but Tellos's chainblades dug deep into the plasticrete and he hauled himself up onto the crest of the wall.

Two autogun shots punched through his abdomen. He felt the pain, but he welcomed it, because that meant his body was healing as quickly as it was wounded. Bolt pistol fire crackled from the Marines beside him and the fire point on the wall fell silent. Tellos barely glanced at the Marines following him up, and he jumped into the compound.

The main barracks was an imposing building of black metal with gunslits for windows, surrounded by a wide plasticrete plaza criss-crossed by fire points on the building and on each corner of the compound's walls. A makeshift village of hovels and tents had grown up around the building and there were scores of Septiams here, massed near the main blast-doors in the opposite wall, ready for the Jouryans to blow the doors and try to take the compound.

If the Soul Drinkers hadn't been there, perhaps that was what would have happened. But with Tellos leading the assault from an unexpected direction, every one of those Septiams was dead.

Tellos hit the ground running and twenty Marines followed him. Every second he spent here was a second when the enemy were beyond his reach and so he charged headlong through the jerry-built shanty-town. He ran heedlessly through the walls of flimsy dwellings and brushed hovels aside with his chainblades, barely breaking step to slice through the few defenders who managed to turn and face him.

The Septiams – several hundred of them, clustered around barricades to form a killing zone inside the blastdoors – barely had time to notice the assault charging in behind them.

Tellos was a good dozen paces ahead of the assault squads. When he hit the Septiam lines, he didn't stop to fight. He dived into the mass of Septiams and kept going, carving deep into their ranks, twin chainblades swinging in great arcs that severed limbs and head with every stroke. The Septiams turned and tried to counter-charge but they just ran straight into the storm of death.

Tellos strode deeper into the Septiams, leaving a gore-soaked channel of broken bodies that gave the Assault Marines a crucial gap to get a foothold against them.

Rotting faces lolled as they died a second time. Knobbed, grey-skinned limbs swung clubs and knives uselessly. Short-range lasbursts and auto-gun shots spat from the throng but Tellos ignored them, absorbing the ill-aimed shots with his mutated flesh and slicing off the hands that tried to bring weapons to bear too close.

It was the purest butchery. The rage came on Tellos again, the same rage that had first been sparked in him when he lost his hands on the Geryon weapons platform, and had continued burning inside him as he stormed the beaches of Ve'Meth's stronghold and battled daemons on the deck of the *Brokenback*. It took hold of him and pushed him further than any Marine could go. It was the fuel that fed his mutated flesh and the impossibly fast, deadly strikes he made with the improvised weapons thrust into the stumps of his wrists.

Tellos didn't live for much else – the rage was the only thing that could make him feel worth anything. Killing in the name of the Emperor was the purest form of service, and when His spirit took over Tellos there was nothing that could stop him.

His chainblades were clotted with blood. He was covered in gore from head to toe, occulobe organs secreting fluids to wash the blood out of his eyes, blood raw on his pale skin and slick against the armour on his legs. Hundreds of faces merged into one as he thrust in every direction, the

Septiams trying to surround him just walking into the killing zone that radiated from him.

The more mindless Septiams were driven forward to surround and swamp him. He batted them aside or cut them in two, clambering onto the rampart formed from their bodies to hack down at the tainted troopers from above. Scores died around him, hundreds, every cut ending an undeserving life. The Assault Marines pushed the Septiams back against the gates and forced them into Tellos – those who tried to counterattack found themselves trying to duel with superhuman warriors whose armour turned away bayonets and rifle shots and whose chainblades cut through flesh, bone, and salvaged Elysian armour alike.

Tellos saw Jouryan helmets, Elysian fatigues, senators' finery and Enforcement Division uniforms, all wrapped around subhuman corpse-creatures, faces twisted with hatred and disease. Their desiccated tongues moaned and gurgled as they died. Their bones cracked and skin split, muscles ripped to rags by the chainblade teeth. It was the purest slaughter of all, corruption and decay vanquished by the Emperor's strength, Tellos's rage a link to the Emperor like a vox-line to the Golden Throne.

A heavy hand clapped down onto Tellos's shoulder and only the reflexes hard-wired into Tellos's brain kept him from driving his chainblades into the body of a fellow Marine.

Captain Karraidin's leathery, battered face snarled out of the hood of his Terminator armour. 'Damn it, Tellos! The enemy's broken! Blow these doors and get to the brig entrance!'

For a moment Tellos was enraged that the Emperor's work had been so rudely interrupted. Didn't Karraidin realise they were surrounded by slavering, corrupted enemies?

Then he saw what Karraidin saw – Tellos was just a few metres from the inside of the compound wall, standing on a pile of bodies twenty men high, with the Septiams broken and cowering around him.

Karraidin was right. The rage could wait a while before taking over again.

He waved the two assault squads forward from where they had formed a line of steel backing him up. All carried frag and krak grenades and several had melta-bombs designed to melt through armoured hulls. The Assault Marines sprinted across the blood-slicked ground to the huge double blastdoors and attached bundles of grenades to the hinges and bolts.

Meanwhile, Karraidin's command squad swapped bolter fire with the fire points on the walls and in the barracks buildings, covering the Assault Marines as they rigged the doors and fell back before blowing them.

The blastdoors fell open in a shower of sparks, sheets of steel crashing to the rockcrete ground.

Squads Luko and Hastis entered under Karraidin's covering fire. With them was Sarpedon. 'Good work Karraidin, Tellos,' he voxed. 'We've cleared out the buildings around the perimeter. The Jouryans are holding them. The Septiams are trapped between the Stratix and the Jouryans and they'll try to break out at any moment, so we have no time to waste. Hastis and Luko, you're with me into the holding cells. Karraidin, hold the doors. Tellos, you're reserve. Cold and fast, Soul Drinkers, move out.'

The small strike-force Sarpedon had managed to smuggle into Septiam City split in two, Karraidin and Tellos to take up positions in the compound amongst the broken bodies of the Septiams, Sarpedon and the two tactical squads heading towards the barracks building from which intermittent fire still spattered down from roof and gun-slit windows.

Somewhere beneath that building were the holding cells, where the criminals of Septiam Torus had been held before the plague took a hold. If they had not been emptied in the chaos that gripped the city, and if there was anything left alive down there, then somewhere in those cells was Adept Karlu Grien.

CHAPTER NINE

FROM THE OBSERVATION deck of the yacht, the warzone seemed calm. The stars were as hard and cold as they were anywhere else in the galaxy, and had Thaddeus not been so familiar with the torments of Teturact's rebellion it would have been easy for him to assume that all was right in the heavens.

But he knew that one tiny winking red star was actually the forge world of Salshan Anterior, where half a million Guardsmen had been surrounded and butchered on the oxide-rich plains and where the Navy was now primed to bomb the hardened workshop-bunkers into dust. One constellation was composed of unnamed dead xenos worlds where Guardsmen and tech-guard warred with tens of thousands of Teturact's cultists, battles flowing like water over planets of frozen oxygen. Gigantic fleet actions were being enacted right in front of his eyes, the blackness between the stars scattered with battleships maintaining blockades and forming up from orbital barrage runs.

The yacht's observation deck was a crystal hemisphere blistered out from the upper hull, providing an unbroken panorama of space. Several drinks cabinets and reclining couches rose from the floor and a trio of personal servitors waited attentively in case their masters showed any signs of needing something. It was an easy place to forget about war.

But Thaddeus could not forget. Lord Kolgo was probably right – he was far more experienced an inquisitor than Thaddeus would probably ever be. However, Thaddeus still had a job to do. He had made a private vow, and he could not betray himself by breaking it now. No matter what the cost.

A circular hole hissed open in the floor and a platform rose up. On the platform was an impossibly slight figure, a man so insubstantial it seemed he hardly cast a shadow. He wore a cobalt uniform trimmed with silver bullion and his frail body was topped with a curiously featureless face, smooth jet-black skin almost unbroken by eyes, nose and mouth. A length of white cloth embroidered with High Gothic devotionals was tied around his head, and the blistered, charred skin just showing on the man's forehead indicated the stresses regularly placed on the warp eye underneath.

'Navigator,' said Thaddeus. 'I am glad you could join me.'

The Navigator smiled. 'Your invitation took me by surprise, my master. I am not much used to social functions. I hope I am not found lacking.

'Not at all,' replied Thaddeus with his friendliest smile. 'There are trillions of souls in this galaxy, it is only right that you should get to meet a few of them. Amasec? Assuming you're not on duty, of course.' He held out a decanter and glass.

The Navigator accepted a glass of the rich, treacly amasec, which Lord Inquisitor Kolgo had probably had imported at a cost Thaddeus couldn't imagine. The Navigator took a tentative sip and seemed to appreciate the nicety.

Thaddeus looked up at the starscape. 'What do you see, Navigator?' he asked. 'Does it look anything like this in the warp?'

It was a risk. Navigators rarely spoke of what they saw when they led ships through the dreams and nightmares of the warp and there was an unspoken taboo against asking them about it. Thaddeus reasoned that this meant Kolgo's Navigator had probably never been asked, and that it would be a relief for him to tell someone.

'It… sometimes. At first. We want it to look the same, you see. Everyone knows what space looks like, everyone who has ever seen the night sky. But after the first few moments you have to let it change. You have to begin to see the warp as it truly is. There are no rules to it – half of it is inside your head – but that doesn't make it any less real. Just by looking at it, you change it. The Astronomican is the only constant and even then it can flicker and leave you alone. All the things you see when between sleeping and waking, those are real in the warp. There are colours you can't make with light and every now and again, something… looks back at you…' He smiled again, taking another swallow of amasec. 'And you can call me Starn. Iason Starn.'

'And you can call me Thaddeus, Starn.' Thaddeus placed the decanter back into the gold-plated hands of the servitor that glided silently over to him as he sat down on one of the couches. 'I imagine Kolgo places great value on you.'

'Indeed. I have been with him for twenty-three years.'

'It sounds like we are both prisoners of a sort.'

'There are worse things.'

Thaddeus sat up suddenly, as if in surprise. 'Starn... isn't the Starn clan related to House Jenassis?'

'We are a sub-clan,' replied Starn. 'We are proud to be one of the constituent parts of House Jenassis. Few outsiders know much of our Houses, Thaddeus, you must be most learned.'

'I'm sorry, I didn't realise you counted House Jenassis as your patrons. You must all be mourning your patriarch.'

Starn nodded, looking mournfully into his amasec. 'Yes, a terrible thing. Chaos Marines, they say. The Enemy, in House Jenassis itself. Many of us do not believe it, others know it must be true but cannot fully understand it.'

'And you?'

'This is a dark galaxy, Thaddeus. Terrible things do happen. The Emperor knows I have seen enough of them with Kolgo over the years.'

Thaddeus let the silence mature. The subtle mutations that accompanied the Navigator gene hid the fact that Iason Starn was more than eighty years old, and he had probably been in service since adolescence. How often had any non-Navigator talked to him like this? Let alone an inquisitor, someone with authority, even if he was very much subordinate to Lord Kolgo.

'Phrantis Jenassis was not the best of leaders,' said Starn at last. 'But without him the House has no leadership at all. There will be another round of politics, and how we hate it. Some of us will die, inquisitor, though we are forbidden to admit it. Even Navigators have their factions.'

'So do inquisitors, Starn. But we are forbidden to mention it, too, so don't tell anyone.'

On cue, a servitor hovered up to Starn and refilled his glass. The beauty of amasec was that it didn't taste strong, but it was.

Starn was not a stupid man. He accepted the refilled glass almost resignedly, as if he had worked out what his part was to be and he was just going through the motions until it was over.

Thaddeus knew his role, too. 'If there was someone who knew who had killed Phrantis Jenassis – imagine that! Perhaps it was something slightly more complicated than a raiding force of Chaos Marines. It would almost be comforting to know that Phrantis wasn't just a random killing, wouldn't it?'

Starn took a deep swallow. 'I should have guessed this wasn't a social call. Why would a man of your station associate with me out of choice?'

'Why would a man of your quality associate with your master's prisoner? That's what I am, Iason, and you are well aware of it. You don't want to spend the rest of your life flirting with madness. Perhaps you were once content, but not any more. You find yourself dreaming of the life of a common citizen. You wish you could be something more than you are, because what you are is a piece of someone else's machine. Lord Kolgo considers you a part of this ship. Why shouldn't he? You've never claimed to be anything more. But if you could do something meaningful, something that would affect the whole of House Jenassis – that would be worth something far more.'

'I have heard… stories.' Iason Starn's eyes were suddenly alive, as if he were finally aware of himself. They formed an incongruous focus in his featureless face. 'Inquisitors can have a man skinned alive with a word. They can kill thousands, millions if they think they have to. It would be nothing for Lord Kolgo to have me killed if he thought I was betraying his trust.'

'It is too late for that, Iason. Kolgo has this place bugged, of course. He knows every word we have said. If he wants to have you liquidated he will have made the decision already, no matter what you do. You know I am right, Iason. And you should consider yourself fortunate – now you can make your decision without worrying about what Kolgo will do, because he will have made up his mind already.'

Starn was shaking, and almost unconsciously bolted the rest of the amasec to calm his nerves. 'I can see why you inquisitors are so feared.'

'You should see Kolgo in full flow. He does the same thing to fellow inquisitors. Now, the choice.'

'The choice.'

Thaddeus reached inside the plain clothes he had been given in the infirmary. He took out a small, folded letter. 'This document is in cipher, you need never know what it says. All I need is for you to make sure it is transmitted to the correct astropathic duct. Nothing more. I have no access to Kolgo's astropaths but you do. Kolgo will consider me a potential ally for the future and will let me get away with this, because crossing me now could come back to haunt him in the unlikely event I rise to a similar rank as he. He will not let me get away with a blatant abuse of his hospitality, however, since that would hardly be playing the game. So I must use you.

'Kolgo cannot get rid of you immediately since that would leave him in largely uninhabited space without a Navigator and his work within the warzone is too important for him to spend months marooned. Once he has returned to the fortress you will be surrounded by fellow Navigators and can doubtless organise some protection from other members of your House. This game is not without its risks, but you see how you have a relatively low-risk part to play.'

Starn waved away the servitor that came to refill his glass once again. 'What a complicated game.'

Thaddeus smiled, genuinely this time. 'Politics, Iason. I'm just learning myself.'

The Navigator stood, smoothed down the flawless uniform of Clan Starn and took the letter from Thaddeus's hand. 'I am afraid, inquisitor, that my time is short. There are charts to be drawn up and courses to plot, you know how it is.'

'Of course, Navigator Starn. I wouldn't want to keep you from your work. The Emperor protects.'

'That he does, inquisitor.' Starn stepped onto the platform and disappeared back through the floor. If Thaddeus was lucky, he would soon be delivering Thaddeus's message which, if again he was lucky, would reach the *Crescent Moon* shortly.

Not only would his strikeforce be able to act on the information he had recovered from the cathedral, but it would also demonstrate to Kolgo that keeping Thaddeus a virtual prisoner on his yacht served very little purpose. Kolgo couldn't visit anything outrageous on Thaddeus – the Inquisitor Lord had only as much authority as his fellow inquisitors let him have and he needed lesser men to defer to him. Thaddeus could be one of those lesser men, which meant it wasn't in Kolgo's interests to have him imprisoned, killed, or anything else.

Thaddeus hated the idea that infighting and point-scoring should be as large a part of the inquisitor's world as fighting the Emperor's foes. But the game was there to be played, and if he had to play it to fulfil his vows, then play it he would.

And no matter what Kolgo wanted, Thaddeus had a critical advantage. He had Stratix Luminae. Very soon, he felt that little else would matter.

THE MESSAGE HAD been simple. There were two locations – the first was Stratix Luminae, a location which was absolutely not to be approached without Inquisitor Thaddeus himself. The second was Septiam Torus, last recorded location of Adept Karlu Grien, which could be the last chance the strikeforce had to intercept the Soul Drinkers before Stratix Luminae, after which they might be lost forever.

Colonel Vinn and the storm troopers, minus the recon platoons lost at Pharos, were waiting in deep system space for Thaddeus's next communication. Septiam Torus, meanwhile, belonged to the Sisters.

Sister Aescarion slipped the restraints of the grav-couch and reached up to grab the handrail mounted onto the ceiling of the Valkyrie's passenger compartment. Aescarion had bullied the three Valkyrie aerial transports plus crews out of the rear echelon Jouryan forces, knowing that fifty battle-ready Sisters and the mention of Inquisitorial authority was more than enough to secure anything she might need.

By the time she had made it to the surface of Septiam Torus the battle for Septiam City was almost a full day old and she needed to get into the thick of it quick. They said there were Space Marines spearheading the Jouryan assault, and even if they did not turn out to be the Soul Drinkers, it seemed the Imperial forces could do with a force of heavily-armed battle-sisters fighting alongside them.

The Valkyrie lurched as it switched to defensive manoeuvres. Aescarion couldn't see out of the passenger compartment but she could hear the anti-aircraft fire punching up past the Valkyrie from enemy-held sections of the city, and knew the ruins of Septiam City would be streaking by below. One good hit now and the twenty Sisters with her would die in an instant, regardless of training, armour, or even faith. But that was the way war went. Aescarion had taken a vow long ago to wait for death and welcome it, when the time came.

Her battle-sisters felt the same. She had her own Seraphim squad and two more squads, Retributors carrying three heavy flamers led by Sister Aspasia and a ten-strong unit under Sister Superior Rufilla. Two more Valkyries carried similar complements – whether it would be enough to face the Soul Drinkers would be in the hands of the Emperor.

'Black Three's lost an engine, ma'am,' came the tinny voice of the pilot through the ship's vox. 'Says he's going down.'

'Can they land?' replied Aescarion, the image of a score of valiant dead Sisters flitting through her mind. Black Three was the lead Valkyrie in the formation, heading for the plaza near the senate-house which the Jouryans had just liberated from the enemy.

'They can bring her down but they're well short. They're going to hit the slums.'

'We can't be spread out. Follow them in and prepare for deployment. From the Enemy will the Golden Throne deliver us, citizen.'

'Whatever you say, ma'am,' replied the pilot. 'Hold on.'

Bad news. The designated landing zone would have put the Sisters behind the last reported location of the Marines, in a position to assault them if they were the Soul Drinkers or reinforce them if they were loyalist Marines. The situation in the city was fluid and confused, but from what Aescarion understood the slums were seething with close-quarters battles between the benighted Septiams and the Stratix XXIII. Aescarion wasn't sure which would be more dangerous to her Sisters.

'Coming down, ma'am. Doors away,' said the pilot, his voice strained as he fought to pull the Valkyrie's nose up after a steep descent.

'Sisters!' yelled Aescarion. 'Prepare to deploy! Aspasia, I want fire before we hit the ground! Rufilla, secure our zone and cover us!'

The Sisters Superior saluted in acknowledgement, and then the rear ramp juddered open.

The Valkyrie was swooping down an avenue of shattered slum buildings, little more than shacks piled on top of one another until they spilled into the road and crushed the lower layers into strata of rubble. More solid buildings were pocked and scorched by small arms and artillery. Greying tangles of bodies lay clustered around intersections and barricades. Smoke plumed up from below, filling the compartment with the stink of fuel and las-burned air. Tracer fire streaked from every other window and explosions crumped beneath the sudden roar of the Valkyrie's engines.

Black Three was already down, one engine billowing black smoke, the bulk of the ship laid crossways across the road where it had crash-landed and skidded to a halt. The black-armoured forms of Sisters were deploying rapidly from the stricken transport, using the hull itself for cover or sprinting through a shower of enemy fire into the ruins at the side of the road.

Aescarion saw they were coming down almost on top of Black Three. The Valkyrie dipped lower, downward thrust driving up thick clouds of dust and debris. Without waiting for the pilot's signal, she ran onto the ramp and jumped.

She flicked a switch and her Seraphim jump pack kicked in. Useless on Eumenix, she and her squad had equipped with the jump packs knowing how useful they could be deploying from the air. Her squad followed, Sister Mixu right behind her, all with bolt pistols drawn and cocked.

Aescarion hit the ground and managed to keep her feet. She was about thirty metres from Black Three, a smouldering dark shape through the swirl of dust. The engine roar was suddenly replaced with gunfire, crackling from all directions. The distinctive report of bolt weapons told her that the Sisters were leaving Black Three and returning fire from the ruined buildings that lined the road. Smaller-calibre weapons blazed down from the buildings all around and Aescarion knew that while they didn't have the discipline of the Sisters, they had far greater numbers. She glimpsed muzzle flashes and oddly twisted, loping humanoid forms through the chaos.

A single report sounded and a las-flash, white-hot, speared through the air next to her. Aescarion glanced behind her in time to see one of her Seraphim fall, shot through the throat by a long-las shot.

Snipers.

Aescarion loosed off a few shots at the closest attackers and ran for the nearest cover. She couldn't get pinned down here. She had to get clear, then gather the Sisters and break out. If she paused for a moment they could be surrounded and bogged down, and not get out of here until the whole city was won. That was not an option.

The collapsed building offered scraps of cover, half-toppled walls and piles of rubble. Aescarion dived for cover as a volley of shots tore down from the other side of the street. Autogun and las-fire kicked up sprays of broken stone and wood around her as she hit the ground.

More fire followed, this time from directly above. Sister Mixu skidded in beside her, twin bolt pistols drawn, and both Sisters returned fire into the remains of the ceiling overhead.

They had taken cover directly beneath an enemy fire point. Through the ragged hole twisted faces leered down, rotten jawbones hanging, skeletal hands aiming their rusted guns down at the Sisters.

Shots rang off Aescarion's armour. She and Mixu returned fire, pumping bolt shells through the ceiling into the attackers, sending showers of debris falling. Aescarion felt a shot crease her cheek. The fire fight drew more attackers in, sharpshooters picking shots through the swirling dust and more Septiams crawled through the ruined buildings to face this new threat. Mixu fired upwards with one hand and sideways with the other. Aescarion drew her power axe but even her power armour could be overwhelmed by the sheer weight of fire coming at her if she were to stand up and charge.

A sheet of pure white flame tore through the building at head-height, then swung upwards to fill the building above with billowing flame. Burning skeletons fell down from above, and the gunfire was replaced with the strangled screams of burning men.

Aescarion looked up to see Sister Aspasia directing her Retributor squad's heavy flamers as they hosed the building around Aescarion's Seraphim with fire.

Aescarion saluted Sister Aspasia as the Retributors and Sister Rufilla's squad moved in to secure the ruins.

'Seraphim,' she yelled, 'with me! Forward!' Aescarion charged through the rubble, towards where the Sisters from Black Three were holed up. She and her Seraphim blasted the Septiams who rounded a ruined doorway in front of them at close range, shattering half-a-dozen diseased bodies before Aescarion lunged through the door and laid into the Septiams beyond. A sharpshooter, long-las still clutched in his gnarled hands, fell headless to the rubble. Aescarion's axe cut the arm off another Septiam and her boot shattered his spine as he fell. One of her Seraphim vaulted over the wall beside her, grabbed the closest Septiam and hauled him off his feet, shooting two of his comrades through the man's stomach.

Aspasia's squad followed Aescarion through the ruins. 'Rufilla's secured a landing zone for Black Two,' voxed the Sister Superior as she hurried over the rubble. Aspasia was a true veteran, older than Aescarion who was no young woman herself. Her power maul steamed with the caked blood burning in its power field, and her armour was pocked and smouldering with bullet scars.

'Casualties?' asked Aescarion.

'Three Sisters lost, commended to the Emperor. Tyndaria lost a hand. We can fight on,' replied Aspasia.

'Good.' Aescarion voxed all the Sisters within range. 'When Black Two is down the whole strikeforce will advance southwards! This area is held by the Septiams and we will have to go through them first. Aspasia, I want you to the fore. With flame shall the unholy be cleansed.'

Aescarion switched her vox-receiver through the Guard frequencies, tapping into the tangle of transmissions blaring from all over the city. It was a chaotic mess, with two major regiments in the city and a third, the Gathalamorians, trying to coordinate artillery strikes that more often than not killed as many Guardsmen as Septiams.

Snatches of battlefield communication filtered through static. The Stratix regiment were pushing hard, butchering their way through the ruins of the residential areas in a tide that swept towards the centre of the city, the senate-house and temples.

The Jouryans, Aescarion knew from the sketchy reports she had got from the Jouryan rear echelons, formed a massive wedge thrust deep into the heart of the city as far as the Enforcement Division barracks. It was a wedge tipped by the Space Marines, who had arrived so suddenly nobody knew who they were or why they were here. To reach that position the Sisters had to get through the battle lines to the cluster of temples that cast a shadow onto the edge of the residential district, then through the heart of the Septiam defence to reach the Arbites precinct.

The roar of engines drowned out the transmissions as the shadow of Black Two passed over the road. It turned and descended, back ramp dropping and squads Tathlaya and Serentes jumping into the edge of the ruins. The Valkyrie swivelled to bring its chin-mounted guns to bear and blasted hundreds of rounds into the buildings opposite, scouring the upper floors clean of the sharpshooters. Boltguns blasted at the few Septiams still in the area, the return fire scattered and feeble. The Sister carrying Squad Serentes's heavy bolter paused at the threshold of the ruins and sent a volley of shots across the road, and Aescarion spotted broken figures flailing in a ground-floor window.

'Move out!' ordered Aescarion. Squad Aspasia broke cover under Rufilla's fire, sending sheets of flame in front of them as they moved off through the ruins, aiming to flush waiting Septiams into the teeth of Rufilla's guns.

Black One and Black Two were gone, soaring up away from the vulnerable position over the road. The Sisters were alone – but that was when they always fought the best.

THE UPPER FLOORS of the barracks building were infested with the enemy, toting weapons stripped from the precinct's armoury, many wearing patchy ill-fitting armour over their hunched bodies. Sarpedon didn't care about them. Everything he cared about was beneath the building.

Blue-white light flared in the confined basement stairwell as Sergeant Luko's lightning claws leapt into life. Squad Luko was in the front with Sarpedon, and Squad Hastis would form the rearguard to see off any Septiams coming down from the upper floors.

The door at the bottom of the stairwell was of massive plasteel, with a huge mechanical lock. Septiam City was like any other place in the galaxy, with its own criminals and petty heretics. This was where they were kept, and such people could not be allowed out.

'Mine,' said Luko with some relish. 'Back me up, men.' The sergeant lunged forward and punched both sets of claws into the metal of the lock, the talons sparking as they bored into the metal. He planted one foot against the base of the door and tore the whole locking mechanism out, ripping a ragged hole in the door, spitting with molten metal.

The door swung open and Squad Luko trained their guns into the darkness behind. Sarpedon hung back as they moved into the darkness beyond the doorway, keeping his force staff drawn. His autosenses peeled away the dark to reveal the grim grey plasticrete walls of the cell block beyond, glowstrips on the ceiling burned out, floor and walls stained with age and blood.

'We're in, no contacts,' came a vox from Squad Luko. Luko himself followed, his lightning claws casting flickering lights across the walls.

There was no sound from inside, just the rumble of battle from above. But the place stank: of sweat, decay, rotted filth. Sarpedon's engineered third lung kicked in to filter out the worst of it but it was still the stench of pure death.

The prison held two hundred inmates, mostly in solitary confinement, in cells fronted with tarnished steel bars. The first rows of cells were empty – they must have been released when the plague's madness had first gripped Septiam City.

Karlu Grien was probably among them. But Sarpedon had known that before he had come to Septiam Torus, and he had come anyway. There was always hope, no matter how slim.

'Kitchens up ahead,' voxed one of the Marines from Squad Luko.

'Move in,' said Sarpedon. Nothing moved in the shadows. The Marines trained their guns over the insides of filth-spattered cells. Sergeant Luko pushed through the large double doors into the kitchens, with long benches and tables beneath a high ceiling. Lines from Imperial psalms were carved into the plasticrete of the walls and ceiling and a pulpit stood at one end of the room where the preacher of the Enforcement Division would inform the inmates of the gravity of their sins as they ate. Like the rest of the prison the place was empty, with the kitchens ransacked and pages of devotional texts torn up and lying around the pulpit.

Luko glanced at the auspex scanner he carried, checking the layout of the brig. The Enforcement Division barracks were based on a Standard Template, the same as thousands of similar buildings on frontier and low-population worlds. 'Cell 7-F,' he said. 'Through this room and to the left, in the moral criminal wing.'

Karlu Grien was a moral criminal, a tech-heretic, guilty of making forbidden technology. He had been stationed on Septiam Torus to oversee the refining of the Soulfire crop, but what he had seen on Stratix Luminae had driven him to dabble in dark things and the Enforcement Division had locked him up. If he was still down here, he would be in cell 7-F.

'We've got movement,' voxed Sergeant Hastis from outside the kitchens.

'Karraidin?' voxed Sarpedon to the squads on the plaza above. 'Do we have hostiles coming in behind us?'

'None, commander,' replied Captain Karraidin. 'We've got them pinned down.'

'Hastis, get your men into this–'

Sarpedon was interrupted by a terrible sound, a dozen voices screaming at once, and a hideous cracking like hundreds of breaking bones. Hastis yelled an order and bolter fire roared, but the screams grew louder in reply. Luko rushed up to the door into the area, ready to take on anything that came through the door that wasn't a member of Squad Hastis.

Three Marines burst through the door at once, running backwards and firing into the corridor on full auto. They were followed by something Sarpedon could only think of as a wave of flesh, a tide of melded human forms, dozens of bodies welded into a single wall of muscle and breaking bone that erupted through the door. Twisted faces leered from the mass, hands reached and organs pulsed through rips in the taut skin. Every mouth was screaming, an atonal keening that cut through even the roar of gunfire. The stench it carried with it would have been enough to knock out a lesser man, and even Sarpedon felt it driving him back from the beast.

Sergeant Hastis was half-swallowed by the mass, too, bones snapping as the mass extruded limbs to drag him face-first into it. The Marines of his squad already swallowed were still fighting back, the flesh splitting and ripping as bolters and combat knives slashed at it from inside.

Bolt shells pumped into the mass as Squad Luko and the remaining members of Squad Hastis fell back into the dining area. Sarpedon held his force staff tight and felt the force of his will flooding into its psychoactive nalwood, the wood hot and thrumming in his hands as it focused the psychic power flowing around his body.

The mass already filled half the room and there seemed no end to it. Bolt shells seemed to have no effect.

'Mine again,' said Sergeant Luko. He spread his lightning claws and dived into the mass, the claws slashing deep scorched furrows in the flesh. Sarpedon reared up on his hind legs and leapt across the room, following Luko into the mess of melded corpses. He clambered up the front of the roiling mass and tore deep gouges with his front legs, before plunging his force staff and letting all his psychic force rip through it and into the flesh. Skin and muscle boiled away leaving a huge scorched pit beneath Sarpedon, burned deep through layers of melded bodies, sending a shower of ash bursting from the wound.

Luko ripped the slabs of flesh apart and hauled Sergeant Hastis out of the gory mass – but the front of Hastis's head had been dissolved and a bloody skull's face stared blindly out, long service studs still embedded in the bone of the forehead. Luko threw Hastis's remains behind him and slashed away the tendrils of muscle trying to entwine his legs.

The mass surged forward again and filled the room. Bolter fire poured into it and didn't seem to slow it down – tainted blood was ankle-deep in the room and chunks of shredded flesh were spattered across the walls and ceiling.

Sarpedon could feel the disease inside it, like a ball of white noise somewhere deep in the heart of the corpses. It was dense and evil, something he saw with the psychic eye inside him and felt through the skin of his mutated legs where they touched the unholy flesh. Here the supernatural disease that infected Septiam City had taken the prisoners in the cells and, in that confined space, it had worked its corruption on them until they had gathered around the carrier into this ball of melded corpses.

The carrier – the first to be infected down here, now the host for the disease – lay in the very centre of the mass. Sarpedon felt this with his mind's eye, the seething knot of disease sending out a mindless psychic scream as it powered the exertions of two hundred bodies melted into one.

Sarpedon raised his force staff and cut downwards, opening a three-metre slash in the skin. With his front legs he pulled the wound wide open, drew his bolter with his free hand, and with his hind legs powered himself into the wound. Sarpedon heard Luko yell something as he dived in. But the room would soon fill with the mass and only Sarpedon stood a chance of stopping it in time.

He couldn't see, but he could feel. Corruption flowed through the veins around him. Walls of flesh pressed against him and he held his breath to keep from inhaling the foulness of the beast's innards. He tore his way through towards the carrier, pulling himself forward with his front legs and free hand. The wound closed behind him, so he was encased in a cocoon of muscle. Bones snapped as limbs turned inward and reformed to grasp at him. The heat was intense and the darkness complete.

But he could feel the carrier, the still-human shape hunched and foetal in front of him. He gouged and clawed his way closer to it until its seething corruption was bright against his mind. With two legs he speared the body and dragged it closer to him. With one hand he grabbed it by the back of the neck, and with the other he put the bolter against the forehead and fired.

The body spasmed and the flesh surrounding it shuddered in unison as the monstrous intelligence inside was shattered. The mass released its grip on Sarpedon and he pushed himself backwards. The flesh liquefied behind him until he burst back out through the skin again, sliding to the floor on a wave of gore.

He still had the body of the carrier in one hand. It was mostly intact, save for the gaping bolter wound in its forehead and the severed arteries extruded through its skin where it had been connected to the other bodies. The prisoner's electoo was still on the back of the neck, with the prisoner's name, number, and bar code.

Somehow, it didn't come as a surprise that the carrier had been Karlu Grien.

'Take the gene-seed of the fallen,' said Sarpedon, dropping the deformed body to the ground.

One of Squad Hastis – Brother Dvoran, the youngest – removed his helmet and drew his combat knife. He kneeled down by the ruined body of Hastis and began to cut out the gene-seed organs, the twin glands in the throat and chest that controlled all a Space Marine's other augmentations.

Sergeant Hastis had been at the forefront of the assault of Ve'Meth's fortress, one of the Marines who had joined Sarpedon after the catastrophe of the Lakonia mission and Sarpedon's defeat of Chapter Master Gorgoleon. He had been as loyal as any Marine, one of the solid veterans Sarpedon relied on as much as they relied on him. Now he was dead, and so went another man who could not be replaced. They would have to cut off Hastis's head when the gene-seed was taken, to stop him from turning into a walking corpse like those that infested Septiam City.

Of course, Hastis's gene-seed couldn't then be implanted into a novice, as the Chapter traditions required. Not now. But it was still a powerful symbol, and it was symbols that held the Chapter together – so Dvoran cut the sacred organ from the sergeant's throat for transport back to the Chapter.

'It was always a long shot, commander,' said Luko, looking down at the body of Karlu Grien, the only man who could have told them the information they needed.

'Secure this area,' said Sarpedon, heading for the doors beyond the pulpit.

He tore the doors off their hinges and strode into the corridor beyond. This was where the prisoners had gathered as the madness first took them – deep gouges marked the walls where the prisoners had tried to claw their way out. Teeth and bone shards were embedded in the plasticrete and everything was stained brown-black. Bars on the cells were bent out of shape. Sarpedon could feel the madness imprinted on the walls. He could still hear the screams.

Cell 7-F was a pit of stained darkness, blood and filth crusted up the walls, the bars so corroded that they shattered as Sarpedon tore them aside. The pallet Karlu Grien had used as a bed was a slab of decay and Sarpedon's talons sunk into the caked filth on the floor as he entered the cell.

It was barely two metres square and into that space was packed so much malice and despair that Sarpedon could taste it, acrid and metallic in his mouth. Karlu Grien had probably been insane before he ever came here – Stratix Luminae had seen to that. When the plague came it sought out the most receptive carrier and found the mind of a mad heretic.

Sarpedon reached up and scraped away the hardened gore. Beneath were deep scratches in the walls, like in the corridors outside – but more ordered, forming patterns against the plasticrete. Sarpedon scraped the wall clean, revealing a pattern of straight lines and arcs that covered the whole back wall.

'They've taken Hastis's gene-seed,' said Luko. Sarpedon turned to see the sergeant standing in the corridor behind him. 'His was the only seed intact.'

'Good,' said Sarpedon. He pointed at the image gouged into the back wall. 'Record this on the auspex. Then get ready to move out, there's nothing left for us here. Send the message to Lygris to bring us out.'

'Yes, commander,' said Luko, and headed back to join his squad.

Sarpedon stared for a moment at the image, carved by a madman using the bloody stumps of his fingers. Techmarine Lygris would know if it meant anything. It was these tiny hopes that kept Sarpedon going, and the Chapter with him. They all looked to him for leadership, even born officers like Captain Karraidin or Chaplain Iktinos. If he gave in to despair then the Soul Drinkers would all give in, too – but they had followed him through the Chapter's greatest crisis and embarked with him on a mission which forced them to give up almost all they had – he owed them more than failure.

AESCARION SUSPECTED DeVayne wasn't a genuine officer. Like almost all the Stratix troopers he didn't wear the jacket of his fatigues, the loaded ammo webbing taut over a bare torso covered with gang tattoos. He wore several desiccated scalps on his belt and carried a pair of ivory-handled hunting laspistols that surely more properly belonged to a real officer. But his platoon of near-savages evidently had enough faith in DeVayne's leadership and, on the ground, that was enough for Sister Aescarion.

'Storm 'em, you sons a' hrud-lovers!' yelled DeVayne as he directed the men of his platoon into the shattered temple grounds and towards Septiam City's forum, where public buildings clustered around a wide marble-tiled plaza broken by gilded statues of Imperial heroes. The forum had become the focus for a brutal Septiam counterattack against the foremost Jouryan forces – most of the statues lay toppled by explosions and the tiles had been hurled up by artillery strikes to fall back down in a lethal stone rain. Basilica and shrines were burning shells. Jouryans and Septiams were dug in on either side, the blasted expanse of the forum a no-man's land for which thousands of men were dying.

The largest concentration of Septiams were in the grounds of the Macharian Temple, where a giant porphyry statue of Lord Solar Macharius looked out over ornamental gardens, now a mess of dug-in fire points and trenches swarming with corpse-like Septiams. It was this position that the Stratix forces were assaulting from the rear, with Aescarion's Sisters lending bolter and flame to the Stratix lasguns.

The Stratix broke cover from the tangle of minor devotionals and shrines behind the temple, heading for the rear wall of the temple grounds. They sported several exotic, salvaged guns – hunting rifles, hellguns, well-worn shotguns with hive ganger kill-marks – alongside their standard issue lasguns, and they wore a patchwork of salvaged, stolen and patched-up fatigues and body armour. They looked more like feral world savages than Guardsmen, but after Aescarion had linked up with DeVayne's men she had watched them carving their way through the Septiam defences with the added firepower of the Sisters. They ripped their way out of the slums at last and made a massive push to link up with the Jouryans in the centre of the city. Now they were assaulting the last strongpoint between the two forces.

'Seraphim, to the fore!' yelled Aescarion and followed the Stratix out of cover and up to the wall.

The Stratix were clambering over the sagging brick wall. Aescarion glanced back to ensure her squad was with her, then thumbed the inhibitor switch on her jump pack and let it propel her clean over the wall. She landed in a roll, crashing through the woody plants at the base of the wall. She glanced around her, trying to build up a rapid picture of her surroundings – a pair of ex-Enforcement Division field guns had been manhandled hurriedly into position leaving deep gouges in the turf, and a gang of Septiams were loading massive shells into the breaches.

Aescarion broke into a run, a round clunking home into the chamber of her bolt pistol, her Sisters landing and following her. The Seraphim were on the gun gang before they knew they were even under attack, Aescarion blowing holes through one before beheading another with her power axe, Sister Mixu unleashing a volley that stitched bloody ruin through three more. The Sisters killed so quickly and efficiently that by the time the Stratix caught up with them the fire point was denuded of Septiams, bodies draped over the gun emplacement and the makeshift barricades.

DeVayne took one look and ordered a detail of his men to man the guns. Within minutes the field guns were blasting at near point-blank range into the Septiam trenches and dugouts. The shells ripped huge plumes of pulverised earth out of the ground, raining debris and bodies back onto the temple gardens.

'Nice work, Sisters,' called DeVayne as he led the rest of his men into the shattered Septiam lines. Aescarion followed him, Sisters at her side, the air filling with lasblasts and autogun rounds as the Septiams tried to return fire.

Aescarion and DeVayne charged into a Septiam position that, facing fire from both directions, rapidly disintegrated into chaos.

SARPEDON LEAPT OVER the pedestal, which had once held a monumental statue of Ecclesiarch Pulis XXIXth, landing squarely in the middle of the Septiams dug into a shell hole in the middle of the forum. He lashed his force staff into the midriff of one even as Tellos dived in beside him, twin chainblades ripping arcs of gore from the Septiams. Rotted jaws dropped in horror as Tellos's Assault Marines followed, bolt pistols and chainswords spattering the Septiams across the torn marble.

'Tellos!' yelled Sarpedon. 'Take the autocannon!' He pointed towards a quad-mounted autocannon dug in just inside a shattered basilica – it was pounding fire into the Jouryan positions, but it could easily be re-sighted to bring down any ship trying to land on the forum and that was why it had to go.

Tellos seemed not to hear, intent on butchering the Septiams he had beaten down to his feet.

Sarpedon grabbed Tellos's shoulder and picked him up, holding him level with his own face.

'Take the autocannon,' he snarled. 'Now!'

Tellos glared at him through a mask of Septiam blood and found his feet, sprinting through a hail of fire, taking shells and lasblasts to his body as he ran for the autocannon mount. His assault squad followed, just as Squad Karraidin and the survivors of Squad Hastis vaulted into the shell hole.

'Karraidin, spread your men out and keep some heads down.'

'Can Lygris land here?'

'It's hotter than he'd like but he'll do it. Now get to it, Soul Drinker.'

Karraidin sprayed with his storm bolter at the source of the heaviest Septiam fire, and led his squad out of the shell hole to cut down the enemy crossfire as much as possible. Squad Luko had spread down one side of the forum and were exchanging fierce fire with the Septiams cowering in the law courts, and the Jouryans behind the Soul Drinkers were adding what fire they could to cover the Space Marines.

If the Guardsmen had known the Space Marines were securing a landing zone for extraction, they might not have been so enthusiastic about supporting the Soul Drinkers' drive for the forum. But Sarpedon wasn't here to fight their battle for them – the success of his mission depended on what fate dealt to them, and getting off Septiam Torus was the only objective left.

A vicious gun battle erupted at the Septiam-held far end of the forum and spilled out onto the forum itself. Septiams broke cover as gunfire and flashes of flame chased them out of their positions. Sarpedon snapped off shots at a couple of unwary targets. Luko's guns chewed through several more. It was a counterattack – Sarpedon saw that some of the troopers vaulting over barricades and struggling with each other at close quarters were not Septiams, but soldiers from the Stratix XXIII that barely resembled Guardsmen at all.

'Tell Lygris to move it,' called Luko over the vox, 'We're taking fire!'

'From the Septiams or the Stratix?'

'Neither,' came the reply. 'Adeptus Sororitas!'

SISTER AESCARION DUCKED into the cover of a column as a spray of fire spattered against the front of the basilica. She paused for a second and charged out again, firing as she went, the boltguns of her Sisters covering her as she led the way to the next patch of shelter. The Stratix and the Septiams were locked in a mad, swirling melee behind her, two sets of savages getting to grips with knives and rifle butts, and if she and her Sisters got dragged down into it they would never get out.

'Marine!' yelled Sister Mixu behind her. Aescarion glanced and saw a flash of deep purple as a Space Marine blasted at them with his boltgun, ducking back in time to avoid the return volley of bolts that shattered the marble around him.

It was the first living Soul Drinker that Aescarion had ever seen, the first glimpse of an enemy her faith required her to fight. More fire lanced from the sheltered Marine squad and Aescarion heard a scream as one of her Seraphim died, drilled by a bolter round through the abdomen that found a weak spot in her armour and blew out her lower back.

'Aspasia! Get the flamers to the fore and pin them down!' ordered Aescarion as her Sisters dived for cover, a whole Space Marine squad now blazing away at them. The dying Seraphim was dragged into shelter and Aescarion threw herself against the closest column, feeling bolter shells impacting against the other side of the stone.

She could see across the forum from where she sheltered, and she quickly scanned the expanse of broken marble for more Marines. She spotted some battling amongst the ruins of a shattered basilica, swarming over an autocannon artillery piece, cutting through the Septiams defending it. Another was in massive hulking Terminator armour, something Aescarion had never seen before, and more were moving out of a shell hole by a statue plinth to find better cover as Septiams tried to push onto the forum away from the assaulting Stratix.

Mutant. The glimpse she got of it was so fleeting she couldn't believe it was real – but when the Soul Drinker dodged from cover again her suspicions were confirmed. The Marine's legs were like those of a huge and monstrous spider, insectoid and tipped with long talons. The Soul Drinker's armour was more ornate than that of his battle-brothers, and from the force staff he wielded Aescarion recognised a Librarian, keeper of the Chapter's psychic lore and power.

The Sisters of Battle despised witches, and regarded even those in the employ of the Imperium with suspicion. Aescarion had never seen the psyker's art result in anything other than corruption and Chaos. The Librarian would be a target even if he wasn't who Aescarion suspected: Sarpedon. Commander of the Soul Drinkers, leader of the rebellion, and the primary target of Strikeforce Thaddeus.

'Rufilla, Aspasia, give us cover!' yelled Aescarion over the din of gunfire and the whistle of bullets. Sister Mixu dived down to Aescarion's side.

'That him?' she gasped.

'Do not pause to rescue me if I should fall. He will not fail to kill me and we need lose no more Sisters here than we have to.'

'Can you take him?'

'Probably not. Keep the other Marines away, the only chance is for me to catch him alone.'

Aescarion charged, firing at Sarpedon with her pistol in her left hand, her power axe in her right. Sister Mixu and the three remaining Seraphim charged out behind her, twin pistols blazing at anything that threatened their Sister Superior as flame from Squad Aspasia washed over the Marine squad in the ruins. Rufilla's Sisters sent sheets of rapid fire across the forum. On the other side of the battlefield, the autocannon mount was shattered by krak grenades and the Soul Drinkers assault squad fell back from the collapsing artillery piece as Aescarion sprinted the last few paces through the bullets to reach Commander Sarpedon.

* * *

SARPEDON SAW THE shimmering diamond of the power axe before he saw the Sister herself. He knew no Septiam, and precious few Guard officers, would ever have a power weapon – the charging figure was a Sister of Battle, a soldier of the Imperial Cult, fanatical and fuelled by pure faith.

If he was lucky, she would think he was a Chaos Marine, mutated by exposure to the magics of the Enemy. If he was unlucky, she would be a part of the Inquisitorial taskforce that Sarpedon had known was following the Soul Drinkers since their assault on House Jenassis.

He dug a talon into the ground and pivoted, his great weight – Marine, armour, altered legs – swivelling on a pin. One hand gripped the force staff and he let it swing out in a wide arc. The staff met the axe in a huge flash of sparks.

The Sister was a true veteran, with a lined, strongly-featured face and red-brown hair streaked with grey. Her armour was glossy black with no order markings, free of ornamentation. She swung away from Sarpedon, reversing the swing of her axe and trying to bring the butt of it into Sarpedon's ribs. He raised a leg and deflected the blow but the leg's joint folded under the impact and he lurched to one side, almost forced to put a hand down to the ground to steady himself. He rolled with the motion and lashed out with two legs, catching the Sister with a glancing blow, and knocked her back a pace. There was a pause, a fraction of a second, as the two sized one another up and tried to anticipate the next move.

'Traitor,' hissed the Sister, hefting her axe from one hand to the other, her pistol holstered and forgotten.

'No traitor,' said Sarpedon levelly. 'Just free.'

The Sister struck first, an easy feint, striking at Sarpedon's head in the hope that he would raise his guard and open himself up to a chop to the legs. He deflected the high blow with the head of the staff and the low blow with the other end, handling it like a quarterstaff. He struck back with a leg, stabbing at the Sister's throat with a blow she dodged with enough speed to instil some respect in Sarpedon. She was a born fighter, this one, with her instincts honed across scores of battlefields until she had the faith to take on a warrior like Sarpedon.

Faith was power. Faith was the straitjacket that had held the Soul Drinkers prisoner since the days of their founding, and faith was the force that kept them fighting now even when so much of their world was gone. Sarpedon had learned long ago to respect faith, and to treat it as the deadliest weapon there was.

There was a roar overhead and Sarpedon didn't have to look up to know it was Lygris in the fighter craft. The Sister hacked down at him with a lack of finesse that was well beneath her, driving the shimmering axe blade down at the Soul Drinker. She stamped down on Sarpedon's front foreleg – the one that wasn't bionic – with her foot and Sarpedon felt the joint wrench, ligaments torn inside the chitinous exoskeleton. Sarpedon parried her next blow and reached out with his free hand, grasping her armour at the collar. With strength even a normal Marine didn't have, he picked her up and swung her over his head, smashing her body into a huge chunk of fallen masonry.

The glistening, metallic fighter craft above sent incandescent lances of energy burning into the buildings along one side of the forum. It dipped low, openings forming in the side and a tongue of metal flowing from the hull to let Marines of Squad Luko scramble on board. Sarpedon spotted the Assault Marines following Tellos from the wreckage of the autocannon mount as the fighter swooped low again, close enough to the ground for the Marines to run onto the lowered ramp. Small arms fire rattled along the hull of the fighter and bolter fire ripped back from inside the passenger compartment.

The Sister crashed to the ground, winded but not broken. Sarpedon swung the force staff round and drove it, head-first and double-handed, towards the woman's midriff. She rolled aside and grabbed one of Sarpedon's legs, using it as leverage to swing herself up and ram an armoured elbow into the side of Sarpedon's head.

Sarpedon reeled. For a moment he was open and vulnerable, and a quick blade would have taken his head off. But instinct took over and he jabbed forward and down with one of his powerful hind legs. The axe blade whistled past his face, blistering the skin of one cheek with its power field, as he fell backwards. One hand planted on the ground to support him as the talon of his hind leg sheared through the Sister's armour and impaled her through the muscle of her thigh.

Two more legs stabbed into the ground to give him leverage and he flung the Sister across the forum, the talon ripping out of her leg as she flew through the air trailing an arc of blood.

'Sarpedon! Karraidin!' came Lygris's urgent voice over the vox. 'We've got Guardsmen coming your way, you need to get on board now!'

Sarpedon looked away from the Sister's prone body and saw the troopers – Stratix XXIII, tattooed hive-scum to a man – pouring through the Septiam lines and over the ruined forum. There were hundreds of them, and in Sarpedon they saw a mutant who had just defeated one of their Sororitas allies.

Lasgun fire ripped towards Sarpedon and Karraidin, whose squad was taking cover in ruins a hundred metres away. Sarpedon vaulted over the closest statue plinth but fire was coming from everywhere,

scoring deep scars in his armour, several lasbursts burning through the
chitin of his legs. One Stratix followed him into cover, combat knife
clutched in his hand. Sarpedon punched him hard in the face – his
head snapped back and he flopped brokenly to the ground. Sarpedon
fired twice with his bolter, blowing the torso of one Guardsman apart,
before impaling another on his force staff as he fell.

'Damn it, taking fire! Get us some support!' voxed Karraidin over the
chatter of his storm bolter, but Lygris's fighter was yawing upwards as
Stratix anti-tank teams got into position and started sending lascannon
blasts up into the gleaming hull.

Without warning there was a titanic flash and a searing wave of heat.
Sarpedon saw charging Stratix reduced to ashen skeletons as his own
autosenses forced his pupils almost shut against the glare. The blistering wave of energy washed over him, scalding the skin of his legs and
peeling the paint from the edges of his armour.

He glanced behind him and a saw the source of the blast – a Leman
Russ Executioner tank, huge plasma blastgun glowing from the sudden
discharge of power, white smoke billowing from the energy coils.

For a moment there was silence as the glare on Sarpedon's retinas
died to reveal a huge hole blown in the Stratix attack, dozens of charred
bodies filling a massive scorch mark across the stone.

A huge Jouryan attack filled the vacuum, grey-fatigued troops rushing
to blunt the Stratix charge. Guardsmen or no, they had seen the Soul
Drinkers as allies and the Stratix as the enemies of their friends. Many
of them could probably not tell the difference between a Septiam and
a Stratix in the heat of battle anyway, and though some saw Sarpedon's
deformities and faltered in their charge most hurtled into the fray.

A brutal close-quarters fight erupted in the forum, Stratix against
Jouryan, looted knives against bayonets. Heavy weapons teams opened
up against the Executioner but other front-line tanks, Exterminators
and Leman Russ battle tanks, rolled through the rubble to support the
infantry.

Lygris saw his opening and the fighter lurched downwards again, hull
opening up to let Karraidin drag his massive armoured frame on board
followed by his squad. The fighter turned and dipped low enough for
Sarpedon to leap up on his powerful legs. He grabbed the edge of the
opening and pulled himself up into the passenger compartment. The
fighter aimed its nose upwards and Sarpedon could see the huge
swirling melee filling the forum, Stratix and Jouryan Guardsmen killing
each other, the surviving Septiams caught up in the butchery.

Something flared below the fighter and Sarpedon looked over the
edge of the doorway to see the Sister he had beaten, rocketing upwards

on her Seraphim jump pack. She came up just short and grasped the edge with one hand, the other holding her power axe.

Sarpedon saw she was was streaked with grime and blood, her face set with faith and zeal.

He had to admire her determination.

'For the Emperor, Sister,' he said, and with a flick of his powerful bionic foreleg he kicked her off the edge of the ship to fall helplessly into the heart of the battle.

'Get us out of her, Lygris,' he voxed, and felt the fighter tip back as the metal flowed back over the opening. The last impression he had of Septiam Torus was the mingled cries of thousands of men as they fought, killed and died. Just as it had been for thousands of years the Imperium was destroying its own, although Sarpedon had rarely seen the idea so vividly come to life.

'Did you see the image we sent you from the auspex?' voxed Sarpedon as the engines kicked in and he strapped himself back into the grav-restraints. He looked around the passenger compartment and saw that the Marine force on Septiam Torus had lost over a quarter of its number, with almost all of Squad Hastis gone. Had it been worth it? Was anything?

'Received intact,' replied Lygris from the cockpit.

'Do you know what it is?'

'Looks like a cogitator circuit, something to recall information from a mem-bank. Probably the key for a security system.'

The main engines took over and the sound of the atmosphere rippling on the hull dropped away as the fighter passed out into space.

It had been worth it, Sarpedon told himself. It had to have been. Otherwise, not one of them would survive Stratix Luminae.

CHAPTER TEN

FOR THADDEUS, SPACE travel was the most frustrating part of his work. The time spent between the stars was time wasted, and even when the warp meant a century's worth of travel took only days those were still days he wouldn't get back. Patience was perhaps his greatest strength but space travel, more than anything, made it wear thin.

He knew the *Crescent Moon* was fast, that was one of the reasons he used it. But he had no way of knowing how quickly the Soul Drinkers could move. Presumably the alien fighters Aescarion had reported were warp-capable, since they would be the perfect way to sneak past the warzone's blockades with the minimum of risk – perhaps they were already on Stratix Luminae, and Thaddeus was already too late. Perhaps they had to enact some other part of their plan before they could reach the planet. Perhaps Stratix Luminae was already lost – Stratix, after all, was in the same solar system and Teturact could have decided to despoil and garrison the planets bordering his homeworld.

At least Thaddeus had some idea of what the place looked like. He had Captain Korvax's pict-recording playing on a personal holo-servitor. The image was paused as Korvax looked across the defences towards the outpost – a simple, low plasticrete building with massive blast doors and fire points on the roof. It didn't look like much but, for whatever reason, Sarpedon had risked his own life and the lives of his Chapter to get there.

Lord Inquisitor Kolgo had released Thaddeus without actually admitting he had ever been held prisoner, simply docking his ship for

435

refuelling and maintenance and letting Thaddeus walk out. It was just the next stage in the game, a favour done to secure a favour in the future when Thaddeus might be worth something. However, Kolgo and Thaddeus would never be allies, because Thaddeus would destroy the Soul Drinkers or die trying. Neither option would endear him much to Kolgo.

Thaddeus had used the time he had spent waiting to meet up with the *Crescent Moon* researching Stratix Luminae, but there hadn't been much to find out. It was an Adeptus Mechanicus Genetor facility, where biological experiments had been carried out by adepts seeking to delve further into the secrets of genetics and mutation. Such outposts were usually isolated and Stratix Luminae was no exception, being a world of frozen tundra with no population aside from the outpost staff. Ten years ago eldar pirates, who had plagued the Stratix system intermittently, were fought off by a force of Space Marines who responded to the Adeptus Mechanicus's distress call. There was, of course, no record of who the Chapter involved might have been, which led Thaddeus to conclude that it had been the Soul Drinkers well before their break with the Imperium.

What had Korvax found there that had interested Sarpedon so much? Thaddeus could only hope he got there in time to find out.

'Inquisitor?' came a polite voice from the door.

Thaddeus looked up to see Sister Aescarion in the doorway. Thaddeus's quarters on the *Crescent Moon* weren't spartan but were still towards the simpler side of what an inquisitor could become accustomed to – there was little more than a bed, his trunk, a couple of chests of clothes and belongings and his desk with its shelves of books above. The large viewport looking out onto space was one of the few obvious luxuries – hidden in the room were also a poison-sniffer servitor, an anti-transmission field generator and a small void safe in which Thaddeus could transport sensitive or potentially tainted items.

Aescarion wore the simple white robes of the Sisters – without her armour she seemed half the size, little more than an ageing woman with an unusually proud bearing. So puritanical was the aura she seemed to project that she made Thaddeus's rooms seem positively decadent.

'Sister,' said Thaddeus. 'I hadn't expected you to leave the infirmary so soon.'

'I have had worse wounds that this,' replied Aescarion, limping slightly as she walked over to take a seat at Thaddeus's desk. That she chose to sit at all illustrated her discomfort, but she refused to show it otherwise. 'The bone was broken but there was little muscle loss. And I have learned to heal quickly.'

'I can imagine.'

'I wanted to speak with you, inquisitor. Something has been troubling me.'

'About Sarpedon? He is a Space Marine Chapter Master and a powerful psyker. There is no point in chastising yourself for not defeating him.'

'It is not that, inquisitor. I have lost in battle before, it is part of what makes us strong. It is just... he could have killed me, and he did not. The ways of the Enemy are many and strange and heretics might spare those who they think will suffer more from living than from a quick death – but he had no idea who I was. I was just another soldier in a city full of soldiers.'

'Do you believe he knew you were part of my strikeforce? That he let you live to send a message to me?'

'Perhaps. I just think that Sarpedon is no normal enemy. The Guardsmen genuinely believed that the Soul Drinkers were Imperial Marines and fought alongside them, even against their fellow Guardsmen. I fought Brother Castus and Parmenides the Vile, inquisitor, I was at Saafir and the Scorpion Pass. I know many of the forms of the Enemy, but the Soul Drinkers are the subtlest yet. They are not just animals to be hunted. This pursuit could cost us more than just our lives.'

'Sister, you have done what I have not. You have seen the Soul Drinkers up close and you have fought with their leader. You must be at the forefront on Stratix Luminae. As always, you may be required to give up your life and you will very probably have to face Sarpedon again. Be honest with me, Sister – does this scare you?'

Aescarion smiled, a rare thing. 'I am terrified, inquisitor. The Enemy has always terrified me. It is through faith that I live with this fear. If I was not afraid, then what would there be to believe in? I know the Emperor is with me because without Him I would be paralysed with fear. But with him, I can fight the Enemy in spite of it.'

'Very enlightened, Sister.'

'It took me most of my life to understand, inquisitor. And it has not been a short life.'

Thaddeus reached down and adjusted the holo-servitor's controls. The image flickered and changed to an old Mechanicus file. Once he had known the name of Stratix Luminae he had been able to find some rudimentary information on the place, and the newest layouts dated from a few months after the Soul Drinkers had driven off the eldar there. The surface building was a simple one-storey entrance to the lower levels. Hastily-improved defences ringed the outpost entrance, consisting mostly of plasticrete blocks placed on the frozen, broken earth.

'The entrance is just one floor, probably no more than security station,' said Thaddeus. 'Assuming the installation is on Standard Template Construct lines there will be at least two levels below the surface. Probably a laboratory level, maybe containment on the lowest floor where it's easiest to isolate. Apart from that we know nothing, except that somewhere in there is an objective that Sarpedon considers important enough to risk the life of his whole Chapter.'

'Unless we get there first,' said Aescarion.

'We may not have that luxury. The Soul Drinkers have a head-start and they know what they are looking for.'

'I and my Sisters are ready. I know that Colonel Vinn and the storm troopers would say the same. I have just one question, inquisitor.'

'Ask, Sister.'

'Stratix Luminae is evidently deserted. Do you know why it was closed down?'

Thaddeus shrugged. 'No, Sister, I don't. Aside from these final schematics Stratix Luminae will cease to exist as soon as the Soul Drinkers turn up. I have noticed they seem to have that effect.' Thaddeus picked up the decanter that stood on a side table. 'I would offer you a glass of devilberry liqueur, Sister, but I would imagine you abstain.'

'The human form is the form of the Emperor and to poison it willingly is a sin,' said Aescarion.

'We are all sinners, Sister,' replied Thaddeus, pouring himself a measure.

Aescarion stood, smoothing out her simple robes. 'There are some things that it is pointless to lecture on,' she said. 'Many are the times I have extolled the virtues of abstinence to the laity. Few are the times I have been listened to. In this case it is enough that I follow my vows myself.'

'I am glad I do not offend your sensibilities.'

'You know as well as I do there are far graver sins you could sink to. Now, I should minister to my Sisters, I have not led their prayers for several days.'

'Say a few words for me, Sister. We must all prepare as best we can.'

Thaddeus watched Aescarion leave, seeing for the first time not a warrior but an old woman who had seen rather too much of the universe.

He switched the holo-servitor back to Korvax's pict-recording, reviewing for the hundredth time the same file that had perhaps sent Sarpedon deep into the warzone. As it had done every time before, the file cut out just before Korvax entered the installation, but the original file must have shown the inside of the installation and the work the

Adeptus Mechanicus had done there. Whatever it was, Stratix Luminae had been closed down soon afterwards and of the two known surviving staff members one had gone insane and the other had been relocated to an outpost almost hidden beneath a hive city.

Thaddeus switched off the holo. He knew as much about Stratix Luminae as anyone could now. He poured the liqueur back into the decanter and headed up to the bridge.

It would only be a few more days before the *Crescent Moon* reached the Stratix system, but in the back of his mind Thaddeus knew every intervening moment was wasted.

THE SPACE AROUND Stratix was diseased. A miasma of pestilence hung in the space between planets, like an almost imperceptible gauze turning the distant stars sickly colours and colouring the worlds of the Stratix system strange hues of decay. Stratix's sun was paler, and anyone who looked at it through the right filters would see sunspots, like black scabs, festering on its surface. So strong was Teturact's influence that it had even infected the star that shone on his homeworld.

The system's blockade was a shoal of rotting ships, launched from Stratix's dockyards and cannibalised from merchant and outpost fleets throughout the system, or brought in from the fleets of worlds conquered in Teturact's name.

Squadrons of escorts were fitted to function as fire-ships, rigged to burst like seed pods in huge clouds of space-borne spores that would eat their way through portholes and bulkheads and infect enemy crews. Larger cruisers teemed with crew who needed neither heat nor air to work, making for ships that could only be disabled by complete obliteration, while other near-derelict cruisers had massive armour plates welded to their prows so they could act as suicidal ram-ships like giant hypodermics loaded with disease. Monitoring stations and orbital defence platforms turned weaponry outwards, cyclonic torpedoes and magnalasers now hard-wired into crewmen whose minds were the only parts of them left alive.

Stratix itself was a giant gnarled ball of charred blackness, studded with glowing spots like embers where hive-forges still burned. The hives covered almost the entire surface of the planet and were charred with exhaust fumes, and whole swathes of city were obscured by thick streaks of toxic cloud. Here and there low-orbit docks broke the atmosphere like tarnished metal thorns.

The other worlds were just as touched by Teturact. The whole system had warped according to his will. Locanis, closest to the system's star, had a thick greenhouse of an atmosphere that had turned from pale grey to rotten black overnight. Callicrates was rich in the ores that Stratix used in its industries, but the silvery metallic surface was now pockmarked with patches of rust hundreds of kilometres across. St Phal was a graveyard world now, so thick with walking skeletal dead that from space its surface seemed to squirm as if covered with maggots.

Stratix Luminae was even colder and whiter than ever. The gas giant of Majoris Crien was covered in swirling storms of sickly browns and purples where once it had been vibrant green, and its many moons were drifting away in erratic orbits as though the giant world was too weak to hold onto them any more. The Three Sisters, the tiny, far-orbit ice worlds of Cygnan, Terrin and Olatinne, were pulling further and further from the distant sun as if trying to escape from the infection spreading across the system.

Teturact's tombship dropped back into realspace; it was like a home-coming. The comforting glow of disease surrounded the planets with haloes of pestilence. Somehow, space smelt different here. It was redolent with life. Even through the many layers of armour between the void and the bridge of the tombship, the stench was there: the stench of home.

The crew of servitors and menials who had been jacked into the bridge had degenerated to the point where only fragments of their minds still worked. So the crew had brought more in, plugging their minds into the consoles and heaping more and more bodies against the banks of readouts and controls until the bridge was a single charnel pit, three deep in writhing corpses like a carpet of skin and muscle.

It was the ultimate slavery, for these near-dead to surrender their very humanity to Teturact. No one else was allowed on the bridge aside from Teturact and his bearers, because it was a place where anyone in control would be worshipped and that honour was only permissible for Teturact himself.

The front of the bridge gave way to a massive viewscreen through which Teturact could see the beauty of the Stratix system stretching in front of him. Stratix represented more than just another world, it was the first, the heart of his corruption and the first proof that he truly had the power to rule worlds. He had done much good work on Eumenix and the place would be as solid a bastion as any in his empire, but the Stratix system was home.

Wordlessly, he urged the bridge crew to turn the ship towards Stratix. The bodies writhed beneath his feet and moaned as their minds were connected through the bridge cogitators to signal the main engines and thrusters.

Teturact let his mind sweep out. With every new world he became stronger, and his consciousness was no longer bound to his wizened body. He let it flow through the tombship, washing over the bright, roiling pits of corruption that were the minds of his wizards. He felt the fractured pride of the Navigator above the prow, still trying to hold on to the idea of the old naval aristocracy even as his flesh melted off his bones.

He could see beyond the ship, past the ripples it left in realspace as it passed out into the void. It was warm and welcoming, tinted with disease, and he could hear, like the echoes of a distant choir, the voices clamouring for him to come and save them all over again. He could drink that feeling, their desperation and their gratitude, and the pleading that followed as they came to realise they would always need him to keep their slow deaths at bay. It was what fuelled him. It was why he had built a war machine out of his empire and engaged Imperial forces in grinding campaigns of attrition that only he could win.

He felt the desperate dimming of Stratix's star and the warping of the gravitational web between the worlds – so powerful was the concept of Teturact as a god that it deformed the universe around it. He could taste the dark, rich taste of corruption so pure it could bleed across the void in a stain that would eventually cover his whole empire.

Stratix itself was a glorious beating heart of suffering, St Phal a suppurating wound in reality, Stratix Luminae a hard white pearl of dead ice, Majoris Crien a bloated spectre. Teturact could feel them distorting space around them, so powerful was the taint he had left on them. Spacecraft like swarms of locusts or huge lumbering monsters patrolled the system, and Teturact could hear them calling his name.

The beauty of it all still had the power to astound him. Teturact had seen extraordinary things and become immune to all of them but this – these billions of souls in pain and rapture, pleading for his touch and singing praises in gratitude, all forming a psychic tide that flowed into Teturact's mind.

But there was something else here, something that wasn't here before. Something pure and untouched by Teturact. Different, yes, shifted sideways from reality – but not diseased.

Teturact focused his will on the intrusion. Tiny and metallic, they were like needles sewing a wound back together, piercing the gauze of suffering and driving deep into system space. There were several tiny craft, faster than any Imperial ships of comparable size.

Teturact felt a cold, affronted anger. These were his worlds. The Imperial spearheads that had tried to punch into the Stratix system at the start of the rebellion had paid for their boldness with madness followed by servitude in Teturact's armies. No one had dared poison this cauldron of disease with their cleanliness since then.

Teturact could smell a hot, bright bolt of psychic intelligence in one of the ships, something subtly different than a normal human psyker. It was taut, focused, and very, very powerful.

Teturact pulled back from the shoal of bright slivers and let the whole system fill his mind. He could see the trails of near-normality that the ships left behind them and estimated the course they were taking, straight as an arrow into the heart of the system.

Their route would take them to Stratix Luminae.

Teturact's consciousness snapped back into the confines of the bridge. The bodies piled up around him shuddered as even they felt the resonance of their lord's anger. He spat out an order with his mind to switch the tombship's course towards the frozen planet and intercept the intruders.

Stratix Luminae – no, thought Teturact, that could not be allowed.

KORVAX SLAMMED *a new magazine into his bolter and heard half his squad doing the same. He glanced at Sergeant Veiyal – the sergeant's helmet had been damaged and he was bare-headed, his breath coiling white in the cold.*

'The others have our backs,' said Korvax. 'Sergeant Livris, your squad has the point. Veiyal, with me. Advance.'

Korvax levelled his bolter and followed the Assault Marines as they charged into the darkened heart of the outpost…

The air was close and Korvax recognised the smells that got through his helmet filter – gun smoke, blood both alien and human, unwashed and terrified men. His autosenses adjusted quickly to the darkness and Korvax saw techguard bodies lying where they had taken up fire points near the blast doors. Automated guns hung limp and shattered from the ceiling, and a gun-servitor lay dismembered on the makeshift defences.

The blast doors led into a single large, low room with a smouldering rectangular hole in the floor where a cargo elevator had once been. The security stations that covered the blast doors and entrance chamber were heavy constructions of ferrocrete with firing slits and automated guns – Korvax saw tech-guard bodies slumped at the fixed heavy stubbers and blood spattered across the walls and floor.

'They've been shredded, captain,' voxed Livris, who was moving rapidly into the entrance chamber with his assault squad.

'Shuriken fire?'

'Something else.'

Korvax's squad moved in behind the Assault Marines, training bolters on the dark corners that pooled where glowstrips had failed.

Livris peered over the edge of the cargo lift, auspex scanner in hand. 'Do we move in, captain?'

'Go, Livris. Cold and fast.'

Livris dropped down the smoking hole, followed by the assault squad. Korvax could still hear the gunfire from outside as Squad Veiyal held off the remains of the eldar forces from the blast doors. If the xenos had got inside, they were doing a good job of hiding it – hardly any sound seemed to filter from the outpost's lower floors.

'It's a lab floor,' said Livris. 'Wait, the auspex is…'

Gunfire erupted below. Chainblades chewed into metal.

'Squad, with me!' yelled Korvax and followed Squad Livris onto the floor below, power sword hot in his hand.

The darkness below was punctuated with strobing muzzle flashes. Heavy gothic architecture was crammed into the low-ceilinged lab floor, with ornate workstations covered in complex machinery and webs of glass tubing. Korvax saw tech-guard and lab personnel still living, and many more lying dead slumped on seats or consoles. Tech-guard were taking cover and firing almost blindly with lasguns.

Korvax couldn't see the enemy. Squad Livris were sending out suppressive volleys of bolt pistol fire and Korvax's tactical squad lent their own fire, spitting explosive bolts in all directions.

A battle-brother's scream ended in a choked-off gurgle, and in the flash of gunfire Korvax saw him fall, a shining web of silvery filaments billowing over and through him, slicing through armour plates, coiling into armour joints and unravelling to shred the flesh and bone inside.

Korvax got a glimpse of the aliens – they had heavier armour suits than the warriors Korvax had fought at the barricades, with a large carapace over the back and large, thick forearm plates that helped support massive weapons with spinning barrels that wove spirals of bright threads. The eldar aimed and a bolt of filaments shot out, bursting against one of Livris's Marines and reducing his pistol arm to a mess of loose armour and shredded muscle.

Korvax fired but too late, the eldar had disappeared, winking out of existence with a clap of air rushing into the space he left behind.

'Teleporters!' yelled Korvax as gunfire continued to spatter across the darkened lab floor. A surviving tech-guard screamed as an unseen enemy shredded him with a monofilament burst. Something flitted into view and disappeared, almost catching Sergeant Livris with its lethal web.

Korvax kept his head down and moved past his battle-brothers, trying to gauge the angle he would take if he were trying to kill as many of them as possible. He had to trust the alien attackers would be too distracted by the other Marines and their gunfire to notice him until it was too late.

He backed up against a pillar, listening carefully, trying to filter through the din of bolter and lasgun fire. He heard, very close, the burst of air as something materialised on the other side of the pillar.

He lashed round the pillar with his power sword and felt it cut through something, armour plate and flesh, not deep but enough to impose a split-second of pain and confusion. The eldar warrior turned in surprise, the emerald eyepieces of its conical helmet staring out at Korvax as the Space Marine grabbed it by the throat with his free hand.

He hauled the alien off its feet and slammed it hard into the pillar, then powered it up into the ceiling so the carapace on its back hit the low fluted roof. The carapace fractured and blue flashes of escaping energy confirmed Korvax's suspicion that the carapace housed the teleport-jump device. Korvax lifted the xenos again and, before it could bring its flailing gun to bear, plunged his power sword through its chest. The flashes of the sword's power field illuminated the several warriors who jumped in to surround Korvax, perhaps half-a-dozen of them, moving to kill the Soul Drinkers' obvious leader and avenge their fallen.

Livris's Assault Marines jumped the eldar from behind, chainblades glancing off carapaces. Livris himself beheaded one and Korvax took another, breaking its leg with a stamp of his foot and cutting the alien clean in two. The surviving xenos jumped again, flitting out of reality not to surround the Marines but to flee.

Korvax pulled his sword from the remains of the eldar at his feet. He saw a couple of surviving tech-guard still hunkered down amongst the equipment. There was a technician, too, a woman in an adept's robes, peeking terrified from beneath a lab bench, doubtlessly not knowing whether to fear the aliens or the Soul Drinkers more.

Korvax walked over to the closest tech-guard and hauled him to his feet. The man's face was laced with blood where he had caught the edge of a filament burst and the barrel of his lasgun was warped, overheated from continuous firing.

'Are there any more?' asked Korvax sternly.

The tech-guard nodded and pointed to the far end of the lab floor, where a set of doors had been blown off their mountings leading to a dark corridor beyond.

Korvax dropped the tech-guard and led his Marines into the corridor. It was low and close, too narrow for two Marines to stand abreast. The air stank of something rotting and biological, and his helmet pre-filter was flashing up warning runes to mark the toxins it was keeping out of his system. The corridor sloped downwards and curved sharply back on itself, leading towards the next floor down.

Korvax looked down to see the floor ankle-deep in milky fluid, swimming with scraps of muscle tissue. It reflected the wan light from ahead, filtering weakly from the entrance to the next floor down. Normally security doors would have sealed off the lower floor, but they were open now.

Through the doorway Korvax glimpsed drifts of shattered glass and thick ribbed cables lying across a floor awash with the fluid, the drainage channels clogged with clotted wads of flesh. Glass cylinders three metres high stood in rows along the length of an enormous hangar-like room, some intact and full of fluids, others shattered.

Korvax slowed, edging towards the entrance, ready for that shuriken shot or energy blast. The eldar down here would have heard the battle above, they would know the Soul Drinkers were coming.

'Any movement on the auspex?' he voxed.

'Nothing,' came the reply.

The first body Korvax saw was slumped over the shattered remains of a cylinder, its abdomen impaled on jagged shards of curved glass still stabbing up from the cylinder's base. It was an eldar, in a blue armoured bodyglove with the helmet removed. The features of its slender, angular face were slack in death, its large dark eyes open. A shuriken pistol lay by its limp hand. Another body lay nearby – or most of it at least, Korvax saw. This eldar's body had been bisected at the waist, and the lower half lay mangled several metres away.

Korvax waved his squad forward and cautiously they entered the room, Livris alongside him. There must have been five hundred of the cylinders here, arranged in rows like standing stones, with a clearing in the middle where cold vapour coiled off a huge hemispherical machine.

'Spread out!' ordered Livris, and his Assault Marines broke formation as they entered, moving between the cylinders in ones and twos. Korvas kept his squad closer, and as he advanced towards the centre of the room he saw more and more eldar bodies, mostly warriors but also one or two xenos in elaborate robes whose enclosed helmets had complex crystalline arrays built in. The eldar leadership caste, all psychic, the guides of their species on the battlefield and off it. The Imperial studies of the eldar named them warlocks, and several had met their end here beneath Stratix Luminae. One body was full of shuriken discs – this was not the result of a tech-guard last stand. Something else had happened here.

'Something's alive,' voxed Livris curtly. Korvax looked across to see the sergeant consulting his auspex scanner.

'Where?'

'Everywhere.'

There was a strange, faint buzzing in the air now, like a failing lumoglobe, almost imperceptible but coming from everywhere at once.

Bio-alarms flashed on Korvax's retinal display. Toxins were building up in his blood now. His armour integrity was in the green so it was as if the poisons *were spontaneously appearing in his organs. His oolitic kidney kicked in to filter it out but if it kept increasing...*

'I see him,' voxed the point Marine of his squad. Korvax looked through the cylinders and saw what the Marine was indicating – in front of the huge metallic hemisphere was a figure, kneeling as if in supplication, its warlock's robes spattered with blood.

'In position,' voxed Livris. Korvax knew he could give the word and the assault squad would be on the stranger in a heartbeat.

'Hold,' he replied. 'Squad, cover me.'

Korvax stepped slowly towards the figure. The area around the hemisphere was like a clearing in a forest of glass, and thick cables ran from ports all over the curved panels. The tingling, buzzing sound grew stronger and Korvax could feel the strain on his internal organs as more and more exotic poisons synthesized themselves in his bloodstream.

The figure stood. It was tall and slim, and even from behind Korvax recognised the elongated skull of the eldar. It turned around. Its long face was mournful and its eyes were weeping black blood. Korvax levelled his bolt pistol at the alien's head. 'Why are you here, xenos? What do you want?'

The alien spoke a few hushed syllables, then as if suddenly remembering the Marine could not speak its language–

'I could not hold it, brutish one. I thought... we could take it with us and keep it from you. We could destroy it. But we were too late, you have let it grow for far too long.'

'What? What did you come for?'

The eldar smiled. The skin of its face was taut and it split hideously, weeping watery gore. Korvax saw blood running down its wrists to drip off its fingers and realised the alien was coming apart under some great force.

'You tell me, low creature. It was your kind that made it.'

As Korvax watched, the eldar's skin turned mottled and dark, tendrils of blackness tracing out its veins. It slumped back down to its knees and its body sagged grotesquely, its skeleton coming apart under the same forces that were starting to prey on Korvax and his Marines.

'Squad Veiyal?' voxed Korvax, 'get onto the crews on the Carnivore. Have them prep the infirmary, we'll need every man checked out. Inform the Chaplain there is a potential moral threat on Stratix Luminae.'

'Understood,' came Sergeant Veiyal's voice, filtering down through the sound of static and muted gunfire.

'Marines, fall back!' ordered Korvax as the eldar warlock collapsed in a welter of blood.

The eldar was dead, its remains twitching inside its stained robes. The plates of the hemisphere were pulsing in and out like a ribcage drawing breath, cables popping from the sockets.

Korvax turned and jogged with his squad as they fell back, then broke into a run as a terrible creaking roar began from the hemisphere and the floor and walls began to warp. The remaining cylinders shattered one by one, filling the air with showers of liquid and glass, spilling malformed humanoid shapes out on the floor. A plate burst off the hemisphere, spinning across the huge room and embedding itself in a wall.

The buzzing became a scream and warning telltales flashed all over Korvax's retina. He saw battle-brothers flagging as they ran, the terrible influence of whatever lurked in the centre of the room working on their systems. The eldar warlock had held on with his mind, the Marines had their bodies, but the eldar had been defeated and so could they.

Korvax was one of the last through the doorway. Livris, beside him, slammed a palm into the door controls and the massive security doors began to yawn closed.

'Move!' yelled Korvax. 'Get to the surface, this battle is over!'

Before the doors shut Korvax saw the hemisphere erupting in a huge gout of cables and machinery like metallic entrails, biomechanical equipment pouring up from a lower level and bringing a force with it that Korvax could feel in his very bones. The gene-seed organs in his throat and chest burned, his third lung and second heart were like lumps of molten metal in his chest.

Korvax just had time to see a human form rising from the middle of the destruction.

The eldar had come to Stratix Luminae to kill it. They had been too late. As Korvax rushed towards the surface, he hoped the Imperium would not make the same mistake...

THE IMAGE FROZE, with Korvax's pict-recorder looking out on the destruction of the lab floor.

'This,' said Sarpedon, 'is all we have. Stratix Luminae was closed afterwards and forgotten about. There are no plans or records within our reach. Captain Korvax's record is the only visual of the facility that exists. So this is what we will use.'

Sarpedon stood on a pulpit looking out on the Marines of Squads Luko, Karraidin and Graevus. In front and below him was the focus of the briefing sermon – the projected pict-recording that Captain Korvax had taken during the first assault on Stratix Luminae. The image, and Sarpedon's voice, would be transmitted to the other ships in the tiny fleet, where the Soul Drinkers would be stood as here in the cargo bay of the alien fighters.

'It is a testament to the strength of your will, brothers,' continued Sarpedon, 'that you have fought alongside me though very few of you know our ultimate goal. The truth is, we are fighting for survival. We are fighting for the Great Harvest, when the Soul Drinkers will take novices and begin the process of transforming them into Marines. The Harvest should be underway already, with our Chaplain and our Apothecaries forging another generation to take the fight to the Enemy. It has not happened.'

Sarpedon spread his arms, indicating his mutated legs. 'This is why. There is not one Marine that has no mark of mutation upon them. Many are stronger because of it, as am I. But the blood of Rogal Dorn is poisoned.

'Our blood, the gene-seed taken from Dorn's own body, is corrupted down to its basest elements. The Chapter is a chalice of that blood, and each drop poured out is the seed of another battle-brother. But the chalice is bleeding dry of Dorn's blood and soon there will be only corruption left. Our gene-seed is tainted, it cannot be used to create new Marines.'

The image rewound suddenly, flitting through the moments of destruction as Korvax retreated. Then it paused again, looking out on the glass cylinders and their obscure contents, as Korvax saw them when he first entered the lower floor.

'The adepts at Stratix Luminae were trying to control mutation. They were growing mutated flesh and trying to make it whole again. I, and the highest officers of this Chapter, believe they succeeded. The evidence Korvax gives us shows that the experimentation was in its final stages and was only halted by the deaths of the adepts at the hands of the eldar. It is waiting there to be recovered and used. Used by us, brothers, to reverse the poison that is killing the Soul Drinkers.'

Karraidin stepped up to the pulpit, the boots of his huge Terminator armour clunking on the metallic floor. The Soul Drinkers Chapter had never possessed many suits of the advanced armour and Karraidin's was one of the few left. He had earned it, though – a resolute and fearless assault leader he had proved himself capable of leading the hardest ship-to-ship attacks. He had joined Sarpedon in the heat of the Chapter war and there were few veterans in the Chapter that Sarpedon trusted more.

'The first force will be under my command,' began Karraidin. 'Our objective is the lower floor of the facility. The force will consist of my squad along with Squads Salk and Graevus. The mission is to recover experimental material and data – Techmarine Lygris and Solun and Apothecary Pallas will go in with us as support. You do not need to be reminded that whatever Korvax found may still be there.'

'The second force,' said Sarpedon, 'will be commanded by me. We will secure the surface and the exterior of the facility, and hold it until the assault force is extracted. Stratix Luminae is located in one of the most heavily enemy-infested systems in Imperial space and we will be seen, if we have not been located already. It is likely the facility will be attacked and we must ensure the facility and our landing zone remains secure at all costs. Luko, Krydel, Assault Sergeant Tellos and myself will be in command on the ground. All Marines not in the assault or the ground force will remain on the fighters as interception and reserve.'

Every Marine would know what that meant. Up until now Sarpedon had not risked the whole Chapter at once – Marines could not be replaced and there would be no edict from the Adeptus Terra to resurrect the Chapter if it was all but destroyed. The mission was about survival, and the future of the Chapter could be risked because it was that future they were fighting for.

Sarpedon took out his battered, well-thumbed copy of Daenyathos's *Catechisms Martial*. 'Emperor, deliver us,' he began, 'so that we might deliver creation from the Enemy...'

Together, solemnly and all aware that it could be for the last time, the Soul Drinkers began to pray.

STRATIX LUMINAE WAS pale as a cataract stricken eye, several thousand square kilometres of frozen tundra broken only by rare rock formations and the single incongruous structure of the Adeptus Mechanicus Biologis installation. From above, it was barely a pinprick of artificiality in an infuriatingly dead world. But Teturact could feel the life within, a life rather like himself that seethed with potential.

He pulled his consciousness back through the hull of the ship and into the ritual chamber. Deep in the heart of Teturact's ship, this was a secret place he had forbidden anyone to enter.

It was the only part that was clean and free of the corpses that littered the rest of the ship. Lacquered, decorated panels of exotic hardwood covered the walls and ceilings. Tapestries hung from the walls, covered in images of Imperial heroism that seemed desperate and comical now so much of that Imperium had turned into Teturact's nightmare. The floor was tiled with mosaics of devotional texts, and the air was perfumed by censers that swung slowly from the ceiling.

Glow-globes concealed in chandeliers produced a light that made the shadows harsh. The light glinted off relics assembled in alcoves set into the walls – the finger bones of a saint, the hereditary power axe of Stratix's priesthood chased with silver and set with gemstones, the furled banner of the Adepta Sororitas, sacred works of art from the distant Imperial past and powerful symbols that had seemed vital to its future. Teturact had gathered them from Stratix itself and holy places his forces had conquered. Their influence was a painful veil over the brightness of his power, as if some new gravity was dragging his mind back down to mortality – it pained Teturact to enter the room, but it existed for a reason.

This was the only place that Teturact had ordered kept pure in his entire empire. Its components had been looted from luxurious upper spires and sacred conquered places, and assembled here into a place of purity that Teturact had ordered kept inviolate. The reason was simple – the most powerful magics required something to be defiled as part of the enactment, and nothing was so powerful as the defiling of purity.

Teturact's wizards were ranged before him, hooded and deformed, their heads hunched down in reverence because it was to him that they owed everything. This unholy nugget of purity must have been painful for them, too, a sharp painful obstruction to the complete corruption of the ship, but they were bound to Teturact's will and took the pain as he demanded.

You know what you must do, he thought at them. *Make it happen.*

One wizard shambled forward. He pulled down his hood and Teturact saw he had not one face but several, melded together as if they had melted into one. Several malformed eyes blinked in the light of the chamber's chandeliers. One of its mouths opened and began to keen, a low, buzzing drone. Its other mouths joined in, weaving a grotesque harmony that would have reduced mortal men to tears.

Gnarled limbs reached out from beneath its tattered robes, some arms, some pincers, some tentacles. Each hand made a different sign of blasphemy in the air, trails of red light spelled out symbols of heresy.

The other wizards shuffled into a circle around the singer. Teturact's brute-mutants carried him back out of the circle and each mutilated mind began to enact a separate part of the spell. One was a pure stab of rage, a bright red spire of burning hatred that provided fuel for the ritual. Another took that hatred and wove it into a tapestry of suffering, the chamber resonating with psychic after-images of torture and despair.

The lacquer on the walls began to peel. Images of the Emperor's sacred armies tarnished and were obliterated. The tapestries began to unravel and a patina of age and corruption spread across the gleaming relics. Even the light changed, gradually becoming dimmer and yellower, making everything in the room seem older.

Shapes began to appear, broken spectres drawn by the ritual's power, shadowy forms that stood hunched over the circle. The magic was drawing curious warp-creatures like blood draws scavengers. Monstrous things were watching. Perhaps the gods themselves, who would look down on Teturact with jealously that he had achieved what they could not and built an empire of suffering in the heart of the Imperium.

He could taste it, like old blood. This was one of the oldest magics, and it was his to command.

The keening rose, becoming louder and higher. Another wizard entered the circle and drew a knife of blackened iron from its robes. This wizard was larger than the rest, broad-shouldered with a musculature that showed even through its robes. It threw its head back, revealing a face with shredded skin that hung like ribbons over the red wet features beneath, and plunged the knife into its stomach.

Ropy purple entrails slithered out and where they hit the floor a dark stain spread like rust, warping the mosaics until the devotional High Gothic texts were squirming symbols of disease and death. The wizard sank to its knees and scraped the point of its knife through its spilled entrails, divining the course of the magic now coursing around the room. It carved a final sigil in the floor and the symbol lit up.

The walls themselves were peeling away in layers, revealing what lay beyond. The room had been set up in one of the ship's fighter decks. Where once hundreds of attack craft had been parked on the wide expanse of rusted metal, now heaps of thousands upon thousands of bodies festered. Pasty, desiccated limbs lay across dead faces staring blindly. The heaps were dozens deep, mountains of death, harvested from the hives of Stratix and heaped as an offering to Teturact's mercy.

Teturact had been glad of them, not just as a symbol of his own power. They had a practical purpose, too, as did all the bodies crammed into every spare corner of the tombship.

The walls of the room fell away and its ceiling broke into flakes of rust that fluttered away. The spell was all but complete. The chanting grew higher and the air burned with power, black sparks leaping from the cowls of the wizards, half-formed shadowy observers flickering in and out of sight.

The first of the bodies stirred, dragging itself from the side of one of the corpse-mountains and tumbling down the slope. It knocked other bodies down with it and they stirred, reaching out dumbly with gnawed fingers. Limbs reached from the slopes until whole mountains were stirring and the first of the bodies struggled to its feet and began to walk.

Teturact could feel the seething as the whole ship began to awaken. The people of Stratix had pleaded, begged, for him to save them from death, and he had done so in return for their souls. Now he was extending the bargain to those he had not saved the first time round, the dregs of Stratix's charnel pits. The tombship was more than a place of worship for Teturact – it was a weapon of war, the deadliest he could create. It was the vessel for an army that did not need to eat or sleep, that would follow unquestioningly, that would never flee and could fight to the death because they were already dead.

Teturact's master plan, the infection and salvation of an empire, could only go so far. Sometimes, he had known all along, he would have to intervene directly and take the fight to the enemy. The tombship was his means of doing so. Now his enemies had struck closer to home than even he had imagined, driving into the Stratix system itself, daring to defile Stratix Luminae – and Teturact had created the tombship for just such an offence.

The mountains were now shifting heaps of human beings, struggling to clamber from beneath one another, teeth and nails gouging, brackish blood running in streams across the fighter deck floor. Many of them shambled closer, dressed in the rags of workers' overalls, regal finery, soldiers' fatigues and everything in between. Teturact's brute-mutants raised him high and his vast mind took in the faint pinpricks of guttering light that were the minds of the dead.

He took every one of those points of light and snuffed them out one by one, replacing them with the unblinking black pearls of his own mind. The final phase of the ritual was Teturact's own – to make these awakened dead answer solely to his will. They were now no more than his instruments, to be controlled as if they were his own limbs. He stretched his mind out and did the same to the bodies waking throughout the ship, until he felt tens of thousands of mind-slaves connected to him like parts of his own shrivelled body.

The pitiful resistance of the Imperium seemed more laughable than ever. How could anyone claim Teturact was not a god? He had created an army and controlled them utterly. He was master of billions and billions of worshippers. There was no greater calling. Soon, when his empire stretched across the stars, it would be complete and Teturact would take his place in the pantheon amongst the gods of the warp.

A tiny part of his mind reached out to the controllers on the bridge. His orders were the last they would ever receive.

He commanded that the tombship be taken into low orbit around Stratix Luminae. Then he demanded that the shields be dropped and the hull of the tombship be allowed to disintegrate in the planet's atmosphere. He already knew how the ship would break up, the parts that would land intact and the remaining fighter craft and shuttles that would fly out of the wreckage. He knew which parts would split open and rain down an army on the frozen surface.

It was a beautiful thing, his tombship. But it was just a single building block in the immense cathedral of his empire. It was a small thing for it to be sacrificed, when the prize would be the sanctity of the world where Teturact himself was born.

CHAPTER ELEVEN

'EMPEROR PRESERVE US,' said Sister Aescarion. 'That's the ugliest thing I've ever seen.'

Inquisitor Thaddeus had to agree. The long-range sensors on the *Crescent Moon* were transmitting a visual composite directly onto the viewscreen on the bridge, and it was not pretty. Stratix Luminae was in the background, looking like a huge eye without a pupil. In the foreground hung a truly hideous thing, a ship that was as diseased as any of the unfortunates on Eumenix. Pustules the size of islands spat plumes of bile out into space. Hull plates oozed out of the superstructure, straining under the ship's corpulent mass. Lance batteries were rusted gun barrels sticking out of orifices ringed with scabs. The engines bled pus and the entrances to the fighter decks had deformed into lipless drooling orifices that mouthed dumbly and vomited clouds of debris, corpses and filth.

The ship was huge, larger by magnitudes than the *Crescent Moon*. It had to be a full-scale battleship – there might have been an Emperor-class under there somewhere.

'Bridge, do we have this profile stored?' asked Thaddeus.

The servitors at the consoles spent a moment calculating, wire fingers clattering on the keyboards of their mem-consoles.

'Battlefleet Stratix had three Emperor-class battleships,' came a tinny, synthetic voice. 'The *Ultima Khan* was reclassified heretic and reported destroyed at Kolova. The *Olympus Mons* and the *Dutiful* are unaccounted for.'

'It doesn't matter what it used to be,' said Colonel Vinn unexpectedly. 'It's orbit is too low. It'll be breaking up within the hour.'

'Maybe so, colonel,' said Thaddeus, 'but this is too much to be a coincidence. Bridge, what do we have following us?'

Another moment's pause. Then, 'Two light cruisers, designation unknown, heretic probable. Cobra-class escort squadron, again heretic. Unknown attack craft and merchantmen.'

'If we're being trailed by that many and we're still this far out,' said Thaddeus, 'then the Soul Drinkers will have been spotted, too. They're on Stratix Luminae already and the Enemy is close behind them.'

'Let them fight one another?' suggested Vinn.

'Unless they're in league,' replied Aescarion with bitterness, spitting out the words as if she longed for the Soul Drinkers to be under Teturact's command so she could destroy them all the more justly.

'Agreed,' said Thaddeus. 'We will not have another chance to bring them to bear. But we can't land right on top of them. If they're landing troops we'll be blown out of the sky even if this ship has broken up by then. Bridge, get me landing solutions, far away from that battleship to get down in one piece. Colonel, how's our armour?'

'Enough APCs for the Sisters and remaining men,' said Vinn. Thaddeus felt the sting even through the man's expressionless voice – the best of his men were dead, shot or frozen stiff at Pharos. 'We weren't expecting to run a mechanised assault, inquisitor.'

'It'll do, colonel. We just have to get there, the rest we'll make up as we go along. Sister, colonel, you both understand the enemy we will be facing. The Soul Drinkers are probably under-strength but they are still Space Marines. We cannot destroy them all, but we have an advantage in that they want something at Stratix Luminae and must make themselves vulnerable to get it. They will probably be engaged by other forces so we will have the luxury of picking our targets.'

'The first of those targets,' came that familiar half-machine voice from the rear of the bridge, 'is Sarpedon.' The Pilgrim emerged from the bridge entrance. Thaddeus didn't know how long he had been there – though every member of the strikeforce had to be fully briefed, he had privately wished to have this talk with Aescarion and Vinn alone. But the Pilgrim seemed able to shadow everything he did.

'Sarpedon is the key,' continued the Pilgrim. He walked slowly up the bridge until he stood between Aescarion and Vinn, and Thaddeus saw the repulsion pass over Aescarion's face. 'Sarpedon is their weakness, and he knows it himself. Without him there will be no purpose. Without him, even if he is the only one to die here, the Chapter will fragment to be hunted down one by one. All other targets are secondary.'

'I have command here, Pilgrim,' said Thaddeus sternly, more as a show to the others than in any real hope of reining in the creature. 'We know there will be other key Marines. Any specialists or officers are to be considered vital targets. But agreed, Sarpedon is high on that list. At least he should be easy to spot.' Pict-recordings from House Jenassis had been issued to every Sister and storm trooper – every one of them knew that amongst the Soul Drinkers was a monster with spider's legs who was to be destroyed at all costs.

'There is a good chance the Soul Drinkers will be fighting another enemy when we engage,' repeated Thaddeus. 'This is the best advantage we have, and we will use it. They will not know we are coming and we will strike as hard and fast as the Soul Drinkers themselves. Have your troops pray, both of you, and never forget we are here to do the Emperor's will.'

The strikeforce's leaders left the bridge and suddenly the whole area was bathed in a red glow. The engines below roared into life, immense plasma turbines grinding into action as the primary engines fired.

The motley flotilla tracking them was left behind as the *Crescent Moon* powered away from them. The thruster solutions took over and the ship began the descent to Stratix Luminae.

THE FIGHTERS SCREAMED into the planet's upper atmosphere, the surface a frozen desolation beneath them, Teturact's flagship a still vaster slab of pure rotting malice above them. The xenos fighters slid through Stratix Luminae's atmospheric envelope like knives through silk, forewings flowing into shining blades that cut through the strong, freezing air currents.

The ship – and it had to be Teturact's flagship, nothing else could radiate that aura of corruption and evil – didn't fire on them. Perhaps its crew and systems were too far gone to be able to track them and fire effectively. But it had certainly seen them – every Marine, even those with no psychic ability, felt the dark eye of something within focusing on them as if they were samples on a microscope slide.

The ten fighters carried the whole of the remaining Soul Drinkers Chapter, down to barely six hundred Marines and a handful of Chapter serfs. Sarpedon along with Squad Krydel and Squad Luko were in one craft, with one given over entirely to Tellos and his Assault Marines who Sarpedon suspected wouldn't follow anyone else. Another carried the force that would strike directly into the facility –

Ben Counter

Squads Karraidin, Graevus and Salk along with Techmarines Lygris and Solun and Apothecary Salk.

Apothecary Karendin and the Chapter Infirmary took up a fighter craft along with Techmarine Varuk. Chaplain Iktinos had a craft of his own along with those Marines whose squads had lost their officers and chose to follow the Chaplain into battle. One fighter held Tyrendian, the Librarian who was effectively the Chapter's chief psyker after Sarpedon himself. The remaining three contained the squads earmarked to form a mobile reserve – Sevras, Karvik, Corvan, Dyon, Shastarik, Kelvor, Locano, Preadon and the Librarian Gresk.

When assembling the force it had been brought home to Sarpedon just what a state the Chapter was in. Less than half the Marines were still organised into squads along the old Chapter lines – Marines whose squads had lost their officers joined other squads or formed around leaders like Iktinos, Tellos or Karraidin. The Chapter had always had a more fluid organisation than the Codex Astartes had set out but it was now in a constant state of flux. There had simply not been enough time to organise it properly, not when every passing hour made their irretrievable genetic corruption more likely.

It was Techmarine Varuk who noticed the disintegration first. The scanner signature of the flagship above began to become more indistinct, as if there was some kind of interference covering it. Rapidly the truth became apparent – the ship was coming apart, shedding hull sections like scabbed skin. Whole decks peeled away and began to fall into the atmosphere, bloated hull sections rupturing and spilling clouds of debris. The rearmost fighters began to report near-collisions with chunks of debris streaking down from above. The scanners on the fighters, even though they were advanced xenos tech, were quickly blinded by the mass of signals suddenly pouring into orbit.

Teturact's flagship was coming apart above them. Varuk voxed Sarpedon to tell him, and Sarpedon knew better than to assume the death of the ship was good news.

TETURACT WATCHED HIS ship rupture and it tasted good. The ship had once been a mighty battleship, carrying enough firepower to raze a city to the ground. Teturact had not only corrupted it until it served him, but had proven he could destroy such a thing with a thought. A symbol of Imperial might had been captured, deformed, and then destroyed, all because Teturact wished it.

If anyone had needed proof that Teturact was a god, this was it.

He felt the plasma reactors overloading and breaking up, sending shockwaves through the hull that fractured the stern and sent the engines spiralling downwards towards the surface. The tang of escaping fuel plasma was a metallic, chemical taste of Imperial doom.

Already sections of corridor and gun deck were falling, packed with the living dead. Some would not make it to the surface intact but enough would to disgorge an army onto the ground. He reached out with his mind and felt the wizards, held in a near-indestructible plasma conduit, waiting in the belly of the ship to be vomited onto Stratix Luminae. Teturact, as was proper for the master of the dying ship, waited on the bridge. The bulkheads nearby had already failed and hard vacuum had turned the slave-bodies beneath his feet rigid and cold, but Teturact kept himself and his brute-mutant bearers intact with a barely-conscious effort. The hardness of space was a reminder of the purity of death he would leave at Stratix Luminae.

The gods were watching. Teturact could feel their eyes on him, both curious and jealous, and fearful that he would rise and join them. The gods were no more than ideas made real in the warp, and Teturact had created ideas of his own – servitude through death, purity and corruption made one, the subjugation of souls through suffering and deliverance. Those concepts would be coalescing in the warp even now, and when they became strong enough Teturact's mind would be divorced from his body completely and he would join the kingdom he had created in the warp as its god.

He could feel the universe flickering at the edges of his consciousness, like an endless harvest of souls begging to be enslaved, delivered from their suffering by the servitude and oblivion Teturact offered.

But there were matters closer at hand. He drew his mind back in, the sensation almost painful. He watched the first wave falling towards Stratix Luminae and the hard bright darts of the intruder craft flying through the first curtain of debris.

His army would be on the ground waiting when the intruders landed. If they ever got to land at all.

THE FIGHTER LURCHED suddenly, throwing Sarpedon against the curved metal wall. The instrument panels flared brightly as damage signals from the fighter's systems flooded into the controls. The viewscreen flickered and was suddenly full of debris shooting down past them, chunks of blackened metal and showers of torn corpses.

'Keep us straight!' yelled Sarpedon to the serfs wrestling with the alien controls. 'Get us down!'

Comms runes flickered on Sarpedon's retina. Several Marines were voxing him at once.

'...Karvik's down, sir, lost its engines...' the voice was Lygris, whose craft was closest in the formation to the fighter carrying Squads Sevras and Karvik.

There were thirty Marines on the fighter. They would not be the last to fall – Sarpedon could see the life sign monitors going haywire in the confusion and guessed that the falling storm of wreckage was Teturact's way of landing an army.

'Sarpedon to all squads,' he voxed. 'Break formation and take evasive action. Do whatever you have to.' He turned to the serfs at the controls of his fighter. 'Find Karvik's fighter, I want to know if anyone could have made it.'

Another jolt and the fighter banked to avoid a falling torrent of wreckage, slabs of hull plate streaking past the viewscreen. Karendin's craft, which housed the infirmary, would be busy even before the fighters landed, guessed Sarpedon.

'Crash us if you have to,' said Sarpedon to his crew. 'Just bring us down.'

'Crash-land in thirty seconds, commander,' replied the serf at the navigation helm.

'Do it.' Sarpedon switched to the channels for Squads Krydel and Luko in the fighter's passenger compartment. 'We're coming down hard, sergeants.'

LUKO CHECKED THE restraints on his grav-couch, his hand dextrous in spite of the massive lightning claw gauntlets he wore. 'You heard the man,' he shouted to his men over the din of wreckage slamming off the fighter's hull. 'Buckle up.'

KARVIK AND SEVRAS'S fighter hit the ground too steeply, one wing catching in the frozen earth and flipping the fighter end over end. It came to rest upside-down within sight of the facility, spewing strange alien fuel onto the tundra.

Theirs was the first down, though not intentionally. Even as the craft was still slewing to a stop the first elements of Teturact's army were picking themselves from the fallen chunks of wreckage and piles of bodies, their flesh burned and frozen by the fall, bones broken, minds jelly. The will of their master demanded that they stand on broken legs and take up twisted shards of wreckage as weapons. Their master had shown them salvation, even holding back death itself – so what could they do but serve?

Their master, their god, demanded service in return for everything he had given them. There was no reason for them to resist as they shambled towards the fallen fighter and towards the landing spots of other silver craft now streaking towards the ground, nothing remaining in their ruined minds but the resonating order to kill.

SERGEANT LUKO'S RESTRAINTS only just held as the fighter slammed into the ground, the frozen surface scraping agonisingly against the hull, the alien entrails of the craft shaking loose under the impact. He was thrown around in his restraints until he thought his reinforced ribcage would collapse.

He knew how important this mission was, and that to die during it was a more honourable death than any of the billions of Imperial citizens could hope for – but he did not want to die like this, out of sight of the enemy, the victim of chance and gravity.

The howling stopped. In the moment of silence that followed Luko checked his autosenses and tested his muscle groups for injury. Bruises, strains: nothing he couldn't ignore.

'We're down,' came the vox from the bridge.

'Soul Drinkers, move out!' ordered Sergeant Krydel from the other side of the compartment. The metal of the hull flowed and peeled back from an iris that opened in the fighter's side. Freezing air flooded in.

Krydel was out of his restraints and already leading his Marines out. Luko snapped off his own restraints and the power fields of his lightning claws were alive before he hit the ground.

'Look lively, men, it's not a happy welcome!' he voxed as he saw the first enemies scrambling towards him. Bolter fire snapped and several of the living dead came apart.

Sergeant Krydel set off headlong to secure the fighter's landing site. Luko ran to the nearest cover – a gigantic fallen chunk of machinery – and sliced the first few corpses that crawled out of it to ribbons with his lightning claws.

Good. He was blooded. Now the real business could begin.

Debris was still falling. Some was recognisable, landing craft or jerry-built drop pods, more was just random chunks of the diseased flagship. Bodies were falling, too, and very few stayed lying down where they landed. Luko could see the facility, smaller than some of the fallen wreckage, a single-storey building pockmarked and scorched by small arms fire.

'Get me a fire point here! I want fire arcs covering the approach, Karraidin's coming in on our tail!' Luko's Marines scrambled onto the wreckage, forming a hard point where they could find cover and form a disciplined fire point to keep the approaches to the facility clear of enemies.

Luko glanced up and saw the sky dark as if a thunderstorm was brewing. A bright streak of light was another fighter coming in and dark specks were more of Teturact's army coming down.

The first wave was just a harrying force to keep the Soul Drinkers from getting dug in. What followed would be the real test. Vermin like this had killed Dreo, they said, a man Luko had served alongside as a brother and who he could not imagine dying. The heart of that corruption was above them, and Luko hoped that whether the Chapter succeeded or failed, they could do some damage to that heart.

Maybe even stop it from beating. But for the moment Luko had more immediate concerns.

'We're clear to thirty metres,' voxed Krydel over the chatter of bolter fire.'

'We've got you covered. Start the push on the facility,' replied Luko, barely flinching as a building-sized chunk of engine crashed to the ground nearby.

Luko glanced round to see Sarpedon emerging from the craft, moving swiftly on his eight legs, beheading a corpse-mutant that loped towards him without breaking his stride.

'Karraidin, we're down. What's your position?' Sarpedon was voxing. Then a scream and the descending silver dart of a fighter cut through the air overhead in answer, the craft banking sharply and looping down into a perfect short landing between Sarpedon's position and the facility.

Sarpedon hurried into cover beside Luko, snapping off shots with his bolt pistol as he went. 'Hold this position, sergeant,' said Sarpedon. 'Cover Krydel and Karraidin's force.'

'Where will you be, commander?'

'Everywhere. Same as the enemy.'

Luko nodded and clambered onto the smouldering wreckage where he could direct his squad's fire. Already, thick swarms of enemies were pouring from fallen landers, their numbers denuded by disciplined fire from Luko and Krydel. But there were so many of them…

And there would be more. It was raining corpses, and not one of them would stay dead for long.

EVEN FROM THE *Crescent Moon's* landing site the fallout was clearly visible, a dark torrent pouring onto the horizon like a storm of black rain. The blurred black smudge in the sky that was the enemy battleship was fragmenting even as Thaddeus watched, sections of the hull peeling away to reveal the ship's skeleton.

The cargo ramp of the *Crescent Moon* touched the ground and Colonel Vinn, in the lead APC, gave the order to roll out. The column of vehicles

– refitted Chimera transports with reinforced armour and overcharged engines, along with a couple of Sororitas Rhino APCs – roared out of the *Crescent Moon* and onto the surface of Stratix Luminae.

Thaddeus, from his Chimera towards the back of the column, looked out from the commander's hatch as the vehicle rolled down the ramp. The air was freezing and he was glad of the heavy blastcoat he wore – he could see his breath coiling in the air. Every planet, he had learned in his short Inquisitorial career, had its own smell, and Stratix Luminae smelled empty and secretive like an abandoned house. The colourless landscape of endless tundra seemed to hold something more than just desolation, as if something had happened long ago, or was sleeping beneath the surface, that resonated through the air and the barren earth.

'Rein in the front vehicles if you have to,' Thaddeus voxed to Colonel Vinn. 'I don't want us blundering into someone else's fire fight. Halt at the first contact and keep me posted.'

An acknowledgement signal was Vinn's only reply. He was a man of few words, perhaps because he knew that even if he survived he would probably be mind-wiped and unable to remember any conversations he had had.

Thaddeus ducked back down into the body of the Chimera, where the Pilgrim sat in the darkness, filling the passenger compartment with its aura of menace. Thaddeus would rather not have travelled with the creature but he didn't yet trust it to be out of his sight.

'We can kill them, inquisitor,' grated the Pilgrim. 'You know that, don't you? We are not just here to find them and report back. We are soldiers. We can kill them with our own hands.'

'I am not here for your revenge, Pilgrim,' said Thaddeus darkly. 'I have vowed to do my duty. I will bring the Soul Drinkers to justice but that doesn't mean I'm going to get this strikeforce destroyed in the attempt. If it takes me decades then I will wait.'

'There will not be another chance.'

'If I cannot finish it here then I will make another chance.' Thaddeus sat back in the juddering APC and checked the load in his autopistol. He had very few of his custom bullets left but if there was ever a time to use them it was on Stratix Luminae. If the Pilgrim was right then one of those fearsomely expensive shells would be enough to kill Sarpedon and behead his Chapter. If the Pilgrim was wrong, and Thaddeus had to admit it tended to be right, then just getting close enough to take the shot would be enough to get Thaddeus killed and end any hope of the Inquisition ending the threat.

'Vehicle on point reports small arms fire,' came a vox from Vinn.

'Any hostiles?'

'Not yet.'

Good. At least it seemed the strikeforce wouldn't be heading into a combined force of Teturact's followers and Sarpedon's Marines. Thaddeus suspected this would be the only good news he got that day.

KARRAIDIN'S POWER FIST ripped through two enemies, blasting their rotting bodies apart in showers of spoiled meat and bone. Bolters chattered and chewed through a dozen more as Sergeant Salk blew another apart. What had been a barren wasteland minutes before was rapidly turning into a landscape of twisted, blackened metal, stinking smoke billowing off the fallen wreckage, enemies clawing their way towards Karraidin's spearhead from every angle. Bodies fell from the sky, thudding into the ground, and more often than not something ragged and broken rose up to carry on fighting.

Salk couldn't even see the facility now, with towering engine stacks and hull segments embedded in the ground in front of him.

'Salk! We need to split the force, get through any way we can and rendezvous at the blast doors!' bellowed Karraidin, storm bolter blazing away at a knot of creatures that had once been Guardsmen, some still holding lasguns and combat knives.

Salk nodded and waved his Marines forward, Trooper Krin blasting into the shadows with his plasma gun and being rewarded with a shower of broken bodies illuminated by the plasma flash. Small arms fire – lasguns, autoguns, stub pistols – was spattering against the wreckage around them. Salk knew they had to keep moving or the sheer numbers now being thrown against them would trap them.

'After me! Krin, pick your targets and go for clusters!' Salk drew his chainsword and jogged forward, slashing at the emaciated faces that loomed through the wreckage and smoke. The fight was getting closer by the second, limbs reaching out for him, bolter fire spattering from behind him into anything that moved. A lasgun shot speared past his head and another burst against the ceramite of his chest armour – he stamped down on a corpse-soldier crawling in front of him and rammed his chainblade through the abdomen of another who fell gibbering down at him from above.

A plasma blast roared overhead and incinerated half a unit of enemies, dressed in the tatters of Naval Security uniforms, emerging from a crashed lander. They were more intact than most of the enemies Salk had faced so far, the cold hatred still legible on their faces, assault shotguns in their hands. Salk snapped off bolter shots at them then dropped into the cover of a hull section as shotgun fire ripped back at him, filling the air with a storm of shrapnel.

Bolter counter-fire tore back and Trooper Karrick dived into the fray, charging into the security troopers followed by the rest of the squad. Salk clambered to his feet and joined the melee, beheading one enemy and crushing the ribcage of another with the pommel of his chain-blade. Karrick, a tough veteran with more experience than Salk but who seemed to accept the younger man's authority without question, grabbed one trooper by the wrist and hurled him against the hull plate with enough force to break his back.

The surviving troopers tried to fall back but Squad Salk never left the front foot, and in a final volley of bolter shots the Naval Security unit lay shredded and smoking on the ground.

'Keep going,' voxed Salk. 'There'll be more.'

Salk led the way through the labyrinth of wreckage, heading towards where he knew the facility should be. He checked the squad icons – a couple of battle-brothers were wounded but it was nothing they couldn't fight through.

Salk got his first glimpse of the facility building and it was nearly his last. The single-storey building was swarming with enemy troopers of higher quality than the shambling corpses that had fallen so far. They were not resurrected dead but fanatic troopers, scores of them manning the fire points on the roof and clambering up the walls. They fired from behind the makeshift barricades still remaining from the assault ten years ago. Heavy bolter shells tore down from the roof and Salk ducked rapidly back into cover, hearing the too-familiar report of shells through ceramite as one of his brothers lost a limb to the large calibre fire tearing through the wreckage.

They had to get out. The first line of defences would be a safer place to fight from than here, but the squad had to get there first.

'Grenades!' called Salk and the Marines who could do so pulled frag grenades from their belt pouches. 'Krin, give us a covering shot!'

Plasma fire erupted over the closest barricade, white-hot liquid fire rippling over the barbed wire and into the trench behind. Several Marines hurled grenades a split-second afterwards, multiple reports adding to the plasma shot and throwing plumes of pulverised earth into the air.

'Now!' ordered Salk and led the charge, sprinting the few metres over the ruined barricade and into the same trench that Captain Korvax had taken from the eldar a decade earlier. This time it was not xenos but corrupted heretics the Soul Drinkers were fighting, still wearing the uniforms of their original units, Imperial Guard and PDF troopers, even private militia – Salk recognised the emerald uniform of Cartel Pollos before he cut the man wearing it in two. Teturact's army had come from

all over his empire, and doubtless every world he had visited had provided a tithe of armed worshippers to their master.

Karrick was at Salk's side in the trench, hauling an ex-Elysian
Guardsman towards him and cutting his throat with a combat knife.

Salk glanced down the trench and saw other Soul Drinkers doing
what they did better than almost any other force in the galaxy – close-
quarters battle, cold and fast, toe-to-toe with the enemy where they
were safer than anywhere else in the battle.

Salk checked the icons again – it was Brother Vaeryn they had left
behind, his life-icon flickering to show great blood loss and trauma.

'Vaeryn, come in,' voxed Salk.

'Lost a leg, sergeant,' came the crackly reply.

'Can you fight?'

'Fight but not move. I'll have to do my bit from here.'

'Fates be with you, brother.'

'The Emperor protects.'

Maybe they would be able to pick up the stricken Marine on their
way back out of the facility, but Salk doubted it.

Heavy bolter fire was still streaming down, throwing up chains of
explosions along the rear parapet of the trench. The sudden whine of
a heavy weapon and a bright orange explosion on the roof of the facility told Salk that his was not the only Soul Drinkers squad moving on
the facility. Salk took the brief respite in firing to look up over the
parapet at the facility – one corner was down but there was still a dual
heavy bolter mount facing them, along with the small arms fire streaking down from either end of the trench where heretics were trying to
win back their defences by firing blindly down from both corners.

A plasma shot ripped down the trench on cue and blew another
three men into the air at one end of the trench, Krin's shot freeing half
the squad to fire up at the remaining weapon mount. Bolter shots
spattered against the plasticrete of the building and a gunner's shattered body tumbled off the roof.

Salk led the charge over the rear of the trench and into the next,
vaulting over makeshift barricades to cut down the few cultists huddling for cover from the bolter fire. Salk could see the blast doors now,
through the web of tracer fire and the gauze of falling earth from the
explosions now bursting all around the facility.

The towering form of Karraidin appeared as the captain strode
towards the facility, storm bolter firing. Small arms shots bounced off
his thick armour as the Marines around him snapped off shots at the
roof, bringing down more and more shooters. Salk ran forward again
and his squad met Karraidin's in the shadow of the facility as the last

fire point was cracked open by a well-aimed frag grenade. Salk saw that Apothecary Pallas and Techmarine Lygris were with Karraidin's squad – Lygris, Salk remembered, had suffered severe wounds early in his career and now wore a near-expressionless mask of synthetic flesh instead of a face.

'Well met, brother,' said Karraidin with a grin creasing his battered features.

Salk drew his squad up in cover around the blast doors. 'I'll get grenades. We'll blow the door.'

Karraidin just walked up to the doors and, the power field around his gauntlet flickering to life, punched his power fist into the metal. Arcs of light spat as the field ripped through the metal and Karraidin tore great strips from the door until he had gouged a hole large enough for even him to walk through.

'Squad Graevus, where are you?' voxed Karraidin.

'Got tied down, we're on your heels. Solun's with us.'

Salk saw Squad Graevus heading through the wreckage of the defences, the white diamond of Graevus's power axe blade shining.

Karraidin switched to the vox for all the squads and specialists under his command. 'Spearhead, we've made the facility. We're going in.'

The captain ducked through the ragged hole and into the facility. Salk followed, chainsword drawn.

The first thing that hit him was the smell, a stench so awful that it almost made Salk reel. It would have been enough to drive back a normal man and even with a Marine's constitution Salk felt his additional organs and filters kicking in to prevent the stench from leaving him nauseous and dizzy.

His autosenses rapidly adjusted to the darkness. The first floor was the security station he remembered from Korvax's pict-recording, the shattered automated defences spilling metal entrails onto the floor, stark plasticrete construction pocked with bullet scars.

Where the cargo elevator had been there was now a solid metal slab with a security console nearby, blocking the way down.

'Can you get through it?' asked Salk.

Karraidin shook his head. 'It's wired. Probably to blow if it's tampered with. Get a techmarine up here.'

Lygris came to the fore and began to work with the security console. 'Time to see what Adept Aristeia taught us.'

Squad Graevus and Techmarine Solun were entering through the breach. Solun hurried up to help Lygris input the complex code that Aristeia had provided them with. Solun's mem-gear made quick work of the complicated algorithms that generated the entry code, but even

so there was a painful delay as the techmarines worked on the interface.

The few minutes were agonising. Cultist counter-attacks came to the
breach and were swept away by pin-sharp bolter fire from Squads Karraidin and Salk. Lasgun shots spattered in from ex-Guardsman cultists
and Salk drew his men up in front of the console to shield its delicate
working with their bodies from any stray shots. This could be it – Sarkia
Aristeia could have been mistaken or lying and everything would end
here, on this Emperor-forsaken snowball of a planet which had nothing to give them.

A Space Marine never gave in to despair, but in those moments Salk
felt the enormity of the task weighing on him – the Soul Drinkers were
finally free after thousands of years of servitude to the Imperium, and
now a tiny thing like Aristeia's memory would decide if they survived
to use that new freedom.

'Done. Stand back!'

A spiral crack appeared in the slab and slowly it opened, segments fanning open like an iris. Half the Marines pointed their
bolters into the growing hole in the floor as corroded motors
strained to open a hatch that had been sealed for ten years. A thin,
stinking fog coiled up from below and Karraidin held up a hand to
fend it off while his sensors adjusted. Salk glanced at his squad's
auspex to see what was beneath them, but there was just a mass of
static swirling. They knew it was a four metre drop into the floor
below, but that was it. There could be anything down there.

'Graevus, do you object to having the point?'

'It's what I'm here for,' replied Graevus. He hurried up to the opening
with his squad. It was absolutely pitch black inside.

'Cold and fast, we get in and we secure whatever we find. Karraidin,
get the specialists in afterwards, if there's anything in here I don't know
how long we can hold it off. Squad, move!'

Graevus holstered his bolt pistol to hold his axe two-handed, then
dropped into the hole. His assault squad followed him rapidly, each
man dropping into the unknown with weapons drawn.

'Damnation!' came a vox almost immediately, half-scrambled by
interference but definitely Graevus's voice. 'What is… Get down here,
everyone, I can't…'

Static howled over the vox. Without pausing Salk jumped in after the
squad, knowing that his squad would be right behind him.

He landed on something hot and soft, squirming and undulating
beneath him. Something twisted past his face and his autosenses
picked out a tentacle, as thick as a Marine's waist, squeezing the life out

of one of Graevus's Assault Marines before cramming the remains into a giant circular maw big enough to swallow a tank. Yelled orders and cries of pain were everywhere, along with the roaring of something inhuman that seemed to be coming from everywhere at once.

Salk's squad were dropping in all around him. He flicked the selector on his bolt pistol to full auto and dived into the fray.

SARKIA ARISTEIA GULPED *down the pure, freezing air, trying to get the stink of mutation and burning flesh out of her lungs. She stumbled from the open blast doors and fell to the ground, grazing her palms on the frozen earth. It was ruination outside the facility, with the tech-guard defences reduced to rubble and heaps of pulverised earth. Barbed wire was wrapped around broken bodies of men and eldar. Corpses lay everywhere, their blood already freezing hard – Sarkia even saw the armoured form of a fallen Marine. Plumes of smoke rose from craters and, as Sarkia looked up at Stratix Luminae's pale blank sky, she saw the twirling contrails of the Soul Drinkers Thunderhawks as they returned to their ship in orbit. She had seen them fight, and by the Omnissiah they were awesome, a head taller than the tallest normal man, fast and ruthless, deadeye shots and ferocious in hand-to-hand. Truth be told they had scared her more than the quick, skilful eldar. She supposed that the Soul Drinkers had saved her life from the alien menace, but it was a hollow feeling.*

The Marines hadn't bothered with the survivors. An Adeptus Mechanicus ship would probably come, carrying adepts that would use Sarkia and the other survivors to seal the facility and label it Interdictus. The work they were doing there had been revolutionary, even Sarkia knew it. But it had been dangerous, and even if the eldar raid had been a coincidence (it couldn't be, the aliens had to have known what they were doing here and come to stop or steal it) the mutagenics could easily have got out of hand. Now the containment around the primary samples had been breached – Sarkia might be killed and incinerated to prevent contamination, or she might be interrogated until she gave up what little she knew about the program in an investigation into possible corruption or incompetence. It all depended on the unknowable logic of the Archmagus in charge.

Something stirred in the entrance, moving out of the shadows. Another survivor? A few tech-guard and adepts had survived, Sarkia was sure she had seen old Karlu Grien hobbling out of the wreckage below. But no… it was a survivor, perhaps, but not one she wanted to see.

It was naked, humanoid but not human. It was so emaciated it couldn't possibly be alive – pallid skin stretched taut over a vestigial ribcage and a stringy abdomen. Its limbs were too long and it had too many fingers and toes, which had too many joints apiece. It looked too weak to stand but it strode confidently out of the blast doors and into the light. Its face was no face but a knot of hanging skin, with a pair of stern triangular eyes that glowed faintly. It looked at her, once, and Sarkia could feel the menace, like a lasgun beam right into her soul, burning those eyes and that nonexistent face into her mind forever.

It looked at her like she looked at cells under a microscope. In that moment she knew what it was – one of the experiments from the lowest level, perhaps a success, perhaps a failure. The adepts had been trying to unlock the human genetic pattern so they could halt, reverse, or create mutations at will – this was one of the things they had made. By the way it moved without enough musculature to support itself, Sarkia presumed that it was one of the psychic creations she had heard rumoured darkly by the menial staff.

A wave of revulsion rolled over her and she scrambled away into a half-collapsed trench as the creature walked by, forgetting her as it looked out over the remnants of the defences and the gory relics of the battle. She could feel its hatred and corruption, she could feel her very soul becoming filthy with its presence. She fought the urge to vomit, to grab sharp chunks of frozen soil and scrape herself bloodily clean.

She tried to tear her eyes away but couldn't, as the creature lifted off the ground and shot towards the sky, leaving behind an invisible but powerful stain of hatred and corruption that Sarkia Aristeia would never be able to wash off.

HE WAS BORED *by this world, where the sum of living things wasn't even worth the effort of killing. Filled with the hatred of life that was hard-wired into a soul that should never have been born, Teturact looked up at the darkening evening sky, took hold of his feeble body with his awesome mind, and flung himself up towards the heavens.*

He could feel life out there. And life meant death, and death meant power, and power was the closest thing in the universe to the sacred. For Teturact had known, since the moment he had been born in a test tube crammed with mutating clone-cells, that he was a god, with a god's power and a god's ambition. Now he just had to let his worshippers know they had to worship him, and as he plunged through the vacuum towards the teeming life-light of Stratix, he knew exactly how to make them kneel.

THE HELL WAS lighting up the sky. The psychic circuit raged around Sarpedon's body, cold fire against his skin, and he felt as if his blood would boil trapped inside his armour. He poured every last drop of his willpower into the Hell, the unique power that had brought him into the fold as Chapter Librarian a lifetime ago. The same power was now drawing stern spectres of order and justice in the sky, throwing down lightning bolts of purity at the hordes pouring from crashed landers and fallen piles of bodies. The nalwood force staff was hot in his hand and Sarpedon had to force back the Hell, rein it in before it demanded all his focus and blocked his capability to lead his Marines.

He let the psychic fire die down to a bearable level and clambered up onto the pile of wreckage he was using for cover, climbing to a vantage point where he could get some overview of the battlefield. A short distance away Squad Dyon was taking ranging shots at distant groups of enemies, and nearby Librarian Gresk was leading the prayers of Corvan's assault squad as they prepared for the counter-attack they would soon drive into the heart of the enemy. Sarpedon looked out over the battlefield at the force his Marines were facing and though he did not accept despair, he got some idea of the sheer scale of the fight to come.

Traitorous Guardsmen jumped from Valkyrie transports so twisted with corruption that they looked like huge flying beasts. Shambling dead groped their way from drifts of broken bodies and were whipped into advancing waves by cadaverous taskmasters. The sky was thick with falling debris, and Sarpedon knew the force had already lost Marines to the wreckage dropping from orbit. He could not begin to estimate the numbers of Teturact's army. He knew that a battleship could hold upwards of twenty thousand crew, but there was no telling how many cultists and living dead could be crammed into the same space.

The Hell was throwing some of the enemy back, forcing the still-sentient troops of Teturact's horde to falter as they charged. But the dead and the fanatics kept coming, and with each passing moment a hundred more emerged, formed huge bloodthirsty mobs, and advanced.

The Soul Drinkers were drawn up in a rough defensive circle around the facility. The barren tundra had become a landscape of broken metal and dead bodies, where the Soul Drinkers' superior firepower mattered less than brutal close combat. Several squads were already fighting hard within the position, hunting down and crushing the pockets of attackers that fell close to the facility, and already there were tales of brutality and bravery being written in the bloodstained maze of wreckage.

Sarpedon held the front and Iktinos the rear, and it was from the far side of the facility that Sarpedon could see the flashes of psychic fire from the Librarian Tyrendian. Two fighters were still airborne and functioning as a mobile reserve, but Sarpedon knew they could not stay in the air much longer. All he could see of Sevras and Karvik's fighter was a pall of smoke hundreds of metres away. If anyone had survived, they would have to fend for themselves.

Sarpedon dropped back down to the ground as the first lasgun shots from the advancing horde spanged off the twisted metal around him.

'Range?' he asked of the closest sergeant, Dyon.

'Give the word and we can give them a counter-volley.'

'Let them get closer. I want rapid fire, we need to thin them out, not scare them.'

'Understood.'

The vox crackled with gunfire. 'Commander!' came Chaplain Iktinos's voice. 'The heathens have assaulted with armour. We are engaging.'

Iktinos was cut off before Sarpedon could reply, the sky past the facility flashing scarlet with Tyrendian's psychic lightning.

Sergeant Luko's voice came over the vox a second later. 'Tellos is counter-attacking, sir. We can't hold him back, we're advancing to give his men covering fire.'

'Do it, Luko. Just don't get cut off, they're coming in everywhere.'

'Understood.'

So battle was joined. Sarpedon knew the Hell would be little use against the mindless hordes at the forefront of the attack. He let the psychic circuit die down to a faint dull glow against his skin and holstered the force staff on his back.

'Dyon, bring your men forward and engage. We'll throw them against the men behind them. Pass the order on, give me solid rapid fire and cover the assault squads.'

Dyon ran forward through the growing storm of las-fire, his Marines snapping bolter shots off at the hordes that were even now breaking into a run as they began to charge.

Sarpedon followed, cycling through the vox-traffic, ready to intervene when a flashpoint erupted. He could feel the psychic feedback like a million buzzing insects as Gresk started to quicken the reactions and thought speed of the Marines around him and Tyrendian continued to fling mental artillery at the forces charging the rear of the facility.

This was where the future of the Soul Drinkers would be won or lost. He checked the magazine in his bolter, and drew the Soulspear.

TETURACT'S SHIP WAS a ragged skeleton around him, sheets of hull flapping uselessly like torn skin, the inner decks exposed like the cells of a beehive, bleeding the living dead into the upper atmosphere. The ship was shedding its last few scales, and Teturact willed his wizards down to the surface one by one where they could direct the battle and lend the power of their minds to the vastness of his horde.

There was a sudden flare of power far below, right in the heart of the growing battle. It coincided with a flare of hatred and grim determination as the two sides met, tinged with a delectable joy as someone who loved bloodshed charged into the fray. But the flare of power remained, hard and bright, something old and powerful and tinted by the taste of humanity. A relic, a weapon, the presence of which suggested that someone down there could be powerful enough to put a dent in Teturact's glorious army.

That could not be allowed. And furthermore, it was in itself a disadvantage. Because Teturact could see it, a bright black light on the surface of Stratix Luminae, and if he could see it then he could deal with it personally.

His brute-mutants, drifting aimlessly since the ship's gravity had given way, were drawn to him to act as bearers once more. They lifted Teturact's wizened body onto their broad shoulders and with a thought he willed them downwards, through the disintegrating body of the ship, and into the upper atmosphere of the planet.

The freezing, thin air whipped around him as he descended, extinguishing the fear flickering in the bovine minds of his brute-mutants. His senses flowed out and he saw the tiny force, just a few hundred Marines, surrounded by the legions of his loyal worshippers. Where the two forces met combat blazed and the hot, spicy taste of lives lost flooded the wreckage of the battlefield. The Marines could fight, but the fire of that combat would eventually consume them. With the wizards even now landing amongst their flock, Teturact had more than enough raw manpower to make it happen.

The hard nugget of raw power shone directly beneath him. Teturact smiled, if it could be called a smile, and plummeted downwards.

CHAPTER TWELVE

MUTATION HAD RUN unchecked through the stores of sample tissue for ten years. The lower basement had been full of refrigeration units containing sheets of cultured skin and cylindrical slabs of artificial muscle and, when containment broke down the unleashed half-humans absorbed it all. Now there was barely any difference between the individual organisms – several had joined into huge gestalt creatures and, aside from the strongest who had left them so long ago, they thought with one mind.

They had been starving for some time. Now, they were hungry. In the lab floor just below the surface, many were loose, and at last they had some new game on which to prey.

Sergeant Salk hacked down with his chainsword and severed a long, articulated tentacle-limb as it tried to wrap itself around Techmarine Solun's throat. The beast reared up twice as tall as a Marine, its head a writhing knot of tendrils surrounding a round muscular lamprey's mouth, its body a pulsating column of oozing muscle. Its head touched the low vaulted roof of the dark, nightmarish laboratory before it bellowed and crashed down on the spot where Solun had lain a moment before.

Salk dragged the techmarine aside just in time. Both Solun's legs were gone, chewed off by the same beast that had swallowed half of Salk's squad. The beast thundered in rage as it lumbered forward – Salk jabbed at the gaping maw and stabbing tentacles, keeping the thing at bay as Solun tried to fend off the claws of its lower limbs.

The lab floor was a nightmare. The vaulted ceiling was crusted and discoloured. Banks of corroded machinery and shorted-out command consoles provided scores of hiding places for mutant creatures and obstacles for the Marines. Bolter shells were zipping across the room and globs of brackish mutant blood spattered from gunshot wounds and chainblades. Salk's own chainblade was so clotted with gore that its motor whined and smoked angrily. The lights were out and the gauze of filth and corruption that lay over everything cut down the visibility like fog, so that all Salk could see were huge mutant forms looming all around and glimpses of his battle-brothers in muzzle flashes and the detonations of grenades. The din was terrible, gunfire and bestial howls, the crack of fractured ceramite and the cries of the dying.

It was all but impossible to keep cohesive. The vox was distorted and near-useless. Salk's own squad was scattered, many of them dead, others wounded. Brother Karrick would be lucky to keep the arm that had been mangled by something unspeakable that struck from above. Salk knew that any of them would be lucky to get out alive.

There was a flash of white armour and Apothecary Pallas was diving onto the beast from behind, punching his carnifex gauntlet through the mutant's hide. The array of chemical vials emptied through the gauntlet's injector spike and a black stain of necrotic tissue spread. The huge mutant convulsed, forcing Pallas to hold on to avoid being thrown across the room. Salk ducked forward and drove his chainblade into the mutant's head, again and again, feeling the weapon's motor straining under the weight of tissue clotted around its teeth.

The beast stopped thrashing. Pallas rolled off it and landed beside Solun, the white sections of his armour now dark and slick with corrupted blood.

'Thank you, brother,' gasped Salk.

'Don't thank me yet,' replied Pallas. 'We still have to get onto the containment level. That's where the samples will be kept.'

'Where's Karraidin?'

'Down. He and his squad are making a stand but they're trapped. Graevus is holding the way down but he can't make it without help. Lygris is with them, trying to get the blast doors open.' Pallas used one of his few remaining vials to inject Solun with powerful painkillers and coagulants, restricting the blood flow to his ruined legs.

'I'll take what men I can and help out Graevus,' said Salk. He looked down at Solun.

'I'll do what I can here,' replied Pallas.

'They'll need you down there,' said Solun, his voice weakening. 'There isn't much you can do for me, Pallas.'

'I can stabilise you so we can pick you up on the way out. We need you alive.'

'Good luck, brothers,' said Salk, knocking the worst of the gore off his chainblade before heading into the foetid gloom to gather the remains of his squad.

'Wait!' said Solun. 'What... what's yours?'

'My what?'

'Your mutation. We are all changing, that's why we are here.'

Salk thought for a second. To tell the truth he had been ignoring it. Pretending to himself that it wasn't real. 'Karendin says it's metabolic. My body chemistry is changing. I don't know the details.'

'And it's getting worse?' Solun was going into shock and his voice was faltering.

'Yes, brother. It is.'

'So is mine. It's my memory, you see. I can... remember things. I'm starting to remember things that I never learned. Ever since the Galactarium... please, we have to finish this. Even if we die trying, we can't turn into one of these creatures.'

'Don't speak, Solun,' said Pallas. 'Drop into half-trance, you're in shock.' He looked up at Salk – his face was streaked with mutant blood. 'Get to Graevus. Don't wait for me, I'll make it if I can.'

Salk nodded once and sprinted into the gloom, the deformed monstrosities of Stratix Luminae closing in from the darkness around him, and the secret of survival somewhere below.

THADDEUS HIT THE floor of the Chimera APC as it roared over piles of wreckage, storm trooper driver grinding the gears as the vehicle almost overturned trying to scale the unexpected obstacle.

'Tanks are ruptured,' said the driver from up front. 'Bail out!'

The rear hatch swung down and Thaddeus jumped out, followed by the Pilgrim, who showed agility beyond his ragged appearance as he scuttled down the wreckage to ground level.

Towering twisted piles of wreckage had turned the barren tundra into a maze. The sound of battle came from all directions: hellguns and bolters, the booming amplified voices of cultist taskmasters, storm trooper sergeants yelling orders. A couple of storm trooper squads were nearby trying to clear out a cordon to mount another push – the vehicle column had broken up completely, the APCs rendered all but useless by the rapidly changing, lethal environment.

Thaddeus snapped off a couple of autopistol shots, knocking down a couple of cultists who had taken up a firing position high up in the closest wreckage. He saw as they fell that they were Guardsmen, damned souls whose will had proven too weak and who had been corrupted into the service of Teturact. This was the worst kind of evil, the kind that took dutiful Imperial citizens and turned them into the tools of Chaos.

'Sister! Colonel! What's our situation?'

The vox was a mess of warped static. Sister Aescarion's voice came through first. 'We're not going to be able to break through here, inquisitor. We're facing some kind of... moral threat. Heresy and daemonology.'

'Sarpedon?'

'I think not. Witches, inquisitor. We have lost many already.'

'Fight on, Sister, I will see if there is another way.'

Thaddeus couldn't raise Colonel Vinn at all. The storm troopers were moving forward, battering their way towards the facility with volleys of hellgun fire, but they could not move fast enough to keep from being surrounded. Thaddeus recognised the advancing hordes from the battlefield reports that had come in from all over the warzone – vastly superior numbers, most of whom were barely sentient and so felt no pain or despair, who could be defeated only by killing them all. The same armies that had carved out Teturact's empire were here on Stratix Luminae, and they wouldn't be any easier to kill.

Thaddeus and Pilgrim ducked into cover as lasgun fire spattered towards them from ex-Guardsmen traitors duelling with the closest storm troopers.

'Do not feel sympathy for the Soul Drinkers,' said the Pilgrim, as if reading Thaddeus's mind. 'Evil will always fight with itself. Just because Sarpedon battles this same corruption does not mean he is our ally.'

Thaddeus looked over the twisted hull fragment he was using as cover. He saw heretics crouched in the wreckage, swapping fire with the storm troopers – hellgun blasts took off heads and ripped torsos apart but there were just too many of them.

'We cannot make it as one,' Thaddeus said.

'The strikeforce was never anything more than a decoy,' replied the Pilgrim. 'Though you may be loathe to admit it, it was only us who could face Sarpedon. Let them fight, it takes the eyes of our enemies away from us.'

Thaddeus looked at the Pilgrim, its hooded face as sinister as ever, its grinding voice like a warning in his head. 'Not without Aescarion.'

'Teturact's witches are here. There is much power in them, I can taste it. If Aescarion is facing them then she is lost. We are the only hope.'

Thaddeus gripped his autopistol tight, sweating in spite of the freezing cold of Stratix Luminae. Aescarion was as loyal a Sister as he could hope to have on his side, and the storm troopers were some of the best-trained troops the Ordo Hereticus could field. But men like Kolgo had taught Thaddeus that even loyal citizens like these were secondary to the ulti-mate goal of doing the Emperor's will. If they had known, they would have understood.

'Agreed,' said Thaddeus. 'We two can slip by when a hundred are halted. Lead the way, Pilgrim.'

The inquisitor and the Pilgrim moved quickly towards the facility, always keeping the wreckage between them and the concentrations of enemy troops, leaving the strikeforce to draw away the enemy while they searched for their true quarry.

Whatever Sarpedon wanted, it was in the facility. And that was where Thaddeus would find him.

PERHAPS KARRAIDIN WAS dead. Perhaps Solun was, too, trapped and all but helpless on the floor above. It didn't matter. What mattered was that the future was below them, trapped in the festering heart of an evil that had grown unchecked for a decade. Salk still lived, along with a handful of his squad. Graevus and many of his Assault Marines, too, along with Techmarine Lygris and Apothecary Pallas. It would have to be enough, because they had one chance and this was it.

Techmarine Lygris, covered by the bolters of his brothers crammed into the corridor behind him, had opened the control panel of the blast doors and was rewiring the security circuits. The data-slate showing the scrawl-ings from Karlu Grien's cell was his guide – the diagram was the most secret thing the mad adept had known, the key to the blast doors fitted to the containment floors after the facility had been hurriedly sealed.

A fountain of sparks burst from the door controls and the doors jud-dered open, smoke pumping from the corroded servos.

'Cover!' yelled Graevus and the bolt pistols of his squad were levelled at the opening doors as Lygris scrambled back and drew his own pistol.

Salk watched as he prepared to enter the place that had almost killed Captain Korvax ten years before.

The floor of the facility's second underground level was gone, eaten away as if by acid, a ragged ring of blackened metal all that remained. In the centre, where it would have been bisected by the floor, was sus-pended a huge sphere, corpulent and rotting, seething flesh pulsing between the rusting metal plates. It hung from the ceiling by a web of raw tendons and rained a steady shower of filth down into the lowest level below.

It was there, at the deepest point of the facility, that the containment had failed and where the worst of the corruption waited. The released mutagens had knitted the raw tissue into a thick pulsing mantle of flesh that lay over everything like a blanket, rippling like water, boils as tall as a man spurting hot pus like geysers, the remains of hulking biocontainment units like islands surrounded by bleeding scabs and writhing proto-limbs.

In the centre, breaking the surface of a small lake of brackish blood rained down by the sphere above, was a structure that Salk guessed was a control room or tech-shrine. Thick cables snaked away from it, and the windows now clouded with corrosion would once have looked out across the whole containment floor.

The Soul Drinkers looked down on the scene from a thin ledge of crumbling metal that clung to the wall just beyond the exit of the corridor leading to the floor above. The sounds of battle coming from the lab floor made it clear that they couldn't stay there – they could be trapped and butchered by the mutated beasts charging down the corridor from above.

Salk glanced across at Graevus. The veteran's power axe, clutched in his huge mutated hand, still fizzed and crackled as its power field burned off the blood crusted on its blade.

'One way,' said Graevus simply.

'Agreed,' said Salk. 'Lygris?'

Lygris nodded. 'You need me down there.'

'Pallas,' said Graevus, 'you stay here. Someone has to get to the surface if we don't make it. Get Sarpedon to evacuate the force as best he can if we can't find anything or get back up. Whatever happens, we'll need you to fix us afterwards.'

'Just make sure there's enough left of you to patch up,' replied Pallas.

Graevus smiled, hefted his power axe in both hands, and jumped.

SARPEDON SAW THE dark star as it fell, a weeping open eye that bled malice as it plummeted down from the sky. It warped everything around it – with sight alone Sarpedon could tell it was something of terrible power.

But his mind confirmed it. Sarpedon was a telepath who could transmit but normally not receive – but even so he was receptive enough for the new arrival's sheer malevolence to burn itself into his mind. He felt filthy, as if some physical corruption were washing over him, and his mutated genes seemed to squirm inside him as if trying to escape. He heard screams as the traitor horde surrounding the facility keened in worship or despair, or perhaps both. The sky was turning dark and for a moment everything seemed to tilt as reality itself buckled under the strain of containing such a power.

The falling object landed a few hundred metres away in an explosion of shattered metal and earth. The Soul Drinkers firebases were holding well against the advancing masses of enemies, except where Tellos to the front and Iktinos to the back were embroiled in brutal swirling hand-to-hand combat. This would turn the tide, Sarpedon had no doubt – the leader of the horde had decided to take a personal hand in the battle. Sarpedon hurried through the closest cover, where several Marines had taken up firing positions. He didn't know which squad they were from – organisation was breaking down and officers were in charge of whichever Marines were in earshot.

'We need to put together an assault force,' he called to the nearest Marine. 'Round up as many brothers as you can and…'

The Marine turned to speak just as his head snapped to the side and a ragged hole appeared in his temple. A report sounded over the din, the sharp crack of an autopistol. Sarpedon ducked into cover as more pin-point shots rang out, one punching through the chitinous armour of his leg, another zipping past his head far too close. He saw the attackers closing in from behind. There were two of them, one a hooded, hunched figure prowling forward like an animal, the other an unaugmented man in a long blastcoat with a heavily modified autopistol in one hand.

Sarpedon brought out the Soulspear and it responded to his grip, his genetic signature unlocking its pre-Imperial technology and sending twin blade-shaped vortex fields out from either end. The Soulspear had served him well so far in this battle, but these new enemies were no traitors or mutants.

With sudden, shocking speed the cowled figure leapt forward, great strength propelling it as it pounced. Sarpedon slashed with the Soulspear but the cowled monster was too quick, ducking beneath the vortex blade and batting aside the front legs that Sarpedon jabbed up to fend it off.

Sarpedon was thrown back onto a mass of wreckage, the foul-smelling creature pinning him down with strength that Sarpedon had only witnessed in a fellow Space Marine. The arm that held the Soulspear was pinned – he reached round with his free left hand and tried to grab the attacker by the throat but it lunged back and drove an elbow into Sarpedon's face. His mouth filled with blood and he spat out a tooth bitterly, reaching out with two legs to get some purchase on the wreckage. He dug his talons into the torn metal and hauled himself over, rolling to the side and using the momentum to push the attacker off him. He grabbed a handful of the rags that covered it, and pulled.

The cowl tore away, and Sarpedon saw his attacker's face. Its skin was dead and pale blue-grey, red-raw where thick cables snaked into interfaces in the scalp. Its eyes were pure black. Its nose, mouth and throat were gone, replaced with brass-cased augmetics, metallic gills that fanned open and closed as it breathed and thick cylindrical filtration units where its throat should have been.

Sarpedon recognised that hate-filled expression, eyes burst black from the sudden pressure drop, twisted with loathing for the betrayal it felt. 'Greetings, Michairas,' said Sarpedon, and cracked a vicious head butt into his enemy's face.

Sarpedon had killed Brother Michairas once before during the Chapter war. When many of the Soul Drinkers had rebelled against Sarpedon's ascension to the post of Chapter Master, Michairas had been one of their leaders. He had been a young but excellent warrior, novice to Commander Caeon, and had even participated in the rites that followed victory on the Lakonia space fort. When Sarpedon had tracked Michairas down on the strike cruiser, he had torn out his rebreather implants, throttled the life out of him and hurled him out of an airlock. Those hate-filled eyes had stared at him from through the porthole even as they filled up with blood and turned black.

Sarpedon had a moment to admire Michairas's toughness and resourcefulness. He had no idea how the Marine had survived – perhaps the damage done to his rebreathers hadn't been enough and he had somehow managed to get his helmet on and drift until picked up. Probably he had clawed his way back on board the strike cruiser and stolen a saviour pod. It didn't really matter – it must have taken massive strength of will to not only survive, but set out on a path of revenge that had brought him to Stratix Luminae.

The blade of the Soulspear hummed through the air and Michairas ducked it as Sarpedon knew he would – he stabbed deep into Michairas's shoulder with his front leg and felt the talon slide through muscle, bone and augmetics.

But Michairas didn't feel the pain. He probably couldn't feel anything any more, with so many of his organs replaced with augmentics and bionics. Instead he grabbed hold of the leg embedded in his shoulder and used its leverage to throw Sarpedon clear over his shoulder, slamming him into the rock-hard earth.

Michairas leapt onto Sarpedon like a predator, fingers reaching out to gouge at Sarpedon's eyes. It was only when his limbs suddenly refused to obey him that he realised the blade of the Soulspear was stabbing through his stomach, shearing through his spine. Sarpedon kicked him off to roll onto the ground beside him, withdrawing the vortex blade of the Soulspear.

'The Soul Drinkers you knew are gone,' Sarpedon said grimly. 'That Chapter dies with you.'

The black eyes were still staring at him when the Soulspear sliced Michairas's head off. Augmetics shorted as the headless body fell back, bionics sparking and cables spewing black conductor fluid.

Sarpedon turned to the second attacker, the normal man who had hung back while Michairas attacked. Wordlessly, the man took aim and fired. The bullet hummed like an insect as it whipped through the air – Sarpedon ducked it but he could hear it as it zipped back towards him. A guided round, rare and lethal.

Sarpedon's wrist flicked and the Soulspear cut the bullet in half in mid-flight.

The man lowered his weapon.

'Inquisition?' asked Sarpedon, the Soulspear still alive and thrumming in his hand.

'Yes. Ordo Hereticus, sent to kill you.'

'Are you going to stand there wasting bullets on me, or are you going to fight an enemy worth fighting?'

The inquisitor stared at Sarpedon and paused for what seemed like forever. Sarpedon could see the tendons in his hand and neck tensing as he prepared for the next move – to attack or flee, to demand Sarpedon's surrender or to negotiate for his own safety.

Before the inquisitor could act a shockwave tore across the battlefield, tearing from the traitor leader's landing site through the wreckage and barricades. Sarpedon turned and saw showers of earth and shattered metal fountaining as something powerful and fast hurtled straight towards him, carving a furrow through the battlefield, throwing traitors and Marines alike into the air as it passed.

Sarpedon dived to one side as a wall of flying debris ripped over him, covering his legs with deep slash marks down to the muscle and knocking the inquisitor flying. Sarpedon hit the ground hard and rolled quickly, planting his leg under him to spring up and face whatever new monstrosity had sent itself against the Soul Drinkers.

Metal and soil fell like rain. In the centre of the destruction, in a zone of calm like the eye of a hurricane, was Teturact.

No descriptions existed of Teturact but Sarpedon knew straight away who he was facing. Sarpedon could feel his augmented organs straining to keep diseases from erupting throughout his body at the enemy's mere presence. Strange sounds rolled just beneath his range of hearing, the taste of rank blood filled his mouth. His autosenses could barely contain the sight in front of him.

Teturact was a thin, wizened humanoid form perched like a malevolent carrion bird on the shoulders of four immense, brawny brute-mutants. The faces of the mutants were swamped with muscle until their features hardly showed, and their trunk-like arms ended in fists as large as a man's torso. Teturact probably couldn't walk on his own, but even in that deformed, dried-out body Sarpedon could taste the vastness of Teturact's mind and the immense power it could bring to bear.

Teturact reached out and Sarpedon was held in a psychic vice that reached through his armour and began to crush his solid bone ribcage as it hauled him high into the air. A white wall of pain crushed inwards as he struggled against bonds that only existed in Teturact's mind. The battlefield whirled underneath him and Sarpedon could see the facility, the isolated pockets of Soul Drinkers holding back the tide, the vast swarms of traitors wading through the volleys of bolter fire and the piles of their own dead. He saw the snarled knots of slaughter where Tellos and Iktinos were engaged in savage hand-to-hand fighting on opposite sides of the battlefield. He could even pick out, through a whitening gauze of agony, the battle on the edge of his vision where black-armoured Sisters and Hereticus storm troopers were fighting tides of zombies and wizards whose corrupt magic Sarpedon could taste.

Sarpedon's ribcage fractured. A warm wave rode through him as internal organs ruptured and his insides were flooded with blood. He tried to reach through Teturact's grip deep into his own mind, to dredge out the power of the Hell that might distract Teturact long enough for Sarpedon to strike back. But Teturact was powerful, more powerful than anything Sarpedon had felt before, a vessel of pure hatred and corruption focused through an utterly malevolent mind.

With a flick of his will, Teturact threw Sarpedon down to the ground. Somehow, Sarpedon forced his legs underneath him and spread them enough to cushion his landing, otherwise his armour would have been cracked clean open by the impact. As it was he felt the muscles tearing in their armour of chitin and his single bionic leg shorted out with a flash of pain.

Teturact lifted him up again, legs dangling uselessly, and brought Sarpedon through the air towards him. Sarpedon saw Teturact's ruin of a face, flaps of ragged skin for features, weeping raw pits for eyes.

'You are different,' said Teturact's voice in Sarpedon's head, thick and treacly, like acid corroding his brain. 'My worshippers have faced the Astartes many times, but they tasted pure and misguided. You are tainted. You are like I once was, a man flawed down to the genes. Ah, but I took those flaws and made them my reason for being. You are afraid of them, however. You want to turn yourself back. How can you turn back when you are already so much more than a man?'

Teturact drew Sarpedon closer. It felt like his mind was on fire.

'If you could only see what is possible when your own body is no longer a prison, then you would really know what freedom is. That is what you want, isn't it, flawed man? To be free? Yet you search to rebuild the prisons of your flesh.'

Sarpedon knew he couldn't take Teturact on, not when the vast fortress of the mutant's mind stood before him and Sarpedon himself was, ultimately, little more than a man. But Sarpedon could taste somewhere in Teturact a single weakness, the same weakness that was killing the Imperium and which the Soul Drinkers themselves had possessed until Sarpedon had shown them the way out.

It was arrogance. Teturact believed he was a god, and his victims were worshippers. When he looked at the Soul Drinkers he saw more fodder for his worship, strong and skilled men but men nonetheless. Sarpedon was not much more than a man but he was more, and what set him apart was the strength of will that had seen him fight against his Chapter and his Imperium, accepting the hatred of the universe in return for a fleeting taste of freedom.

A white stab of psychic power was driving forth from Teturact's mind, boring into Sarpedon's own mind the same way it had done to untold billions of desperate plague victims, to plant in him the seeds of worship and bind him to Teturact's will. Sarpedon let him in, pulling back his psychic defences just enough to let Teturact think he was winning.

Cold horror washed through Sarpedon. He could feel the exultation of a god and the billions of minds united in worship. He could see a universe where stars were weeping sores and planets teemed with life like spores of a disease, all singing the name of Teturact. He could feel the Imperium he hated crushed beneath the weight of worship, the minds of its citizens liberated even as their bodies decayed and the armies of the Emperor died in their trillions...

Sarpedon opened his eyes. He could swear he detected rapture in that near-featureless face, the face of a god being fed the worship he craved.

With a strength he didn't know he had, Sarpedon snapped his mind away from Teturact, the images of glorious decay receding with impossible speed and leaving him dazed and near-blind with the effort. But Teturact was stunned, too, his mind losing its grip on Sarpedon and dropping him to the ground. Sarpedon landed hard on his back, exhaust gases hissing from the fractured power plant in his armour's backpack.

He fumbled with numb fingers for his boltgun. His hands shook as he brought it to bear on the indistinct shapes towering over him, and his trigger finger spasmed as he willed it to pull down on the trigger.

Half a magazine of bolts sprayed out. Every one ricocheted off an invisible shield of will, space warping where they hit.

The brute-mutants leaned down and Teturact leaned with them, his spindly form tottering directly over Sarpedon.

Traitor! it screeched into his head. *I am a god, you are vermin! Vermin! And you deny me, believer of nothing? I will give you something to believe!*

A red spear of psychic hatred shot down and held Sarpedon to the ground like an insect pinned to a board. Spite poured into him, hot and livid, the rage of a god denied. Just once it had been denied, once in its lifetime, and its response was to annihilate the mind that denied it in a tide of hatred.

Sarpedon was strong, stronger than a man, stronger than even any Marine. That meant he would survive a split second more before his mind gave way and his body became just another shell in service of Teturact the God. The last thing he would see would be the ruined mutant face, those bleeding eye-holes narrowed in hate. It gave him a strange satisfaction, in those last moments, that he could force even that unreadable face to give away its emotions.

'In the name of the Immortal Emperor,' cried a voice from nowhere, 'I dub thee Hereticus!'

A shower of blood and flesh was the head of a brute-mutant disintegrating. A falling shadow was the mutant's body falling and the spindly shape above it was Teturact falling with it, wizened limbs flailing.

Sarpedon forced himself to roll through the pain as Teturact and his mutant bearers fell to the hard earth around him.

INQUISITOR THADDEUS FELT the kick of the autopistol in his hand and was grateful that he could feel anything at all. He had been frozen in place as Teturact had seemed about to tear Sarpedon apart with psychic power, but whatever Sarpedon had done had worked and in the split second Teturact's attention was diverted Thaddeus had taken aim and blown apart the head of the closest brute-mutant.

He yelled out the protocol forms of the Inquisition as he fired. He was going to do this properly.

'By the edicts of the Conclave of Mount Amalath I claim your life as forfeit and cast your soul to the mercy of the Emperor!' Thaddeus pumped shells towards Teturact's spindly, momentarily vulnerable body but one of his mutant bearers got in the way and the explosive-tipped shells blew fist-sized lumps of flesh from its hide. Thaddeus had spent the last of his precious tracker-shells on Sarpedon, and seen it swatted out of the air before it hit – he had to rely on old-fashioned hand-aiming now.

Thaddeus ran towards Teturact, trying to draw a bead on his cowering mutant form, snapping shots between the brute-mutants sheltering him. The hammer fell on an empty chamber and Thaddeus holstered the pistol quickly, for he was out of ammunition and his remaining spare clips lay back in the storm trooper Chimera.

He still had one more weapon. He reached inside his flak-coat and drew out the massive, boxy bolt pistol Aescarion had brought back from Eumenix, its casing decorated with the golden chalice of the Soul Drinkers, half a clip of explosive bolts in its curved magazine. He had to grip it with both hands to take aim.

Teturact's wits were gathering and the cold, greasy feel of its deformed mind was evident in the air. The surviving mutants were rearing up to defend their master – Thaddeus's first shot missed high as the pistol's kick deceived him but the second hit, blowing a mutant's throat out. It fell backwards against its brother mutant and in a flash of strange black light the second mutant's body was sliced clean in two in a welter of strange-coloured blood.

Sarpedon, battering and bleeding, was back on his many feet, his armour scored and dented, the strange weapon with its twin shimmering black blades in one hand.

Thaddeus raised the bolt pistol. His opponent was battered, shocked and slowed, but would not remain so for long. 'By the authority of the Holy Orders of His Inquisition and the Chamber of the Ordo Hereticus,' he said, 'I execute the destruction of your body and the release your soul for judgement. May the Emperor have mercy on you, for His servants cannot.'

His trigger finger pressed down and his whole body shook as the bolt pistol juddered, hot cases spilling to Thaddeus's feet. The pronouncement of execution ringing in his ears, he emptied the rest of the pistol's shells into Teturact.

SARPEDON HAD BEEN ready to die. But the final shots were not for him. The inquisitor fired off the last of his bullets into Teturact who was sprawled on the frozen ground beside Sarpedon, showered in the blood of his brute-mutant retainers.

You couldn't kill something like Teturact just by destroying its body. Sarpedon could feel the malevolent mind reaching out even now, seeking for some other living thing to take up roost, so it could escape and begin its reign again.

Sarpedon reared up on his back legs. Forgetting the pain of his torn muscles and ruptured organs, he took one last look at the ruined non-face of Teturact.

I serve the Emperor, mutant, he thought, knowing full well that Teturact could hear him. *I need no other god.*

He stamped down on Teturact's head, talons shearing through the feverish brain, and the dark light of Teturact's soul was extinguished forever.

TECHMARINE LYGRIS TORE the mem-circuits from the archive console. There was no time for finesse, they would just have to trust that enough would survive. From inside the command room he could hear the vicious din of battle and he knew that every second here cost more battle-brothers their lives.

Beside him, Sergeant Salk plunged a hand through the window of the command structure and, bracing his legs against the plasteel wall, hauled Apothecary Pallas out of the pulsing sea of rotting flesh that pressed in on the structure from all sides. Pallas was covered in filth, smoke rising where his armour's exhausts were clogged with gore, and somewhere he had lost his bolt pistol in the mire.

He held up a hand, and it held a specimen cylinder with a clot of pink, uncorrupted flesh inside.

'Got it,' he said, almost out of breath. 'There was one containment unit intact. I think Graevus is still out there, he...'

That was all he could say before everything erupted in white noise. It was a scream so loud it filled the heads of every Soul Drinker, blocking out every sense. It was the death-scream of something vastly powerful, a keening of absolute rage and despair. The walls of mutant flesh shrunk back as they felt the death of one of their own.

Squad Graevus were revealed, hacking their way from beneath a web of flesh, where they had held position around the last functioning containment unit. The heaving mass of muscle and skin spat back Marines, some still alive, others half-digested. The mutant sea spasmed and the whole containment floor churned like a sea in a storm.

'Salk to all points,' yelled Salk over the vox, which was barely functioning any more. 'It's over, every man out!'

He clambered onto the roof of the command structure where he could see Graevus's squad battering a path across the floor. The survivors of Salk's own squad were fighting their way up onto the top of the rolling mantle of muscle. They had seen him and were forging their way towards him, slicing and shooting through the malformed limbs that reached for them.

'I don't know if this is getting through,' voxed Salk through the static on the command channel, 'but this is Squad Salk and we are withdrawing from the facility. If there's an army still up there we will need extraction in about five minutes. Salk out.'

No ONE KNEW where Colonel Vinn was. Inquisitor Thaddeus and the Pilgrim hadn't returned. Aescarion now had command of the Inquisitorial troops and she was organising them into a withdrawal. The Soul Drinkers were on the other side of an immense mass of walking dead and fanatical traitors, led by powerful witches who threw lightning or turned men inside-out with a look. Many of the storm troopers were dead or cut off, but the Sisters had formed a formidable hard core of warriors against which wave after wave of enemies had broken, chewed up by bolter volleys or blasted into guttering valleys of fire by flamers and melta-guns.

'Squad Rufilla, secure the Rhinos and cover us as we embark,' voxed Aescarion as she snapped shots at traitors clambering over burning barricades of their own dead. She had personally led counter-attack after counter-attack into the shattered traitor lines, and her axe arm ached with the jarring of power blade against bone. Her Seraphim had fought as well as any troops on Stratix Luminae but in spite of the pride the warrior in her felt, the Sister saw only failure. The Soul Drinkers were on the other side of an army she could not hope to cut through, and no matter how many enemies of the Emperor fell here the strikeforce would not corner their quarry today.

The dead had not died for nothing. She would never forget that, for every one died in the service of the immortal Emperor and that was an end in itself. But the Soul Drinkers would escape their justice, and their treachery would stay an open wound in the soul of the Imperium.

Squad Rufilla was pouring fire over the heads of the Sisters and storm troopers as they ran back towards the Rhinos and Chimeras. Several of the vehicles were out of action, tracks ripped apart by sharp ridges of wreckage or hulls dented by collisions. The strikeforce crammed into the surviving transports, small arms fire spattering against the hulls, the traitorous hordes taking the opportunity to press on through Rufilla's fire.

Aescarion was on the front lines with the Sisters around her rapidly falling back. She followed them, snapping shots into the shambling dead tumbling down the valleys of twisted metal around her. A hand reached out and she sliced it off with a slash of her power axe.

'We have you covered, Sister, get on board now!' Rufilla's bold voice sounded over the vox and Aescarion picked up her pace, the vehicle convoy beginning to roar off back towards the distant *Crescent Moon*.

'Sister!' someone yelled, not over the vox but out loud, out of breath and close by. Aescarion paused and looked back to see Inquisitor Thaddeus struggling across the blasted battlefield, firing with a bolt pistol he held with both hands, shooting his way through the living dead of Teturact's army. His face was streaked with blood and his flak-coat was torn and burned at the edges. He broke into a run when he saw Aescarion and she thought for a moment that there were troops with him lending him covering fire as he ran towards Aescarion and the convoy, but Squad Rufilla's fire was soon ripping over his head and into the living dead.

'Sister,' he said as he got close, 'we are done here.'

'I am pulling the troops out,' she replied. 'We thought you were lost.'

'I was,' he replied. 'Teturact is dead, we have done enough here.'

'And the Soul Drinkers?'

Thaddeus reloaded his bolt pistol. Aescarion wondered where he had got it, and the ammunition for it. 'Teturact's wizards are still in command here?'

'They are. I have seen them, they are foul things indeed.'

'They command this army now. They are our target. Without Teturact they will have nowhere to flee to. If we can hunt them down quickly their armies will fall and the warzone will be cleansed.'

'But the Soul Drinkers will have to flee this planet too, inquisitor, surely we will never have a better opportunity to...'

Thaddeus blasted a volley of bolts into the closest few traitors as Rufilla's covering fire lanced down over his head and scoured a zone of safety around them. 'Aescarion, one day I will teach you about politics. But for now I must exercise my authority as an inquisitor and demand you do as I instruct. We can argue when it is all over.'

Rufilla yelled a final plea and Aescarion turned, leading Thaddeus back to the last Rhino where they clambered in beside Squad Rufilla and, still snatching shots at the enemy through the firing slits and hatches, roared bruisingly across the battlefield towards the *Crescent Moon*.

THE AIR WAS full of the stench of gunfire and rotting flesh, but Salk still gulped it down in relief as he led the bedraggled spearhead from the ruins of the facility. The sound of battle raged not far away and Salk knew that bitter close combat was waged just behind the facility, where the lives of Marines had bought the spearhead the time to snatch the Chapter's future. The facility smoked from thousands of small arms hits and the area around it was a dark twisted nightmare of wreckage and craters. Above, Salk could see the dark form of the battleship still ghosted against the sky, its skeletal frame disintegrating.

Behind Salk and the survivors of his squad was Graevus, supporting Karraidin with his mutated arm. One of Karraidin's legs was gone at the knee and his storm bolter hand was a gleaming red ruin, but he was alive, and his squad formed a cordon around him. Pallas and Lygris were with them – they had tried to find Techmarine Solun as they charged through the mutant-infested laboratory level, but he was gone.

'Soul Drinkers, this is Sergeant Salk. Mission fulfilled, get us out of here.'

Static. Then – 'Salk, stay in cover we're coming in.'

The seconds were agonising. Lygris and Pallas carried the only chance the Soul Drinkers had of genetic survival. A single well-timed assault or lucky impact could wipe out the future.

With a roar of engines and a flash of silver a fighter shot down from above, impossibly bright against the darkening sky. The lower portals yawned open and the fighter dipped so low its belly scraped the piles of wreckage.

Pallas and Lygris went first, dragged into the passenger compartment. Somehow, Graevus got Karraidin onto the top of a pile of wreckage and purple-armoured hands reached down to haul the wounded old captain aboard. Salk covered Graevus as he and his men went next, and finally Salk boarded, bolter chattering to the last. The portal began to bleed closed and the last Salk saw of Stratix Luminae was a blackened ruin, a twisted metal hell swarming with enemies that formed a writhing sea around an impossibly thin cordon of purple.

'Librarian Gresk to Commander Sarpedon,' someone was voxing, and Salk realised it was one of the reserve fighters that had picked them up. Gresk – one of the Soul Drinkers' pyskers, a Marine who could throw fireballs with a look – must have dropped off most of the Marines with him already as only his retinue and the survivors of the spearhead were in the passenger compartment. 'We have the spearhead. Mission concluded. Repeat, mission concluded.'

'Understood,' came the reply vox, which Salk could just hear over the growing whine of the engines. 'All squads, fall back and extract. All squads...'

Salk fell back against the grav-couch. He ached all over and, as his metabolism came back down to near-normal, he would feel a dozen new injuries he didn't know he had.

He was alive, and somehow it hardly seemed right. He could see Solun, as if he were there in front of him, lying crippled on the floor. He could see Marines pounded to bits by the tide of mutant flesh. He could see Captain Dreo lying mortally wounded in the Mechanicus lab on Eumenix, and he remembered the account of how Hastis had died on

Septiam Torus. How many of the Chapter had died? He didn't dare think. Only the Chapter's true leaders, like Sarpedon, Karraidin and Lygris, would dare to comprehend the price they had paid, and Salk knew that it would weigh them down like death itself.

If it was worth it, though, if the Chapter had a future, then there was hope. Sarpedon had not cursed them with hope until he had known they had a real chance, and now that hope was all the Chapter had left.

The Marines struggled into their grav-harnesses and Gresk gave the order to the bridge. The fighter's engines kicked in and it shot through the atmosphere, out into the hard vacuum and away from Stratix Luminae at last.

THREE OF THE fighters were lost, the one that had crashed in the first moments of the assault and two more that had been brought down by fire from the ground as they swooped low for extraction. The rest picked up the Soul Drinkers even as they fought. With the squads of the cordon gone, the traitorous, leaderless hordes poured over the facility like a tide of hungry vermin, there to fight against the mutated inhabitants until there was nothing left at the facility but death.

Iktinos was one of the last to be picked up. He and the squads with him were surrounded, and he was still battering traitors back from the lower hatch with his crozius as the fighter lifted off. The fighters broke formation and swooped out into space, weaving through the remnants of Teturact's flagship and leaving the Stratix system far behind. They evaded the *Crescent Moon* as they went, as its weapons shot down the transports trying to leave Stratix.

As the squads counted off, Sarpedon estimated that about four hundred and fifty Soul Drinkers had got off Stratix Luminae, leaving the Chapter at less than half its original strength.

THE LAST FIGHTER, having picked up Iktinos and his men at massive risk, made one last pass over the battlefield. Iktinos himself called out over the vox as the craft searched for Tellos and his Assault Marines, last seen cut off and surrounded, taking on tens of thousands of mutants and traitors face-to-face.

The battlefield was in such chaos that it was impossible to find anything, let alone a last stand of so few men against so many. As the fighter was ordered to give up the search and escape before it was shot down, Iktinos found Tellos's vox-channel and tried to contact him one last time.

But all he could hear was screaming.

* * *

'NOT ONE AMONGST you does not know fear. If you say any different, then you lie. You are terrified. You are assembled on a space hulk, surrounded by rebel Space Marines, being lectured by a mutant and a witch. Yes, I am well aware of what I am, and I am also aware of what the Imperium would say if they knew what I was. They would find strong, young, free men like you and they would point me out as a warning of what you might become. Traitor, they would say. Heretic. Unclean. And so another generation would be poisoned against freedom and become a part of the corrupt, crumbling Imperium, a breeding ground for Chaos, built on the backs of slaves.'

Sarpedon gripped the pulpit. He felt the burning of pride on the back of his mind, and though it was pride that had cost the Soul Drinkers so much in the past, he knew that here he had something he could truly be proud of. The novice candidates, three hundred of them, were stood in ranks on the gun deck of a battleship deep in the heart of the *Brokenback*. They were all towards the older end of recruitment age, beyond which the implants and operations that turned a man into a Space Marine would fail. All were strong and fit, not necessarily great warriors but – much more importantly – youths who had proved their bravery and their willingness to face any odds for what they believed in.

Iktinos had selected them, with Sarpedon's approval. After Stratix Luminae the Soul Drinkers had taken back the *Brokenback*, taking their alien fighters close enough to activate the many combined machine-spirits and causing the hulk to break from its moorings and rendezvous with the fighter fleet again. It had been the best part of a year since then, during which time the hulk had visited hotbeds of rebellion and secession, finding those who had banded together against the might of the Imperium and selecting the bravest of their young fighters.

Many who fought against the Imperium were just bandits and tyrants. But some were driven by an all-pervading hatred of oppression, and it was those that had provided the recruits Sarpedon now addressed. Chaplain Iktinos had selected them for courage, intelligence and dedication, and so the Great Harvest had begun again.

'You will not all survive,' continued Sarpedon. Three hundred pairs of eyes watched him intently. 'The implant procedures alone will account for some. Training will account for more. But those who survive will be ready to understand some of the truths about mankind and the threats it faces. The Imperium is one of those threats, for it is too obsessed with its own tyranny to face what is truly dangerous to humankind. Daemons, powers of the warp, dark magics and gods you will be forbidden to name – these are the enemies we fight against. These, and no other. For this is the will of the

Emperor untainted by the ambitions of the power-hungry. I can offer you a lifetime of battle and pain and the promise of a violent death, and I demand of you your every waking moment. But you will die knowing you have lived fighting for what the Emperor stands for, and that is more than anyone in the Imperium can claim.

'Soon the blood of Rogal Dorn will run in your veins and you will learn of your place in the unending defence of mankind. Until then, think on the unforgiving future I am showing you. If it was easy, it would not be worth doing. I trust that when you take on the mantle of novice and eventually the armour of a battle-brother, you will understand some of what I have told you, and the legacy of the Soul Drinkers will live on in you.'

They were afraid, and they had every reason to be. They were facing the long and trying process of becoming a Space Marine, and Sarpedon could not properly explain to them the constant hardship and pain combined with the ever-present fear of failure. But Iktinos had chosen well, and Sarpedon felt that few of them would fall before they took up the armour and boltgun of a Soul Drinker.

It was a miracle they were here at all. The existing mutations of the Soul Drinkers, including Sarpedon's arachnoid form, could not be reversed, but the accelerating mutation had been halted thanks to the tireless efforts of Pallas and the apothecarion, using the information they had found on Stratix Luminae. The gene-seed organs recovered from the many dead had been stored and eventually their mutations had been regressed, to the stage that they could now be implanted into the recruits who passed the first stages of their training. The carnage that culminated on Stratix Luminae had been for one reason, and that was to purify the Chapter's gene-seed and make the Great Harvest possible again – it would take a long time before the Chapter approached full strength again, but it would happen, and of that Sarpedon was proud.

Under Iktinos's gaze, the novices filed off the gun deck towards their first training sessions. Graevus would teach them hand-to-hand fighting while Karraidin, who could do little else until the techmarines and apothecaries fashioned some bionics to replace his lost hand and leg, would school them in the ways of Daenyathos and the sciences of war. Sarpedon wished Dreo was still there to teach them marksmanship, but there were enough crack shots still alive in the Chapter to do an admirable job. Sarpedon himself would have a role schooling that handful of recruits who showed some psychic potential, testing their mental resilience and training them in the use of their powers. And, of course, he would regularly expose all the recruits to the horrors of the Hell, so they would be able to face their fears and keep on fighting.

Sarpedon knew the Soul Drinkers were utterly alone, surrounded on all sides by those who hated them. The Inquisition would not give up hunting them and the daemonic foes they faced would only get more savage. There were doubtless forces more deadly even than Teturact out there, and the Soul Drinkers would have to seek them out and face them if they were to stay true to their purpose. But in spite of it all, Sarpedon knew how grateful he should be. How many men in the galaxy could claim they were truly free? Sarpedon could, and so could his Marines, and in time so would his novices.

In the end, there was nothing else that mattered. The Emperor's message was one of freedom – from the warp-spawned and the tyrannous alike. mankind was in chains all across the galaxy, and Sarpedon swore to himself that the Soul Drinkers would free it.

Sarpedon stepped down from the podium and began the long walk through the body of the *Brokenback* towards the bridge. The hulk was to head for a silent sector, light years from habitation, where the training and slow rebuilding of the Chapter could begin.

Freedom. It had taken Sarpedon so long to find out that it was the only thing worth fighting for. Freedom was what both the Imperium and the warp feared more than anything. It would take thousands if not tens of thousands of years but if Sarpedon could wield that freedom like a weapon to destroy the enemies of humanity, then the Soul Drinkers might truly be victorious and the Emperor's will might at last be done.

CRIMSON
TEARS

CHAPTER ONE

ENTYMION IV WAS quiet.

Colonel Sathis couldn't even hear the insects here. The indistinct rumbling of his Chimera APCs, following some way behind his command vehicle squadron, all but drowned out the faint wind. Even the hoofbeats of the Rough Riders' mounts were louder than the sounds of the planet itself. Sathis could see the Rough Riders scattered up the sides of the valley through which his force was travelling, men from the 97th Urgrathi Lancers, whose supposedly obsolete methods of cavalry warfare made them excellently suited to scouting out unknown territory. And everything about Entymion IV was unknown.

Sathis took a practiced look at the terrain. He had good all-round visibility here, but further ahead that became less and less likely. 'Stop us here,' he ordered to the driver of his command-pattern Salamander.

The vehicle ground to a halt and the silence was almost total. Sathis climbed down from the Salamander as the engine's vibrations ceased. He took a breath of the air – every planet smelled different and he thought the air of Entymion IV was clean, quiet, as if it was old and proud and resented the marks of pollution that human habitation always left. The purplish sky overhead, the dark ragged ribbons of mountains before them, the thinly grassed valley slopes – it was easy to imagine that this was an unspoilt world. Of course, Entymion IV was nothing of the sort – Gravenhold was a large and populous Imperial city and large sections of the planet's surface were given over to the intensive agriculture that gave it such importance. But at that moment,

Colonel Sathis imagined that there were perhaps some places the Imperium would never completely tame.

And always, the silence.

Sathis tried to imagine what was so damned important about this planet. The truth was hidden somewhere in segmentum-level economics. Entymion IV was a major agri-world and if the crop here failed it would have a knock-on effect across scores of other worlds. But a failure was a distinct possibility because the planet had fallen silent – completely silent, both to long-range astropathic communications and short-range vox and radio transmissions. If that meant something grave had happened to the planet's population then Sathis was to reach the capital, Gravenhold, find out what was wrong and report back. Entymion IV was certainly important, but Sathis couldn't imagine why such a bluster seemed to have blown up amongst the Administratum when the planet fell off the map. For the moment, the world was quiet.

Beneath the darkening dusk sky the tops of the valley slopes were knife-hard silhouettes. Ahead the terrain changed gradually, first becoming foothills and then great rearing slabs of rock. Colonel Sathis's immediate objective was to make his way through the Cynos Pass to the other side, where the way would be clear for a drive on Gravenhold. To do it he had the Steel Hammer detachment of the 2nd Seleucaian Defence Force, a formation of Chimera APCs teeming with almost a thousand battle-toughened and well-disciplined Guardsmen assisted by an artillery and anti-tank section, and enough bloody-mindedness to get them through anything. The Urgrathi cavalry were his scout force, and he was supported by tanks from the Jaxus Prime Siege Regiment. It was a fine force, compact and highly mobile. It was fortunate the right troops had been available, because the force had been assembled in a damned hurry by Guard standards.

'Everything alright, sir?' asked Sathis's driver.

'It's fine, Skarn,' replied Sathis. 'I don't want us hitting the pass at night. We should corral here and move on it at dawn. Get me comms.'

Sathis waited for a few moments while his Salamander crew raised the force's officers on the vox-net. Sathis had been on the planet for two days and one night, and he still didn't entirely trust it. The valley pass would be the best place by far for an ambush and at night the chances of such a thing happening increased drastically. Sathis had been in a similar position at the Hellblade Mountains years ago, when as an infantry lieutenant with the Balurians he had been pinned down for eighteen hours by a smattering of eldar troops who had the higher ground. He didn't want to end up in the same situation again – it could take just a few secessionists or rebels to force his advance to a halt and that wasn't in his battle plan.

He worked out the standard pattern in his head. The Seleucaians would form a formidable APC laager in which the men would spend the night, with the tanks and Sathis's command post in the centre while the Urgrathi rode patrols throughout the night. The few hours lost would be repaid with reduced risk to his force. Soon he could report back that all was well on Entymion IV, and he could go back to some real war or other.

'Marshal Locathan,' said Skarn, passing Sathis the vox handset.

'Locathan,' said Sathis brightly, knowing the grizzled old Jaxan tank commander would want to press on through the night.

'Commander?'

'We're going to wait out the night here. Go in with fresh men and daylight at dawn. Bring your tanks up past the Hammers and make sure your men get some sleep.'

Locathan was preparing to argue the point with Sathis when the first shot rang out.

THREE MONTHS BEFORE Sathis's force landed, all communication had been lost with Entymion IV.

Long-range communication, which was transmitted by psychic astropaths through the warp, died out without warning. Astropaths described a sudden dark blanket of silence falling, often in mid-sentence, which remained resolutely impervious to any attempt to penetrate it.

Entymion IV, and the whole Entymion system, was well-known in the sector for the vagaries of the warp space that lay just beneath its realspace, and so patchy communications were nothing new. Greater attention was paid when in-system communications dropped out as well, rendering the planet both deaf and dumb. Entymion's star was likewise prone to electrical disturbances and short-range comms had failed before, but a total silence was something new.

The Administratum, wary of losing whole agri-crops as transport ships could not organise landings on the planet, sent in a team to find out what was going on. The twelve-man surveyor team, which included an Arbites liaison to ensure punishment for whoever was to blame, entered the atmosphere of Entymion IV and was never heard of again.

The possibilities of rebellion, natural disaster or self-imposed quarantine had been raised and hopefully ignored. The Administratum could not risk ignoring them any longer. If Entymion IV stayed silent then billions of credits worth of food would never be harvested and delivered. Every scenario they created suggested resulting famines in the nearby worlds that relied on Entymion IV for sustenance. The Entymion Expeditionary Force was assembled rapidly and Colonel Sathis was given overall command, with orders to land on the planet, make his way to the capital Gravenhold, and bring back the news that all was well.

The consuls of the Administratum crossed their fingers.

Two days after making landfall on the relative safety of the great rolling plains beyond the mountains, the Entymion Expeditionary Force finally made contact.

ANOTHER BULLET SMACKED into the side of the Salamander before Sathis reacted.

'Taking fire!' he shouted and vaulted over the side of the Salamander as the rest of the crew took cover behind its high armoured sides.

He dropped the vox handset and scrabbled for it as shots whipped through the air above him and slammed into the vehicle's armour.

'...repeat? Colonel, repeat!' Locathan's voice was sharp and businesslike.

'We're taking fire,' said Sathis. 'Small arms, sounds close. Stand by.' Sathis reached over and switched the frequency to that of the commanding officer of the Steel Hammers. 'Commandant Praen. Commandant, do you have any men ahead of us?'

Praen's voice sounded surprised. 'Colonel? No, none of our lads.'

'Then who the hell is shooting? Get your forward platoon up here and give us some support!'

The gunfire suddenly thudded down heavier, chains of automatic fire juddering through the air and ripping up plumes of dirt where they stitched along the ground.

'Get us back. Now, into cover.'

The driver, still hunkered down, ripped the Salamander into reverse and the vehicle lurched backwards. Sathis could see the fire now, streaking down above him from the top of the valley. A thick bolt of energy fizzed past and Sathis was sure he could make out the roar as it vaporised a chunk of the opposite slope. Heavy weapons, weight of fire – who was it? And how could they have hidden?

Something was shrieking down at them with a sound like a thousand voices screeching at once, the sound of metal carving through the air, layered beneath a dark stuttering of gunfire.

A force like a huge invisible hand slammed Sathis so hard against the side of the Salamander that his head cracked back and forth and he felt sure he would pass out. The purple sky whirled above him and for a moment it was beneath him, swinging down so he thought he would fall into it, tumbling forever.

The Salamander came to a rest on its side, gouging a deep furrow of earth as it slid to a halt. Sathis's vision swam back just in time to seen Skarn crushed beneath the lip of the armoured compartment and the hull. Another body fell brokenly past him – Lrenn, the gunner.

Sathis scrambled out, leaving his officer's cap behind in the wreckage. The ringing in his ears died down to be replaced with the sinister sound of bullets and las-fire thumping into the earth around him like rain, reports of gunfire and shouting filtering through from further away. He heard the whining of engines and looked up to see the craft that had strafed the Salamander – it was a sharp crescent shape, bladed and savage, that twirled upwards on twin white flames from its engines.

Rebels normally used obsolete marks of Imperial aircraft. This wasn't one of those.

The vox was still in the wreckage. The rest of Sathis's command squadron – a Chimera with a veteran squad from the Seleucaians and two more Salamanders – were retreating rapidly as volleys of enemy fire ripped down at them in white-hot ribbons.

Sathis's mind was in a whirl. He had been under fire dozens of times before, of course. He wasn't scared. He had been shot at, bombed, burned, betrayed and stranded. He had shrapnel in his leg from a rebel artillery barrage on Cothelin Saar, he had nearly died from a bayonet wound when the greenskins stormed his bunker at the Croivan Gap. He had joined the Planetary Defence Force at fourteen, been drafted into the Guard two years later, and killed and fought and eventually led for his Imperium, and he had earned every stripe on his sleeve. But he had never seen a silent planet become a battleground so quickly.

He had never fought an enemy that could get so close, so silently. He didn't think he could lead his men to fight an enemy they couldn't see.

He could see Rough Riders wheeling on the valley slopes, scattering as fire criss-crossed between them. There were silhouettes at the top of the nearest slope, but Sathis couldn't see if they were dismounted riders or the enemy.

Sathis began to run for the closest Salamander but a bolt of liquid fire tore down and bored right through the vehicle, turning its crewmen into guttering figures of flame, blowing its tracks out and sending a blue burning pool of promethium belching out beneath it. The sound and heat hit Sathis like a wall and he fell back onto the smoking earth, the flash of the explosion burned red against his retinas.

Sathis scrambled back towards the wreckage behind him, his nostrils clogged with the stink of burning grass and cannon smoke, his skin raw hot from the plasma flash.

This was worse than the Hellblade Mountains, worse than Cothelin Saar. Hell, it was the worst yet. It wasn't just pain, or fear, or the sight of his men dying, it was the humiliation. He had been caught cold, surrounded, beaten by an enemy that could pick its shots, that could wait to strike instead of being forced into battle against the superior Guard numbers and discipline.

For a moment he was back to his first actions, a boy soldier hearing hostile fire for the first time, seeing the first bloody bodies being dragged back from the battlements and seeing the look in his comrades' eyes that said: *I don't think we're going to make it out of this one.* Sathis had left the boy behind a long time ago but now he was back and with him the doubt, the fear.

A hand grabbed at him and Sathis knew he was dead.

He looked up at the aristocratic face of Hunt Leader Grym Thasool, commanding officer of the 97th Urgrathi Lancers, just before Thasool hauled him up off the ground and onto the back of his Urgrathi charger.

Sathis grabbed on tight to the elaborate tack that kept Thasool strapped to the back of the heavy, muscular charger. Thasool dug his heels in and the charger, bulkier and surlier than a Terran standard horse, shot forward, slaloming between the bolts of falling fire.

Sathis choked down the fear and confusion. He was an officer. This was where he earned that status.

'Get to a vox. Bring up the Hammers, get the… get the armour to pin the enemy down and counter-attack…'

'Bloody xenos, sir!' said Thasool, wrenching on the reins to haul his mount around the burning Salamander wreckage. He was heading towards the rear of the formation, where the Steel Hammers in their Chimeras would mount a massive counter-charge if someone could get there in time to give the order. 'Seen 'em before. The shadows, you see? They had to wait for the dusk. It's the shadows they hide in.' Thasool, Sathis knew, was utterly fearless, from a long line of aristocratic warrior-officers who had had all the cowardice bred out of them. He might have been recounting an anecdote over a glass of devilberry liqueur, were it not for the way he had to raise his voice over the gunfire.

A charger galloped by with a headless rider. Thasool charged on past a tangled knot of bodies, three or four men who had been caught by the same energy bolt and burned into a red-black mass in an instant. A horse lay sheared clean open by las-fire, shredded entrails smoking.

Men were yelling. Rough Riders wheeled in confusion through a savage latticework of fire.

The sound of men dying was everywhere.

'Company, wheel twelve left!' bellowed Thasool. 'Close and give them the blade!' Sathis realised Thasool was giving orders through his unit's vox-net, trying to bring the scattered Rough Riders together so they could use the speed and strength of their charges to batter back at the enemy.

Riders in the green-and-gold Urgrathi uniforms were galloping heads down through the storm of fire, converging on their leader. They were as fearless as Thasool himself. Sathis didn't think he had ever felt greater respect for fellow soldiers than he did for the Urgrathi Lancers in that moment.

A figure coalesced from the dusk shadows at the foot of the valley slope. It was humanoid but its skin drank the light, so it seemed to be pure liquid blackness spilling through from another reality. As the weak sunlight hit, the features emerged – corded muscles, hands encased in sickle-like blades, the face hidden by straps and buckles as if it was trying to hold something in. It was tall and slim but powerful, moving quickly and smoothly as its skin shimmered between sickly pallor and pure blackness.

The thing made of shadow dropped and rolled between the stamping feet of the charger that rode at it. One curved blade flashed out and the charger pitched nose-first into the ground, throwing its rider. The figure seemed to flow over the ground to plant its blade between the rider's shoulder blades before melting back into the shadows.

Sathis let go of the charger's tack with one hand and took out his sidearm, a standard pattern autopistol. He could see more of the enemy. Figures flowed blackly along the lengthening shadows, blades cutting through the riders and their chargers as they swept down towards the valley floor.

The fire kept coming. The shadows further up the slope hid an army, and Sathis picked out a curve of glossy, beetle-black personal armour lit by muzzle fire. Enemy infantry with body armour – aliens if Thasool was right. Sathis spotted something flitting through the air out of the corner of his eye, something that left a glittering crescent of glowing black energy bolts as it passed. The enemy were everywhere, barely visible against the gathering darkness, just a suggestion of movement all over the valley slopes.

Thasool had his power sword drawn, a heavy thrusting blade encased in elaborate gold decoration.

A shadow congealed around the charger's feet – Sathis fired twice at the face that shimmered into view beneath him, its eyes sewn shut, a bloodied metal bar between its teeth. The shots went wide but Thasool swivelled in the saddle before spearing the thing through its throat. The sword's power field flashed and Sathis saw limbs broken beneath the charger's hooves in a wash of blood.

'Mandrakes,' spat Thasool. 'Scouts. We never forgot 'em, disgusting xenos assassins.'

'Xenos? You mean… Hrud? Tau?'

'Eldar,' replied Thasool grimly, slashing down at the black shape flowing towards them. 'The pirate kind.'

The charger rounded a bend in the valley and Sathis saw two forward Chimeras of the Seleucaian Steel Hammers, their veteran Guardsmen dismounted and firing disciplined volleys up the sides of the valley. Their officer – a Lieutenant Aeokas – saluted hurriedly as Thasool slewed the charger round to a halt in the cover of the nearest Chimera.

'We've got two hundred plus!' shouted Aeokas over the volley of lasfire. 'Hostiles on both sides. They've got us surrounded!'

'Comms,' said Sathis as he slid down off the charger. There was a body at his feet, a Seleucaian with a cluster of bloody crystal shards studded over his face and upper chest. The crystalline fire was like a rain of razors here. Sathis felt tiny fragments slicing into the exposed skin of his face and hands like papercuts. He heard a scream as a crystal shard pinned a Seleucaian Guardsman to the side of a Chimera through one bicep.

Someone handed Sathis a vox-handset. 'We're under attack!' he said, trying to keep his voice level. 'Praen, bring everything you've got forward for a counter-attack. Locathan, cover them and get that air power off us!'

'Understood. Saddle up and full charge!' ordered Praen, the engines of his Chimeras juddering behind his voice. Further back the sound of quad autocannons thudded through the air as the Hydra anti-aircraft tank began to fill the sky with shrapnel.

Lieutenant Aeokas yelled something at Sathis, but his voice was lost in a sudden shriek of white noise that blotted out even the gunfire. The air just behind the closest Guard squad's position blurred and puckered, warping the light as if something was scrunching up the background like a picture. A pinpoint of blackness in the centre of the disturbance flooded open like a dead pupil.

The first attacker out of the portal wore glossy purple-black armour with a bone-white face mask, wicked green eyes shining with malevolence, the plates of the armour swept into sharpened curves. Taloned gauntlets held a halberd with a blade that shone and rippled, shifting between one reality and the next. More followed, each one with a speed that, when coupled with the heavy armour and savage hacking weapons, made them as inhuman as the most horribly misshapen alien.

The Guard squad didn't even have time to turn and face them. Halberds bit through Seleucaian uniforms, cutting so cleanly that the bodies didn't even bleed until they hit the ground – they just fell, arms sheared off, torsos slashed in two, heads falling free, looking for all the galaxy as if they had never been alive.

Sathis had faced the eldar before, and he knew they were tricky, treacherous creatures who could turn from allies to savages without warning. But he had never seen anything like this.

The second Guard squad turned and fired instinctively. Las-bolts fizzed and burst against armour. More enemies were coming through the portal, these ones wearing lighter armour and carrying shard-firing rifles. They were spreading out and Sathis ducked down by the Chimera to shelter from the chains of shattering crystal, firing all but blind with his autopistol as the air was clouded with crystal shards.

Thasool waded in without a thought, vaulting down off his charger and stabbing left and right with his sword. He speared one enemy through the chest and lashed out at an armoured eldar, swiping off its arm. It stumbled to the ground, Thasool stamped down in its shoulder and, with a practiced downwards thrust, impaled it through the head. Las-bolts and crystal shots were streaking by him, shredding the hem of his hunt leader's greatcoat. Thasool ignored them. His men were dying and according to the code of the Urgrathi lancers, that meant Thasool was dying too, and physical danger didn't matter any more.

'Fall back and mount up!' yelled Aeokas, gesturing with his chainsword as he fired at the lighter-armoured eldar with his laspistol. 'Get us out of here!'

One of the Guardsmen, his uniform spattered with gore and grime, ducked the hail of fire and unlatched the rear ramp of the Chimera. Aeokas waved the surviving men towards the APC, half of them giving covering fire as the rest fell back.

For a moment Thasool was holding up the aliens on his own, cavalry sword flashing as he kept the armoured eldar at bay. Then one stepped forward into the arc of Thasool's blade, turning the power sword on the haft of its halberd. The butt of the halberd snapped up and cracked into Thasool's chin – the hunt leader stumbled back and the reverse stroke of the halberd brought the heavy shimmering blade carving up into Thasool's stomach, up through his ribcage and out in a crescent of blood. Another eldar stepped up behind Thasool and struck off his head so neatly it was like watching an execution.

A hand grabbed Sathis's shoulder and dragged him backwards into the body of the Chimera. The last Guardsman in was hauling an unconscious comrade with him and threw the body in after Sathis before clambering in himself.

'Go!' yelled Aeokas over the din of crystal fire shattering against the side of the Chimera. Sathis looked around and saw blood-streaked faces, eyes hollow with shock, some bringing their lasguns to bear to fire out of the back of the Chimera as the eldar followed them.

'We have to get to higher ground,' said Sathis, shifting the weight of the dying Guardsman off him. 'Get a vox-link to orbit so they can pick us up. And where the hell is Praen?'

There should have been several Chimeras full of vengeful Guardsmen here to bail them out. What was happening? Where had the xenos come from?

The answer was obvious. They had been there all along, waiting.

The driver of the Chimera was either brilliant or crazy; the engine complained loudly as the vehicle slewed round a bend in the valley, almost flinging men out of the back. Crystal rained down as eldar warriors on the slopes fired at the vehicle, lances of energy weapons bored deep smoking holes in the ground just centimetres away from the hull.

'There's an outcrop about half a kilometre up the valley,' shouted Sathis. 'It's defensible. We get there, raise the alarm and wait for Praen!'

The rear doors of the Chimera were still swinging open. Sathis half-expected to see the xenos fighter craft again, sweeping down on bat-like wings to stitch a line of fire through the Chimera. But instead he saw the first of Praen's Chimeras, kicking up a trail of churned earth as it sped down the valley after them.

Then, Sathis heard the sound. It was a thousand voices – more – all howling at once. It began quietly, a reedy wail somewhere beneath the gunfire and the engine and the breathing of the angry, wounded men around Sathis. But then it grew into a dull roar flowing down the valley like a wind, and grew further still until it seemed to be coming from everywhere at once, from the very earth and sky. Arcs of purple lightning crackled up the sides of the valley and pits of pure blackness were opening up in the air as the second Chimera roared past.

Then there were bodies almost tumbling out of the very air itself, out of holes in reality that opened above the valley floor. Dozens of bodies, alive and evidently human, pale and flailing. The Seleucaian Chimera zoomed past most of them, some disappearing under its tracks, a few somehow clambering over the bodies of their dead to cling grimly on to the hull. Sathis saw sparks as they tried to lever off panels to get inside. Sathis saw they definitely were human, half-naked and armed with shards of metal, bones, crude clubs. More were tumbling in the Chimera's path and Sathis saw the APC ride up over the mass of bodies, tracks whirring helplessly in the air as it lost traction.

The pause in its charge was all the enemy needed. Suddenly there were ten, twenty, more of them swarming over the tank. The APC's engines croaked horribly and it lurched forward, the throng forcing it over onto its side. A top hatch came off and as Sathis's Chimera zoomed away from the wreck he saw the feeding frenzy as the enemy got inside.

Emperor alone knew what the enemy were doing to the crew. It was too late for them now. But the whole valley behind Sathis's Chimera was choked with the enemy, a horde of them. The eldar did not attack like that – they used stealth and guile, moving their specialised elite forces into place before attacking. This was more like the headlong charge of the greenskins. This was all totally, totally wrong.

Lightning flashed down past the open rear hatch.

'Get us up the slope!' yelled Sathis. 'Higher ground! Now!'

He knew what had happened to the Seleucaian Steel Hammers. A massive horde of xenos attackers had flooded the valley, bogged them down, and probably killed them all. Locathan's tanks had probably suffered the same fate. If any had escaped it would have been in the opposite direction, back the way the convoy had come, towards the open plains. It was the better option, thought Sathis, but he didn't have the choice now.

The Chimera turned and ground its gears as it started up the slope. Pits of blackness were opening up in the air.

'Guns forward!' shouted Aeokas, and the able-bodied Guardsmen wrestled themselves into position so they could fire out of the back of the Chimera.

'Lasgun!' shouted Sathis, and someone handed him a well-used Triplex pattern lasgun, its barrel still hot from firing. He felt like a recruit again, the weapon heavy and sinister in his hands for the first time. Sathis had gone through the same basic training as any Guardsman and somehow he had always known deep down that, in the end, it would come down to how well he could shoot and fight just like the men under his command.

It was right. It was natural. One man fighting for the Imperium, and for his own survival. It was the way to fight an abomination like the one that was ambushing them on Entymion IV. Sathis pushed the doubt down further. He was an Imperial citizen sworn almost by definition to fight the Emperor's wars and meet his end uncomplaining, only grateful that he had been given the chance to live a life that meant something in this cold galaxy.

The Chimera was slowing as the slope got too much for it. More portals were opening up, irregular splotches of blackness like spatters of dark ink laid across reality.

More bodies poured out in a torrent. The eldar elites had jumped down in a regular practised formation, like grav-chuters dropping from a transport plane. This was a rabble, herded into the portal somewhere else to be thrust unceremoniously out into battle. They were armed with knives, clubs, iron bars and the occasional low-powered laspistol some civilians owned. There were straps buckled over their eyes and their cheeks were slit so their mouths were wide red flapping grimaces.

And they were not eldar. They were human.

The good men and women of Entymion IV.

'Fire!' shouted Aeokas, but he needn't have bothered. Lasgun shots spattered out in a fan, punching red holes through the mass.

They were getting closer. Sathis pulled the lasgun's trigger and the gas kick from the power converter was familiar; he could imagine the rectangular bruise below his shoulder in the morning. Not that there would be a morning.

The enemy were getting closer. Sathis could see their pale, malnourished bodies, the rags they wore around their waists, the scars and crude self-made tattoos on their naked torsos. Another las-volley chewed through them but those behind were climbing over the dead so that they rose up like a wave about to break.

A metallic shriek signalled the end of the Chimera's gearbox. Sathis heard the top front hatch open and more las-shots open up as the driver added his laspistol to the carnage.

Brave chaps, thought Sathis. All of them. Such a shame.

Sathis hauled himself forward out of the Chimera. The APC was stuck now and it was no more than a tomb. The horde was close enough for him to smell the sweat and blood. Outside the APC their howling was the only sound. He couldn't even hear his own voice as he ordered the Guardsmen out of the APC.

The Seleucaian Guardsmen dropped out of the rear hatch, Aeokas yelling to leave the wounded. Sathis flicked the lasgun selector stud to full-auto, knowing that it didn't really matter if the power pack ran out now.

It was strangely comforting, he thought, to know that he was going to die. The certainty was warm and encouraging. An officer could rarely be certain about anything – he had to have fall-back plans, contingencies, reserves. Now, he could concentrate the last few seconds of his life on killing as many of these alien-loving scum as possible.

The Guardsmen were going to make a stand on the ridge. Good for them. Sathis clambered up on top of the Chimera as the horde surged closer, las-bolts still blowing sprays of blood from them. One ran forward and tried to jump up after him but Sathis shot him through the throat, imagining his old parade-ground instructor clapping him on the shoulder for such a good shot.

Sathis looked up and saw the valley stretching out behind him. It was thronged with crowded white bodies, like squirming maggots. Thousands of them. Hundreds of thousands. No wonder Entymion IV had fallen silent – its population was insane.

The eldar were waiting on the slopes and watching them, almost invisible, their dark armour mingling with the lengthening evening shadows. Their plan had simply been to stop the convoy and break it up, so that when their horde of slave-soldiers arrived the end would come the quicker.

They probably thought they had won. But no alien could win against the Imperium. Trillions of citizens, billions of soldiers, thousands of forge-worlds pumping out tanks and guns and spaceships, the Imperial Navy, the Adeptus Ministorum to marshal their faith, the Adeptus Terra to guide them – all the eldar had done here was to make them all angry.

Portals were opening up over Aeokas and the Guardsmen. Their lives were measured in seconds now. Aeokas would lead them to the last, not because he had to, but because there was no meaning left in his life except to lead his men in dying.

The horde were scrumming around the Chimera now, trying to clamber onto it. Sathis kicked one in the face and shot another, wishing he had a bayonet. He sprayed a fan of las-fire that knocked two or three more off the Chimera.

The evening sky was now a deep, vibrant purple. The distant mountains were silver-edged teeth of black in the distance. What did the eldar want this world for? Why was it so important? Why here, and not somewhere out on the frontier where the Imperium might never intervene? Why not some fat sweating hive world where the xenos could herd millions of underhivers through their portals without anyone even noticing? Why here? Why Entymion IV?

A handmade knife plunged between Sathis's shoulder blades. Sathis's hand spasmed and he dropped the lasgun as more of the subjugated humans surrounded him. Something heavy and metal slammed into his ribs. His vision swam as the blood flowed out of him.

Colonel Sathis's world ended on the slopes of Entymion IV. And even as he died, he knew that his death would not be the last.

CHAPTER TWO

LIFE, IF YOU knew how to look, was a field of stars. If you could see past the mundane backdrop of the galaxy and tune in to the lights that everyone carried around in their minds, then you would see a million shining beacons of humanity. Most were virtually static, milling around in cities on tight endless circuits from homes to manufactoria and back again. A few ranged over their worlds, aristocrats or lawkeepers, criminals or wanderers. Some orbited planets in smugglers' scows or planetary defence platforms, and some zipped between worlds on spacecraft – they were the soldiers, the messengers, the adepts, the Imperium's lifeblood pumping through the arteries of space.

This particular system, Diomedes Tertiam, was well-populated so the task would be difficult. There were about twenty-three billion inhabitants spread across two hive worlds and a multitude of colonies and off-world stations. How was it possible to sort one lifelight out from all these?

It was certainly the right system. One of the hive worlds sported the psychic scars of sudden, inhuman violence. All hives were shaded with the mental crimson of bloodshed but that was like a dull glow, almost comforting in its normality, signalling that the underhivers were culling each other as effectively as they had ever done.

But one hive was different. Bright slashes of carnage were still written across the upper spires of one particular hive, throbbing with the shock that had yet to wear off, seeded with the residue of death and watered with intense white fear that ran like foul water down the levels of the hive.

There. It had happened there. It matched up with what they already knew, and confirmed they were in the right place.

There was another world, equally important as a landmark in their quest. It was a smaller planetoid where the lives were penned into tight regular clusters – they barely moved, and so they formed geometrical ranks rising in pyramids from the surface. Prisoners in their cells. A prison-world, the sinkhole for the most dangerous criminals that the Diomedes Tertiam could produce. Beneath the upper levels were empty spaces in the pattern, larger cells with no prisoners. The life-lights present on those levels flickered with pain or throbbed dully with desperation. Glowing splashes of death were overpowered by the ice-cold rime of suffering.

Interrogation cells. Highest security. And one of them was full of bright lives, milling around as they made preparations. Reinforced doors, adamantine restraints, medical servitors to deliver massive doses of hypno-sedatives into the prisoner to be kept there. They knew what they would have to hold, and they knew what it could do. Perhaps they had been to the hive and seen the results first-hand – either way they would be under no illusions. They were preparing to receive one life-light that could never again leave the pattern of the prison world. It would grow dim and die there.

The view pulled out again. The object of their scrutiny would not be there, but the knowledge of the prison world helped pin it down. Seen from a distance, the system had patterns of its own. Some lives – smugglers, fleeing criminals, deep system patrols – moved seemingly at random around the planets and their star, but most followed fairly regular routes between the worlds. Thin arteries picked out by the psychic echo of those who plied them, the standard routes were relatively safe and well-patrolled. That meant the highest chance of getting their prisoner back if he escaped. That meant he would be there, somewhere.

The collective scouring intelligence lined up the violence-marked hive and the prison world, and found a thread that connected them – a short, straight, direct route with few travellers but plenty of static waypoints where monitoring stations were marked out by the lives of those who kept watch.

There. It had to be. The secure route the system authorities used to transport their prisoners. It was probably watched over by the Adeptus Arbites, watching out for treachery or incompetence. Perhaps some of those hard, bright, disciplined points of light were the life-echoes of the Arbites officers, stern and upright, giving leadership to the Imperium's policing.

The watchers had killed more than a few Arbites in their time. They had not relished it, but it was necessary. The Arbites were just one arm of the Imperium, just one cog in the huge machine that ground Mankind down into a helpless, pliable mass of weakened minds. The lights of the population were dim and dying, susceptible to rebellion or suggestion from dark powers. If more men and women of the Imperium could see the population as the watchers saw them, then perhaps the Imperium would be no more and there would be freedom. Or perhaps just mindless anarchy – they all knew the solution for the galaxy would not be an easy one.

These were all questions for another time. Together the watchers peered down closer at the inter-system route between the hive and the prison planet. The prison planet, they noticed, was small and its gravity would be low. That way the prisoners' muscles would be wasted and stringy after a year or so, making it more difficult to escape if they got onto a ship or made it as a far as a standard-gravity world. It was an old trick, and it worked. It probably wouldn't work on the prisoner they were surely transporting at that moment, though. There would be no choice but to restrain him permanently, and kill him when they were done with him. This was because their prisoner, in body and especially in mind, wasn't really human.

One ship carried several hundred despairing souls. The result of an underhive sweep, rounded up to fill some conviction quota. Another had a few hard-bitten criminal minds sedated and kept in restraints. Killers. Seditionists. The Imperium's worst, as much a result of the Imperium as the bustling hives and iron-hard discipline of the Arbites. Interesting, but not what they were looking for.

One ship was small, holding barely a dozen life-lights. It was the crew that gave the first clue. They were afraid. Fear was a strange thing that made a soul stronger and weaker at the same time, and you couldn't hide the stain it left on your soul. A thin, reedy flicker hovered at the heart of their minds, fluttering away behind everything they did. They were afraid because they knew their ship could be scuttled at any moment if their prisoner looked like he could escape; their lives were not valuable enough to be spared if it looked like they might lose their cargo. They were afraid, too, that they would do something wrong in the long, complicated dance of red tape that surrounded the transport of a prisoner like this. Adepts from a dozen organisations would have to be notified, and each would have to ratify some part of the process. Maybe even the Inquisition would be involved, demanding one of their

observers be present, perhaps even insisting on conducting some inter-
rogations of their own.

The Inquisition would have a lot of questions to ask the prisoner.
Most of them would be about the watchers themselves.

Most of all, of course, the crew were scared of the prisoner himself.

A hard red-white point of boiling hate, so sharp and stark it looked
like it had been nailed into the backdrop of space. A bullet wound of
madness. The depths of primal emotion had bubbled up to the surface
and swallowed the conscious mind. It was unmistakable. Even from
this distance, even with only the psychic residue to go by, there could
be no doubt. This was their man. The violence on the hive had been of
such intensity that only several men like this could be responsible.
Most of them had escaped to ply their carnage in some other system,
but something extraordinary had happened at Diomedes Tertiam – one
of them had been captured. Probably at great cost, he had been sub-
dued, restrained, processed through many layers of bureaucracy, and
assigned a grim drawn-out death of interrogation on the prison world.
It was extraordinary, one in a million. But it had happened. And it was
the chance the watchers were looking for.

The hating soul writhed in its restraints. At its heart it was a paradox
– everyone was, but the paradox here was stark and obvious. It was
boiling over with hatred, the uncontrolled outpourings of a broken
and degraded mind. But all that was doubly dangerous because it was
bound in the iron-hard bands of discipline – that same discipline that
bound the soul of every Space Marine.

THE CERTAINTY WAS enough to break the contact. The Diomedes Tertiam
system snapped back, the billions of life-lights whirling away into the
distance as Sarpedon's perception pulled back from the psychic landscape.

The swirling blackness dissipated and Sarpedon was back in the
chamber on the *Brokenback*. Librarian Gresk sat just across from him,
sweat running down his dark skin. The Chapter's third Librarian, Tyrendian, sat stock-still and meditative, his breathing controlled. He looked
too young and handsome to be a Space Marine, let alone a battle-hard-
ened outcast like a Soul Drinker.

Each Librarian did things differently. Gresk's power tuned into the
metabolisms of his fellow Marines, quickening their reactions and
movements to make them more effective fighting machines. Tyrendian's psychic power was raw and unchannelled – he hurled lightning
bolts across the battlefield. Sarpedon, meanwhile, was a telepath who
could transmit but not receive, and so he sent hallucinations and

unwanted primal emotions straight into the minds of his enemies. And just as they differed on the battlefield, so the three used their own techniques and skills when it came to the meditation.

Sarpedon had found a large, lavish ballroom in one of the spaceships that made up the twisted hulk of the *Brokenback*. It was dim and shadowy now, its chandeliers burned out and its furnishings mouldering. It was large, dark and quiet, perfect for the meditations.

Gresk shuddered and leaned forward over the table. He had focused his power inwardly, forcing his mind into ever-faster cycles of activity until he had projected his perception out into space and into the Diomedes Tertiam system. It took its toll – Gresk's breathing was heavy and laboured. Gresk was old, and meditation was a paradoxically exhausting activity for him.

'It was him,' he said.

'He was further gone than we thought,' replied Sarpedon. 'You felt the hatred. I couldn't feel anything else in him.'

'But it was definitely one of them. One of our own.'

'Yes, yes. It was.' Sarpedon shifted uncomfortably. The meditative session had lasted several hours and, even without his power armour, he had become stiff and aching. 'They have almost put him past our reach. We will have to be quick.'

'Perhaps it is best to leave him be,' said Tyrendian. The Librarian's eyes slowly opened as he brought himself out of the trance. 'There is nothing in this brother that can be reasoned with. He is just an animal now. Think what Tellos himself would be like! Perhaps it is better to let him run amok. The Imperium will find him and put him down.'

'Think, Tyrendian.' snapped Gresk. 'Tellos had the run of this place. He knows the *Brokenback* better than any of us. He might know how to hunt it down, or cripple it. Even Techmarine Lygris doesn't know what all its strengths and weaknesses are. If the Inquisition got to Tellos it could be the end of us.'

'And if we go after him, Gresk, we might deliver ourselves to the Inquisition regardless. Don't you think they're after him, too?'

'Enough,' said Sarpedon. 'We haven't got that close yet. We will make the most of the lead we have. Thank you for your meditations, brothers. Now rest and prepare. If we recover this one we might need both of you to break him open.'

Sarpedon stood up from the table, and an ignorant observer would see for the first time one of the reasons the Soul Drinkers were excommunicate. Sarpedon was a mutant, an obvious and powerful one. Eight segmented arachnoid legs sprouted from his waist, a relic of the Chapter's most shameful actions. Taking advantage of a schism

between the Soul Drinkers and other Imperial authorities, the Daemon Prince Abraxes had corrupted the Marines' bodies and very
nearly done the same to their souls. Abraxes was dead and the Soul
Drinkers were treading the long path of redemption, outcast by the
Imperium they had once served but sworn to fight the powers of
Chaos that had so nearly claimed the Chapter itself. The mutations
remained, and though Apothecary Pallas was well on the way to halt-
ing the degeneration they were causing, they would never be
completely cured. Most of the Soul Drinkers had mutations somewhere, but none so dramatic as Sarpedon's own. As Chief Librarian
and de facto Chapter Master of the Soul Drinkers, Sarpedon was their
greatest hero and their greatest failure. It was he who had led them
into the Chapter War that left so many of their own dead at a
brother's hands, who had almost led them into the worship of
Abraxes's patron god Tzeentch, who had left them with a mutative
legacy that had almost claimed all their lives.

And Sarpedon was responsible for Tellos. That might be his greatest
failure.

Sarpedon activated the vox-bead in his throat with an unconscious
impulse. 'Lygris?'

'Commander?' Techmarine Lygris's voice crackled through the vox.

'We've got a location. A transport heading for the prison planet in
the Diomedes Tertiam system. Get some sensors on it and put us on
our way. I'll need intercept plans.'

'Understood. Boarding torpedoes?'

'No, it's a well-policed route. They could be shot down. Use one of
our Imperial ships. We'll send in the scouts.'

There was a slight pause. 'Understood.'

'This is what we trained them for, Lygris.'

'Can they handle one of Tellos's men?'

Sarpedon smiled. 'Ask Karraidin.'

It was all the answer Lygris needed. The hoary old Captain Karraidin, the Chapter's hardest-bitten assault officer, was the Soul
Drinkers' new Master of Novices and he was an even harder taskmas-
ter than Sarpedon had expected. The scout-novices had hated him
when they were first recruited, now Sarpedon knew they would follow Karraidin through the Eye of Terror itself.

Gresk had stalked off through the decaying finery of the ballroom,
beginning the long trek through the hulk to his cell where he would
run through mental exercises to recover his strength. Tyrendian had
stayed behind, contemplating the once-beautiful gilt murals that covered the room's walls.

'Aekar would have been so much better at this,' said the Librarian quietly. Tyrendian seemed to say everything quietly.

'We did well enough,' said Sarpedon. Aekar had died of psychic feedback while probing the atmosphere of a world where the Soul Drinkers had fought the Daemon Prince Ve'Meth. The rest of the Chapter's Librarians had been killed in the subsequent battle against Abraxes, on Stratix Luminae, or from uncontrollable mutation. Now Sarpedon, Gresk and Tyrendian alone made up the whole Chapter Librarium.

Tyrendian turned to Sarpedon, his face was normally unreadable but there was something earnest in it now. 'We all need to know you understand the risks, commander. The Imperium is hunting Tellos as closely as we are. We will put ourselves in plain sight if we move on him.'

'I can't leave one of our own out there,' replied Sarpedon. 'Tellos is my responsibility. I was the one who let him get so far.'

'You,' said Tyrendian. 'Not us. You have led us this far, commander, but remember this Chapter is still bigger than you. We have the scouts and the novices to protect, too. We only have – what, four hundred Marines left? And just the three of us Librarians. We cannot afford another Stratix Luminae.'

Sarpedon nodded sadly. 'You're right. A Space Marine Chapter should consolidate after our losses. Build up a scout company, fortify, re-equip. But Tyrendian, the Soul Drinkers are not a Chapter any more. We are not an army. We are nothing but the principles that bind us together, and one of those principles is that a brother is a brother and we have a responsibility towards him. If we can get Tellos and his Assault Marines back then we have to try. And if we can't, it is our responsibility to see that the Dark Powers do not get him first. Besides, Gresk is right. If the Inquisition gets hold of Tellos they could hunt us down.'

'We might not survive, Sarpedon. You know that.'

'If we forget why we are fighting then we will be just one more band of renegades. Remember what we once were, Tyrendian. We fought for the Imperium to prove how superior we were. Now we fight because it is the work of the Emperor. Rogal Dorn was the man he was because of the strength of his will. We have to be the same.'

Tyrendian shrugged. 'We could leave. Take the *Brokenback* to the other side of the galaxy. Tellos is the Imperium's problem.'

'The people of the Imperium have to live with a corrupt regime that would see them dying before it admitted it was wrong,' replied Sarpedon. 'They don't deserve Tellos butchering his way through them as well. He's our problem and I intend to see that we solve it.'

For a moment it looked like Tyrendian would say something in reply, but whatever it was he bit it back.

'The scouts will have to be everything we hope they are,' continued Sarpedon. 'How are the Librarium recruits doing?'

Tyrendian thought for a moment. 'Scamander will join the Librarium eventually. Nisryus too, perhaps. None of the others are strong enough to be certain, but there may be a couple of capable psykers still amongst them.'

'I want Scamander going in with Eumenes's squad.'

'Then we'll see if I'm right.'

With that, Tyrendian left. The Soul Drinkers' Librarians, even before the Chapter's excommunication, had served as advisors to the Chapter Master, always open and honest with their advice. Sarpedon was glad there was one still left who felt he could speak his mind. The Soul Drinkers had followed Sarpedon almost religiously since the schism and he knew that he needed a foil for his command. The Primarch on whom the Soul Drinkers' geneseed was modelled, Rogal Dorn, had himself been wilful and headstrong. That was his strength, but also his weakness, a weakness shared by every Chapter Master since and compensated for by the counsel of the Librarium.

What if Tyrendian was right? Sarpedon could tear the Chapter apart, pursuing battles they couldn't win. But what else was there? How many times had Sarpedon sworn to die in the service of the Emperor? What would the Soul Drinkers themselves say? They would walk into hell if it seemed the best way to do the work of the Emperor and bring the fight to the forces of Chaos. But then, Tellos had once been the same.

These were questions for later. Sarpedon had to brief the scouts for their first true mission, one that would go some way to deciding the Chapter's future.

THE DESTRUCTION OF the Entymion IV Expeditionary Force did not go unnoticed. The sketchy reports from orbit showed a massive enemy force cutting Colonel Sathis's command to ribbons in a matter of minutes. No one had any idea anything like that could be present on the planet – any potential resistance had been expected on the plains outside Gravenhold, consisting of rebellious guerrilla fighters or, in the worst case scenario, household troops and rebellious Planetary Defence Force units commanded by Gravenhold's hereditary aristocracy.

The reality had been impossible to understand. The sheer numbers were dizzying. A minimum of ten thousand enemy soldiers had packed the valley, having seemingly appeared from nowhere. Warpcraft or hitherto unknown xenos technology were the only explanations for the sudden appearance of the army. Worse, the only place an enemy could have mustered an army of that size was from the population of Entymion IV itself.

The Adeptus Terra had to assume that Entymion IV was under the control of a hostile force, a moral threat, something that could use Imperial citizens as a weapon against the Imperium.

The message reached the dusty ancient halls of Terra itself. Lord Commander Xarius, hero of the Rhanna Crisis, was swiftly appointed command with orders to recover the planet at all costs. Xarius appropriated all the available Guard units for several sectors around and had, in a little under two months, assembled a force that most commanders would need years to pull together. The entire Seleucaian Fourth Division, more that seventy thousand men, demanded that Xarius take them to Entymion IV to avenge the dead of their brother regiment. Xarius also brought the regiment with which he once served, the elite heavy infantry of the Fornux Lix 'Fire Drakes'. The sector battlefleet was less rapid to answer the call but still seconded a cruiser, the *Resolve*, and escort squadrons along with a fleet of transports to get Xarius's army to the Entymion system and maintain a blockade to keep the rot on Entymion IV from spreading.

Xarius was a hard and unrelenting man, especially with himself. He called in every ally and favour he could to bring the army together, but if he wanted a rapid, effective invasion of Entymion IV then he had to have a cutting edge. The Seleucaians and the Fire Drakes were tough troops but they weren't the tip of the spear, the surgical strike-capable assault troops he needed to crack open Gravenhold. For a moment he paused before he ordered the troop-laden fleet to move into the Etymion system. He had seen the hazy, flickering sensor images of what had happened to Sathis. He knew he needed an edge before he would send a hundred thousand Imperial lives into the teeth of that kind of war.

At the last moment, answering the request of the Senatorum Imperialis itself, a strike cruiser arrived then left just as suddenly, leaving behind several Thunderhawk gunships carrying the men Xarius needed to lead the charge on the walls of Gravenhold. Those men were the Space Marines of the Crimson Fists' Chapter.

GRAVENHOLD WAS A masterpiece.

It was an old city that had survived the best efforts of the Administratum to Imperialise it. The existing histories of Entymion IV had the city dating back to the Great Crusade, and the city now standing on that site was several hundred years old. Some passing fashion for simple pale elegance had coincided with a drive by the planet's aristocracy to build themselves a capital worthy of the name. The result was Gravenhold as it now stood. Broad decorative arches straddled mosaiced thoroughfares that ran between the grand exchanges and trading-houses of the nobles. The River Graven that cut through the city from east to west was straddled by several bridges, each a work of fine decorative engineering, the most impressive being the Carnax bridge that connected the government district to the city's wealthy north.

Each estate in the north was like a city of its own in miniature, as if the aristocrats who once ran the planet liked to imagine themselves as the monarchs of tiny empires. The senate-house where the Gravenhold's plutocratic government once met was a handsome circular building, all columns and galleries, located on a bend in the river so the Graven almost surrounded it like a moat. The city's amphitheatre dominated the southern portion where the houses of the workers and minor adepts became picturesque slums, winding streets raidating away from the arena.

It was a shame, reflected Commander Reinez, about the mills. The large, ugly buildings were typical of the kind the Administratum inflicted on cities under its ultimate control, as Gravenhold had been. The knotted industrial piles were crammed up against the eastern wall, and around them were encrustations of shanty towns where an unwelcome underclass of sub-menial workers had taken root over the last few decades. The spaceport just beyond the eastern wall was an eyesore, too, a network of concrete landing hubs and maintenance yards that sprawled obnoxiously on the city's doorstep.

All this information was of secondary importance to Commander Reinez as he looked over the city from the south-western gate chapel. His Space Marine's eye had first noted the military implications of invading Gravenhold. He had seen worse places for cityfights – immense urban hives, crumbling hollow city-corpses riddled with craters and enemy foxholes, even cities seething with the influence of Chaos right down to the very stones. But Gravenhold had been built with an eye towards defensibility – certainly the city's walls were firm and unbreached, the gates easily-defended. The River Graven was as big an obstacle as any. And, like every city Reinez had fought over, the most well-ordered streets could become warrens of barricades and firing points without notice, suddenly plunging a placid cityscape into an unending labyrinth of warfare.

But what struck Reinez most was the same thing that had puzzled everyone since Cynos Pass. The city was, as far as his augmented and well-trained eyes could see, deserted.

Sergeant Althaz hurried up to Reinez, the pre-dawn light casting a greyish sheen over his dark blue power armour. 'The lower levels are clear, sir. The chapel is secure.'

'Good. Tell the Guard command the gate is theirs.'

Althaz saluted. 'Yes, sir. For Dorn.'

'For Dorn, sergeant.'

The gate chapel was a finely-made temple that formed the end of the city's wall just before the south-eastern gate. Its clergy had once performed rites to bring the Emperor's blessing on those passing through the gate below, casting holy water from the marble balconies and making benedictions on those who stopped at the city's threshold to pray. The chapel was now abandoned but perfectly intact, pale grey marble cherubs held up the ceiling of the top floor where Reinez stood, flanked by High Gothic inscriptions cut deeply into the walls. There was room enough in here for a congregation of a couple of hundred, kneeling before an altar of carved obsidian, their faith focused by the aroma of incense from the censers on the ceiling and the way the sunlight fell in shafts between the columns around the balcony.

The chapel covered several floors, down to the ground level where the city's population once walked out to begin the journey to the fields to the south. The chapel itself was the top floor, with the belfry just below, then a winding spiral staircase connected half-floors and mezzanines down to street level. Three squads of Crimson Fists held the chapel: Reinez's own command squad, Althaz's Tactical squad, and the Devastator squad of Sergeant Caltax. The Crimson Fists were the lynchpin of the first Imperial drive on Gravenhold – the heavy infantry of the Fire Drakes Guard regiment would enter the city through the south-eastern gate, and the Crimson Fists had to keep that gate open at all cost. If the enemy turned the broad thoroughfares beyond the gate into a killing zone, using the towering administrative blocks as firing platforms, then even the tough Fire Drakes would be thrown back in disarray. The Crimson Fists were to prevent that from happening.

Not that any enemy had yet shown his face. The invasion force had landed in the hinterland of Gravenhold itself, but neither the southern landing fields of the Fire Drakes or the Seleucaians to the city's east experienced any kind of resistance – Entymion IV was quiet and welcoming. The only hint that anything was wrong lay in the complete abandonment nature of the small settlements outside the capital, some left with food decaying on tables.

The Imperial forces had warily approached the city, every Guardsmen watching for omens of bad luck that would confirm his suspicions that the city was one big trap. The veterans of the Seleucaian Fourth Division had successfully invested the spaceport through which the eastern thrust would be mounted, while the Crimson Fists had taken the chapel with nothing more than a handful of orders and the cold-blooded efficiency that was the legacy of Rogal Dorn.

Reinez knew better than to assume the Imperial drive would be uncontested. But he also knew he was above the superstitions of the Imperial Guardsmen who saw imminent death in every shadow and idle remark. The population of Entymion IV had been corrupted and made rebellious by xenos or Chaotic influence, that didn't mean the heretics would contest their city. They might have abandoned the place, perhaps left a few booby traps to keep the troops busy for a while, intending to make their stand in the mountains or the rugged, untamed forests that straddled the planet's equator.

Either way, no matter how Reinez might want to get to grips with the enemy here, the Crimson Fists had a job to do. When the gate was forced, the Fire Drakes had taken their section of the city and Gravenhold was back in Imperial hands, then they would worry about taking back the rest of Entymion IV.

As if on cue, alert-runes flashed on Reinez's retinal display.

'They're in the wall,' came a vox from Caltax two floors below, just beneath the belfry floor. Then an explosion rocked the chapel and sent the limbs of stone cherubs raining from the ceiling. Deep cracks snapped through the floor and ceiling and the whole chapel shifted suddenly as if it was about to topple into the gateway.

The Fire Drakes were making their move even now. Chimera APCs, a handful of support tanks, and hundreds of men were marching across the city's threshold, relying on the Fists to support them. The enemy had struck at the Fists first, so that when the real slaughter began there would be no one to stop it.

Bolter fire chattered up from below, from the belfry level with its huge adamantium bells, from the crypt floors with entombed clergy.

'Caltax! What are we fighting?' Reinez jumped down the flight of stairs to where his own squad was stationed, in the main chapel with its rows of pews and grand lectern. They were fanned out with bolters ready, prepared to sell their slice of the gate chapel dearly. Already the chemical tang of gunsmoke was in the air.

Bolter shots rang off marble. Blades clashed with ceramite armour. The fight was inside the chapel, but that made no sense. The city wall was made of solid stone blocks several metres thick – there was nowhere for the attackers to have come from.

'Marines!' yelled Caltax over the vox. 'Traitor Legions!'

Then the back wall of chapel fell in, the stone blistering and rotting to reveal a cavity melted deep through the rock. And the Chaos Marines poured in.

A storm of bolter fire filled the chapel floor. Black wooden pews were chewed into kindling. Marble columns became clouds of spinning shrapnel. The world snapped into slow motion, a result of the combat-hormones now pumping through Reinez's body. The enemy were Space Marines, the worst of the worst, those who had turned their back on the Emperor and given themselves to the dark gods. Their armour was deep, vibrant purple, trimmed in bone. They carried chainblades and bolt pistols, and they were adorned with body parts – hands, heads, ears, skins – nailed to the plates of their armour. Few wore helmets and their faces were pale, drawn visions of soulless malice: eyes wild, hair unkempt, skin tight and scabby. One had eyes that stared madly from stalks jutting from sockets, another moved on cloven hooves with legs that were jointed the wrong way.

The storm of bolter fire tore one Traitor Marine to shreds and ripped the arm off a second. But there must have been a dozen piling into the room. Reinez's senses were working faster than his body and he fought the inertia of his limbs to draw the heavy thunder hammer from its scabbard on his back and charge through his squad into the fray.

Marines. Chaos Marines. No one had suggested it might be this bad.

Then he saw the golden chalice symbol on the shoulder pads of the enemy Marines, and Reinez realised how bad it really was.

The two sides clashed and the chapel was suddenly a mad, swirling cauldron of violence. Chainblades drew showers of sparks against ceramite. Reinez saw Brother Alca die, his head cracked against the stump of a pillar, skull split open by a traitor's boot. A Chaos Marine was impaled through the shoulder joint of his armour by Brother Paclo's bayonet – Paclo heaved the Marine into the air and fired half a clip of bolter shells through the traitor's ribcage.

Reinez's hammer slammed into the mass of enemies. He didn't care which of them he hit.

A Fist fought with his combat knife against a Chaos Marine with a chainsword. The chainsword won, carving off the Fist's leg before spearing through his gut.

Reinez struck again and felt ceramite break. He could barely see anything – the air was seething with smoke, gunflashes, debris and sprays of blood. The sound was immense – men screaming and yelling, gunfire, the shriek of chainblades, the thunderous strike of his hammer.

The world howled and fell apart. The ground fell away. Everything tumbled end over end, darkness alternating with the shafts of sunlight, purple and blue armoured bodies falling past one another.

The floor of the chapel had given way. Reinez realised this just as he landed two floors down, in the belfry.

Reinez had suffered worse. He had come through this horror and confusion before, and always survived, always been there at the end to drag some victory from the jaws of Chaos. He was the first up – he had to be, otherwise a single bolter shell or well-placed chainblade thrust could kill him on the ground.

Sounds filtered through the white noise of shock. A gunfight on the lower levels was sending stray bolter shots up to ring a strange rapid crescendo from the half-dozen massive grey metal bells hanging in the room. A stairway ran around the inside of the column that made up the chapel building at the end of the city wall. Crimson Fists were pressed against the wall, firing almost blindly down at enemies on the levels below. Reinez had landed badly on a platform stretching across the stairway, level with the bells – many Marines must have fallen past him to the bottom of the shaft.

Reinez dragged himself to his feet. Bolts of pain shot through him but they were comforting – none of his injuries were too severe. He could forget them.

His thunder hammer vibrated gently in his hand, its power field eager to crash into another enemy. A Chaos Marine, half his face a massive oozing wound, ran at him before Reinez could take proper stock of his situation.

The Marine knocked Reinez back onto one knee, slashing with his chainblade before trying to bring his bolt pistol level with Reinez's head. Reinez grabbed the gun wrist with one hand and lashed out with the hammer, knocking the Marine's legs out. He used the momentum to bring the hammer back up again and let it fall in a slow, brutal arc, slamming into the Marine's head and carrying on through the skull into the floor. Reinez had to haul on the hammer to keep it from carving through too much of the platform and bringing the whole thing down.

'Commander!' yelled someone behind Reinez. He looked up from the dead Chaos Marine to see Sergeant Caltax clambering up the last flight of stairs to reach Reinez's position. 'There're at least twenty of them, sir. Came in through the wall. Half my men are down or cut off.'

'Take everything you can and win back the stairs.' Reinez glanced around, several of his squad were on their feet around him. Brother Paclo's crimson gauntlets glistened with the blood of the Marine he had killed, Arroyox had probably broken a leg but was living with it, and Kroya was calmly finishing off a wounded Chaos Marine at his feet with a bolter round to the neck. 'We'll force them down to Althaz, crush them between the two.'

Caltax nodded quickly. He turned back to yell down at his men. 'Force them back! Get that heavy bolter to bear and–'

Reinez barely saw the blade. It was too quick to see, the only evidence of its passing the sudden sharp crescent of blood and the way Caltax's head rolled sideways to fall free of his neck.

The enemies of the Imperium took infinite forms and Reinez had fought thousands of them. Savage orks. Heathen eldar. The robotic constructs of dead empires, mindless hordes of ravenous aliens, the dead come back to life, Emperor-fearing citizens seduced into rebellion, the legions of Chaos itself, and more besides. He had come to recognise when a foe was something he couldn't face himself, a sixth sense that had kept him alive long enough to rise through the ranks of the Crimson Fists.

The sixth sense was screaming now. The thing that had killed Caltax paused for a fraction of a second and Reinez took that time to evaluate it as an opponent. From the waist down it was a Space Marine, in the purple of the Chaos Marines now sheened with blood. But its upper half was different. Its torso was so packed with muscle it seemed about to burst, and its skin was so pale and translucent that Reinez could see the thick bundles of muscle and white tendons bunching up beneath. The skin was covered in threadlike white scars, thin and neat enough to mark the surgical implants that turned a recruit into a Marine. But if this thing had once been a Marine it wasn't any more – its head turned towards Reinez and all the Crimson Fist could see in that face was hate. The eyes were black pearls staring from between strands of unkempt black hair, the teeth bared and bestial.

Reinez barely had to think it and his bolter hand squeezed the trigger, pumping two shots into the Chaos Marine. There was no blood, just puckered white wounds appearing in the skin. The flesh flowed around them, sealing off the wounds as if they had never been there.

Mutant. A powerful one – fast, strong, and bulletproof. The only way to kill it was to tear it apart piece by piece, and Reinez didn't know if he could do that.

The Chaos Marine charged. Reinez saw its weapons were not swords it held, but chainblades jutting directly into the severed stumps of its wrists. It had no hands, because it didn't need them – it existed to kill.

Reinez put everything he had behind his thunder hammer, swinging it low into the Marine's unarmoured midriff. The Marine twisted as it ran, moving out of the arc of the hammer's head. One blade speared towards Reinez's face and Reinez, dropping his bolt pistol, dropped to one knee and grabbed the Marine's bare arm.

His fingers sank into inhuman flesh that closed over them.

Reinez turned to match the momentum of the Chaos Marine, planting his foot on the floor and adding his own weight to the Marine's charge. The two careered headlong together, slamming into the stone wall of the belfry.

Reinez couldn't defeat this enemy. Everything he had learned in decades of service had told him that. But he could kill it, if he paid a high enough price .

Reinez felt them smash into the wall and keep going, the stone blocks ripped out of the wall before them. The light that swept over him was the dawn light of Entymion IV – they were several floors up, just empty air between them and the ground.

The south-eastern gate whirled around Reinez as he tumbled downwards with his enemy.

A broad avenue ran between the two gatehouses, one of which was taken up by the gate chapel. Statues of devout pilgrims and past aristocrats lined the avenue, figures rendered in multicoloured marble with details picked out in gilt. Down this avenue were advancing the Fornux Lix Fire Drakes, hundreds of men moving warily in their body armour and gas-helms, between rumbling Chimera APCs and Hellhound support tanks.

They knew that something was wrong. They had heard the storm of bolter fire. Some of them were even now scattering into cover, knowing that they might be next. Many of them turned and watched as Reinez and the Chaos Marine burst out through the wall of the gate chapel and tumbled the long drop to the ground.

Reinez clung to the Chaos Marine, feeling the muscle squirming beneath his gauntlet. This creature would die with him. No Space Marine feared death – but every one feared dying without doing their duty to the God-Emperor. Reinez inwardly rejoiced that he would not have a pointless, unsung death.

The dark green oblong of the Chimera whirled up towards him, and with a scream of torn metal Reinez and the Chaos Marine smashed into it like twin meteors.

Reinez's vision blurred and swam. He was in a deep sharp pit of shredded metal, the tall towers of the administration district swirling high above him. The pallid bulk of the Chaos Marine hauled itself over him, blocking out the blue-grey morning sky of Entymion IV.

The Chaos Marine looked down at Reinez. There was no soul in its eyes. It raised an arm above its head, ready to piston the long rusting chainblade down through Reinez's throat.

Reinez ripped his pistol hand free of the wreckage and emptied the magazine into the Chaos Marine. The shells ripped through it, tearing bloodless wounds so deep Reinez glimpsed lungs and veins pulsing before the wounds closed up. The Marine reeled, its weight falling back off Reinez.

The half-second it bought him was enough. Someone shouted an order and suddenly dozens of las-shots were slashing through the Marine, battering it back. It roared horribly and launched itself off Reinez, into the shelter of the wrecked Chimera.

Reinez tore himself free. His thunder hammer was still in his hand – its power field ripped through the torn metal and Reinez was free.

More las-fire. Thudding into the Chimera, splintering the stone of the chapel tower, fizzing trails of superheated air.

The Fire Drakes weren't just shooting at the Chaos Marine. They were firing everywhere, and that fire was answered from the tower blocks surrounding the Fire Drakes' entry point.

Reinez could see the enemy. They had infiltrated the tower blocks in their hundreds, firing from dozens of windows. They were tiny pale shapes – even from this distance Reinez thought they looked human. The fire was small arms – lasguns and autoguns, with a few heavy stubbers sending chains of fire rattling down. The Chaos Marine attack had been the first move in a massive counter-attack.

The gunfire was like hot, deadly rain. If the Crimson Fists had still held the chapel, Caltax's Devastator squad would have sent heavy weapons fire ripping through the administration towers. But the Fire Drakes were now trapped beneath the weight of enemy fire, pumping useless lasgun shots up at the windows.

Reinez saw a Hellhound's flamer tanks blow, swallowing up several men and an officer in a mushroom of flame. 'Scatter!' yelled Reinez at the Guardsmen, hauling himself out of the Chimera's wreckage. 'Get to cover! Now!'

The Fire Drakes nearby heard him, running heads down to take shelter behind statues or at the foot of buildings. There were bodies already scattered – flailing forms fell from windows where a lucky hit brought down an attacker. One landed wetly nearby and Reinez saw they were indeed human, naked to the waist, their faces wrapped in leather straps and their skin pierced all over.

Cultists. Heretics. The lost and the damned, beyond all hope. Which meant that there was no hope for Gravenhold, either.

The Chaos Marine reared up monstrously and lashed out, taking off a Guardsman's head and bisecting a second man. Reinez hefted his thunder hammer and prepared to die there, beating back the thing that could wreak bloody ruin through the Guardsmen.

He charged, and fell. Pain rifled through his body. His vision greyed out and he looked down to see a shredded mess of blood and ceramite where the armour around his foot had split – the adrenaline and combat hormones had blocked out the pain and he hadn't even noticed.

Reinez dragged himself towards the Chaos Marine, las-fire boring through the paving around him. The Chaos Marine was heading for the closest tower block – there were other Chaos Marines in the lower storeys, rattling bolter fire down at the Fire Drakes.

Reinez knew he wouldn't reach the Chaos Marine, but he had to keep going. Because this wasn't just another traitor to him, as foul as that was. This was something even worse.

Reinez recognised the golden chalice the Chaos Marines bore on their shoulder pads. He knew that purple and bone livery.

'I know what you are!' yelled Reinez, trying to prop himself up on his thunder hammer. 'I know! Traitors to the blood of Dorn! Excommunicate and damned!'

The Chaos Marine seemed to hear him. It looked round, once, but Reinez couldn't read the expression on its face. Then it was gone into the shadows of the nearest building, and a scattering of las-fire threw Reinez back onto his face.

Engines roared nearby. Tracks chewed into the paving slabs.

'Medic!' someone yelled. Hands reached down and Reinez felt himself hauled by several Guardsmen into the back of a Chimera, a medical officer with hands full of blood packs leaning over him.

'I don't need blood,' he said bitterly. 'Help your men.'

The medic, who had probably never seen a Space Marine before in the flesh, turned back to men moaning in the back of the Chimera. Reinez didn't need a medic, he had survived much worse. He would be back on his feet within the day with the attentions of a competent Apothecary. His pride was more injured than his body. He had been prepared to die, and he had failed. He had come face to face with the traitors who had left a stain on the name of Rogal Dorn himself, and they had escaped.

But he would redeem himself. Because as soon as he was back with his battle-brothers, he would contact the Chapter Master of the Crimson Fists and tell him that he had found the Soul Drinkers.

CHAPTER THREE

EIGHTY PER CENT of the Fornux Lix Fire Drakes made it out of the south-eastern gate, falling back in good order. They regrouped and by nightfall had counterattacked with armour and Hellhound flame support tanks, fighting bitterly through the lower floors of the closest tower blocks until they had a foothold just inside Gravenhold.

As the attack had got under way, the surviving Chaos Marines had melted away into the city, taking their dead and disappearing. As they were ordered to pull out of the chapel, the Crimson Fists reported the supposedly solid city wall that backed onto the chapel was riddled with a warren of tunnels. Before they left, the Fists used some of the Fire Drakes' demo charges to bring the whole gate chapel down, sealing off that avenue of attack. But they had killed only a handful of the traitors in the few minutes of the gunfight – the enemy had now melted back into the city, ready to burst out and strike at the invading Imperial forces.

Captain Reinez survived. While the Crimson Fists' Apothecary tended to him, he demanded a high-level astropath from Lord General Xarius and got it. He sent an astropathic message to the Crimson Fists' Chapter Master on the Chapter fleet several sectors away, and informed him that the Soul Drinkers were in Gravenhold. Shortly afterwards Reinez ordered his remaining Marines to withdraw from Gravenhold to the Fists' command post south of the city, and to await further orders.

The Seleucaian Fourth Division's drive into the west of the city went better, at first. Even as the enemy were turning the canyons of tower blocks into a killing zone for the Fire Drakes, the Seleucaians moved in rapid order through the massive landing decks and maintenance sheds of the city's spaceport. Access to the city was through a series of huge arches cut into the wall, leading to the dark industrial mill district crowded into the eastern edge of Gravenhold. Xarius's own Baneblade super-heavy tank formed a command post in the centre of the Seleucaians, and from its heavily armoured interior Xarius listened to the desperate reports from the south-eastern gate as his own side of the pincer rolled rapidly through the abandoned spaceport unopposed.

The enemy were behind them. The fuel sumps had been drained and, risking the suffocating and flammable fumes, the Gravenholders erupted from beneath the ground to swarm over the rear echelon elements following the main body of Guardsmen into the city. Medical units, artillery, half-tracks loaded with ammunition, fuel and food, the small Adepta Sororitas preceptory that administered to the division's spiritual health – they fought a savage close-quarters battle they were ill-equipped for.

Xarius turned the formation around to strike back but by then all order was gone. The tanks at the forefront were held up by the infantry that had been marching behind them. The heavy guns were useless with so many Imperial units mixed up in the melee. Somehow, Xarius forged a meaningful counterattack from the chaos and sent several thousand men and scores of tanks rolling into the enemy.

But the damage was done. The Seleucaians won back uncontested landing pads streaked with blood and burning vehicle sheds draped with the bodies of their support units. The enemy left their dead and headed back underground. Xarius forbade reprisal attacks down the miles of filthy fuel tunnels. Those who disobeyed never returned, many drowned or incinerated when the tunnels were flooded again.

The Seleucaian thrust never got into the city. Night fell over the spaceport on the first day, Entymion IV's evening sun reflecting off the sheen of clotting blood that marked where the enemy had torn Sisters Hospitaller and divisional file clerks apart in the melee. There were hundreds of the enemy dead, but no one had any illusions that there weren't plenty more where they had come from.

THE ENEMY. WHEN the stream of wounded finally ran drier, divisional medics received some relatively intact corpses to examine. Xarius himself made sure he was present, the dissections carried out in the shadow of his Baneblade.

Beneath powerful arc-lights the enemy was revealed. It was quickly established that they were human. They seemed heavily worked and borderline malnourished, their skin was pale from a lack of light suggesting an almost completely underground or nocturnal existence. The faces of some were wrapped in thick metal straps buckled around their heads, others were so covered in self-inflicted scars that they formed masks of scab tissue. A couple had the skin of the face entirely removed – the more extreme mutilations should have led to rapid sickness and death, but these had survived.

Their bodies were scarred, too. Most were pierced. Some had evidently carved messages into themselves, either in too eccentric a hand to read or in a language foreign even to the Sister Dialogus who was brought in from the survivors of the preceptory.

The dissection continued and the evidence mounted. The enemy had enlarged hearts or apparently superfluous organs grafted into them. Many had been repeatedly cut open and sewn back together with crude, almost frenzied stitches.

But they had survived. They should have been killed by whatever procedures they had suffered, yet these men and women had survived long enough to die beneath the lasguns and tank tracks of the Seleucaian Fourth Division.

The weapons were mostly the expected mix of lasguns and autoweapons looted from the Planetary Defence Force supplies, with a few hunting rifles and other aristocratic pieces thrown in. But there were some of apparently xenos design, too – some kind of rifle made of irregularly-shaped material like hardened black glass, that fired streams of razor-sharp crystal shards. A stubby bulbous weapon that looked somehow organic, which shot bolts of blackness that burned through armour. Some of the rebels had glossy black armour plates, like segments of beetles' carapaces, fused with their skin.

Aliens, the rumours had said. Some kind of corruptive xenos influence had taken hold of Gravenhold. It was clear by now that the enemy was the one-time population of the city and that they had sunk far too deep to ever redeem themselves. There were even reports of Traitor Marines from the Fire Drakes, but inevitably no bodies had been recovered to confirm them. Xarius watched the gruesome dissection silently as the divisional medicae peeled back the layers of horror, and thought how the enemy must have been begging their gods for him to send in spearheads of Guardsmen for them to ambush.

But Reinhardt Xarius had been an Imperial soldier for his entire life and a commander for most of it. He knew exactly what advantage the Imperium had. They had determination, tenacity, bravery and above all, numbers. He spent the rest of the night working out defensive strategies for the troops camped in the spaceport and the south-eastern gate, but he knew that the next day his first task would be to demand all the sector authorities send him every reinforcement they could.

The enemy knew the city, and the Guard would have to kill every single one of them to winkle them out. But the Imperium's crucial advantage was that they could muster enough Guardsmen and tanks to do exactly that.

WHEN THE PLANET Veyna was annexed by the Imperium in 068.M41, it was a Halo Zone world marked out only by the lakes of liquid nitrogen at its polar caps and the small civilisation that clung to survival near the equator. These people were the descendants of settlers from the Scattering, the great drive of colonisation that seeded the galaxy with humanity after the discovery of warp travel. Veyna was one of the many worlds that had been forgotten for thousands of years, cut off by the Age of Strife and bypassed by the Great Crusade, only to be rediscovered in the second half of the forty-first millennium.

There were hundreds of worlds like Veyna. Most of them never even had names. Isolated and backwards, feudal or blackpowder-level worlds, gradually drawn back into the fold by the ravenous Imperium that considered itself to own every community of humans in the Galaxy – including those they hadn't discovered yet. Normally Veyna would be given an Imperial designation and perhaps a handful of hardy activists from the Missionaria Galaxia to convert the heathens, and then left alone aside from the occasional tithe demands from the Administratum. The Imperium would add a handful of new citizens to the immense population labouring and fighting under the aegis of the Emperor, and the people of Veyna would have been granted theoretical protection against the many ravening forces that might creep across the galaxy to consume them.

But Veyna had its polar caps. It was cheaper to ship pure liquid nitrogen from Veyna's polar lakes than to manufacture it, and so Veyna's only natural resource was quickly claimed by the Adeptus Mechanicus for the factoria on its forge-worlds.

The only habitable land was earmarked for the great processing plants and spaceport that the Mechanicus would need to take their harvest from Veyna. The natives were displaced, offered one-way passage to the closest forge-world where they would live short but productive lives in the lightless workshops and factory floors. Slow death in the name of the Emperor beckoned them, and they were assured by the missionaries that they would do better to die young for the Lord of Mankind than to die old heretics.

Most believed them and the civilisation of Veyna disappeared overnight, herded into the bellies of Mechanicus cargo ships. Many survived the trip only to die in industrial accidents or simply get so ground down by the unrelenting toil until it was difficult to tell the living from the dead. The last of them survived long enough to see the dregs from other worlds, more slaves in all but name, brought in to replace them at the machine face. Each one was just one more link in the endless chain of suffering that greased the wheels of the Imperium with the blood of the hopeless, and as they themselves prepared to die they longed for the brutal frozen haven of Veyna.

But some did not agree.

The hardiest and proudest of the Veynans survived out on the tundra, raiding and harassing the Adeptus Mechanicus garrison, sabotaging pipelines and spacecraft before disappearing into the wilderness. Sporadic tech-guard patrols could do little against an enemy that could live off the tundra and disappear at will.

Within thirty years of the first shipment the polar lakes were drained and the Adeptus Mechanicus withdrew from Veyna. The only survivors of the once-proud Veynan civilisation were by then the dwindling tundra raiders who saw their chance as the Mechanicus evacuated their equipment and personnel. They stowed away on cargo ships and hijacked shuttles, determined to take revenge on the Imperium by attacking the valuable cargoes travelling the ill-guarded space between outlying systems. The Veynans would become pirates, waging a symbolic war to honour the memories of their dead.

The Mechanicus convinced the Imperial Navy to nip this threat in the bud. The Imperium did not want one more nest of pirates preying on vulnerable space traffic. A squadron of escorts was diverted to surround the Mechanicus ships and destroy those Veynans who had taken the crews hostage. The Navy offered an ultimatum. The Veynans could free their Mechanicus hostages and abandon the ships they had taken, to be taken into custody, given the opportunity to renounce their sins in the sight of the Emperor, and be executed. Otherwise, they would be blown out of space, hostages and all.

The escorts had been about to open fire when the *Brokenback* arrived.

THE TRANSPORT SHIP's outer maintenance corridors were as cold as the Veynan winter. Eumenes saw his breath coiling in front of him as he clambered down through the ragged metal hole bored by the boarding pod and drew his bolt pistol.

He had braved those Veynan winters as a boy, all but naked on the tundra. Now he had an enhanced metabolism and augmented organs so new he still ached from the operations to implant them, and wore a carapace of padded semi-powered armour. Cold couldn't kill him any more. It felt like nothing could.

Eumenes's enhanced vision picked out details from the darkness. Steel struts, heavy segmented pipes, spurts of coolant, the occasional inscription promising to honour the ship's machine-spirit if it kept working. One wall was the curved metal skin of the inner hull surface. The thrum of the ship's engines rumbled through everything.

'Squad Eumenes down,' voxed Eumenes, the feel of the vox-bead still unfamiliar in his throat. He had been trained with all this equipment over and over again but it was still relatively recently that he had taken up all the equipment and augmentations of the Space Marine he would one day become.

He would be a Soul Drinker. He had prayed for salvation from the souls of his dead ancestors on Veyna, and they had led the Soul Drinkers to him. He and the other scout-novices were recruited from those who had suffered at the hands of the Imperium, and none had a bigger grudge than Eumenes. One day, he would lead his excommunicate brothers against the darkness that grew from the Imperium like cancers in a sick body.

Eumenes had memorised the likely layout of the transport ship. Each ship was different but the transport was built around a plan that meant the differences would be minor. He heard the feet of his scout squad hitting the floor behind him and he began to lead them forward into the closest access duct.

'Selepus, get up here,' said Eumenes. 'I want you up front.'

Selepus, thin-faced and quick, was instantly at Eumenes's shoulder. 'If we get a contact, I'll keep it quiet.'

'Good man.'

Scamander, the Librarium novice, was last out of the boarding pod. Eumenes's six-man squad wore dark purple carapace armour over bone-coloured undersuits. Since they weren't physically full Space Marines they could not yet wear the armour of a full battle-brother, but it had its blessings – it meant they were smaller and quieter, perfect for sneaking into an enemy spacecraft.

The squad moved quickly and quietly through the inner hull skin and into the ship proper. Selepus was on point, his monomolecular fighting knife in his hand and his bolt pistol holstered. Selepus was more dangerous that way. Scamander brought up the rear. He was there in case the plan went wrong and they needed some psychic artillery.

The transport was cramped but well maintained. A niche in the wall held a libation of scented machine-oil and a prayer typed out in binary, forming a tiny shrine to the ship's machine-spirit. Selepus ducked around the corner up ahead, and waved the rest of the squad forward.

'Crew quarters ahead.'

Eumenes nodded, and the squad moved on.

The corridor opened into a low-ceiling room, partitioned by columns and low walls. It was divided into a kitchen and mess, dormitories with rows of bunks, a small shrine with a gilded icon of an Imperial saint, and an area with seating and a few books.

Selepus had killed the first contact before Eumenes even noticed him. It was a menial in grease-stained coveralls, with half of his head shaved and the other half covered in long braids. Hive gang stock probably, press-ganged or conscripted into menial service. The man's head lolled back too far as Selepus drew his knife through his throat from behind – the menial had been sitting at one of the mess tables, eating a bowl of something grey and stringy.

Selepus lowered the body silently to the floor. The squad spread out through the crew quarters, Nisryus, Thersites and Tydeus flanking Scamander.

Once the sweep was done, Eumenes had the squad pause.

'Anything, Nisryus?'

Nisryus's own grudge with the Imperium was that it had murdered his family. Nisryus had narrowly avoided being burned at the stake, he had been the son of an aristocrat whose family hid the psyker-taint in their bloodline. Nisryus had watched his family scourged and burned alive. It was the Soul Drinkers's attack on the Sothelin prison world where the executions were held that saved him. The Soul Drinkers had drawn may recruits from the rebels held prisoner on Sothelin, and Nisryus was one of those who had proven able enough to take on the mantle of Chapter novice.

Nisryus closed his eyes. His precognitive powers were immature, but he was strong enough to use them without risk of corruption. His eyes were too old for his face, surrounded by crow's feet, and they wrinkled up as he concentrated.

'He'll think we're enemies,' said Nisryus. 'To him, everyone's an enemy.'

'And the crew?'

Nisryus shook his head. 'I can't see them. His presence blocks them all out.'

It made sense. From what Sarpedon had said, the strength of the captive's emotions had broadcast his location to the Librarium from several systems away. It was a miracle Nisryus could see anything at all.

Selepus indicated a narrow archway leading towards the stern. 'Cargo bay that way.'

'Let's go.'

BEFORE EUMENES'S TIME, when the Soul Drinkers still fought under the Imperial banner, the Great Harvest was held every decade to bring new recruits into the Chapter. Since the Chapter had been fleet-based, the Great Harvest saw them visiting scores of planets over the course of a year, picking a handful of the best and youngest warriors and running them through a brutal meat grinder of a selection process. Those the Chaplains selected as suitable were given endless psycho-doctrination sessions, surgical implants and enhancements, and intensive combat drills. They lived as novices, attending upon the Marines to forge respect for the soldiers they would one day become.

The Soul Drinkers had finally begun to arrest their genetic decline a little more than a year ago, and had restarted the Great Harvest to recover the losses they had suffered at the hands of both Chaos and the Imperium. The Chapter, now residing on the space hulk they had christened the *Brokenback*, travelled to worlds where rebellion had flared against Imperial repression. Their new recruits came from the ranks of those who had dared to stand against the Imperium, not because they thought they would win but because they valued their freedom more than their lives. They saved the best of them from corpse-strewn battlefields or Imperial prison ships, from desperate last stands and mass executions. Eumenes had been rescued from the last stand of the Veynan rebels, Nisryus from execution as a psyker-witch. Scamander had been saved from the duelling pits of Thrantis Minor where he had been sentenced to die in the arena for joining a movement in support of the planet's persecuted psykers. There were just over a hundred fighting novices in the Chapter now, and Master of Novices Karraidin had judged many of them ready to take up active duty alongside their battle-brothers.

They were not yet fully Space Marines – there were many more surgical adaptations to take place before then – but in a sense they never would be. The Soul Drinkers had spent almost all of their history as Imperial lapdogs and only the leadership of Sarpedon himself had brought them into the light. Sarpedon had decreed that the Chapter's novices would no longer undergo the rigorous psycho-doctrination that all Soul Drinkers before them had. The novices would fight as the Chapter's existing Marines did – because they were in a battle worth fighting, against the forces of Chaos instead of at the whim of the corrupt Imperium. Not because endless sleep-training had broken their free will.

The scouts were the future. There were only around four hundred Soul Drinkers left and the scout-novices would be the ones to repopulate their ranks. It was a new Chapter being born from the ashes of excommunication. An army of free men, fighting because it was right.

No wonder the Imperium feared them.

THE LAST FEW crewmen made their stand in the engine block.

The adept, on secondment from the Officio Medicae hospital on Diomedes Tertiam, clutched his slim black case to his chest with one hand while the other held a shaking laspistol. The case contained his medical implements with which he had been carrying out tests on the prisoner.

It was a fascinating subject, after all. But now all that was forgotten.

Most of the crew were probably dead. The bridge hadn't answered the ship's vox. The adept himself had seen some of the ship's crew lying with slit throats. He had seen one of the invaders – quick, shaven-headed and wearing heavy purple armour that didn't slow him down one bit, firing rapidly with a bolt pistol and blowing a menial's torso apart.

The adept and two of the ship's armsmen had fled here, to the engine block, where they had taken up a vantage point on the gantry halfway up one of the generatorium stacks. Even a small ship like this needed vast amounts of power for its sub-warp engines and the result was this cavernous space, dominated by the engine stacks. The vantage point was excellent; they could see across the oil-stained floor of the engine block below and the solid humming mass of the engine tower protected them from behind.

One armsman, an excellent shot who had sniped tharrbeasts for sport on the ash wastes of Diomedes Tertiam, scanned for targets, pulling back the hood of his pressure suit to get an unobstructed view through the sights of his long-las. The other armsman stuck close to the adept and racked the slide on his shotgun.

For a moment there was silence except from the adept's shuddering breath. They would be safe here – they had plenty of ammunition and no one could sneak up on them. The armsmen would protect their adept. It was their job. Whoever it was who had taken the ship, they would suffer when the ship's autopilot brought it to the orbital checkpoint where their prisoner was to be transferred out. The adept only had to survive for the half hour or so before that happened, then security troops would storm the ship and save him.

He was an old man. He wasn't supposed to do this kind of thing any more. But he felt the comforting weight of the laspistol in his hand. No one could get him here. The armsmen would die first. But it wouldn't come to that.

'Movement,' said the armsman with the rifle. 'I've got it...'

That was when the adept burst into flames.

SCAMANDER'S BLOOD RAN cold. It always did when he used the power the Emperor had given him. It took all the fire in his soul and siphoned it out into the outside world where it took the form of leaping flames that appeared as if from nowhere. But it had to come from somewhere – somewhere inside Scamander, in the depth of betrayal he had suffered. The Emperor had looked out from his Golden Throne and granted Scamander pyrokinetic powers with which to scourge the Emperor's enemies, and yet the Imperium had condemned Scamander, that same Imperium that claimed to do the Emperor's work.

He remembered that betrayal and let it flow from the depths of his soul and out through his outstretched fingers, through the air to the cluster of figures huddled on the gantry above.

Bright orange flame blossomed. A man screamed as his clothing suddenly caught fire. Scamander forced the fire out of himself, feeling a psychic cold like a spiral of ice coiling down through him. He played the fire across the other targets, too, a pair of armed crewmen. One of them had seen Scamander and had been preparing to shoot, but that only made the psychic path between him and Scamander shorter. The sniper spasmed as fire boiled up from inside his lungs – he flailed and toppled over the gantry rail, falling to the floor far below.

Scamander let the fire fall. His frozen breath glittered as he exhaled, crystals of ice were hard slivers in his mouth. He couldn't use his power for long periods of time yet, and would have to train long and hard to become living artillery on a par with Tyrendian.

With the psychic flame gone, the adept and the second armsman were wreathed in black smoke as the fire guttered. They were no longer screaming.

'Are they dead?' asked Thersites, who was hunkered down behind Scamander covering the approach behind them.

'Better check,' replied Scamander, panting with the effort. He was radiating cold.

Thersites nodded and hurried towards the stairway leading up to the gantry. A quick glance told him the armsman on the floor was very dead indeed – Scamander had felt the man die, his death a flicker of feedback as the flame coursed through him. The other two might need a bolt shell to be sure.

'Eumenes? We've got the last of them in the engine block. They're gone,' voxed Scamander.

'Understood. Get back to the engine block entrance and be ready to fall back to the pod. How are you?'

'It took a lot out of me. But Thersites is covering me.'

'You rely too much on your power, Scamander. There won't always be another scout there to back you up. It doesn't matter how many men you can burn, as long as it leaves you vulnerable you're better off shooting.'

'I have to learn, Eumenes…'

'And I have to lead. The galaxy hates us enough without you knocking yourself out trying to incinerate everything.'

'Of course. Of course you're right.'

'Good. Stick to your gun except in extremis. Now get back to the pod, we're entering the cargo hold.'

No wonder Nisryus had been all but blinded. Eumenes didn't have his fellow scout's precognition, but even he could feel the force of raw emotion that bled out of the captive.

The cargo hold was mostly empty, with a few crates and void-boxes piled up against the walls to leave a single wide space. In the centre of that space was a metal frame, evidently purpose-built to hold an over-sized human figure spreadeagled, angled forward so it was forced to stare at the floor. A block of steps led up to a pulpit overlooking the prisoner's back. Several jointed armatures reached out from the pulpit, each tipped with a syringe or scalpel.

The captive was two and a half metres high. He was stripped naked and his body was so crammed with muscle that it seemed ready to burst. Dark grey oblongs under the skin of the pectorals and abdomen marked where the black carapace had been implanted, and neuro-jack sockets in the biceps and chest once linked the captive's nervous system to his power armour.

His torso was covered in scars. Many were thin white surgical scars, showing where organs had been implanted or internal injuries had been healed at the Chapter apothecarion. Others were thick wounds, many recent, plastered over with the fast-forming scab that resulted from a Space Marine's augmented blood. Other, fresher surgical scars covered his back – the crew had been busy taking samples and testing the captive's metabolism to see if he really was who they thought he was.

A Space Marine. A soldier of the Adeptus Astartes, one of the legendary giants of the battlefield that every Imperial citizen had heard of but so few had ever seen. They were the stuff of stories, the fabric of the Imperium's legends, and now there was one here, mad and captive.

But more than that. The prisoner was that rarest of creatures – a renegade Marine, one that had broken his psycho-doctrination to rebel against the Imperium itself. A Soul Drinker.

A Soul Drinker gone mad.

The prisoner looked up. A rope of spittle hung from his lower lip. His eyes looked heavy and exhausted. But as soon as he saw Eumenes crossing the cargo bay towards him something woke up inside him. Eumenes saw the Marine's hair, once shorn close, was growing out – sweat and grime had turned it into rat's tails. He was unshaven, too.

He growled and the frame shook as he tried to break free. Runnels of dried blood crusted the manacles around his wrists and ankles.

'Brother,' said Eumenes carefully. 'We have come to take you back.'

The rage in the Marine's eyes died for a moment. 'I have no brothers,' he said.

Eumenes had not seen the battle on Stratix Luminae. That had been before he and the other novices were recruited. But he had heard that it was terrible indeed, and at its climax the Soul Drinkers had been forced to leave behind more than thirty Assault Marines under Sergeant Tellos. Tellos, they said, had gone mad in the battle, and he had taken with him the Assault Marines who had chosen to follow him.

The Chapter had known better than to assume Tellos and his battle-brothers had died. But it was still a shock when the scattered reports of renegade Marines from across the Imperium, filtered through the many cogitators on the *Brokenback*, had indicated that Tellos was not just alive but possessed of a mindless lust for destruction. He and his Assault Marines had blazed a path of destruction, indiscriminate and pointless, raiding Imperial settlements and killing anyone they found. On Diomedes Tertiam one of them had been captured and that Marine was here, being transported to the system's prison planet.

But he would never get there. Sarpedon needed him, because he might know where Tellos was headed next.

'Nisryus,' said Eumenes. 'Is there a Marine in him somewhere?'

Nisryus walked forward carefully. The Marine looked at him with undisguised hate. Nisryus held out a hand, gingerly probing the emotion that saturated the cargo bay. Those emotions echoed backwards as well as forwards, giving Nisryus limited precognitive powers – here, they were strong enough to hint at the mental landscape hidden within the Marine's madness.

'Just,' said Nisryus.

'Good. Selepus, Tydeus, unclamp the frame and take it back to the pod. We need to be out of here before the checkpoint.' Eumenes flicked on the vox. 'Scamander, Thersites, get back to the pod. We're done.'

Soon the scouts would be gone and the ship would be devoid of life when it was recovered. The system authorities would believe that their prisoner had escaped and killed the crew, before disappearing. They would scour the nearby intrasystem space for a saviour pod or shuttle that the prisoner might have used to escape. They would, of course, never find him.

The lost battle-brother would not be broken for the good of a corrupt Imperium. Instead, he had an appointment with his Chapter Master.

CHAPTER FOUR

SARPEDON LOOKED ACROSS at Brother Lothas. He was reminded that all the Soul Drinkers had very nearly fallen as far as Lothas, and Sarpedon had led them to that brink.

Lothas had been sedated and taken to the apothecarion, located inside a hospital ship that made up part of the *Brokenback*'s immense bulk. His wounds had been healed and he had been cleaned up, but he still looked every inch the monster Eumenes had found. Unbound but separated from Sarpedon by a near-invisible power field that crossed the interrogation cell, Lothas almost vibrated with pent-up energy.

Sarpedon was alone in his half of the cell, but he knew that Chaplain Iktinos and other senior Soul Drinkers were watching. Lothas didn't know that, however. Sarpedon wanted this to be man to man, a soldier to his commander, face to face.

'I have seen the records of your service with the Chapter,' said Sarpedon. 'Eleven years as a son of the Emperor. Assault honours at Diocletian Dock. Purity Seal granted after the Quintam Minor. Sergeant Graevus recommended you as leadership material after the Chapter War.'

Lothas spat into the power field, which flashed slightly and fizzed. Sarpedon ignored it.

'It is said that Tellos valued you very highly.'

Lothas paused at that. Tellos, the most severely mutated of the Soul Drinkers except perhaps Sarpedon himself, had been a heroic and skilled Assault Sergeant before the Chapter's downfall and a talismanic, seemingly unkillable soldier after it. Assault Marines who had lost their sergeants had often chosen to follow Tellos into battle, he was a symbol of the Soul Drinkers' triumph over corruption and perhaps the most naturally gifted warrior the Chapter had. Lothas had probably all but worshipped the man.

Then, on Stratix Luminae, Tellos and his Assault Marines had gone insane.

'Is Tellos still alive?'

Lothas clenched and unclenched his fists. His desire to break through the power field and strangle Sarpedon was palpable. 'Tellos can't be killed,' he growled.

'Was he with you on Diomedes Hive Prime?'

'Ha! If he had there wouldn't be a Hive Prime! We are the seeds of destruction. We are the new scourge. Some of us he scattered. Some of us still follow him.'

'Why follow him? Why not return to your Chapter?'

'Because you were weak!' Lothas lunged forward and punched the power field, sending out a red flash and a spray of orange sparks. The field was configured to administer a neural shock on contact but Lothas's enhanced metabolism shrugged it off, he hardly seemed to notice.

Sarpedon was physically stronger than perhaps any of the Soul Drinkers, a legacy of Abraxes's mutations. Presumably the weakness Lothas mentioned was mental. 'What could Tellos do, Lothas, that we cannot?'

Lothas sneered. 'He could see beyond. There are billions of vermin in this galaxy wasting their lives fighting for an empire that doesn't care about them. Do you think you are any different? What can you do? You are fighting a war you can never win, as if you could destroy Chaos, cleanse the galaxy, with four hundred mutants and a space hulk!'

Sarpedon knew it would do no good to argue with Lothas. He wanted the man to rant at him to tell Sarpedon everything that was bubbling over in his mind. 'So why does Tellos fight?' he said calmly.

Lothas barely needed prompting. His eyes were afire like a preacher's. 'To fight! Because there is no right and wrong, there is no freedom, there is no Emperor's light! The only meaning in life is to leave a scar on the galaxy that will never heal. In the moment of destruction is exultation, and Tellos taught us to make that moment last forever.'

Sarpedon leaned forward, one bionic leg clicking on the pitted metal floor. 'Pure destruction. Nothing else.'

'Pure,' said Lothas. 'True purity. None of the excuses, none of the limitations. These are the things that make you weak. Everything you could be is bound up in this crusade that you cling to.'

Sarpedon guessed that Lothas was repeating Tellos's own words. Lothas had no will left of his own, only the seeds planted there by Tellos after Stratix Luminae. Perhaps he had been corrupting them even before that, on the *Brokenback*, under Sarpedon's nose.

'But it will have to end, Lothas. Everyone dies eventually.'

Lothas shook his head, smiling grimly, revealing broken teeth. 'No, Sarpedon. The bigger the scar, the longer you live. And Tellos will live forever, because after Entymion there will be no greater scar.'

Sarpedon leaned back on his hind legs. 'Is that all you see? Purposeless destruction?'

'I see you lying to yourselves. You will die as if you were never here while we will let the galaxy burn. I see a universe so drowned in blood that it will never forget us. Blood, Sarpedon. Blood for the Blood God.'

Sarpedon rapped sharply on the door behind him. He could hear Lothas's breathing, heavy and deliberate, as the door ground open and Sarpedon walked on his eight clacking talons out into the corridor beyond.

The cell was located in the belly of an Imperial battleship, an old mark that had seen service well before the Gothic War. The black iron formed an oppressive vaulted ceiling and false columns down the walls. Dozens of brig cells led off on each side – a ship this size might have had twenty thousand crew, with its own criminals, police force and prison. With the addition of the power fields set up by Techmarine Varuk, it was secure enough to hold a Space Marine.

Chaplain Iktinos, as normal wearing full armour and skull-faced helmet, was standing just outside the door. The door clanged shut behind Sarpedon.

'He's gone,' said Iktinos.

'But Tellos might not be. We have a name: Entymion. Probably a place, maybe a person.' Sarpedon thought about the immense size of the Imperium and the difficulty of finding out what one word meant amongst those thousands of worlds and trillions of people. 'I'll put Techmarine Varuk on it.'

'If only we still had Solun,' said Iktinos.

Solun had been a specialist in information. The mem-banks implanted in his armour had given him a formidable capacity for processing information. He was dead now, left beneath the surface of Stratix Luminae.

'What about Brother Lothas?' Iktinos's voice was grave. He already knew the answer.

'Shoot him,' said Sarpedon. 'Incinerate the body.'

Iktinos turned aside and Sarpedon heard him voxing Sergeant Locano, whose Marines would function as a firing squad. It was

Iktinos's duty to administer the final rites to a condemned battle-brother, not that Lothas would appreciate it.

Yet again a battle-brother would die a death that had nothing to do with the Emperor's will. Sarpedon had lost too many that way already. It was time to lead his Marines into a fight that meant more than survival.

Tellos was a force for Chaos now. The Soul Drinkers had created him, they would bring him back, or they would destroy him trying.

'THIS IS WING Epsilon out of the *Resolve*, reporting on G-Day plus seven.' The voice was weary, vox-echoed from some flight officer who had badly needed sleep after a long, hard sortie. 'Seven Marauder fighter-bombers with three Thunderbolts flying cover approached Gravenhold from the south-east and broached enemy airspace in good order. Anti-aircraft fire was sporadic until within one point five kilometres of the target, when flak-batteries of the same pattern assigned to the Entymion IV PDF opened fire. Thunderbolt Epsilon-Red suffered minor flak damage. Marauder Epsilon-Green suffered the loss of the starboard waist gun and two crew casualties.'

There was a pause, perhaps as the officer remembered the dead and wounded. 'The target co-ordinates were for Gravenhold's sporting arena. The target was well-lit by tracer bombs and clearly visible amongst the surrounding buildings. Marauder Epsilon-White began the bombing run. Epsilon-White's radio transmissions became erratic. Epsilon-White overshot the target and Epsilon-Green took the point for the bombing run before suffering heavy damage from Epsilon-White's tail armaments.'

Another pause. The officer took a couple of breaths. 'Epsilon-Green was lost with all hands. The Marauders Epsilon-Blue, Black and Grey began transmitting erratically. As squadron commander I ordered all craft to withdraw from the target area and return to the *Resolve's* ground base. Only Thunderbolt Epsilon-Red and the Marauders Orange and Indigo responded to this order. Um... I was on Epsilon-Indigo. The... the transmissions... I considered the transmissions coming from the rest of the squadron to constitute a moral threat. I... I lost control of Epsilon-Indigo. When I returned... when I regained control the Marauder was over the north of the city. Its bomb load had been dropped, I don't know where. Crewman Trevso was still alive, I think I had, um, executed the other four, or perhaps they had turned on one another, I don't know... Trevso and myself turned Epsilon-Indigo back towards the ground base. There was no further anti-aircraft fire and we landed successfully. Crewman Trevso and myself were separated upon landing and taken to separate monitored medicae-cells where I was asked to make this report. I haven't seen Trevso and I don't think the rest of the squadron came back...'

Lord General Xarius flicked off the recording. He had heard enough. The same kind of thing was happening all over Gravenhold. The place was crawling with moral threats. He leaned back in his chair, wishing there was enough room in the sunken command office to stretch out in. He was an old man now, he needed to get out and stretch his legs.

The inside of Xarius's Baneblade was plush compared to a front-line tank, but it was still cramped. Gunners sat in cradle-seats, suspended almost upside-down, thick cables running from their skulls into machine-spirit ports. The Baneblade's enginseer stood at the command pulpit, the thin metal tines that had replaced his fingers working on the keyslate in front of him as he adjusted the tank's systems and typed binary prayers to the Machine God. Xarius's flag-commander Hasdrubal was near the Baneblade's brutal sloping prow, watching the pict-screens that formed the eyes of the super-heavy tank. The flag-commander was a man perfectly suited to his job, good at repeating Xarius's orders in an ear-splitting yell and filling in the gaps with his own common sense. Servitors hung in two rows, massive bronze-cased arms contrasting with their grey dead flesh. They were still now, but when the Baneblade was in combat they would haul the massive shells into the breech of the tank's forward gun. Up in the turret, perched on top of the Baneblade, more gunners and loader-servitors waited for the next time Xarius ordered the tank to move.

Right now it was still parked in Gravenhold's spaceport. It was comparatively safe there, since the makeshift mortars that the enemy sometimes fired from the eastern wall could not penetrate the Baneblade's massively thick armour.

Gravenhold. Xarius would have to take every stone of the city the hard way. After the initial thrusts on the city had been repulsed, he had asked for reinforcements and got them: fighter and bomber wings from the naval cruiser *Resolve*, the reserve elements of the Fornux Lix Fire Drakes, and the Algorathi Janissaries to reinforce the Seleucaians in the west of the city. But they weren't enough to break into the city and crack open the hard core of rebel resistance. Armoured thrusts were surrounded and cut off, infantry assaults charged only into empty buildings while their flanks and rear echelons were swamped by cultists. The Naval bombing runs were supposed to have reduced the enemy strongholds to rubble, but they had found it hard to pin down the enemy, even when warpcraft was not ripping the minds out of their crews.

Emperor's teeth, they didn't even know what they were fighting! The Seleucaians had been grinding slowly through the industrial sector in the west of the city and many men were swearing that they has fought xenos there – probably eldar, maybe something else, highly-trained and lethal. The human enemies, on the other hand, fought in desperate hordes, and the priests who heard the Guardsmen's confessions had reported to Xarius that the hand of the dark gods was laid heavy on Gravenhold. There were even Traitor Marines in their somewhere, waiting to launch terror strikes the moment the Guardsmen got too deep into the city. The enemy, whatever they were, had the run of the city and knew it inside-out to the extent that they could appear and disappear at will, laying ambushes and confounding Imperial patrols.

Chaos. Chaos and aliens. Xarius shook his head and tried to remember the many enemies of both that he had fought. Aliens were lying and devious, Chaos was abominable and destructive. Sometimes, Xarius thought he would give anything for an honest enemy.

Nothing in Gravenhold made sense. Whatever was killing his men in the massive ugly mills, or forcing the Fire Drakes to buy every inch of the south-eastern district in blood, it wasn't made up of the rebels and degenerates Xarius had fought so often. Something very, very terrible had happened to the city and Xarius had only just scratched the surface of it. There were hints of it in the battlefield reports he had piled up on the desk that took up much of his command office – the statements from soldiers who had fought super-fast xenos killers or mind-warping heretic sorcerers. Amongst them was an old archaeological intelligence report that suggested Gravenhold's supposedly solid outer walls were actually honeycombed with thousands of cramped tunnels. The same report had conjectured that Gravenhold was built on the site of several pre-imperial settlements. Emperor only knew what was lying under the streets, and how the enemy was using it to avoid the Naval and artillery strikes that should have pounded them into submission.

'Lord general?' Flag-commander Hasdrubal looked down into Xarius's command office. His voice was clipped and nasal, typical of the sleep-taught diction of the Seleucaian officer class.

'Hasdrubal. What is it?'

'Developments at the south-eastern gate, sir.'

'Are the buggers counterattacking?'

'It's not the enemy, sir. We've got it on the holo.'

Xarius grunted in annoyance and switched on the tactical holomat, which unfolded from a brass-cased console like a metallic flower. The old machine shuddered and a flickering three-dimensional map of Gravenhold appeared in the air. Xarius oriented it so it was lying on one edge and he could see the whole plan of the city. He noted the arena, surrounded by the southern hovels and stubbornly still standing after the destruction of Squadron Epsilon. Enemy contacts were sinister yellow triangles, covering the industrial and administration sectors. Massive swathes of the north and centre of the city hadn't even been touched by Imperial forces, and the map was infuriatingly featureless in those areas.

Xarius spotted the new development straight away. 'What are these?' he said, pointing to a cluster of dark blue squares that had appeared just outside the south-eastern gate, forming an island in the Fire Drakes' rearward supply areas.

'That's the thing, sir,' said Hasdrubal with a smile. 'They're Thunderhawks.'

COMMANDER REINEZ WATCHED the Thunderhawk gunship descend, its downthrust throwing up a wall of dust and debris off the hastily-cleared landing zone, battering the barracks tents and medical posts of the Fornux Lix regiments. The Thunderhawk was painted in the dark blue and crimson livery of the Crimson Fists, and bore the personal heraldry of the Chapter Master himself.

Reinez's squad stood to attention. Four of them had been lost in the Soul Drinkers' attack – Caltax's squad had suffered worse, including the death of Caltax himself. Sergeant Althaz's squad had held the lower floors bravely but had still lost two Marines. Reinez and the six surviving Marines of his squad saluted as the Thunderhawk touched down, joining the four others that had already made landfall, and the deployment ramp ground open.

Chaplain Inhuaca stamped down the ramp, black armour polished and gleaming, the silver skull of his helmet face mirror-bright. The dark red tabard over his armour matched the traditional red gauntlet of the Crimson Fists and at his waist hung the crozius arcanum, an eagle-topped icon that served as both weapon and badge of office. Censers mounted on Inhuaca's backpack released strong, spicy incense that cut through even the swirling dust of the Thunderhawk's landing. A pair of servitors tramped along behind Inhuaca bearing two banners, one was Inhuaca's personal heraldry, and the other was that of the Chapter Master. Inhuaca's banner showed a skull burning with silver flames, over a field shaped like a gauntlet to symbolise the hand of Rogal Dorn that was recovered after his death. The Chapter Master's heraldry was the red gauntlet with laurel wreath that had been carried by successive Chapter Masters for three thousand years.

Inhuaca's squad followed him. They were Tactical Marines with dark red robes over their armour – veteran battle-brothers who had been inducted into the Chaplain's seminary, and from whom would eventually be chosen a successor to take up the crozius when Inhuaca was gone.

'Commander,' said Inhuaca, his voice steely and stern through the rictus of his skull-mask. 'Well met.'

Reinez inclined his head respectfully. Inhuaca was a senior member of the Chapter, and this day he carried the authority of the Chapter Master with him. 'Well met, Chaplain. I think Entymion IV could do with some spiritual strength.'

'The Chapter Master was most concerned with your report. He asked me to confirm it with my own eyes.'

'Of course.' Reinez turned to his squad, still at attention behind him. 'Paclo!'

Brother Paclo picked up the ammunition crate at his feet and walked up front. Reinez opened the crate and took out the item inside.

He held it up for Inhuaca to see. The Chaplain inspected it for a few moments, no emotion visible through the opaque green eyepieces of his skull-mask.

It was a shoulder pad, ripped from a suit of power armour. The purple ceramite was chipped and bullet-scarred, but there was no mistaking the symbol painted onto it. The golden chalice of the Soul Drinkers.

'Then it is true,' said Inhuaca at length. 'The blood of Dorn itself has become corrupted.'

'Mutants and traitors, Chaplain,' said Reinez. 'I saw them with my own eyes.'

'And you will have your chance to avenge the honour of Rogal Dorn, commander.' Inhuaca took a rolled parchment from his robes and handed it to Reinez, it bore the Chapter Master's seal in crimson wax.

Reinez unrolled it and read quickly.

'The Chapter's instructions are simple,' said Inhuaca as Reinez read. 'You have the second battle company along with myself, armour and support units. Your mission is to locate the Soul Drinkers in Gravenhold, cripple them and prevent their escape from Entymion IV. If he is here, you are to bring back the head of Senior Librarian Sarpedon.'

'The second company? But what of Captain Cazaquez?'

'The Chapter Master decreed that as the first to face this enemy you were best to preside over their destruction. Captain Cazaques is agreed upon this and relinquished command of the second company. I and my retinue shall act in the Chapter Master's stead regarding the interpretation of his orders but shall defer to your command in all other things. This is the will of the Chapter. The blood of Dorn must be made pure, commander.'

Reinez kneeled, as he would before the Chapter Master himself. The servo-assisted brace encasing his wounded foot whirred to compensate, reminding him that in the moment of retribution he had been found wanting. With a whole company under his command, he would not fail like that again. 'By my honour as an Astartes and an inheritor of Rogal Dorn, I submit to my Chapter Master and am bound to the will of the Crimson Fists,' said Reinez, following a traditional Chapter form.

'Good. Arise, commander, I am under your orders now.'

Reinez was under no illusions as to how important his task was. The Crimson Fists were still rebuilding themselves after the disaster that had destroyed their fortress-monastery on Rynn's World, and were barely above half their peak strength. The second company, a flexible battle-company with a hundred Marines and enough firepower and expertise to equal ten times that number of Guardsmen, represented an enormous slice of the Chapter's fighting strength.

But it made sense. Reinez had felt it when he first saw that golden chalice on the shoulder pads of traitors, and he still felt it now; the Soul Drinkers were an abomination in the face of Rogal Dorn. Their continued existence prejudiced the Crimson Fists' place as defenders of the Imperium as much as the Rynn's World disaster had done. Every moment the Soul Drinkers abused Rogal Dorn's legacy was a moment of defeat for all Dorn's sons.

No doubt the other Chapters that bore Rogal Dorn's geneseed – the Imperial Fists, the Black Templars – would have felt the same. At full strength and with the backing and respect of the Adeptus Terra, they probably would have believed they were the proper choice to act as executioners in Dorn's name. But they were not here. The Crimson Fists were, Reinez was, and it was a responsibility he welcomed.

'Your first task,' said Reinez, 'will be to assemble the battle-brothers and ensure they understand the nature of this enemy and moral threat it poses. You can speak to their souls as I cannot.'

Inhuaca inclined his head in acceptance. 'And you, commander?'

'The Soul Drinkers deserted the Imperium in their entirety and they may have more than one company at their disposal. I am going to secure us some allies.'

THE SELEUCAIAN REINFORCEMENTS had included, at Lord General Xarius's specific request, a great deal of armour. Demolisher siege tanks for turning Gravenhold's picturesque architecture to rubble, Basilisks and Griffons to shell anything that looked suspicious, Hellhound infantry support tanks to fill streets and alleyways with burning promethium. Xarius's battle plans called for plenty of tanks, even hard-bitten, heretics thought twice about fighting on when faced with las-proof armoured hulls and saw their comrades crushed beneath rumbling tracks. But while a soldier could scavenge food and ammo from the battlefield, and even fight on with a bayonet if it suited the Emperor's will, a tank could not drive on unsupported.

The coming drive into Gravenhold needed fuel and ammunition. It needed spare parts. The most valuable part of the force's Naval component wasn't the *Resolve* or its Marauder fighter-bomber squadrons, it was the dozens of supply ships. Fuel landers disgorged bellies full of promethium into hungry tanks, armoury shuttles dropped off loads of Griffon shells and lascannon batteries. Xarius knew, as all the best commanders did, that an army starved of support was just a herd of helpless men at the mercy of the Emperor's enemies.

Most of the craft made landfall at the Imperial-held spaceport, where the rearward elements of the Seleucaians and the newly-arrived Algorathi Janissaries bullied Officio Munitorum adepts over who got which crates of ammunition, rations and medical supplies. A few landed to service the Fornux Lix Fire Drakes, although that particular regiment was known for its self-sufficiency and ability to do with men what most regiments had to do with tanks. Some wounded officers left on the support craft, heading up to the medical suites up on the *Resolve* where the conflict had yet to reach, although most wounded men had to make do with the casualty posts manned by regimental medics and Sisters Hospitaller.

Just after midnight, a few minutes into G-Day plus eleven, two fuel transports went off-course and veered eastwards, away from the spaceport and over the stony mass of Gravenhold. It wasn't the first time – some transports had been lost to the warpcraft that had so confounded the Marauder squadrons, others to old-fashioned malfunctions or human errors as there were in every war.

No one, including Lord General Xarius, thought much of it. The Officio Munitorum factored in such losses: a few aircraft, a tanker full of promethium, a spacecraft that was mass-produced on a dozen forgeworlds. No great loss.

Except they were not lost. Over the centre of Gravenhold, in the very shadow of the senate-house, the two wayward craft came in to land.

TECHMARINE VARUK PRESSED his bolt pistol hard against the side of the pilot's head.

'There,' he said coldly. The mechanical servo-arm attached to the backpack of his power armour pointed at the wide avenue beneath the ship, between the senate-house. 'Land us there.'

The terrified pilot shakily brought the lander down between rows of buildings that rose like marble cliff faces. This district had housed the offices of Entymion IV's ruling senators, and the streets had served their horse-drawn carriages and sedan chairs along with long trains of scribes, assistants and hangers-on. There was no one there now, and barely anything to indicate the malice that infested the city. The windows were dark and doors hung open, and just down the road the paving was scarred with a long burned crescent leading to the smouldering wreck of a Naval fighter craft. Aside from that, nothing.

The lander was only just wide enough for the avenue. The pilot, some Officio Munitorum lower adept, had no doubt landed the craft in worse terrain than this but never with a Space Marine threatening to blow his brains out. The lander's stubby wing scraped down a building, knocking down chunks of masonry and splitting the columns that held up a carved pediment. The ship's proximity alarm made an annoying pinging noise as the landing gear descended automatically, crushing a wrought iron streetlight.

The lander settled uncomfortably on the paved surface of the avenue.

'We're down,' said the pilot. He was pale and in poor shape, sweat rolling down his face and gathering in the folds of his neck. The shirt of his Munitorum-issue uniform hung open over his ample belly and the vest underneath was dark with perspiration.

'Open us up,' said Varuk. 'The lower hatches.'

The pilot scanned the instrument panel as if seeing it for the first time, then flicked a couple of switches.

'We're down,' came Graevus's voice, voxed from inside the lander's cavernous fuel tank. Through the lander's front window Varuk saw the first couple of squads hitting the ground and spreading out under the nose of the lander, taking cover behind the landing gear and closest columns.

'Good,' said Varuk. He took his bolt pistol away from the side of the pilot's head and holstered it. 'Stay here.'

Varuk pulled himself through the rear hatch of the tiny cockpit, clambered down the short access ladder and found the lower hatch open. He swung out onto the ground below and took his first breath of Enytmion IV's air. It stank of fuel from the lander. Not a good omen.

Squads Graevus, Salk, Luko and Corvan were on the ground. Apothecary Pallas and Librarian Tyrendian were with them. The second lander, a larger ammunition carrier, was landing at the intersection a hundred metres away, crushing a grand ornamental fountain beneath its weight as it came down. As a Techmarine, Varuk was a specialist in machine-lore, and to his trained eyes the landers were both ugly, inefficient things. Watching the ammo carrier shifting its ponderous bulk onto its landing gear reminded Varuk of the high risk Sarpedon had taken – trusting the better part of the whole Chapter to these crude machines that might have been shot out of the sky, or simply crashed through mechanical failure, at any moment.

Before the ammo lander was fully settled the rear loading ramp was down and, instead of crates of lasgun power packs and autocannon shells, Soul Drinkers dropped out onto the ground. Sarpedon himself was first out. Sergeant Krydel's squad followed close behind and ran ahead to secure the intersection along with Squads Dyon, Kelvor and Praedon. Iktinos was next out, along with a mob of more than forty Soul Drinkers who had lost their officers and chosen to follow the Chaplain as they had done on Stratix Luminae. Varuk himself was one of the last out: he was accompanied by the remaining specialists, Apothecary Karendin and Librarian Gresk, and the two scout squads under Senior Novices Eumenes and Giryan.

More than two hundred Soul Drinkers, including most of the Chapter's officers and specialists. Those left on the *Brokenback*, including the senior Techmarine Lygris, had simple orders: don't get spotted, and be ready to carry on the Chapter's work if the force on Entymion IV failed to return.

'Varuk! Are we alone here?' The vox was from Sarpedon. Varuk checked the dataslate mounted on the back of his wrist as the clamp on the end of his servo-arm rotated away to be replaced by a bundle of sensor tines.

He waited a few moments as the screen of the dataslate swirled with interference.

'Nothing,' he said at length. 'But it might be these buildings.' Varuk wasn't used to being the lead technical specialist in the field. Lygris normally took that role, but as effective captain of the *Brokenback* he was more valuable in space, keeping the space hulk hidden in the darkness outside system space.

Sarpedon switched to the all-squad channel. 'Sarpedon to all squads, we need hard cover. Get to the chamber mercantile alongside the senate-house.'

There was a sound like a lightning strike and Varuk saw Sergeant Graevus shattering the heavy wood door of the closest building with his power axe. A hardy close combat veteran, Graevus bore one of the Chapter's more obvious mutations in the form of his grossly enlarged and powerful hand. 'Through here!' he yelled and led his Assault Squad into the building.

'What do we do about the pilots?' asked Varuk.

Graveus glanced back at the lander. 'They can fend for themselves.'

Varuk followed Graevus through along with Squad Luko, the massive armoured bodies of the Space Marines only just fitting through the frame of the broken double doors. Varuk's eyes adjusted to the darkness instantly and he was almost stopped in his tracks.

The building had presumably once been a meeting-hall or council chamber where Gravenhold's ruling class had negotiated over control of the trillions of credits' worth of agricultural produce that Entymion IV exported. Now, it was something quite different.

A pedestal of deep green stone stood topped by a throne rendered in black metal, twin crescents rising from the back like huge sickle blades. Seating had surrounded it in concentric rings but the seats had all been torn out and replaced with heavy metal rings hammered into the floor. Each ring fastened a set of manacles to the floor, and Varuk could imagine hundreds of hunched forms kneeling in chains before whoever had sat in the throne. There were deep scratch marks on the tiled floor, dark brown with dried blood. There were more manacles on the pedestal where the enthroned creature had kept slaves or captives chained at his feet.

The walls had been stripped of whatever decoration they previously held, and were now covered in a deep black and silver mural. Heavily stylised beings, tall and slender and wielding curved blades and whips, stood over endless rows of human figures kneeling with their faces turned to the floor. Complex, curved lettering ran in friezes, spelling out some xenos language.

Varuk looked upwards. Hundreds of severed human hands hung from chains from the ceiling.

'By the throne,' said Sergeant Luko, making the sign of the aquila with his lightning claws.

'Grox-born xenos,' spat Graevus. 'Heathens.'

'We've found something,' Luko was voxing. 'Looks alien.'

'Recent?' came Sarpedon's reply from outside.

'It's been here a while.'

'Then we've probably found this world's source of corruption. But it's Entymion's problem, keep moving.'

'Understood.' Luko jogged to the far side of the room, activating his lightning claws and tearing out the far door. Beyond was the massive stone construction of the chamber mercantile, a semi-circular building in the shadow of the senate-house. It was fronted with massive columns carved to look like giant stacks of archaic one-credit coins and covered in sculptures of stern-faced adepts holding scales and quills. Gravenhold's commodities were once traded there between the various power groups – now the windows were dark and there were a few smears of long-dried blood on the front steps.

Varuk caught something moving at the edge of his vision, his ocular enhancements magnifying the small, sudden motion.

'Contact,' Varuk voxed to the three squads beside him.

'How many?' asked Graevus.

'Not sure.'

'I didn't see anything,' said Corvan, whose Assault Squad was right at the doors.

Sarpedon's Marines were crossing the street, already securing the steps and the shadows beneath the chamber mercantile's pediment.

'Be advised,' Sarpedon was voxing, 'Novice Nisryus reports possible hostiles.'

Nisryus – the precog. Varuk was not seeing things after all. The shape had been dark and darting and though Varuk was sure he had seen it, it had dissolved into the shadows before he could focus on it.

Varuk unholstered his bolt pistol again. Luko led the way across the street and Varuk folowed close behind. He could taste it, the alien wrongness of the place, the eyes upon them.

A Marauder squadron streaked overhead and as Varuk watched, one of the craft banked sharply and lost control, locked in a death spiral. He could feel a dark, sinister pulse beneath his feet or perhaps in the back of his mind, waves of faint madness. There was something terrible underneath Gravenhold, something that had snared Tellos, knocked that Marauder out of the sky, perhaps even drawn the Soul Drinkers themselves to the city.

'Heads up!' came Sergeant Krydel's voice over the voice. 'Charges set!'

In a plume of fire and rubble, the stone doors were blown off the front of the chamber mercantile and Sarpedon was leading the way into the building, ready to face any heretic or alien that might be waiting for them.

Varuk could see the scout squads following Sarpedon, Novice Nisryus hollow-eyed and intense. He could see it, the evil all around them. What was happening on Entymion IV? What did it want with the Soul Drinkers?

Varuk followed Luko into the shadows of the chamber mercantile, and Gravenhold swallowed them all whole.

CHAPTER FIVE

'THE THING ABOUT Space Marines, Threlnan, is that they're all brain-washed psychopaths.' Lord General Xarius walked lopsidedly with a cane. His troops tended to assume it was an old war injury but the truth was Xarius was an old man and his hip was giving out.

'Sir?' Colonel Threlnan was a large and brutal-looking man who looked almost comical following on the smaller, almost feeble-looking Xarius.

'I'm glad they're here, certainly,' continued Xarius. 'The Crimson Fists were an essential part of the battle plan. But you see, now the first battles have been fought I'd rather have a few more decent men who can be counted on to follow orders and run away like proper soldiers.'

The two were walking through the spaceport, where the maintenance sheds and docking clamps were overrun with supply yards, machine pools and endless dark green tents in which the Seleucaians snatched a few hours of sleep before being rotated back into the city. One of the landing pads had been appropriated by the Algorathi Janissaries and several units of them, in their archaic uniforms with bullion and epaulettes, were drilling on the cracked concrete surface. The Janissaries were a museum piece, their previous duties had involved the pacification of backwards worlds and they still fought as if forming a square and fixing bayonets could win a battle.

'Marines are good for morale,' said Threlnan.

'Hah! That they are, as long as they're fighting on the same side. Don't look at me like that, Threlnan, I know what they're like. The Dark Angels were supposed to spearhead our assault on the Dragon Archipelago on Balhaut, and when the order came down they were nowhere to be seen. Off fighting their own little war, never mind the men dying in the surf to win a beach the Marines should have taken. Never mind the rest of us lesser men.

'No, when they do what they're told they're the best, I know that. But just because we've suddenly got a company of Crimson Fists doesn't mean they'll fight where I tell them. They should be helping the Fire Drakes get a decent foothold in the south but I can't even contact the Fists' commander. They've got some private war here, Threlnan, and you're a fool if you're hoping it will coincide with ours.'

'I still think we should do our best to get them on-side, lord general,' said Threlnan. He nodded in return to a salute from a group of Seleucaians loading ammunition onto a Leman Russ battle tank. 'They're the best soldiers the Imperium has.'

'Soldiers? I hardly think they fit that description. Do you know how they make them, Threlnan? No, of course you don't. They find some barbaric planet where children fight before they can walk, and they hunt down the most bloodthirsty killers. They recruit them when they're twelve, thirteen, fourteen, with all that hate and that arrogance, just at the age when you think you're bulletproof and nothing can kill you. Then they keep them like that, give them a gun and some armour, and point them at the nearest enemy. They're not soldiers, colonel, they're maniacs. They won't answer to anyone save their own kind. And have you seen how they fight? They find the closest enemy and try to cut them up with swords.' Xarius shook his head. 'Madness. Just madness. Just so there can be something to carve on the cathedrals and put in children's stories. Now I've got a hundred of them just waiting to bend all my battle-plans out of shape.'

They walked for a few moments. Xarius watched the troops going about the real business of war: tending to the wounded, keeping the tanks running, distributing rations and ammunition. 'At least with soldiers,' he mused almost to himself, 'you know they'll fight until they break and then run away or hide in a fox-hole. You know when it'll happen so you can pull them out before they break. You know when they think they're safe they'll go off drinking and whoring, you know they'll brew rotgut and steal rations and gamble and get into knife-fights. You can plan for those things, Threlnan. Space Marines you can't plan for.'

A mortar round landed somewhere on the spaceport, throwing up a cloud of smoke and debris. There were still rebels hiding in the looming curve of the outer wall, using the tunnels to move. The Seleucaians were putting teams into the tunnels but they were short-lived, and there were too many places for the enemy to hide. Most of the soldiers were content to ignore the mortars and hope they never ended up a tunnel rat.

'We can do this without the Marines,' said Threlnan. 'An armoured thrust will puncture the heart of this city. Move up artillery and pound whatever's in front, then do it again. Keep going until we've driven them onto the Fire Drakes.'

Xarius sighed. 'I know. Armour, and lots of it. Followed up by plenty of poor dead boys. How long until the artillery train is down?'

'Departmento Munitorum says it'll be available within forty-eight hours. They're loading the landers now. Medusas and Basilisks, plenty of mobile firepower.'

'Good. Keep your boys in good spirits, Threlnan. Tell them they're going to get a chance to take the fight to this enemy, to do what they're trained for, fight the Emperor's fight, all that.'

'Yes, sir.' Threlnan saluted and walked off towards his staff tent, where he would finalise the plans for the drive into the heart of Gravenhold. Emperor alone knew what they would find, but Xarius knew he had the galaxy's ultimate weapon – tens of thousands of soldiers, none of whom the Imperium would greatly miss. What did they matter when there were trillions without number under the aegis of the Imperium? Xarius looked at them, fresh-faced near-recruits and scarred veterans alike. None of them deserved to die in Gravenhold, but a lot of them would. They were the fuel that kept the Imperium going, of course – without their sacrifice the Empire of Man would fall to ravening aliens, heresy, and worse. But that he should be the one to condemn them all! Him, one man out of all those trillions to have the deaths of so many laid at his door!

That was why he was a lord general, of course. Few men could understand the burden of command. Fewer still could handle it. That was what separated a Guardsman from a Space Marine; the Marines didn't understand death. To them it was nothing, just a stage in universal justice delivering heroes to the Emperor's side and heretics to the many hells of the Imperial Creed. But Xarius knew that death was the end. He was facing his own death and he felt the impending deaths of his men as keenly as his own. When you died, you turned to dust, and no matter what the preachers said the Emperor never noticed.

For the Emperor, he thought. In the hope that He might one day do something for them.

For the Emperor, they would all die.

* * *

NEITHER PILOT SURVIVED. As they tried to raise someone, anyone, on the long-range vox they were swamped by pale-skinned, half-naked enemies, faces marred by ugly piercings and masks of leather and metal, bloody hands prying off hatchways and hull plates.

Pilot First Class Edorin managed to open up a vox-channel to the *Resolve* just in time for them to hear his screams as he died, his ammo lander lurching off the ground as he desperately gunned its takeoff engines in an attempt to take flight and escape. The yowlings of his killers sounded through the vox, bestial and inhuman, before the lander turned slowly over and fell back into Gravenhold's streets. Its fuel cells ruptured and burning promethium poured out onto the road before igniting and immolating both Pilot First Class Endorin and the insane cultists who had killed him.

Pilot Second Class Kallian lasted a bit longer. He opened a vox-channel while his fuel lander was still intact, but he couldn't take off – enemies were jammed in his landing gear and tearing open transmission lines. He broadcast feverishly to anyone who could listen as he drew a sidearm he had never fired and hoped it would let him take a few of them with him.

He had been hijacked by Traitor Marines, he said to anyone out there who could hear him. Mutants. Heretics. There were hundreds of them, and they were in the city, last seen in the mercantile district by the senate-house. He described the purple and bone of their armour, the mutations he had seen, their cold-bloodedness and determination. Now he was useless, and the Traitor Marines had sent near-naked Gravenholder cultists to come and finish him off.

Then they tore the rear cockpit hatch out. Pilot Second Class Kallian saw the straps and spikes they wore like bridles and blinkers, the patterns of the wounds on their skin, the bloodstained rags they wore and the crude weapons they carried. He took aim and fired.

He had never fired the autopistol he had been given as a sidearm. He had never cleaned it, either. The weapon jammed solid in his hand.

Pilot Kallian died a short and bloody death, not knowing that his franctic vox-transmissions had been received. But they had not got through to the receivers on the *Resolve*, or to the command posts of the Seleucaians or Algorathi Janissaries at the spaceport. Instead, they had reached the comms post of the Fornux Lix Fire Drakes.

'HOW LONG AGO was this?' Reinez held the printout in his massive gauntlet and glared down at Lieutenant Elthanion.

'Twenty minutes,' replied Elthanion. He was something of a rarity, a genuine assault veteran who had both the tenacity to survive up-close combat and the level-headedness to become a worthwhile officer. He was the front-line commander for the Fire Drakes, with Colonel Savennian a figurehead and administrator. Elthanion's bionic eye and mouthful of broken teeth told Reinez everything he needed to know about the man.

'Do we know where?'

'Naval command say there were two landers that went down by the senate-house. They weren't destroyed on impact so it looks like one of them was our man.'

Reinez glanced through the body of the transcript. The pilot had evidently been terrified. As a Space Marine, Reinez was always vaguely mystified to see a man's fear laid out before him. To think that the threat of physical harm should drive a man to babbling near-incoherence – it reminded Reinez of why the Imperium needed the Space Marines. They were the Emperor's chosen, and they knew no fear. But the dead pilot had at least been lucid enough for Reinez's purposes.

'Lieutenant, you remember what I said to you earlier?'

Elthanion nodded. 'That we are on the same side. And that you and your men can take the fight to the enemy as we alone cannot.'

'Do you believe it?'

'My men are some of the toughest in the Guard, commander. I have the greatest respect for them. But yes, I believe what you said.'

'Good.' Reinez crumpled up the transcript. 'I need Colonel Savennian to give me command of his fastest and hardest-hitting elements. Your Armoured Fists units. Your veterans. Assault specialists. Tanks.'

'You're going in?'

'There is no choice to be made, lieutenant. We have only one shot at this enemy. My Marines can take it but only with your support. Will your men fight alongside us?'

Lieutenant Elthanion paused. No doubt he was thinking about the thrust the Crimson Fists and Fire Drakes would have to make into Gravenhold., further than they had gone before into the city's most important district where the enemy no doubt held sway. But he was also thinking about the chapels he had worshipped in with their statues of Astartes heroes, the stories the preachers had taught him of the Space Marines who won the Imperium for Mankind and put normal men to shame. He was thinking about the legends he had read, and of how he might be a part of one of them.

'Yes, they will fight,' he said.

'Excellent.' Reinez held his hand out to shake, Elthanion took it, and Reinez had to make a conscious effort not to crush the man's hand with his instinctive strength. 'The colonel will relinquish command of his forward assault units and have the force assembled within two hours. We will move then with or without the Fire Drakes.'

'You will not be failed, commander. You have my word as an officer.'

Elthanion saluted, turned on a heel and strode off. He would keep his word. Secretly, somewhere deep inside him, he had longed to fight alongside the Emperor's chosen. Reinez had seen it before. He knew that Lord General Xarius would not allow his Guardsmen to be diverted into the Crimson Fists' war – but Xarius wasn't there, and he didn't know. Gravenhold was damned and for Reinez the only thing worth fighting for on Entymion IV was the destruction of the Soul Drinkers. If he had to spend the lives of every Guardsman here to achieve that goal, he would do it.

If the Guardsmen could understand what it meant to be a Space Marine – the traditions and principles they were protecting, then they would gladly lay down their lives.

'Reinez to all units,' he voxed. 'We have them. Prepare to move.'

NIGHT WAS FALLING. They all knew they were being watched.

The chamber mercantile was a long, curved high-ceilinged hall, its broad, mosaiced floor broken by dealing-tables and auction-pulpits, heavy carved wooden thrones for important delegates, fenced-off pens for display livestock, small side-offices for scribes and adepts and ledger-stations with script-servitors still bent dormant over well-thumbed account books.

The Soul Drinkers had secured the building quickly, the scouts searching the offices and private dealing rooms, and it was again deserted. The Marines had taken up defensive positions behind the stone columns and hardwood dealers' desks, and settled in until they understood their surroundings better.

Sarpedon's gamble had paid off. Whatever force had summoned Tellos to the planet had recognised the Soul Drinkers and hadn't attacked them on sight as they would have any Imperial troops. The landers they had taken down to the city had been swamped and destroyed by cultists who had waited for the Soul Drinkers to be clear before attacking. But clearly the enemy did not fully trust the Soul Drinkers just yet, because they were watching.

Scout-Novice Nisryus could feel them all around. He knew a second before when they would show themselves and so only he had seen them clearly – xenos, probably eldar, wearing close-fitting elegant armour and lurking on the rooftops or between the columns of nearby buildings. They were silent and almost invisible, and Nisryus guessed at several dozen of them moving just out of sight, both alien and human, able to melt into the city apparently at will.

Sarpedon knew they were testing the Soul Drinkers, waiting for them to make some move that would mark them out as the enemy. Sarpedon wasn't going to give them that chance. He sent out patrols to monitor the closest buildings and maintain a perimeter, and sent the scouts up onto the chamber mercantile's roof to keep watch. The xenos had not tried to destroy the Soul Drinkers as they landed so they must suspect they were here to join their cause, but that didn't mean Sarpedon could risk breaking the fragile truce by tearing up the city looking for an alien to interrogate.

Eldar. That made things more complicated. The eldar were deceitful, untrustworthy and arrogant in the extreme. The Imperium had stopped short of a campaign of genocide against them because the eldar were an ancient race and knew secrets about the galaxy that the Imperium wanted to know – and the eldar were as implacable foes of Chaos as the Imperium itself claimed to be. But they were still aliens, heathens and pirates. Sarpedon had fought them before and he remembered a species who would gladly lead a billion humans to their deaths to save one of their own. Sarpedon didn't blame them for not trusting the Soul Drinkers, he would certainly never trust the eldar.

The uneasy quiet was broken by the crackle of the vox from Squad Eumenes on the roof.

'THEY'RE APPROACHING,' voxed Eumenes, peering through his magnoculars at the plume of dust and smoke to the south-east. Small arms fire was spattering, tiny flashes of auto- and las-weapons through the smoke. 'Looks like armour and troop carriers.'

'Xarius is driving on the city at last,' voxed Sarpedon in reply.

'Doesn't look like it, commander,' said Eumenes. He handed the magnoculars to Selepus, who kneeled beside him behind the marble parapet of the building's roof. Without them Eumenes got a better sense of the approaching force. 'It's on a narrow front and it's moving too quickly. I don't think this is in Xarius's battle plan.'

'Marine armour,' said Selepus, sharp-eyed as ever. 'They've got Vindicators and Rhinos.'

Eumenes smiled. 'It's the Fists,' he voxed.

BULLETS THUNKED INTO the side of the Rhino APC, sounding like massive fists battering the vehicle as it churned through Gravenhold's streets. Las-bolts whined in reply, and vehicle-mounted autocannons thudded shells into the buildings on either side.

Reinez's squad, cramped in the hardened passenger compartment of the Rhino, had been through infinitely worse. Reinez stood and threw open the Rhino's top hatch, three of his Marines stood with him, bolters ready to counter any fire that came their commander's way.

The street was full of churning engine-smoke. The Rhinos carrying his strike force thundered alongside Chimeras and Leman Russ tanks stencilled with the insignia of the Fornux Lix Fire Drakes, the monstrous roar of their engines punctuated by gunfire streaking in from the buildings on either side of the broad avenue. The towering buildings of the administration district had given way to marble and white stone, carved friezes and statues, monuments and columns. The enemy had been caught cold by Reinez's bold gambit, and the force he had assembled: eleven Rhino and Razorback APCs, several Vindicator and Predator support tanks and the Fornux Lix armour of a dozen Chimera-mounted squads and half as many Leman Russes and Hydra flak-tanks were driving at prodigious speed through Gravenhold. Reinez could see the indistinct figures of enemy troopers in the windows and on the rooftops, firing at the vehicles as they roared past. The Fire Drakes had lost two Chimera squads to rocket launchers and small arms, and one Crimson Fists' Predator was stranded, crippled beneath the south-east gate.

'How much further?' he voxed on the Fire Drakes' channel as the convoy tore through an intersection, gunfire stitching lines of scars across the road.

'Five minutes,' came the reply from Lieutenant Elthanion, who was in a Chimera at the front of the convoy. Behind his voice on the vox was the roar of a Vindicator shell blowing the front wall out of a building. Reinez saw the thunderhead of dust and debris blooming up ahead.

'Good. Crimson Fists, prepare to disembark! Assault units, we're going in hot! You are the spearhead!'

A chorus of acknowledgements sounded over the Fists' vox channel from the sergeants under his command.

'In the name of Dorn and the immortal Emperor,' intoned Chaplain Inhuaca over the vox. 'By the Hammer of the Primarch and the Sword of Him on Earth, through pain shall we know Him, through death shall we exalt Him…'

As Inhuaca's prayer echoed through the vox, autogun shots spanged against the upper hull of the Rhino. Reinez's Marines returned fire, snapping off bolter shots. The massive architecture of the merchant's district loomed and the weight of fire increased. Pallid figures scampered between the buildings, silhouettes against the roofline or scraps of movement in the near-dark shadows. 'Faster!' yelled Reinez, banging on the roof of the Rhino. A bolt of pure blackness whipped down from a rooftop and blew the track off a Leman Russ. Reinez's Rhino slewed wildly to avoid the wreck. A Chimera up ahead overturned spectacularly as the convoy gunned engines and made a final charge towards the objective.

Every gun was blazing now: sponson-mounted heavy bolters, Marines' boltguns, even the lasguns of the Fire Drakes taking pot shots from their Chimeras. A tank commander leaned out of the turret of his Leman Russ and loosed off a plasma pistol shot. A battle cannon ripped the heart out of a building, sending broken bodies flying from the upper floors. Hot trails of gunfire streaked through the gathering darkness, and the streets were illuminated by the massive muzzle flashes of the tanks' autocannon.

The resistance was fearsome. But Reinez had fought through worse. The shock of the attack, the element of surprise, had achieved what Xarius's initial thrust on the city had not. The enemy were just humans, unaugmented heretics, amateurs and fanatics who were breaking against the sheer resolve of the Adeptus Astartes.

The curved mass of the chamber mercantile appeared down the next avenue, ornate and imposing. The convoy passed an overturned Predator battle tank and another burned-out Chimera as the convoy gunned down the avenue, Reinez's bolt pistol kicking as he fired into the shadows. Reinez saw Inhuaca, standing proud from the top hatch of his Rhino, the crozius in his hand crackling blue-white in the gunsmoke and flying debris.

'KELVOR, DYON, GIVE me a firing line at the windows. Graevus, Krydel, counter-charge. The rest of you, I want a crossfire, massed bolter fire.' Sarpedon stood in the centre of the chamber mercantile as his Marines scattered to take up defensive positions. 'Luko, where are you?'

'The street to your left flank,' replied Luko over the vox. 'We've got movement everywhere, xenos crawling all over the damn place.'

'They're not our problem right now. Get behind us and keep the route out of here clear.'

Librarian Tyrendian stomped up, his force sword in his hand. 'Where do you want me?'

'With Graevus.'

Stray shots were spattering in through the front windows and the roar of engines set the massive marble architecture and hardwood fittings trembling.

'For Dorn!' yelled Sarpedon, his eight legs taking him swiftly towards Squad Dyon hunkered down beneath the front windows. 'For the Emperor and for freedom!'

None of them had asked why they weren't falling back. They all knew why; the Soul Drinkers weren't running any more.

'…count ten Rhinos, support armour, at least eight Chimeras, probably Armoured Fist squads…' Eumenes was voxing from the roof. 'First coming in now.'

A Chimera in the colours of the Fornux Lix regiment slewed to a halt outside the chamber mercantile's ruined front doors. Guardsmen in heavy flakweave body armour were piling out of the back.

'Wait for the Fists,' voxed Sarpedon, the psychic circuit of his aegis hood heating up as his telepathic powers boiled below the surface of his mind.

THE FIRST CHIMERA shrieked to a halt.

'We're there!' voxed Elthanion. 'Fire team seven down!'

Fire was hitting the convoy hard from behind, xenos energy weapons now, bolts of power that sliced through hulls.

'This is the place,' relayed Elthanion as the squad reported their location. 'Suggest we give 'em a taste of battlecannon!'

'No!' ordered Reinez, flicking on the energy field of his thunder hammer. 'They're not that easy to kill, the rubble will just give them cover. Just back us up and pin down their flanks.' Reinez switched to the Fists' vox-channel. 'Second Company, charge!'

THE FIRST RHINO tore through the front wall of the chamber mercantile in a waterfall of shattered marble, riding high on a wave of rubble and plunging into Squad Kelvor. Soul Drinkers disappeared beneath its tracks as the rear and side hatches swung open.

Squad Dyon opened fire as one. Bolter fire riddled the side armour of the Rhino and shredded the first man out, an Assault Marine in the dark blue and red colours of the Crimson Fists. The rest of the Fists leaped out and Sarpedon saw a chainblade dispatch one of Squad Kelvor, another sliced the leg of Sergeant Kelvor himself.

Bolter fire streaked in from the rear of the hall as the Fists dived into Squad Dyon, blades shrieking. Sarpedon jumped forwards and stabbed with his force staff like a spear at the closest Assault Marine, the aegis circuit burning white-hot as he focussed his psychic power through its tip.

The press of power-armoured bodies turned the blade aside and the butt of a chainsword smacked into the side of Sarpedon's head. Sarpedon reeled, reached out with his free hand and grabbed the edge of the Crimson Fist's shoulder pad. He planted his legs firmly, talons cracking the tiled floor, and threw the Assault Marine clear over his head. He reared up on his hind legs and plunged the force staff two-handed through the Marine's chest, psychic energy discharging in a bright white flash that split the Marine's breastplate in two.

Another Assault Marine squad was vaulting in through the front windows, then another. A section of the front wall blew in to a Vindicator shot, scattering chunks of masonry all over the place. A wall of bolter fire ripped in through the gap followed by two units of Tactical Crimson Fists Marines – one carried a flag depicting a red gauntlet surrounded by lightning strikes, the standard of the Crimson Fists' Second Battle Company.

'Graevus! Now!' voxed Sarpedon frantically as a bolt pistol shot punched through one of his back legs and Brother Thorinol's severed head smacked into the wall beside him.

From the darkness in the back of the hall, lit by the strobing gunfire, Sergeant Graevus led the charge.

EUMENES SPOTTED A Guard officer cut down as he directed his troops, head snapped back by a shot from Sniper-Novice Raek of Scout Squad Giryan. A detonation from below shook the building and several of the scouts were knocked to their knees.

'The Guard are trying to flank us,' said Eumenes, lining up a bolt pistol shot and firing. His first went wide, his second blew the leg off a Fire Drake toting a grenade launcher. The Guardsmen were swarming all over the place, jumping from the Chimeras to take up cover beneath the thick columns and ornate statues that lined the front of the buildings. Las-fire was streaking up at the scouts, tearing chunks out of the lip of marble sheltering them.

'Giryan! Take the right, I'll take the left!' shouted Eumenes. The two squads broke up and headed for the sides of the buildings, where the chamber mercantile was separated from the neighbouring buildings by narrow alleys. Eumenes skidded to a halt and glanced down into the alley, drawing his head back from the replying barrage of las-fire. 'Scamander!' he yelled. 'Give us some room to work!'

Scamander dived into cover beside Eumenes. He took a deep breath and held out his hands over the edge, the spaces between his fingers glowing with licks of flame. There was a flicker of heat in the air and suddenly a rush of fire blazed down indiscriminately, pouring like liquid over the Fire Drakes massed below.

Scamander grimaced as his mental energy poured out through his mind. He let out a long juddering breath that was white with frost crystals as all the heat bled out of his body, and was multiplied by his psychic focus to turn the valley into a blazing orange furnace.

Men were screaming. An officer was shouting for calm, firing warning shots. Ammunition from a grenade launcher cooked off in a deafening crescendo of explosions. Flesh sizzled and popped.

'That's enough, novice!' ordered Eumenes before Scamander drained himself completely.

Scamander shuddered and the flame stopped falling from his hands.

'Squad, move!' called Eumenes. Scamander was falling backwards, exhausted, as Eumenes vaulted over the parapet and dropped into the alleyway.

There was nothing to burn in there now Scamander's psychic fire had been withdrawn and only bodies were blazing. Eumenes landed well enough to snap off a shot that took off the officer's hand, Selepus dropped straight as a dagger behind the officer, stabbing his combat knife through the man's neck and turning to plunge it into the chest of the Guardsman behind him. Nisryus followed, then Thersites and Tydeus. Tydeus fired a round from his grenade launcher, filling the least charred end of the alley with smoke and shrapnel, throwing two Fire Drakes out onto the street. Scamander was last, landing badly, his body limp with exhaustion. He would recover in a few moments, but for those few moments he was vulnerable.

The sound of a tank rumbled close. 'Hellhound,' said Nisryus. 'They're going to smoke us out.' His stilted body language told Eumenes that Nisryus's precognitive powers were kicking in.

'They wish it was that easy,' said Selepus, knife still in hand in preference to his bolt pistol.

'They think we'll fall back,' said Nisryus. 'So they can follow us.'

'Then we won't,' said Eumenes. 'Tydeus! Cover us! Let's move!'

THERE WAS NO room to bring pistols to bear in the savage press of armoured bodies. Sergeant Graevus wielded his power axe with his left hand and punched with his mutated right, the close quarters magnifying his strength as every blow struck a Crimson Fist.

He was surrounded, he was all but blind. The air was full of shrapnel and smoke and even his enhanced hearing couldn't make sense of the screaming din. Gunfire, yelling, shrieking chainblades, the blade of his own power axe biting into ceramite, bones snapping, thunderous explosions as the Guard armour continued to demolish the far end of the chamber.

He was drowning in a sea of bodies. Soul Drinkers and Crimson Fists fought in a brutal scrum. It was ugly and savage with no room for skill – but if the Crimson Fists piled into the chamber the weight of their gunfire would scour the Soul Drinkers off the face of Entymion IV. Graevus had to stop them. He had to buy his battle-brothers time.

Graevus shoved with his right and an Assault Marine stumbled back, opening up enough space for a good swing of Graevus's power axe. Another blue-armoured arm punched out to block his blow and the axe blade severed it above the elbow in a flash of sparks. The Assault Marine regained his footing and lunged with his chainblade, Graveus turned it with the haft of his axe and suddenly they were face-to-face, wrestling, Graveus's face reflected in the red eyepieces of the Marine's helmet. He saw his own gnarled veteran's face was spattered with blood.

Bodies pressed in around him. A bolt pistol rattled off its whole magazine and someone slumped against Graevus, held upright by the press – he couldn't tell if it was a Fist or a Soul Drinker who had died.

The Assault Marine had his arm around Graevus's neck and was dragging him down. Graevus shifted his weight and reached down with his deformed hand, its enlarged, elongated fingers wrapping around the Marine's leg armour. He pulled and the Marine was pitched onto his back, Graveus on top of him, Graevus forcing a knee onto the Marine's chest and punching again and again, the ceramite denting and cracking under the huge mutated fist that pistoned into the Assault Marine's face and chest.

Someone kicked Graevus in the head and a chainblade just missed a slice at his head. Graevus swung his axe wildly, the power field carving a shining blue arc. He couldn't tell if he had hit anything. The world was just a mass of armoured limbs and the deafening scream of a fight he couldn't win.

There was something else. Held high above the melee, tattered by gunfire, was the banner. The battle standard of the Crimson Fists Second Company. The image brought home the fact that the Fists hated the Soul Drinkers so much they had sent an entire battle company after them, the Fists, who were themselves severely depleted, had been willing to risk perhaps half of their fully-trained veteran manpower on destroying the Soul Drinkers.

The standard.

The Marine beneath Graevus hadn't tried to kill him in the last few seconds so Graevus assumed he was unconscious. Graevus swung again, trying to clear a space in front of him. The Soul Drinkers of his squad behind him rattled bolt pistol shots over his shoulder to batter back the Crimson Fists and suddenly there was a space in front of him to charge into, swinging a lighting-quick figure-eight with his axe. A chainsword shattered somewhere in the throng and sparks showered where the axe's power field met ceramite.

Graveus couldn't tell his battle-brothers apart through the veil of shrapnel and smoke. He could barely tell friend from foe. He just hacked and barged forward, the weight of his brothers behind carrying him forward. There were dead Marines beneath his feet and the floor was slick with blood. A Soul Drinker fell to a plasma pistol blast from a Fists' sergeant; Graevus ignored him, concentrating on pressing forward.

A lightning bolt split the air above him and a Fist was thrown into the air as if from a catapult, electricity arcing off him. Graevus glanced behind him and saw Librarian Tyrendian backing them up, his aristocratic face lit by the flickers of power playing around his head.

Graevus saw a Crimson Fist in lighter blue armour, a high aegis collar obscuring his helmeted head, his armour inscribed with protective sigils. A Crimson Fists' Librarian.

The Fists' Librarian raised a hand and dark ripples flowed from his fingers. They punched through the air in writhing darts and Graevus saw them swirling around Tyrendian, forming tendrils of shadow that tried to snare his arms and drag him down, envelop his head and blind him. Blue-white power flickered around Tyrendian's hands and with a blast of electricity the shadows were suddenly shredded.

Graevus was caught in the middle of a psychic duel. It meant he was in an even more dangerous place than before, but he couldn't worry about it now.

A bolter shot hit his greave and almost pitched Graevus onto his face. Splinters of ceramite were driven into his shin but he strode through the pain. The world was dissolving into dark chaos, with only the Battle Standard of the Second Company to focus on. Another lightning bolt slashed by from Tyrendian and the Crimson Fists' Librarian sent black tendrils spiralling through the air, lashing out at Soul Drinkers, ensnaring flailing limbs. Graevus saw the wounded Sergeant Kelvor ducking in front of him, only to have his chainsword snatched out of his hand by the shadow tentacle, another snagged his remaining ankle and threw him on his back. A Crimson Fist loomed over Kelvor but Graevus put his shoulder down and barged into the Fist, knocking him back into the throng to disappear between the jostling bodies.

Kelvor was back on his remaining foot and firing with his bolt pistol, but the momentum of Graevus's charge was gone and the crowd pressed in again. Graevus, back-to-back with Kelvor, held his power axe like a quarterstaff and blocked a chainblade strike. He took a bolt pistol shot to the chest, his internal breastplate of fused ribs cracking, compressed gas spraying from his armour's ruptured exhaust.

Lightning tore past Graevus and suddenly Tyrendian himself was in the press beside him, purple shining in the strange light pulsing from his temples.

The Fists' Librarian was fighting through the melee, too. Two psykers, lit up to one another like beacons on the battlefield, each one an affront to the other. It was inevitable they would ignore the rest of the battle to kill one another.

Bolter fire ripped in a disciplined volley from the Soul Drinkers in the rear of the chamber mercantile, thudding into the bodies of the Crimson Fists trying to force their way in. The battle standard dipped as the Marine holding it fell, only for it to be snatched up again by another Fist. Return fire streaked over as Crimson Fists pulled back from close combat to snap fire back, and the press eased off around Graevus.

There were too many Crimson Fists. A whole company could tear the building down if they had to. The bolters of the Soul Drinkers had bought a few seconds, and Graevus had to use them now or he might as well roll over and die.

Tyrendian and Graevus charged as one, Graevus's axe and Tyrendian's force sword hacking to force a path through the Crimson Fists. Someone swung a power sword at Graevus and it met the head of his axe in a terrific spray of sparks – Sergeant Kelvor dived on the attacker and Graevus pressed on.

Tyrendian broke free and sent a bolt of psychic lightning straight into the ground, knocking back the closest Fists and clearing his path to the Librarian. Hands of shadow were reaching from the ground but Tyrendian kicked free of them, the Crimson Fist Librarian stopped projecting his power and drew his own force sword, a long rapier of burning light, putting up a guard just in time to turn Tyrendian's lunging strike.

Graevus's head whirled. He was all but surrounded now, only momentum keeping him going. He could see the Marine who carried the Second Company's standard. The bearer was standing on the slope of rubble that had once been the chamber mercantile's front wall, holding his bolter in his free hand and firing off rapid volleys into the Soul Drinkers taking cover behind rubble and furniture in the back of the hall. The Fist's white-painted helmet and the golden honour studs marked him out as a recognised veteran, someone who had lived through the Rynn's World disaster and come out driven by bitterness and vengeance.

The battle was lit in staccato flashes as force swords clashed, Tyrendian's sword and the Librarian's rapier clashing and discharging their pent-up psychic power into the air. The Librarian saw an opening and lunged – Tyrendian sidestepped and closed the gap, trapping the Librarian's head in the crook of his elbow and kneeing the Crimson Fist in the face. He dropped his sword and with his free hand ripped the Librarian's helmet off, revealing a dark-skinned face distorted with effort.

Tyrendian threw the Crimson Fist backwards and before the rapier could be brought to bear Tyrendian held out both hands on either side of the Librarian's bare head. With a final yell of effort, power leapt from Tyrendian's palm and a lightning bolt ripped right through the Fists' Librarian's head, coursing into Tyrendian's other hand to form a continuous current of looping psychic power.

The Crimson Fists' Librarian was bathed in hot blue light as he threw up a psychic shield to keep his mind from being shredded. But Tyrendian, while he lacked subtlety in the application of his psychic talents, had immense reserves of raw power. The Crimson Fist spasmed wildly, foam spattering from his lips, his force sword falling from his shuddering hand.

The Crimson Fist's head exploded in a massive wash of psychic feedback, ripping out from him like the shockwave from a bomb blast. The Fist's body was ripped apart in a welter of gore and a storm of shattered ceramite, throwing Crimson Fists and Soul Drinkers onto the ground. The sound was like a thousand screams, a psychic death cry that speared straight into the mind of every Marine.

It felt like Graevus had run into a wall of solid force. He was battered backwards and fell to his knees, the Librarian's death a spear of white noise transfixing his mind.

He forced his eyes open, the scream still reverberating through his head. A huge hole had been blasted in the middle of the battle at the breach, with Soul Drinkers and Crimson Fists thrown to the ground or blasted back out onto the street.

The standard bearer was on his knees.

Graevus forced himself to his feet. He ran the last few paces as if in slow motion, his limbs complaining, every breath agony through his cracked ribs. Fallen Crimson Fists reached out to grab him but he hacked down on either side of him with his axe; he sliced off a hand, kicked a Fist out of his way. A Soul Drinker at the back of the chamber mercantile saw what he was doing and bolter fire snapped over his shoulder, beating back the Crimson Fists' Assault Marines who tried to reach him.

The standard bearer was on his feet. Graevus knew he only had one shot. He swung back his axe and dived, bringing the axe in a glittering arc heading for the Crimson Fist's neck.

The Marine brought the haft of the standard up to block the blow, just as Graevus knew he would. The axe blade carved downwards, passing under the standard and cutting clean into the Marine's waist. Graevus felt the blade jarring as the power field forced its way through the ceramite of the Marine's abdominal armour, sliced through his spine, and passed clear out the other side.

The Marine's upper half toppled to the ground. Vermilion blood fountained. Graevus caught the standard as it fell, the banner falling over him like a shroud.

The Librarian's death throes had cleared the space for Graevus to take the banner, but it had also removed the brutal melee that was blocking the Crimson Fists' route into the chamber mercantile. Two squads of Crimson Fists were even now scrambling over the rubble into the hall to bring their bolters to bear.

Graevus knew they would get in. There were just too many of them. The Soul Drinkers could not outgun the Crimson Fists, the only way to beat them was to break their spirit. Space Marines were the most unbreakable troops the Imperium had, but the Soul Drinkers had no choice.

Graevus had struck one blow by snatching their standard. If he made it out of the chamber mercantile alive, he would strike another. And as he ran through a storm of bolter fire, he prayed that Sarpedon would strike the third.

His prayers were answered, because that moment the Hell began.

CHAPTER SIX

'THEN WHERE THE bloody hell is he?' snapped Lord General Xarius. He stood up sharply, ignoring the familiar pain in his hip, and knocked the makeshift table of ammo crates so several of Colonel Threlnan's situational maps fell onto the floor.

'We're not sure,' came the vox reply from Hasdrubal. Hasdrubal, the flag-commander of Xarius's Baneblade, functioned as Xarius's adjutant mainly because he was there. Xarius didn't maintain a personal staff of his own, preferring the resources to go to the front line where they might actually make a difference. 'He's commanding a force of armour in the south of the city but Colonel Savennian says he doesn't have an accurate location for the convoy.'

'St. Aspira's teeth!' hissed Xarius into the vox-set. Colonel Threlnan and his adjutant officer looked up in surprise at the minor blasphemy. 'Tell me the Crimson Fists haven't gone with him.'

'We're... again, we're not sure...'

'Find out. Get an eye in the air, a Thunderbolt or something.' Xarius flicked off the vox-channel.

'Trouble?' said Threlnan.

'Lieutenant Elthanion and half the Fire Drakes just drove into Gravenhold without thinking to mention it to anyone else.'

'Couldn't Savennian order them back?'

'Damn it, Threlnan, how do you think I got where I am today? By making sure I sure as hell know what kind of men are supposed to be fighting for me. Colonel Savennian earned his rank by being the half-brother of the governor-regent of Fornux Lix. He's a politician. He's only there because protocol needs a colonel's signature on everything. It's Elthanion that runs that regiment and he's swanned off.'

'Where does that leave all this?' Threlnan indicated the maps and plans Lord General Xarius had been poring over before Hasdrubal had informed him of the Fire Drakes' unauthorised mission. They were the troop dispositions of the Seleucaian and Fornux Lix troops and those Algorathi units who had been rotated into the field. They also described the troop movements that would lay the foundation for the next phase of the war for Gravenhold. A huge drive into the city, masses of infantry and armour, moving forward according to intricate patterns to bring massed firepower against every intersection and likely strong-point. Other plans were backups, describing how forces were to react to bottlenecks or bypass potentially fortified strongpoints.

They relied, of course, on Imperial forces rolling in from both directions, splitting the enemy forces. That meant the Fire Drakes had to play their part, winning the whole administrative sector and then the governmental quarter culminating in the senate-house itself. It was a goal they could not achieve if they were storming about the city getting killed in some private war.

'It leaves all this a mess,' replied Xarius. 'The Departmento Munitorum say they can't get us any more Guard units. If we lose the Fire Drakes then we don't have a battle plan. We just let this city bleed our forces dry until they pull us out.'

Threlnan shook his head. 'If they didn't care so much about getting this damn city back the Navy could have just have fragged it from orbit…'

'No one could care less about the city, Threlnan. The reason we haven't hit it from orbit is that an orbital strike would have levelled the city and left the enemy intact. They're underneath it, hiding. There are sewers and ruins and Throne knows what down there. We'd just be giving them a ruined city to hide inside. Our men are not dying just because someone admires Gravenhold's architecture, colonel, they are dying because that's the only way we can get this planet back. I would thank you to remember that.'

Threlnan was about to answer, but the vox-set bleeped. Xarius picked it up.

'Lord general?' It was Hasdrubal. 'The auspex crews on the *Resolve* are picking up activity near the senate-house. Plenty of it, too. It's lighting up all the sensors.'

'The Fire Drakes?'

'Yes, sir. Them and the Crimson Fists.'

'The Fists? Wonderful. Now we've got two armies running wild.' Xarius rubbed his eyes, trying to force back the headache that was building behind them. 'How many?'

'It looks like all of them, sir.'

THE BURNING WRECK of the Hellhound filled the streets with billowing red-black smoke, choking back the dozens of Guardsmen who must have thought they were facing a force with massive numerical superiority. In reality it was just the six men of Scout Squad Eumenes, snapping off bolter shots while Selepus dragged any Guardsmen who got too close into the shadows and slit his throat. Eumenes himself was crouched down beside Novice-Librarian Scamander, directing the bolter fire through the smoke. He hadn't received all the implants of a full Marine but his eyesight was still considerably augmented. It cut through the smoke so his scouts were shooting at Guardsmen who couldn't fire back. From the cover of the rubble by the entrance to the alleyway, Scout Squad Eumenes was holding back the Fire Drakes troops who were supposed to be surrounding the Soul Drinkers and attacking from the back of the chamber mercantile.

A unit of Guardsmen, veterans with melta guns and plasma weapons, was moving rapidly around the pool of burning promethium to pin down the scouts. Eumenes indicated them with a sharp stabbing hand signal and Scamander, now recovered from his exertions, holstered his bolt pistol. He took a deep breath and raised his hands, teeth clenched with effort as he coaxed a long tongue of flame from the blazing wreck.

The flame lashed out like a whip, wrapping around three of the veterans and setting their fatigues ablaze. They fell to the ground, rolling in an attempt to put the flames out but Scamander concentrated on them instead, making the flames grow until the superheated air scalded their lungs and stopped their screams. The other Guardsmen ran for cover on the far side of the street – in retreat and unable to return fire, they were wide open to the volley of bolt pistol shots the rest of the squad snapped off at them. One was struck in the back of the head by a well-placed sniper shot, sending him somersaulting forward.

Scout-Sniper Raek ran from the still-smouldering alleyway and hit the ground by Eumenes. His armour was charred and smouldering, and the supressor on the end of his long sniper rifle was dull red with heat. His face was dark with grime and bled from a dozen minor shrapnel wounds. 'Squad Giryan's falling back,' he said. 'The Guard have got the alley on the far side.'

'Losses?'

'We've lost three. Including Giryan.'

'Get to the back of this alley and keep them away for as long as you can, we need that street clear.' Eumenes switched to the command vox-channel. 'Sarpedon, this is Eumenes. We've lost Squad Giryan and the Guard are going to flank us.'

The vox-net was full of static and background bolter fire. 'Fall back,' came the reply. 'All squads, retreat to the senate-house. Luko, Eumenes, cover us. For Dorn!'

SARPEDON WAS A telepath. He had always been extremely powerful, powerful enough to join the ranks of the Chapter Librarium, and following his mutation his mental strength had grown to heights rarely achieved by even the most renowned Librarians of the Adeptus Astartes. But he was a telepath that could only transmit, not receive – he made up for this flaw with raw power, and the intensity of the images which he forced into the unwilling minds of his enemies.

The power was referred to as the Hell. In the carnage of the chamber mercantile, it was a vision of corruption. If the Crimson Fists wanted to find Chaos amongst the Soul Drinkers, then Sarpedon would give it to them.

Tortured daemonic faces howled from the shadows. The ceiling of the chamber dissolved into a swirling black cloud from which huge taloned hands reached down, blazing with corruptive power, pulsing with waves of decay. Sarpedon ripped out of his memory every daemonic abomination he had encountered in his long career as a Space Marine and painted them on the walls of the chamber mercantile – sorcerous runes that refused to be read, raw naked souls burning in the madness of the warp, scabrous daemons capering in the darkness, voices that whispered blasphemies from every direction.

The Soul Drinkers had all trained with Sarpedon, subjecting themselves to the full force of the Hell in the depths of the *Brokenback* so they would be able to tell Sarpedon's illusions from reality. The Crimson Fists had not.

They had seen Graevus snatching their standard from under their noses. Now they faced this daemonic assault, as if a horde of daemons was suddenly manifesting from thin air all around them. The Emperor himself had decreed that a Space Marine should know no fear and the Crimson Fists were no exception, but it wasn't fear that Sarpedon needed. It was just that one moment of doubt, the realisation that they might be fighting something they couldn't beat, something that could steal their sacred standard and conjure daemons all around them. It wouldn't last long, but it did not have to.

'For Dorn!' Sarpedon yelled again, and broke cover, followed by Squad Dyon and the remains of Squad Kelvor. Graevus was already heading in the same direction with the scattered brothers of his squad, Tyrendian just behind him. The Crimson Fists poured bolter fire after them and Sarpedon saw one of Graevus's Marines struck down by a bolter round through the neck, but the Crimson Fists weren't following, not yet. For a couple of seconds they would pause at the breach, unsure whether they should dive into the fight or hold back in the face of superior opposition.

The Soul Drinkers were falling back through the exits in the back of the hall, the many smaller entrances once used by the lesser adepts and retainers. Sarpedon reached the back of the hall, running past Squads Corvan and Praedon who were lined up behind the heavy wooden fixtures of the chamber to provide covering fire.

'Get out!' Sarpedon yelled as he ran past, his eight talons splintering the mosaics on the floor.

He was forcing every foul image out of his mind and into the storm of illusions behind him, as much to cloak the Soul Drinkers' retreat as to keep the Crimson Fists back. Already the Fists were advancing – they were mostly veterans who had seen worse things before and after Rynn's World than anything Sarpedon could conjure up and the ruse had only worked for a few seconds. But already most of the Soul Drinkers were out into the street behind, heading for the senate-house under cover from Eumenes and Squad Luko.

Sarpedon burst out into the street. The air was full of smoke and las-fire was streaking down at him now, whipping by from one end of the street where the Guard had got men through the alley. Squad Luko was gathered on the steps keeping up a volley of bolt pistol fire. Squad Dyon's Tactical Marines took their place and their more effective bolter fire battered back the Guardsmen already sheltering behind a pile of their own dead.

Squads Corvan and Praedon were out, followed by volleys of fire from the Crimson Fists. Two battle-brothers from Squad Praedon were caught and tumbled down the steps – one had lost the better part of his leg but the other had suffered a massive head shot. The still-living Marine was hauled to his feet by Sergeant Praedon as the Marines made a break for the buildings opposite where the rest of the Soul Drinkers were already taking cover.

The Guardsmen at the alleyway scattered, but not for cover. With a roar of collapsing masonry, a Leman Russ Demolisher ripped out through the alleyway, shunting aside massive piles of rubble with the huge dozer blade fitted to its front. The turret turned and the huge main cannon fired, blowing a tremendous hole in the front of the building opposite.

Sarpedon was almost thrown to the ground.

'Get out of here!' yelled Sarpedon to the Marines still in the street. 'Move! They're coming through!'

Guardsmen were pouring through the widened alley, using the Demolisher for cover. A bolt from Squad Dyon's plasma gunner streaked into the side of the Demolisher, blowing the side weapon off in a welter of fire and sparks, but it wouldn't help much.

Sarpedon was out in the middle of the road, running and shooting. All the Soul Drinkers were out of the chamber mercantile and were making a dash for the buildings opposite.

'Varuk!' yelled Sarpedon into the vox. 'Now!

Somewhere in the complex of buildings, Techmarine Varuk activated the detonator signal keyed to receivers in bundles of krak grenades hidden against the back wall of the chamber mercantile.

The wall of force hit Sarpedon before the sound did, a blast of expanding air like a shove in the back. His eight legs kept him upright but the sound was deafening, followed by the blinding cloud of dust and debris that billowed across the street as the rear wall of the chamber mercantile collapsed.

Sarpedon kept going, the pre-filters in his throat keeping the choking marble dust out of his lungs. The Fire Drakes were protected by respirators and as they recovered they kept up their las-fire, sending scarlet streaks of laser through the dust, but it wasn't enough to slow the Soul Drinkers down now. Sarpedon thudded into the side of the building and scrambled along the front, finding the huge jagged hole the Demolisher had blown and pulling himself inside.

The Crimson Fists would be slowed down by the explosion, but nothing else. It took a great deal more than a well-timed booby trap and some flying masonry to dissuade a Space Marine. At the most, it bought the Soul Drinkers a minute or so more time to get out, and Sarpedon knew they had to make the best use of it they could.

The plan was simple. With the Fists and the Guard broken up and slowed down at the chamber mercantile, the Soul Drinkers were to retreat, force their pursuers to follow them through offices and meeting-halls, until they got to the senate-house.

The senate-house. The location Sarpedon had chosen for the Soul Drinkers' last stand.

No HUMAN WOULD understand the thoughts that went through the mind of the alien.

On one level, they were driven by the same desires that defined the actions of all living things. To survive. To achieve, and attain superiority. To stave off suffering. But below that layer of instinct was something else entirely, something that was made up of both pride and desperation, an obsessively free will and a grim pre-ordained, almost biological imperative to prey on lesser species. The alien was monstrously proud, and yet he acted out of fear. He was cruel to the point of abstraction, as if the infliction of suffering fulfilled an aesthetic ideal – and yet every cut and kill was in deference to forces it could not control and that it had to bow before, no matter how it refused to accept the domination of another. A human could not possibly understand all the contradictory layers that made up its consciousness. All they ever saw were the results: the dead, the enslaved, the broken.

This was what it meant to be one of the eldar, the galaxy's chosen race, the heralds of creation, the masters of reality. Freedom and enslavement, cruelty and deference, arrogance and desperation. The minds of the eldar were based on an unending cycle of cause and contradiction that would drive the primitive-minded humans insane.

Akrelthas of the Kabal of the Burning Scale crouched down behind the elaborate carving that jutted from a corner of the rooftop. Only the faintest of evening light remained and night was rolling across Gravenhold, but there was plenty of illumination below. Muzzle flashes and explosions lit up the streets of Gravenhold's ruling district as bright as day, and Akrelthas could clearly see the human soldiers gunning each other down, tearing each other apart.

There were two sides to the conflict but Akrelthas had to look carefully to see how the fight was playing out, because to Akrelthas they all looked the same.

Akrelthas leaned forward, the interlocking beetle-black plates of his armour flexing over his close-fitting bodysuit. He left the splinter rifle slung on his back as he crawled a little way down the wall like a large and spindly spider – they couldn't see him up there. He had been watching them here before the fight had begun and they hadn't seen him then, when they had been on the lookout. They were all but blind, these humans, blind and stupid. It was only their sheer numbers and wide distribution across the galaxy that meant the species had survived this long.

The unarmoured humans were fit only to fight the subjugated warriors who had once made up the population of this city. They were beneath eldar notice, no better than cattle driven forward to die. The armoured humans, however, were something else. Their specialisation approached the skill of the Kabal's own incubi – these humans were shock troops, built to fight with up-close savagery. It was crude but beautiful, for the sight of such destructive power brought to bear in one place pleased Akrelthas's aesthetic senses as much as a well-placed blade strike or a horde of slaves bent down beneath the lash.

It was nothing compared to the honed prowess of the Kabal, of course, but it was impressive nonetheless.

Akrelthas had a job to do. His master, and the mistress above them all, wanted information. Gravenhold was a complex pattern of forces, both military and metaphysical, and the Kabal had to know everything it could about the human armies and how they interacted. The purple-armoured humans were an independent force, their motives unknown, their allegiances undecided. If the Kabal's plans were to unfold in such a way as to please She-Who-Thirsts, then those questions had to be answered.

The unarmoured humans – the Imperial Guard, whose billions of soldiers marched to their deaths to maintain some hopeless vision of humanity's future – and the blue-armoured soldiers fought together. That much was simple enough. Those in blue and those in purple were Space Marines, soldiers vaunted as heroes of legend by the rest of humanity, and which were in reality just another bludgeoning weapon the Imperium of Mankind used to clumsily imitate the true patterns of warfare. Akrelathas watched as the Marines in blue surged forward out of the contested building, their gunfire throwing a purple Marine to the ground. The fallen Marine was set upon and quickly despatched where he lay, the ugly chain-toothed weapons of the Marines cutting him in two on the ground.

The two armies of Marines were not allies, then. This would interest the Kabal greatly. This was the sign Akrelthas had been told to look out for, it meant that both forces of Marines would play their assigned part admirably well in the eldar victory.

Akrelthas sprang lightly back up onto the roof, glanced once more down into the melee where humans killed one another to unknowingly exalt She-Who-Thirsts, and sprinted off into the gathering darkness.

CHAPLAIN IKTINOS LED the charge through the offices of Gravenhold's proxy cardinal. Where once Gravenhold's great and good had come to beg counsel or indulgences from the Ecclesiarchy's representative, now the armoured boots of the Soul Drinkers crunched through scholars' cells and racks of illuminated scrolls. Pistol fire from more than twenty Crimson Fists Assault Marines, who had used their jump packs to take the first floor of the building, streaked down from the first floor balcony, where the grand staircase lead up to the chambers once occupied by the Proxy Cardinal's own staff.

Iktinos didn't yell the devotional prayers a Space Marine Chaplain was supposed to as he drew his Crozius Arcanum and headed for the stairs. He didn't have to. He was the spiritual heart of the Soul Drinkers – the only Chaplain the Soul Drinkers had, the principal advisor to Sarpedon and the spiritual mentor to every Soul Drinker.

Brother Falcar, who had fought under Sergeant Hastis before Hastis's death on Septiam Torus, dived in front of Iktinos, taking the full blast of a plasma gun shot that was meant for the Chaplain. Falcar was thrown off the grand staircase, a smoking hole ripped through his torso.

More Soul Drinkers surged forwards, taking volleys of bolt pistol fire. Some fell, tumbling down the stairs, others sprinted ahead to come to grips with the first of the Crimson Fists.

Iktinos's crozius arcanum blazed, its power field reacting with the veil of shrapnel hammering down. Another Soul Drinker fell shielding Iktinos – Brother Thorical this time, whose squad leader had been the late Sergeant Givrillian.

Iktinos charged up into the Crimson Fists, crozius shattering ceramite and bone. He did not feel the hot fury of a warrior or the dry desperation of a man fighting for his life – he fought deliberately and calmly, knowing the Soul Drinkers around him would hold off the chainblades and bolter shots that were meant for him. On Stratix Luminae, when the whole Soul Drinkers Chapter had faced destruction, he had forged a bond between him and the Soul Drinkers who followed him. They had died to keep the Chapter's figurehead alive. They had walked into the jaws of death because he was leading them.

A Crimson Fist drove his chainsword through the shoulder of the Soul Drinker who pulled him out of Iktinos's way. Another Fist fell back, one side of his helmet's faceplate blown off by a bolter shot.

The Crimson Fists Assault Captain was in front of Iktinos now. Iktinos recognised him – Assault-Captain Arca, one of the Second Company's real veterans. Iktinos had met him briefly when the Chaplains of the Imperial Fists' successor Chapters had gathered at Rynn's World. That had been before the Crimson Fists' fortress-monastery was destroyed, before the Soul Drinkers were excommunicated.

It was a long time ago.

Arca must have recognised Iktinos, because the Fist paused for a second. In the middle of the melee at the top of the stairs, the two Marines regarded each other for a moment. One thought how such a brave and noble man could still fight in the name of a corrupt and monstrous Imperium. The other wondered how a guardian of the Chapter's faith could have fallen so far into corruption and rebellion.

But then the moment was gone. And the fury of their combat lit up the building like a lightning storm.

'THREE SHOTS. LASCANNON. Then we're clear.' Nisryus, his eyes glazed with concentration, crouched with his back against a half-ruined wall, the rest of the scouts hunkered down behind him. The shouts of the Fornux Lix Guardsmen and the hissing las-fire filtered through the background of rumbling tanks and falling masonry as the Guard units advanced.

On cue, three fat bolts of crimson energy hissed overhead, sending out a wash of stinking ozone.

Nisryus hadn't been wrong yet.

'Now!' yelled Eumenes and the scouts ran forward, crossing the gap in cover. Tydeus fired a grenade to cover them and the scouts made it to the cover of the next ruined building intact. The Guard's Demolisher siege tanks were rapidly reducing the district to rubble, blasting siege cannon shells into the buildings in the hope of slowing down the Soul Drinkers so the Crimson Fists could force a stand-up fight. The scouts, in return, were doing their damndest to hold up the Guardsmen, and Eumenes had little doubt that his handful of scouts were the only obstacle between the Fornux Lix Fire Drakes and a complete encirclement of the Soul Drinkers.

'The Fists!' shouted Nisryus. 'They're here...'

Eumenes caught sight of something in the ruined building looming over them, its internal architecture laid wide open by Demolisher fire, its floors sagging and shedding drifts of rubble and broken furniture. There was someone on the upper floors – bolter fire flashed from within, the whine of bolter shells zipping through the air and the smack as they hit masonry.

Eumenes saw with a glance that the Fire Drakes covered everything past the rubble cover, their fire fields overlapping with a completeness that reminded him that he was up against professional soldiers. 'Where do we go?'

Nisryus looked up at the firefight bleeding out of the ruined building. 'Nowhere.'

A Crimson Fist smashed through the masonry two floors up and fell, gunning the exhausts of his jump pack to land square in the middle of the scout squad. It was an Assault Marine, with chainsword and bolt pistol, his chest armour scarred and smoking from the hit that had knocked him out of the building.

Thersites was closest. His two bolt pistol shots rang off ceramite and the Fist ignored them, stabbing out with an inhumanly quick lunge of his chainsword. Thersites didn't realise he had been struck until he hit the ground, a huge wet ragged hole where his chest had been.

Selepus leapt at the Fist from behind, his knife stabbing down at the neck join of the Fist's armour. The Fist turned, caught Selepus by the throat and threw him hard against a half-toppled column.

Nisryus crashed against the Fist's leg, knocking the huge Marine down onto one knee. Eumenes dived out from cover, lashing out with a kick to the faceplate of the Marine's helmet to knock him onto his back. Eumenes was suddenly on top of the Marine, his bolt pistol jammed into one eyepiece, pumping shell after shell, point-blank. Splinters of shell casing and ceramite spat up at Eumenes, cutting hot weals across his face as the faceplate split and the Marine thrashed as he died.

The gunshots gave way to silence inside Eumenes's head. It took a few moments for the din of battle to flow back in. The ruined face of the Marine, all shattered ceramite and blood with one smashed eyepiece glaring at him blindly, was all he could see.

A strange warmth washed through him. It was pride. He had killed his first Marine.

He looked up from the dead Crimson Fist. He still had men to lead. 'Selepus?'

Selepus was picking himself back up off the ground. 'I'm fine.'

'Thersites?'

'He's gone,' said Scout-Sniper Raek, kneeling over Thersites. Thersites was letting out a final rattling breath, blood flecking his lips. His tattered lungs were pumping weakly, visible through the red-black hole in his chest.

'We're clear,' said Nisryus, pulling himself from under the dead Marine.

'Good.' They could mourn the dead scout later, when there were fewer people shooting at them. 'Selepus, carry Thersites. Raek, on point. Let's move.'

APOTHECARY PALLAS CROUCHED down, las-shots zipping through the plush audience chamber from the demolished far wall. Here, among the burning drapery and bullet-riddled upholstery, Brother Kirelkin was dying, multiple las-burns scoring his fractured armour. Kirelkin's squadmates in Squad Kelvor were covering Pallas, but Pallas knew right away there was nothing he could do. One of Kirelkin's hearts was punctured and his torso was filling up with blood – his lungs had collapsed and in a few moments he would be gone.

Las-bolts thwacked into the lushly upholstered seating, arranged in rows around a throne from which one of Gravenhold's aristocrats held audience. Bits of burned hardwood showered Pallas as the top of his Apothecary's gauntlet slid back to reveal the thick gleaming needle of the reductor unit inside.

Kirelkin's lifesigns were zero. Pallas thrust the reductor into Kirelkin's throat, feeling the unit thunk forward and snip closed around the gene-seed organ. The unit slid back, drawing the precious organ with it.

'Is it done?' asked Sergeant Kelvor. Kelvor's leg had been severed scant minutes ago but already his augmented blood had crusted into a hard seal around the stump.

Pallas nodded.

'Then we're gone. They're trying to surround us.'

Pallas ducked beneath the random gunfire and followed Squad Kelvor into the building, towards where the senate-house loomed.

Another good Marine gone. Many more of Sarpedon's little wars, and there wouldn't be a Chapter left.

SQUAD LUKO AND Sarpedon reached the steps of the senate-house first.

Sergeant Luko, his lightning claws smoking from the Guardsmen he had cut through to get there, ran up the steps and stopped with his back against the pillar.

The senate-house had dozens of entrances, to make sure that no one senator had to follow another into the building. Arches ran right around the circular wall of the building, each one carved with the names of past senators. With so many entrances the exterior was barely defensible but inside, hidden now in darkness, was a warren of offices, seating, auditoria and annexes clustered around the senate chamber itself. It would take the Crimson Fists and Fire Drakes a long time to winkle the Soul Drinkers out.

'Clear!' called Luko, and his Marines ran up past him, bolters trained, moving through the archways and into the building.

Sarpedon scuttled up the steps and took cover with Luko behind one of the pillars. Already Chaplain Iktinos and his mob of Marines were coming out of the Ecclesiarchical building across the street, Iktinos's black-painted armour smoking from scars inflicted by a power weapon. The Soul Drinkers were all closing in on the destination and the Fists and Guardsmen were coming with them. Gunfire was drawing nearer and every building seemed to be sporting battle cannon wounds belching smoke.

'Anything in there?' asked Sarpedon.

'No contacts,' replied Luko. 'No one's home.'

The vox crackled. 'Brother Faerak here,' came the transmission from inside the building. 'We've got a situation.'

'Frag,' spat Luko. 'They've got there first.'

'I don't think so, sir. You'd better see it.'

Luko and Sarpedon entered the building through the closest arch, the darkness closing around them. Sarpedon's eyes automatically adjusted to the low light, revealing carved hardwood partitions, handsome bronze sculptures of past senators, inscriptions and prayers of diligence and temperance pinned to the walls. Squad Luko had smashed through the closest wooden walls, Sarpedon and Luko followed in their wake.

Inside the senate-house there should have been a massive auditorium surrounded by private chambers and adepts' offices. Instead there was a yawning pit, a dark ragged shaft sinking through layers of stone foundations and earth, straight down so far Sarpedon couldn't see the bottom. Broken beams and pipes jutted from the crumbling sides, and the shaft cut through several levels of basements so keenly that there were still items of furniture and piles of old senatorial records threatening to topple into the pit.

Sarpedon glanced up – the roof of the senate-house was intact so this wasn't bomb damage. It had been dug deliberately, and recently.

'More xenos?' asked Luko.

'I don't think so,' said Sarpedon.

Then, there was the sound of voices. Someone was shouting down in the depths of the pit in a language Sarpedon could not quite understand; it had the tone and inflection of Imperial Gothic, as if the language itself had mutated. Then there was movement: pale, skinny shapes scrambling up the sides of the pit. There were hundreds of them. Thousands.

The Marines of Squad Luko aimed their bolters into the pit, ready for Luko's order.

'Hold your fire!' yelled Sarpedon. He flicked on the vox. 'Sarpedon to all squads, take cover and hold fire.' The other Soul Drinkers, those now advancing towards the senate-house and those still fending off the Guardsmen and Crimson Fists, broke off and headed for cover. There would be no last stand. They were about to find out if Sarpedon's plan had a chance of success.

Luko looked around at Sarpedon. 'This had better damn well work.'

Sarpedon said nothing. The voices grew louder and sparks of sorcery lit the inside for a split second. Thousands of creatures – humans – were scrabbling up the ladders and handholds, their skin pale, their faces obscured by straps and disfiguring piercings. They had every kind of weapon – knives, clubs, lasguns and autoguns looted from the Entymion IV PDF soldiers, bare hands, teeth. Some figures were floating up the middle of the pit, robed sorcerers with witch-born magic crackling around their hands. The gibbering and screeching grew louder and Sarpedon could make out looping patterns carved into their bodies, hands stripped of skin with metal shards for talons, facial features obscured by scraps of metal seemingly hammered into their skulls.

With a sound like death itself, the army of Gravenhold swarmed up out of the ground.

CHAPTER SEVEN

LORD GENERAL XARIUS watched the holomat projection grimly. Those few who came to know him well soon understood that it was a bad sign for him to be silent, and he didn't say a word as the previous three hours were played out on the holographic map projected into the heart of his Baneblade. The super-heavy tank was hull down in the very shadow of the western wall, ready to grind along behind the Seleucaians behind the advance, that advance had, of course, been postponed until Xarius had regained control of all the forces that were supposed to be fighting for him. The sound of mortar fire and occasional battle cannon shots from forward armour patrols filtered through the massive hull of the Baneblade – Xarius ignored them. He had more important things to worry about.

The holograph was zoomed in on a portion of Gravenhold to the east – the governmental sector, centred around the grand senate-house that stood on the shore of the River Graven. It was covered in scores of blinking icons, dark blue for the Crimson Fists, light blue for the Fornux Lix Fire Drakes, red for the enemy.

Xarius shook he head and wound back the projection, zipping through the last three hours of combat in reverse. It still didn't make sense. It had all happened, certainly – but it couldn't have. It shouldn't have.

The recording was back at the beginning. Xarius watched it unfold again – the blue column of icons snaked from the south-eastern gate towards the governmental district – Elthanion had rounded up the

cream of the Fire Drakes' armour, Leman Russ main battle tanks and
Demolisher seige variants, even Hellhound flame tanks, to support the
Chimeras full of troops. The Crimson Fists had brought their own
armour – Space Marines were far too proud to be anything but self-suf-
ficient – mostly their Rhino APCs and some support tanks.

Red blips flickered where the long-range sensors on the *Resolve* had
spotted enemy fire streaking towards the convoy. The convoy was
mounting a classically stupid drive, completely unsupported, relying
on speed to get through unscathed and without any apparent concern
about getting surrounded or, indeed, getting back to the south-eastern
gate again. Some tanks were destroyed or crippled, their icons dim,
their passengers and crew probably picked off by isolated pockets of
Gravenholders.

Then the convoy reached the governmental district itself. What followed, even in the clinical holo-display, was a murderously brutal close
firefight. Xarius could only assume that the Traitor Marines that the
Fists had encountered in the first moves into Gravenhold were holed
up in strength, because suddenly the red icons of the enemy were a
tight knot of resistance and the light blue of the Guardsmen were dying
in their dozens. It was savage. Xarius had seen this kind of fight before,
and sometimes found himself too close to them. He could feel the men
dying out there. He could taste the smoke in the air and feel the heat
of the flames.

There must have been two hundred Traitor Marines. If it had been a
case of them against the hundred-strong Second Company of the
Crimson Fists the numbers would have told – but the Fists had armour
and the support of the Imperial Guard. The Traitors had fallen back,
fighting bitterly every metre, to the senate-house itself. The senate-
house should have been one of the centrepieces of the recapture of
Gravenhold, where the Fire Drakes planted the flag of the aquila on
the roof to signify that the city was almost won. Instead, it had erupted
with a massive flood of enemy troops.

Xarius had never seen so many Space Marines in one place, but even
that was nothing remarkable compared to the army that came out of
absolutely nowhere. The sensors on the *Resolve* suggested between ten
and twenty thousand enemy troops, a tidal wave of red icons swamping the Crimson Fists and the Guardsmen. The only possibility was that
they had been travelling underground, gathering under the senate-
house and colluding with the Traitor Marines to launch an immense
trap.

What had been a rapid, unstoppable drive by the Imperial forces
turned into a rout in a matter of seconds. Xarius slowed the projection

down to real-time, watching the enemy pour out across the streets, through the now-ruined Ecclesiarchical offices and the chamber mercantile, spilling down along the banks of the Graven. He switched on the vox-recorder unit, hearing the fractured transmissions of the Fire Drakes as the disaster unfolded.

'...sweet Throne of Earth, there are thousands of them... fire team nine, team nine where the hell is my cover fire?'

'... witchcraft! It's damned witchcraft, they've got the Hellhound crew and they're coming for us...'

'Retreat! It's a frag-up, follow the Fists and get out of here...'

Guardsmen were frantically reciting prayers from the *Uplifting Primer* that every Guardsman was issued with, in the hope of keeping enemy sorcery out of their minds. Fire teams were shooting at one another, either through psychic domination or sheer panic. The Crimson Fists were putting out massive volleys of bolter fire and falling back to their APCs, leaving the Guardsmen to extricate themselves. Xarius saw and heard more than a thousand Guardsmen die in the first few minutes, dragged down by the baying hordes, trapped like rats in closed-off streets, shot by their friends or crushed by the tracks of their own tanks. One vox-burst ended as a Leman Russ exploded, cutting off the voice of its commander in a wave of static. Many others ended in screams. Xarius didn't need anything more to imagine what was going on in those streets – the *Resolve* would probably send him pict-steals of the streets in the morning but he could see, in his mind's eye, the charred bodies and paving sticky with blood.

In his younger days, Xarius would have chased the image away with a good shot of something alcoholic and spicy. He would have pretended that a lord general did not see the men under his command as men at all, but as numbers, weapons, statistics to be stacked and sacrificed until they added up to a victory. But he did not believe that any more. The Imperium was built on death, and it was his job to feel every single one of those deaths in the hope that he could win a victory that did not cost the very lives it was supposed to save. He wasn't a soldier. He was the opposite. He was fighting a war of his own, to keep the suffering from swallowing up what humanity the Imperium had left. It was a war he would one day lose, but that didn't mean he should stop fighting.

Wearily, Xarius flicked off the holomat and felt the claustrophobic interior of the Baneblade looming down on him.

'Hasdrubal?' he voxed.

'Sir?' replied the flag-commander.

'Get this damn coffin back onto the spaceport. The push will have to wait.'

'Yes, sir.'

The engines growled into life as the command tank began to turn and head back out from the shadow of the wall to where it would be safer. Damn the Fire Drakes, damn Elthanion and the bloody Crimson Fists. If a general lost control over his armies he wasn't fighting a war any more, he was just presiding over a disaster. Xarius tried to imagine what kind of disaster could erupt in Gravenhold if he let it happen, and he was glad to find that his imagination wasn't that good.

THE RAZORBACK ASSAULT APC juddered as it crashed over the remains of an administrative building shattered by Demolisher fire. Commander Reinez held on as the vehicle slewed round, gunfire still spattering against its armour.

The back hatch was hanging open and the Crimson Fists were firing out, keeping the hostiles out of the road behind them in case one of them had a rocket launcher or a demo charge. Through the hatch Reinez could see absolute desolation – plumes of smoke, wrecked tanks, piles of bodies, buildings ablaze or already gutted, the broken remnants of the once-handsome governmental district. Fornux Lix Chimeras and Fists' Rhinos ran a gauntlet of small arms fire and suicidal attacks from the corrupted soldiers of Gravenhold, who ran into the streets and seemed determined to take on the surging tanks and APCs with nothing more than bare hands, knives, teeth and fury.

'Inhuaca?' Reinez voxed through the static that accompanied any battle. 'Chaplain, come in!'

'… receiving you, barely,' came the stern voice of Chaplain Inhuaca.

'Where are you?'

'Ahead of you. Approaching the gate.'

'They killed Captain Arca,' said Reinez, unable to keep the anger out of his voice. 'They took the banner.'

Inhuaca paused. 'Then we have much to avenge.'

Reinez flicked off the vox in anger. He had thrown everything he had into taking the heads of the Soul Drinkers and he had failed. He had been thrown back in disarray. He had lost Crimson Fists, most of them veterans and many of them heroes of the Chapter like Assault-Captain Arca. And he had lost the standard of the Second Battle Company, which had been entrusted to him by the Chapter Master himself.

He had seen the Soul Drinkers. He had seen their mutations and their treachery. He had seen the trap unfold, where hordes of the enemy poured out to swamp the Fists and the Fire Drakes. He had faced them, and he had lost.

Reinez fired off a volley of bolter shots at hostiles in the street, seeing their pallid limbs flailing as they died. The Razorback's turret ground round on its bearing and launched a glittering las-blast into a building as the APCs rushed past it, boring through solid marble and sending out a shattered plume of masonry dust. The Marines crowded into the APC beside Reinez fired too, their guns chattering, sending the Emperor's wrath down on the only targets they had after the Soul Drinkers had cheated them out of delivering justice.

'Enough!' yelled Reinez, too disgusted with the wretchedness of the enemy to even look at them. 'Driver! Close the hatch and get us out of here! Catch up with the Chaplain at the gate!'

This battle was over. The APC's rear hatch closed, shutting out the grim aftermath of defeat. The engine revved up and the vehicle surged forward, forgoing firing for extra speed. The enemy couldn't hurt them. It was better to leave them behind and plan to bring the Emperor's vengeance down on them all at once, not waste lives and ammunition on skirmishing with them in the street.

The other Marines knew better than to complain. Reinez was furious, and they knew it because they all were. The shame of defeat had rarely been more acute, even for those who had lived through the loss of the Chapter's fortress-monastery.

The Fire Drakes were faring far worse than the Crimson Fists. They must have left hundreds of dead men in the streets of Gravenhold, with more doomed to die cut off and trapped within the city. But it was the insult that hurt more than the knowledge of those deaths. An insult that had to be avenged, even if it meant Reinez wouldn't get off Entymion IV.

He would kill them. He would kill them all, and it would be his hand that took the head of Sarpedon. He had seen the mutant witch, the arch-heretic, lit by the gunfire in the chamber mercantile. Reinez knew then, crammed into the back of a Razorback with a handful of defeated Marines and fleeing like a whipped animal, that the Emperor's will would only be done on this planet when Sarpedon was dead, and when it was Reinez who did the killing.

IT WAS A TIDE of corruption. It was an endless nightmare of broken minds, men and women robbed of their souls, reduced from humans into a near-mindless horde. The sorcerers were worse – magicians, rogue psychics, witches who sailed above the churning crowds of Gravenhold's unfortunate citizens and directed them like choirmasters. They wore flapping robes of emerald and black, or foetid wrappings of piecemeal leather that dripped bile as they flew.

Runes of power were scorched into the air as they cast their spells, sometimes so bright they were burned into the walls. Their orders, transmitted by thought or magic, rippled through the enemy like waves, drawing the teeming army one way or another. Drifts of bodies built up beneath the windows of Guard-held buildings until the enemy could clamber over their own dead and into the lower floors. Guardsmen were dragged out into the streets and torn apart, tanks were mobbed until their tracks were clogged solid with bone and gore and the Gravenholders pried the hatches open. Guardsmen blew themselves up with demo charges rather than die at these hands – others were mentally dominated by the sorcerers as if for sport, shooting their comrades or jumping out of top-floor windows.

'Are we just going to watch this?' said Luko grimly, hunkered down behind a pillar at the front of the senate-house, watching Gravenhold burning. The rest of the Soul Drinkers were scattered through the surrounding buildings and the Ecclesiarchical offices opposite the senate-house, probably all itching for the command to open fire. The Soul Drinkers had sworn that though they had turned their back on the Imperium they were still dedicated to eradicating the enemies of the Emperor; which definitely included the corrupted Gravenholders. It was an affront to them to be forced to stand by when they could kill thousands of them before being overrun, but Sarpedon was their leader and his word to them was law.

'Yes,' replied Sarpedon. 'We watch.'

'Iktinos here,' came a vox from the Chaplain, in cover on the far side of the senate-house where the river Graven ran in a wide loop around the government district. He had Marines on what remained of the senate-house's upper floors, watching the slaughter unfold. 'The Crimson Fists have pulled out and the Fire Drakes are in full retreat. The enemy is following them.'

'Good.' Sarpedon switched to the scouts' vox-channel. 'Eumenes? Get your squad into the senate-house and into the pit. We're going to where these creatures came from. Report all contacts, fire only when fired upon. Understood?'

There was a pause, slightly too long. The scouts, like all the Soul Drinkers, wanted to fight this enemy, not oblige them. 'Yes, commander,' came the eventual reply.

'Good. Luko will be behind you, find out what's down there and make sure we can traverse it safely.' Sarpedon nodded to Luko, who got to his feet and turned to hurry back into the senate-house where his Marines were watching over the pit in case something else came out.

'Luko,' said Sarpedon. 'Did you think it would work?'

'Honestly?' replied Luko. 'No. I thought it was too much to expect they wouldn't kill us.'

'Something is controlling them, Luko. Something that Tellos was fighting for. As far as they are concerned we're just more of the same, come to die for them. If we look like we're here to fight them instead then they really will kill us.'

'I understand, commander. But I'd be happier if I knew who "they" were.'

'I think we'll find out soon enough. Back up the scouts, and keep your eyes open. No one knows what's under this city.'

Luko saluted with a lightning claw and ducked down into the shadows of the senate-house.

Someone had called Tellos to Entymion IV to fight. Who, and why, were the questions Sarpedon was risking his Chapter to answer. So far Sarpedon had shown his Marines were on the side of the enemy in Gravenhold, they had fought the Guard and the Fists, and let the army of debased citizens run riot through the Imperial forces. Now he had to get close enough to begin the hunt for Tellos.

IMPERIAL HISTORY WAS a fiction. Eumenes had known this even as a child on Veyna, when he heard tell of the Imperial preachers who likened him and his people to vermin to be exterminated. He had seen it when he compared the sanctioned Imperial histories in the *Brokenback*'s Librarium to the recollections of the Soul Drinkers who had lived through betrayal and excommunication.

The history of Entymion IV said the Imperial presence was the first, last, and only human civilisation on the planet. Gravenhold had been planned and built by the first settlers, led by the original explorators and missionaries, to codified Imperial architecture and Standard Template Construct blueprints. There had been nothing there before the city, created on virgin earth for the convenience of the Administratum.

The truth, realised Eumenes as he clambered down the rickety makeshift ladders into the depths of the shaft, was that there had been something here long before the current Gravenhold. Layers of architecture, crushed into contrasting strata of stone, marched past before his eyes. Chunks of recognisable structures loomed out of the crumbling earth wall. Sometimes, Eumenes could just make out, with his still-improving eyesight, carvings or inscriptions in languages he couldn't read. Gravenhold was old – or at least, whatever was beneath it was old.

'Clear!' came the vox from Selepus, twenty metres below.

'Nisryus, anything?'

'They've gone,' replied Nisryus, who was just below Eumenes. 'Most of them won't come back this way. It's confusing down here – the way they think – it's not like human beings. There's something else in there.'

'If you start to lose control, Nisryus, you shut it down,' said Eumenes sternly. 'I don't care how good a precog you are. This city's one big moral threat and I don't want you compromised on my watch, understand?'

Nisryus knew full well what would happen if his psychic powers made him a conduit for some daemonic entity or mind-controlling alien. He wouldn't be the first psychic recruit to be put down by his comrades.

Selepus was on the ground, which was knee-deep in foul water where floated the bodies of the Gravenholders who had fallen during the climb up. Eumenes and Nisryus followed him down, the scout squad dropping into the water. There was only one scout squad now, the survivors of Squad Giryan fought under Eumenes. The eight-strong unit included Eumenes's scouts, Raek the sniper, and scouts Laeon and Alcides from Squad Giryan.

Selepus turned over one of the bodies. Its eyes were covered by a strip of metal that seemed to have been pressed to the skin while red-hot, burning its way through the muscle and melting into the bones of the skull. Rivets were driven into its scalp and it had rusting, jagged talons sprouting from its fingertips. It was dressed in battered leather, the remains of a forge worker's gear.

Nisryus walked up to the body and held a hand over it, letting the sensations of its death flow into him.

'Careful, Nis,' said Scamander. 'They were crazy, even I can feel it.'

'This isn't a human mind,' said Nisryus, his eyes closed. Eumenes saw he was trembling slightly and there were dark lines around his eyes, the marks of psychic fatigue. 'It's xenos. The people weren't just dominated. Someone… someone tore out their souls and put something else in there.'

Several tunnels led off from the bottom of the shaft. Selepus was already at the largest, carefully peering down it. It seemed to have once been a service shaft or sewer, there were lead pipes running along the ceiling and the walls were of slimy brick.

'Clear,' he said.

'Luko,' voxed Eumenes. 'We're going in.'

'Take care, lad,' replied Luko, whose Marines were just reaching the shaft floor. 'I'd hate to have to shoot something through you.'

There was a whole city beneath Gravenhold. Probably several. It was obvious – it was served by half-collapsed sewers that had been dug out to form broad half-flooded avenues under the city. Even with the water it was easy enough for a trained scout to follow the path the Graven-holders had taken – they had crowded the sewers and left scratches on the walls and occasional bodies floating, each bearing the same extremes of self-mutilation as the one Nisryus had inspected. There were tunnels leading everywhere and the horde had been fed from many different parts of the undercity, but the main mass had come from somewhere to the north, beneath the noble estates of Gravenhold. The Soul Drinkers had only seen that part of the city from outdated pict-steals during the briefing sessions on the *Brokenback* – lavish villas, each trying to outdo its neighbour, the largest sporting whole villages of ser-vants' quarters and even the smallest cramming statue gardens and courtyards around houses that ranged from the elegant to the grotesquely tasteless.

It was easy to imagine the aristocracy of Gravenhold too wrapped up in their petty games to bother noticing what lay beneath their feet. Now they were either dead or transformed into a mindless army, controlled by an unholy alliance of corrupt sorcerers and aliens.

The Soul Drinkers moved down the shaft and followed in the scouts' footsteps. Eumenes reported everything he saw to the units behind him, knowing they were spreading out to secure the route his scouts were forging. Sometimes there were inscriptions carved roughly by the builders of the tunnels, graffiti in some pre-imperial dialect.

There were surviving Gravenholders, too, crippled or lost, keening alone in the darkness. Eumenes instructed Raek to take each one down from a safe distance – the scout-sniper was quiet and unassuming, but he was as efficient a killer as Selepus.

Eumenes had moved through the tunnels for almost an hour when he saw the main tunnel ahead was collapsed, leaving a huge rent in the ceiling and a long drift of fallen masonry. The bricks and rubble were smeared with blood from the thousands of bare feet that had charged down it into the tunnels from a huge cavity above. Eumenes could see the ceiling of the cavern above – it looked like a low stone sky, dark rock braced with curving columns of white stone like ribs.

'Stop,' said Selepus.

'Movement?'

'I think so.'

It wasn't like Selepus not to be sure. Eumenes waved for the squad to halt. 'Eumenes here,' he voxed to the squads behind him. 'Stop, we've got contact.'

Selepus was scanning the shadows, knife in one hand and pistol in the other. He indicated one of the side tunnels with the point of his knife. 'It was through there.'

Scamander had his pistol holstered and had his hands held up, ready to fill the confined tunnel with fire. The rest of the squad were clustered in the centre of the tunnel, weapons drawn, covering every angle.

'Don't,' said Nisryus. 'I don't think it wants to hurt us.'

'This would be a bad time for you to be wrong, Nis,' said Eumenes, and then he saw it. There were footsteps in the water, but the creature making them seemed composed of shadow, bleeding into the darkness around it. The barest hint of a lithe, humanoid shape was cast onto the wall before it flickered out of view again.

Eumenes glanced down the tunnel and saw Squad Luko assembling at the next junction back, bolters ready. Luko himself had his lightning claws activated, the power field casting strange reflections on the water.

'Scamander?' said Eumenes. 'More light.'

Scamander brought his hands together and in his cupped palms a white-hot ball of flame appeared. He opened his fingers and the shuddering white light filled the tunnel.

With no shadows to hide in, the alien appeared.

Most Imperial citizens had only seen eldar in pictures or carvings. Even those that were accurate told a lie. The eldar were broadly humanoid – they had two arms, two legs, a head and a recognisable complement of facial features – and so most citizens probably thought they appeared a lot like humans. Eumenes knew different, for he had seen pict-recordings from the battles the Soul Drinkers had previously fought against the eldar and now he finally saw one up close, he understood what 'alien' really meant.

The eldar's proportions were totally, horribly wrong. Its skeleton was jointed wrongly, its pigeon chest flaring into broad shoulders with long arms and fingers like spiders' legs. Its legs were thin but seemed wound up ready to spring at any moment and its face was elongated, with a small mouth and tapering nose. Its eyes were the worst – large, soulless, with huge glittering pupils. The utter inhumanity of the thing was accentuated by the way its skin shimmered and shifted – it was supposed to blend into the shadow but under Scamander's harsh light it squirmed like something trapped, rippling between black and white. On its lower half it wore a tight-fitting bodysuit with curved armour plates, its torso was bare and it carried a strange crystalline pistol in one hand. The other hand held a dagger with an elaborate guard that encased the alien's fist and a long, curved, jagged blade. It was slightly taller than an average man, but the comparison meant little. Every muscle and movement was alien.

There was a second eldar crouching down at the next junction, but though exposed neither one ran. There was an uneasy pause. Eumenes didn't have to tell his scouts not to shoot, but it would only take one threatening move for all that to count for nothing. These were aliens. They were practically born to betray Mankind.

'Good,' said a smooth, dark voice with enough of an accent to tell Eumenes it wasn't from a native speaker of Imperial Gothic. 'Then you are curious, and you are willing to talk, not just fight. Both these things are good. Don't you agree? Youth of the living race, youth of the strong, don't you agree?'

The third alien was different. As it walked into view Eumenes saw it wore full armour, black and glossy, worked into elaborate curves and spikes with plates that locked together to allow full movement. Its weapon was slung over its back, a long crystal rifle. It had a tall helmet with bright jade eyepieces hanging at its belt – its bare face was so pale it looked dead and jet-black hair hung down over its shoulders. 'Forgive my pets, my bloodhounds,' it said, indicating the two other eldar. 'Your soldiers named them "mandrakes" and they fear them greatly, but you have nothing to fear.'

'They're not our soldiers up there,' replied Eumenes. 'But then you knew that.'

The eldar smiled in deference. The expression was as wrong as the rest of it, and Eumenes guessed it was mimicking a human smile to put the scouts at ease. It wasn't working. It had black predator's eyes and a sneering little slit of a mouth, and nothing it did would make Eumenes trust it.

'Please,' said the alien, indicating the path ahead that sloped upwards into the cavern. 'Come with me, sons of the strong.'

'Sir?' voxed Eumenes on the command channel.

'Go with him,' replied Sarpedon. 'Luko, Graevus, join them. Pallas too. If you get the slightest hint of an ambush, get back here shooting. We'll be right behind you.'

Luko's tactical squad and Graeveus's Assault Marines, along with Apothecary Pallas, moved down the tunnel. They were wary but their weapons weren't raised. Eumenes waved at his scouts to lower their own pistols, and Selepus holstered his knife.

'Excellent,' said the alien slimily, seeing that the Soul Drinkers were co-operating. 'The prince has long wished to meet with you.'

'GUILLIMAN'S ARSE,' swore Luko in quiet awe as the Soul Drinkers saw the palace for the first time. They had realised by then that there were cities lying in layers beneath Gravenhold, but none of them had suspected anything might survive this intact. And yet it had, and suddenly what had happened to Gravenhold made a little more sense.

The cavern was not natural. It was a handsome scalloped hemisphere, carved with huge and precise geometry, the dark stone braced with struts of white that formed an enormous vaulted ceiling so high it looked like a dark grey sky.

'They must have known,' said Pallas quietly as the Marines spread out from the entrance formed by the collapsed sewer. 'Whoever was here before the Imperium, they must have built it like this because they knew it would be buried. They had to make sure something survived.'

'Or else it's a tomb,' replied Graevus. Graevus still carried the banner of the Crimson Fists Second Battle Company, rolled up around its standard pole and held in his unmutated hand. He had lost three Marines in the chamber mercantile and he and his squad were badly battered.

The palace itself was even more extraordinary than the chamber it was hidden in. It sat surrounded by lavish stone gardens, marble and jade carved to resemble trees and flower beds, cold and astoundingly lifelike as if a real garden had been suddenly petrified. Marble fountains sprouted flowing torrents of glass. Lawns of emerald crystal were broken by stands of black stone trees with jade leaves.

The building was of dark green veined stone, deeply lustrous, drinking in the light from the glow-globes that hung like fat shining fruit from the stone trees. It was an extraordinary conceit, with bone-coloured marble picking out its battlements, tall fairytale turrets, a massive portcullis of mirror-polished gold and a wide moat full of what had to be quicksilver, churning and swirling around the base of the palace's outer wall. The palace had been built to look like a castle and though it was more a decorative folly than a fortification, the Soul Drinkers, being soldiers, still noted the firing slits and the formidable overhangs of the battlements. They saw the way the corner turrets jutted out to force attackers into overlapping fire fields and the simple difficulty of crossing the moat. If things turned bad, the palace could be a hellish place to attack, especially if it was defended by anything like the forces the aliens could evidently bring to bear.

The alien, with its two mandrake companions loping alongside it, led the way. With Scamander's blinding light withdrawn they shifted in and out of view, their forms blending into the shadows of the trees and fountains. The main path towards the palace wound past statues, oddly stylised depictions of Gravenhold's earlier inhabitants apparently, but not definitely, human.

The golden portcullis ground open as a bridge extended from below the main gate. The interior of the palace was dark with a dim glow from somewhere inside, purplish and uninviting. The Soul Drinkers followed the aliens across the bridge and through the outer wall. The air was as cold as a tomb, the stone sweating slightly, the armoured footsteps of the Marines echoing.

In the courtyard beyond, an expanse of crystalline lawn surrounding the palace's inner keep, hundreds of eldar stood as if to attention. They wore black glossy armour and carried weapons varying from the crystalline rifles to long barbed whips to curved, serrated swords that gleamed with venom. Behind the front rows of warriors were more heavily-armoured eldar with full helmets, thicker and more elaborate armour, and massive halberds with energy blades. There were dark shimmering forms slinking along the battlements above them, more mandrakes no doubt, along with more eldar warriors this time carrying heavier weapons: long-barrelled guns made of something gleaming and black, multi-barrelled versions of their crystalline rifles, and stranger-shaped weapons besides.

The eldar were raiders and bandits, rarely mustering in any number, striking in small co-ordinated bands. It was rare to see so many in one place, let alone in the presence of Imperial troops. The eldar were silent as they stood to attention, eerie and intimidating. There was little doubt how much killing power this army possessed, and the numbers assembled probably counted for only a fraction of their full strength in Gravenhold.

The alien accompanying the Soul Drinkers spoke a few words of the sibiliant eldar language and the assembled warriors parted before the black stone doors of the keep. The doors opened and the alien led the Soul Drinkers into the keep.

Inside, a second large door led into an enormous throne room. Lying prostrated on the floor, facing the throne dais, were scores of the Gravenholders, their faces pressed against the cold stone floor, crouched in silent adoration of the figure on the throne.

Even seated, the prince was obviously tall, and the long halberd leant against his tall throne of green marble was evidently there for more than show. His armour was even more elaborate than that of his elite soldiers – the shoulderpieces curved so high they formed a crescent moon behind his head and dark red silks embroidered with silver billowed from between the interlocking armour plates. A brilliant green jewel was mounted in the centre of his breastplate, illuminating his face from beneath and picking out his long, cruel features. His skin was pale and his shaven head was covered in intricate tattoos, dozens of characters from the eldar language probably recording his many works of depravity.

Behind his throne stood a group of the prince's personal warriors. In contrast to the warriors in the courtyard these were stripped-down, their armour designed more to show off their snakelike muscles and perfect alabaster skin than to provide any actual protection. The reason for their lack of armour was soon obvious. At an almost imperceptible signal from the prince one of the warriors backflipped off the dais and scampered up to the Soul Drinkers with lightning speed and incredible grace, picking its way between the prostrate Gravenholders with such ease it was as if they weren't there.

The lithe eldar exchanged a few words with the Soul Drinkers' guide. Eventually the guide turned to the closest Marine, which happened to be Luko.

'The Pirate Prince Karhedros of the Kabal of the Burning Scale, Lord of the Serpent Void, Victor of the Wars of Vengeance, First Scion of Commoragh and Beloved of She-Who-Thirsts, bids welcome to his allies the Drinkers of Souls, exiles from the Beast Race, loyal to the Prince and devoted to his glory.'

'It is an honour,' replied Luko uncertainly.

'What offering have you brought the prince, that he might know the path of your souls?'

The Marines shot a few uncertain looks between themselves. No one had said anything about an offering. Space Marines were not diplomats, and Sarpedon the Chapter's leader was not there.

Eumenes stepped forward and took the banner from Graevus's arm. 'Here,' he said to the eldar guide. 'We have brought this. The prince's enemies are our enemies.'

The prince saw this, and stood up on his throne, Regally, with the long strides of someone indeed taller even than a Space Marine, he strode across the throne room past the prostrate Gravenholders and took the banner from the guide. It unrolled in his hands and the bloody, bullet-charred standard of the Crimson Fists Second Company stared out at the prince. The red gauntlet icon was embroidered above a scroll listing hundreds of engagements where the Second Company had distinguished itself, a list that should have had Gravenhold added to it.

Pirate Prince Karhedros regarded the banner for several long moments. 'It seems,' he said in flawless Imperial Gothic and a silky voice, 'that my enemies would dearly love to see you dead for what you have taken from them. Those that hate you also hate me, and I hate them. That makes us allies. Bring your warriors to my palace, we have much to discuss.'

Luko looked round at Eumenes. 'Well done, lad,' he said with obvious relief. Then, he flicked on the vox. 'Sarpedon, we're going to need you here. Bring everyone.'

CHAPTER EIGHT

COLONEL SAVENNIAN HAD, at least, answered the summons when Xarius had sent it out. More importantly, he had brought Lieutenant Elthanion with him on the Aquila-pattern shuttle that zipped from the south-western gate to the eastern spaceport, giving the city and its baleful influences a very wide birth. Along with Colonel Threlnan of the Seleucaians, Colonel Vinmayer of the Algorathi Janissaries and Consul Kelchenko, who effectively commanded the 4th Carvelnan Royal Artillery, Savennian completed the complement of commanding officers under Lord General Xarius.

Xarius met them as the shuttle touched down. Elthanion was still smoking slightly and stank of gunsmoke and sweat, an old soldier in marked contrast to the almost doll-like Savennian, an elderly aristocrat who had gradually shrunk in his old age until from a distance he looked like a regimental mascot in a colonel's uniform.

There had been a time when Xarius would have bawled out both men there and then for dereliction of duty, for wasting the valuable lives of Imperial citizens to go chasing after some Space Marine's personal vendetta. But Xarius knew it wouldn't do any good. Ethanion and Savennian knew damn well they would be lucky to get away without a court martial after Gravenhold was won, and if they stepped out of line again, Xarius would be well within his rights to have them both shot.

So Xarius said nothing, and let his makeshift adjutant Hasdrubal make with the niceties and lead the colonel and the lieutenant to where the commanders of the Entymion IV strikeforce were gathered.

'THIS,' SAID XARIUS, indicating the artillery train with a sweep of his arms, 'is the beginning of the end.'

The huge circular landing hub in front of him was full of artillery tanks. Basilisks with long-range Earthshaker cannon stabbing upwards, Griffon mortar tanks with elaborate hull-mounted cranes to load their wide-mouthed mortars. Medusas with huge forward-firing guns to crack open bunkers and gun emplacements. Even two Deathstrike missile launchers, devastating strategic weapons which launched vortex warheads – they only got one shot, but by the Emperor they could make it count. The air around them was shimmering with the downdraft of another lander, carrying a pair of Basilisks in its skeletal hull as it descended. Crewmen were scrambling all over the tanks, loading fuel and ammo, finding their favoured machines, checking gunsights and steering.

'This is the 4th Carvelnan Royal Artillery, gentlemen,' continued Xarius. 'Courtesy of the consul here.'

Consul Kelchenko, a fat man in the deep blue uniform of the Departmento Munitorum, nodded smugly. Kelchenko's tiny corner of the Departmento Munitorum was responsible for deploying, fuelling and arming the Carvelnan Royal Artillery, which meant that he was effectively the unit's commanding officer even though he hailed not from the Guard but from the Administratum.

Xarius turned back to the colonels, sitting in a large supply tent that had been cleared out to provide seating for the officers, their various adjutants, and a large holodisplay. 'We now possess the most effective way of killing our own men and creating plenty of rubble for the enemy to hide behind.'

The holodisplay flicked on. Images of the first few hours of campaign flickered past, eerily silent pict-steals of the murderous fighting around the industrial mills and the south-eastern gate. 'The campaign for Gravenhold will require a systematic and relentless drive across the city on a wide front. Our Guardsmen will be advancing into enemy-held areas within moments of artillery barrages. There is ample opportunity for our own men to be shelled, for the line to break apart, for Guardsman to kill Guardsman in the confusion.

'This campaign will only hope to succeed if there is absolute co-operation between all branches. Between the artillery, the men of your regiments, and the observers on the *Resolve*. The battle will be decided at squad level, at which your sergeants will excel because you will have chosen, briefed and directed them according to the extremely close-range combat likely to occur in this environment.'

The holodisplay was showing the Fire Drakes being driven back at the south-eastern gate, fire streaking down at them, bodies and gutted Chimeras littering the broad road. 'But this will not be enough. The Guard advance and the artillery must be co-ordinated with absolute diligence and precision. This operation will be assembled and put into action within the next twenty-four hours so you do not have much time to get your aim in. I suggest you make the most of it.' The holo changed to a map display of Gravenhold and its most prominent features – the River Graven, the arena in the heart of the slums, the massive black iron mills, the lavish homes of the aristocracy.

'Gentlemen, your first impressions. Colonel Threlnan?'

Threlnan stood. 'I believe our first target is the industrial sector. We have been reducing the enemy presence with aggressive patrolling. It will need a major footslog to drive them out and these are large industrial buildings, they won't react well to shellfire. Bringing down a couple of troublesome enemy strongholds is about our limit until we break through into the slums.'

'Which we can happily pound to rubble?' interjected Xarius.

'Yes, sir.' Tactical arrows were appearing as Threlnan spoke, marking out the various paths the Seleucaian units would take. It would be a gruelling, building-by-building grind as the Guardsmen cleared sharpshooters from the towering mills and warehouses. 'If we bypass the mills we'll be handing the enemy a haven too tough for us to crack. Once we drive them into the slums we can push them eastwards with the artillery.'

'Good. Gentlemen, what of the Fire Drakes?'

'I shall allow Lieutenant Elthanion to explain our battle plans,' said Savennian. His voice was thin and nasal, as if he had never had to raise it in his life.

Savennian looked even more brutal than Threlnan and, unlike Threlnan, he had none of the officer's polish to take the edge off it. He was still fresh from battle and he had not had all his minor shrapnel wounds dressed. His heavy dark grey body armour was dulled with grime from engine smoke and spotted with more than a little blood. 'Recon has suggested a large body of enemy light infantry between the governmental district and the south-east gate,' said Elthanion.

'So we noticed,' said Xarius, but choked back the instinct to say more.

'The Fire Drakes are at about sixty per cent full strength,' continued Elthanion, ignoring the insult. Enemy icons swarmed around the governmental district, barring the path of the unit icons representing the depleted Fire Drakes. 'We lost a lot of armour. But we're planning an infantry drive with full artillery support from the start. We'll pound them against the River Graven, then meet up with the Seleucaians to cross the river. Long, hard assaults are what the Fire Drakes do best. The enemy has the numbers but not the quality, we'll break them and chase them into the river.'

Xarius eyed the plans. They were straightforward enough, but the advance from the south-east gate would have had twice the momentum had the Fire Drakes' armour not been so badly mauled haring after the Traitor Marines. Xarius's plan was to have the Seleucaians and the Fire Drakes meet in the centre of the city's southern half, then turn northwards to cross the Graven en masse and surge into the north of the city. The north, with its sprawling noble estates and adepts' quarters, had seen barely any combat and it was anyone's guess as to what might be in there. It was hoped that victory in the south would cripple the enemy hold and leave the north vulnerable, and the colonels' contributions so far seemed adequate. But there was still too much the Imperials didn't know. Xarius wished very dearly that Gravenhold really could be destroyed from orbit, but he knew better than anyone that this battle would be won the old-fashioned way.

'Adequate,' said Xarius. 'Colonel Vinmayer?'

Vinmayer wasn't the source of the problem with the Algorathi Janissaries. He was just a symptom. The Janissaries had, for more than three hundred years, served as a garrison on a feudal world where forming a square against nomadic cavalry or swatting aside spear-armed peasants with parade-ground volley fire was enough to do the Emperor's will. Vinmayer wore a fine powder blue uniform with breeches, shako, gold bullion in neat rows across his chest, a dress sword scabbarded at his waist and only a pearl-handled duelling laspistol holstered on one hip to suggest he belonged in the forty-first millennium. 'My men are the best-drilled you'll find this side of Cadia, sir! Our Seleucaian friends will have nothing to fear, we'll back them up every step of the way. There will be no enemy counter-thrusts, of that you can be sure.'

The arrows on the holo now showed where the Algorathi units, hopefully furnished with some Chimeras and a few grim war stories about what real battles were like, would advance into the wilderness left behind by the Seleucaian thrust. Their job was to form a barrier against the most obvious counterattacks, from enemies driven into the extreme south of the city's slums where they might reform at the southern wall and drive into the Seleucaian rear. 'As you can see, I have worked carefully with Colonel Threlnan to ensure his every move is shadowed by my men.'

'Good,' said Xarius. 'Then the Janissaries will be where they can be of the most use. Gentlemen, all this is good enough in practice but if we treat Gravenhold like the seat of some petty rebellion then this plan will break down and we will fail. Make no mistake, if the city is not taken by us, in this way, then we will lose the whole planet. The Administratum would rather write it off as lost than have a major military catastrophe on their hands, and I will not have that magnitude of failure under my command. You answer directly to me, and if discipline breaks down in those streets, you'll be busted down so far you'll be carrying ammo to the men you now command. Questions?'

No one made a sound.

'Good. Get these plans finalised, I can see gaps big enough to drive a Baneblade through. Go to your men and see to their morale, they'll take a battering in there no matter how it goes. And for the Emperor's sake, don't forget we're all on the same side. Dismissed.'

'I have... I have one question, sir,' said Consul Kelchenko.

'Yes, consul?'

'What about the Crimson Fists? I had expected their commander would be here.'

Xarius sighed. 'The Fists can join in if they want. Perhaps you might even find some orders they can follow. Now dismissed.'

Kelchenko looked disappointed as the assembled officers broke off to return to their men. Doubtless he had hoped since childhood that one day he would meet one of the armoured heroes of the Imperium. The Marines had that effect. Used right they were a powerful psychological force.

Xarius hoped the Fists would play along. The invasion needed all the help it could get. The Seleucaians were competent and numerous and the Fire Drakes were quality troops, even the Algorathi Janissaries has their uses, but the Crimson Fists could form a cutting edge that Xarius knew could make the difference.

But the Crimson Fists wouldn't listen to him, he knew it. In their own way they were as lost to him as the Traitor Marines they were so eager to kill.

Accompanied by Hasdrubal, Xarius walked back to the squat, monstrous shape of his Baneblade, oddly comforting for all its ugliness. The truth was, when the engines were powered down it was probably the quietest place in the spaceport, and Xarius was an old man who needed some sleep.

BETRAYAL HUNG AROUND the palace like radiation. Sarpedon could feel it. As a telepath, even one who could not receive or read minds, he could sense the heavy dark weight of it tainting everything. The other Soul Drinkers, temporarily barracked in a wing of the palace, could feel it too – they were surrounded by hostile xenos of the kind they were honour-bound to kill, holding off enacting the Emperor's will because Sarpedon knew the aliens were his only link to Tellos.

Sarpedon hated it, too. He hated it more, because he was responsible for it. He had delivered his Marines into the stronghold of eldar far more sinister and cruel than those he had fought before, even on Quixian Obscura where he had first earned his spurs in the eyes of the old Chapter. The mandrakes were silent killers who could probably sneak up on even a Marine in the gloomy depths of the palace. The incubi, as the prince's heavily armoured elites were known, were the equal of an Assault Marine in close combat, and no one knew what other secrets the xenos might unleash at the first opportunity.

The eldar were warriors, aesthetes, pirates, philosophers and killers. But most of all, they were liars.

'Our meeting is fortunate, Lord Sarpedon,' said Prince Karhedros. 'We two are cast out. Hated by our species, no? Betrayed. And forced to fight the cancer that is Mankind. Forced! Surrounded by death, compelled to slaughter. This is your story as well as mine. So we are the same.'

Karhedros reclined on a long couch of carved black wood, some alien creature lying dissected and raw on a low table by his head. As he spoke he picked fleshy scraps from the creature and swallowed them. The circular chamber, on the lower levels of the palace and evidently somewhere beneath the stone gardens, was so lavishly upholstered and strewn with gold-embroidered cushions that it threatened to swallow the silent eldar body-servants that followed Karhedros everywhere. They wore little more than strips of black silk, but that same silk covered their faces completely. They kneeled silently around the room.

Sarpedon declined to take the second couch. With eight legs and power armour, reclining was not an option. 'It is true,' he said, swallowing the filthy feeling it gave him to talk with this creature. 'We are both excommunicate.'

'Ah, yes. A fine way to put it. Your language is painful to us, strong one, but it does have its little gems. Excommunicate we are.' Karhedros glanced at one of the body slaves, who slunk forward and wordlessly poured a long, fluted glass full of something amber-coloured and effervescent. Sarpedon thought the body-slave was a female eldar but he found it difficult to tell with a species whose every muscle and sinew was wrong.

'Try some,' said Karhedros. 'It's not the best, but it's as good as you'll find on this planet.'

Sarpedon accepted the glass from the slave. Even if it was poisoned, his many internal augmentations and redundant organs would filter out anything harmful. It would be more dangerous to refuse it and risk causing suspicion. 'My battle-brother fights alongside your warriors,' said Sarpedon. 'That is enough to convince me we are on the same side.'

'Ha!' Karhedros let out a strange barking laugh. 'I have eyes and ears throughout this city, they more than convince me we are fighting the same enemy. Many died that would otherwise have lived to blight me. We honour our fellow sufferers, Lord Sarpedon, and I feel this city will be won all the sooner. You speak of your brother Tellos, I assume? I understand now where he learned to make war.'

'We fight the same enemy,' said Sarpedon, 'but I still do not know why we fight them here. What do you want on this world? It must have been good enough to convince Tellos.' Sarpedon took an experimental sip of the liquid. It was wine, doubtless looted from some aristocrat's cellar. Sarpedon's metabolism broke down the alcohol instantly but even his unsophisticated palate could tell it was very good indeed.

Karhedros leaned forward conspiratorially. 'I want this city, Sarpedon. I want this world. Think about it. We both wish to hurt the Imperium. For revenge, for gain, for whatever reason. Hurt it. But it is huge. Why, you know better than I what a monstrous thing this empire of Mankind is. I have tried to hurt its citizens, I have. I have enslaved and tormented them by the thousands, but it does not notice! They send warfleets to chase me away but dare not bring me to battle to avenge the insults I do them. They treat me like vermin to be swatted away when I annoy them, but not worth the bother to kill.

'Now tell me, what is the point of that? I have killed more of them than I can count, and believe me I tried to keep a tally, Lord Sarpedon. And then I started to think. What is the Imperium? What is it made of? It cannot be made of its citizens, because I have tortured countless numbers of them to death and not made this empire bleed. What else is there?'

Sarpedon couldn't help considering this question. The Imperium was vast and corrupt. In serving it for thousands of years, the Soul Drinkers had become a part of that corrupt machinery, and it had taken a direct betrayal by the Imperium to force Sarpedon to realise it. It cared only about maintaining its own survival, and certainly had no regard for its masses of citizens. 'Its fleets? Its armies?'

'No, Lord Sarpedon. It took me a long time to understand it, too. The answer, excommunicate one, is its worlds.' Karhedros took another morsel of his meal, this time of pink, gelatinous brain material. The creature had been something like a hairless dog, but it had been elaborately dissected and laid open like a bed of glistening, fleshy flowers. 'The monster you call the Imperium is made of nothing. It does not value its people or its spaceships. The only thing it cares about is the most insubstantial thing of all: the claims it makes to the worlds under its shadow. Take that away, and they swarm like angry insects. And so they become the vermin, Lord Sarpedon. Nothing but vermin.'

'So you want to take a world from them?'

'Of course. What other way is there? I exist, I think, to cause suffering. The Imperium has proven impervious to all the wounds I have caused, and so this is the only way I can do what I am here to do.'

'You know, Prince, that many have tried to make claim to Imperial worlds. Too many for anyone to count, in fact. I once fought them. The Imperium has many rebels and usurpers. Aliens, too. Greenskins, Tau, worse things. And there are some who hold them still, I will admit, but they are few in number and all, if I may say so, have far greater resources than you appear to. You might take Entymion IV and maybe even hold it for perhaps decades, but the Imperium will eventually tire of the insult and send enough Guardsmen to drive you out. Or simply send a battlefleet to irradiate the planet.'

'But that is the point. Strong one, child of Mankind, you are too close to your species to understand. I will not send my warriors to hold every street and hill like common soldiers! I am not some ork warlord. I do not fight, not when I don't have to. I control. The people of Gravenhold are just mindless slaves now, but when my haemonculi are finished they will be able to act and think for themselves, with my will imprinted on their minds. I and my court will dissolve away.' Karhedros swallowed the last dregs of his wine. He dropped his glass, and a slave darted forward to catch it before it landed on the deeply carpeted floor. 'They will lose their world. It will be reduced to a lifeless ball of rock by their own weapons. But they will not have won, and they will know it. They will never forget. Entymion IV will be a cancer, a reminder of their weakness. Suffering, Lord Sarpedon. It will eat away at so many of them, there will at last be a scar of suffering on the Imperium to which I can lay a claim.'

Sarpedon could feel the prince's emotions bubbling away just beneath the surface. They were horrible, twisted parodies of human hatred and joy, completely alien but so strong that they battered at Sarpedon's mind. It took a lot to register with Sarpedon – though he was a psyker he was virtually a 'blunt', someone who could not receive telepathic information. Prince Karhedros's emotions were intense and offensively alien enough to force themselves into Sarpedon's consciousness. Karhedros was driven and dangerous, but then,

Sarpedon had seen and heard enough to have come to that conclusion anyway.

'So you will leave Entymion IV and watch the Imperium destroy it themselves,' said Sarpedon. 'I would imagine that would be very satisfying. But what then?'

Karhedros plucked what looked like an eyeball from the glistening carcass, and popped it in his mouth. 'I will find another world, important but underpopulated, just like this one,' he said as he chewed. 'And then I will do it all again.'

Sarpedon sat back on his haunches. His skin wouldn't stop crawling. Sarpedon had fought all manner of monsters but rarely had he come across a creature who inflicted suffering purely for its own sake. It was a religion for Karhedros, and murder and torture were rituals to the She-Who-Thirsts deity Karhedros had hinted at.

'And the human sorcerers you brought here,' said Sarpedon. 'Do they share this dream?'

Karhedros shook his head. 'Their gods are cruel and brutish. Have you heard them pray? They beg for insanity, so they will have the strength to commit ugliness. I need them to control the Gravenholders. Magic does not come easy to my kind and we do not wish to attract the attention of the warp with our recklessness. This is just another crusade for the sorcerers. I give them the chance to fight in the name of their gods, they want nothing more. Soon they will cease to be useful. I must confess I would rather it was sooner.'

'And Tellos is the same?'

'Your brother Marine? He is not like them. He is honest. He does what he does because he enjoys it. It was why I was so honoured that you came to join him. I trust you fight for the same reason? For the joy and the exhilaration of doing violence to something you hate? No base gods.'

'No, prince, no gods. Where is Tellos now?'

Karhedros waved a hand dismissively. 'He has the run of the city. His purpose is to go where the fighting is thickest and kill what he can. The humans in this city are terrified of him, you know. Absolutely awestruck. I see your race is divided into the strong and the weak, and you strong ones strike such utter fear into the weak. When you are on the same side they clamour around you like children, hoping your strength will rub off. When you oppose them they run screaming. Most amusing!'

'But you don't know where he is.'

'You will know as well as I do that this Tellos is not a creature to be kept on a leash. I am sure you will find him soon enough. The truth is,

Lord Sarpedon, your arrival is most fortunate. The Imperials intend to launch a major operation. They were reinforced by artillery and are massing men on both sides of the city.'

'A rolling advance. Artillery and men.' Sarpedon nodded. 'Typical Guard. Old-fashioned and costly, but it'll work.'

'Exactly. There is a chance they might be able to actually win this city if we are not prepared. But that won't happen if my warriors and your Marines hold them up long enough.'

'Long enough for what?'

Karhedros's smile looked almost real. 'Do you really think I will tell you all my secrets at once, Lord Sarpedon?'

Sarpedon had never been so close to an eldar, and never spoken to one at all save to admonish one for daring to exist before trying to kill it. But here he had to converse with one, and act as if he was a heartfelt ally – Sarpedon was sure that he must appear as alien to Kahedros as the eldar did to him, and that it was only this that kept Karhedros from seeing right through him.

If, of course, Karhedros hadn't guessed the truth already, and was just setting up the Soul Drinkers to betray them.

'Now,' Karhedros was saying, 'we have much to do. My advisors are drawing up plans for your deployment. Your Marines will have to move at a moment's notice.'

'They are eager to go,' said Sarpedon, which at least was true.

'Good.' Karhedros indicated the glistening carcass. 'Please, Lord Sarpedon. Try some. It is only right that my allies should enjoy the pleasures I do.'

'It is pleasure enough to fight,' said Sarpedon, which thankfully was diplomatic enough a refusal.

By the time Sarpedon left Karhedros's chamber, leaving the alien dining with his retinue of masked slaves, he felt so filthy and sinful that it took an effort of will just to keep going. He was not a servant of Karhedros, he was not fighting for She-Who-Thirsts. He was here to find Tellos, redeem or kill him, and get out. And if Sarpedon got the chance to betray Karhedros along the way, then all the better.

'Looks even worse from the inside,' said Luko darkly. The wing the Soul Drinkers were using as a temporary barracks looked out over the stone garden. No doubt it had been an artistic marvel in its day, but now it was dark and sinister. The way the mandrakes could occasionally be seen, bleeding from one shadow to the next, didn't help.

'You hate this place too,' said Eumenes. Eumenes's squad had been barracked with Luko's, which Eumenes felt was fortunate. He liked

Luko – aside from Karraidin (who was back on the *Brokenback*, looking after the remaining novices), Luko was the Soul Drinker Eumenes probably respected more than any other.

Luko shrugged. 'Not just the palace. This whole city is wrong.' Luko looked round from the glassless window looking out over the garden. 'Can you feel it?'

'Like it'll turn around and stab you in the back? Like it'll swallow you? Yes, I feel it.'

'It's these damn aliens. You've never faced the eldar, have you, Eumenes?'

'I've read about them. The old Chapter fought them many times. But no, I hadn't seen a live one until today.'

Luko sighed, and Eumenes saw how old he looked. Normally, armed with his lightning claws and revelling in face-to-face fighting, Luko radiated confidence. Not now. 'Most xenos are born just to survive. Some are born to be predators, like the tyranids or the greenskins. You can understand that. It's what the Imperium does – hells, it's what we do. But the eldar are different, novice. They're all born to lie.'

'And we're lying to them? Sounds dangerous.'

Luko smiled grimly. 'I'd rather be back on Stratix Luminae. Back in the Chapter War, even. Anything rather than sit here waiting for them to kill us. The eldar don't know what the truth means – they'll fight alongside you one moment and slaughter cities full of innocents the next. That's one thing the old Chapter would have agreed with, never trust the eldar. I just hope we get to turn on them before they turn on us. Don't turn your back on them, novice, and I mean it.'

The palace wing behind them had once been lavishly gilded but its walls were tarnished and brown, peeling to show the bare stone beneath. Squad Luko and Eumenes's scouts were taking shifts to drop into the half-sleep, not wanting to let down their guard in this nest of aliens but knowing they needed all the rest they could get. A couple of Luko's Marines were stripping their boltguns, while Nisryus was leafing through a battered set of the Emperor's tarot he had taken from the Chapter librarium. Selepus was in half-sleep but Eumenes knew, from experience, that anyone trying to creep up on him would have got a blade in the gut before they got into pistol range. Scamander was resting, too – he needed it more than any of them, because repeated uses of his powers had drained him more than he would admit. His skin was probably still cold to the touch.

'We killed a Fist today,' said Eumenes.

'So I heard,' said Luko.

'He killed Thersites.'

'And you wanted to make him pay? Show him the Emperor's justice?'

Eumenes nodded. In truth he hadn't been thinking of the Emperor at all – he had been thinking of his dead battle-brother and the insult the Fist had done by daring to attack them. But it was close enough.

'Remember how that feels, Novice Eumenes. Eventually it'll be the only thing that keeps you going.'

'But you have more, don't you? I've seen you fight, I've heard you. You love it.'

'One day, novice, you'll be a leader. Everyone can see it. You're the lead scout here and you'll have your own Marine squad if you want it and you get out of this alive. So I'll let you into a secret.' Luko leaned closer. 'I hate it. Fighting is what animals do. It's the most base and ugly thing a human being can stoop to. But you don't chose whether to fight or not in this galaxy. If it's not the Imperium it's the dark gods, or it's the xenos, or it's your own battle-brothers. So I make out that I enjoy it, and most of the time I manage to convince myself as well as the men I'm leading. I can live the lie as long as it's keeping me alive. But take me out of that and make me look at it from the outside, like now, and I hate it.

'I can't tell you why to fight, novice, that's up to you, but if you do it for its own sake then you'll end up no better than that creature you took off the prison ship.'

The two men sat in silence for a few moments, the only sound the clacking of metal on metal as Luko's Marines finished refitting their boltguns.

'Nisryus,' called Eumenes. 'What are the omens?'

Nisryus looked up from his tarot, the dog-eared cards lying in a semi-circle around him. The Emperor's Tarot was an ancient tradition but Space Marine Librarians didn't use it very often, they rarely possessed the precognitive skills required to make the most of the Tarot. It was said the Emperor himself spoke through the cards, if only the user listened hard enough. Nisryus held up the first card he had laid. It depicted an archaic Mechanicus war machine, a massive castle that ground across a battlefield on immense tracks, raining death from its battlements. The Destroyer.

'There will be battle,' Nisryus said.

Luko smirked. 'Don't need the Emperor to tell us that.'

Nisryus held up the next card. It was the Jester, inverted. 'A battle you will lose, Sergeant Luko.'

Luko stared for a moment at the card, knowing that of all the Soul Drinkers it could only represent him. 'That is good to know, novice. Thank you.' He sounded serious.

Eumenes saw the Constellation was also inverted, along with the Arrow of Fate. He wasn't an expert but he knew it meant great confusion and reversal, with whole strands of fate changing with the slightest action.

There was a clattering at the door to the wing that could only be one thing and sure enough Commander Sarpedon walked in, his eight talons clicking on the stone floor. He was in full armour and carrying his force staff. 'Luko, Eumenes. Make ready to move out.'

Luko sprang up and shouted heartily to his men, grinning. 'You heard, Marines! Your dreams have come true!' With a flourish he pulled on one of his lightning claws, the bright talons catching the dim light. 'We're going to give this city some real soldiers to fight!'

Eumenes watched Luko marshal his men, and knew he had a lot to learn. He would have to lead, and leadership meant refusing to let your men down.

At least Eumenes knew now what he really wanted. It had flickered in him when he had killed the Crimson Fist, and it burned inside him now he had seen what drove men like Luko. The Imperium took human beings and it turned them into the things they would ordinarily hate, and only the lucky ones among them ever realised it. Sustained by war, the Imperium had ground up whole populations and turned them into soldiers, so they could die in places like Gravenhold to preserve the principles of oppression and tyranny. Eumenes wasn't a Soul Drinker just out of chance. It felt like he was there for revenge against the Imperium, on behalf of the whole human race.

'Your scouts have excelled,' said Sarpedon, standing just behind Eumenes and rising almost twice the scout's height on his insectoid legs. 'But I need you out there, too.'

'Where do you need us?' asked Eumenes.

'Everywhere, Scout-Novice Eumenes. The Soul Drinkers will have to face the Imperial Guard, there's nothing I can do about that for the moment. But you won't be with them. Eumenes, I need you to go out there and find Tellos.'

CHAPTER NINE

THE TRACKS OF the Baneblade ground through the wreckage of the battlefield. Lord General Xarius, theoretically safe in the belly of the super-heavy tank, watched the destruction unfold through the pict-recorders on the outside of the tank that sent images to the many screens surrounding him.

It was bad. Seleucaians lay dead in drifts where the enemy had been dug in, around towering skeletal factories and material silos. Many buildings were blackened husks, all were damaged, some were still ablaze and a few had been completely bulldozed to the ground by the Seleucaian armour.

'Keep up with them, Hasdrubal,' voxed Xarius, straining to hear his own voice above the relentless thudding of the Baneblade's massive engine pistons and the din of wreckage, masonry and bodies being ground to dust under the tracks. The Baneblade lurched as it dragged its bulk over the uneven ground, and over the noise Xarius heard heavy weapons fire chuddering away somewhere nearby. And behind that, ever-present as it had been since the first moments of the operation, was the constant booming of the artillery as it ground along behind the first waves pummelling Gravenhold into dust.

'Yes, sir,' replied Hasdrubal, commanding from within the blunt bulldog nose of the tank. 'Driver! Get us up closer, lean on the infantry line!'

Xarius could see the men advancing. Threlnan had been thorough, sending out his men in waves to make sure that dug-in enemies could be dealt with while the first waves pushed on. Several Sentinels, spindly two-legged walkers that could pick their way rapidly across the shattered industrial landscape, accompanied squads of men creeping warily through the wreckage and gun smoke. Immediately in front of the Baneblade a squad of Guardsmen checked the inside of a burned-out Leman Russ, their lasguns with bayonets fitted ready to impale any Gravenholders using the wreck as shelter to launch an ambush. There had been enough such ambushes already – the Gravenholders really didn't care about dying, and when their original savagery was spent the survivors went to ground to emerge several waves later and kill advancing Guardsmen who thought they had the easy job.

The effect, of course, was to make every Guardsman alert. Las-fire sparked on one pict-screen and Xarius turned to see Gravenholders pinned down in a ruined factory workshop, swapping fire with Seleucaian infantry until a Leman Russ Demolisher blew the whole building apart with a shell from its siege cannon.

Xarius switched to a feed from one of the forward units, the Sentinel-mounted pict-stealer shuddering as the walker lurched forward firing sprays of crimson fire from its multi-laser. Without sound it was an eerie sight. Seleucaians were diving for cover amongst the smouldering ruins of hovels, hurling themselves into the open channels of filth that ran through Gravenhold's southern slums, huddling down behind half-toppled walls. Gravenholders were fighting for every scrap of ground, fighting through the remains of their own past lives. Crumbling buildings full of dirt-cheap tenements had been blasted open, spilling broken furniture into the streets. Rusting groundcars lay on their sides as makeshift barricades, riddled with las-blasts. A Seleucaian officer yelled, the sound cut off from Xarius but the meaning clear, as he waved his men into the dubious cover of a ruined building. An enemy heavy weapon sent ricocheting fire ripping through a unit of Seleucaian veterans who scattered like fleeing rats into the shadow of any cover they could find.

The Sentinel turned to face the gun emplacement – a heavy stubber, belt-fed, with a gunner and an ammo handler – and sent a sustained burst of las-fire into the Gravenholders. One died straight away, the other lost an arm, and the Guardsmen rushed forwards to finish him off.

Murderous street-to-street fighting, hand-to-hand, room-by-room, across hovels reduced to ruins by the rolling bombardment of the big guns. Xarius shook his head, it was always the worst when the enemy were crazy, because then they didn't run away. You had to kill them, all of them, and that was how you got battles like this.

'Threlnan,' voxed Xarius to the Seleucaian colonel. 'Have you got a tac report up yet?'

Threlnan's voice crackled back over the command vox-net – he was with a forward command post, huddled down in a Salamander as his guard of Leman Russ tanks thundered away to keep counter-attacking Gravenholders away from him. 'It's sketchy, sir, but we've got some steady reports coming in from the latter waves. We're getting a decent picture.'

'Good. Send it.'

'Understood. I'll give it you as a burst transmission.'

'Stay safe, colonel.'

'And you, sir. Threlnan out.'

Xarius looked up from his tiny tactical office – above him the ammo-servitors hung from the ceiling, jointed metal arms poised to lug shells into the breeches of the Baneblade's massive guns. Xarius knew the tank's three auto-targeting heavy bolters would be more useful here than the big guns – a stream of fire, targeted by the tank's ancient machine-spirit, would shred any Gravenholders who got close. He doubted the tank's main armaments, the immense mega-battle cannon and the squat-barrelled Demolisher that jutted from the slope of the front armour would even be fired on Entymion IV.

The holo flickered to life, its large display making the inside of the tank feel even more claustrophobic. The map of Gravenhold was streaked with static, the tank's motion upsetting the delicate workings of the holoprojector.

Xarius's position was marked by its own icon. Xarius knew it really signified the Baneblade itself, not him. He was halfway through the industrial district, on ground that had been won early on in the grand push. The Gravenholders' hold on the area had been weakened by aggressive patrolling and the bombardment had chased thousands of enemies out of the area, leaving only a few nests to resist the first waves of men and armour as they swept westwards from the wall. The Baneblade had been untroubled by enemy counter-attacks and the Seleucaians were showing an admirable level of discipline in smoking out the Gravenholders still intent on making their lives dangerous in the shadow of the massive agri-mills. The first waves of the Seleucaians were exhausted and the second and third were the ones now fighting for Gravenhold's slums. The progress was bloody but it was steady. The enemy had nothing that could hold back the tide of tanks backed by men, rumbling through the hovels.

Xarius did a few mental calculations. There were probably something in the region of five thousand Seleucaians lying dead, dying or

permanently disabled in the ruined streets of eastern Gravenhold.
Xarius was forced to admit to himself that it wasn't too bad, so far. He
didn't know yet how the Fire Drakes were doing to the east, or whether
the Algorathi Janissaries were running into counter-attacks yet as they
formed their line to the south, but the Seleucaians were acquitting
themselves acceptably.

Which begged the question, why was the enemy letting them get away
with it? The only reason the Seleucaians were here at all, barring a little
string-pulling by Xarius, was that one of their sister regiments had been
completely wiped out by the presumably alien forces on Entymion IV.
There was plenty of horror unfolding in the raw red line of the Seleucaian advance, but there didn't seem to be any aliens involved. Or Chaos
sorcerers. Or Traitor Marines. Gravenhold was welcoming them in a little too eagerly.

Xarius scrutinised the holo again. The slums were bad ground to hold
– few hardpoints to take and hold, riddled with alleyways and tunnels
even after bombardment. A difficult place to make your own, to impose
your will over. The city's main arena, positioned in the midst of the
slums so the city's poor could flock to its spectacles and vulgar enter-
tainments, was the only building of any real size until you got to the
government district.

'Threlnan,' voxed Xarius again. This time he heard more fire in the
background of the vox; Threlnan was closer to the fighting.

'Sir!'

'I have your tac report. Make the arena your objective.'

'Sir, yes sir, I've got units making for it now.'

'It's the only defensible structure in the south-east of the city. Priority
target.'

'Understood!' Threlnan paused amid the unmistakable sound of small
arms fire smacking against the side of the Salamander. 'Priority one! I'll
get the Carvelnan artillery to soften up its surroundings and concentrate
the third wave on it.'

'Make it happen, Threlnan. We need somewhere to anchor the line.'

'Yes, sir! Threlnan out.'

'Try not to die, colonel.'

'No, sir! Threlnan out.'

THE SOUL DRINKERS were scattered throughout Gravenhold's undercity.
The tunnels were not just sewers but underground thoroughfares, crypt
corridors, winding alleyways through half-collapsed buildings and
whole landscapes of stone and earth. But for the Space Marines'
enhanced vision the undercity would have been pitch black – as it was,

armour lamps and flares were needed to negotiate the most inhospitable routes through flows of mining spoil and rushing underground rivers.

Gravenhold had not been settled by the Administratum, as its official histories indicated. It had not been purpose-built to manage the agricrop, its stones laid into virgin soil. Gravenhold was very, very old. There had been several settlements on the same site, and when the Administratum first demolished whatever stood there to lay the foundations for Gravenhold they had not thought to dig too deep. Probably they had used parts of the old city in the construction of the new. Certainly the city walls were riddled with old passageways, burial chambers, and narrow twisting stairways that had nothing to do with the Imperial population. It had been an insignificant detail of history in the grand scheme of the Imperium, but for a great many men it had proved a fatal one.

Prince Karhedros had given the Soul Drinkers their orders, but it was not he who was in charge – that was still Sarpedon, and it was at Sarpedon's insistence that the Soul Drinkers followed intricate crystalline holo-maps or shadow-skinned eldar guides through the underground city. Karhedros had given them key points to hold to keep the massive Imperial drive at bay, and Sarpedon needed the malevolent alien to trust them for just a little while more until Tellos showed up.

Of course, he didn't have to like it. Truth be told, his skin was still crawling from having to talk to the heathen – it was even worse that he was actually in league with it, even if he had no intention of keeping his word when the endgame began.

Luko had been sent to hold a medicae station, a solid building at the northern edge of the industrial district. Graevus was leading a force to the eastern walls to engage the Guardsmen pushing into the city from the south-east – probably, Sarpedon guessed, the Fornux Lix Fire Drakes. Iktinos and the Marines who were now resembling his personal retinue were commanded to lurk on a vital bridge across the River Graven, and throw back the Guardsmen (Fire Drakes or Seleucaians, whichever got there first) who would doubtless try to cross. Karhedros had agreed to give the scouts the run of the city on the pretence that they were gathering intelligence on Guard movements – they would, of course, be hunting for Tellos.

Sarpedon, meanwhile, was headed for Gravenhold's arena.

'You KNOW WE'RE too late,' said Librarian Gresk as Sarpedon's force moved through the dripping half-natural caves beneath Gravenhold's slums. 'The Guard have it already. The arena would have been the first location the Guard drove for. It's the only firm foothold in the slums and they need a point to anchor the line.'

'I'm sure you're right,' replied Sarpedon. Squads Krydel, Salk and Praedon were advancing behind him, guns ready, along with Apothecary Pallas. 'But we're not here to take it. We're here to take it back.'

'Movement,' came a vox from a sharp-eyed Marine in Squad Krydel. The force took cover behind the folds of flowstone and the giant stalagmites, eyepieces glinting in the darkness. Sarpedon held up a hand to indicate they should hold their fire. Even with his limited psychic reception he could feel what was approaching.

The sorceress was carried on a litter by a dozen slave-cultists whose faces were masses of scars and stitches. The bearers's hands had been tied together so they melded into single large fleshy claws suitable only for lifting the poles of the litter. The sorceress herself was a petite thing, with skin the colour of hardwood and eyes so green they shone in the darkness. She was naked, but her body was featureless, as if she was a facsimile of a human being, a women-shaped vessel into which the spirit of something far more malevolent had been poured. Only her face seemed to have been finished, high-browed and full-lipped. Her hair hung in faintly writhing dreadlocks and her fingers ended in long golden claws.

The sorceress waved a hand and from the shadows slunk her cultists, not the mindless creatures of Gravenhold but her own personal retinue. Like her bearers their facial features were sewn up with such crudeness that their faces were just masses of bloodied twine and scar tissue, with malformed eyes staring out of oozing gaps in the skin at insane angles. They wore close-fitting black bodysuits studded with gems as green as their mistress's eyes and they were armed with lasguns, standard-issue. They had either once been renegade Guardsmen or the sorceress had the resources to equip her private army properly.

Sarpedon could make out a couple of hundred cultists. She probably had more.

'The prince had told us to expect you,' said Sarpedon carefully. 'Highmistress Saretha?'

Saretha's mouth opened and a long organ slid out from deep within her throat, a sharp-pointed scaly tongue like the tail of a rattlesnake. She let out a long, rattling hiss.

A slave scampered forward. This one had been permitted to unpick the stitches that had sealed its mouth, leaving a wide drooling slit.

'Highmistress Saretha, Most Chosen Scion of the Lord of Unspeakable Pleasures, though her name be unworthy in the mouths of slaves. You are here as appointed?'

'Yes, highmistress. I am Sarpedon of the Soul Drinkers.'

Another long, horrible rattle.

'The pleasurable dead speak of you, Lord Sarpedon. Through you the Lord of Pleasures gives death to many.'

The sorceress was so corrupted she couldn't even speak. Perhaps her mutated tongue was a deliberate affectation, begged from her god so she could demonstrate her superiority by using a slave to interpret for her. In any case Sarpedon choked back the urge to kill every single one of these vermin there and then, and he knew that his Marines could only do the same for so long.

'I do not stand on ceremony, highmistress,' said Sarpedon quickly. 'The prince wants the arena. I intend to deliver it to him.'

'Indeed, as do I.' Sarpedon had to force himself to look at Saretha when her slave was speaking, and not at the slave itself. 'The Lord of Pleasures has eyes above us. The servants of the corpse-emperor believe they have won it but do not suspect us below them.'

'What are they moving into the arena? Artillery? Tanks?'

'Men. And supplies.'

'The Guard have standard procedures,' said Sarpedon, comforted by the fact that he was talking on military matters, something he could be sure of. 'They'll put the ammunition dump underground to keep it safe from mortar hits. An arena like this will have plenty of space for it, with cells and barracks under the arena floor. Which is where we come in. Saretha, you take the surface. Draw the Guard onto the arena floor. My Marines will take the ammo dump underneath.'

There was a pause, then a short spitting hiss.

'The highmistress defers.'

Saretha began clicking and hissing at her cultists, who scuttled forward with curiously insectoid movements and surrounded her, bearing her into the shadows.

'Throne of Earth, Sarpedon, did you feel it?' said Gresk as Saretha disappeared from sight, her cultists carrying her up towards where the arena loomed over the ruined slums. Even the grizzled old Gresk looked perturbed by what he had just seen.

Sarpedon nodded. 'Chaos. Pure Chaos.'

'Xenos and the dark ones, in league. I didn't think you would go this far, Sarpedon.'

'We could hit out at them now, Gresk, and we'd last a few moments doing the Emperor's work until we died. But if we get close enough we could find Tellos and hurt these vermin badly.'

'But the Guard…'

'The Guard want us dead, Gresk. As long as that is true, they are our enemy. There's nothing we can do about it now. And believe me, Gresk, I intend to hurt that creature just as much as you do.' Sarpedon turned and waved his squads forward. 'Salk,' he voxed, 'You have the point. Take us up into the lower reaches of the arena, no contacts, just get us there.'

Sergeant Salk paused for a split second then moved forward with his squad, ready to lead the way out of Gravenhold's underbelly and into the makeshift Guard strongpoint of the arena.

Sarpedon knew the Soul Drinkers trusted him. But they had to keep on trusting him, just a little bit longer. They were in Gravenhold not because they had to be but because Sarpedon had chosen to be, because whatever happened to Tellos was something Sarpedon had to see with his own eyes and because any force powerful enough to turn Tellos to its cause was something worth fighting. He could explain it to them, but he couldn't be sure they would understand like he did. They just had to trust him. That was all.

'We've got something here,' voxed Salk from up ahead. 'Looks like cells cut into the rock. There's a spiral passage leading upwards.' The thuds of lifter-fitted Sentinel walkers echoed down along with the distant crumping explosions of mortar fire.

'Good. Krydel, Praedon, stick close. Gresk to the front, Pallas with me. Our objective is the central ammo dump the Guard will have set up under the arena floor. This is what we will do when we reach it...'

'I'VE GOT A shot,' said Sergeant Kelvor. He was lying on his front, bolter pointed down through the hole in the inside of the Gravenhold's massive wall, the crosshairs of the scope hovering over the throat of a careless Guardsman officer who was pausing to consult a map without taking cover first.

'Hold,' said Graevus.

'You're sure?' Kelvor was a very good shot, a fact that had not been compromised by the loss of his leg at the chamber mercantile. He could take the Guardsman as a matter of course, and draw several units of the advancing Fornux Lix Fire Drakes into a firefight instead of winning back more of the administrative district.

'We're not here to fight the Imperial Guard,' said Graevus. 'Karhedros can't watch us here.'

'You're sure of that, Graevus?'

'No. But I am sure we're not fighting for the xenos just yet, so they can win their own battle for the time being.'

'Fair enough.' Kelvor pushed himself away from the hole. Gravenhold's old city walls had been riddled with tunnels and stairways, so although the xenos guide had melted away soon after they had reached the wall the Soul Drinkers still had little trouble in reaching a good sniping spot. The Marines of Kelvor's squad were positioned in firing spots along a section of the wall very high up. The Assault Marines of Squad Graveus were there as a reserve, to face down any Guardsmen who might try to flush out the snipers. In the tight confines of the wall, there was little doubt that Graveus's chainswords and his own power axe could hold off the bayonet-armed Guard almost indefinitely.

But Graevus's small force wasn't about to start risking their lives for Prince Karhedros just yet. Both Graevus's and Kelvor's squads had been badly battered in the chamber mercantile – Kelvor had just three Marines left, Graevus six.

Librarian Tyrendian walked from the shadows inside the wall. He was the final member of Graevus's force, someone who in the old Chapter would have outranked Graevus. 'Do you know what I think, sergeant?'

'Enlighten us, Tyrendian.' Graevus, if he was being honest with himself, did not like Tyrendian. He looked too young and too unscarred. Tyrendian was as brave and dangerous as any Soul Drinker, but he just didn't look like the mangled old veteran he should have been. There was something not right about him, something too perfect.

'I think, sergeants, that Karhedros knows exactly what Sarpedon intends to do. He knows we will betray him. The eldar know things they shouldn't, it's what they do. The reason he tolerates us is because he fully intends to betray us first.'

'That is not comforting to know, Librarian,' said Graevus. 'What do you suggest we do about it?'

'Find out what he wants.' Tyrendian knelt down at the wall, careful to keep his armoured body in the shade so the Guardsmen advancing through the city far below wouldn't spot him as he looked down through one of the holes. 'Karhedros didn't come to this city by accident. The eldar don't conquer, they raid and destroy. This city is important to him for some reason.'

'Emperor knows there's enough about it the Guard never anticipated,' said Kelvor, who had taken the scope off his bolter and was using it like a telescope to peer down at the Fire Drake units skirmishing with scattered Gravenholders far below. 'There must have been cities here for thousands of years before Gravenhold was founded. Maybe there's something old under all of that. Pre-Imperial, even.'

'If there is, then Karhedros has had enough time to find it,' said Tyrendian. He was watching the Fire Drakes, too. Their line was holding well, the front advancing gradually as the commanders sent reserves through to help clear out the knots of Gravenholders who opposed them. 'I think it's something more complicated than just some old artefact. Look, Karhedros could have the Fire Drakes bogged down in these streets for days on end if he threw enough men at them, but he's practically giving them the administrative district. Either he needs them to be in the city or he doesn't care how far they get.'

'That might be the reason,' said Kelvor, pointing to where the administrative district broke into the highrises fanning out from around the south-eastern gate. The Fire Drakes had used their remaining armour to batter the highrises into glassless steel skeletons standing over avenues full of rubble and the enemy had fled them, but it wasn't an enemy Kelvor had noticed.

Graevus hunkered down beside Kelvor and took a pair of magnoculars offered by one of Kelvor's Marines.

The dark blue Rhinos of the Crimson Fists were grinding through the rubble, following in the wake of the Fire Drakes' advance. The Fists were going back into Gravenhold, this time slowly and deliberately, along the trail blazed by the Guardsmen.

'They're bringing the Fists in,' said Kelvor. 'They must still think there are Traitor Marines in the city.'

'Technically speaking,' said Tyrendian, 'they're right. But the Fists aren't following the Guard, they're coming to get us on their own.'

'Fine by me,' said Kelvor with relish. 'I owe them a leg.'

'How long was it since we and the Fists were brothers?' asked Graevus. Tyrendian and Kelvor looked back at him. 'There was a time when the two Chapters would have gone in together to kill something like Karhedros. Instead we're here killing each other when the real enemy sits back and waits for us to do whatever it is he needs for his plan to work.'

'It's a bad time to start doubting, brother,' replied Kelvor. 'Sarpedon broke with the Imperium because the Imperium is as bad as Chaos. It might not be easy but it's right.'

Graevus sighed. 'That's the point. Think on it. What was it that pulled us apart in the first place? Chaos? Some xenos? No. It was the Imperium itself, just ordinary human beings. The Crimson Fists are some of the bravest soldiers humanity has but we are forced to kill them because the Imperium needs them to be as blind as we once were. If Mankind could just see what we all saw then perhaps these wars would be over.'

Tyrendian raised an eyebrow. 'A Marine who longs for peace? I don't think you would enjoy it, sergeant.'

Graevus scowled back. 'I don't think there's much danger of that, Tyrendian,' he said. 'I just wish mankind could all fight on the same side without having to be deceived into doing it. Fight because it's right, not just to keep the Imperium alive.'

'Looks like they're all on the move,' said Kelvor, quickly counting the Rhinos streaming through the south-east gate. 'I'm sure what you say is right, Graevus, but if the Fists find us they're not likely to let us convince them. Sarpedon should be in vox range if he's close enough to the surface, I'll let him know the Fists have arrived.'

'Good. My squad will take the first watch, yours take the second. Tyrendian, get some halfsleep so you're fresh if we need you. Hold your fire unless we get spotted, Kelvor, I don't want us starting any wars for the prince just yet.'

THE GUARDSMAN SLUMPED to the ground, his throat neatly slit. He hadn't made a sound.

With a practised motion Selepus withdrew the knife, grabbed the body by the collar of its elaborately brocaded uniform and hauled it into the shadows of the abandoned slum building. The building, largely untouched by the brief firefights this area had seen, was a pile of dirt-cheap apartments piled on top of one another, a filthy sagging deathtrap typical of Gravenhold's slums.

In the warren of rooms that made up the ground floor, Scout Squad Eumenes waited out of sight. Scout-Sniper Raek kept watch, his keen eyes scouring the cityscape along the barrel of his rifle.

'Another Algorathi?' asked Eumenes.

Selepus nodded. 'Haven't had one of these put up a fight yet. Something's spooked them, though. Looks like they were just supposed to be watching the backs of the Seleucaians but now they're patrolling deeper and deeper. They're scared of something and they're sending patrols to flush it out.'

'Is it us?'

'No. They don't know we're here.'

'Tellos?'

'Could be.'

The scouts had been trying to pick up Tellos's trail since Karhedros had cut them loose. Eumenes was proud that his scouts were the only Soul Drinkers to have the run of the city instead of running around pretending to follow Karhedros's orders, but theirs was still a daunting task. If Tellos was in the city at all he could be anywhere in or beneath it. The only hope the scouts had was to assume Tellos wouldn't be content to stay in hiding. Tellos's Marines, if they were as crazy as the one Eumenes had recovered from the prison ship, would be eager to go a-hunting through the ranks of the Guardsmen and it was amongst the Guard that the scouts were most likely to find Tellos.

In the southern slums there were plenty of Guard, but little fighting against the Gravenholders, so Tellos could hunt undisturbed. So that was where the scouts had started looking.

Scout Alcides had turned over the still-warm body and was rifling through the pockets and pouches of its uniform. The Algorathi Janissaries wore ridiculous powder blue fatigues with silver brocade. This soldier, like the rest of them, had managed to keep his uniform clean for about thirty seconds and it was now a shade of muddy blue-grey with dirt ground in around the ankles and cuffs. The Algorathi Janissaries, the scouts had quickly ascertained, might have been fine for garrisoning some backwater world but were in over their heads in Gravenhold. It was why the Guard were using them for patrolling rather than fighting, but even so, booby-traps and occasional knots of Gravenholders had started to take their toll. Not to mention the scouts themselves. Alcides pulled a folded sheet of paper from one pouch. 'Looks like standing orders,' he said.

'Let's hear them,' said Eumenes.

'The enemy is underhand and will not hesitate to strike at you with ambushes and other deceit,' read Alcides. 'Every Janissary is to uphold the spirit of his regiment by remaining absolutely on guard, watching over his fellow soldiers, and most of all remaining dutiful and honour-bound even in the face of such ungentlemanly provocations. Platoons are to be rotated into aggressive patrols to hunt down the creatures responsible and every Guardsman on those patrols will consider their eradication his personal responsibility. The enemy are thought to be heavily armoured and skilled in close combat, they are therefore to be greeted with overwhelming fire whenever they are spotted! Dangerous they may be but they are also few in number, not to mention degenerate heathens who shall not prevail in the sight of the Emperor. Every man will do his duty by the Regiment and by his Emperor, signed, Colonel Vinmayer.'

'Sounds like Tellos,' said Scamander.

'Sounds like us,' added Raek, his aim not wavering as he spoke.

'Whoever it is we're going to find them before the Janissaries do,' said Eumenes. 'Next, we get an officer. Can you manage that, Selepus?'

'No problem with the kill. But getting close won't be as easy, even if these guys are amateurs.'

'Good. We need to move closer to the Algorathi lines, then. Nisryus, I want you up front with Selepus, make sure he knows if anything's going to stumble into us. Everyone else stay back and spread out. We want the Algorathi to do our hunting for us, then we sneak in and take the kill. If it turns out to be Tellos then we'll have to go in fast and hard, and I don't need to lose anyone beforehand. Keep quiet, low, and fast. Move out.'

Without another word the scouts moved out of the crumbling tenement, all but invisible in the tangled streets of southern Gravenhold, knowing that they were not the only army in there capable of putting the fear of the Emperor into the Guard.

SERGEANT LUKO AND Techmarine Varuk watched through the cracked window of the medicae station at the approaching walls of dust that signalled the advance of the Seleucaians.

'How many?' asked Luko.

'Hard to tell. If they're just Chimeras then there are a hell of a lot of them. But I think they'll have artillery mixed up in there, which would probably be worse. What they'll do to us when they get here is your department, sergeant.'

Luko smiled. He always seemed the Soul Drinker who most relished the prospect of a good scrap. 'Tons of shells followed up with tons of men. It's practically the Guard's motto.'

Luko walked back from the window. He and Varuk were on the first floor of the medicae station, in one of the surgical theatres where devotional scripts were carved into walls painted just the right shade of dark green to hide the blood. The station was covered with carved prayers, devotional graffiti, tiny makeshift shrines and piles of offerings to the Emperor and his many saints, both patients and the medicae staff they relied on tended to be religious types. The theatre contained a large polished metal operating slab, an autosurgeon with several folded metallic arms like the legs of a dead spider, and a couple of large tanks of anaesthetic gas. Gravenhold's elite were well cared for in airy, spacious hospitals dotted around the north of the city, but when the city had been normally populated this medicae station would have been heaving with the sick from the slums and those mangled by the ceaseless machinery of the industrial district. The devotional items were a last desperate offer to the Emperor to save them, but scores must surely have met their end in that theatre or in the cramped, bleak ward-house on the lower floor.

'All squads,' voxed Luko, 'They're coming. Prepare for an artillery barrage and then an infantry assault. They're not expecting us to be here but they'll throw everything at us once they realise we are so I don't want anyone acting like this is their last stand. We draw them in, hold them up, and get out of here.'

'This would be a bad way to die,' said Varuk, almost idly. Techmarines could be an odd lot, before the Chapter broke with the Imperium

Varuk, like most Techmarines, he had made the pilgrimage to Mars where he had been instructed in some of the secrets of the Machine God. Exposure to the mysteries of the Adeptus Mechanicus wasn't exactly conducive to normal behaviour. 'Just for appearances. Just so some xenos will trust us a little longer.'

'It's not just so Karhedros will think we're good little Marines,' said Luko, slightly annoyed. 'We don't want the Guard to take this place too fast, otherwise they'll get to Tellos before we do. And besides, if Karhedros doesn't trust us then none of us will get off this planet alive.'

'On Mars they teach you about logic,' said Varuk. 'I've been trying to think how any of this is logical, but none of it is.'

'That's where you and I differ,' said Luko. 'I just fight. You have to think about it.' He flicked back to the vox. 'Squad Dyon, have you got the front of the building covered?'

'It's locked down,' came Sergeant Dyon's reply.

'Good. If you can immobilise one of their tanks with plasma fire you could get them snarled up in gridlock. Squad Corvan?'

'Sergeant?'

'Get a couple of Assault Marines out into the alleyways. We could draw a lot of men into bolter range that way. And my lads, hold the basement. We need to keep our escape route clear and I wouldn't put it past those damn Guard to send some poor boys in through the storm drains. Any questions?'

There were none. 'Excellent. Check your guns and praise the Emperor, we're going to give them hell!'

'Got them,' said Varuk. 'At least three Chimeras with a lot of men on the ground. That engine note is a Basilisk, I'm sure of it, probably two or three.'

'Then we should be downstairs,' said Luko. Just then, the first artillery shot landed just short of the medicae station, kicking up a vicious plume of shattered pavement and earth, and the fight was on.

CHAPTER TEN

SARETHA THE BITCH-QUEEN, the Whore-Priestess of the Dark Prince of Chaos, did not believe in leading from the front.

'Onward! For lust and the end of their world!' she hissed, a spell woven around her words that sent them darting into the minds of her slave-warriors. Around her, leather-clad cultists surged forwards, muscling through the lower reaches of the storm drains towards the surface.

The filthy water in the conduit was chest-high but Saretha was held well above it by her cultists, who would rather die a hundred deaths than allow indignity to touch the skin of their mistress. They loved her, every one of them. And love, like every emotion, created ripples in the warp where her lord Slaanesh lived. The love her cultists had for her was so strong that it created a billowing tide of emotion in the warp, enough for Slaanesh himself to notice it and give His blessing to Saretha. It was why she had been gifted with sorcery, a subtle magic that wormed its way into the minds of men and women and convinced them that they had loved her all along.

The conduit sloped upwards and Saretha saw the drain covers ripped from the concrete by the strong hands of her most able assault-cultists, and the human tide swarmed out of them. She was carried along on that tide, the stench of the sewers mingling with the ever-present sweat and gun smoke on the surface, clashing with her perfumed oils. The voices of her cultists were raised in wordless praise of the Dark Prince and Saretha echoed them, shrieking with lust as she was carried out onto the surface and through the grand entrance gates of Gravenhold's arena.

In a very literal sense, the Imperial Guard of the Seleucaian Fourth Division never knew what hit them.

The arena's many entrances, broad archways around the outer edge of the coliseum, were barricaded against attacks but none of them had been built to withstand a tide of thousands of men and women who were desperate to die. Coils of razor wire were crushed beneath dozens of bodies, all writhing and squealing at the novelty of such pain. The sentries manned mounted heavy bolters to send chains of massive-calibre fire through the horde of cultists, but they just kept on coming, howling with joy as their bodies were blown wide open. The stitches in their lips were torn open as they were finally permitted to scream their pleasure to the sky.

Those gunners who saw Highmistress Saretha could not bear to shoot at her. They could never fire upon something of such overwhelming beauty, something too pure to ever harm. So they fired into the swarm of cultists even as the entranceways were choked with bodies that toppled like a landslide over their guard posts.

These were not just Gravenholders. These cultists mixed the blind fanaticism of the city's slave-soldiers with martial prowess and brute strength. Lasgun fire rattled back from the centre of the hordes as the crowd pressed against the barricades, streaking the old sandstone walls with trails of las-fire.

A squad of Guardsmen tried to engage the cultists, snapping off volleys of lasgun fire to keep the horde out of the arena. But Saretha's beloved did not fight by hiding and scurrying away when death was in the air. Death was the ultimate thrill, the final and most sacred experience granted them by Slaanesh, and the Guardsmen learned this the hard way as the cultist dead were carried forward by the momentum of the charge.

Fire raked back at the Guardsmen. That was nothing compared to the raw, shrieking, bleeding mass of bodies that poured towards them, clambering over one another, stacking the entrance tunnel almost to the ceiling. The Guardsmen fled, and the battle for the arena was on.

SARETHA RODE OVER the shattered remains of the Guard defences. Staked barricades lay in splinters, their spikes impaling a dozen of the ecstatic dead. The walls were painted with blood that shone as brightly as the gems on her cultists's bodysuits. The din of screams was an awful and magnificent music, and for a few moments Saretha just basked in it, the waves of cacophony washing over her. She could lose herself in it, drinking deep of the pleasure that Slaanesh taught was present in all experiences. But she was a fighter as well as an aesthete, there would be plenty of time to indulge her lusts after the battle, for now her duty was to take the arena.

'Weak-souls! Small-minds!' spat Saretha at a group of cultists who had paused to dismember a Guardsman. 'To indulge your basest when there are deaths to be lived through! The Prince spits on you!' Thoroughly chastened, the cultists dived back into the charge, eager to realise their love of their mistress through the sacred experience of battle.

A fire-team of Guardsmen was gathering in the rafters above her, ready to launch volleys of fire down on the cultist mob. Saretha spotted them and, picking a moment of the most extreme pleasure from her memory, hurled it out of her mind at the insolent unbelievers. With the spell still on her lips those memories surged into the Guardsmen's minds. Unprepared for a vision of such pure Chaos, they spasmed violently as their nervous systems overloaded. Bones cracked as their muscles contracted violently, organs ruptured, and they were granted one true glimpse of the Dark Prince's power before they died.

The bodies fell from above to be trampled under the feet of Saretha's palanquin bearers.

The cultists had broken through to the tunnel's exit, where they were emerging in a heaving mass into the arena's dizzying banks of seating. Beyond that was the arena floor where drab green tents were pitched side by side around gun emplacements and vehicle repair yards, muster grounds and medical stations. Guardsmen were running into formation as officers yelled, bringing heavy weapons to bear, forming firing lines to receive Saretha's horde.

So many tiny, closed minds, blind to the promises of Slaanesh. So many lives pleading to be ended, so they could get their one vision of the Dark Prince's power. Death was the final experience, the final moment of transcendental pleasure-pain that converted everyone into a believer in the end.

Highmistress Saretha smiled to herself. This was the part she looked forward to the most, when they made a stand and tried to resist her.

'THEY'VE STARTED,' SAID Sergeant Krydel. An instant later the sound rumbled down through the many layers of cells and chambers: the thud of heavy weapons, the faint white noise of men shouting and screaming, the fizz of las-fire.

Krydel's squad was in front, stalking carefully through the decaying network of cells beneath the arena. The cells had once held the worst of Gravenhold's small but persistent underclass, captured and sentenced to fight for their lives for the entertainment of the workers in the slums. There were also larger cells, stained black-brown with blood, where wild creatures had been held for the prisoners to fight. The place smelt of old sweat and death.

'Then we need to move faster,' said Sarpedon, who was following between Squads Salk and Praedon. Sarpedon would rather have brought some Assault units than the three Tactical squads, but Assault Marines were becoming a luxury amongst the Soul Drinkers after so many had been lost on Stratix Luminae.

Squad Krydel shoved their bulky armoured bodies through the narrow stairwell that led to the next layer up. 'Activity here,' voxed one Marine, Brother Callian.

'Guard?'

'Yes, sir.'

Sarpedon followed, just squeezing his many-legged form through the gap. He saw the floor on the next level up had been scuffed by Guard boots. They must have taken one look at the stairwell and decided it wasn't worth going any further down.

'Why didn't they seal it?' asked Krydel.

'This is recent,' said Brother Callian, kneeling to inspect the disturbance. 'Perhaps they were called up when Saretha attacked.'

'Good luck for us,' said Sarpedon. 'Don't waste it.'

This level had more room and higher ceilings, and larger rooms without bars over the doors led off from the wider corridors. This must have been where the free fighters, men who fought for pay or to earn off a debt, slept or prepared for their fights.

There was an explosion somewhere far above, a dull thud that shook runnels of dust from the packed earth walls. Something big had gone up.

'The Guard cleared out of here in a hurry,' said Sarpedon, 'which means there won't be sentries or booby-traps. Salk, take us up, double-quick.'

Salk was tough in close combat; he had proven that in a short career as a sergeant that had culminated on Stratix Luminae. He was the best choice to have up front in case the Marines blundered into any remaining Guardsmen down here.

The psychic shriek from above shuddered through the earth straight into Sarpedon's soul. It was the filthy, corrupted pleasure-shriek of an individual so debauched by Chaos that they welcomed it into their soul. It had to be Saretha, and she had to be in the thick of the fighting.

'It will be over soon,' said Sarpedon. 'By then it'll be too late. Let's move.'

SARETHA WOULD NOT be touched. Only the consecrated hands of her most trusted cultists, whose touch carried with it the blessings of Slaanesh himself, were permitted to make physical contact with her. The enemy, the weak-minded followers of the corpse-Emperor, were too crude and vile to even contemplate the honour of touching her.

'Die!' she hissed into the face of the closest Guardsman.

And he did, his heart stopping in shock at the vividness of the psychic images that knifed through his mind. The images flooded through his ruptured mind and a dozen more Guardsmen, counter-charging down the rows of stone seating, saw a fragment of what he had seen. They screamed, stumbled, vomited. A few were able to put up a fight as cultists streamed past Saretha and into the middle of them.

Saretha's cultists were streaming down the lower rows of seating, scrambling over the carved benches to get to grips with the rows of Guardsmen who were thinning out their ranks with volleys of las-fire. Return fire was evening the odds but the cultists had to get up close. More Guardsmen were mounting valiant counter-charges from further up the arena's sloped seating area, trying to get close to Saretha herself.

The insult was appalling. Saretha lashed out with her mind again, feeling the dirty little life-lights of the Guardsmen go out as she overloaded their senses.

She turned her attention back to the battle. The cultists were surging closer, clambering over their dead. They were badly thinned out but the dead had done their duty to their god, dying so those behind could swarm closer. The first ranks of cultists were over the lowermost rows of seating onto the dirt surface of the arena. A firing squad of Guardsmen sent a sheet of crimson las-fire into them, cutting them to shreds, but the gap closed in a second and before the Guard had time to take aim again the cultists were amongst them.

The effect was instant. Guard units fell back between the tents and temporary buildings, the weight of their las-fire faltering as they ran from the fanatics bearing down on them.

Cultists tore through billet tents, smashed through the windows of medicae and command huts, swarmed screaming into the Guard camp on the arena floor. An old, battered Chimera APC rolled towards the cultists and exploded, its fuel tank sabotaged by Guard mechanics in an attempt to slow the cultists down. It didn't work.

This was the beginning of the end. Saretha had seen it several times before. The Guardsmen above her had not, and they swore in horror as the fall of their base camp began. They were supposed to be safe, they were supposed to form a strongpoint in the Guard line. Now they were being eviscerated by a foe that even death could not hold back.

'Now take your reward!' called Saretha, her voice coursing into the minds of every cultist. 'See now your reward! Slaanesh sees your devotion and see how he repays you! Take their lives, drink of their blood, draw such pleasure from the slaughter!'

She wished she was young again, new to the extremes of pleasure the Dark Prince promised. She wanted to be down there, among her warriors, revelling in the blood and death. The memory of it filled her with a poignant ecstasy, she could never feel that thrill of discovery again, for she had experienced so much that simple joys like maiming and killing meant little to her. The memories would always be there, but now only the extremes of devotion to Slaanesh gave her the intense doses of pleasure she needed to survive.

But there was nothing to regret. She knew the heights the human soul could reach, and now she herself was more than human. What more could anyone ask?

'Take me down,' she commanded to her palanquin bearers, and they bore her down over the rows of seats towards the brutal close-quarters melee that was erupting in the Guard camp.

One more time into the heart of the slaughter, she told herself. For old time's sake.

'HEADS DOWN, LADS! Now!' Sergeant Luko charged down the stairway into the ward floor as the first shells slammed home. His squad and Squads Corvan and Dyon hit the floor of the medicae's main ward, the walls shuddering around them.

The first shell tore through the upper floors and ripped open the operating theatre. Techmarine Varuk was thrown down the stairwell in a shower of debris.

'…know we're here, we've got to–' Luko's vox-message was blotted out by the second shell that hit the outside of the building and rocked it to its foundations. Slabs of ceiling fell down.

'Don't you curl up and hide, lads!' shouted Luko between the explosions. 'The infantry'll be next!'

Varuk slid onto the floor beside Luko. 'Griffons and Basilisks,' he said as crunching explosions sounded from the surrounding slum buildings as they were blasted apart.

'How many?'

'Support unit. Not a saturation barrage.'

'Good. Then we'll get something to fight.'

With a tremendous crash, the side wall of the ward caved in, the foundations of the building pulverised by a Basilisk shot that tore deep into the ground.

The morning light flooded in, choked a dirty grey by billowing clouds of dust. Luko glanced up and spotted tanks through the swirling debris. And on an urban battlefield, tanks never advanced on their own.

'On your feet!' he barked. 'Guns up!'

The first Guard squad into the medicae building were met with a hail of bolter fire. They didn't stay to duke it out, they broke and fell back, diving behind chunks of fallen masonry as Luko's Tactical Marines sprayed fire at them. The tanks halted and ground behind cover and the accompanying Guard scattered into the shadows. Bad news could travel faster than a bullet and every one of them soon knew that they had stumbled across the Traitor Marines.

Luko knew how powerful a rumour it could be. In the days before excommunication, the Soul Drinkers had turned battles just by the rumour of their involvement. That was why Karhedros needed the Soul Drinkers. If the Imperial Guard thought they were up against Traitor Space Marines then they would falter in their advance, no matter how brave and determined they might be. Officers would wait for reinforcements. Commanders would divert resources. Space Marines were a terror weapon, and Marines who followed Chaos were, if anything, even more terrifying.

'That's enough! I'm not killing these boys for that damn alien's sake,' voxed Luko. 'Dyon, cover us. The rest, fall back to the cellars. We'll give them a firefight then get out of here.'

'I hear that,' said Varuk. Luko heard the unease in his voice. Sarpedon could be enthusiastic about fighting the Imperial Guard when he had to, but here in Gravenhold, at the behest of an alien, it didn't feel right to be killing Guardsmen who thought they were fighting Chaos.

Las-fire was streaking back now, the weight of bolter fire holding back the worst but not for long. Assault Squad Corvan was first into the cellars, Sergeant Corvan's bionic leg clacking against the tiled floor as he hurried down the narrow stairwell. Varuk followed them then Squad Luko. Dyon's fire kept the worst of the Guard firepower off the Soul Drinkers before Dyon followed the others down.

With luck, the Guard would be tied up at the medicae station long enough for Karhedros to be satisfied. In any case, Luko wasn't willing to let his Marines die in a fight over nothing.

The cellar was a grim place, once antiseptically clean but now dark and evil-smelling. The medical waste stored here had been left to decay as the refrigeration units had failed, along with the corpses in the facility's morgue. The back wall and half of the floor of the morgue had collapsed, revealing a passage into Gravenhold's undercity which Luko had earmarked as the Marine's escape route. The Soul Drinkers hurried through the morgue as a couple more Basilisk shots shook more bodies out of the mortuary shelves.

'Dyon here,' came Sergeant Dyon's vox from above. 'No sign of them following. Looks like we scared them off.'

'Make the most of it,' said Luko. 'Get down here and do not engage.'

The uninviting darkness of the undercity was better than the prospect of a firefight with half the Seleucaian 4th Division. Luko led the way downwards, the malodorous darkness enveloping him as the gunfire from above became distant and dim. Squad Corvan took the rear; if the Guardsmen followed them, the Soul Drinkers would need Assault Marines in the rear to hold them off.

'Varuk, get back to Corvan and help him collapse the entrance,' said Luko. 'No need to help them follow us.'

Luko heard Techmarine Varuk calling for krak grenades from Squad Corvan's Marines.

This part of the battle was all but done. Soon Luko would leave the war for Gravenhold behind, help find Tellos, do whatever he had to and get off this damn planet with its aliens and its sorcerers. It couldn't come soon enough.

The shockwave thudded down the tunnel as the entrance caved in. Ahead was a half-crushed tangle of black iron, some forgotten part of a civilisation that no longer had a name. Luko flicked on the power field around his lightning claws just in case, and walked on into the darkness.

'SAY AGAIN?' CONSUL Kelchenko frowned as he concentrated on the vox, the message obscured by static and the sound of the long-range artillery thundering away behind him. A messenger hurried up in the crimson uniform of the 4th Carvelnan Royal Artillery. Kelchenko waved him away as the message repeated.

'Marines, sir… Space Marines, honest to the Throne, I saw them with my own eyes…' The voice was that of an officer with the Seleucaians, bypassing the normal com-channels to talk with Kelchenko directly.

'Calm down, soldier,' said Kelchenko. 'How did you get on this frequency?'

'…my vox-man patched in, consul, I thought normal channels would take too long… need support here, I'm not taking on Marines in this hellhole, not without some of your boys' muscle…'

Marines. Kelchenko had heard them mentioned in a couple of the briefings but he had never really thought about what would happen if the Seleucaian push crashed into them. Kelchenko had heard the stories about what a single squad of Space Marines could do. If there were Marines to be fought in Gravenhold then Xarius's grand push was in trouble.

And then it hit him. He could take them out. The most feared creatures in Gravenhold, and Kelchenko could be the one to destroy them. As far as the Imperial Guard were concerned, Kelchenko was nothing more than a glorified civilian, an interloper from the Administratum playing at soldiers. Never mind that it was men like Kelchenko that kept the Guard supplied with ammunition and rations, never mind that formations like the Carvelnan Royal Artillery couldn't exist without Kelchenko and other consuls martial like him.

And now the battle would be turned by a single order from Kelchenko. Because Consul Kelchenko had brought one of his rarest and most spectacular weapons with him to Entymion IV.

'What are your co-ordinates?'

'Transmitting them now...' For a few moments the vox was lost in static but Kelchenko heard the piercing tones as the officer's co-ordinates were sent in a burst of information over the vox-net. '...looks like they're well dug in, we need this place given a damn good strike to blast them out...'

'Withdraw your men,' voxed Kelchenko. 'Get them all out of there. Now.'

'...understood... repeat, message understood... rather like to know what you're planning, consul...'

'Just fall back and get into cover. Kelchenko out.'

Kelchenko looked down the line of artillery pieces he had drawn up just inside Gravenhold's eastern wall – Griffons, Basilisks, even a couple of Hydra anti-aircraft pieces should the Gravenholders prove to have air power at their disposal. The artillery tanks were all blasting away, throwing shells into the city in front of the Guard advance to keep the Gravenholders on their toes. But the combined power of every artillery piece in the city couldn't match the weapon Kelchenko had in mind for the Marines.

Kelchenko switched to a heavily encrypted vox-channel.

'Standing by, sir,' came the reply, crisp and clear.

'Good. Stand by for co-ordinates.'

'Co-ordinates received.'

'Good. Go to code black.'

'Sir, we have had no confirmation from Lord Commander Xarius. Are you sure...'

'Quite sure, crewman. Code black and prepare for launch.'

There was a long pause. Then–

'Launch locked.'

'Good. Go to code red. Deathstrike away.'

The vox howled with a sudden vibration. 'Deathstrike away.'

Kelchenko looked up to see the glittering crescent described by the Deathstrike missile as it streaked over the city towards the heart of the battleline.

'That'll show the bastards,' said Kelchenko quietly. He wasn't sure himself if he meant the Traitor Marines, or the rest of the Guard.

'CODE BLACK ON the Deathstrike, commander,' said Brother Paclo, crouched down in the hull of the Razorback.

'Are you sure? Have they launched?'

'Yes, commander.'

'Damnation. Then they know where the Soul Drinkers are.'

Commander Reinez had been frozen out by Lord Commander Xarius. After the battle with the Soul Drinkers Xarius had taken to leaving the Crimson Fists out of all communications, as if he thought they were a burden on his command. But Reinez wasn't prepared to hunt the Soul Drinkers on a battlefield he knew nothing about, and so he had instructed the Techmarine that accompanied Chaplain Inhuaca to set up a link into the vox-net. The Crimson Fists were monitoring all the command channels used by the officers of the Imperial Guard in Gravenhold, including the encrypted channel that Paclo had just listened in on.

'Gunner, make way!'

Brother Arroyox, functioning as the Razorback's gunner, dropped down and let Reinez pull himself up into the open turret. The Crimson Fists' column was stationary, waiting in ground cleared by the Fire Drakes less than an hour before. The Fire Drakes were progressing rapidly, with the majority of the resistance further east where the Seleucaians were grinding through the slums. The Razorback, an APC with less transport capacity than a Rhino, but with twin turret-mounted heavy bolters, was towards the head of the column containing the remaining strength of the Crimson Fists.

Reinez looked up into the morning sky. It was a drab grey dawn and the trail of fire was clearly picked out against the milky sky, the train of a rocket, arcing up from the east of the city. He followed the trajectory and a practised eye told him the rocket was heading towards the centre of the slums, an area currently contested by the Seleucaians.

'Paclo, are there any reports of xenos resistance in the slums?'

'Not yet, sir. Human-equivalent only, a few sorcerers. Tough, but no xenos.'

'Good.' Reinez flicked to Inhuaca's vox-channel. 'Chaplain, we have an objective.'

'I see it too,' came Inhuaca's stern voice. 'You are certain it is the Soul Drinkers?'

'What else would they be firing at? If it's the xenos then we'll kill some aliens, to which I assume you have no objections. But if it's the Soul Drinkers then I want us to be there when they are blasted out of whatever hole they are hiding in.'

'As you wish, commander.'

'All squads,' voxed Reinez. 'The Guard are smoking the enemy out and we must be there to finish them off. For Dorn and for the Throne, bless your weapons and move out.'

With a roar of engines the Crimson Fists Second Company, humiliated once against the Soul Drinkers, stormed into Gravenhold determined not to be beaten a second time.

SQUAD SALK WAS first in.

'Now!' yelled Salk and his Marines vaulted the improvised barricade across the entrance of the practice ring.

The Guardsmen reacted too late. A squad of them, eight-strong, held the underground practice ring with its heap of tarpaulin-covered ammo crates and las-cells. The first thunderous bolter volley threw them to the ground – one was hit, blasted wetly against the far wall and the others dived into cover.

Most troops would have used their surprise attack to get into the practice ring, find cover of their own, keep firing on the Guardsmen and work their way into the room until all the Guardsmen were dead or had surrendered. Space Marines were not most troops. The philosopher-soldier Daenyathos, the legendary tactician of the old Chapter, had written in his *Catechisms Martial* that a Space Marine's strength was magnified when up close, face-to face. Salk didn't have to order his squad to charge across the ring, jumping supply crates, trusting in their armour and their faith in the Emperor to protect them from the frantic las-fire streaking back at them. The veteran Brother Karrick was first in, shattering a Guardsman's jaw with his bolter stock, kicking over a pile of crates onto a second man. Karrick was one of the few of Salk's Marines who had survived Stratix Luminae, he had nearly lost an arm there, but Apothecary Karendin had rebuilt it and Karrick now used it to pick up the Guardsman on the floor and throw him against the near wall.

Brother Treskaen barged one Guardsman to the ground, knocking him aside and blasting a chain of bolter shots through another.

'Back! Back!' yelled the Guard sergeant, a tough-looking shaven-headed man whose left arm had been replaced by a crude bionic.

'Let them go,' voxed Salk from behind his Marines. His chainsword was drawn but he knew he wouldn't have to use it. The Guardsmen fell back under more bolter fire, fleeing full-tilt back into the network of cells and workshops. 'Sarpedon? We've taken the practice ring but we'll only have a few moments.'

'Good,' replied Sarpedon over the vox. 'Can you rig it to blow?'

'Karrick can. Then we need to be gone, there's a lot of stuff here.'

'Make it happen. We'll keep back.'

Salk glanced at the ammo dump. The practice ring was a large circular room cut out of the stone with a floor of beaten earth, where the more well-regarded gladiators would hone their skills between spectacles. The Soul Drinkers' best guess had been right, this was the only place beneath the arena big enough to store the Guard's ammo dump. The Gravenholders had made a habit of lobbing mortars at the Guard's staging areas by the south-east gate and in the spaceport, so they had to keep their ammunition beneath the ground and the arena was the only place in the slums with an underground complex the Guards knew about. There were a couple of hundred crates under large green tarpaulins, they contained las-cells, rounds for missile launchers, heavy bolters and autocannons, tube-charges, grenades, replacement lasguns, and all the other bits and pieces needed to keep several thousand Guardsmen armed and fighting.

'Karrick! Rig this up.'

'Yes, sir.' Karrick was an older man than Salk, a Marine who had fought for so long on the front lines that he could turn his hand to any battlefield task. He seemed to have accepted the old Chapter's view that his leadership skills didn't match his ability to fight. Salk was only promoted to sergeant just before the Chapter War and he was glad to have an old warhorse like Karrick to lend his squad some experience. Perhaps that was why Karrick had never been given a squad of his own – because his experience was more valuable within a squad than leading it.

Karrick broke open a couple of crates, pulling out demolition charges and las-cells. 'Give me a couple of minutes. Then we will have to move, this place is all packed earth and the whole floor will collapse at least.'

'Fine. Treskaen! Get a couple of men on the exit. The rest get back to the barricade.'

Salk looked down at the dead Guardsmen on the floor. The Soul Drinkers had once fought on the same side as the Imperial Guard, taking their place in the immeasurably vast army of the Imperium. The irony was, the old Chapter would have had even less compunction about seeing a Guardsmen dead by their hand. They had been arrogant in the extreme – superior to the rest of humanity, the elite, the shepherds manoeuvring the human race towards the lofty goals of the Emperor. The Imperial Guard were just lesser men, normally useful, sometimes obstructive, always disposable.

Now the Soul Drinkers were forced into conflict with the Guard, and yet Salk saw them more and more as human beings than he ever had when he was trained and deployed by the old Chapter. The Soul Drinkers didn't fight to justify their opinions of superiority any more. They fought against the same enemies the Guard should be fighting: the Ruinous Power of Chaos. Instead, the Guard, like the old Soul Drinkers, were compelled to fight the Imperium's wars to the exclusion of everything else. Sometimes they coincided with the war against Chaos. More often they were just to quell rebellion, to terrorise citizens into abandoning their ideals of secession, independence and freedom. The men and women of the Imperial Guard died, not to fight the Dark Powers that were on the brink of devouring humanity, but to keep the ancient, corrupt edifice of the Imperium from collapsing under the weight of its own citizens.

And so the Soul Drinkers had to kill them, when they should have been fighting the same fight.

'It's done,' said Karrick. 'How long do we need?'

'Five minutes,' replied Salk.

'It's done.'

Salk flicked onto the all-squads channel. 'Soul Drinkers, we're gone.'

SARETHA DIDN'T NEED to touch them to feel the pain. Their suffering bled out of them, like a rain of razors against her skin. Her service to Slaanesh had left her so sensitive that emotions strong enough could radiate out and sear her like the heat of a star.

She had almost forgotten how good it could feel.

Her cultists crowded around her, forming a wedge of willing bodies trampling through the tents of the Guard encampment. They were almost at the centre of the arena camp, at the heart of the cultist thrust that had driven the Seleucaian Guardsmen out to the edge of the arena. Las-fire was sporadic and broken – the horror of the assault had thrown the Guardsmen into disarray. Saretha could hear their officers yelling, trying to drag the terrified Guardsmen into a firing line.

Their minds were so closed, thought Saretha. So blind. They really think they can survive.

Another Guardsman died nearby, trampled beneath the feet of her bearers. But they were running out. It was the curse of Slaanesh that victory meant there would be no more deaths to savour, and Saretha, on a deep and half-realised level, was addicted to the suffering of others.

'Forward!' she hissed, her long spiny tongue rattling fearsomely. 'Take me closer!'

She lashed out with her mind, sending a psychic knife slicing through the tents and heaps of equipment, the abandoned weapon emplacements and corpse-choked barricades. She felt the flickering life-lights of her own men go out but the shuddering, blind panic of the dying Guardsmen was in short supply now.

'Damnation,' she snapped to herself. 'We killed them all.'

When the arena was won in the name of Slaanesh, and until the alien came to claim it, she would have to satisfy herself with her own followers.

She saw the last knot of Guardsmen crouched among the far seating behind piles of supply creates, swapping las-fire with the cultists that surrounded them, unable to see even the beauty of their deaths.

And then the world exploded around her.

LUKO'S LIGHTNING CLAWS flashed as he ripped through the rusting iron bulkhead that blocked his way. His Marines had found their way from the medicae station down into the guts of some old industrial district, all staircases and corroded metal, some layers crushed almost flat by the weight of the city above. It was tight going, but if the Marines could get down here then so could the Guardsmen, with a few demo charges and some guts.

Luko ripped a V-shape into the iron then slashed again, slicing out a triangle from the bulkhead that slammed to the floor.

'We're going to have to cut our way through, lads,' he said, indicating the tangle of metal that lay beyond. 'I make it two kilometres north and seventy metres down to the palace.'

'We're clear behind,' voxed Sergeant Dyon.

'Good. Keep the plasma gun to the rear. Squad Corvan behind me, and get your chainswords out. It'll be tough going.'

Then the shockwave slammed into him, and the darkness erupted from everywhere at once.

* * *

Two EXPLOSIONS WITHIN seconds, like punctuation marks in the battle. The force shook down crumbling hovels in the slums and crystal chandeliers in the mansions to the north. The *Resolve* saw them both from orbit, sudden plumes of destruction amongst the warfare.

The explosion in the centre of the arena sent a shaft of fire a hundred metres into the air, showering the surrounding area with cultists and Guardsmen's bodies. The massive stonework of the arena was fatally fractured and half of it collapsed, the column of fire followed up by a roaring cloud of dust as the masonry crashed down.

The second explosion was a bolt of purest blackness that streaked into the heart of the slum district, blooming into a dark sphere that swallowed up the medicae station and three surrounding blocks of ruined tenements. The silent, hungry void consumed anything it rolled over, and where its furthest extent reached it left men, buildings, and tanks sliced neatly apart.

The vortex missile that had hit the medicae station was normally mounted on the Titans of the Adeptus Mechanicus Legions. It was the only example of vortex technology the Imperium could reliably replicate in any numbers and even then its use was rare. The vortex it created was a chained pocket of no-space, a miniature black hole, an anomaly of physics that sucked anything it touched into the annihilation of the warp. It even sucked in the morning daylight, casting premature dusk over Gravenhold's slums.

THE ARENA FLOOR sunk thirty metres, the cells and training rooms flattened. What remained of the Imperial Guard camp was dragged into the churning mess of pulverised earth and broken bodies, and now lay at the bottom of a huge ragged pit blasted by the detonation of the ammunition dump.

The cistern beneath the arena floor, once used to flood the arena for mock water battles, had been used by the Guard to store promethium tank fuel. It had gone up along with the ammunition and the result was a massive crater where the arena floor had once been, surrounded by a few tottering columns of seating like teeth in a broken jaw.

'There,' said Brother Karrick. The tunnel into which his Soul Drinkers had escaped had collapsed just behind them and now looked onto the bottom of the crater. Smashed tanks lay half-buried in the heaped rubble, tattered bodies were strewn everywhere. In places the dust was stained black with blood, so the slaughter above must have been tremendous.

'Where?' asked Sergeant Salk, who had been the last out of the arena cells and whose squad had narrowly avoided being buried.

'Movement,' said Karrick. 'See it? One of them's still alive.'

'Damn, I thought we'd got them all.' The plan was simple: wait until Saretha's cultists were in the arena and then blow the ammo dump, wiping out her personal army while attracting the least suspicion. It would buy the Soul Drinkers time; the longer Karhedros's army could be forced into a stalemate against the Guard, the longer the Soul Drinkers could hang on and make themselves useful, giving them more time to find Tellos before Karhedros inevitably betrayed them.

It was a shame about the Guard. But they would have died at Saretha's hands anyway and at least this way, death was the worst thing that had happened to them.

'Check it out,' said Sarpedon. 'Be quick.'

The Soul Drinkers spread out across the heaped wreckage, picking their way past upturned tanks and knots of corpses towards the tangle of supply crates and weapon emplacements. Salk saw the way the cultists' stitched mouths were burst open, and he had heard their ecstatic cries from below the arena. They were fanatics, extremists who would never give up. So were the Soul Drinkers, except the Soul Drinkers knew they were right.

'It was here,' said Karrick, stalking past an upturned weapon emplacement built of lashed-together sandbags it was stuck end-on in the heaped rubble, a shattered heavy bolter hanging from its mount.

'I don't see anything,' said Salk. 'Squad? Contacts?'

'Nothing here,' said Brother Golus, who was pushing mangled bodies aside with the muzzle of his bolter in case one of them was just playing dead.

'Clear here, too,' said Brother Skael, sweeping his bolter over the expanse of rubble. The rest of the squad sounded off. There was nothing but death there. Except Karrick wasn't a man who jumped at shadows.

The sound like a striking rattlesnake was the only warning. All Salk saw was a bolt of blackness streaking up from the ground in a shower of debris, spinning through the air as it threw itself at Brother Golus.

The psychic attack that followed it was a wave of foulness. Pure corruption. Salk felt tendrils of something writhing and obscene reaching through him and caressing his soul, a cacophonic choir shrieking in his ears. He saw the blessed debaucheries of the Whore-Priestess Saretha, the mountains of squirming bodies, the taste of refined blood in his mouth, the gentle touch of daemons.

He screamed as he ripped the images out of his mind. His vision swam back and he saw Saretha the Bitch-Queen, the muscles of her naked ebony-skinned body gleaming, her razored tongue punching repeatedly into Brother Golus's chest like a rapier's blade.

Salk dragged himself upward, his hand on the hilt of his chainblade. Saretha's hateful eyes glanced at him and the wave of filth roared through him again – the smell of burning flesh, the feel of cold entrails against his skin, the choir of voices raised in agony, thousands of sensations crammed into one bolt of unholiness.

He moved in slow motion, like a man swimming against the current, the force of Saretha's evil pushing him back. He had faced moral threats before and he knew the depths to which Chaos could sink. But to feel the experiences of the enemy flooding through him, to have memories of debauchery welling up from inside him as if they were his own. He didn't think he could cope with that. He fought on, but he could feel his soul slipping away. He could see the blackness that would remain when his mind was destroyed.

A burst of blue-white light knifed out of nowhere. Golus thudded to the ground as Saretha was hurled through the air, slamming against the burned-out hulk of a Leman Russ tank.

Sarpedon's nalwood force staff was still glowing with energy as his eight legs carried him over the rubble towards Saretha. The Chaos witch sprang to her feet and moved too fast for Salk to see, but Sarpedon was faster; no one, not even Apothecary Pallas, fully understood the extent of Sarpedon's mutations but they had left the Librarian lightning-fast and monstrously strong. With a blur of movement he flipped Saretha onto the ground, slashing out with one of his taloned forelegs. Saretha caught the leg, thinking for a moment that she had left Sarpedon vulnerable before Sarpedon stabbed a second leg through her stomach.

Saretha's blood was clear, like water. Sarpedon lifted her up and caught her by the throat with his free hand.

Salk pulled himself to his feet. He looked down at Brother Golus – the Marine was still alive but badly hurt. The rest of Salk's Marines were on the ground, too, their minds reeling from Saretha's assault. She had nearly taken the whole squad down. Nearly.

Saretha squirmed in Sarpedon's grip, colourless blood spurting from her wound.

'What does Karhedros want?' said Sarpedon evenly.

Saretha hissed violently, her tongue lashing out, but Sarpedon's long reach kept her out of range.

'What does the alien want? What did he promise you? I know you can speak.'

He has you already, came Saretha's voice, a thick syrupy sound broadcast directly into Salk's mind. She was a telepath, of course. She couldn't speak normally because she didn't have to. *He had you from the beginning. You. Your mad cripple. All a part of it.*

'A part of what?'

I can taste the death on you. There are many dead men in the warp who speak of you. Your deformed body, your revenge, as strong as the will of the gods, as strong as us...

Sarpedon was squeezing.

The sacrifice has already begun. Nothing will get off this planet alive. Nothing. Oh, all that death... it was why he chose you...

Something cracked in Saretha's skull. Sarpedon knew better than to try to force something like Saretha into cooperating through mere pain, Salk realised – his grip was tightening involuntarily as he resisted the way her words were worming their way into his soul. She wanted to break him. Even facing death, she wanted to take one more soul for Slaanesh.

He is clever. For an alien.

Another crack, louder this time. Saretha's body fell limp, only her eyes still moved, glinting up at Sarpedon, as if daring him to finish the job.

Salk drew his chainsword. 'Permission to kill it, commander?' he said.

Saretha's body spasmed. Her ebony skin flowed, turned liquid, and slipped through Sarpedon's fingers. She lost her shape, her eyes becoming two burning points in a formless boiling mass, twisting in on itself.

Sarpedon's force staff stabbed out but the mass parted before it. The thing that was Saretha formed up around a bone-white spear that had been her tongue.

When it charged, it came quicker than anyone could see. But Sarpedon didn't need to see. Saretha was a psychic beacon, emblazoned on the minds of everyone nearby. Sarpedon's reflexes were faster than thought.

The force staff shone brighter than a lightning bolt as it slashed down. Its described an arc that hung in the air behind it as the two halves of Highmistress Saretha flopped to the ground in a slithering mess of transparent entrails, the bone-hard spiny tongue split neatly lengthways.

Sarpedon wiped Saretha's clear blood from his eyes.

'Permission denied,' he said.

CHAPTER ELEVEN

'INTERFERENCE MY ARSE,' snapped Xarius, looking up from the reams of cogitator printouts that all but filled his command office, the chattering of an autostylus merging with the rumbling engines of the Baneblade. 'Get him on the vox. Better still, find the idiot and bring him here. I'll give him the old field punishment number one, that little rotmaggot, Munitorum or not.'

When Xarius got really angry, he became quiet and intense. Hasdrubal probably knew the warning signs by now, but that didn't make his job any easier.

'He's somewhere in the industrial area, the second front,' said Hasdrubal. 'Directing the long-range artillery. There's something wrong with the vox-net…'

'Nothing wrong with it when he called the codes in, was there? Worked perfectly well when he decided to start throwing vortex missiles at my battlefield. You don't deploy ordnance like that without the commander's say-so, even Consul bloody Kelchenko knows that. I'm doing him the undue courtesy of assuming he's not just showing off, which means that something spooked him and that's the kind of thing a commander needs to know about. Emperor's teeth, does he think this isn't difficult enough? Maybe he thinks we should be giving the enemy a sporting chance? Maybe it's fairer if we don't all work together. Do you think that might be it, Hasdrubal?'

Hasdrubal had the intelligence not to answer.

Xarius sat back. The office in the heart of the Baneblade was in danger of becoming completely flooded with paper. Transcripts of vox-casts were being forwarded to him by officers all over Gravenhold – he was grateful for the information, but the old, unwelcome feeling of managing a massive human tragedy was well bedded in now. That was what none of them understood: a single battle was an immense disaster. A capital ship lost in the warp, an outbreak of a plague in a hive city, a reactor breach on a forge-world, none of these compared to the toll in human lives that accompanied any major battle of the Imperial Guard. Even when they won, they lost.

Xarius shook his head. 'They've lost the arena, you know. The whole Seleucaian front is unsupported. The enemy could flank them in an instant, they could cut them to pieces. The Janissaries are running from their own damn shadows. And now Kelchenko is throwing my Deathstrikes at some bogeyman or other.'

'With respect, sir, Kelchenko must have had some reason to–'

'Oh, certainly. Aliens, wizards, Traitor Marines, the whole damn city is brimming with them.' Xarius held up a handful of printouts. 'They're seeing everything out there, Hasdrubal. It's a called a battle, it does that to people. The truth is that the much-vaunted aliens haven't shown up yet, which means they're underneath us, waiting for us to walk right over them. That's how they got the arena, mark my words. No one knows what's under this city. I wouldn't be surprised if the real enemy had the run of this place. They're laughing at us, Hasdrubal, and it's morons like Kelchenko that are doing their best to help them.'

Xarius eased his old body out of his chair and clambered out of the sunken office, up into the main hull compartment with its servitor-loaders and clanking engine housings. 'I'm going to get this thing moving so I can find Threlnan, sit him down and work out this mess. We've got enough of the city to redeploy, and if we don't those alien groxhuggers will lead us by the nose into whatever trap they sprung on Sathis at the Cynos Pass. Can we get to Threlnan's position?'

'Yes, sir. But I can direct the driver…'

'Humour me, Hasdrubal. I need to see this battle through my own eyes for a change. Besides, there's more legroom up front. Just get me a fix on Colonel Threlnan. I can make it an order if it would make you happier.'

Hasdrubal ducked into the vox-operator's tiny cubbyhole to scour the vox-net for Colonel Threlnan's location, which was probably somewhere between the first and second Seleucaian waves, if, of course, he hadn't died at the arena. Xarius pulled himself into the tank commander's seat, in the brutal blunt nose of the tank next to the driver, who looked uncertainly up at Xarius.

'Keep up with the infantry and make ready to change course,' said Xarius, noticing the badge of the Steel Hammers of the Seleucaian 2nd. The Seleucaians, Xarius reminded himself, had flocked to join his command to avenge the Steel Hammers who had died at Cynos Pass.

Xarius saw the infantry up ahead, advancing through the battle-ground that had chewed through the limits of the industrial sector and into the slums. Some of them would be driven on by revenge, the score to settle now including the men and women who had died at the arena. But most of them, Xarius knew, would only be caring about their survival. Xarius knew this because he had been a soldier, too, and all he had ever wanted to do out there was get back alive.

The Gravenholders were relinquishing their city bit by bit, knowing the Guard were too unwieldy to react to them and the aliens that Xarius could feel lurking beneath him. Xarius had to get together with Threlnan and work out a way to get the Seleucaians ready for the final attack, which would cut them to pieces if they were caught unawares. It was, of course, an impossible task.

But then, Lord Commander Xarius had become a lord commander precisely because he could do the impossible. It always cost thousands upon thousands of lives, but that was a price the Imperium had always been most willing to pay.

THE VORTEX PULSE had turned Luko's world into a nightmare of torn metal, a black and swirling madness with a razor-edged wind tearing through it. The world collapsed in on itself, sucked into a black maelstrom that bore down on him and his Marines like a dark sun dawning above them.

The warp-stain rippled at the edges of his mind. As he fell he heard daemons cackling, He saw their tiny, baleful eyes through the darkness. He felt the winds of the immaterium battering against him, and glimpsed the psychic thunderheads of emotion that towered in the warp.

He hit the ground and the warp let go of him to be replaced with a ringing concussion. The world was now full of pain, sparks and white noise.

There was dark reddish stone, smooth with age, beneath him. Walls of the same stone rose around him, soaring up into domes and minarets, decorated with bands of brass and sculptures of strange, stylised faces.

It was one of Gravenhold's previous incarnations, a dark temple-city, this part of which had survived intact beneath a sky of rusting metal. Luko pulled himself up to his knees and glanced behind him.

An immense sphere had been bitten out of the undercity, extending from the surface down to the temple-city. It was a perfect spherical space, cutting through towers and minarets, its sides striped with the various layers of Gravenhold it had sliced through. Where there had once been thousands of tons of metal and stone, now there was just a giant echoing space. A shaft of grimy grey light reached down from where the sphere met the surface.

The space was beginning to collapse under its own weight. Debris was tumbling down, the start of a landslide.

'Luko to all squads,' voxed Luko. 'Who's alive?'

Acknowledgement runes flashed in Luko's vision, projected by his armour onto his retina. All of his own squad. All but two of Squad Dyon, who had been in the rear. All but one of Squad Corvan. Varuk was alive, too.

'Brothers Muros and Pamaeon are gone,' voxed Dyon.

'Brother Thallion, too,' voxed Sergeant Corvan. 'Tell me that wasn't a vortex detonation.'

'Either it was a Deathstrike missile or a Titan,' replied Luko. 'I like to think we'd have noticed a Titan, though.'

'They must really hate us,' said Corvan.

'The feeling is becoming mutual.'

Techmarine Varuk stomped up, his armoured form and servo-arms silhouetted against the shaft of light from above. 'It's all going to collapse,' he said. 'One half is going to slide and then they'll have a path down. If the Guard are pursuing then they'll be on us in minutes.'

'Agreed,' said Luko, waving his scattered squad towards him. Their armour was battered and scorched, but they were unharmed. 'These damn streets are wide enough for a Leman Russ.'

'There's a canal here,' voxed Corvan. 'Less than a metre deep. Looks like it flows underground and out of the city. There's room for us but I'd like to see them get a tank down here.'

'Good. Then you're in the lead. Soul Drinkers, underground isn't safe any more. That alien owes us three deaths now but we'll have to survive this before we can make him pay. Look sharp and move out.'

CHUNKS OF MASONRY and debris rained down as Gravenhold shifted, filling the huge sudden void carved by the vortex missile. The Imperial Guard waited at the lip of the crater, waiting for the landslide to leave a negotiable path down to the undercity. It was their first glimpse of what waited for them beneath Gravenhold. What should have been solid rock was shot through with tunnels, chambers, whole subterranean cities, abandoned for thousands of years and now infested by the enemy they were here to fight.

Many felt they had been lied to by the Seleucaian officers, who had ordered them into a battle where only the city of Gravenhold was being fought over, not the endless layers of ruins that lay beneath it. The officers felt they had been let down by their intelligence, led into a city that, it turned out, no one really knew anything about at all. Gravenhold itself was bad enough, but at least they knew where it was and how it fitted together. But downwards – there could be anything. And there was nothing more dangerous than fighting a battle through the unknown.

But few Guardsmen had time to voice these concerns. Because just as the landslides picked up enough pace to make a first tentative descent viable, there was a roar of engines from the west. A column of vehicles crashed through the slums, running the gauntlet of the Gravenholders and making straight for the missile site.

Rhinos and Razorbacks crashed to a halt, scattering the Guardsmen assembling to begin the pursuit.

This quarry was reserved for the Crimson Fists.

'TAKE HIM,' SAID Scout-Sergeant Eumenes.

Scout-Sniper Raek didn't reply. Instead, his finger tightened on the trigger and an Algorathi officer's head snapped back, clear and brutal through the lenses of Eumenes's magnoculars.

The Algorathi Janissaries, the scouts had quickly realised, relied on their officers. The Janissaries were an aristocratic regiment at heart, drawn from a world where class and privilege were reflected in their ranks. The masses followed society's leaders, in battle as they did on Algorath itself. Eumenes had never been to the planet of course, never even heard of it before except as the homeworld of the men his scouts were hiding amongst, but he felt he knew the place all the same. There was little question that one class led and the rest followed, it was more Imperial than the Imperium itself.

It also bred men who had a fundamental battlefield weakness. Take out the officers, and their ability to fight was significantly diminished. They could still shoot straight but anything more complicated than sitting tight and keeping their heads down was beyond them.

The Algorathi Janissaries in Gravenhold were currently suffering a severe shortage of officers.

'Nisryus, are they onto us?'

The precog shook his head. 'They could have passed right by but they would have missed us. Which means they're not looking.'

'You're sure? This place is thick with patrols.'

'I'm sure. I can see their future footprints, they're fading out now their plan has changed but it's clear enough.'

'They're moving for a reason. Either they're redeploying or they're running.'

Eumenes pulled back from the window, leaving Raek to watch the squad of Guardsmen who had thrown themselves into cover. The building his scouts were hiding in had been hit by an artillery shell and lost its roof and back wall, but it was well-positioned to watch the wider avenue that cut through the piled-up hovels. The Janissaries had been scouting the avenue, presumably to prepare for a large troop movement. The scouts had slowed that process down but the patrols were still coming.

'Running from what?' asked Scamander, watching the back of the first-floor room.

'Tellos, maybe,' said Eumenes. 'Which is why we're here.'

'I've got something,' came a vox from Selepus on the floor below. 'The third tenement on the the south side. On the roof.'

Eumenes ducked to the window. He could see the building, but there was nothing there.

'I've got it,' said Raek, looking through the scope of his rifle. 'On the corner.'

Eumenes looked closer. There was just a tiny dark shape at the parapet. He looked at it through his magnoculars.

He saw the subtly bladed armour of an eldar. It was crouching down, taking aim with one of their strange crystalline rifles.

'Want me to take it?' said Raek.

'Wait. We don't want a fight with those things, not yet.'

'More,' voxed Selepus. 'Lots more.'

He was right. Dark shapes danced at the windows. With movements too fluid to be real they vaulted out into the open, sprinting and flipping over obstacles so quickly Eumenes couldn't pick any one of them out of the sudden rush of blurring shapes.

They seemed lightly-armoured, all but naked, the pallid eldar flesh white in the morning sun. Eumenes saw blades, whips, as they descended on the Guardsmen whose officer Raek had killed.

Blades sliced. Guardsmen came apart. There were barely a handful of las-blasts before the eldar were crouched amongst the bloodstained rubble the Guardsmen had been using as cover, and Eumenes saw them clearly for the first time; lithe, snake-muscled eldar, their movements so fluid it was hard to imagine they were real creatures. Their scanty purple-black armour contrasted with their pale skin and their too-large eyes shone.

One of them, wielding a whip, yelled an order in their xenos tongue and the eldar melted away, just sinking into the rubble and disappearing.

'Looks like we've found a whole new war,' said Raek quietly.

'Then why are they bothering the Janissaries? The Gravenholders are getting crushed between two fronts in the city. These slums aren't worth anything, that's why they sent their most useless Guardsmen here.'

'They're just in it for the hunt, then?' voxed Selepus. 'Easy prey.'

'No, it's not that.' Eumenes put down his magnoculars. The avenue was now effectively cut off. No Janissary officer would lead his men down there now, not with patrols being reduced to bloodstains on the rubble. That meant the Janissaries would have to avoid the thoroughfare entirely. They would have to head north.

'I think the eldar are herding them.'

LUKO JUST RAN.

Space Marines, the Emperor himself had decreed, knew no fear. That was why they existed, they fought on when other men would run and die, and it was due to this more than anything else that a Marine was the deadliest thing the Imperium could put on a battlefield. But they were not stupid, either. And Luko knew when to stand and fight, and when to run.

The Soul Drinkers could hear the voices of the Crimson Fists, flinging curses into the darkness. They could see the muzzle flashes as the Fists snapped off sighting shots at them, white-hot bolter rounds cutting streaks through the shadows.

'Dyon! How many?' voxed Luko, following Squad Corvan through another waist-deep watercourse.

'Can't tell,' came the reply from Sergeant Dyon, whose squad was last in the formation. 'Looks like Assault Squads, two at least. They're just the vanguard.'

Even a conservative estimate put the number of Crimson Fists pursuing them at most of the surviving Second Company. The Soul Drinkers hadn't been able to stand up to them in a straight fight at the chamber mercantile. Now they were just running like rats across a seemingly endless underground river delta. Dozens of rushing watercourses split off from the main river, and it was across the resulting delta that the Soul Drinkers were forging, hoping to find some way down deeper into the undercity. Luko silently cursed himself for the heretical thought that he was entertaining, he would do anything to see the eldar right now. Whatever side they were on, his Soul Drinkers could do with someone else for the Crimson Fists to fight.

'Got something,' voxed Corvan, whose Assault Squad took up the lead in case they stumbled into something that needed the attention of their chainswords. 'It's deeper but it's heading down.'

Luko's enhanced vision picked out white water up ahead. 'Take it,' he said.

A few strides later he was up to his chest in fast-running water, following Corvan's Assault Marines down into a channel that dove beneath the delta plain into a water-smooth stone tunnel.

Gunfire chattered behind him as Dyon's Marines swapped a few volleys of bolter fire with the Fists. The Crimson Fists Assault Marines were armed with bolt pistols so Corvan's Tactical Marines had the greater range with their bolters, and a few volleys bought them the time to get into the tunnel without losing ground to their pursuers.

White noise of rushing water filled the tunnel. Luko fought to keep his footing; a normal man would have been swept away.

'It widens up ahead,' voxed Corvan.

'Use the space,' said Luko. 'Throne knows what's down here.'

Squad Corvan spread out, as did Squad Luko behind them, several Marines were now wading downstream abreast with their guns held up out of the water. The blackness ahead of them swallowed everything as the tunnel forged downwards.

'Contact! Throne of Earth, what…'

Pistol fire echoed, bolter rounds smacking into the stone walls. Glass broke.

Luko barged forwards past the Assault Marines to see what Squad Corvan had blundered into, water hissing on his lightning claws as he activated the power field.

'Hold it!' Sergeant Corvan was yelling, his power sword a bright stab of light held above his head. 'Hold fire!'

Luko saw what they had found. And slowly he began to understand what Gravenhold was all about.

The rushing river emerged into a wide space, a swirling cauldron of shoulder-high water, too big to see the far walls. Hung in racks fixed into the ceiling were translucent cylinders, and in each cylinder was the smudgy, indistinct shape of a human form. Corvan's Marines had shattered one cylinder with gunfire and its contents lay draped over the rack, glistening with some thick, clear liquid: a pallid, hairless human form, naked and raw.

Corvan reached up and pulled down one arm of the body. There was a tattoo on the bicep.

'It's Guard,' he said. 'Seventeenth Iocarthian Regiment.'

'That doesn't make any sense,' said Luko. 'Iocarth is three systems away. What's he doing here?'

'She,' said Corvan.

'Varuk!' called Luko. The Techmarine forged his way through the water towards him. 'What the frag are these things?'

Varuk struggled through the Assault Marines and took a closer look. 'Not cryogenics,' he said. His servo-arm reached up and a tiny drill whirred at its tip, boring through the side of a cylinder. A threadlike probe spooled out into the liquid, then withdrew. 'Something chemical. Metabolic deadeners, preservatives, conductive saturates. This body was alive until we came along, just.'

'Is this Imperial tech?'

'It's not Adeptus Mechanicus. This is advanced, if it was them there would be prayers and incense everywhere. There might be private industries which could make this, but... well, they've got no business being on Gravenhold at the best of times. And this needs maintenance to keep all these bodies alive. But...'

'But what?'

Varuk examined the base of the closest intact cylinder, where bundles of wires fed into it. 'There should be a power source. This whole place should be lit up like a battleship's bridge. Otherwise they'll shut down.'

'And then what?'

'The bodies either disintegrate or they wake up.'

'Care to guess which?'

'Fifty-fifty.'

'I think we can do better than that,' said Corvan. He had lifted the hand of the corpse and was examining its fingers. The tips were split at the end. Corvan squeezed one finger and a long, thin metal claw, like that of a feline predator, extended. 'Not Guard issue,' he said.

'All this is Karhedros,' said Luko. 'The eldar are raiders. Slavers. He could have taken shipfuls of captives, brought them to Gravenhold, installed them down here. And now he's waking them up.' Luko walked forward a few paces, trying to get a feel to see how many bodies were stored there. He counted a dozen racks, each holding cylinders stacked three deep, stretching off into the darkness.

There were hundreds of bodies. Thousands. And this was just one location. Karhedros had the whole city to hide them under. 'Varuk, how long before they start coming round?'

'Looks like they've been powered down for a couple of days. Some of them are already twitching. I'd guess a matter of hours.'

'Then I think I know what this battle is about,' said Luko. 'Why the aliens are letting the Gravenholders lose the city for them. Why Karhedros wanted us here at all. This isn't about conquest, Soul Drinkers, that damn alien doesn't want to conquer anything. This is about sacrifice.'

TWENTY-THREE MINUTES later, the vox went down across Gravenhold.

The Imperial communications had been patchy at the best of times, cutting in and out at random, but aside from the inevitable confusion of combat, information still found its way through the chains of command up to Lord General Xarius's Baneblade. And suddenly, it was completely gone.

Vox-operators in Guard command squads frantically checked their equipment as their handsets went dead. The forward spotters of the Carvelnan Royal Artillery were cut off from their artillery units and the Imperium's big guns were suddenly silent.

The Crimson Fists, their communications already strung out since they were underground pursuing the Traitor Marines, were suddenly without the vox-net that co-ordinated the charge through the endless subterranean darkness. The attack foundered as the Fists crossed a raging underground river delta, the Assault Squads stranded unsupported on the very heels of the Soul Drinkers. Chaplain Inhuaca demanded they continue, Commander Reinez refused to lose any more of his Marines to an obvious trap. It was clear that both men were livid, but Reinez was haunted by the loss of his standard at the chamber mercantile and was damned if the Soul Drinkers would pick off the rest of the Crimson Fists piecemeal.

The *Resolve* was all but blinded. Communications to the surface were gone. The few spotter-ships out over Gravenhold wheeled in confusion, flitting between bearings and altitudes, trying to find pockets of clear air where they could send and receive. The clever ones gave up and returned to the *Resolve*, hoping to make a visual landing in the cruiser's fighter bays. The rest flew around until their fuel ran out and they had to ditch. Some made it into the abandoned agri-wastes outside the city, but most crashed into the war-torn streets themselves. Captain Caislenn-Har on the *Resolve* itself powered up all weapons and put all crew on full alert, more to reassure the crew that they were doing something positive than for any practical reason. All the ship could do was maintain visual contact with the city and try to pick out what was going on from aerial pict-steals. What had never been a particularly glorious campaign for the Imperial Navy became a maddening stalemate, with even intra-orbital communications cut off so the supply ships and escorts that surrounded the *Resolve* were equally deaf and dumb.

The Soul Drinkers were cut off from one another, too. But then, it was something they were getting used to.

'DIE ON YOUR knees or send me back to Dorn!' yelled Librarian Tyrendian, and the catacomb tunnel was lit bright acid white by the claws of lightning that leapt from his hand. A dozen creatures were blown apart, sallow grey flesh and thin blood plastered over the ancient tomb-niches and worn inscriptions that covered the walls.

Graevus glanced behind him at the Librarian, whose aegis collar burned with blue-white light that bled from Tyrendian's eyes.

'Charge!' shouted Graevus and his squad ran into the gap Tyrendian had blasted. Clawed hands were reaching from everywhere, as if the Soul Drinkers in the eastern wall were fighting not a mass of separate creatures but an amorphous, multi-limbed creature surging up the tunnel at them. Graveus lashed out with his power axe, the muscles of his mutated hand carving a great shining arc through them. Old bones scattered as the axe blade bit clean through the stone of the tomb-niches. The Assault Marines behind Graveus stabbed with their chainblades, turning leering faces and blade-tipped limbs into shrieking masses of shredded flesh.

Apothecary Karendin was there, bolt pistol blasting. One of the creatures clambered over Graveus's guard and dove down on Karendin; the Apothecary thrust his medicae gauntlet into its chest and impaled it with a dozen syringes and reductor probes. Combat hormones pumped through it and the thing shook itself to death in a mad welter of blood.

It was bad. Worse than they could have expected. The enemy was coming up from below and this time they weren't on the Soul Drinkers' side. They were making for the surface through the undercity and, in the east, that meant going through the wall and through Graevus, Kelvor, Tyrendian and Apothecary Karendin.

These weren't Gravenholders. These things weren't even human any more. The Gravenholders fought in a mad human flood, but they were still people. These were something utterly bestial. Graevus saw fingers that ended in razor-like blades, mouths that opened to reveal sharp metal tongues like swords, torsos that burst like seed pods crammed with shrapnel, suicide creatures who tried to grab hold of a Marine before their bodies were torn apart by blades and spikes ripping out from inside them.

The Soul Drinkers forged their way further down, Squad Kelvor in the rear as the sergeant fought to keep up on the makeshift prosthetic leg Karendin had fashioned from lengths of wood and bones. The Soul Drinkers' vantage point further up the wall was already swamped, and these monsters seemed to be coming from everywhere at once. The only way out was to get to the foot of the wall and take their chances in the streets of the administrative district.

Graevus literally waded in, stamping down and lashing out at the same time, feeling the weight of the enemy. It was like cutting through dense jungle, like swimming against the current. Brother Vargulis died by his side, faceplate sliced open.

Graevus wasn't going to die here. He was going to get off this dung-pile of a planet. He was a Soul Drinker. He had defied the Imperium and spat in the eye of Chaos. He could damn well do anything, and that included surviving.

The tide gave way to light. Graevus's axe gouged through the crumbling stone and he half-fell into the street, where administrative office blocks crowded up against the eastern wall. His squad fell out with him, Squad Kelvor followed, fighting to keep the creatures from flooding out after them.

'Back!' yelled Tyrendian, and Graeus led his Marines further down the alleyway before another of the Librarian's psychic lightning bolts shattered the ancient stone and a landslide of rubble buried the breach the Soul Drinkers had made.

For a moment there was relative quiet.

Karendin withdrew the probes and reductors of his medicae gauntlet. It was slick with gore. 'Alien tech,' he said darkly. 'Nothing Imperial could have made them.'

'Eldar?'

Karendin shrugged. 'Throne knows.'

Squad Kelvor moved forwards to the entrance of the alleyway. The east wall was behind the Fire Drakes' lines, the Soul Drinkers had tangled with the Fire Drakes at the chamber mercantile and had no intention of doing so again.

'Are we clear?' asked Graevus.

'No,' replied Kelvor. 'We are not.'

Graevus hurried up to the entrance of the alleyway. In front of him was a road wide enough for the mag-tractors that hauled loads in from the fields or the truckloads of workers leaving through the south-eastern gate. The road was filling up with Fire Drakes, running out of the alleyways or the lower floors of the towering administrative blocks. They were falling back, officers yelling orders that kept the men in a steady line. Chimeras rumbled backwards, multi-lasers or pintle-mounted storm bolters facing the way they had come.

Kelvor and Graevus crouched back, but there was no danger of their being seen. The Fire Drakes' line was retreating, several hundred men all training their weapons on the road.

Someone's nerve slipped and a las-shot spat out. A dozen more followed, then a hundred, lasguns on full auto kicking out a storm of crimson bolts and a stinking metallic cloud of burned air. The din of the fire was broken only by the whirring of the multi-lasers as they fired.

The enemy poured like a flood out of the lower windows of the buildings up ahead, burst like fountains out of manhole covers and storm drain gratings. They flowed over obstacles, poured out of alleyways, fell like waterfalls from the crumbling face of the inner wall. Thousands of them. Tens of thousands. Trying to kill them was like a cruel joke, like throwing pebbles into the sea.

The Fire Drakes broke and ran.

'Into the building!' shouted Graevus. 'Up! Go up!'

The Gravenholders were just a garrison force. They were the men and women who had been in the city when Karhedros had come, their minds addled and their bodies pressed into service. This was Karhedros's real army, a slave-army tens of thousands strong, the killing blow from an immense trap that comprised the whole city.

Squad Kelvor quickly broke the closest ground-floor windows and the Soul Drinkers vaulted in. The only safety from the flood was the high, defensible ground of the administrative blocks, the same ground the Gravenholders had struck from in the earliest days of the battle. Graevus followed them in and Karendin was on their heels.

Librarian Tyrendian was the last. With a glance back, he sent out a bolt of blue-white lightning that plunged into the advancing horde, slicing them open in a gigantic wound, reducing a dozen subhumans to charred skin and scalding steam. But the flood quickly filled the wound it left. Tyrendian hauled himself through the small window, and the administrative district of Gravenhold was swallowed up by the slave-army of Karhedros.

THE UNDERGROUND PALACE was just for decoration. It was the topmost tower, built for show, just to prove that whoever had built it could control the skyline of the city at a whim. The wings the Space Marines had used, the courtyard the warriors had ranked up in, even the stone garden with its frozen beauty, these were just the extra flourish that completed the palace of one of Entymion IV's long-forgotten pre-Imperial kings.

The real palace was further down. And while the topmost elements were dark and stern enough, the main body of the palace was utterly brutal. Massive bulbous columns reared up against cliff-like walls of chiselled onyx. Battlements of jade frowned over slit windows like scowling eyes. Ivory inlays surrounded immense verdigrised bronze doors, bright teeth framing a yawning mouth. Karhedros's personal army was stationed in the palace and around its imposing stony hinterland. The wyches lounged by the massive front steps, their languid half-naked bodies giving no hint of the sheer fury and combat skills they employed in battle. Several squadrons of Reaver jetbikes were lined up in the shadow of the front wall, their fanatical riders tinkering with the anti-grav motors or concocting new forms of combat drugs to heighten their senses and reflexes. The eldar warriors were uneasy, barracked in their camp outside the palace, the sentries cradling their splinter rifles wishing they could get a piece of the real battle raging far above them. They would get what they wanted soon enough. They would get far, far more than they imagined. A great many of Karhedros's eldar were on the surface herding the human prey into the path of the slave-army, but there was still a formidable force at the palace.

Inside, the palace seemed even more vast. The ceilings were so high and lost in shadow that to look up was like looking into the night sky. Whoever the king had been, he had wanted to intimidate anyone who came near him. His throne room, larger by far than the audience chamber where Karhedros had first received the Soul Drinkers, placed his throne on a platform backed by huge sweeping wings of dark green stone. The floor and walls constantly sweated beads of water so the air was damp, as if the whole place had risen from beneath the sea, an effect compounded by the dim greenish lights that glowed from luminescent patterns carved into everything.

A hundred of Karhedros's incubi, the heavily-armoured eldar elites who had cost him a great payment of souls and sacrifice to acquire, stood at permanent attention outside the throne room. The throne room itself was the province of the sorcerers and haemonculi. The sorcerers were a dark and hated breed, all of whom had joined Karhedros's pirate fleet to escape the persecution back on Commorragh. They were the ones who gazed into the warp beyond the eldar webway, and sought to draw power from it. The warp was the domain of She-Who-Thirsts so their sorcery was considered the foulest of heresy – but Karhedros needed them, as did all eldar on some strange philosophical level, and though they were tortured and abused they needed him just as much.

The haemonculi were a caste of torturers who set themselves aside from the rest of Commorragh, and pursued the arts of torment. They offered their services to anyone who needed experts in the intricacies of pain, and Karhedros – whose pirates had enslaved prisoners of every species – was an excellent employer. That the haemonculi could become a privileged class within eldar society spoke much of the way Commorragh was. There, suffering was a currency, almost literally a building block of society, to be traded, fought over and stolen. A society based around the concept of suffering was too lofty a concept for the minds of species like humanity to understand, and so the eldar knew that they were the ultimate expression of sentient life in the galaxy.

And Karhedros's kind, those who had embraced what they were instead of fleeing from it, were the ultimate expression of the eldar.

Karhedros himself sat on the throne, watching the sorcerers work.

Their ritual dance began.

'Who will see the end of days? Who will be there when all is come to nothing?' cried a voice from amongst the ranks of the sorcerers.

One of their number ran forward, a gangly, misshapen creature dressed in clanking jointed armour like an insect. 'We see it, we all, with every moment, for time is already ended, and nothing remains...' The eldar in the throne room danced in a complex pattern of intersecting circles, further embellished by the many strange forms of the sorcerers. Magic did strange things to the body and mind. The warp always took its price.

Another sorcerer stepped forward, this time stooped and wizened yet moving with the litheness and speed of a wych. 'Nothing but will, for the will of the sentient mind is all, for understanding is creation, for without it, there is nothing...'

Karhedros watched as the dance became quicker, the circles tighter, like packs of predators closing in on the same prey. The dance was at once a mockery and a refinement of the dance-cycles the eldar had used before the Fall, and were still used by those lesser eldar who hid in their craftworlds. It was itself not magic, but there could be no magic without it because it focused the vast consciousness of each eldar on the part they had to play.

'But what will? What will can make a universe? What intellect comprehends us? What gives us form?' The voice was shrill, the speaker a stunted wretch of a creature carried aloft by her fellow dancers. 'Which dreamer dreamed Commorragh?'

The voices of every sorcerer and haemonculus were raised in unison.

'She-Who-Thirsts!'

Then, the spell began.

Karhedros's kind were wary of sorcery. She-Who-Thirsts was jealous, and magic drew on the power of the warp that belonged to her. But away from Commorragh, Karhedros could take the risks his fellow eldar would never countenance. And besides, the earliest stages of the sacrifice on the surface would be enough to appease her for a few moments.

The circles of dancers were suddenly linked by a purple-blue tongue of fire, streaking through their bodies like a winding sea-snake. The pattern they formed became more and more complex until Karhedros could see the images reflected in its coils: the battlements of the palace around him, then the layers of Gravenhold's undercity streaking past, layers of history dripping with the memories of war and revolution.

The spell tapped into all the death and violence, drawing its power from a hundred generations of war.

The city was a focal point for misery, not a constant, relentless background but sudden bursts of violence that razed one city and built another on the ruins. The pulses of hate were more powerful than weak-minded humanity could ever understand. Reality was weakened around Gravenhold, shot through with cracks that bled pure emotion from the boiling psychic ocean of the warp. It was one of the reasons Karhedros had chosen the planet, it was closer to She-Who-Thirsts than most of realspace.

In fact, if Karhedros listened hard enough, he could hear her calling him.

The shape of Gravenhold was illuminated by the whirling tongues of fire now. The smouldering arena with the massive crater at its centre, the murderous heights of the mills to the west, the sprawl of the slums with their gorgeous taint of misery, the decaying decadence of the nobles' villas in the north.

One sorcerer died, the tongue of fire wrapping around it and shaking it to pieces. The others ignored it and carried on their agonising, spasming dance. Death was a good sign, it meant that She-Who-Thirsts was watching, and had reached out to snatch up the soul of the weakest.

Not long now.

The battle was outlined in fiery reds and purples. The Guardsmen by the east gate were being pushed back in a burning line of dying men. The tide was spreading through the hovels, swirling around the humans in the centre of the slums. They didn't know it yet, but they were preparing for their last stand. The south of the city was populated by the least competent of the Guardsmen, and they were up against a more horrible foe than even the slave-army, but like the rest of the humans, they had no idea what they were up against.

The haemonculi knew their cue. When the dying began, that was where they had to be.

Each haemonculus was a result of his own experimentation – here a sewn-up torso with entrails snaking in and out of artificial orifices, there an extra pair of arms tipped with syringes and scalpels. Hunched backs, multiple glinting eyes, skins turned inside-out and rippling with nerve endings, a hundred different abominations the haemonculi visited on themselves to prove their worth.

Karhedros could taste the pain even from his throne. The haemonculi ran amongst the sorcerers, cutting, killing. One slash of a scalpel-tipped tentacle left a wound so painful it lasted for an age, echoing around in the mind of the sorcerer. Blades were much favoured by the haemonculi and they wrought exquisite slaughter among the willing sorcerers. Knives and scalpels flashed like lightning, staining the blue fire a deep lustful blood red.

As they died, Karhedros saw their souls dragged out of their bodies. The writhing, yowling spiritual heart of an eldar was the purest receptacle of suffering, filled to the brim with the undiluted pain of a lifetime. The sorcerers were shunned and abused, living grim and painful lives even by the standards of Commorragh, and so they were particularly incandescent with agony as She-Who-Thirsts reached through the medium of the spell and ripped their souls away.

In their last moments before annihilation, Karhedros knew they would be grateful. They had become more than they ever could be in life. They were an offering to She-Who-Thirsts, to prove to her that Karhedros's devotion was true.

The haemonculi were almost done. The throne room was buzzing as reality wore even thinner. Karhedros felt the gaze of She-Who-Thirsts upon him and it filled him with awe. It was fitting that he should be the one to make this offering to her, for he was the greatest of Commorragh's children, who were the greatest of the eldar, who were the greatest of all the living things that populated reality.

The fire imploded and the eye-searing scarlet afterglow was swallowed in blackness. The fabric of reality bowed outwards and flowed back and everything rippled as if through a heat haze.

Reality reset itself, and the sorcerers were gone. The haemonculi now stood around a huge circular vortex composed of every colour, shot through with the purple-black of lust – the emotion of She-Who-Thirsts herself, the colour of her desire to consume.

'She-Who-Thirsts!' called Karhedros, standing up from his throne and throwing his hands in the air. 'Consume you shall! Devour! Gorge on their pain! For I give you this world, a world I shall rule in your name! A new Commorragh, perfect in its suffering! For this is my offering to She-Who-Thirsts, the dreamer who dreamed us all!'

A new Commorragh. Karhedros carried on living, which meant She-Who-Thirsts approved.

The first part of the spell was complete. The warp portal had opened. Now all that remained was for the sacrifice to be completed, and the suffering it created would flood into the portal. Soon it would swallow up the whole planet and the new Commorragh would be born.

And Karhedros, the pirate prince of the eldar, would become a king.

CHAPTER TWELVE

'THEY'RE ABSOLUTELY BLOODY everywhere,' said Threlnan.

'Thank you. I like it when tac reports are to the point,' said Xarius. The Lord General pulled himself up out of the tank commander's hatch. Colonel Threlnan helped him down the Baneblade's front armour and onto the ground. Xarius looked around at the shattered buildings and dust-choked air, the darkening sky and the hundreds of Seleucaians hurriedly setting up makeshift fortifications to stem off the tide. Threlnan's command post was in the heart of the slums, in one of the more built-up areas where the buildings were relatively solid, but the place would still fall if enough human waves hit it.

'We're pulling back from the front,' continued Threlnan. 'We drew the front elements back after we lost the arena and I had them just keep going. We're looking at a tight line through the heart of the slums, anchored by the river to the north. Anything solid the men find, they fortify it. We're in for the long term.'

'And the enemy?'

Threlnan took Xarius's arm and led him across the cratered ground towards the shadow of a local Enforcer watchstation, probably the most intact building left in the slums. 'They're mostly coming from the east but they're cropping up everywhere. Damn lot of them came up through the vortex crater to the west of us, although there wasn't much left of them after the Crimson Fists were finished. We're trying to hook up emergency comms to direct Kelchenko's artillery but... well, I think Kelchenko's having problems of his own, sir.'

'And yourselves? How are you going to keep you and your officers alive?'

Threlnan shrugged. 'Get some guts behind a few lasguns, throw down some sandbags, hope for the best. To be honest, lord general, I'm not confident that your coming here was the best move. I mean, the comms being down is killing us and I won't be able to call for extraction if it gets too hot down here.'

'Nonsense! Don't tell me you're not glad to see a Baneblade.'

'Well, of course, sir, but there's a limit to how many of them one tank can kill...'

'It's not for the enemy, Threlnan. It's for your boys. Give them a good old-fashioned symbol of the Emperor's wrath and they'll last twice as long. As for me, you said so yourself, the comms are down all over the city. I'm not much use giving orders from somewhere safe if there's no way anyone can hear me. I'll be doing more good as an extra gun than as a lord commander, don't you think?'

Xarius sat down on a fallen chunk of masonry. The Enforcer watchtower behind him had once been a stern symbol of Imperial authority, it was sheer brutal rockcrete with fire points on the corners and firing slits lower down, and was already populated by most of the heavy weapons units attached to Threlnan's command. The rest of the defensive position was taking shape: a line of ruined buildings was being built up with rubble and sandbags while the gap made by a wide crater-ruined street was being plugged as Hasdrubal drove the Baneblade into position. The fourth side of the position was bounded by a line of Chimeras with flak-board propped in the spaces between them, again manned by Seleucaian troops. A couple of Leman Russ main battle tanks and a single Hellhound flame tank stood in the middle, ready to blast shells or pour flame into whatever enemy managed to break through, And if they got that far, break through they definitely would.

It was a picture that Xarius knew was being repeated all across the Seleucaian line, Guardsmen finding the toughest-looking locations amongst the shattered buildings and racing to fortify them before the swarm reached them. Tiny islands of order in a sea of chaos, nuggets of the Emperor's light in the coming darkness. How many of them would survive?

'What do we know about the other regiments?' Threlnan asked.

'The others? Not much more than you, I'd imagine, which is to say barely anything. There are still shells coming over from Kelchenko so presumably he's got some artillery in reasonable shape. But the Janissaries were under attack from something before the comms went down and it looks like the Fire Drakes are getting the worst of it. Haven't heard from the *Resolve*, but presumably they're fine unless these grox-lovers have learned how to fly.'

'What are the evacuation plans?'

Xarius took off his officer's cap and undid the top button of his dress uniform jacket. His uniform wasn't meant for fighting. 'All evacuation scenarios assumed the main Guard concentrations to be in the space-port and outside the south-eastern gate. From within the city, and assuming the comms come back on at some point, I'd say we can get maybe twenty per cent of personnel out of this city before it falls. Most of them will be the rear echelons. From within a contested city... no, not many will get out. The *Resolve* had landers and shuttles but can you imagine them getting enough craft close enough, under fire, to lift us out of a contested location like this? The Battlefleet Solar couldn't do it.'

'So we sit tight and hope,' said Threlnan.

'And fight, colonel.'

'I shall find a priest. Have him read a few prayers.'

'Good idea, Threlnan. Best one I've heard today.' Xarius took out his sidearm, a handsome antique autopistol he kept holstered at his belt. 'Do you think you could rustle up a lasgun? Something with a bit of range. This fellow's just for show and he doesn't pack that much of a punch.'

'If I may speak freely, sir,' said Threlnan officiously, 'you really should be back at the spaceport. Hells, you should be up on the *Resolve* by now. There's no need for you to be down here. Leave it to the soldiers.'

'I am a soldier, Threlnan.' Xarius leaned forward, suddenly serious. 'And every soldier here knows what a tragedy this is. It's a shambles. Our mission here was to find what had taken over the city, kill every-thing that moved and avenge Sathis and his men. It was a simple bloody mission. One city! We even had the gakking Space Marines tag-ging along! There are a thousand battles like this being fought right now, Threlnan, literally a thousand all over the Imperium, most of them bigger and more complicated. And no one wants to hear about Traitor Marines or cheating aliens or any other excuses. We were given a simple job and we couldn't do it.

'Have you any idea what they'll do to me if I get out of this? They'll look at a whole agri-world and thousands of Guardsmen lost, and all for nothing. I'll be busted back down to spitoon boy. Hells, they'll probably send me to Mars and replace my innards so I can live another century or two, just to pay them off for what happened here. It will be as if nothing I've ever done had happened. I'll be less than nothing. Tell me how the Emperor treats failures, Threlnan. He commands us to put bullets in their heads or hang them at dawn. They won't kill me but they might as well do. I'm not scared of dying, Threlnan, and to tell the Emperor's honest truth I've been looking forward to it for a while now. But I am scared of being nothing. That's what they'll make me after this. Going down fighting alongside these boys here is a good way to go, considering all the other ways there are. That's the choice I'm making. I can make that an order if you want.'

One of the Seleucaians hurried over from the barricades. 'Sirs, the lookouts have spotted something. Looks like they're coming.'

'Make sure each squad has a runner for ammo and wounded,' said Threlnan. 'And... didn't Corporal Karthel teach at a seminary?'

'Karthel? Yes, sir.'

'Good. Get him and three men into the centre, men not manning the barricades can pray with him.'

'Yes, sir. Anything else?'

'Yes. Get the lord general a lasgun.'

Xarius looked up at the Seleucaian Guardsmen. 'Scope and Mars-pattern stock, please, if you have one.'

'You heard him,' said Threlnan. 'Get to it.' The colonel took out his own sidearm, a rugged laspistol with a hotshot pack sticking out of the cell slot. 'They'll need me at the barricades, lord general. Where will you be?'

'Oh, around,' said Xarius. 'Wherever you need an extra man.'

'Best of luck, lord general. By the Throne, for the Emperor.'

'For the Emperor, colonel.'

The sky over the city was darkening, as if Entymion IV's sun was turning its face away.

Xarius knew what it would be like. He had been there before: the stifling tension, the way it knotted your guts up, the way it added years to you before the battle took them away. The knowledge that so many of these men would die. The taste of fate, heavy like a thick blanket over everything. Xarius had been sure that he would die before, many years ago, more than once, when he had shared the battlefield with the men he led instead of directing anonymous unit markers around a holo-map.

It was strangely comforting, knowing he was going to die. The Emperor had had more than His fair share of battles out of Reinhardt Xarius, so Xarius didn't really mind it. He just hoped it wouldn't hurt, not that it was likely to take long, given that Xarius was an old man with brittle bones and a heart that probably wouldn't last a decent drinking session nowadays.

Someone handed him a lasgun. It had a scope but only a wire Rhyza-pattern stock. It was good enough, he supposed. Somehow Xarius had always known that it would end like this, no matter how high he rose or how many campaign medals he amassed, it would always end on a planet he hated, wondering if his gun would take one of them out before they got him. The Emperor had decided, before Reinhardt Xarius was even born, that Xarius would die like that. So it didn't matter. None of it mattered.

The only thing that really mattered was the horde that Xarius could just hear, screeching and hollering a few streets away. If they wanted the life of Lord Commander Reinhardt Xarius, they would have to earn it. However he did it, with las-bolt or rifle stock, with his hands or his teeth, or just by being there, Xarius would make them suffer.

THE FAR SOUTH of the city was turning into hell.

It had started when the sky went dark. Purple-black clouds boiled out of nowhere, blotting out the sun of Entymion IV and casting a ghastly twilight over everything. With the comms down it was as if the planet was suddenly cut off and plunging downwards, the air turning chill, the shadows deepening, the ragged mess of the slums becoming a sharp and menacing labyrinth of ambushes.

Then the news arrived. How it got to the Algorathi Janissaries, huddled in the heart of the slums fleeing from a series of sudden and brutal assaults, was unknown. But suddenly, like bad news always was, it was on the lips of every Janissary. Crouched in cover, some still sticky with the blood of their fellow Guardsmen, they told one another of the massive enemy forces that were bubbling up from the ground elsewhere in the city. Thousands of them. Hundreds of thousands. A hidden army, come to encircle and slaughter every Imperial soul in Gravenhold.

The Janissaries were still being nibbled away. Men were dying by the minute. The last man on every patrol seemed to disappear, snatched away by something swift and unseen. Sniper shots snapped into any Guardsman who showed his head; the shooters fired razor-sharp shards of diamond-hard crystal, and those they did not kill outright were paralysed by the pain. Colonel Vinmayer tried to keep a tally of the dead but they were dying so quickly, and in so many ways, that it was all he could do to keep his men together. Their position was hopeless – a block of half-ruined tenements that had been deathtraps well before anyone had started firing artillery at them – but it was all they had. It was an island of hope in a city that wanted them dead. The Algorathi Janissaries learned urban combat very, very quickly, trying to maintain a perimeter while the men on the outside were being swallowed up by the lengthening shadows.

The comms flickered back on. It was as if the city was waiting for them to take their place in the trap before it let them talk to one another. The communications between the Janissaries and the other forces in the city, with Lord Commander Xarius or the *Resolve*, were still denied, but Vinmayer could at least talk to his men directly.

It was no fun if the men could not share the fear. It was no tragedy if the sons of Algorath could not think they had hope, before they found out that they still had to die alone.

Vinmayer, however, was not a man bred to give up. He had carried the banner of Algorath into its first true combat assignment in several centuries and those unlucky generations before him had prepared their sons for the time when the Algorathi Janissaries would meet their fate in the fire of battle.

He switched to the all-squad vox-channel.

'The company,' he began, 'will form a square. The officers in each corner will be responsible for holding the line. Squads eleven through nineteen will form a mobile reserve, bayonets fixed. The enemy are all alien liars and will falter at the resilience of our formation. I shall take my place in the line where the fighting is fiercest, for so do the sons of Algorath fight. These are your orders. Do not stray from them while but one of us remains. For the Emperor, Colonel Vinmayer out.'

The enemy must have had access to the Janissaries' vox-net, because they used Vinmayer's speech as their cue.

'THEY'RE ON THE move! There!' Eumenes ran down the rubble-filled street, pointing up past the chewed-up skyline. Clouds of thrown-up dust and the crash of collapsing rubble were marking a course parallel to the scouts as something massive and powerful barged its way through the slums.

'Dorn's hand, what is it?' asked Scout Laeon, who was just behind Eumenes.

'The end for the Janissaries, that's what,' replied Selepus.

'They're heading north,' said Eumenes. 'Fast. Keep moving.'

The scouts ran full-tilt through the ruins but they could barely keep up. Even Selepus, who could move through this difficult ground as easily as if he was walking, could only just keep the enemy in sight. The remnants of Gravenhold's shattered lives streaked past, however Karhedros had taken over the city's population it had happened overnight, for here and there collapsed walls revealed a snapshot of lives frozen in time. Tables were laid out for meagre meals. Beds were still made. The families that had lived crammed into these hovels had been snatched away in the middle of eating or sleeping or praying, to become part of Karhedros's army.

'There!' called Selepus. The scouts had come to an area all but shelled flat, affording them a glimpse of the enemy force charging northwards.

Eumenes could see just the suggestion of dark, armoured shapes, and then they were gone.

'Small force,' said Scout-Sniper Raek from behind Eumenes. 'But tough.'

'Eldar?'

'Maybe.'

A hundred metres ahead the terrain broke up, alleyways becoming roads, hovels becoming blocks of tenements. Eumenes reached the edge of one road and skidded to a halt.

'Stop! It's the Guard.' The powder-blue uniforms of the Janissaries, now filthy with dust and mud, were poor camouflage against the dismal dark grey tenement blocks they were using as cover. Eumenes could make out the city block they had chosen, not good to defend, but better than anything within spitting distance.

They had set up a weapons point on one corner of the block, with a couple of heavy bolters and what looked like a lascannon on the first floor of a half-collapsed block. Eumenes spotted men crouching behind makeshift cover in a long, straight line down both sides of the block away from the corner. They had bayonets fixed.

'Selepus,' said Eumenes, 'take Laeon and see if you can get across the road to spot for Raek, I want us across on the east side of–'

A force like a battering ram smashed out of the ruins twenty metres up the road. At first Eumenes thought it must be a tank, barrelling at full speed through the crumbling building and ripping out into the street in a cloud of dust.

The Janissaries had known it was coming but they barely had a handful of las-shots before the enemy was among them, smashing into the line. Blue-uniformed bodies were thrown into the air. Something exploded. Screams were drowned out by gunfire and the sound of armour on stone.

'Closer!' shouted Eumenes. Fear rippled through the Janissaries and they were all shooting at anything that moved, las-bolts spattering against the wood and brick around the scouts. Selepus led the way, hugging the crumbling walls, keeping the scouts in shadow as chaos erupted all around them. Sniper-shots spat from somewhere far off and Janissaries died, shredded by crystal shards.

'Down!' shouted Nisryus suddenly. The scouts had learned to listen to the precog. As one, the scouts hit the ground a moment before something cut the air knife-sharp above them, shrieking on grav-engines over the street and into the Janissaries. Eumenes glanced up, eldar jetbikes, almost too fast to see, streaking in a wide loop back through the Algorathi line. Long curved blades jutted from every surface of each jetbike's long front fuselage, slicing heads from bodies, arms from shoulders, the bare skin of the riders spattered with blood.

Eumenes had seen pict-steals taken during battles with the eldar. They were lithe, lightly-armoured warriors, each specialised in a particular form of warfare. They were deceitful heathens, and the Soul Drinkers had fought them before and after the excommunication, but these were different. The eldar were manipulative and inscrutable. These aliens were just cruel. They revelled in blood. They fought for torment's own sake. Eumenes saw one biker spear a Janissary on the nose of his jetbike then gun the engine and sweep upwards, letting the air resistance drag the man further down the hull, splitting him open. Another had long chains trailing behind his bike that snagged uniforms and skin, yanking two men out of the line then swooping low so they were broken to pieces along the ground.

'Oh, sweet hands of Dorn,' swore Laeon. 'It's them.'

Eumenes scrambled to the edge of cover, following Laeon's gaze.

The force that had first smashed into the Janissaries was playing merry hell. The Janissaries had thrown men forward from the centre of the block but they were just more meat for the slaughter. Eumenes saw purple armour slicked black with blood, chainblades rising and falling, helmetless heads with mad staring eyes.

He saw something more. He saw massive muscles writhing under deathly pale skin. Arms punching into fleeing Janissaries, lifting them up and hurling them through the air off the ends of long whirring chainblades. Blades jammed into the stump of severed wrists.

The Soul Drinkers. The renegades lost at Stratix Luminae, turned mad and brought into the service of a mad alien.

And Tellos.

THE SLAVE-ARMY hit the river first. The River Graven was the anchor point for the northern end of the Seleucaian line, and the massive well-built warehouses by the docks made for an excellent defensive position. The Seleucaian units there who fortified them considered themselves to be luckiest in the city, they were protected on one side by the deep river, while the huge dock buildings could be turned into a formidable fortress. They were the keystone for the whole Seleucaian regiment, forming a fastness to which other units could fall back, a solid foundation for the enemy wave to break against.

They thought they would be the last to fall. Which, presumably, was why the enemy hit them first.

The first truly great battle of the campaign's closing stages erupted on the south bank of the River Graven as ten thousand slave warriors poured into the eastern side of the position. The Seleucaians had covered the roads approaching the docks with scores of firing positions and volleys of las-fire and heavy weapons cut the first ranks of the enemy to shreds. Thousands died in a few minutes, the already dark sky becoming as black as night as las-smoke and debris blotted out what light remained.

The slave-army piled its dead up into bloody ramps of corpses and scrambled up them over the Seleucaian barricades. The Guardsmen saw clearly for the first time what they were fighting, humans who were not human, their bodies deformed into living weapons. Some exploded into shards of bone spikes, others turned berserk and ripped Guardsmen apart with talons or spiny whip-like tongues. The Guarsmen fell back from the first positions in disarray and the slaves swarmed into the shadow of the warehouses, charging heedlessly through crossfires and minefields.

They couldn't outflank or outthink, and normally they would be easy prey for a competent and well-drilled regiment like the Seleucaians. But the slave-army had two advantages: it had the numbers, and it had the element of sheer horror. The Seleucaians had already weathered the unnaturalness of killing soldiers who had once been citizens of the city they were supposed to liberate, but this was something different. These were the slaves taken by xenos raiders over many decades, the sons and daughters of the Imperium who had been twisted into something so inhuman it was blasphemy. The Guardsmen saw their own faces in the creatures they killed. In the monsters that tore their comrades apart they saw friends and loved ones they thought they had forgotten. Karhedros didn't need any alien sorcery to shatter the resolve of the Guardsmen. The Guardsmen did it themselves.

The Imperial Guard communications flickered back on just in time for officers up and down the Seleucaian line to hear the river position falling. The warehouses fell, the disciplined Guard fire breaking down in the face of the assault. Thousands of enemy bodies choked the eastern barricades but they just made it worse, the foul chemical stench of the bodies as they broke down deepening the nightmare.

The Seleucaians were up against the river itself. There, some order was whipped back into the men and they made a last stand, taking cover around the huge mechanical docking cranes, firing from behind giant exposed cogs or banks of container crates. But the ground there was too open, and the Guard fire couldn't thin out the charging ranks quickly enough.

Men turned their lasguns on themselves before the enemy clawed their way over the machinery and into the final Guard positions. The few remaining heavy weapons were surrounded by oozing piles of bodies before they were overrun and their crews torn apart. The final slaughter was the most terrible; so many bodies fell into the river that even the observers on the *Resolve* could make out the Graven running red.

The officers of the regiment heard it all. They heard the lieutenant in charge of the position pull a pin on a frag grenade and blow himself up as the final crane mountings were overrun. They heard the last survivors up on the crane assemblies themselves, sniping at the slave-warriors climbing up the structure towards them. They heard the final prayers of men who might have hours left before their las-cells ran out, but who would definitely die no matter what.

The keystone of the Seleucaian position had fallen. Every officer, and most of the men, knew what the situation was now. There were only two ways out of Gravenhold – die at the hands of the aliens' slave-warriors, or kill every single one of them. The Seleucaians checked their las-cells for the hundredth time, and got ready to do the latter.

'Sacrifice,' said Sarpedon.

'Sacrifice,' replied Luko. 'It's the only thing that makes sense. And it's happening now, all over the damn city. We're only seeing a fraction of what must be happening but there are thousands of them. They're hitting the whole Guard at once, the Seleucaians, the Fire Drakes.'

Sarpedon had met up with Luko beneath the city as soon as the comms had come back, hurrying from the undercity just beneath the ruined arena to the underground river, roughly parallel with the Graven, to which Luko had fled from the Crimson Fists. The river rushed along beside them, winding through chasms of spectacular rock formations and plunging down sudden waterfalls. This part of the undercity was mostly natural, but there had been some kind of primitive troglodytic civilisation here, probably living off the strange pale blind fish that writhed through the waters. Crude stone burrows were scraped into the earth, and the abstract but somehow still disturbing runes carved into the thick bases of stalagmites suggested a dark and benighted people. Gravenhold had not always been a place of power and riches. Bit by bit the undercity was suggesting a grim, complex history of conquest and downfall.

'The eldar don't conquer,' said Sarpedon. 'They don't hold ground. At most they take slaves and move on. You're right, Luko, he needed this city for something. He needed this battle. He knew we'd turn on him all along. He was counting on it. I can't think of a force in this city more capable of raising hell than us and hell is exactly what he needs.'

'You didn't see them wake up,' said Luko. 'He must have kept them there since he took the city over. Maybe even longer, if he got under the city before the Gravenholders ever knew about him. Just like a damn alien. You know, I'm starting to get a feel for what you've led us into.'

'Really, Luko? What is that?' Sarpedon folded his arms and sat back on his eight haunches.

'Karhedros lured Tellos here because, like you said, he needed hell-raisers, people who could be guaranteed to fight and kill no matter what. He probably would have been content just with Tellos and his slaves to mix it up with the Guard. He must have thought it was his lucky day when we turned up. Hells, we've carved our way through more than our fair share of Guard. We've soaked this city in enough blood. As far as Karhedros is concerned we're his best men. We're on his side, Sarpedon. We're doing just what he wants us to do.' Luko spat. 'Used by a damn xenos.'

'We're here for Tellos,' said Sarpedon. 'Not Karhedros. We will find our brother and do what we have to do. Then, if it is necessary, we will punish the alien for what he did to him.'

'How, Sarpedon? How? I've followed you from one side of the galaxy to the other, I've fought the wars I hate because I knew it was the right thing to do. But I don't think we can win this one.'

'I have given you free rein to speak your mind to me, Luko. That is not a privilege I can extend forever.'

'We won't forgive you, Sarpedon, if you throw us away here for nothing. Remember what happened the last time you forced this Chapter to fight itself.'

There was a pause. For the briefest moment, an onlooker might have thought the two could end up in a shouting match, even a brawl. In the old Chapter, they probably would have. But the Soul Drinkers under Sarpedon and Luko were out of earshot, keeping watch over the banks of the river and the dense forests of stalagmites. The fighting on the surface had begun to spill into the undercity and the Soul Drinkers had to be vigilant for both slave-warriors and Guardsmen even down here.

'I know what you are saying, Luko,' said Sarpedon. 'I came here to find Tellos. Our battle-brothers have died and we haven't found him. But we have found something else, Luko. This Chapter is sworn to do the Emperor's will. Tell me His will is being done in this city. Tell me that.'

Luko had no answer.

'You said Karhedros created this battle as a sacrifice, and we're a part of it. As long as we're a part of it that means we can do something about it.'

'This is not our fight, Sarpedon.'

'That's the point. This Chapter does not fight just to survive. We have done too much of that already. These eldar are devoted to their god, She-Who-Thirsts. They worship and fear it, I could sense it. I just had to get close to Karhedros to know. When this sacrifice is completed, the city is dead. This planet is dead. And Karhedros will be much, much more than just another xenos pirate. It became our fight the moment he promised this world to She-Who-Thirsts.'

'When did you decide this, Sarpedon?'

'What does it matter? What else are you going to do but fight?'

'Commander,' came a voice over the vox, faint through the static, filtering all the way down from the surface. 'Eumenes here.'

Sarpedon turned away from Luko, straining to hear the scout's voice. 'Eumenes?'

'We've found him, commander. Tellos. He just chewed his way through the Algorathi Guardsmen.'

'Where is he now?'

'Slaughterhouse district, near the river.'

'Don't go near him. You can't take him on your own, trust me on that. Can you get back to the government district?'

'Maybe.'

'Good. Do it. I'll gather all the Soul Drinkers who can make it under the chamber mercantile.'

'Understood. Eumenes out.'

Sarpedon turned back to Luko. 'You've got what you wanted, Luko. It's coming to an end.'

'Karhedros has an army to spare in that palace. I'll wager we only saw a fraction of it. Do you really think you can take him on and still have anything left over for Tellos?'

'No, I don't. But the Emperor doesn't listen to excuses.'

CHAPTER THIRTEEN

CAPTAIN THORELLIS VEL Caislenn-Har of the Imperial cruiser *Resolve* walked onto the bridge of his ship, wreathed in a cloud of chemical smoke.

'Navigation,' he said, his voice grating through the heavy-duty rebreather collar that circled his lower face. 'Please, please for the love of the Emperor and all his saints tell me we know where the rest of the fleet is.'

The navigation helm was wrought into the form of a massive cathedral organ, its processing stacks shaped like the pipes and the control console of a long keyboard with hundreds of keys. Data-servitors shaped like gilded cherubs clung to the sides of the organ, whispering strings of co-ordinates to one another. The navigation officer, sitting in the position of an organist, turned sharply at Caislenn-Har's approach, the officer was pure naval academy product, starched collar and all.

'Direct comms are still out,' she snapped, 'but the sensorium has confirmed the positions of escort squadron *Vestal*, primary fueller *Sacred Truth* and seventy per cent of the system support fleet.'

'And?'

'They are somewhat out of position.'

'Good enough.' Captain Caislenn-Har waddled over to his command chair, a massive throne of brass and jade that reared from the scalloped floor of the bridge like the head of a sea monster.

The bridge of the *Resolve* was fitted out in the highest Imperial style, like a baroque nightmare of cathedrals and graveyards crammed onto the banks of an artificial lake fifty metres across. It was onto the surface of this lake that the information from the ship's sensors were broadcast – but now, with most of the comms still down, the surface was just a rippling mask of static. The twin organs of the navigation helm and the communications hub stood on opposite banks of the lake, while behind it a giant tomb complete with guardian statues housed the ship's bridge cogitator. A construction of gold and silver slabs cut into the shapes of stylised clouds hung from the ceiling overhead, on top of which was Master of Ordnance Crinn bent over his readouts and controls.

Banks of cogitator stations lined the walls where petty officers and flight controllers sat, their faces lit eerily green by the data streaming past their eyes. The ship's tech-priest complement were housed in a crown-shaped structure that jutted from the back wall of the cogitator-tomb, constantly rotating like the cog symbol of the Mechanicus itself. The priest currently on duty was enthroned surrounded by silver-plated angels, thick ribbed datafeeds snaking from beneath his robes as they fed information on the ship's systems into his mind.

It was all as ornate and cumbersome as Caislenn-Har himself. The captain himself should have been long dead from multiple and ravenous cancers, but instead the Imperial Navy had fitted him out with so many rebreathers and blood purifiers that he waddled obesely everywhere surrounded by fumes from his artificial lungs.

'I want a full situation report,' said Caislenn-Har. 'Navigation, I want evasive solutions in case all this nonsense is the prelude to a full-scale attack. What about long-range sensors? Could something sneak up on us? Are we bothering to look over our shoulders while all this is going on?'

The navigation officer keyed in a subtle tune and the servitors drifted down on their stubby little wings, whispering a chorus of information as they worked out the various evasive routes the *Resolve* might take. Images flickered by on the surface of the viewing lake, fuzzy, shaky pictures from the *Resolve*'s scanners. The babble of activity got louder as crewmen and officers struggled to make sense of the few working sensors and communicators they had.

'And can we see the city, please? That is why we're here, after all.' Caislenn-Har threw his hands in the air. 'Are they all dead down there? Is the damn place on fire? I don't know because we're completely fragging blind up here! I don't want aerial pict-steals, I want to know where the Guard are!'

'I recognise this,' came Master of Ordnance Crinn's voice over the bridge vox. 'We got some anomalous readings just before the comms went down. Looks like quantum radiation. Probably a vortex detonation.'

'So the Deathstrikes worked after all. Ha! I owe Consul Kelchenko a drink. What else?'

'Orbital comms are still out,' said the officer at the communications helm, the organ's pipes thrumming mournfully as they reported signals not received. 'The emergency channels are up but they're beacons only. We know the *Truth* and the *Vestals* are still there but no details.'

Caislenn-Har leaned forward and tapped his grey-skinned fingers on the arm of his command throne. This was bad. The Navy had been ineffective at best throughout the campaign for Gravenhold but now it was completely blind. The ship might as well not have been there. Anything could be going on down in the city, and judging by the suddenness and completeness of the blackout it probably was. The main task of the *Resolve* had been to watch out for xenos ships coming to aid the aliens that had taken over Gravenhold but as far as anyone could tell the long-range sensors weren't working so the eldar could be right behind the *Resolve* and no one would know it.

'Not good,' the captain muttered to himself. 'Not good at all.'

Something occurred to him. He straightened up and flicked on a little-used vox-channel. The ship's own vox had only just come back on-line and it was through a howl of distortion that a voice answered.

'Ship's archive.'

'This is Captain Caislenn-Har. Are the mem-banks affected by all this?'

'No… no, sir. They're up and running.'

'Good. What's your name?'

'Ensign Castiglian Krao, sir.'

'Ensign, I want to know what could have done this. Weapons, creatures, warp phenomena, anything that could knock out everyone's comms. Can you do that?'

'I'll make a full search, sir. I'll need permission to second one of the tech-priests onto it.'

'You shall have it.'

'Thank you, sir. Ensign Krao out.'

The surface of the lake flashed again and an aerial shot of Gravenhold appeared. Caislenn-Har could make out the glowing black-hearted crater where the Deathstrike had gone down. A cluster of dockyard buildings on the south bank of the Graven was burning and there was a ragged dark hole where the city's main arena had been. A basic overview of troop dispositions was superimposed over the image, Caislenn-Har made out the concentration of Seleucaians in the compact line from the river down to the southern slums, the artillery bunched around a couple of the old mills, the Fire Drakes in the middle of the administrative district in the shadow of the wall.

'Where are the Janissaries?' asked Caislenn-Har of no one in particular.

'Forward sensors back on-line,' came a vox from someone in the *Resolve's* prow sensorium. 'Severely anomalous readings, running diagnostics.'

'Plasma flux past the limits,' came yet another vox from the reactor core. 'Venting coolant... emergency auxiliary shutdown in operation...'

Caislenn-Har shook his head. His ship was feeling as knocked about as the Guard in the city. Either the sensors were still on the blink or there was something down there pumping strange readings into the ship's sensors. Caislenn-Har wasn't sure which was more likely.

The barely-contained chaos of the bridge played out as Caislenn-Har watched. Runners from all over the ship carried orders or reports to and fro. A gaggle of tech-adepts descended on the communications helm and started taking it apart, levering off its gilded panels, calling down the heavy servitors mounted on the walls to remove the datastacks and remonstrating with the communications officer. A priest hurried in, ascetic brown robes at odds with the massive glory of the bridge, and intoned prayers for the soul of the ship and her crew. Something ancient and electrical finally blew in the cogitator-tomb and ratings hurried in with extinguishers to douse the small fire.

The worse the situation, the more they invented new distractions for themselves. Caislenn-Har wasn't a ship's captain because he was an efficient leader – he wasn't even very ruthless and even before he had become a waddling mass of medical equipment he hadn't been that charismatic. He was there because when everyone else was running around exasperated, he could stay relatively calm and remind them of the tasks that really needed doing. Like getting the ship's sight back, and getting back in touch with the rest of the small fleet.

'Captain?' came a new vox. 'Ensign Krao. We've got our initial results back.'

'Good-good.'

'Well... most disruptive weapons would have inflicted massive physical damage too and, well, I think we'd notice if that had happened.'

'Indeed.'

'And without any nebula clouds or quasars nearby it's not likely to be stellar phenomena, unless Entymion's star had just exploded. Aside from massive technical failure on our part the only remaining options are very unlikely. Sir.'

'Entertain me, ensign.'

'Well, there was one thing.'

'What?'

'Magic.'

'I see. Thank you, Ensign Krao.'

Caislenn-Har flicked off the vox. 'Magic,' he sighed to himself. 'Gakking wonderful.'

Then the view-lake blazed as a large chunk of Gravenhold's wealthiest district erupted into a column of purple-white fire.

'WHAT IS THE weapon that will never fail?' asked Iktinos gravely.

'My soul,' replied Brother Kekrops. 'My soul that will never run dry or falter. That will never be taken and turned against me.'

'Good,' said Iktinos. He moved on down the line. 'Where will the final battle be fought?'

'In the minds of Mankind,' came Brother Myrmos's answer.

'When?'

'We fight it even now.'

'Good.'

Iktinos touched the small leather-bound copy of the *Catechisms Martial* that hung from his waist by a silver chain. The words of Daenyathos, the legendary philosopher-soldier of the Soul Drinkers, were as relevant to the Chapter now as they had been before the excommunication. It was Iktinos's duty that the Marines of his flock should know them off by heart. These were his Marines, the ones with whom he had forged a spiritual bond on Stratix Luminae, and he intended to condition their souls for the struggles the Soul Drinkers would have to endure in the future.

Carnax Bridge was relatively quiet. Seleucaian scouts had tried to cross the previous day when they were at the limit of their westwards push. Their bodies still lay sprawled on the road where Iktinos's Marines had picked them off with bolter fire. The Seleucaians had evidently decided there was some invincible force on the north bank of the River Graven, and had not sent anyone else over.

The bridge was a handsome piece of engineering, a suspension bridge spanning the sheer-sided river with the cable towers in the centre topped with spread-winged eagles. The gate houses on either end were meant to monitor the traffic between the poor south of the city and the wealthy north, and the northern gatehouse was correspondingly more lavish. The tall square marble tower frowned with statues and plaques dedicated to the aristocrats to whom the city had owed its gratitude, and inside it was a complex of ballrooms and reception halls to give an appropriate greeting to dignitaries who needed welcoming into Gravenhold's better half.

Iktinos's Marines were stationed in the lower two floors – the two battle-brothers Iktinos had questioned were keeping a watch over the bridge. A mix of Tactical and a few Assault Marines, Iktinos's Marines had lost their own officers and chosen Iktinos to lead them. Normally they would make for an unacceptably unwieldy formation, but Iktinos used them like a weapon. His Marines did not need the tactical independence their previous training had taught them, they just needed to follow him.

'What news?' he asked.

'Very little,' replied Kekrops, an Assault Marine. 'There is a lot of activity on the south side, though. And it looks like a fortification has gone down north of the river, lots of gunfire and explosions. Karhedros is striking back.'

'With what?'

'We haven't seen any xenos, chaplain. More like... humans. Rebels. Maybe even fellow Guardsmen.'

'Hmm.' It was frustrating that Iktinos's Marines had not fought a true fight since the chamber mercantile. He had been tending his small flock only since Stratix Luminae and they had had precious few exposures to battle since then, and battle, of course, was the only place where Daenyathos's words could truly be understood. 'What a fascinating place this city is becoming. Like the Imperium in miniature. Humanity killing humanity with aliens and witches looking on. What would Daenyathos have said?'

'Nothing, chaplain,' replied Kekrops. 'He would have watched until he understood, and then he would have acted.'

Iktinos nodded. 'Indeed. Give the watch to Thieln and Apollonius and enter half-sleep for three hours. This battle may yet reach us and I want you all rested for when the time comes.'

The two Marines saluted and left to summon their two replacements. Iktinos looked out through the grand picture window that looked down on the expanse of the bridge, the Graven was tinted pink with blood and there were dozens of bodies now floating by. He saw some of them were all but naked, with abnormal growths of flesh and metal forming weapons fused to their bodies. Some foul xenos-tech, no doubt. He shook his head. In spite of all, in spite of everything the Emperor had wished and that His faithful had done, aliens and heretics still nibbled away at Mankind's future.

Iktinos had sided with Sarpedon's revolt because even after the intense psycho-doctrination and religious instruction, he had never been completely satisfied with the way the Emperor's will was done. Sarpedon had convinced him that the Imperium was built to serve its rulers and not the Emperor, and everything Iktinos had seen since then had proved that correct. But there was more. The Emperor did not just want humanity to go on surviving. Mankind was not just another animal, there was more to the constant struggle than simply continuing to exist. The Emperor had a grand path for mankind to follow, but instead it was just stagnating, fighting the same wars, living and dying without ever taking that step forward.

It had taken excommunication to suggest the way. Iktinos wasn't sure yet, but he had read the works of Daenyathos and researched the history of the Chapter, and moreover looked into the teaching he himself had received. He was beginning to understand what he had to do, and the first step was to pass that on to his Marines.

He was a Chaplain of the Soul Drinkers, and as such there was perhaps no one in the galaxy who knew the Emperor's Will like he did.

'Disturbance to the north,' came a vox from Brother Octetes.

'Troops?'

'No,' replied Octetes, whom Iktinos had placed on watch at the northern wall of the bridge gate house. 'It's... maybe another Death-strike...'

Iktinos ran through the ballroom, stomping down into the orchestra pit and over the stage that dominated one end of the room.

Behind the stage backdrop, Brother Octetes was looking out over a view of the north of the city, with its sprawling villas and mock castles competing for obviousness of wealth. In the middle of it all was a strange pulsing purple-black mass, a black glow shot through with purple lightning strobing upwards. 'Iktinos to all Marines,' voxed the Chaplain, wishing that he was still in contact with the other Soul Drinkers below ground. 'Possible moral threat, take cover and steel your souls, this is some xenos trick...'

Then the portal opened.

FROM THE HEART of Gravenhold's northern estates, a lance of purple-streaked blackness ripped up through the ground and up into the darkened sky. Handsome villas were vaporised, their marble walls and gilded friezes dissolving against the raw force of dark magic. Mystical symbols from an alien language flickered in a circle around the crater torn by the magic, echoing the complex patterns of the ritual enacted far below.

The blood that had soaked into Gravenhold, the blood from the thousands dying in its streets, burst upwards and fountained like lava from a volcano, coursing through the streets in a horrendous flash flood, crashing in foaming waves against the buildings. It was as if a massive bullet wound had been torn out of Gravenhold, sending gouts of blood hundreds of metres in the air.

A shockwave rippled out, swamping an area a dozen streets across with evil magic. The magic flooded into the imprints left by savage emotions, leering faces bulged from polished hardwood walls, formed by the arrogance and disdain of Gravenhold's ruling class. The resentment of their downtrodden servants became spectral hands that reached grotesquely from floors and roads. Wherever violent death had blossomed, foul gibbering creatures budded off from the mutating nightmare, capering and screeching down the twisting streets.

The bolt of dark sorcery lanced up through the black clouds, sending thunderheads recoiling. It scoured right through the atmosphere of Entymion IV and boiled up into the black vacuum of space. It streaked past the *Resolve*, blistering the outer hull. Some unfortunate maintenance teams in the outer hull layers were struck mad with visions of alien sorcery, of a great world hanging in the warp where an eldar prince ruled an empire of torturers and magicians.

The magic hit the fueller ship *Sacred Truth* full amidships and sliced it in two. Its enormous fuel cells were breached and exploded, their death a speck of white light in the dark column. Purple lightning arced off the remains of the forward half, incinerating its five hundred-strong crew who were immersed in a torrent of pure madness before they died. Supply ships and landers were scattered by the force of the eruption, spinning out of control into outer orbit or into the deadly gravitational pull of the Entymion system's sun.

In the city, everyone felt it. Pain burst behind the eyes of every Guardsman, followed by a spike of pure evil stabbing at their souls. Lord Commander Xarius saw the fields of dead on Valhalla, endless mounds of frozen corpses that he had put there by ordering the advance. Commander Reinez saw a Traitor Marine he had fought when barely a full battle-brother of the Crimson Fists, and recalled the horror of a fellow Marine choosing to die for the dark gods. Sarpedon saw the face of Michairas, the Marine he had hurled out of an airlock during the Chapter War and who had survived to face Sarpedon again on Stratix Luminae – Sarpedon was filled with shame that he had killed a battle-brother twice over.

Lieutenant Elthanion of the Fornux Lix Fire Drakes saw his men suppressing a rebellion on a far-flung Imperial world, his men dragging women and children from their homes to teach their seditious fathers and husbands about the Emperor's justice. Consul Kelchenko saw his predecessor to the office of consul, an elderly man pleading for clemency as Kelchenko read out the charges of corruption and incompetence that had seen the old man hung and Kelchenko elected to the consulship.

Fear. Shame. Hate. These memories bubbled up from the minds of every human in the city, feeding on the magic now infusing the city. Most men choked them back down, forced them into the depths of their minds where they belonged. For a few they were the last straw and yet more of the soldiers in Gravenhold went insane.

At the very centre of the black column, like the eye of a hurricane, was the true product of Karhedros's spell. It was a tiny window through reality that looked directly into the endless psychic landscape of the warp, and it was growing.

PRINCE KARHEDROS STOOD on the lip of a bottomless pit in the centre of his throne room, a shaft sunk right through the bedrock of reality into the warp. Looking down, he could see a magnificent universe boiling away, seas of molten emotion, floating mountains where roosts of daemons nested. His sorcerers had just opened the gate. The portal was now self-sustaining, the warp energies rushing out of it too vast for it to close.

He could hear a cacophony of daemons' whispers and the screaming of the damned who had become lost in the warp. He could hear the words of gods and amongst them She-Who-Thirsts, first amongst them and the patron of the true eldar. With an open warp portal on its surface Entymion IV would soon be suffused with warp energies and would sink out of real space into the warp in its entirety. A whole world, delivered intact to She-Who-Thirsts.

A human mind would just revel in the knowledge that it would rule a planet where it could mould the continents and populate the continents with subjects drawn from the endless menagerie of the warp. But Karhedros had something more than a human mind. He could understand the cosmic consequences of his actions. He would be a new power in the warp, a creature that had crossed the boundaries between one reality and the next. Whole threads of destiny, so beloved of eldar who cowered away from She-Who-Thirsts, would be snapped. The future history of the galaxy would end and new fates would come into play.

A new Commorragh, no longer hiding from the eyes of the craftworld eldar but a proud beacon shining upon the whole of the warp, illuminating every corner of its reality with the purity of its cruelty and the magnificence of its ruler. No one knew where such an abomination would end. The balance between the warp and realspace could be shattered, one could bleed into the other, and eventually reality as it was known would change into something new. Karhedros didn't know what form any of it might take, but he could feel the savage delight rising in him that he would have been the author of it all.

Karhedros looked over at the haemonculi standing around the portal. Their already twisted faces were contorted with pain. The portal was using the power of their memories to remain stable. They hadn't expected Karhedros would use them that way when they had agreed to join his mission to Entymion IV, but then their minds were too small to understand the true consequence of what Karhedros was doing. They were the torturers of eldar society, each and every one had memories of the most horrendous torments. Many, having experimented on themselves, offered a unique concoction of suffering and cruelty perfect for Karhedros's needs.

Karhedros walked around the portal with its captive haemonculi. The incubi, the heavily-armoured eldar elite who served Karhedros as personal bodyguards and retainers, were standing in black-armoured ranks outside the throne room.

'Captain, our time here is short,' said Karhedros to the leader of the incubi.

'So it has been decided,' said the captain. The incubi were a breed apart from the eldar, and no one really knew what they were or how they thought. 'The call of She-Who-Thirsts becomes ever louder. Now we cannot ignore her.'

'Our hand is now played and the animals on the surface may try to find this place. Grant them death before they see our new world.'

'Of course, my prince,' replied the captain. The swirling column of warp energy cast strange reflections in the eyepieces of his otherwise featureless mask. 'So do the incubi serve their mistress.' The captain – who like all of Karhedros's incubi had never divulged his name – turned sharply and along with his armoured warriors marched out towards the palace gates, where any assault would have to try to breach the palace's frontal defences.

The incubi marched past the wyches, who in contrast waited in a languorous mob apparently without any discipline. It was a completely false appearance, because every single one of them could turn into a lightning-quick killer in a heartbeat.

'And you,' said Karhedros, smiling with what an ignorant observer might think was fondness. 'Children. Blessed of my blood. You killers, you beautiful things.'

The wyches stirred. A couple drew weapons or contorted their bodies as if idly practising the movements of death. One flipped onto her feet. Karhedros couldn't name her, because the wyches chose their leaders anew every day to keep themselves on their toes. 'The games are over, aren't they?' she said. She was as fine a specimen of eldar as existed, with huge green-flecked black eyes and near-white skin pulled taut over snaking muscles. 'We had so little play. And these animals are sometimes good sport, when they have warning. A few of them can fight, and sometimes they don't give up. Is there no more sport here?'

'The games,' said Karhedros, 'are only just beginning, especially for you. You have followed me since I first left Commorragh, do you really think I would cut you down, chain you up and let you never fight again? You shame me. Atone in the streets. Keep the blood flowing. I fear the destruction might end and that will do us no good. Keep the killing hot, blood of my blood. Make them bleed, and I shall see to it that the blood on our new world will never stop.'

The lead wych flipped backwards, drawing a pair of twin-bladed weapons as she did so, she whooped once and the other wyches echoed, following her as she ran for the front entrance. They had permission to kill, those were the only orders Karhedros had ever had to give them.

The eldar warriors were holding the regions around the palace, aside from those that were still out in the city herding the warring human factions towards one another. The palace was hidden and its guardians were Karhedros's best. He could feel the touch of She-Who-Thirsts even now, reaching down from the heavens to caress him in thanks for her dark new world. What things she would show him, for the goddess who wanted to devour the souls of other eldar would instead welcome him as her right hand.

Karhedros ascended the tight winding stairs that led to the chambers once occupied by the palace's king. This king had liked gold and ebony and the walls and floors of his chambers were solid shiny black, covered in delicate inlaid patterns of creamy white. Unusually good taste, for a human.

Akrelthas sat at the large black hardwood desk in the study. Long ago, when Karhedros had been an Archon of the Kabal of the Burning Scale on Commorragh, Akrelthas had been a lieutenant he had almost trusted. Now the Kabal was Karhedros's personal army of pirates and slavers and Akrelthas was still there, Karhedros's eyes and ears.

'Will it stay open?' asked Karhedros.

Akrelthas thought for a moment. 'If the slaves we made keep fighting, as we created them to do. And if the humans don't surrender and die too quickly.'

Karhedros smiled. 'I don't think there's too much danger of that. They have strange ideas about when it is right to die and when they should fight. I understand them well enough, I think. If you place too little pressure on them they become complacent, too much and they give in to despair. But just enough, and they will never give up. Hope is the key. As long as there is a little hope, but not too much, they fight to the death. Every time.'

'You know them well, my prince,' said Akrelthas. 'Perhaps half of them remain and they are resisting hard.'

'And Sarpedon?'

'We do not know. Some of his troops remain on the surface but most are evidently beneath the ground.'

'I should very much like to know where he is. He will be feeling greatly betrayed, and that is something humans take very personally. I should not be surprised if he was heading towards us to fulfil some honour by dying beneath our battlements, which is a complication I would do without.'

'I shall set the mandrakes onto him, prince.'

'Good. We probably have a handful of hours left, ensure the blood does not stop flowing and we shall be done.'

'Of course.'

Karhedros left Akrelthas to his duties. The ancient king had evidently liked to look out over his kingdom because the chambers opened directly onto the palace battlements, which in turn looked onto the immense natural cavern in which the palace stood. The mass of the palace bulged out from one wall with the rest of the cavern stretching out before it, eventually breaking into dozens of smaller tunnels. The ceiling of the cavern hung with stalactites and streams of water spattered down from watercourses on the levels above. Karhedros's eldar warriors were garrisoned on the rocky plain, with a few jetbikes still idling in case anything really did manage to get down there and threaten the palace. The warriors were well aware of their real purpose, however, they were to witness Karhedros's ascension to lord of their new world, because many of them had been there from the beginning. They had been part of Karhedros's pirate fleet when She-Who-Thirsts had first planted in him the desire to leave Commorragh and found the true home of the eldar race.

Karhedros found this underground fortress lacking. It was as good a seat of rulership as existed on Entymion IV, but it had been conceived by brutish human minds. Karhedros would raise a new bastion from the sea, a city-fortress to put the towers of Commorragh to shame, riddled with torture chambers and fighting arenas, pleasure-pits and temples to his goddess. His alien mind could pick out the threads of fate that would lead to him sitting on a throne atop its pinnacle, able to see his whole world at once. Every one of those threads was intact, winding through the next few hours and into the coming dawn.

On the surface, the blood was flowing. Beneath, the portal was sucking the matter of Entymion IV into the warp. As far as Karhedros was concerned, he was already the prince of the warp. All it needed was time.

CHAPTER FOURTEEN

THE JETBIKE STREAKED overhead so close it nearly took Eumenes's head off. He felt the air sliced apart centimetres from his face. A shot from his bolt pistol went wide and the biker wheeled insanely low, jinking between severed stumps of streetlights as he banked his bike around in a long arc for another pass.

The government district had received a thorough bombardment from the Guard artillery after the battle in the chamber mercantile and the scale of the destruction was impressive. Where once there had been seemingly solid blocks of buildings there were now warrens of half-fallen walls and rooms blasted open to the air. Between the Fire Drakes and the Seleucaians, this area was no-man's land and the eldar were all over it, spoiling for a fight, hunting for things to kill. The Soul Drinkers scouts were a prime target, but Eumenes didn't mind so much. He liked being underestimated.

Eumenes snapped off three more shots at the low dark shape streaking around behind him, the shots spanging off charred support columns or drifts of rubble. The bike's long armoured nose flipped over and the bike rolled crazily, using the roll to turn so sharply it was suddenly knifing straight at Eumenes, its rider's teeth bared beneath its green-eyed goggles. Hooked chains streamed behind it, and blades flaring out from the bike's nose sliced off chunks of masonry as the engine screeched into its highest gear.

Eumenes could duck. He could dive to the ground, hoping that the bike would pass over him instead of dipping lower and eviscerating him with the blades hooking down from its underside. He could do what the biker expected, and die. But he did not.

Eumenes stepped out from cover, offering himself up to the biker's blades. The biker had probably seen Guardsmen doing the same, mesmerised by the speed and grace of the jetbike, laid open to a spectacular kill. The biker saw his chance. The bike tipped to one side, the biker reaching out with his own sickle-bladed knife to take the scout's head personally. Eumenes would become a new trophy to be impaled on the spiked chains, a new plaything for when the games were over.

Eumenes, however, didn't fight alone.

The biker suddenly snapped to one side, wrenching the controls as he did so. The jetbike banked too hard and spun out of control, swinging round and round as it careered through the ruins. It smacked into a half-toppled column and broke in two, throwing the nose section and the engine in opposite directions with the biker sailing across the cratered street beyond.

Scout-Sniper Raek slipped out of the shadows a short distance away. 'Good kill,' he said with a smile

'Kill's not done yet,' replied Eumenes. He held out his bolt pistol, drawing a bead on the biker who was trying to crawl away, dragging his broken legs behind him. Eumenes put a bolt through the eldar's neck. 'Never turn your back, Raek, until you see them die.'

The scouts were coming together as a team. Raek's sniper rifle and Eumenes's cunning made for a formidable killing team without adding Selepus's knife or Nisryus's precognitive edge. Scamander hadn't had to use his pyrokinetics for a while, the scouts were moving quickly through the governmental district without needing heavy firepower, dealing quietly with anything that got in their way. The eldar thought they were hunting frightened, stray humans, and more than just the biker had died for that assumption.

'We're there,' voxed Scout Tydeus from up ahead. The vox-channel was still distorted but at least it was working. Eumenes peered through the ruins and saw what had once been the chamber mercantile up ahead – now it and the senate-house behind it were charred shells criss-crossed with smouldering support beams.

'Keep moving.'

As the scouts moved into the ruins of the chamber mercantile they saw some remnants of the battle against the Crimson Fists. A red-gauntleted hand stuck out from beneath a fallen slab of stone. Dead Fornus Lix Guardsmen lay, mouths dry and open, eyes staring. Flies were starting to settle on the dead. Eumenes recognised one dead Soul

Drinker as one of Graevus's men, an Assault Marine whose loss the Chapter couldn't really afford. The fresh open wound on the Marine's throat marked where the gene-seed had been removed by one of the Apothecaries – if the Soul Drinkers got off Entymion IV that gland would be implanted in one of the next novices to be inducted into the scouts. Eumenes himself had one, taken from a sergeant named Givrillian who Sarpedon had considered one of the Chapter's finest Marines.

The chamber mercantile's basements were laid open by an artillery strike, the crater gouging down two floors. Charred paper lay everywhere, the rooms beneath the chamber mercantile had evidently been used to keep all the financial records that Gravenhold generated. Eumenes saw the Marines of Squad Graevus, posted as sentries. There were few of them left now, and Sergeant Graevus was looking the worse for wear himself, his armour was pitted and smoking, and the fittings of his power axe were clotted with drying gore.

'Scout-Sergeant,' said Graevus. 'Good. Sarpedon was waiting for you.'

'From where we were standing it didn't look good on the east wall.'

'No, not good. They went right over us into the Fire Drakes. We had to fight our way through both of them.' Graevus led the way further down, through burned-out studies and libraries.

'The Guardsmen in the south are gone,' said Eumenes. 'The xenos dealt with them directly.'

'There's nothing to stop them any more. Whatever Karhedros is doing with this city, he's nearly finished. Now they can just have their sport. I'll be glad when we're off this damn planet.'

Eumenes looked at him. 'I don't think we're done here.'

Sarpedon was waiting in an almost intact study, antique glow-globes casting yellowish light over walls crammed with mouldering books and the large desk which Sarpedon stood behind, alongside the two other Librarians, Gresk and Tyrendian.

'Scout Eumenes,' said Sarpedon. 'Excellent. We need you to pinpoint Tellos's position.' Sarpedon had an old map of Gravenhold unrolled on the desk. He had already marked the places where the city had been rearranged by artillery or explosions, like the obliteration of the arena and the new crater in the city's north.

'Good to see you alive, Novice Nisryus,' said Gresk.

'Thank you, sir,' replied Nisryus.

'Staying sharp?'

'Very. The fighting helps, I think. I'm not seeing much further but it's getting clearer by the hour. Eumenes will need to know which of the bridges on this map has the twin gate houses before he can tell you where Tellos is.'

Eumenes looked up from the map. 'He's right.'

Sarpedon smiled and pointed at one of the bridges across the River Graven: Carnax Bridge, the same one Iktinos was still holding.

'Then he's here,' said Eumenes. Close to where the slums met the edge of the governmental district was the slaughterhouse district. One of Entymion IV's main exports was the livestock that grazed on its immense grassy plains, some of which were held back to feed Gravenhold's population. Eumenes was pointing to one of the warehouses where they were slaughtered. 'Once the Janissaries were broken we followed his Marines here. I hung back and didn't get any closer but it looks like he's got more than thirty Marines with him.'

'You're certain it's Tellos that's leading them?'

'Half-naked? Chainblades for hands? Yes, I'm sure.'

'Good. You did well not to face him yourself. Tellos has been changing for the worse ever since the star fort.'

'Commander, why... why is he like that? What happened on Stratix Luminae?'

'Two questions, novice, and I am afraid I don't know the answers. Tellos himself probably doesn't know.'

'Will you need me to lead you there?'

'No, Eumenes, we can make it quickly enough. There is something else I need you to do. Rather easier, in a way.'

'What?'

'I need you to find the Crimson Fists.'

'PUT YOUR BACK into it! Throne of Earth, I'm one hundred and seventeen and I'm not ready to give in yet!' Lord Commander Xarius ignored the pain in his joints and heaved another sandbag onto the barricade. Slave-soldiers had scrabbled up the barrier as they swarmed through the ruined buildings that bordered one side of the position, now the sandbag wall was soggy with their blood and the dead lay three deep just beyond it. The smell was appalling, many of the Seleucaian Guardsmen were wearing their rebreather masks.

'Yes, sir.' The soldier next to Xarius heaved up a couple more sandbags, helping to plug the gap where the slave-soldiers had broken in. He had seen the soldier next to him dragged over the wall by steel-taloned hands and ripped limb from limb in front of him. Xarius knew that men who saw such things could clam up, fall almost comatose, and when that happened they might as well be dead.

'Scared?' asked Xarius.

'Yes.'

'Use it.'

In spite of Threlnan's protestations, Xarius had hurried forward with the few reserve men to plug the gap. The men had tried to hold him back but he was sure he had plugged a couple of those deformed freaks before the Seleucaians had formed a second line and massacred the enemy with volleys of las-fire. Now Xarius had his place in the line, preparing the defences for the next surge.

Threlnan's position had been held by about two hundred men half an hour before. Now Xarius guessed they had about a hundred and fifty.

'How is your side looking, Hasdrubal?' voxed Xarius.

'Good, sir,' came the reply. The Baneblade, under Hasdrubal's command, had used its heavy bolters and the odd Demolisher cannon shot to rip the street in front of it to shreds, wiping out the gaggles of enemies that tried to charge down it. The Seleucaians hunkering down beside it had picked off survivors with las-fire. 'We've got enough ammo to keep going all night.'

'I think we're going to have to.'

'And yourself, sir?'

'I'm safe enough, Hasdrubal.' One of the Guardsmen threw another enemy body over the rebuilt sandbag wall, landing with a wet thump on the blood-soaked earth and ash. 'Worry about yourself.'

Likewise the heavy weapons in the Enforcer watchtower kept the third side of the position clear, turning the tangle of ruined hovels in front of it into a blistered, bullet-scarred killing ground littered with bodies. The fourth side was commanded by Threlnan himself – two of the Chimeras forming a defensive line were burned-out but the line had ultimately held.

The small rectangle of bloodstained rockcrete was Xarius's whole world. Beyond it was no-man's land, haunted by enemies who, even if they had once been human, were now alien-wrought fighting animals. Somewhere out there were other islands of Guardsmen, and communications from them occasionally got through to the Baneblade's vox-receiver. But mostly, Threlnan's Seleucaians were on their own.

They had all seen the billowing red-black smoke when the docks had fallen. They all kept glancing up at the shaft of purple-black energy coursing up into the sky. They knew the end was coming soon.

'I'm pretty certain there's a rule against your being here,' said Threlnan. Xarius looked round – the colonel was standing just behind him. His skin and uniform were a charred grey-black. 'There's a directive somewhere about commanders keeping themselves out of harm's way. I'm sure of it.'

'Don't worry, colonel,' replied Xarius, picking up his lasgun again. 'I imagine they'll save that court martial for last.'

'I let a lord commander into the front line, sir. I won't be able to explain that one away.'

'I'll put in a good word for you.'

'Not much good if you're dead. I'm serious, if any of us survive it should be you.'

'Why? This is my fault, Threlnan. That's what the chain of command is for. The buck stops at the top and that means with me. I'm just trying to put it right. And it doesn't look like you're playing the rear-echelon officer yourself, Threlnan.'

'Ah, I can't ask these boys to die on their own.' Threlnan held up the melta-gun he was carrying. 'Besides, it's been a while since I toted one of these. Brings back memories.'

'Acranthal?'

Threlnan nodded. 'Three days and those damned xenos tau never stopped coming. We held that valley until the Navy sent a flyer down to pick us up; I must have gone through a dozen of these power packs before the end. Won me my commission.' Threlnan shook his head, the memories of a soldier's life flooding back. 'And you?'

'Second Battle of Armageddon.'

Threlnan cocked an eyebrow. 'You were there?'

'Tartarus Hive. Nothing like a dying hive city to make you feel small. Calxian Seventh, you know. They made me an officer because I got out alive, that was pretty much how you got promoted by that stage.'

'Well, at least we've both been there before.'

'It's a first for most of these lads, though.'

'Best of luck, sir.'

'And to you. Fight hard enough and maybe they'll put up a statue.'

Threlnan saluted and walked back to his men. Xarius saw the last few bodies being pulled away from the centre of the position, while the two remaining medics tended to the dozen or so wounded. Guardsman Karthel, who had been given chaplain's duty, was doing the rounds taking last-minute confessions and offering the Emperor's blessing to anyone who asked for it. Men reloaded the pintle-mounted weaponry on the Chimeras or ran heavy bolter ammo to the Baneblade's sponson gunners. One trooper took a swig from a canteen, another wiped his gory bayonet blade on the trousers of his fatigues. The nerves were dissolving by now, to be replaced with a grim refusal to die.

'They're coming again!' yelled a trooper on the roof of the watchtower, pointing over the ruined buildings.

'Saddle up!' shouted a sergeant on Xarius's line. 'You! Get your jacket back on. You're on duty, soldier!'

Xarius leaned his old, complaining body against the sandbags, squinting through the tangle of ruins along the barrel of his lasgun. It was still warm from the last volley of shots. Someone moved past him and threw a couple of spare las-cells at his feet. The Guardsman next to him took a deep breath, muttered a prayer and took his position alongside Xarius.

'Gak on a stick,' said a soldier down the line. 'I can see them.'

'More of the same?' said another soldier with mock weariness.

'I don't... no, different.'

'Xenos,' said Xarius wearily. 'At last.'

Then Xarius saw them, too. But they weren't xenos.

At first he thought he saw a woman, but only for a moment. Then he saw the huge ugly claws, the scaled and taloned legs, the pale blue-white skin and the noseless face with its malicious slit of a mouth and black liquid slashes for eyes.

The smell hit him. Musk, heavy and thick, a cloying invisible mist of pheromones. He felt his head swimming and his muscles relaxing, his fingers demanding they be allowed to uncurl from around the trigger of his lasgun. His legs wavered. His eyelids drooped. Did he really need to carry on breathing? Wouldn't it be simpler to lie back and let this beautiful, lethal creature cut him apart?

'Rebreathers!' he gasped, and pulled his own mask out of its belt pouch to pull it over his head. There was a commotion on the line as other men did the same. For some it was too late as they stumbled back, eyes rolling, blind with confusion.

'Medics! Get them out of here!' shouted one of the sergeants. Xarius got the rebreather over his head in time to see more of the creatures advancing, their skins shimmering strangely as if they were just out of phase with the physical world.

He spotted the malevolent reflection of the column of magical energy, pulsing its way into the sky. Warp-magic. The black arts. The xenos were in league with the dark powers, after so many years in command Xarius had suffered his brushes with the agents of Chaos.

'Daemons,' he hissed.

The Seleucaians couldn't take this. Hells, the Space Marines would be hard pushed to fend off a daemonic assault. Xarius had never been in thick of one but he had seen the aftermath, and signed the orders to execute the men who had witnessed enough to break their minds.

The daemons were coming closer, darting between the charred timbers and half-collapsed walls. Some wore scraps of silvery mail or interlocking armour plates, others were completely naked, a horrible parody of female beauty with snaking muscles and teeth glinting in their shark-like mouths.

'O Emperor, though sin calls its siren song and the ways of the corrupt be tempting, shield our souls from perfidy...' Xarius raised his voice as he prayed, hoping the men near him would recognise they weren't fighting rebels or xenos any more and take up the prayer with him.

'...and ...and may your saints come to us, and new saints be born from us...' The Guardsman next to Xarius spoke with a wavering voice as he watched the daemons advance. The Seleucaians, like Xarius, had been taught the simple prayers common to seminaries and chapels throughout the Imperium. Now, suddenly, those words started to actually mean something.

Xarius was leading the prayer, aware of how old and frail he must have sounded calling on the grace of the Emperor as creatures like nothing the Seleucaians had ever seen before moved lethally towards the line. But the prayer was a weapon, it was a shield for their souls, and without it many of them would already have gone mad or died in horror as the pure evil of the daemons's substance made contact with their minds.

There was more movement, further back. Something was bounding closer with sudden, unnatural speed. Xarius spotted long avian limbs pistoning through the shadows, monstrous tubular heads with long sharp ribbons for tongues. Then the daemon cavalry burst out through the ruins, hurtling at supernatural speeds towards the line, daemons were riding the monstrous creatures bareback, claws held out ready to slash and behead, black liquid eyes huge with hate.

'Oh, frag!' shouted the sergeant. 'Fire! Bloody well fire!'

Las-shots whipped out, slicing through the ruins. Daemonic flesh was seared to ribbons and reformed, leaving new deformities on the daemons as they charged. A couple were knocked down, their flesh dissolving as their hold on reality was broken. But the rest – maybe twenty daemonic cavalry – slammed home into the barricade.

Iron-edged tongues lashed out, impaling. Claws snapped off heads and arms. The daemons screamed as they hit and the din was appalling, shearing through Xarius's senses and becoming a wall of hateful white noise.

'Tower!' he shouted, though he couldn't hear his own voice. 'Covering fire! Everything you've got! Everything!'

One of the beasts leapt the barricade right over his head. He let a dozen shots fly on full-auto, searing the mount's underbelly, but it landed intact. The creature wheeled and the daemon on its back plunged its claw into the back of a Guardsman, lifting him high and flinging him back over the sandbags into no-man's land. One Guardsman, his mouth working as he yelled the words of the prayer, jumped onto the daemon's back and stabbed again and again with his bayonet, blue blood spraying all over him. The daemon swivelled round and opened its mouth so widely its jaw must have dislocated like a snake's before it leaned forward and bit half the Guardsman's head off. Another handful of Guardsmen turned their fire on the beast, Xarius lending his firepower to theirs as they speared the daemon with dozens of las-shots. Wet blueish clots of flesh spattered out of the spasming daemon's body as it came apart, its mount slumping to its knees as it melted in a pall of stinking vapour.

Stupid, proud old man. He could have got out of this and yet he insisted on that one dramatic gesture to show what a good man he was. Now he was going to die.

It was the daemons' musk talking. The Dark Powers didn't just send foul monsters to kill everyone, they messed with your mind. Turned you into one of their own. Frag that, thought Xarius savagely, and shook the traitorous thoughts out of his head.

He glanced up and down the line and saw it was in tatters. Half the cavalry had made it over the barricade. A couple were heading for the wounded, the medics and the ad hoc chaplain trying to fend them off with laspistols and bellowed prayers. The men of the line were back-to-back in desperate knots, trying to batter the daemons back with lasgun fire as they were picked off by slashing claws and stabbing tongues. There was nothing to hold back the daemons on foot save for a couple of feet of sandbags and the Emperor's grace, and Xarius knew they had asked about as much from the Emperor as they could. It was down to guts now.

The heavy weapons on the tower opened up as one, and heavy bolter shots stitched down, raking down through the front rank of daemons interspersed with crimson lascannon shots and explosive autocannon shells. Some of the daemons made it through and into the men making their last stand by the barricade, claws sparring with bayonets. The white noise was dying down to be replaced with the clashes of steel on claws, gibbering daemonic screaming, howls of dying men, hopeless orders yelled by officers demanding that their men do the impossible.

Xarius wheeled. He was alone. The men on either side of him were dead and he was stranded between two knots of desperate men, the space between them criss-crossed with las-fire. Xarius dropped down into the cover of the half-collapsed sandbag wall, wishing he could

disappear, the customary ache from his old body replaced with twitching floods of adrenaline.

Please, Emperor, please make it quick. I don't mind your taking me
now. I have failed you completely enough. But make it quick.

A shadow fell over him, edged red by the strobing las-fire. Xarius saw
the writhing fleshy horns on its head and the gnarled crescents of its
claws. Even its shadow was unnatural, seething and changing. Silhouetted by the fire still stuttering down from the tower, the daemon was
a black shape above him. He saw the distorted reflection of his face,
staring down from the inky curved surfaces of its eyes.

He knew then that it wouldn't be quick.

A white-hot wall of heat thudded into him, slamming him down into
the sandbags. Scalding liquid spattered over him. He scrabbled to wipe
it off his face, out of his eyes.

A second shadow fell. Something grabbed the front of his uniform
and dragged him to his feet. His lasgun was shoved back into his chest
and he grabbed hold of it instinctively.

'Saw you kill that thing,' said Colonel Threlnan. The melta-gun in his
free hand was thrumming as its core came back to critical mass.
'Thought I'd get in on the action.'

Xarius blinked the daemon's blood out of his eyes and the shape of
Colonel Threlnan emerged. 'Daemons, Threlnan. Not just xenos.
Throne of Earth, I've marched you all into hell.'

There were other soldiers with Threlnan, members of his command
squad, surrounding the two officers to keep the daemons away with
volleys of las-fire. They might have bought thirty seconds or so.

Xarius thought wildly. No matter what, it was over. He only had to
worry about his duties as a lord general of the Imperial Guard.

'Hasdrubal!' shouted Xarius over the vox. 'Battle cannon, five o'clock!
Thirty metres!'

'But sir, that's where...'

'Bloody do it! Now! And then get into reverse!' Xarius looked back
up at Threlnan. 'This place is done. I've seen daemons fly and walk
through walls and all kinds of crap, we can't hold them here. Fall back
to the tower.'

The grinding of the Baneblade's tracks cut through the screaming.

'We need to move now,' said Xarius.

'Right.' barked Threlnan, vox on the all-squad channel. 'All troops,
back to the tower. Now. Tower, covering fire. Get the Chimeras back to
block us in.'

The thirty seconds were up. Threlnan, Xarius and the surrounding
troops broke into a run, las-fire snapping half-blind. The Seleucaians

who could were doing the same thing, and the position was gone completely. The daemons running in through the buildings were sprinting unchecked into the heart of the position.

'The Emperor be my guide!' someone was yelling. 'The Throne be my beacon!' Xarius saw it was the makeshift preacher, Karthel, who was kneeling over the wounded with a laspistol in each hand. He was trying to fend off the daemons scrabbling towards the wounded.

The medics were with the troops running for the tower.

Someone screamed and a daemon impaled the man just behind Xarius with its claw, lifting him clean up into the air where he wriggled like a stuck fish, blood spurting. A stray las-shot took down someone else. Guardsmen's hands kept pulling Xarius forward and suddenly all those years were catching up with him, the weight of decades trying to crush him down to the floor.

Threlnan fired again and the daemon's midriff was vaporised. The dying Guardsman thudded to the floor. No one tried to help him. Like the wounded, like the crazy, he was just one step removed from dead.

The sheer grey sides of the watchtower, now peppered with las-shot holes and spatters of gore, loomed up ahead. Seleucaians were scrambling in through the open front doors, tripping over one another. Some of them were firing from the cover of the doorframe, teeth gritted as they sprayed full-auto lasgun fire at anything that wasn't human. If a single daemon got in, the slaughter would be even more terrible.

The Chimeras were trundling closer, ready to block the doors once enough men had got inside. All the Guardsmen knew they weren't important enough to wait for. Once the doors were closed, that was it.

Threlnan fired again, the wash of heat almost knocking Xarius onto his face.

Xarius heard the Baneblade tracks stop grinding. That was the only warning anyone had.

The mega-battle cannon mounted on the Baneblade was the biggest gun in Gravenhold save for the single remaining Deathstrike launcher. The explosion was so loud it wasn't a sound at all but a wall of force that threw Xarius the rest of the way into the watchtower. One Chimera was shunted sideways by the shockwave, slamming into the watchtower. Men were thrown to the ground. A daemon's body shattered against the doorframe, spraying shimmering gore everywhere. The heat came next, singeing uniforms and hair, blistering paint, howling over everything. Choking dust and smoke billowed like a sandstorm.

Xarius turned over painfully, every joint a throbbing nugget of pain. He was lying just inside the watchtower. As his senses swam back he saw the huge crater where the ruined buildings had been, now just a massive bowl filled with rubble and splintered wood. Fragments of shell casing were stabbed into the rockcrete, glowing hot. Bodies and parts of bodies were cast around, just more ruins.

Xarius guessed that half the daemons were gone, vaporised in the blast.

Hands grabbed hold of him and dragged him further in as the last few Guardsmen followed, caked with blood and dust. The Chimeras were out of action but the Baneblade would do just as well, reversing into position to block the doors, gun barrel swinging back round.

'Threlnan!' shouted Xarius, barely able to hear his own words. 'Colonel!'

But Colonel Threlnan of the Seleucaian 4th Division was lying on his face, a shard of shell casing speared through him. Blood was spreading from beneath him and Xarius could see his lungs through the massive rip in his back, see them as they stopped pumping.

'Close them,' said Xarius, his voice barely making it out of his body. The doors were heaved shut as the Baneblade backed closer. Xarius could see men still out there, blinded or crippled, writhing through the wreckage. One Guardsmen fell brokenly from the front hatch of a shattered Chimera, crawling towards the watchtower as the doors closed.

The watchtower had been too small to hold the hundreds of Seleucaians, which was why it had only formed one part of the position. Now there could only be fifty or so Guardsmen left. Plenty of room for everyone to die.

Xarius tried to drag himself to his feet as the Guardsmen barred the doors. There were wounded and dying men lying all around the bleak, bare rockcrete ground floor, which was featureless save for the narrow stairway leading to the upper floors and a couple of cells for prisoners. One of the Seleucaians helped Xarius up.

'Is there a medic?' asked Xarius. His ears were ringing and he could barely hear himself.

'One got through, I think,' replied the Guardsman.

'Good. Good, get some painkillers into these men. And into me, if there are any to spare.'

Xarius could hear gunfire still stuttering from the upper floors. He heard the daemons, too, keening madly as they tried to climb the sheer walls. Eventually, Xarius knew, they would succeed.

Xarius looked at the Guardsman who had helped him, it was a sergeant.

'What's your name?

'Sergeant Gabulus, sir.'

'Good. Gabulus, we need to get all the men off this floor. They'll come through the walls.'

'I think the wounded are too...'

'They will come through the walls, sergeant. I know about these things. It's my job. Move them. All of them. And get some guns on the stairs.'

Xarius was too shaken and numb to feel anything apart from a faint annoyance that he wasn't dead yet. It wasn't so bad, dying on the barricades. But now he had to go through another last stand, a wretched final handful of death before it was done.

He had been right all along. He had asked too much of his Emperor. It wouldn't be quick after all.

CHAPTER FIFTEEN

THIS WAS NOT like killing the Janissaries. It was on a different level than hunting even the eldar, expert hunters themselves. Eumenes could feel the danger, the place was steeped in it, drumming silently in his ears, a faint metallic taste in his mouth. Everything was brighter and sharper. The fissures that crackled in the earth, massive wounds torn by the Deathstrike impact, filled the air with the smell of heat and destruction. Eumenes could feel it on his skin like a knife held just above him, ready to strike.

Selepus was so silent it was hard to see him even if you looked right at him. Eumenes had to be careful not to lose the scout in the cratered wasteland. Most of Gravenhold was ruined but the area around the old medicae station was absolute desolation. The scouts took cover in shell craters or behind slabs of ground that had been lifted up by the vortex impact. The area had been carpeted by shellfire on the orders of the Crimson Fists, and a greater weight of death had fallen on this section of the slums than on any other. The bleak heart of Gravenhold was laid open, raw and bleeding to the dark sky. The bodies were unrecognisable twists of carbonised flesh. The abandoned tanks were melted heaps of slag. Palls of smoke bled from gouges right down through the layers of Gravenhold's history, and in places the strata of the city could be seen. At long last Gravenhold was displaying its tormented history to anyone who looked.

Not that there were many to see it. The Imperial Guard had mostly been smart enough to get the hell out before the Deathstrike hit. The

Gravenholders had died in greater numbers, thrown into charred heaps by the force of the vortex blast. The smell of cooked meat mingled with the smoke and ash.

The scouts were approaching the vortex crater itself. Eumenes had heard it was bad but he had never seen destruction on this scale from a single weapon. A shockwave had levelled two blocks in every direction and over the crater itself still hung a dense cloud of dust, the remains of pulverised hovels. More permanent structures were just lonely blackened skeletons. As the air thickened and visibility dropped the bodies became fresher, Gravenholders and then slave-warriors with massive wounds from large-calibre guns or close combat weapons. The blood oozing from their wounds mingled with the dust to form a greyish-red gunk that pooled beneath the tangled heaps of bodies.

Selepus was crouching down by one body, a nightmarish creature with a ribcage that gaped open to reveal a maw filled with fangs. It had been all but bisected by a huge wound, still wet and rapidly caking with dust.

'Chainblade,' said Selepus quietly.

The winds blew and the dust swirled, descending like a thick dark blanket over the ruins. The shape of the crater itself was just ahead, like a deep black pool that seemed to suck the rest of the ruined cityscape towards it.

The Crimson Fists had followed Luko's Soul Drinkers through the crater into the undercity, only to be forced back out when the slave-warriors had awoken and coursed out onto the surface. The Fists had held the tide back, plugging the bleeding wound. Without them the slave-warriors would probably have surged eastwards and wiped out what remained of the Imperial artillery.

The Soul Drinkers could listen in to the Guard transmissions, not that there was much to listen to with the Guard army cut to pieces and being ground into the dirt. But the Crimson Fists were something else. By now they had stopped talking to the Guard and their own vox-channels were too secure. No one knew what they were doing or how many of them were left, only that they were probably holding the area of the Deathstrike hit, waiting to link up with a friendly force and blaze their way out of Gravenhold.

Eumenes crouched down by Selepus, knowing that even in the half-light a sharp-eyed Marine could pick out a scout's silhouette against the swirling dust. And they were all sharp-eyed.

'The crater is deep enough for them to hold,' said Selepus. 'The enemy don't have artillery so it can be defended.'

'Agreed,' said Eumenes. 'It's where I'd be. Aggressive patrols, though. Hunt and kill stuff.'

'Assault Marines?'

'Tactical. They'll want to keep the assault troops in reserve in case the eldar decide to make a battle of it.' Eumenes turned back, he couldn't see his fellow scouts but he knew the pattern they would be using, spread out amongst the upheaved ground and piles of crumbling ruins. He waved Raek forward. Raek slunk out of the shadows and slid down on his stomach next to Eumenes. 'Raek, we'll need you to cover and spot for us.'

'Just you two?'

'That's right. Between your eye and Nisryus I want to know of any surprises that are coming our way. Scamander will be our artillery. Tydeus, Laeon and Alcides are backup.'

Eumenes paused, looking again towards the crater. If he was a commander with the best troops in the galaxy, he would want the Fists out in the ruins, sweeping the area, killing anything that shouldn't be there. If you have a weapon like a company of Space Marines, you use them. In Eumenes's mind he could see patrol routes snaking between knots of hard cover, the places where one fire team would leapfrog the other, the fields of fire they would keep.

Space Marines were good. They were the best. But the Soul Drinkers had been the same before the excommunication and Eumenes had studied them as well as he had the way the Chapter currently fought. They were tough, fearless, and disciplined, but they were not creative. They all thought the same way. Eumenes had sat through dozens of pict-recorded tactical sermons and he knew the principles laid down in the *Codex Astartes* of how a Space Marine should fight. He knew how they thought.

'Can we do this?' he asked quietly.

'Yes,' said Raek, drawing his sniper rifle down off his back and putting his eye to the scope.

Selepus nodded. The others didn't reply, which was enough.

'Because it doesn't matter if we come back from this one,' said Eumenes. 'You know what they can do. They did it to Thersites. They know we're here already.'

'Got them,' said Selepus. Eumenes followed his gaze but couldn't make anything out. For now he trusted the scout; Selepus didn't have a habit of being wrong.

'I'll be thirty seconds behind you,' said Eumenes.

Selepus slid forwards and was gone, worming his way through the hard black shadows in the direction of the crater. Eumenes followed, feeling the field of fire from Raek's sniper rifle sweeping over his back.

Eumenes could feel the Fists watching, because the Crimson Fists would be out there trying to hunt the scouts down. Instinct painted every open angle and field of fire over the twilit desolation. Eumenes could all but see the landscape painted with life and death, the places he could hide and the places where a Tactical Marine could see him and direct a volley of pinpoint bolter fire to leave him a steaming bloody mess.

Then he saw the Fist. He was part of a Tactical Squad patrolling in loose formation, each Marine a strongpoint in a widely-spaced line. To Eumenes the Fist's field of vision was like a wide-beam spotlight that would kill anything it touched – if Eumenes wasn't invisible then he was dead.

Now he had the position of one Marine, Eumenes could pick out the others. Five Crimson Fists, a fire team: one sergeant, one with a flamer, and three with bolters. Perfect for running down knots of slave-warriors, herding them into flamer range with bolter fire with the sergeant's chainsword finishing off the survivors. Not, perhaps, so ideal for a squad of Soul Drinkers scouts with a very specific mission.

Eumenes saw Selepus well before the first Crimson Fist did. Even then it was no more than a shadow on a shadow, a faint suggestion of movement blurring behind the Marine as he scanned for targets. It was the knife that let Eumenes know what was coming. Selepus's combat knife, flashing in that familiar arc towards the Marine's throat where even power armour couldn't save him.

The Fist was as quick as the silver slash of the knife. Faster.

An elbow connected and suddenly Selepus was visible, as if the darkness was lifted off him and he was shockingly obvious, reeling back with his knife still in his hand but a spray of blood spurting from his nose.

Eumenes's grip on his bolt pistol tightened. He was a damn good shot but he couldn't take down a Crimson Fist on his own at this range, even if the shot hit home he would draw a punishing weight of fire before he managed to squeeze off a second shot.

The Fist and the scout were grappling. Selepus was stabbing up at the Marine, seeking the few gaps afforded by the power armour. The Fist was lunging down with the butt of his boltgun, looking to crack open Selepus's skull, smash his jaw, cave in his ribcage.

The other Crimson Fists were running to help. Not even Selepus could hold them off on his own.

Eumenes hurried forwards, risking everything for an edge of speed. He wondered what he would say when they took Selepus's geneseed and buried him in the newly-finished vaults on the *Brokenback*. A good scout. A worthy Marine. An example of the future of the Soul

Drinkers and a man who died in the service of his Emperor. How many men died such a death? How many died free, and for a reason?

Selepus rolled away and tried to disappear again. It was almost successful. The Marine snapped off bolter fire at him and the shots strobed through the darkness, lighting up Selepus as he wriggled away.

By now the Marines knew they weren't fighting more slave-warriors, which meant that they would move to take down Selepus with everything they had. It also meant they would know he wasn't alone.

'Three closing in,' voxed Nisryus. 'Then the sergeant.'

Eumenes saw the Fists appear on the dark horizon a moment later, stalking towards the battle-brother who had so nearly died under Selepus's knife.

'Raek?'

'I can take one.'

'Not good enough.' Eumenes kept moving, skirting around the open ground. He knew now that if Selepus made it out then it would be a bonus. Eumenes wanted some of his men to survive to take up the power armour of a fully-fledged Soul Drinker, but even that was a goal he could ultimately fail as long as the mission was completed.

Eumenes saw his chance. A fissure curved around behind the Crimson Fists squad, and Eumenes finally saw what he had been looking for: the final member of the squad, the Fist with the flamer. If Selepus doubled back and fled, the flamer Marine would incinerate him as he tried to escape. Tactically sound Marine thinking straight out of the *Codex Astartes*. Eumenes followed the faint glint of cobalt blue power armour, pistol heavy and ready in his hand.

Bolter fire was streaking out from the other Marines, picking out a zone where Selepus would be pinned down and in cover. Head down, scrambling for safety, he was so much dead meat as far as the sergeant was concerned, a heretic begging to be spitted on a chainsword as he cowered. If the Fists had realised they were up against Astartes scouts then the sergeant would know exactly what he was facing, the exact make and thickness of the armour, the weapons and training of the enemy. Eumenes didn't have to look to know the sergeant would be rushing forward, chainsword raised, already knowing how it would feel as it ripped through armour plates and into Selepus's chest.

Eumenes kept going. The flamer Marine, the unnaturally tall figure silhouetted black-on-grey in the dirty half-light, hadn't seen him.

Now. Now or never.

Eumenes took aim and fired. His bolt pistol barked and the shell smacked into the Marine's shoulder guard, spinning him round enough to tell him where the shot came from but not enough to knock him off his feet.

'For Dorn!' the Fist yelled, and to Eumenes the gout of flame seemed to ripple towards him in slow motion, flowing over the torn ground, reaching for him like something hungry and alive.

Eumenes threw himself to the ground and rolled, flames licking over him, grabbing at his armour, sending searing red tongues over the skin of one cheek and hand. He had hit the ground hard but he kept firing, a spray of shots smacking up into chunks of broken masonry or whistling wide.

The Fist knew his target was dead. He must have seen Eumenes's body picked out by the glare of the flame. He knew that Eumenes was just a scout, outgunned and outnumbered, one of the hated Soul Drinkers ready to die a screaming mess of charred flesh and bones.

'Now,' gasped Eumenes into the vox.

Raek's bullet thunked into the Marine's throat with a horrible wet sound. The Crimson Fist was knocked backward onto his knees, the momentary shock keeping his hand from squeezing the flamer's trigger lever.

Illuminated by the glare of the flames pooling on the ground, the Crimson Fist had been, almost literally, an impossible target for Raek to miss.

Now, there were just a few seconds left.

Eumenes scrambled through the fire, ignoring the pain searing through his hands as he dragged himself through the burning fuel. The Fist hadn't gone down yet. Eumenes threw himself onto the Marine, knocking the flamer away and pushing the Fist onto his back in the dust.

It was a neat wound, right through the flexible throat armour and through the windpipe. Even a Marine had to breathe, and this one would be dead in a couple of minutes. The blood was already clotting in hard red jewels around the wound but it was too late. Only a fellow Marine knew how to kill another Marine, and in Raek's case the target had been the tiny sliver of weakness between the faceplate of the helmet and the collar of the chestplate.

But killing wasn't enough.

'He's down,' voxed Eumenes. 'But he's not dead. We might get something out of him before he dies. We need to get him back to the palace, now. Use the entrance under the senate-house, take the sewers three kilometres north. Make this loyalist vermin suffer for Lord Sarpedon.'

The Crimson Fists knew their battle-brother was down. Fire was snapping towards Eumenes now. Eumenes rolled off the dying Marine, trying to gauge if there was a safe path back towards the edge of the dust pall and into the ruins where he could disappear. It didn't look like it.

He looked back at the Fist. He was still breathing in long, terrible gurgling breaths.

'For Dorn, brother?' said Eumenes quietly as bolter shells thudded into the ground beside him. 'Dorn was never a slave. Dorn never served tyrants and butchers. Nor do we. When you die, brother, you will not be at the Emperor's side. You will be burning in a coward's hell, watching Dorn lead us. We might be excommunicate, but the Emperor turned his back on you a long time ago, and come the end you will know it.'

The Marine took his last breath. It was enough that he had heard. It confirmed what Eumenes had realised when he had talked with Luko at the palace, he hated them. He hated them for what they represented, and for what they could be if they only saw what he saw. Wasted lives disguised as heroic sacrifices. Slaughter and butchery disguised as triumph. If the Emperor could, Eumenes knew, He would step down from his throne and crush the Imperium Himself, winning it back from the tyrants in a second Great Crusade.

Eumenes would have been happy to die then. He had killed two Space Marines, how many men could say that? But he knew he would be more use alive.

The Fists were firing almost blind, the remnants of the flamer's burning fuel their only target. But they were closing fast and soon and once they saw him Eumenes was dead. He scrambled half-crouched through the shadows, knowing that any second a bolter shell could blow his thigh open and leave him writhing in pain, shatter his spine and paralyse him for those last few seconds, blow out the back of his head and kill him before he hit the ground...

He jumped the melted stump of a wall, ducked past charred support beams sticking like burned ribs from the ground. Bullets whistled and cracked around him.

'Traitor! There,' the sergeant was yelling. 'You can't run from Dorn. You can't run from your blood.'

Eumenes hit the ground. He could feel the Crimson Fists close behind him, searching for their target. He could feel the paths of their bolter shells before they fired them, spearing through him and bursting in the ground beneath, blowing him into bloody chunks. He knew how it would feel, the red wash of pain followed by nothingness.

White-hot light erupted in a great flaming sheet behind him, the heat throwing him down again into the dirt. A wall of fire sheared up from the ground, carving crazy swirling patterns in the dust, edging every-thing in sudden unearthly white light.

It was the artillery. It was the biggest gun the scouts had.

Eumenes saw Scamander standing bolt upright, hands held out, the fire rippling out of him, licking out of his eyes, tapering from his fin-gertips. Eumenes jumped to his feet and ran headlong, not caring any more who saw him. He vaulted the last few knee-high melted ruins and barged into Scamander, throwing him to the ground.

Scamander was ice-cold. Eumenes couldn't imagine he was still alive.

Nisryus and Raek ran up to Eumenes. The wall of flame was still burning but it was flickering, without Scamander it would be gone in a few moments. Tydeus, crouched just behind them, loosed off two shots from his grenade launcher to add to the confusion.

'Just go,' gasped Eumenes, throwing Scamander's freezing body over his shoulder. He got his head down and ran, letting the dust and shad-ows envelop him.

One scout left behind. One probably dead. But the mission, Emperor willing, was done.

Eumenes wasn't worried about the craft of warfare any more, about the teachings of Daenyathos or the unique freedom of the Soul Drinkers. With the bullets of the Crimson Fists still streaking wildly through the darkness, he kept his head down and ran.

'AGAIN,' SAID REINEZ. Seated in the back of his Razorback, Reinez fairly itched with the desire to get back into the city and hunt down the Soul Drinkers. Now they had found him, killed one of his Marines, and escaped. The Fists had killed one of the scouts in return, but tit-for-tat killings weren't enough.

The Techmarine ran back the vox-recording, operating a mem-slate fixed to the back of his gauntlet. Sergeant Iago's squad had lost the sur-viving traitors but he had at least had the prescience to keep the recording of Brother Tehuaca's last communication.

'I can clean it up,' said the Techmarine. 'Lose some of the static.'

'Isolate the voice,' said Reinez. 'I have to be sure.'

The Techmarine made a few adjustments and played the recording again.

'...back to the palace, now. Use the entrance under the senate-house, take the sewers three kilometres north. Make this loyalist vermin suf-fer...'

The voice was young. A novice. Emperor's soul, that meant they were recruiting again.

'Again.'

'...to the palace. Use the entrance under the senate-house...'

'That's enough.' Reinez sat back. 'Send Chaplain Inhuaca in here.'

'Yes, commander.' The Techmarine, the servo-arm on his backpack scraping the ceiling of the Razorback, ducked back outside. The Razorback was Reinez's makeshift command vehicle, parked in the centre of the Fists' position in the great Deathstrike crater. The Fists had been effectively stuck there after blunting the tide of subhumans who poured up out of the ground. With the Imperial Guard shattered and the enemy with the free run of the city, Reinez could not just drive his Marines around the city without a target.

Now he had one.

'Commander? What news?' Inhuaca's skull-mask looked into the Razorback.

'We've found them. A palace underground. It's where Sarpedon has been hiding. It's where my standard is. We can reach it through what's left of the senate-house.'

'This is unexpected. What plan of action do you suggest?'

'Forget the Guard,' said Reinez. 'Load the tanks up, drive there at top speed and throw every fragging thing we've got at them. Any objections?'

'None, commander.'

'Good. Tell the men that Dorn and the Emperor have given them their battle at last.'

SOMEWHERE IN THE bitter, bloodstained industrial mills of eastern Gravenhold, Consul Kelchenko died.

It had only been a matter of time. The massed batteries of the 4th Carvelnan Royal Artillery could shatter city blocks from miles away but they could not defend themselves from the hit-and-run tactics of the xenos raiders, especially when the attacks were interspersed with waves of blood-mad slave warriors.

The artillery had ceased to exist as a cohesive formation about fifteen minutes after the first slave-warrior incursions. The xenos who had duelled with the Seleucaian patrols early in the battle now broke cover and cut the artillery line to pieces. Some of them were half-naked acrobat-warriors who seemed to dance rather than fight, flipping through the rubble and taking heads with a flourish. They ran alongside horrible creatures, like skinless attack dogs, that slunk through the shadows and wolfed men down whole.

There were torturers who stalked artillery crews, using retinues of deformed and animalistic eldar to drag men back to their masters. The few men who had any idea what was happening said the torturers had a lab or a temple somewhere, and were using the battle as cover for some kind of sacrificial experiment. The screams certainly carried far enough to suggest the story was true.

A hovering creature slipped out of the shadow of the mills and did for three Basilisk crews, killing them in a few minutes of panic and pain. It appeared mechanical from a distance but up close the bundles of red wet muscles were obvious between its armour plates, as its underside yawned open and its shear-tipped limbs dragged screaming men inside. No one paused long enough to speculate on what it could be, and the few that saw it and lived thought it was just another xenos experiment in the infliction of suffering.

By then the 4th Carvelnan Royal Artillery was no longer a part of the Imperial forces in Gravenhold. Its co-ordinated barrages were impossible now, with one tank crew too desperate for their own survival to talk to another. The functioning tanks still sent single shots arcing over the tormented city, hoping that the mostly random fire would at least help the Imperial Guard who still had a chance for survival. The Carvelnan Artillery had never been a unit of great prestige or with any notable history to speak of, but there were many stories of immense bravery written in the shadow of Gravenhold's mills. There were crews who fought off slave-warriors with laspistols and bare hands as they chambered one more Earthshaker round. Some men volunteered as runners to find help, or just orders, from command posts that no longer existed.

There were, of course, plenty who ran, or went crazy. Some tried to drive their tanks back through the mills, through the arches under the eastern wall and back into the safety of the spaceport. But the spaceport was overlooked by the wall itself which was now home to roosts of eldar warriors. These eldar had strange winged jump packs that let them flit from one battlement to the next, so they could get the best shots with heavy weapons that fired bolts of blackness. The armour of Basilisk self-propelled guns and Manticore missile launchers did little against the xenos weaponry and soon the way to the spaceport was blocked with burned-out artillery pieces. Men drowned in pools of burning promethium. Artillery shells cooked off in the heat and turned the eastern mills into mazes of toxic smoke and guttering flame.

A few Basilisks were dug in and turned into impromptu pillboxes, and a dozen isolated last stands were enacted. Many crews let the slave-warriors overrun their vehicles before blowing them up, sending hundreds of the enemy and dozens of friends to the judgement of the Emperor. In some places the small contingents of infantry actually mounted a meaningful defence, driving waves of attackers into kill-zones where the artillery could blast the enemy into a thin crimson mist with short-ranged shellbursts. One such defence took place in one of the towering agri-mills, amongst the grain silos and conveyor belts where the labour servitors still went through the motions of their daily work ignorant of the carnage around them. This was the site of the Carvelnan Royal Artillery's last reason for existing – the second Deathstrike launcher, this one armed with a multiple warhead with scores of cluster bombs designed to reduce whole infantry divisions to body-strewn wastelands.

No one was sure where Consul Kelchenko was. The last anyone had heard he was in his command Salamander tank, driving along the line checking the efficiency and morale of the gun crews. Wherever he was, he managed to get a vox-message to the Deathstrike crew. It lasted just a few seconds, and not everyone was sure it was really him, but he recited the launch codes, and that was enough.

Perhaps it was another officer, faking the codes and determined to send one last reminder of Imperial spite into the heart of the enemy. Perhaps it was some alien or cultist imitating Kelchenko, or Kelchenko himself controlled by xenos sorcery. More likely it really was Kelchenko, knowing that his life was measured in minutes and wanting to leave some meaningful legacy on the surface of Entymion IV.

In truth, no one cared. The officer in the Deathstrike launcher gave the order and the missile was launched, carving a violent crescent of fire across the boiling dark clouds. The target area was the villas in the north of the city, presumably where the xenos were waiting to stream southwards and claim the whole of Gravenhold for themselves. The Deathstrike broke up above the north of the city, the individual warheads falling in a brilliant curtain of light.

It was the last valiant display of the doomed 4th Carvelnan Royal Artillery, a final act of destructive beauty in the face of crushing defeat. The warheads plummeted into the villas of Gravenhold's elite, smashing through the roofs of estates and miniature palaces already warped by the magic of the warp portal. A few detonated around the column of black magic still pouring up into the sky – some shot into the column itself and became white streaks of fire, spitting up into space. Clusters of explosive blossomed into huge blooms of flame, sending tidal waves of fire through the streets.

A few wayward slave-warriors were incinerated. The daemons had mostly moved southwards to the killing fields of the slums and administrative district, and only a few discorporated in the inferno.

Eldar casualties were nil. A few of them felt the impacts, far below in the upper reaches of Karhedros's palace. None of them was nervous enough to think it was important.

After this final gesture of defiance from his artillery, Colonel Kelchenko was caught somewhere in the labyrinth of industrial mills, his Salamander crippled by xenos energy weapons. He fled the wreckage, firing wildly with his laspistol sidearm while the lightning-quick gladiatorial warriors of the eldar rushed at him from every side. He screamed obscenities at them, but cowardice took over when the first blade cut him. By the time they had surrounded him he was on his knees, crying and pleading, promising he would give up his Emperor, betray his men, serve them for a lifetime and more if they would just let him live.

But the blades didn't stop, and after twenty minutes there was finally too little of him to survive. The last few artillery pieces lasted a bit longer than Consul Kelchenko, but as the night over Gravenhold became a solid black mantle in the sky the big guns were silent and the east of the city had completely fallen to the enemy.

THE STREETS OF the slaughterhouse district ran with blood at the best of times. But now the channels cut into the rough stone streets overflowed with blood, not from slaughtered livestock, but from the men of the Fornux Lix Fire Drakes. Some time in the last few hours the south-eastern gate had finally fallen and the Fire Drakes had been forced further into the city. They had pushed a vanguard as far as the slaughterhouse district, but they in turn had been cut off and slaughtered in the streets. The rest of the Fire Drakes were still in the administrative district, probably holding the high-rise office buildings as they fell floor by floor to a mix of xenos and slave-soldiers. Maybe daemons, too.

Sarpedon looked over the scene. Fire Drakes were lying draped over ruined walls or simply face-down in the streets. Bodies were piled behind cover where units had made final stands, but mostly they were spread out and scattered. It had been a short, brutal, one-sided fight. The looming warehouses of the slaughterhouse district enclosed stockyards that backed onto the River Graven, and normally offal and slurry from the day's slaughtering would have been dumped into the river. Now the river was in much the same state, but the foulness was human instead of animal.

Sarpedon led the Soul Drinkers out of the burned-out accounting house. It was through the charred cellars of the accounting house that the undercity connected to the surface – it was the closest the Soul

Drinkers could get to Tellos's last position. The rest would have to be over the surface. Almost all the Soul Drinkers in Gravenhold had managed to meet up with Sarpedon's force for the final assault on Tellos's Marines. Luko and Varuk had slogged their way through the undercity, Salk and Tyrendian had made it from the eastern wall. Eumenes's scouts were still in the city fulfilling their own mission, and Chaplain Iktinos was still on the north shore of the Graven where Sarpedon suspected he would be most useful – other than that, all of the surviving Marines in Gravenhold moved out into the slaughterhouse district, bolters raised or chainblades held at guard, ready for anything that Gravenhold might throw at them.

'Bolter fire,' said Luko quietly as he led his squad just behind Sarpedon. 'And chainblades.'

Sarpedon didn't answer. As a psyker he was receptive to extremes of psychic activity and Gravenhold was throbbing dully with it, an ache that had been building up since the column of black magic first ripped up into the sky. Reality was breaking down and it was taking Gravenhold with it. It was subtle at the moment but it would get worse. The colour of the sky, the faint whispers Sarpedon thought he could feel just out of earshot, the heavy, electric feel to the air. And every now and then he sensed a spike in activity, a flurry of something coming through from the other side. Karhedros had opened a window into the warp, of that Sarpedon was sure. And the inhabitants of the warp were coming through.

Daemons. Maybe worse. He had to get the job done and get his Marines out as soon as possible. The Soul Drinkers were badly battered and even they couldn't survive for long if the city was flooded by the footsoldiers of the Chaos Gods.

She-Who-Thirsts. Just another name for one of the Dark Gods, worshipped by aliens too corrupt to see they were damned.

'This is fresh,' Luko was saying, kneeling to examine one of the dead Guardsmen. 'Not more than twenty minutes gone.'

'The target is up ahead,' came a vox from Sergeant Salk. 'One of the warehouses. Looks like the fight started here, there are dead everywhere.'

'Good,' replied Sarpedon. 'All units, converge on Salk's position. Stay alert. We all know who these Guardsmen ran into.'

Sarpedon rounded a corner carefully, bolter drawn. A burned-out Chimera stood just past the cover and Sarpedon's eight legs took him quickly up on top of it. He could see the warehouse in question, with the Soul Drinkers moving quickly and efficiently to surround it. Sarpedon saw Sergeant Kelvor keeping pace in spite of the rudimentary prosthesis Pallas had rigged to replace his severed leg.

He had asked so much of his Marines. They had never let him down.
He hoped he would not let them down by throwing their lives away on
this dying world.

Sarpedon hurried down the street into the shadow of the warehouse.
The bodies were strewn about here in a horrendous mess of severed
limbs and loosed organs. The Fire Drakes had probably seen the warehouse as useful cover until they walked into a lattice of bolt pistol fire
followed by a chainsword charge more murderous than anything they
could have imagined. The doors of the warehouse were scored by a few
las-blasts but not many – the Fire Drakes, decent troops that they were,
had been shredded before they had been able to put up a fight.

'Do it,' voxed Sarpedon.

Sergeant Graveus hefted his power axe and smashed the doors aside
with a single swing. His squad and the few surviving Marines of Squad
Kelvor were in first, followed by Luko and Dyon. Sarpedon's augmented eyes adjusted automatically to the dark as he followed Luko in,
several squads of Soul Drinkers charging beside him, all prepared to
meet the counter-charge of Tellos and his renegade Marines.

The warehouse contained a forest of rotting meat, hung from rows of
meat hooks that ran the length of the single cavernous room. The
stench was horrible and Sarpedon's many respiratory filters kicked in.
The rows of meat slabs were strung in several layers, all the way up to
the high ceiling of the warehouse, all of it long spoiled and foul.

Sarpedon moved forward, moving a side of meat away from him
with one of his forelegs. It spilled writhing maggots onto the dirt floor
as he passed.

No wonder Tellos had chosen to hide here. He had wanted to surround himself with death.

'Clear here,' voxed Graveus.

'Here too,' said Sergeant Dyon on the far side of the room.

'Clear,' said Luko, moving carefully between the slabs of meat beside
Sarpedon. 'But they were here.'

Up ahead the slabs of meat had been cut down with chainswords
and were lying in a trampled, maggoty layer on the floor. This was
where Tellos had hidden out, making murderous forays out into
Gravenhold, returning to kneel in prayer to the Blood God.

The Soul Drinkers reached the far end of the warehouse. The far wall
had been torn through, leaving the warehouse open to the courtyard
beyond which backed onto the River Graven itself.

'They came through here,' said Luko. 'Just a few minutes ago.'

'They didn't know we were coming,' said Sarpedon.

'How can we be sure?'

'Because Tellos would have come out to face me. No, they're heading for that.' Sarpedon pointed towards the twisting column of purple-black energy, fat with the power of the warp. Lightning was streaking down it, and all around blood was falling in a rain of crimson tears to mark the death of Gravenhold. 'Tellos has earned his way to the warp. That's where he's headed. That's what Karhedros promised him. Which means he has to get across the river.' Sarpedon turned to Luko. 'How is the vox?'

'It's getting worse. It's fine short-range but I don't think it'll reach much further.'

'Then try. Someone has to let Iktinos know they're coming.'

CHAPTER SIXTEEN

THE FIRST IMPERIAL forces into the north of Gravenhold were the Crimson Fists, crossing somewhere beneath the river in the tunnels and sewers that ran under the city. The Soul Drinker scout would pay for his poor discipline, just like all the Soul Drinkers would. Already some of the traitors's xenos allies had been spotted, creatures with shadow-black skin that could not hide from the eyes and bolters of the Crimson Fists.

Reinez was at the head of the Crimson Fists alongside Chaplain Inhuaca. The battle-brothers were quiet and tense, bolting down their anger with the discipline of a Space Marine. Reinez knew the feeling – their thoughts were turned towards revenge. In most soldiers, that would make them lax and jittery, their anger taking the edge off their skill in battle. But Space Marines were different. When the hatred grew, they fought better. When the pressure was on, they rose to meet it. It was why the Space Marines were the best soldiers in the galaxy, and why the Crimson Fists were amongst the foremost of the Adeptus Astartes. They had a lot to hate.

They had lost Captain Arca and Brother-Librarian Haxualpha, along with enough battle-brothers for the Second Company to bear the scars for a long time to come. They had lost the standard, sacred to the Chapter and to Rogal Dorn himself. They had been beaten and humiliated by traitors. They had taken out their anger on the Gravenholders and slave-warriors, and on the few aliens they had fought. But it wasn't enough to wipe away the shame. Only the death of the Soul Drinkers would do that.

And so the battle-brothers were silent as they advanced through the grim dark undercity, their hatred bubbling just under, waiting to be unleashed when the enemy dared to stand before them.

They hadn't been able to get any of the armour down the pit inside the ruin of the senate-house. The Razorbacks, Rhinos and Predators were back on the surface. But the Crimson Fists had Devastator squads whose firepower had been stymied in the close quarters of the chamber mercantile, firepower that Reinez was determined to see make a difference now. The Soul Drinkers weren't at full strength – they were scattered around the city, as battered as the Crimson Fists and thinking they were safe in their lair. The Fists were a rock-hard sledgehammer of disciplined, hate-filled men who would die rather than give up.

'We are close,' said Chaplain Inhuaca. He had come to the same conclusion as Reinez, the tunnels led towards the column of power in the north of the city. Sarpedon was working some foul sorcery and even Reinez, who had no psychic ability, could feel the power in the air. It was sorcery that required great preparation and concentration, which meant that Sarpedon would be preoccupied and vulnerable. It would be his last mistake.

'Get the Devastators to the front,' said Reinez. 'Follow up with the assault units. Inhuaca, lead the charge.'

'It is an honour, commander. I take it you wish to face Sarpedon yourself?'

'If we have the choice,' replied Reinez. 'Otherwise, feel free to kill him. Just try to keep his head. I would hand it to Chapter Master Kantor myself.'

'Then if we have an agreement, I would face their Chaplain. The one who killed Arca.'

'Feel welcome to him.'

The tunnel opened up ahead. Darkness yawned. Reinez's vision cut through the gloom and picked out a high cavernous ceiling, a sky of stone. He glimpsed battlements, polished stone glinting in the half-light.

'For Dorn, brothers,' said Reinez to the Devastator units as they moved up ahead, their heavy weapons shouldered, ready to lay down the hail of fire that had been denied in the confines of the city.

'We've got targets,' voxed Brother Kroya, who had taken over Caltax's Devastator squad.

'Sergeants, take positions,' voxed Reinez. The sergeants of the second company sounded off, taking their positions in the wide tunnel – the big guns at the front, Inhuaca and the Assault Squads, then the Tactical Marines who would cover the assault with massed bolter fire.

'Good. Kroya, engage. Crimson Fists, for Dorn and your Emperor, flood this city in heretic blood.'

CAPTAIN CAISLENN-HAR rumbled and wheezed as his servo-assisted body waddled through the tight, dark corridors of the ship's astropathic suite. Nestled in the heart of the ship and heavily shielded against all psychic interference, the astropath quarters were avoided by most of the Emperor-fearing crew. Astropaths, though sanctioned by the Imperium and essential to its functioning, were still psykers and most of the crew did everything they could to stay away from them.

Caislenn-Har found the idea of being here at all to be distasteful. There was more than enough psychic madness happening on the planet below. But needs must, he thought, as he lumbered past the many devotional seals and inscribed prayers with which the ship's astropath had warded his quarters.

'Captain. It is a pleasure.' Astropath Torquen's voice was ice-cold and drained of emotion. It clearly wasn't a pleasure at all. Caislenn-Har imagined that nothing pleased Torquen very much.

The captain squeezed his bulk through the doorway and entered the astropath's inner sanctum. Torquen sat at a lectern that filled most of the tiny room, a spider-like servitor clinging to the chest of his robes and turning the pages of a massive prayer-book. Torquen's face was little more than a skin-covered skull with a lipless reptilian mouth and twin vertical slits instead of a nose. A strip of dark red material was tied around his eyes. Astropaths were almost all blind, a result, it was said, of the ritual on Terra itself where they were converted from powerful but uncontrolled psykers into powerful telepathic ducts. From the walls of the cell led cables and wires that plugged into Torquen's scalp like the strings of a puppet, monitoring his brainwaves. Torquen was the ship's main instrument of communication, because only telepathic messages could reach across the immense interstellar gulf.

'Torquen,' said Caislenn-Har. He was still wheezing, his body wasn't suited to walking around the ship. 'No doubt you are aware of our situation.'

'Is it as bad as it sounds?' The servitor turned another page and Torquen's fingers slid automatically over the writing. The writing was not raised; Torquen could feel the ink on the paper, reading the devotional texts as he had been trained to do, keeping his mind pure.

'Probably. All contact with the planet has been lost. We can't even see the city any more.'

'And then there is the… disturbance.' Torquen waved a hand idly, indicating the ribbon of black sorcery rippling through space, too close for comfort. 'I can feel it, though I do not know what to make of it.'

'Nor do we. Which is why I am here.'

'I wondered why you would visit me yourself. You do not trust this message to the ship's comms.'

'No.'

'Very well. Who is the target?'

Caislenn-Har shrugged. 'The nearest world with a sizeable population. Somewhere relatively important.'

'That is unusual. There is normally at least some particular individual or organisation to be contacted.'

'I doesn't matter who it's sent to. They'll hear it whoever receives it.'

Torquen paused. 'I see. And the contents?'

'I suppose I had better make this sound formal,' said Caislenn-Har. 'Please begin, "For the Attention of the Orders of the Emperor's Holy Inquisition…"'

'WE HAVE RECEIVED no orders to relinquish this position,' said Chaplain Iktinos. 'Therefore there will be no retreat. Is this understood?'

The Marines kneeling around Iktinos did not need to answer.

They were on the ground floor of the Carnax Bridge's northern gatehouse, surrounded by the magnificent finery of Gravenhold's elite. The ballroom that made up the lower floor was used to receive dignitaries who came through the city from the south-east gate and it was designed to impress. Immense chandeliers seemed too fat and heavy to hang from the ceiling, tapestries hung on the walls depicting Gravenholder nobility hunting through the forests around the city. Everything was gold and imported hardwood, a symbol of the decadence and decay eating away at the heart of the Imperium.

'Good.' Iktinos glanced up from the kneeling Marines, looking through the grand windows that looked down the elegant iron span of the Carnax Bridge. There were Soul Drinkers on the bridge, and Iktinos could see with one look that they weren't on his side. Their armour was filthy and dented, their helmets gone and their faces wild-eyed. Most of them carried chainswords thick with clotted blood.

'Take your positions. Make a firing line. Steel your souls.' Iktinos drew his sacred crozius arcanum as the Marines he led formed a line of bolters at the windows. The crozius was a Chaplain's badge of office and a weapon in its own right, surrounded by a crackling power field that would shear through armour.

Iktinos was a Chaplain, a guardian of the Chapter's collective soul. He was just beginning to understand the place of the Soul Drinkers in the Emperor's plan, a grand design for Mankind that needed the Soul Drinkers to be free of the Imperium before they could play their part. Iktinos would lead them in that plan, but first he had to survive.

'...aplain... in your direction, be ready to...' Sarpedon's voice crackled over the vox, distorted by howling static.

Iktinos switched it off. This was his fight, these were his Marines. They would die for him, they would die for the Emperor's plan.

'In range,' said Brother Kekrops, squinting down the length of his boltgun.

'Hold.'

'Counting... thirty-two.'

'Then they outnumber us. Good. Where will your soul be thrice-forged like steel?'

'In battle,' replied Kekrops levelly. 'Where the fires are the cold flames of hell.'

'When will our work be done?'

'Not until the end of time,' said Brother Octetes, who knelt in the firing line with his meltagun ready to fire. 'Not until the Emperor is with us again and all the worlds are one.'

'How will the enemy be known?'

'By their works,' replied Brother Apollonius, who was crouched behind the firing line with his chainsword drawn. 'For when the End Times come, they shall line up against the Emperor and beg us for death.'

'Good. Open fire.'

The windows of the ballroom shattered and the Carnax Bridge was a rushing river of hot shrapnel, sheeting into the renegade Marines. Bolter shells spanged around the supports of the bridge, criss-crossing the killing zone with lethal ricochets.

But it wasn't enough. The enemy were Soul Drinkers, driven mad by horrors most could only guess at. It took more than bolter fire, more than discipline.

Iktinos saw Tellos throwing one of his own Marines aside, trampling another underfoot to close with Iktinos's Marines. Bolter shells passed through Tellos's pallid, gelatinous flesh, punching through his horribly exaggerated muscles without slowing him down. His hands were rusted, gore-crusted chainblades, his face an unrecognisable mask of scars and hatred.

This was the reckoning. Two groups of Soul Drinkers, both forged on Stratix Luminae. One, Iktinos's men, had been enlightened, realising a bond that would take them to the ends of the galaxy doing the Emperor's will. The others, under Tellos, had been lost and damned, drowned in violence until their wills were not their own.

Two men. One enlightened, one insane. It was good that it had come to this, thought Iktinos. This battle would have been fought out eventually anyway.

Tellos dived into the firing line first, his fellow renegades on his heels.

Brother Octetes got one blast off from his meltagun, vaporising the arm of a renegade before Tellos was on him. The chainswords went through Octetes's torso as if Octetes's armour wasn't there, spearing out through his back. Tellos did little more than shrug and Octetes was sheared in two, gore showering everywhere, Tellos revelling in the gout of blood. He flung the two halves of Octetes aside and strode further, swiping off Brother Thieln's arm even as Thieln pumped a volley of bolter shells into him.

The other renegades were into the ballroom and it was a murderous close-quarters melee where neither side was willing to die easily. Iktinos felt almost detached from his body as he raised his crozius and charged in. It was as if he was not himself any more but a part of a greater plan. He was a messenger, a symbol, a pawn of the Emperor himself.

The eagle-headed crozius crashed into the torso of a renegade, crunching through armour and the Marine's inner chestplate of fused ribs. A bolt pistol shot thunked into Iktinos's shoulder pad but the impact barely registered with him. He could feel forces controlling him. He could feel the words of Daenyathos welling up from his memory, the patterns of the *Catechisms Martial* fitting the movements of his limbs that sent the crozius shattering the skull of the renegade at his feet and hacking down through the arm of another.

This was the way it would be in the End Times. Brother against brother, and yet no hatred. Just a total sense of purpose, a conviction that Iktinos was playing a part in a grand drama that would always end in victory, had ended, was ending, always.

Brother Apollonius was duelling with Tellos, giving ground as Tellos's chainblades lashed against his own sword time and time again. Sparks were flying. Iktinos watched them dispassionately, noting the bestial strength that forced Tellos's blade through Apollonius's chainsword, the metal teeth that flew from the shattered blade like shrapnel, the way Tellos simply stamped down on Apollonius's leg and the ugly angle of his leg as it snapped.

Tellos didn't bother to kill Apollonius. He just stepped over him, and turned to Iktinos.

Chaplain Iktinos knew that this fight was written already. It was the will of the Emperor that he bring his crozius down onto Tellos, carving down in a great glittering arc that would shear him lengthways in two with such ferocity that even Tellos's mutated flesh could not save him. Tellos's death had always been there, in the northern gatehouse of the Carnax Bridge, replaying over and over again for countless eternities, waiting for Iktinos to take the stage and place himself in the role of the Emperor's servant.

The crozius rose, sparks pouring from its power field. Iktinos put his whole weight behind the downstroke, feeling the strength of the Emperor himself sending the crozius down into Tellos's mutated body.

Tellos caught the crozius in the crook of his crossed chainblades. Iktinos's blow stopped jarringly, sparks cascading off the power field.

Suddenly Iktinos was back in his body, not watching the combat from afar but face-to-face with Tellos, feeling his arm forced back by Tellos's obscene strength, tasting the blood in the air, ears full of gunfire and screams and the whirring of the blades that were about to eviscerate him.

Tellos swung around, forced Iktinos's crozius arm down. He hooked an elbow over Iktinos's head, forcing it down as he brought his armoured knee up into Iktinos's faceplate with shuddering force.

Iktinos reeled back, his senses swimming. Solid red pain flooded his mind.

Tellos crossed his blades and this time closed them like pincers around Iktinos's arm. With a twist he lifted Iktinos clean into the air and threw him with such force that he smashed through what remained of the window frames and flew out onto the blood-slicked surface of the Carnax Bridge.

Iktinos's crozius arm was broken before he landed, the bones snapped in a dozen places by the force of Tellos's grip. But he could use his other hand just fine, take up the fallen crozius, leap back into the fray and deliver the Emperor's justice to the mutant and traitor who had dared kill his battle-brothers.

Tellos's boot stamped down on Iktinos's good hand, splitting the ceramite of his gauntlet. Red gunshots of pain were broken fingers.

Tellos looked down at the stricken Chaplain, his face silhouetted against the purple glow from the warp portal in the city behind him. Iktinos could just see the eyes, two red black-red pools slitted with hatred.

'You didn't think you were the one, did you?' said Tellos. 'The one to finish what Daenyathos started?'

Iktinos struggled. Tellos had him pinned down and he was unarmed. This traitor, this monster, had him at its mercy.

'How you cling to your faith,' continued Tellos. His voice was thick and dark as blood. 'And yet you say you are free. Did you think you would fight to the end of time, Iktinos? Did you think your acolytes here would be there at the Emperor's side? What do you think He wanted for Mankind? He wanted freedom. Only one of us here is free, and it's not you.'

Iktinos had a soul strong enough to go through hell and still let him counsel to the spirits of his battle-brother. But even so his blood ran cold. Tellos was not just a madman. He could see right through Iktinos, through the skull-wrought faceplate of his helmet and right into his soul.

'Tellos,' gasped Iktinos through the pain and shock. 'What did you become?'

Tellos smiled, actually smiled, the mutated flesh of his face opening up into a wide rictus like a shark. He raised his chainblades, poising one over Iktinos's throat and the other over his heart. 'Blood for the Blood God, Chaplain. That's all there is.'

'Tellos!' yelled a voice. Tellos looked up from his butchery at someone further down the bridge.

Iktinos twisted his head until he could see down the bridge. There, standing in the middle of Carnax Bridge, completely alone, was Sarpedon.

'XENOS FILTH!' BELLOWED Reinez. 'Die! For the Imperium and the divine right of Man! Die!'

The palace gardens were a battlefield. Eldar warriors streamed from the doors to be cut down or blown apart by missile launchers and heavy bolters. Crimson Fists fell to energy weapons on the battlements or horrible skinless beasts that coalesced from the shadows to drag them down with teeth and claws. Jetbikes banked at insane speeds, their riders lashing out with energy blades at Marines only to be snatched off their mounts by well-placed bolter shots.

Chaplain Inhuaca led the Assault Squads in a charge that had left a third of their number wounded or dead before smashing into the main body of eldar warriors. Chainblades carved through exotic armour and sheared through the barrels of crystalline rifles in a mass swirling melee against the gates of the palace. The eldar, cheating xenos though they were, could not stand up to Inhuaca's charge and were forced across the bridge leading to the palace's quicksilver moat. With their backs to the wall the eldar were dying in prodigious numbers as the rest of the Fists followed up, swapping fire with the eldar on the battlements, supporting Inhuaca's assault as they tried to crush the defenders and breach the gates themselves. The moat was choked with eldar bodies and some of the Assault Marines were walking across the bodies to get to grips with the enemy.

It was magnificent. It was beautiful. Those Fists who died would be remembered, and it was an honour that their last memories should be of a true honest battle against the foes of the Emperor.

No more lies, promised Reinez to himself as he ran head down behind the shattered walls and strange stone trees of the palace gardens, crystal shards slitting the air around him. No more betrayals. No more trickery. This was the Crimson Fists' time, a time full of nothing but battle. It was the way of the Adeptus Astartes, force would prevail where cunning did not.

The Space Marines of the Imperium did not misdirect their enemies or weave them into plots full of betrayal and deceit. They destroyed them, absolutely. It was the way of Rogal Dorn. It was the way of the Crimson Fists.

Reinez led the Tactical Squads forward towards the gates, bolter fire streaking up at the battlements, eldar scurrying for cover or tumbling off the wall to land crunchingly far below. Shadow-skinned eldar ducked out of the darkness to pick off Marines with fire from their crystalline pistols or impale them on wicked curved blades, only to be lit up by strobing gunfire and smashed aside by bolter impacts. More eldar, close combat specialists who wore next to no armour but moved with astonishing speed and grace, tried to join the warriors at the gate but Reinez bellowed the order to fire. Fifty bolters shredded the eldar, swatting them aside and spattering the obsidian walls of the palace with their blood.

Still moving, the Crimson Fists turned the palace gardens into a brutal crossfire. Eldar reinforcements lay dead, delicate bodies burst open by bolter fire. Jetbikes burned. Power armour turned aside crystal shards fired by eldar snipers from the palace windows, and the Marine's reply was heavy weapons fire. A plasma cannon blast filled the chamber beyond one firing slit with superheated plasma, exploding outwards in a plume of yellow fire.

Reinez led the Marines over the last few metres of palace gardens and joined Inhuaca at the gate. The Chaplain's crozius arcanum smoked as its power field burned away the blood that encrusted it. The eldar warriors were making a last stand behind one of the wall buttresses, swapping pistol fire with the Assault Marines.

'Squad Zavier! Squad Padros!' yelled Reinez. 'Flank those groxfraggers!'

Two Tactical squads ran onto the far side of the moat and, with the Assault Marines, caught the eldar in a savage crossfire. Eldar bodies were slammed against the wall by the force of the gunfire as the Assault Marines strode in to finish off the survivors. Assault-Captain Arca had been beloved of the Chapter, and the Assault Marines had revenge on their minds.

Sarpedon was hiding behind xenos, letting them die to keep the Fists away from him. A coward and a witch, a traitor and a disgrace to the blood of Dorn. All the eldar filth in the galaxy wouldn't save him now.

'Safest place in this damn city,' said Reinez to the Chaplain.

'Agreed. At last we know where our enemies are.'

'Ready?'

The Chaplain inclined his head. 'Always.'

'Devastators! Get this door down!'

The Devastators had been waiting for the order. A trio of krak anti-armour missiles streaked up into the door, reducing it to splinters of charred hardwood. The golden portcullis beyond barely lasted that long as Reinez smashed the bars aside with a swing of his thunder hammer.

Reinez and Inhuaca charged into a storm of crystal gunfire that filled the courtyard. Reinez's armour had been forged by the finest Chapter artificers to have survived Rynn's World and the crystal shattered against it. Some splinters forced their way into his flesh but he had suffered infinitely worse and he strode through the storm, the Crimson Fists following in his wake. The courtyard was bounded by walls on the battlements of which were the warriors who had fallen back from the outer walls, more of them died to bolter fire and missile blasts as the Crimson Fists made rapid work of the courtyard.

The inner doors opened and the eldar that charged out were heavily-armoured, wielding halberds with powered blades that sliced through the armour of the first Crimson Fists to face them. Reinez was in the front rank and caught a blade on the haft of his thunder hammer, feeling strength he had thought beyond the eldar forcing the blade closer to his face. He dropped back a step, pivoted on one heel and brought the hammer smashing up into the face of the eldar – he saw the eldar's facemask, featureless except for its shining green eyepieces, crumple as the hammer's head shattered the side of its helmet and he threw the eldar aside.

Xenos elites. He had fought their kind before, Aspect Warriors who embodied one particular facet of the eldar way of war. These were different, stronger and more heavily armoured. Reinez swept out again, found his thunder hammer parried and a volley of laser stings slicing into his chest armour from a helmet-mounted projector. A white flash of pain stabbed into the wound but Reinez choked it back, kicking out and smashing the knee of the warrior who had stung him. He brought his hammer up and smacked the pommel of the handle into the eldar's forehead, knocking it to the ground. He swung the hammer again at the eldar's head, presented to him like a target in the Chapter training rooms. The eldar was decapitated neatly, another's arm being broken by the hammer's upswing.

There weren't enough of them. They were up against the whole Second Company of the Crimson Fists, and the eldar were forced back into the palace itself.

'Take them!' shouted Reinez to Chaplain Inhuaca and led the way past the battling eldar into the palace. The eldar could evidently see well in the dark but a Space Marine's augmentations lent him even keener sight, cutting through the gloom.

He wasn't here to kill all the xenos. That could wait. He was after Sarpedon.

The palace was a maze. The dynasty that had built it had evidently been unbalanced because dead ends and insane proportions were everywhere, staircases that soared into nowhere and corridors that ended in sheer dark pits.

Reinez led half of the Marines down into the palace, leaving the rest with Inhuaca to keep the eldar from pursuing them. His instincts took him downwards, down tight twisting stairways and through ambushes of eldar warriors. The eldar had not been expecting them and the defence was piecemeal and desultory, gaggles of them ready to die under Reinez's hammer and the bolters of his battle-brothers. The momentum never let up, Reinez knowing that Sarpedon's best chance lay in sending enough troops out to swamp the Crimson Fists while the eldar and Soul Drinkers organised a proper defence.

Down, further. Deformed eldar torturers led packs of fleshy, mutated creatures that shambled forwards through the gunfire, and the Marines had to take them apart with bolter stocks and combat knives. Brother Arroyox was lost, dragged down by the eldar's creations. Reinez shattered the torturer's torso with his hammer and led the way on, saying a silent prayer for Arroyox's soul.

The palace dimensions grew greater, as if a race of giants had built it. Soaring vaults of obsidian. Sweating greenstone walls that reeked of brine, galleries of faceless statues. The eldar were few down here, and Reinez knew they weren't just hiding, even he could feel the air of reverence in the lower levels. He was on sacred ground where few eldar were permitted, and so few had been down there to face the Crimson Fists when they attacked.

He passed the cells of the torturers, where the remains of Guardsmen and Gravenholders lay dissected on tables of bloodstained onyx. Skins were pinned up on the walls. One chamber held two bodies, evidently Guardsmen stripped naked and chained to the floor. It looked like they had been pumped full of combat stimulants and forced to fight one another with bare hands, dying horribly for the entertainment of whoever led the xenos.

Reinez knew that Sarpedon had fallen far. He was only just now understanding exactly how far. He was a heretic mutant who delighted in cruelty, one who had become like the decadent alien in the depths of his debauchery. The annals of the Crimson Fists would record with pride the purification of Dorn's blood that would be achieved when Reinez killed him.

The corridors and anterooms opened up into an immense vaulted reception chamber. A pair of vast studded doors dominated one wall, where the palace opened up into a lower cavern. A second pair of doors, smaller and of veined green stone, were set into the opposite wall. Though not a psyker, Reinez could still feel the power behind them, the aching swell of dark magic billowing up from the depths of some dark soul.

'There,' he said. 'Meltagun.'

Brother Olcama ran forward with his meltagun as the rest of the squad took their places by the doors, ready to sweep into the room and pump bolter fire into whatever they saw. Reinez was ready to charge past them, knowing that only a witch, a debased psyker like Sarpedon, could be beyond there.

Olcama opened fire. White-hot gobs of molten stone spattered as the meltagun's beam bored through the stone. The walls creaked. The door shuddered as the heat forced its molecules apart and then, with a sound like a caged thunderclap it burst open.

Shards of razor-sharp stone span everywhere. Reinez was prepared for that. He was not prepared for the hurricane of magical energies that ripped out, suddenly uncontained. Brother Olcama was picked up and thrown into the huge far doors, plunging through them even as the shockwave ripped them off their hinges and cast them into the vast dark cavern beyond. The Crimson Fists were lifted off their feet and thrown backwards by swirling tendrils of purple-black magic. Their fingers scrabbled for purchase on the smooth stone floor. Reinez was picked up and thrown, raging his frustration. He hefted his thunder hammer and brought it down into the floor, gouging the head deep into the stone. It drew a deep molten furrow as he was flung back but the hammer braked him and he held on, feet dangling as if hanging, staring into the maelstrom of sorcery beyond the door.

There was something in there. Someone. Kneeling as if in prayer in the eye of the storm, surrounded by the energies of the warp portal.

Reinez dug his feet into the floor and hauled himself towards the door, using the hammer to lever himself along. He couldn't see if any other Fists were with him. He couldn't worry about that now. He was the only one who could do it, they had all known that.

Another step. Another metre. It was pure hate keeping him going. Everything he had ever learned, every prayer of rage, every moment of battle, it all fuelled the hate.

He reached the threshold and pushed himself through the door. The paint was flaking off the ceramite of his armour, the clenched fist symbol on his shoulder pad peeling away. It felt like the skin of his face was going with it. With a final effort, he pushed himself through the storm of magic and into the eye of the cyclone.

The figure looked around. It was a tall eldar, with a drawn, pallid, ageless face, pure black pupils. It was bald and its scalp was covered in intricate black tattoos. Its elegant purple armour was hinged like the carapace of an insect, drawn into blade-sharp curves and crescents. It knelt by the edge of a pit that seemed to lead through the floor and straight into an insane galaxy of light-filled nebulae and shifting formless stars. Reinez knew instinctively that the eldar had created a door to the warp, the dimension of madness and evil where the dark powers lay.

Eldar and Chaos. They had been tearing Gravenhold apart since before the Crimson Fists had arrived. Now here was the heart of it, far beneath the city.

Several more eldar stood, motionless and blank-eyed, around the edge of the portal. They were evidently the same kind of torturers that Reinez had encountered on his way down, their skin cut and stitched as if they had experimented on themselves. Black power flickered from their staring eyes. They had given their souls to keep the portal open.

The tall eldar rose to its feet, taking up the long halberd that had lain on the floor in front of it.

'Lord Sarpedon,' it said in a deep and slightly accented voice, its Imperial Gothic crisp and prayer-house perfect. 'I see you have seen the truth at last. I have been ready to receive you a second time, but I know you will not now be so accepting of my hospitality. For your betrayal, you may have the honour of fighting Prince Karhedros, and of being offered to She-Who-Thirsts in defeat.'

Reinez stepped forward, gripping his thunder hammer in both hands. 'Sarpedon is a heretic and a traitor to the blood of Rogal Dorn,' he snarled. 'A creature should know who kills it. I am Commander Reinez of the Crimson Fists, scion of Rynn's World, a son of Rogal Dorn, servant of the right hand of the Emperor.'

The eldar looked Reinez up and down, noticing his normal legs and the deep blue of his armour. 'My apologies,' it said slickly. 'You all look alike to me.'

There was nothing left but the hatred. The xenos, the traitor, the heretic, all wrapped up into one smirking enemy. Reinez couldn't have held back if he had wanted to.

The eldar was fast, fast enough to turn away Reinez's first blow and spin away from the second, the silvered haft of the halberd deflecting the head of the hammer with its crackling power field. Reinez powered forward, swinging wildly, frustrated with every step by the eldar who could see each move before Reinez made it, bringing the halberd around in silver arcs that threatened to slice off Reinez's head.

Strength wouldn't work. This alien was the very soul of deceit, and its feints and parries would bring Reinez down. But it didn't matter. This was the only victory to be had on Entymion IV, and Reinez's duty to the Emperor and the Imperium of Man demanded he fight for it.

'Your etiquette demands that you know who kills you,' the eldar was saying. 'Very well. I am Pirate King Karhedros, lord of the new Commorragh, favoured of She-Who-Thirsts, the Void Serpent, the End of Worlds, Archon of the Kabal of the Burning Scale, and future lord of the planet on which you stand.' Karhedros swept out a leg and knocked Reinez down onto one knee. The Space Marine barely kept the halberd's crescent-bladed head from slicing into his throat, turning it aside with one armoured forearm. 'When your nightmares bleed into the warp, they will be of me. When your dead souls are sucked into oblivion, they will witness me in my glory as they are consumed. I am the future of the eldar race, the culmination of a thousand fates.' Another thrust and the halberd cut through Reinez's chest armour, plunging deep through ceramite and bone, slitting through one of his lungs. 'I am a god born before you, one with the warp, sired by She-Who-Thirsts to herald the rebirth of my race in the true kingdom of the warp.'

Reinez bellowed and swung out, the hammer's head battering Karhedros back in a cascade of sparks. Enough of the force had got through Karhedros's guard to leave his armour split and blistered down one side.

Reinez breathed out a mist of blood as his lung filled up. He felt his artificial third lung taking the strain. Many more cuts like that and it would be over. He didn't let up, forcing the eldar back around the edge of the portal, towards where one of the torturers stood catatonic.

Reinez barrelled forward, knowing that his greater strength and momentum was his only advantage. He crashed into Karhedros, trying to force him back to the edge of the portal. Karhedros stepped aside and Reinez stumbled, letting his hammer swing out for balance.

Karhedros darted to one side and blocked the swing of the hammer just as it was about to knock the head off the torturer.

Reinez got his balance back and grinned savagely. The eldar had to keep the torturers alive. That was why he was in the portal room at all, to make sure they remained until the portal swallowed up the planet.

Now he knew what Karhedros feared.

The eldar's eyes widened with shock as Reinez swung again, this time low, the hammer catching the torturer full in the midriff and catapulting it far across the portal to fall, broken and showering gore, into the bottomless pit of the warp.

This time Karhedros came back in a frenzy. It was not about affirming superiority over the crude, ignorant human any more. It was about the survival of his ascension. The two warriors fought savagely, sparks flying, cutting and bludgeoning until blood spattered from a dozen wounds each. Karhedros ducked and backflipped, Reinez smashed huge holes in the floor so the shockwave battered Karhedros further.

Reinez knocked another torturer into the portal, Karhedros unable to protect himself and the vessels of his sorcery at the same time. An edge of desperation entered the eldar's fighting style: he was trying to hack deep gouges into Reinez, cut off his arms, stab him through the heart. But it wouldn't work. Reinez, as a Space Marine, was the embodiment of raw force focused for victory. Karhedros had been trained to fight with elegance and finesse. Reinez, ducking a swing of the halberd, came up inside Karhedros's guard and headbutted him, following up by ramming the pommel of the hammer's haft into Karhedros's abdomen. Karhedros stumbled back, wide open for just a split second.

Karhedros expected the hammer strike to the head. Reinez didn't oblige. He charged forward again, reaching round with his hammer hand to pin Karhedros's arm against his side. With his free hand he grabbed the eldar's throat and lifted him up off the ground.

Karhedros struggled. The pirate king was reduced to a helpless xenos, just another foe of Mankind staring into the truth of the Emperor's Justice.

'I was hoping to find Sarpedon here,' said Reinez through a mouth of broken teeth. 'But an enemy is an enemy.'

He pulled back his arm and threw Karhedros into the air with all the strength of his enhanced muscles. As the eldar fell back down he drew back the hammer and swung double-handed. The hammer slammed into Karhedros's midriff as he fell and Reinez smacked him halfway across the room, Karhedros yelling a final curse in the tongue of the eldar as he tumbled in a slow arc into the portal.

Reinez watched the eldar fall. He was still alive when he passed from realspace into the pure madness of the warp. He saw shadows coalescing from the shimmering nebulae and swarm towards the eldar, dark spectral hands reaching out, shadowy maws full of teeth gnawing at Karhedros's body.

Reinez was sure he heard the creature scream as it was devoured. The warp was brimming with mindless, hungry predators and without his world, without the blessing of his god, the Pirate King Karhedros was just so much prey.

Reinez watched until there was nothing left of Karhedros, just a swirling pit of darkness. It took several minutes. Then, Reinez walked around the portal and threw in the remaining few torturers. As the last one followed Karhedros into the warp the whole room shook and the walls of swirling dark energy were suddenly pale as death, shot through with white lightning. Reinez stepped back sharply as the edges of the portal began to crack and crumble.

Reinez placed a hand experimentally into the swirling walls of the cyclone. Most of the power was gone. With the spell broken, the vortex of energy was about to collapse – it meant he could get out, but it also meant there might not be much of a city left to escape to very soon.

He holstered his thunder hammer and, head down, ran back through the wall of power to join his battle-brothers.

The battle for Gravenhold was over. Now all that remained was to escape.

CHAPTER SEVENTEEN

Tellos kicked Iktinos aside, satisfied that the Chaplain was no longer a threat, and walked towards Sarpedon.

Sarpedon was alone on the bridge. The rest of his Soul Drinkers were on the south shore, watching the standoff. Tellos raised a chainblade and the sounds of conflict behind him dimmed as the Soul Drinkers loyal to him backed off from Iktinos's Marines.

The sounds of battle elsewhere in the city were faint against the wind and the dull rush of the River Graven below. Otherwise, there was nothing.

Sarpedon walked forward slowly. His force staff was slung at his back and his bolter was holstered. Tellos held his chainblades low, the closest thing he could do to disarm.

'Tellos,' said Sarpedon. 'We thought we had lost you.'

'And you are here to see if you really had?' Tellos had mutated further since Sarpedon had seen him last, his musculature swelling to grotesque proportions, his face was obscured by his lank hair and deformed flesh but there was still the hint of a grim smile there. 'How noble. Daenyathos would approve. Risk your battle-brothers to placate your guilt. Wage war to prove you did everything you could. You are not so different from the old Chapter, Sarpedon. Just killing the same enemies in a different order.'

'And you, Tellos? What do you stand for now?'

'The same thing you claim to fight for. I am free.' Tellos held his arms wide, his still-churning chainblades spraying clots of congealed blood.

'Once you realise that we are all blood, just blood waiting to be spilt, then you really know what freedom is. We are free of honour and duty. We can do as we please, and it pleases us to kill.'

'I know I lost you at Stratix Luminae. I let you go too far. If it is me you hate, Tellos, remember what your battle-brothers fought for. They would have died for you. If there was a way we could have rescued you, they would have defied my every order to get you back.'

'You think this is as simple as revenge? I did not become what I am because I was betrayed. God of Blood, Sarpedon, if you had not left us there we would not have seen the way! We cut through thousands of those creatures to get out. All that blood, all that death. We heard a voice from the warp, calling us. That was when we understood. Everything is blood, Sarpedon. Ourselves, the enemy, you, me, the earth, the stars. And when you realise everything is blood, you know that blood only flows one way. I have seen how it will end. How everything will end. It is blood and death and madness. We are only playing our part. Soon the whole galaxy will look like this city.'

Sarpedon walked a few paces further, his weapons still holstered. 'I know that Chaos came to you, Tellos. We captured Brother Lothas, he said the same things. The Blood God has touched your mind. But Chaos is a lie! You know that, you fought it often enough! You took a vow with the rest of us that Chaos would be the enemy. It is not too late. We can cure your mutations now. And we can cure your mind. It will not be easy, but we can bring you back.'

Tellos shook his head. Droplets of blood sprinkled from his lank hair. 'Is that why you are here? To bring me back? You left me and my brothers to die, and the rest of the Chapter knows it. Are you sure you're not just making sure they know what a fine leader you are?'

'If the Chapter didn't want me they would let me know soon enough.'

'Oh, that they will. Can't you see the cracks already? I knew they were there since before the excommunication. I was the first. My men followed me instead of you, even when I spoke the words of the Blood God. I have seen how this Chapter ends, too, and it's the same blood and chaos that rules everywhere else. You can't control the Soul Drinkers forever, Sarpedon. You can't control them now. Now they're not the lapdogs of the Imperium they need something to keep them fighting and every one of them is searching for something different. Try them. Ask them. You'll have to kill them all, one by one. And then Chaos will have won. It's already happened, you are just too blind to see it.'

'Perhaps you are right,' said Sarpedon. 'But that's the difference between you and me. You were always eager to fight because you knew you would win. Do you remember how you once were? A hero for the future. And you knew it. But now you fear that we might fail, you have given yourself over to the dark gods. I don't care if failure is inevitable, Tellos. I never did. Our purpose is to fight on against the enemies of the Emperor because the fight itself is justification enough. I can show you. We all can. Do not just give in.'

'I saw the end of the galaxy,' said Tellos, almost sadly. 'All my brothers did. We saw it written in the blood of our enemies. We are on the winning side now. That is all that matters. Everything else is just so much dust. Cling to your honour when Chaos rules everything because that is all you will have.'

'Then if you really are lost, Tellos, there is only one way this can end.'

'Ha! Then you see. Everything ends in blood. You will learn, one day.'

Sarpedon took the force staff down off his back, leaving his bolter. With a mental command he willed its force circuit into life, the circuit spiralling round the inside of his armour to channel his psychic power into the nalwood staff. 'For the Emperor, Tellos.'

'Blood for the Blood God, Sarpedon.'

IKTINOS PULLED HIMSELF over onto his front. The painkillers dispensed by his armour were cutting through the fog of agony but he could still barely move. He saw Sarpedon and Tellos charge at the same time, the two mutants slamming into one another. Flashes of lightning lit up the ironwork of the Carnax Bridge as Sarpedon's force staff smashed against Tellos's blades. Behind Iktinos, his Marines and those renegades who had followed Tellos watched the duel.

Iktinos was the one who would have to lead the Chapter towards its role in the Emperor's grand plan. But it was Sarpedon who would have to fight the battle for the Chapter's soul.

'HE WAS TOO far gone,' said Librarian Tyrendian. Beside him on the edge of the River Graven stood Graevus and Salk. 'We should never have come here. Let the Imperium deal with him.'

'Your commander is risking his life,' snapped Graevus. 'Tellos was our responsibility.'

'You think so? Look at the Imperial forces here. They couldn't defend a single street of this city as they had to. We could have just flown the *Brokenback* in and blasted this city off the face of the planet. There would be precious little to stop us. Wipe out Tellos, his renegades, the aliens, everything.'

'Tellos fought his way off Stratix Luminae without us, Tyrendian. It would take more than that to kill him. This is the only way.'

'I hope you're right, Graevus.'

'He is,' said Salk.

LUKO CROUCHED DOWN in the burned-out southern gatehouse, watching through an empty window frame as the fight unfolded. He saw Sarpedon duck a chainblade, counter with a thrust to the chest. The head of the force staff punched into Tellos's chest but Tellos just swivelled out of the way, the staff passing through his gelatinous flesh.

Luko's muscles twitched in time to Sarpedon's attacks and parries. Luko wanted to be out there, fighting with him, but he knew that this was not just another fight against another enemy. Sarpedon took Tellos's fall personally. He had to make amends personally, too.

He had to win. It had to be over, cleanly and for all. Otherwise Luko knew that this scene would repeated over and over again until Sarpedon was defeated or the Chapter was dead.

'Kill him, Sarpedon,' whispered Luko to himself as Tellos struck back, stamping down on Sarpedon's single bionic foreleg and shattering it in a shower of sparks. 'For all our sakes, make it final.'

'LET ME SEE.' Eumenes lay down in the smouldering rubble of the docks alongside scout-sniper Raek. Beside him lay Scamander, still cold to the touch but breathing and occasionally conscious. Nisryus knelt nearby, keeping watch.

Raek handed his rifle scope to Eumenes. From where they were, in the bloodstained ruins of Gravenhold's river docks amid the remains of a terrible struggle, the combat was just visible down the river as a series of flashes as Sarpedon's force staff hit home.

Eumenes peered through the scope and saw Tellos's hugely overdeveloped back, the cords of muscle writhing beneath his pallid skin as he swung a blade that slammed against Sarpedon's guard and knocked him against the railing of the bridge. Sarpedon was fast and strong but Tellos was nothing but raw power. The Hell was no use, Tellos was too far gone to be distracted by fear.

Eumenes looked up from the scope at Nisryus, kneeling with his back to the rest of the scouts. 'Nisryus. Can you tell who will win?'

Nisryus looked round. 'No. They must be too far away.'

Eumenes looked back at the fight. Sarpedon was on the defensive, his back legs bowing under the pressure as he leaned out of the range of Tellos's blades. Tellos took advantage and pressed home, crossed blades pushing down on the force staff. Sarpedon's back was against the railing.

Sarpedon turned the force staff and tried to prise Tellos's blades apart. The blades snapped apart suddenly and sliced down through the railings on either side of Sarpedon.

Sarpedon reached out and got his arm around the back of Tellos's neck as he fell backwards, and the two of them pitched over the side of the Caltax Bridge into the River Graven.

SARPEDON AND TELLOS hit the river bed still locked together. Sarpedon tried to hold on, hoping for some advantage, any advantage that would let him get in the one single telling blow to finally drop Tellos. The foul waters swirled around him, filling his mouth and nose with the stench of filth and blood. Tellos writhed to get out of his grip, to open up enough space for his chainblades to cut Sarpedon apart.

Tellos reached back and slammed an elbow into Sarpedon's chest. The two Marines flew away from each other, almost lost in the underwater gloom. Tellos twisted in the water and his feet connected with the bridge support, stopping him and bringing him round to face his opponent.

Sarpedon reached down with his legs and his talons found the rockcrete bed of the river. The force of the blow had knocked most of the air out of his lungs and he would have to strike now or be forced to surface for air. That would leave him open, blind and vulnerable. There would be nothing he could do against an attack from below as he tried to gulp down breath.

There was one chance. Tellos probably knew it, too. Whatever the Blood God had shown him, it had purported to be a vision of the future. No doubt Tellos thought he knew how this fight would end. Sarpedon would have to prove him wrong.

Sarpedon dug his talons into the rockcrete and pushed himself forward. Forced into slow motion by the rushing water, the two prepared to clash. Sarpedon took his force staff in both hands, ready to stab it like a spear. Tellos was braced against the bridge support, both chainblades up, ready to impale Sarpedon with the force of his own momentum.

Sarpedon sped up. The water rushed in his face, bodies and chunks of debris rushing past. He could see the red hate in Tellos's eyes, the mark of Khorne the Blood God, most bestial of the Chaos Powers.

He tensed for the strike. He could see Tellos's blades churning the blood-laden water pink, could almost feel them carving through his armour and into his body.

With all his strength, Sarpedon struck.

He was a fraction too high for Tellos's blades, which passed under his body and finished destroying his bionic leg. The force staff passed over Tellos's shoulder, spearing right past him into the bridge support beyond.

Sarpedon's force circuit burst white-hot as his psychic strength was channelled through the staff into the support. All his anger, all his frustration, everything he had ever felt was poured into that one strike.

The iron and rockcrete of the support base shattered. The weight of the support thudded down into the river bed and toppled forward towards the two Marines.

Sarpedon dug his talons into the rockcrete again and forced his seven remaining legs to pull him back from the support. But Tellos's body, bloated with muscles, was too unwieldy to get out of the way. He reached out for Sarpedon, trying to grab a leg and drag him back to share his fate, but Sarpedon's mutant body was just that split second too quick.

Tellos disappeared beneath a massive dark cloud of rubble and debris as first the support column, then the Carnax Bridge itself, came down on top of him.

APOTHECARY PALLAS SAW the bridge coming down from the south shore, just beside the gate house, The whole central section sagged and the suspension wires supporting it snapped like a volley of gunshots. The whole section tipped and pitched into the sea, kicking up a huge plume of dust and water as it crashed into the river bed.

For a moment there was relative quiet. Then Pallas heard something moving in the water just below him. He looked down over the edge of the sheer channel and saw an arachnoid leg reach out of the water and spear a talon into the surface of the rockcrete. A hand followed, then another leg, and Sarpedon was pulling himself out of the water, scaling the wall of the channel.

Pallas reached down and grabbed Sarpedon's hand, hauling him up onto the bank.

'Thank you, Brother Pallas,' said Sarpedon, breathing heavily.

'Are you hurt?'

'Yes. But nothing that won't heal. And I'll need another leg.' He indicated the remains of his bionic foreleg, now a chewed-up mess. Pallas looked Sarpedon up and down – there were chainblade scars all over his armour, a massive dent in his chestplate and a dozen minor wounds where Tellos's attacks had got through his ceramite. His arachnoid legs were bleeding in a dozen different places. But a Space Marine could survive worse.

Sarpedon looked towards the north of the city and saw that the column of dark sorcery was now a swirling white vortex, shot through with lightning. 'Good. It looks like Commander Reinez has done his duty, too.'

Luko ran from the gatehouse. 'Commander!' He pointed down to the river, where the water still churned under the fallen bridge. 'Is he dead?'

Sarpedon followed Luko's gaze. 'Probably not. But I have faith.'

Luko cocked a cynical eyebrow. 'You think the Emperor will kill him for us?'

'No,' replied Sarpedon. 'But I have faith in His Inquisition.'

TWO HOURS AFTER the warp portal began to collapse, every communications device on Gravenhold was activated. Vox-sets on dead soldiers and burned-out tanks, the communicators of the Soul Drinkers and the Crimson Fists, even the comm-relays of the support ships still in orbit.

The same voice spoke from them all. It was the voice of Techmarine Lygris, chief tech-specialist of the Soul Drinkers and the de facto captain of the space hulk *Brokenback*. He was coming into close orbit to send transports down, and any Imperial ships who wanted to be shot out of the sky should stay in his way.

THE BROKENBACK WAS followed in by the Crimson Fists' strike cruiser *Herald of Dorn*. The *Herald* quickly ascertained that a single cruiser could barely dent the huge space hulk, and much less survive the barrage of firepower it could probably bring to bear. Even given that the Soul Drinkers were a hated enemy of the Crimson Fists, the *Herald* hung back long enough for the *Brokenback* to depart before sending its own Thunderhawk gunships down to retrieve Commander Reinez and his men.

Reinez was furious. He thought that the *Herald of Dorn* should have sacrificed itself to keep the Soul Drinkers in Gravenhold a couple of hours longer, and give him and his men a chance to reach them. He eventually made a report to this effect to Chapter Master Kantor, who reminded Reinez that he had lost the sacred standard of the Second Company, and no longer had the right to demand the deaths of his battle-brothers.

THE LAST CRIMSON Fists' Thunderhawk over Gravenhold, responding to an Inquisitorial request, made a detour over the slum district and lent its firepower to a struggle between surviving Guardsmen and a pack of daemons which had entered the city through the warp portal. The Thunderhawk picked up Lord Commander Reinhardt Xarius from the roof of an Arbites watchtower. The men around him had to force him into the custody of the Crimson Fists, who reported later that Xarius had demanded they leave him there to die.

THIRTEEN DAYS AFTER the *Brokenback* jumped into the warp and the Crimson Fists withdrew from the system, Inquisitor Ahenobarbus of the Ordo Hereticus arrived with his personal warfleet and declared the planet Entymion IV to be Diabolis Extremis. The warp portal had by then collapsed and taken most of the centre of Gravenhold with it, forming a massive wound in reality that bled daemons and raw energy into the planet's atmosphere. A plume of warp-stuff jutted from the planet like a solar flare and monstrous creatures ran wild through the ruins of the city and forests beyond. Entymion IV was terminally ill, and only one sentence was appropriate.

LORD COMMANDER XARIUS watched as the sentence was carried out. Inquisitor Ahenobarbus, his body completely encased in the gold-plated power armour he wore as a badge of office, sat beside him on a similarly gilded throne on the reception deck of his flagship.

Xarius was not shackled or locked away, but he knew he was nevertheless a prisoner. Ahenobarbus's personal guard of female Imperial Guard veterans would have been only too happy to kill him. He sat on the reclinium couch and watched as the cyclonic torpedoes soared away from Ahenobarbus's gun cruisers, on their way to deliver the Emperor's judgement on the dying world.

'In Exterminatus Extremis,' intoned Ahenobarbus, his voice booming deep and metallic from the mouth-slit of his facemask. 'Domina, Salve Nos.'

'I should never have got off that rock,' said Xarius bitterly.

'It is right that the guilty be alive to face their judgement,' replied Ahenobarbus floridly. 'If it is possible.'

'Have you decided what it is yet?'

Ahenobarbus thought for a moment, resting his chin on gilded knuckles. 'Your crime has been adjudged incompetence in the seventeenth degree, for which the punishment is execution. It has been deemed appropriate by the Orders of the Emperor's Holy Inquisition that this sentence be commuted to eternal service, particulars to be decided.'

'Penal legions? Death world garrison?'

'Those possibilities are being discussed. Amongst others.'

Xarius sat back on the couch. It was what he had expected. Still, maybe he would find a place better worth dying for than Gravenhold.

He allowed himself the small consolation of watching Entymion IV die.

THE BROKENBACK WAS long gone by the time Ahenobarbus arrived. Lygris had connected up enough of the engines of its component ships to make it fully warp-capable and it was currently streaking through the warp, heading for an anonymous tract of space on the other side of the galaxy.

Eumenes watched the Soul Drinkers disembark from their transports onto the fighter deck of one of the *Brokenback's* many warships. The Apothecaries were tending to the wounded, including Scamander, who would survive, if only just. Chaplain Iktinos, though wounded himself, was holding a sermon on the deck, and Marines knelt around him. They had lost several against Tellos's renegades holding the north end of the bridge, but others had evidently joined them.

Sarpedon was talking with the sergeants, confirming the numbers of the dead and wounded, planning already for how the Chapter would be reorganised to take into account the officers and men who had been lost. There would be funerary rites to conduct, gene-seed to place in storage, novices to educate in the lessons that Entymion IV had taught the Chapter. Again, the Soul Drinkers had taken a battering, but again, they weren't dead yet.

Eumenes was disembarking from the last transport, which had swooped low over the docks to pick up him and the surviving scouts. The scouts had a debriefing from Captain Karraidin to look forward to. Karraidin would no doubt be frustrated that he had not been down there with them, but soon Pallas would complete the bionic replacement for his ruined leg. Although, of course, there were many more lost body parts that needed replacing now.

Eumenes looked round to see Nisryus climbing down from the cargo ramp of the obsolete fighter-bomber that had served as one of the transports. 'Scout Nisryus,' he said.

'Scout-Sergeant?'

'You could tell which way the fight would end, couldn't you? You foresaw it.'

'I did. I saw that Sarpedon would lose.'

'So... you were wrong at last?'

'No,' said Nisryus. 'I think that we all lost.'

* * *

TELLOS CROUCHED ON the heap of dead that filled the now-dry River Graven. After he had dug himself out of the rubble the warp portal had collapsed completely and the raw stuff of the warp was oozing through the north of the city, bringing insanity with it. Imperial Guardsmen and slave-warriors alike, driven crazy by the influx of warp energies, had roamed the city looking for something to kill. Daemons had poured through the breach, eager to revel in death and destruction. Those who strayed too close to Tellos had died and were now piled up beneath his feet. The dead were drawing more and more of the living, eager to take part in the latest game of slaughter. So Tellos waited there for something else to come and face him.

He saw the first torpedo streak down through the black clouds and spear into the ground just outside Gravenhold. The shockwave shook the whole city as the torpedo bored its way through the planet's crust. Lava fountained up as it penetrated the mantle and the pressure was released on an endless torrent of magma surging up from beneath the crust.

A hot red plume whipped up into the air. It was blood, thought Tellos. The blood of a planet. More blood for the Blood God, because everything, eventually, was blood.

Thirty seconds later the warhead detonated, timed to go up at the same time as the other torpedoes which had speared the planet all over its surface. The detonation forced the planet's radioactive core into critical mass and the nuclear fire that resulted flash-burned the surface of Entymion IV away.

The bodies burned. The city burned. Tellos burned, letting the pain wash over him, become a part of him, searing away the altered flesh and leaving only his bare soul burning. He had seen this, too. He had seen how his weak body would be stripped away to prepare it for something stronger, something that would bring the dead of empires to the throne of the Blood God.

Everything was blood, in the end. As his soul flitted through the warp to become one with the Blood God, he saw the galaxy drowned in blood, screaming, dying as Chaos took it over.

And then, as Entymion IV finally died, there was nothing.

ABOUT THE AUTHOR

Ben Counter is fast becoming one of Black Library's most popular authors. An Ancient History graduate and avid miniature painter, he lives near Portsmouth, England. His other novels include *Galaxy in Flames* and *Daemonworld*.

More storming action from Ben Counter

in

CHAPTER WAR

The fourth Soul Drinkers novel

DEEP IN THE heart of the hulk, so far from the massive churning warp engines and the tramping of power armoured feet it might have been deep underground on some forbidden planet, lay the sanctum. Its original purpose was uncertain – presumably it had been a part of a spaceship at one time, because the hulk was an amalgamation of spacecraft welded together into strange and ugly shapes by the forces of the warp. But it was stone, not metal, and its elegant, simple temple was not built in a cargo hangar or a ship's bridge, but in a dark half-flooded cave dripping with stalactites. The temple was partially submerged, the roof of a long covered processional leading up to it now forming a tiled walkway just breaking the surface. Dim lights glowed under the water, glow-globes that had been lit when the cave had been discovered and had probably been lit for hundreds of thousands of years, patiently waiting for its worshippers to return.

Chaplain Iktinos walked along the path, the lower edges of his purple and black Space Marine power armour lit strangely by the light from below. He wore a grim skull-faced helmet, its eyepieces black and expressionless, and had an eagle-topped mace, his crozius arcanum, hung at his waist. Iktinos, like any Space Marine, was huge, not much shy of three metres tall in his armour, but even so it was with humility and reverence that he passed over the threshold into the temple itself.

The sanctum within the temple was also half under water, the lights below the surface casting strange shifting lights along the ceiling. The altar, along with slabs of carved stone that had fallen from the above, broke the surface and Iktinos used them to reach the large slab of fallen ceiling in the centre of the temple. Beside it a statue reared up from the water – it had the upper body of a woman and the head and lower body of a snake, and had its arms raised crookedly towards the ceiling. It was from a cult or religion that had probably been forgotten for centuries. Iktinos ignored its broken, accusing gaze as he kneeled down by the collection of monitoring equipment piled incongruously on the platform.

This place was Iktinos's sanctum, as sacred to him as it had been to whichever worshippers gathered there before their ship had been lost in the warp and become a part of the space hulk *Brokenback*. Iktinos removed his helmet to reveal a smooth, unmarked face with larger, more expressive eyes than deserved to belong in the sinister grimace of the skull. Shaven-headed and with light brown skin, Iktinos's real face had just as much presence as the Chaplain's skull. It was rare that Iktinos took off his helmet as it was a badge of office, an indicator that he was a man apart from the rest of the Soul Drinkers Chapter. Here, in his sanctum, it was safe for him to do so.

Iktinos checked one of the monitor screens. A single green blip jumped across it. He pulled a long spool of paper with various read-outs scrawled down its length by the armatures on a brass-cased printing devices and cast his eyes over its information, evidently satisfied. Then he walked to the edge of the platform and reached down into the water.

A Space Marine's strength was awesome. Even for a Space Marine, Iktinos was strong. He planted one foot on the stone and hauled a large rectangular slab of stone from the water. With a bang that echoed off the rocks of the cave beyond, the slab slammed onto the platform, splintering the marble beneath. On the upper surface of the slab was carved the image of a stern-faced, bearded man dressed in ornate, archaic armour, such as might be found on the noble warriors of feral worlds. He had a crown on his brow and his hands were clasped over his chest holding the pommel of a double-headed axe. All around him were carved letters from a language that Iktinos did not recognise, one that had probably been forgotten as long as the temple's snake-headed god. The slab was a stone coffin for a long-dead king, and the image was carved on its lid.

Iktinos opened some metal clasps, evidently late additions, holding the lid closed, and hauled the lid off the coffin. The muffled screaming began instantly.

Inside the coffin was a wretched, skinny, filthy figure. Its robes were black with dirt and it had a bag over its head with tubes and wires snaking from it, wires that were ultimately connected to the monitors beside Iktinos. The figure reached up and groped blindly at the air in front of it, the skin on its hands pallid and sagging from the damp, wrinkled and rotting. The stench was awful.

Iktinos pulled the bag off the figure's head. The face of the man underneath was swollen and white, splitting along the seams of his features. A wide tube ran down his throat and another up his nose. His eyes were wide and blind, pure white without iris or pupil.

Iktinos pulled the tube from the man's throat and the man could scream properly now, howling sobs of desperation and fear. For several long minutes, the man could only scream. Then there was not enough left in him to scream any more.

'Please...' gasped Astropath Minoris Croivas vel Scannien, his voice hoarse and feeble. 'Please... Oh, my Emperor, stop... just... just let it end...'

Iktinos looked down at him, his face as expressionless as the skull-masked helmet at his feet. 'Stop?'

'The nightmares. Let me out. Or... let me die. Please.'

'You begged us for this.'

'I didn't know!' The words came out as a sob, like that of a child. 'How would I know?'

'You begged us to take you,' continued Iktinos. 'You said you would do anything to get away from Dushan, from the Multiplaeion.' He held out his hands to indicate the coffin. 'This is what you are doing.'

Croivas vel Scannien put his hands over his face and sobbed. There was barely anything else left in him, no words, not even terror or hatred now. There had been a man inside Croivas vel Scannien once, but he was almost completely gone now.

'Why?' he asked, voice just a whisper. 'What do you want?'

'You know what I want.'

'Throne of Earth, what... what do you want me to tell you?'

'All of it.'

Croivas took his hands down from his eyes. 'You know I can't do that. I've told you, why won't you listen? It's... every one of us does it differently. It has to be directed at you, you have to know the codes... with me it's dreams, and at the best of times–'

'You said you were the best,' replied Iktinos, interrupting him. 'You said you could do it when I took you away from Dushan. It was why I took you at all.'

'You really… you really think I wanted this?'

'I don't care what you want. You mean nothing. Which is why you will do as I tell you.'

Dushan had been a world of mutilations. Deep scars across its continents, great ravines splitting its cities apart. Volcanic and tortured. Herds of slaves mined the perfect, flawless gems, forged in the fury of the planet's mantle, for use in precision equipment like cogitators and spaceship sensors. Those slaves had revolted and murdered the ruling classes – classes which included Croivas vel Scannien, an astropath, the planet's link to the Imperium at large. The Soul Drinkers had arrived there to draw recruits from the rioting slaves and in doing so, they had been approached by Croivas who wanted to go with them, too. It was the Chaplain, the spiritual leader of the Chapter, that Croivas had gone with his offer. The Chaplain had accepted. The rest of the Chapter had never known.

It took a long time for Croivas to choke back the nightmares. First his begged, offering Iktinos things he could not possibly deliver or claiming he had a loved one, a woman, back on Dushan who might still be alive. Iktinos explained that there was nothing Croivas possessed that Iktinos could want, and that even if there was a woman she would be buried in the mass graves of the mine pits where the Imperials had been thrown by Dushan's slaves.

Then Croivas threatened, and so desperate was he that some of the threats even sounded realistic. He would strip Iktinos's soul away from his body, drive him mad, wipe his memory so he turned into a drooling infant. Tell the rest of the Chapter what Iktinos was doing. But Iktinos knew that, as powerful a psyker as the astropath was, he would have long ago enacted his threats had he really been able to pull them off.

So eventually, Croivas vel Scennian sunk back into the nightmares that had consumed him ever since Iktinos had sealed him in the coffin and left him to stew.

Cadia had either fallen, or was about to. The lynchpin of the Imperial defences around the Eye of Terror, its commander Ursurkar Creed had demanded assistance from all who could render it to fight off the hordes of traitors and abominations spewing from the Eye. But the Eye of Terror was half a galaxy away, and Iktinos demanded that Croivas move on.

Aliens, of a type never encountered before by the Imperium, had carved out an empire for themselves on the southern fringe, among worlds evacuated or devastated by the century's wars against the tyranids. To Iktinos, such things were irrelevant. The millions of citizens begging for deliverance meant nothing. Less than nothing – they were a distraction, Or would have been, to someone without his superhuman dedication.

Croivas's voice was barely a whisper, his lips bloody with the effort of speaking, His body was falling apart in the coffin, but it was his mind that counted, and Croivas's body – his freedom – would have been one more distraction.

Skeletal mechanical creatures were slowly infesting a cluster of stars close to the galactic core in the Ultima Segmentum. An entire empire had seceded from the heartland of the Imperium, along the western spiral arm of the galaxy, and the call had gone out for the upstarts to be crushed. Religious schisms had plunged the planets near holy Gathalamor into war, and the diocese of Gathalamor itself was begging for assistance in keeping the conflict from its sacred shores.

No use. None of it. Iktinos pressed Croivas harder, but Croivas was falling apart. As an astropath, his task was to receive and transmit messages across the Imperium by virtue of his immensely powerful but very specific psychic powers. Each astropath received messages differently, and Croivas did so by means of dreams. On Dushan he had spent most of his time asleep, sifting through the symbols that pattered against his mind. Back then he had discarded the ones which were not relevant to him, but in captivity, Iktinos had forced him to examine them all, to keep a tally of all the general pleas for help that flitted between the Imperium's astropaths. And Croivas was going insane dredging them all up from his mind.

Daemons summoned to the streets of a world isolated by warp storms. Greenskins flooding through the jungles of a planet deep in the Segmentum Tempestus. Mutants rioting, burning the crops of agri-worlds and threatening hive planets with starvation. Fleets of xenos pirates preying on pilgrim ships, devouring the very souls of their captives. Alien gods demanding worshippers, plagues of insanity and heresy, a hundred thousand wars burning across a million worlds...

'Stop,' said Iktinos.

Croivas gasped and coughed up a clot of blood. His lips still worked, his mind festering with the symbols that had bombarded him as he lay in the cold stone coffin.

'Go back. The greenskins.'

'The... the great beast,' gasped Croivas. 'Came without warning. Shattered them. Without help they'll die.'

'Where? What about the black stone?'

'The… symbol. The code. Black stone. Onyx. And… glass.'

'Volcanic glass,' said Iktinos. 'Obsidian.'

'Yes.'

'What else?'

'Now we this land is ours, we shall never mourn again,' said Croivas. It sounded like a quotation from somewhere, not Croivas's own words.

'What else?'

'The world. A grave for heroes. Vo… Vanqualis. A stone serpent rules. Pride.'

'And the beast?'

'Thousands of greenskins raining down from the sky. Too many to count. Destroyed their armies in a heartbeat. And their fleet is… gone.'

'Is it an exaggeration?' Iktinos's voice was not lacking in emotion now. There was steel in it, an implicit threat so powerful he could have been holding a knife to Croivas's throat.

'No. No, they are afraid. But they will die without help.'

'Will they get it?'

'They are far away from anyone. Perhaps there was an answer.'

Iktinos stood back from the coffin. He glanced down at the monitors – Croivas's heart would not take much more.

'I expect more,' he said. 'You told us you were the best.'

'Then let me go,' gasped Croivas.

In reply, Iktinos picked up the tube he had taken from Croivas's throat and forced it back into the man's mouth. Croivas reached up to fend off Iktinos but the Marine simply grabbed his flabby claw of a hand and crushed its softened bones in his fist. Croivas's scream was strangled and weak. His remaining hand flapped against the lid of the coffin as Iktinos forced it over him again and the shadow fell back over Croivas vel Scennian's blinded eyes.

Croivas's whimpering was barely audible as Iktinos put his shoulder to the side of the coffin and pushed it back into the water.

Iktinos glanced back down at the readouts, made a few adjustments to the air mix and sustenance regiments, then walked back out of the sanctum and towards the cave entrance. As he did so he pulled his helmet back on and his face was replaced with the grimacing Chaplain's skull.

Iktinos had served well, and never given up, where even stout-hearted Space Marines, even fellow Chaplains, had chosen to discard the sacred word and turn their back on the traditions of their order's foundation. Now Iktinos would be rewarded – not with riches or peace, but with the chance to play a part in the greatest work all mankind had ever known. Space Marines, and the Soul Drinkers in particular, were immensely proud, but Iktinos had gone beyond that and it was not proud that swelled his twin hearts and he went to do his duty among his fellow Soul Drinkers.

It was the knowledge that when he was done, nothing in this galaxy – in this universe – would remain unchanged.

CHAPTER MASTER SARPEDON of the Soul Drinkers took to the centre of the auditorium, watched by the hundreds of fellow Soul Drinkers. He was a horrendous sight. From the waist up he was a Space Marine, a psychic Librarian, with his purple power armour worked into a high collar containing the protective Aegis circuit and the golden chalice symbol of the Chapter worked into every surface. He was an old man by most human standards and his shaven head was scarred by war and sunken-eyed with the things he had seen. From the waist down, however, he was a monster – eight arachnid legs, tipped in long talons, jutted from his waist where human legs should be. One of his front legs was bionic, the original having been ripped off what felt like a lifetime ago.

'Brothers of the Chapter,' he began, his voice carrying throughout the auditorium. 'We have come so far it is difficult to imagine what we once were. And I am glad, because it shows how far we have left that time behind. Some of you, of course, have never known the Chapter other than as it is now. And I am glad of that, too, because it shows that in spite of everything the galaxy has thrown at us we can still recruit others to our cause. We have never given up, and we never will. The new initiates, and those who have now earned their armour, are proof of that.'

Sarpedon looked around at the assembled Soul Drinkers. There were faces he had known for as long as he could remember, back into the earliest days of his service in the Chapter before he had led it away from the tyranny of the Imperium. Others were new, recruited by the Chapter in the days since the schism. The auditorium itself currently served as the bridge of the *Brokenback* and it had once been a xenobiology lecture theatre on an Explorator ship that had become lost in the warp. Large dusty jars containing the preserved bodies of strange alien creatures were mounted on the walls and Sarpedon himself spoke from on top of a large dissection slab with restraints still hanging from it.

'We have been apart for some time,' continued Sarpedon. 'Captains, make your reports. Karraidin?'

Captain Karraidin was one of the most grizzled, relentless warriors Sarpedon had ever met. A relic of the Old Chapter, he wore one of the Soul Drinkers' few suits of Terminator armour and had a face that looked like it had been chewed up and spat out again. He stood with the whirr or both his massive armour's servos, and the bionic which had replaced his leg after he lost it in the battles on Stratix Luminae. 'Lord Sarpedon,' said Karraidin in his deep gravelly voice. 'Many of the novices have earned their full armour in the Suleithan Campaign. They intervened in the eldar insurgency and killed many of the xenos pirates. They have done us all proud.'

'What are your recommendations?'

'That Scout-Sergeant Eumenes be given a full command,' replied Karraidin. Sarpedon spotted Eumenes himself among the Soul Drinkers – he knew Eumenes as a scout, one of the new recruits of the Chapter, but now he wore a full set of power armour and he seemed perfectly at home among its massive ceramite plates.

'Sniper Raek has distinguished himself in scouting and infiltration duties,' continued Karraidin. 'I recommend that he remain a scout and take command of other novice forces. Given our current situation I believe the Chapter would benefit from veteran scouts like Raek.' The slim-faced, quietly-spoken Raek was the best shot in the Chapter – as good, some said, as the late Captain Dreo.

'Then it shall be so,' said Sarpedon. 'And of the latest recruits?'

'The Harvest has been bountiful again,' said Karraidin with relish. 'They are born soldiers, every one of them.' The Soul Drinkers recruited new members from among the oppressed and rebellious people of the Imperium and turned them into Space Marines as the old Chapter had done, but without such extensive hypno-doctrination – Sarpedon wanted to ensure their minds were as free as the Chapter itself. For the last several months Karraidin's novices had been earning their place in the Chapter, intervening to fight the Emperor's enemies around the scattered worlds of the largely desolate Segmentum Tempestus.

'Then we are winning our greatest victory,' said Sarpedon. 'The forces that deceived once wanted us broken and desperate, whittled down one by one, reliant on those forces to keep us from sliding into the abyss. We have clawed our way out and built ourselves a future. Some of our best have been lost to win this victory. And I have no doubt there are those who will still try to stop us. As long as we take new novices who believe in our cause, and those novices earn their armour fighting the Emperor's foes, our enemies will never win.

'But those enemies never tire. Ever since Gravenhold we have had to rebuild ourselves and now I believe we are ready to fight as a Chapter again. The Eye of Terror has opened and Abaddon has returned, it is said. More and more of the Imperium's military is diverted to countering the tyranid fleets. The underbelly is exposed and the Imperium is too corrupt to defend itself. We are sworn to do the Emperor's work, and that work is being neglected in the galaxy's hidden and isolated places.'

'Such as the Obsidian system,' said a voice from among the assembled Soul Drinkers. It was that of Iktinos, the Chaplain, distinguished by his black-painted armour and the pale grimacing skull that fronted his helmet. He was surrounded by his 'flock', the Soul Drinkers who had lost their sergeants and gone to Iktinos for leadership. They accompanied him in battle and often led the other battle-brothers in prayers and war-rites.

'Chaplain?' said Sarpedon. 'Explain.'

'The *Brokenback* picks up many signals from across the galaxy,' said Iktinos. 'We are far from the Imperial heartland but nevertheless there is chatter, transmitted from ship to ship. I have been sifting through these to find some indication of the Emperor's work remaining undone.'

'And I take it you have found somewhere?'

'I have, Lord Sarpedon. The Obsidian system, in the Scaephan Sector, to the galactic south of the Veiled Region. The planet Vanqualis has been invaded by the greenskin scourge. The people there have begged for assistance from the Imperium but as you well know, the Imperial wheel is slow to turn and the orks will surely devastate their world.'

'So there is the Emperor's work to be done?' asked Sarpedon.

'They are people of an independent spirit,' said Iktinos. 'They have resisted the Imperial yoke and remaining true to their own traditions. They have survived for a long time alone, and we may find adherents to our cause there. Certainly there are many billions of Emperor-fearing citizens who will perish without help.'

'We are not a charity,' said Librarian Tyrendian sharply. Tyrendian was a lean and handsome man, seemingly too unscarred and assured to have seen as many battles as he had. Like Sarpedon he was a powerful psyker – unlike Sarpedon his power manifested as devastating bolts of lightning, like psychic artillery, hurled at the enemy. When Tyrendian spoke his mind it was with a self-important confidence that won him true friends in the Chapter. 'There are countless worlds suffering.'

'This one,' said Iktinos, 'we can help.'

'We should be at the Eye,' continued Tyrendian. 'Chaos has played its hand.'

'The whole Inquisition is at the Eye,' retorted another voice, that of Captain Luko, the Chapter's most experienced assault captain. 'We might as well hand ourselves over to our enemies.'

'It is also the case,' said Iktinos, 'that our Chapter is not rich in resources. We are lacking in fuel and ordnance. The *Brokenback* cannot go on forever, and neither can we. The Obsidian system has a refinery world, Tyrancos, from which we can take what we please. Tyrendian is correct, we are not a charity, but we can both help secure our future and help an Emperor-fearing world survive without being ground down by the Imperial yoke.'

'And it's better,' said Luko, 'than sitting on our haunches here waiting for battle to come to us.' Luko was known throughout the Chapter for the relish with which he approached battle, as if he had been born into it, and Sarpedon could see many of the Soul Drinkers agreed with him.

'Lygris?' said Sarpedon, looking at the Chapter's lead Techmarine.

'The Chaplain is correct,' said Techmarine Lygris. Lygris's armour was the traditional rust-red and his face, and a servo-arm mounted on his armour's backpack reached over his shoulder. 'Without significant resupply soon we will have to reconsider using the *Brokenback* as a base of operations. We would have to find ourselves another fleet.'

'Then I believe the Obsidian system may be our next destination,' said Sarpedon. 'Iktinos, assist me in finding out whatever we can about Vanqualis and its predicament. Lygris, prepare the warp route. We must be ready for–'

'Let them rot,' said yet another voice from among the Soul Drinkers.

It was Eumenes who had spoken, the scout-sergeant who had recently earned his full armour. He pushed his way to the front, close to the anatomy stage at the centre of the auditorium. He was a brilliant soldier and looked it, sharp intelligent eyes constantly darting, face as resolute as it was youthful.

'Scout Eumenes,' said Sarpedon. 'I take it you disagree?'

Eumenes grimaced as if the idea being discussed left a bad taste in his mouth. 'The people of Vanqualis are no better than any of the rest of the Imperium. They will be as corrupt as the rest of them. You say you have turned your back on the Imperium, Sarpedon, but you keep dragging us back into its wars.'

'On the Imperium,' said Sarpedon darkly. 'Not the Emperor.'

'The people are the Imperium! These vermin, these murderers, these are the corruption we are fighting against! If we have to bring the whole damned thing down, if we have to set worlds like Vanqualis aflame, then that is what we do! The Imperium is the breeding ground for Chaos! The Emperor looks upon this galaxy and weeps because none of us have the guts to change it.'

'Then what,' said Iktinos darkly, 'would you have us do?'

Eumenes looked around the assembled Soul Drinkers. 'The underbelly is exposed. You said so yourselves. We strike while we can. Break it down. The Adepta, the bastions of tyranny. Ophelia VII or Gathalamor. Imagine if we struck at Holy Terra itself, blotted out the Astronomican! This tyranny would collapse around us! We could help rebuild the human race from the ashes! That would be the Emperor's work.'

'Eumenes, this madness!' shouted Sarpedon. 'If the Imperium fell the human race would follow. Destroying it is not the way to deliver its people.'

'If what I say is madness, Sarpedon, then a great many of us are infected with that same madness. Do not think I am alone. And we could do it, Sarpedon! Think about it. The Imperium has been on the brink for thousands of years. We are the best soldiers in the galaxy, and we know what the Imperial vermin fear. We could bring it all down, if we only made the choice!'

'Enough!' Sarpedon rose to his full height, which on his arachnoid legs put him a clear head above the tallest Space Marine. 'This is insubordination, and it will cease. I am your Chapter Master!'

'I have no master!' Eumenes's eyes were alight with anger. 'Not you. Not the Imperium. No one. You cling to the ways of the old Chapter so dearly you are no more than a tyrant yourself.'

No one spoke. Sarpedon had fought the Chapter before – he had led the Chapter War when he had overthrown Gorgoleon and taken control of the Soul Drinkers, he had battled adherents to the old Chapter's ways and even faced one of his own, Sergeant Tellos, who had become corrupted by the dark forces against which the Chapter fought. But a conflict like this had never come into the open so brazenly.

'I see,' said Sarpedon carefully, 'that the Chapter does not unite behind me and cast down the rebel.' He cast his eyes over the assembled Soul Drinkers, reading their expressions – anger and offence, yes, but also apprehension and perhaps some admiration for Eumenes's boldness.

'Then you cannot ignore me,' said Eumenes. 'As I said, I am not alone.' The young Soul Drinker smiled and stepped forward into the centre of the auditorium, face to face with Sarpedon himself. 'They used to say that the Emperor would give strength to the arm of His champion. That Rogal Dorn would counsel victory to the just. Do you believe He will lend you strength, Sarpedon, if we settle this in the old way?'

The old way. An honour-duel. One of the Soul Drinkers' oldest traditions, as old as the Imperial Fists Legion, the Legion of the legendary Primarch Rogal Dorn, from the ranks of which the Soul Drinkers had been founded almost ten thousand years before.

'First blood,' said Sarpedon, with a steely snarl on his face. 'I would not grant you anything so noble as death.'

IN THE HEART of the *Brokenback* lay the dark cathedrals, the baffling catacombs and ornate sacrificial altars, that once adorned the *Herald of Desolation*. Nothing was known of the *Herald* except that it had at some time in the distant past been lost in the warp and become a part of the ancient space hulk, and that its captain or creator must have been insane. Hidden cells and torture chambers, steel tanks scarred with acid stains, tombs among the catacombs with restraints built into the stone coffins – the purpose of the *Herald of Desolation* was lost amid the hidden signs of madness and suffering, smothered by the dark, ornate magnificence that blossomed in the heart of the *Brokenback*.

The dome that soared over Sarpedon's head was crowded with statues, locked in a painful, writhing tableau of contortion and violence. Below the sky of stone agony was a thigh-deep pool of water broken by oversized figures who had been sculpted to look as if they had fallen down from above, and reached up towards the figures of the dome as if desperate to return. The dome was vast, easily the size of the Chapel of Dorn in which the last honour duel among the Soul Drinkers had taken place.

The Soul Drinkers standing observing around the edge of the circular pool seemed distant and dwarfed by the strange majesty of the place. In the centre, Sarpedon and Eumenes stood, armoured but unarmed. This was their fight, and theirs alone – when it was done the results would affect the whole Chapter, but for now it was a matter between them.

'Why have you brought us here, Eumenes?' asked Sarpedon. 'You could have come to me earlier. There was no need to bring the whole Chapter into this.'

'It's not just me, Sarpedon.' When Eumenes spoke there was always a mocking note in his voice, as if he couldn't help but scorn those around him. 'There are dozens of us. And you can't hold out forever.'

'Are you just here to threaten me, Eumenes, or to decide this?'

Eumenes smiled. 'No witchcraft, Sarpedon.'

'No witchcraft.'

Eumenes darted forwards. Sarpedon ducked back and raised his front legs to fend off Eumenes but the younger Space Marine was quick, far quicker than Sarpedon anticipated. Eumenes drove a palm into Sarpedon's stomach and though the impact was absorbed by the armour Sarpedon tumbled backwards, talons skittering through the water to keep him upright. Eumenes jumped, span, and drove a foot down onto Sarpedon's bionic front leg. Sparks flew as the leg snapped and Sarpedon, off-balance again, dropped into the water and rolled away as Eumenes slammed a fist into the floor where his face had been. Stone splintered under his gauntlet.

Eumenes had learned to fight twice. Once, among the brutalised outcasts amongst whom he had grown up – and again with the Soul Drinkers, under the tutelage of Karraidin. He was dirty as well as quick, brutal as well as efficient. And he really wanted to kill Sarpedon. Sarpedon could see that in his every movement.

Eumenes followed up but Sarpedon was on his feet, backed up against a huge broken stone arm that had fallen from above. Eumenes struck and parried but Sarpedon met him, giving ground as Eumenes tried to find a way through his defence. Sarpedon's front bionic leg dragged sparking in the water as he skirted around the fallen arm, watching Eumenes's every flinch and feint.

'What do you want, Eumenes?' he said. 'Why are we here? Really?'

Eumenes ducked under Sarpedon's remaining front leg and darted in close, spinning and aiming an elbow at Sarpedon's head. Sarpedon grabbed him and turned him around, using the strength of Eumenes's blow to fling the young Soul Drinker over his shoulder. Eumenes smacked into an oversized sculpture of a contorted figure, his armoured body smashing its stone head into hundreds of splinters. Eumenes slid down into the water on his knees but he leapt up immediately. His face had been cut up by the impact and blood ran down it as he snarled and charged again.

This time Sarpedon reared up, bringing his talons down on Eumenes and driving him down so he sprawled in the water. Eumenes struggled under Sarpedon's weight as Sarpedon reached down to grab him.

A stone shard, sharp as a knife, stabbed up from the water. Sarpedon barely ducked to the side in time as Eumenes tried to stab him in the throat. Eumenes swept his legs around and knocked Sarpedon's talon out from under him and now Sarpedon toppled into the water.

Suddenly he was face to face with Eumenes. Eumenes had the knife at his throat, Sarpedon gripping his wrist to keep the weapon from breaking his skin. He was looking right into the youth's eyes and what he saw there was not the emotion of a Space Marine. Eumenes might have been implanted with the organs that turned a man into a Space Marine, and he might be wearing the power armour so emblematic of the Astartes warriors – but Eumenes was not a Space Marine. Not in the way that the old Chapter understood it. Sarpedon had not understood what he was doing when he began the harvest anew and made Eumenes into the man fighting him now.

Eumenes tried to force the point home but Sarpedon was stronger and the stone blade was slowly pushed away. Sarpedon held up his free hand, which had a dark smear of blood on one finger. Blood from the cuts down Eumenes's face.

'First blood,' said Sarpedon. He held up his hand so the watching Soul Drinkers could see. 'First blood!' he yelled, signifying the end of the fight.

For a few moments Sarpedon saw nothing in Eumenes's eyes but the desire to kill. The honour duel was forgotten and Sarpedon was not a fellow Soul Drinker to Eumenes – he was an enemy, something to be destroyed. Eumenes really believed in his own cause, Sarpedon realised. To him, Sarpedon was as foul an enemy as the daemons that preyed on mankind.

Eumenes's grip relaxed and the stone shard fell into the water. Gauntleted hand took Eumenes's shoulders and pulled him back away from Sarpedon. The hate in Eumenes's face was gone, replaced with something like triumph, as if Eumenes believed he had somehow proven himself right.

'Take him to the brig,' said Sarpedon, pushing himself up out of the water with his seven remaining legs. 'Post a guard.'

Apothecary Pallas hurried up and shook his head at the ragged state of Sarpedon's bionic. 'This will take some fixing,' he said.

'Be grateful it's the same one,' replied Sarpedon. Had Eumenes shattered one of his mutated legs and not the bionic, Eumenes would have won the duel to first blood. It had been that close. Sarpedon might be stronger, but Eumenes's ruthlessness had almost brought him out of the duel as the victor.

'Your orders, Lord Sarpedon?' asked Techmarine Lygris.

Sarpedon looked up at Lygris. Like Pallas, Luko and others, he was one of Sarpedon's oldest and most trusted of friends, veterans of the Chapter War who had been with him through everything the Chapter had suffered. He realised then that such old friends were becoming rarer, and the Chapter would have to rely on its new recruits.

'Take us to the Obsidian system,' said Sarpedon. 'Find out everything we have on it. And make the Chapter ready for war.

The story continues in

CHAPTER WAR

by Ben Counter

Available from the Black Library
in Spring 2007